# LORNA

LOVE SEQUENCE
BOOK 4

DAPHNE LEIGH

MARBLE CITY PRESS, LLC

*For everyone rebuilding their life after goodbye. May you find the courage to say hello again.*

# 1

Headlights slice through the dark at 3:17 AM, washing over my frosty field like a crime scene spotlight.

My pulse kicks hard as a massive pickup barrels up my gravel drive. I've been out here over an hour, fingers numb and useless, fighting a losing battle against an April frost determined to destroy everything I've built. Each crystal forming on my dahlia beds threatens my livelihood, years of work and the only thing that's truly mine. Something I created. Something my children can inherit. Something my bastard of an ex can't touch.

The truck engine cuts out, but the headlights stay on, casting full light on what must be a truly pitiful sight. A thirty-four-year-old single mom in whatever winter clothes I grabbed in the dark, surrounded by frost blankets and the wreckage of a losing battle.

Leo Robinson unfolds from the driver's side, six-foot-four of pure controlled power. Steam rises from his broad shoulders as he yanks open the truck bed, moving like a man who knows exactly how much space he takes up in the world and doesn't apologize for a damn inch of it.

Levi Walker slips out from the passenger side, his slender figure bundled in approximately seventeen layers. Dark curls escape from beneath a knitted beanie, catching the light as he rubs his gloved hands together, breath clouding around a face too pretty for a farmer.

Then there's Hudson. Levi's younger brother and his opposite in every way. Bouncing from the back seat with barely contained energy, like a man who could go ten hours in bed and still be up for more. He practically vibrates as he circles to the truck bed, all coiled readiness and restless movement that makes me think of tangled sheets and stamina I haven't tested in six years.

For years, I've kept these men at arm's length. Polite waves across property lines, quick nods in the village shop, careful scheduling to avoid their truck on narrow island roads. Pretending I haven't noticed the way Leo's quiet authority makes my stomach drop, or how Levi's soulful eyes follow me when he thinks I'm not looking, or how Hudson's laugh does things to my insides that should be illegal.

Two years of protecting my carefully built life from complications I absolutely, positively do not need.

And now here they are, trampling across my frozen field at 3 AM, carrying armloads of frost blankets and heaters like some kind of rescue squad I never called but desperately need.

"Northeast corner looks the worst." Leo's voice rumbles through the darkness, cutting straight through the howling wind and settling low in my belly.

I stand like a deer in headlights, muscles locked, half-unfurled frost cloth clutched in my cramping fingers, pulse hammering.

"What are you doing here?" Surprise and exhaustion strip away my usual armor.

"We're helping, Lorna," Leo says. No explanation, no apology for showing up uninvited at 3 AM, just those three confident words that hit me in the chest like a sledgehammer.

Hudson steps forward, frost crunching under his boots, his blue eyes electric in the beam of the headlights. A grin splits his face, inappropriately bright for this midnight disaster. "Weather alert came through on my phone. Farmers' warning network." He hefts the stack of frost blankets. "Figured you'd need backup."

"I don't—" The reflexive denial springs to my lips, six years of stubborn independence making "need help" physically impossible to utter. My gaze sweeps across acres of vulnerable plants—my future, my children's future, crystallizing in real time. Pride and practicality wage brutal war in my chest. Then a worse thought hits me. "The twins. They're asleep inside alone. I might need to—"

"We know," Levi says. His voice slices through the howling wind despite its softness. "We brought everything we need. Just tell us where to start."

My heart slams into my throat. Every instinct screams that accepting help means failure. Means being that woman who couldn't hack it alone. But a vicious gust of wind blasts across my face, bringing the scent of ice and dying plants, and I decide pride can go fudge itself.

"The hybrid beds." I gesture toward the rightmost field. "Those are experimental crosses. Irreplaceable. If I lose them, I lose an entire year of work."

"Got it," Leo says, already striding away, boots crunching on frosty dirt. "Levi, help me spread the blankets. Hudson, set the heaters."

We fall into a rhythm. I'm wrestling a blanket over one bed when I spot Leo in the dirt, broad shoulders hunched, those massive hands shockingly gentle as he checks each tender shoot. Hudson's already across the field, unplugging lights I forgot existed, all movement and muttered purpose. Levi moves between rows like he was born to this, steady and unbothered, making it look easy.

The silence breaks only for occasional murmured consultations. The crunch of boots on frozen grass. The whisper of fabric unfurling. My own harsh breathing. My body aches, muscles screaming, but having three more sets of capable hands (hands I'm absolutely not thinking about in any other context) transforms certain defeat into something that might work.

By 4:30 AM, every critical bed is covered. Relief hits so hard my knees nearly buckle.

"The western field should be next," I say, straightening. My back screams in protest, and I press a fist into my lower spine.

Leo notices it. "When did you last take a break?"

"Six years ago," I chuckle, already moving toward the next field.

A large, gloved hand catches my elbow, sending heat shooting up my arm despite all the layers. "Five minutes," Leo says. "Drink some water. Check on the twins."

The monitor at my hip crackles with movement. Maternal instinct overrides everything else.

"Five minutes," I agree. "There's water in the shed if you want it."

I don't wait for a response before heading back, headlamp bouncing ahead of me. Inside, I check on the twins before splashing cold water on my face and grabbing fresh coffee and homemade granola bars.

When I return, all three men are gathered by the shed, their low voices falling quiet as I approach. Leo's gaze catches on the thermos and food in my hands. Something flickers behind his eyes. Approval, maybe. Or hunger.

"Are the twins okay?" Levi asks.

"Still asleep," I say, pouring coffee into the thermos lid and handing it to Leo first. Purely because he's closest, definitely not because I've spent the whole night watching his hands and wondering what they'd feel like against my skin. His fingers graze mine, the faintest spark shooting through me, hot enough to chase off the chill. He meets my eyes, holds them for a breath too long, then nods his thanks before taking a slow, steady sip.

Hudson grabs a granola bar and nods toward the covered fields. "The dahlias—are they your main crop?" He takes a massive bite, chews once, and groans like it's a full-body experience. "Holy shiitake. These are unreal."

"Yes, they're my main crop," I answer, trying not to stare at his mouth. "I specialize in unusual varieties and new hybrids."

"You developed them yourself?" Interest clearly piqued.

I nod, suddenly self-conscious. "I've been crossbreeding dahlias for about five years now. I have a couple dozen varieties that are exclusively mine."

"That's impressive," Levi says, and something in the way he's looking at me makes my stomach flip.

"It's basic genetics," I deflect. "Nothing special."

"Nothing special about creating something entirely new that's never existed before?" Hudson raises an eyebrow, grinning around his mouthful of granola bar. "Sure, that's just an average Tuesday for most people."

Heat climbs my neck, unfamiliar and unsettling. I'm not used to compliments without expectations attached. I tighten the thermos cap like it's suddenly the most important thing in the world. "We should get back to it. The western field still needs covering."

Leo drains his water, his expression unreadable in the glow of our headlamps. "Lead the way."

We work another hour, methodically tucking frost blankets over the last rows. Dawn softens the horizon, washing the fields in pale gray light. Frost glitters over everything except the beds we saved.

"We actually did it," I breathe, exhaustion momentarily forgotten.

"The heaters should keep the ambient temperature just high enough," Hudson says, checking one of the units. "Forecast says the cold snap should break by noon."

By the time I finally stop moving, fatigue settles deep in my bones. But when I turn to face the three men for the first time all night, the sight of them makes me forget how cold I am.

Leo's dark eyes lock on mine, his salt-and-pepper beard dusted with ice. He stands solid and steady, untouched by the cold or the hours behind us, his posture still soldier-straight like he could do this all night.

Beside him, Levi looks like he just stepped off the cover of *Hot Farmers of GQ*—curls slipping out from under his beanie, cheeks flushed from cold and effort. He gives me a small, tired smile that hits me square in the chest. And a little lower.

Hudson's still moving, stamping his boots and blowing into his hands, restless energy refusing to die. When he catches me watching, he grins and winks, and I look away before he notices how much that tiny gesture messes with me.

"I don't know how to thank you," I say, voice rough, gaze fixed somewhere over Leo's shoulder. Looking directly at any of them feels risky. "The plants wouldn't have made it without your help."

"Neighbors help neighbors," Leo says. "That's what we do."

"The least I can do is feed you," I blurt. "Once the twins are up and we've all had some rest. Maybe dinner tonight?" The invitation surprises me as much as it seems to surprise them.

Levi recovers first. "We'd like that."

No one moves. The silence stretches. I push a loose strand of hair back under my hat, suddenly aware of how I must look—mud-streaked, exhausted, nothing like the put-together woman I try to present to the world.

"I should go inside," I manage. "The kids will be up soon."

"We'll pack up the truck," Leo says. "Leave the heaters in place for now. We can collect them once the weather improves."

"Right. Yes. Thank you again. Truly." I hesitate. "Dinner at six? Nothing fancy, just... food."

"Six is perfect," Levi says.

I turn and walk back to my house, intensely aware of their eyes on me. Once inside, I lean against the closed door and release a long, shaky breath.

What just happened? In a single night, I went from polite nods across the fence line to working shoulder to shoulder with them through a full-blown frost crisis, then inviting them into my home like it was the most natural thing in the world. The careful boundaries I've spent two years building melted faster than ice cream in summer.

I sit on the edge of my bed and peel off my socks, exhaustion settling into every muscle. I'll keep things friendly but professional at dinner. Say thank you, feed them well, send them on their way. That's the sensible thing to do.

So why is my last thought before sleep filled with three pairs of eyes, each different and dangerous in their own way, and the quiet, traitorous wondering of what it would feel like if they looked at me with more than neighborly concern?

The shrill beeping of the oven timer snaps me out of my salad-making trance. Six o'clock approaches at an alarming rate, and nothing's ready, not the food, the house, or myself.

"Daniel! Lorelai! Please pick up your blocks from the living room floor!" I call, rushing to silence the timer. A wave of heat hits my face when I open the oven, carrying the scent of bubbling cheese and tomato sauce. The lasagna is perfectly golden, and for one blessed moment, something in my life is going right.

"But Mom, we're building a castle for the fairies!" Lorelai shouts, skating dangerously close to meltdown territory.

"The fairies can have temporary accommodations in the toy box," I say, setting the dish on a trivet and trying not to imagine three large men tripping over Lego turrets. "Our guests will be here any minute."

"Are Mr. Leo and Mr. Levi and Mr. Hudson coming to help us build the castle?" Lorelai appears in the doorway, curls bouncing, face proudly streaked with blue marker.

"Sweet pea, what's on your face?" I grab a damp towel and kneel.

"War paint," she says with complete sincerity. "Daniel said we need protection because three men are coming to our house, and in his book, that's usually a raiding party."

I bite my lip to keep from laughing. "Daniel's been reading too many Viking stories. Mr. Leo, Mr. Levi, and Mr. Hudson aren't raiders. They're our neighbors. They helped Mommy save her flowers last night when it got really cold."

"So they're allies, not enemies." Daniel appears behind his

sister, all serious eyes and solemn logic, and for a second, I swear I see my brother in his expression.

"Definitely allies," I say, ruffling his hair. "Now please, both of you, pick up the living room and wash up for dinner."

As the twins scamper off, I pause at the small mirror by the back door. My reflection looks deceptively calm for someone who changed outfits three times. The soft blue sweater makes my eyes look brighter than they should after a sleepless night, and the jeans do a suspiciously good job of pretending I've seen the inside of a gym this decade. My hair's in its usual messy bun, though this time I might've actually tried. Just a little.

"It's just a thank-you dinner," I tell my reflection firmly. "Not a date."

The doorbell rings exactly at six, and my pulse does an unhelpful little leap. I take a breath that does nothing to steady me and start toward the entryway, only for the twins to race ahead.

"Wait," I call, but Daniel already has his hand on the knob, Lorelai bouncing beside him.

The door swings open to reveal Leo, Levi, and Hudson holding gifts—wine, bread, a homemade pie. Leo wears a deep blue button-up that pulls across his shoulders in a way that should come with a warning label. Levi's in a soft gray sweater that looks criminally touchable, and Hudson's sleeves are rolled just enough to make his forearms look like they could split kindling or hearts with ease.

Not that I'm noticing. Definitely not.

"You're the plant rescuers!" Lorelai announces, pointing at each man like she's unveiling superheroes. "Mummy said you saved the flowers. What are they called again?" She looks up at me.

"Dahlias," I supply, coming up behind the twins. "And yes, they absolutely did." I offer what I hope passes for a calm, welcoming smile instead of one that looks as flustered as I feel. "Please, come in."

Leo steps forward first, ducking to clear the doorframe. "We brought a few things," he says, holding out wine in one hand and a small jar of honey in the other. "The wine's from a local winery, and the honey's from our hives."

"You keep bees?" I take both with genuine surprise. "I had no idea."

"Started last summer," he says, brushing against me as he passes into the entryway. "We had our first harvest this fall."

Levi follows, offering a small, neatly wrapped package. "Herb seed," he says, smiling a little too shyly for someone who looks like that. "I noticed you mostly have flowers, but I thought you might like some herbs too."

"That's really thoughtful," I say. "I've been meaning to start an herb garden."

Hudson steps in last, carrying something in both hands. "Made these today," he says proudly. "Plant markers with a waterproof coating. Figured they'd come in handy for all those fancy hybrids of yours."

I turn one over, admiring the smooth grain and clean edges. "These are beautiful," I say honestly. "And exactly what I needed. My plastic ones keep snapping in half."

Hudson grins, and it's unfair how good it looks on him. "Told you she'd like them," he stage-whispers to Levi, who rolls his eyes.

"Can I see?" Daniel asks, reaching up for one of the markers. Usual seriousness replaced with bright curiosity. "Did you make these? With tools?"

"Sure did, buddy." Hudson crouches to meet his gaze. "I've got a whole workshop full of them. You can come by sometime and I'll show you how they work."

Daniel's eyes go wide. "Mom, can I?"

"We'll see," I say quickly, trying not to sound as flustered as I feel. "For now, I need to check on the food. Dinner should be ready."

As Lorelai proudly shows off the playroom, I seize the chance to hide behind dinner prep, even if everything's basically done. Still, I fuss over the salad, straighten the napkins, check the lasagna way too many times.

It's been me and the twins for so long that having company feels strange enough, but having men in the house feels downright disorienting. The air seems warmer, heavier somehow, full of quiet male energy and low voices that make my heart do unfamiliar things.

"Can I help with anything?" Levi asks from the doorway, voice easy, warm. Sleeves rolled to his elbows, the glimpse of his forearms sending my thoughts scattering in ten different directions.

I drag my gaze upward—huge mistake. His eyes are worse. Calm, steady, stupidly gorgeous, and way too focused on me. "You could, um, fill the water glasses," I say, pointing to the cupboard and praying my voice sounds normal. "Plates are already on the table."

We fall into a quiet rhythm in the small kitchen, moving around each other like we've done it a hundred times. When his arm brushes mine as he reaches for the glasses, the contact sends a spark through me so sharp I almost drop the salad bowl.

"Sorry," he murmurs, close enough that his breath grazes my cheek. "Small space."

"It's fine," I say too quickly, pulse disagreeing. "I'm not used to having people in my kitchen."

He hesitates, studying me like he's listening to everything I'm not saying. "It must be a lot. Running a farm and raising twins on your own."

"You adapt," I say, swallowing past the lump in my throat. "They're good kids."

"They are," he agrees. "But that doesn't make it any less impressive, what you've built here."

Before I can think of a single thing to say that doesn't sound awkward or too revealing, Hudson strolls in and the moment snaps, light and fragile as spun glass.

"Something smells incredible in here," Hudson announces, leaning in just enough that I can feel the heat of him at my back as he peers over my shoulder. "Homemade?"

"From scratch," I say, grateful for the distraction but very aware of how close he's standing. "My grandmother's recipe."

"A woman after my own heart," he says, pressing a hand to his chest in mock devotion. "Nothing beats home cooking."

I laugh. "It's only lasagna."

"There you go again," he teases. "Undervaluing your talents. First you grow rare flowers, now you're serving homemade lasagna. What other secrets are you hiding, Lorna MacLeod?"

The way he says my full name makes something clench low in my belly. It's light and playful on the surface, but underneath there's heat, promise, a dare I'm not sure I'm brave enough to answer.

"I'll never tell," I manage, surprised at the spark in my own voice. "Now make yourself useful and take the salad to the table."

Hudson grins, offering an exaggerated bow. "Yes ma'am."

By the time we all sit down, with the twins perched in their booster seats and the three men making my modest dining table look like something out of a dollhouse, I've mostly pulled myself together.

It's just dinner with neighbors. I can handle dinner.

The conversation flows easily. Leo asks sharp, thoughtful questions about my hybridization methods, his grasp of plant genetics far beyond what I expected. Levi talks about the poetry collection he's been working on, voice soft but steady as he describes drawing inspiration from the Scottish landscape. Hudson keeps the twins laughing with wild stories about "accidental" woodworking mishaps that always end with something exploding or catching fire.

It's nice. Too nice, maybe. For the first time in years, my table feels alive in a way that has nothing to do with food and everything to do with the warmth they bring.

"So how did you end up sharing a house?" I ask, setting another serving of lasagna onto Hudson's plate. "It's an unusual arrangement."

A look passes between them, brief but weighted, like there's more to the story than they're ready to share.

"It's a long story," Leo says finally, his voice quiet. "The short version is we've known each other for years. When we all needed a new start, it made sense to pool our resources."

"Leo owned a ranch in Australia," Hudson adds, twirling pasta around his fork. "I worked for him there. My mom, Ruby, and Levi lived nearby. When she got sick...things changed."

His easy tone falters, and for a heartbeat the light in his face dims. Levi's gaze drops to his plate, the shadow mirrored there.

"After she passed," Levi says quietly, "none of us wanted to stay. There were too many memories. Leo had family ties in Scotland, and we all liked the idea of somewhere completely different."

"So you came here and bought the Morrison place," I say softly.

Leo nods. "That's right. Took us three months to make it livable. Angus Morrison wasn't much for upkeep."

"Or cleaning," Hudson adds, grinning. "Pretty sure some of those dust bunnies were old enough to vote."

The sound slips out before I can stop it, light and unguarded, a sound I haven't heard from myself in years. When I glance up, Leo's watching me instead of Hudson, his mouth curved in a smile that reaches all the way to his eyes. The warmth there softens everything about him, and for a moment, it's hard to breathe. I look down quickly, pretending to focus on cutting Lorelai's food into smaller pieces, willing my pulse to settle.

"And what about you?" Levi asks.

"I bought the farm about six years ago," I say, taking a bite of garlic bread to buy myself a moment. "I grew up not far from here. My family has an estate on Harris, but I was living in Edinburgh before—" I snap my mouth closed. I will not ruin this evening by mentioning my ex. "—before the twins were born."

But Daniel, ever blunt, has no such filter. "Our dad doesn't like us very much," he says plainly. "He lives in London with his new wife. We see him at Christmas and sometimes in summer."

The silence lands right in the center of the table.

"Well," Leo says at last, voice steady, "his loss is our gain. Having dinner with you three is the best thing that's happened to us all week."

Lorelai's whole face lights up. "Do you want to see my fairy castle after dinner? Daniel helped build it, but I did all the decorating."

"Wouldn't miss it for the world," Leo says, meeting her gaze with such gentle sincerity that my chest tightens.

As dinner winds down and the conversation drifts to weather forecasts, island gossip, and spring planting plans, I find myself watching my guests when they aren't watching me. There's an ease between them I can't help admiring, the way they trade glances instead of words, finish each other's sentences, move in sync without effort. Hudson and Levi's teasing has the rhythm of something long practiced, and the quiet way they defer to Leo when he speaks makes me wonder what exactly binds them together.

There's something beneath the surface, layered and unspoken. Not just friendship. Not quite family. Something closer, steadier, and I can't tell if it draws me in or makes me want to look away.

When Lorelai's head starts to droop over her half-eaten dessert, I glance at the clock. It's long past bedtime. "I should get these two to bed," I say, reaching for the plates.

"We'll help clean up," Levi says at once.

"Absolutely not. You've done enough for one day," I protest, though my voice lacks conviction.

"Come on," Hudson says, already collecting silverware. "At least let us stack the dishes. It's basic dinner guest etiquette."

Leo's on his feet too, calmly gathering plates with the kind of quiet authority that makes resistance seem ridiculous. The room feels smaller when he stands, his presence filling it completely.

"Go put the twins to bed," he says, his tone leaving no room for argument. "We've got this."

Too tired to argue, I sigh. "Fifteen minutes, tops. I'll be right back."

Daniel and Lorelai move through their bedtime routine with unusual speed. When I tuck them in, Daniel grabs my hand.

"I like them," he says seriously. "They're not scary like I thought."

"I'm glad, sweetheart." I smooth his hair, throat tightening. "They're very nice neighbors."

"Hudson said I can help him build a birdhouse," Lorelai mumbles sleepily. "And Mr. Leo used to have horses in Australia."

"Did he now?" I whisper, brushing her curls back. "We'll talk about it tomorrow. Sleep well, my loves."

I close their door partway and head downstairs, bracing myself for the chaos I left behind. But when I reach the kitchen, I stop short. Everything is spotless. The dishes are washed and put away, the counters gleam, and the leftovers have been carefully stored in neat containers.

They wait by the front door, coats in hand, ready to leave. Something about the sight, so simple and ordinary, stirs low in my chest. It's a mix of gratitude and longing that edges too close to hope.

"You didn't have to do all that," I say, gesturing toward the kitchen.

"We wanted to," Leo replies simply.

"Thank you for dinner," Levi adds. "It was the best meal we've had in months."

"Hey, I made that pot roast last week!" Hudson protests.

"Like I said, best meal in months," Levi repeats with a straight face, leaning just in time to dodge Hudson's elbow.

Their easy banter pulls a smile out of me. "Thank you again for last night," I say, my throat tight. "For saving my dahlias. I don't know what I would've done without you."

Leo studies me for a long moment, his dark eyes steady and unflinching, making it hard to remember how to breathe. "The heaters are still in place. Forecast says it might get cold again tonight, though not as bad. We'll come back in the morning to collect them, if that's all right."

"Of course." Something unspoken passes between us. "It's really good to see you again. It's been a long time."

He nods slowly, something flickering behind his eyes. "Yeah. It has. Whatever happened back then, Lorna—I don't want it to happen again." His gaze doesn't waver. "We've missed you."

The words settle into me, warm and unexpected, filling the hollow spaces inside me. "I missed you too," I admit before I can think better of it. "All of you."

Neither of us moves. Then Hudson glances at his watch, breaking the spell. "We should head out if we want to feed the animals before it gets too late."

"Right," I say quickly, stepping back. "Thank you again. For everything."

They file out one by one, each pausing in that soft, lingering way that makes it impossible not to notice. Leo's hand brushes mine as he passes, the brief contact sending a pulse of heat straight through me. Levi's gentle smile catches me off guard, and I'm grinning back like some giddy teenager with a crush. And Hudson throws me a parting wink that nearly has my knees giving out.

Then they're gone, the front door closing, the rumble of their truck fading down the gravel drive. Headlights sweep across the porch one last time before darkness settles again, leaving me standing there shell-shocked.

How did an unexpected frost turn into one of the most unexpectedly perfect nights I've had in years? Into resurrecting a situationship I'd officially buried ages ago?

And why, despite every logical bone in my body, am I already counting the hours until morning?

I push away from the door and climb the stairs, trying to shake the thought loose. It's only neighborly gratitude. Nothing more. I have the twins to focus on, a farm to keep alive, a life I've pieced together one careful decision at a time. There isn't room for this. Whatever this is.

I brush my teeth, change into pajamas, and slip beneath the cool sheets, hoping exhaustion will finally do its job. But my mind refuses to settle. It replays the evening in stubborn loops—the laughter, the warmth, the way they looked at me. Three pairs of eyes seeing past the mud on my boots and the half-formed to-do lists, finding something in me I'd nearly forgotten was there.

# 2

I blink awake, momentarily blinded by the sunlight pouring through my window. For one disoriented second, panic grips me. It's well past dawn. I never sleep this late, not in planting season. Not when there's dirt to turn and seedlings waiting.

Then yesterday hits me all at once. The 3 a.m. frost warning. The desperate scramble to save the dahlias. Headlights cutting through the dark, and my neighbors stepping out of their truck like some kind of flannel-clad cavalry.

"Mother of pearl," I mutter, flinging back the quilt and swinging my legs over the side of the bed. I rub my eyes as if I can rub away the memories that chased me through my dreams. Three sets of hands working beside mine. The brush of skin against skin that sent sparks up my arms. Leo's low, commanding voice giving instructions through the cold night air.

And then dinner. God help me, dinner. Leo in that blue button-up that had no right clinging to his shoulders like that. Levi's gentle smile as he passed me the seed packets, his fingers brushing mine in a way that felt far too intentional to be an accident. And Hudson, grinning wide, holding up those hand-carved plant markers like a fisherman showing off his biggest catch.

I stand and cross to the window, the floor cold beneath my bare feet. Morning spills over the fields, soft and golden, turning everything it touches into something almost holy. The dahlia beds are still tucked beneath their mismatched quilt of tarps, old sheets, and the thick row covers the guys brought. The heaters hum low and steady, just as Leo promised they would, breathing warmth into the fragile green beneath.

He also said they'd be back this morning to collect them.

Which means they'll be here. Soon.

Fiddlesticks.

"Mummy! Mummy! Are you awake?"

The twins' footsteps thunder down the hall a split second before my bedroom door bursts open. Daniel and Lorelai tumble in, a blur of mismatched pajamas and bedhead curls.

"You slept forever," Lorelai complains, flinging herself dramatically onto the bed. "We've been awake for ages."

Daniel, ever the serious one, stands by the footboard with that quiet intensity. "Are the plant-rescue men coming back today?" he asks, wasting no time. "Mr. Hudson said I could help him build a birdhouse."

So much for them forgetting that promise overnight. I push back the covers and sit up, slipping into mom-mode. "They're coming to collect their equipment, love. We shouldn't impose on their time."

"But he promised," Lorelai protests, her bottom lip trembling in a way she absolutely knows works on me. "And Mr. Leo said he used to have horses in Australia. I want to ask him about them."

"And Mr. Levi said he'd show me his book about rocks," Daniel adds, eyes bright now. "He said some rocks can tell you stories about how old the Earth is."

I cross to the dresser, pulling out my most forgiving pair of jeans and a flannel that's seen better days. "Let's get some breakfast in you both, and then we'll check the dahlias, okay? If the neighbors happen to come by while we're out there, you can say a quick hello."

Daniel frowns, all logic and no chill. "You said they were our allies now."

I sigh. The kid's too clever for his own good. "They *are* allies. They're very good neighbors. But that doesn't mean they want to spend all their time with us."

"Mr. Hudson said he likes us," Lorelai insists, bouncing hard enough to make the mattress squeak. "He said we're better than their sheep because we laugh at his jokes."

Despite myself, the corners of my mouth pull up. That sounds exactly like something Hudson would say, with that irrepressible grin that turns his whole face into an open invitation to join whatever trouble he's cooking up. "Pancakes or porridge?" I ask, steering the conversation away before Lorelai can start plotting a sheep-replacement plan.

"Pancakes!" they shout in unison, the eerie twin telepathy striking again.

"Pancakes it is. But first, wash your faces and make your beds."

They bolt from the room in a blur of chatter and sock-sliding chaos, and I take a steadying breath as I pull on my jeans. My mind won't quit spinning. Last night cracked open the wall I've spent years building between myself and everyone else, and now I can't shove the memories back into that safe corner labeled *don't you dare.* Not after Hudson made my kids laugh until they hiccupped. Not after Levi crouched on the floor with Daniel, examining his rock collection like it was the crown jewels. And definitely not after Leo's eyes kept finding me across the table, steady and assessing, until heat rushed to places I thought had long gone dormant.

The worst part wasn't the attraction, it was the ease. The way they stepped back into my kitchen like no time had passed, sat at my table, and somehow fell right back into rhythm with me. How they cleaned up after dinner without being asked, moving through my house with that same easy familiarity that used to make me forget myself for a moment or two.

Back then, it had never gone past flirting, only long glances that lasted a beat too long, jokes that carried a spark none of us had the balls to acknowledge. But it was enough to scare me. Enough to make me draw a hard line and keep them from meeting the twins, telling myself it was better that way.

But seeing Daniel and Lorelai with them now, laughing like they've known each other for years, I can't help wondering if I got it wrong. If what I was really afraid of wasn't what might happen, but how natural it already felt.

In the bathroom, I splash cold water on my face, hoping it will wash away the thoughts that won't leave me alone. I'm being ridiculous. They're just neighbors being kind. And I'm just a tired woman who's forgotten what kindness feels like. Nothing more.

Twenty minutes later, after the twins happily demolished a gigantic stack of blueberry pancakes, I'm standing in the middle of my dahlia field, lifting the corner of a frost cover. Relief floods my chest when I see the shoots underneath. Minimal damage, even after the hard freeze.

"Thank you," I whisper into the quiet morning, unsure if I'm speaking to some higher power or to the three men who appeared like knights in a rumbling truck when I needed them most.

Somewhere behind me, the faint sound of laughter drifts across the yard. Daniel and Lorelai are down by the hedgerow, baskets in hand, gathering wildflowers for their fairy castle. Lorelai is the creative director, of course, and Daniel is in charge of logistics, specifically, finding "flowers that make good crowns."

I move down the rows, inspecting each section, cataloging progress and potential problems in my head. These plants are more than a livelihood. They're my proof that I can build something that's mine, that I can thrive on my own terms. My independence. My redemption from a marriage that shrank me until I hardly recognized the woman in the mirror.

When I told Richard I was pregnant with twins, his first response was to suggest "options." His second was to remind me that motherhood would end my academic career. And for a while, I believed him. I believed I couldn't be both a mother and a scientist. It was just one of the many lies he fed me until I started mistaking them for truth. My work on women's sexual health became a punchline in his world—"fringe," "unmarketable," "improper." Words that echo sometimes, no matter how far I've come.

Six years ago, newly divorced and raw from everything that came before, I found this homestead on a windswept Scottish island and poured my inheritance into it. I needed a way to save myself, and the dahlias helped me do that. My research took a back seat to survival, but the science never left me. Hybridization, genetics, controlled growth, I understood all of it. The dahlias were a gamble, but one I could quantify.

I built a thriving business on the same scientific principles Richard dismissed. My so-called "little hobby" now supplies florists across Scotland, and I've started fielding inquiries from buyers in London and Paris. I wonder what he'd say if he saw it now. Probably something about luck. But standing here, dirt on my hands and sun on my face, I know better. This isn't luck. It's reclamation.

By the time I head back inside, the morning's already half over. The twins have migrated to the living room, where Daniel is carefully arranging his rock collection while Lorelai adds flowers to her fairy castle, the same one Leo had crouched beside last night, his massive frame bent low as he asked thoughtful questions about each tiny tower like it was a serious architectural project.

I lean against the doorframe and watch them. Six years old and already so different. Daniel, methodical and introspective like me, with his father's dark hair but thankfully none of his arrogance. Lorelai, a whirlwind of glitter and emotion, her chestnut curls matching mine.

"Mr. Hudson's truck is here!" Lorelai shrieks suddenly, abandoning her castle and bolting for the window. "And Mr. Leo! And Mr. Levi!"

My heart gives a ridiculous little jump. I smooth my hair back, instantly berating myself. It's just the neighbors, coming to collect their equipment. Nothing to get flustered about.

The moment I open the door, they all look up. Three pairs of eyes on me, and just like that, the air changes. Heavier. Hungrier. Like I'm the only thing in the room.

"G'day, MacLeods!" Hudson calls, as if we're old friends. "Fine morning after that nasty frost, eh?"

"Good morning," I stammer, though my focus snags on how Leo's shirt stretches across his chest as he slips his hands into his pockets. He looks carved from something ancient and unyielding. "I checked on the plants this morning and they look good. Minimal damage. I can't thank you enough."

"Our pleasure," Levi murmurs, stepping up beside his brother. Where Hudson crackles with energy, Levi carries a kind of steady gravity, the sort of calm that settles over a room the moment he walks in. "How are the twins this morning?"

As if conjured by his words, Daniel and Lorelai dart past me, full of unfiltered joy.

"You came back!" Lorelai cries, flinging herself into Hudson's arms. He catches her effortlessly, and even from where I stand, I catch the scent of sawdust and something citrusy and bright. He spins her in a wild circle that makes her giggle loud enough to echo.

"Course we did, little mate," Hudson says, setting her down gently. "We've got heaters to collect and birdhouse plans to discuss."

Daniel, meanwhile, approaches Leo with his characteristic restraint. "How many horses did you have on your farm in Australia?" he asks. "I meant to ask yesterday, but I forgot."

Leo's face softens, the guarded lines smoothing out. "Thirty-two at our peak," he says, crouching so they're eye to eye. "Mostly Quarter Horses for cattle work. Two Clydesdales for pulling the heavy stuff."

Daniel's eyes go wide. "That's a lot of horses."

"Sure is," Leo agrees, and when he shifts closer, the scent of him, leather, smoke, and something darkly spicy, reaches me. It's unfair, the way it tangles with the morning air and settles low in my stomach. "It took a lot of work to keep them healthy."

"Would you like some coffee before you grab the heaters?" The words tumble out before I can stop them. "It's the least I can offer."

Leo rises to his full height, holding my gaze. "Coffee would be great," he says quietly. "If it's no trouble."

"No trouble at all." I step back, holding the door wider. "Come in."

And just like that, every promise I made to myself about boundaries and control unravels. I wanted to be careful. Professional. Untouched. Instead, I opened the door again—to them, to want, to the reckless comfort of not being alone.

In the kitchen, I busy myself with the coffee maker, trying to ignore the house brimming with their easy, masculine energy. Hudson is immediately dragged to the living room by Lorelai to play fairies, while Daniel moves on from his rocks and shows Levi his sea glass collection.

Leo leans against the kitchen counter, his gaze doing funny things to my insides. "That was some frost," he comments, his deep murmur rolling through me like warm honey. "I'm glad everything seems to have made it through."

"I don't know what I would have done without you three," I admit, setting mugs on the counter with slightly unsteady hands. "The dahlias are my livelihood. If I'd lost them..."

"You didn't," Leo says simply. "And you won't."

The certainty in his tone, the unspoken promise of future help, should make the independent woman in me stand up and say something, but she's nowhere to be found.

"Do you take milk?" I ask, my voice cracking halfway through.

"Black is fine." Leo takes the mug I hand him, his fingers brushing mine for the briefest second. The contact is fleeting, but my body overreacts—electric, traitorous, alive in ways it hasn't been in far too long.

"Dinner last night was really good," he says, sipping the coffee, eyes steady on mine. "Best meal I've had since coming to Scotland."

Heat crawls up my neck. "It was just lasagna, Leo."

"It wasn't *just* anything," he says. "Good food, good company. The three of us don't get many home-cooked meals unless we make them ourselves."

I swallow, wishing my heart would stop trying to sprint its way out of my chest. "Well, I'm glad you enjoyed it." My words come out lighter than I mean them to, shaky around the edges. After years of being Richard's favorite target, simple kindness still feels foreign. Dangerous, even. "It was nice for the twins to have company."

Nice for me too, though I don't dare admit it.

Leo watches me over the rim of his mug. There's a quiet, searching quality in his gaze, like he's cataloging all the cracks I thought I'd hidden. It's disarming. It's thrilling. It makes me want to look away and step closer at the same time.

"We're planning to smoke some fish this weekend," he says after a pause, easing back as though giving me space to breathe. "We'd love to have you and the twins over, if you're free."

I almost drop the sugar bowl. Two invitations in one week? Every instinct screams to retreat, to find safety in the familiar walls of solitude.

But my mouth, apparently, didn't get the memo. "That sounds lovely," I hear myself say. "What can I bring?"

A small smile touches his mouth, softening the sharpness of his jaw. The crinkles at the corners of his eyes deepen. "Just yourselves," he says. "We've got everything else covered."

Before I can second-guess my acceptance, Hudson barrels into the kitchen like a golden retriever in human form, Lorelai perched high on his shoulders.

"Lorna, your daughter is an artistic genius," he declares, ducking under the doorframe with exaggerated care, his passenger shrieking with laughter. "She's designed a fairy village we could actually build. Tiny doors, windows, maybe even chimneys if we're feeling ambitious."

"Is that so?" I arch an eyebrow at Lorelai, who grins down at me with the unshakable confidence of a child who knows she's extraordinary.

"Mr. Hudson says we can use the scraps from his workshop," she reports solemnly. "And make real fairy houses for the garden."

"Assuming we have your blessing, of course," Hudson adds, catching my eye. "Small project. Totally safe. I'll supervise every step."

And there it is again, that instinct to say no. To keep control, to keep distance, to keep everything neat and safe and solitary. But then Lorelai tilts her head, eyes shining, and Hudson looks at me like he genuinely wants this.

"I suppose a few fairy houses would look nice among the dahlias," I say finally, pretending I don't feel that tiny, traitorous flutter in my chest.

Lorelai lets out a triumphant cheer, pumping her fists in the air.

"And Daniel's helping me with a birdhouse," Hudson continues, lowering Lorelai carefully to the floor. "Kid's got an engineer's brain. Sharp eye for design."

"He does," Levi agrees, appearing in the doorway with Daniel in tow. "He's been showing me his sea glass collection. Very organized and methodical. Might have a future in research."

Daniel straightens at the compliment, pride brightening his whole face. It's such a small thing, but it stops me cold, a man seeing my son, really seeing him. The ache that follows is quiet and deep, the kind that sneaks up on you when you realize how long you've gone without what you didn't realize was missing.

"We should probably grab those heaters," Leo says, rinsing his mug and setting it in the sink. "That way you can get on with your day."

"Right," I say, managing a smile. "I've got seedlings waiting for me in the greenhouse."

As we head outside, I fall into step beside Levi while Leo takes the lead toward the fields and Hudson keeps the twins entertained with wild tales of Australian wildlife. His arms sweep wide as he pantomimes drop bears, and the twins shriek with laughter.

"He's good with them," Levi says quietly, nodding toward Hudson. "Always wanted a house full of kids himself."

The comment slips out so easily, but it catches me off guard, a sudden glimpse into something personal, something real. "He seems like a natural," I murmur, watching as Hudson demonstrates a kangaroo hop that sends Lorelai and Daniel into hysterics.

"Leo too," Levi adds, his words meant just for me. "You wouldn't guess it, but he helped raise our neighbors' kids back in Queensland after their dad passed. Taught them to ride, helped with homework, the whole bit."

I watch Leo's broad back as he gestures toward the rows ahead, trying to picture those huge hands tying shoelaces or holding a picture book steady for little eyes. The image stirs a slow warmth in me, laced with an ache that unsettles more than it soothes.

"And you?" I ask before I can think better of it. "Do you like children?"

Levi's smile is touched with wistfulness. "I do. My mum was a teacher. I grew up surrounded by her students. I always thought I'd have that someday. A classroom of my own, maybe, or..." He trails off, shrugging. "Life takes you places you never planned to go."

"Yeah," I say quietly. "It really does."

Like finding yourself raising twins alone on a flower farm. Or sharing a morning with three Australian men who showed up in the middle of the night and somehow made you forget what loneliness felt like.

At the dahlia beds, Leo and Hudson move in quiet rhythm, collecting the heaters, being careful not to disturb the frost covers draped across the rows. They hardly speak, yet every motion is in sync, one lifting, the other steadying, like some unspoken choreography forged by years of working side by side.

"The forecast says we're in the clear now," Levi says, glancing at his phone. "But we're heading into town this afternoon. We could grab some extra row covers for you. Just in case."

"That's very kind, but I couldn't ask you to—"

"You didn't ask," Levi cuts in softly. "We offered. Neighbors help neighbors, remember?"

There it is again. That phrase. The one Leo used last night, as if it's the simplest thing in the world—a full explanation for everything from midnight rescues to dinner invitations to building fairy houses with my kids.

"Well," I say, aiming for casual but not quite succeeding, "if you don't mind, I'd appreciate it."

Leo straightens then, lifting one of the heaters with a flex of muscle that makes my pulse stutter. His shirt pulls tight across his shoulders, and I have to drag my gaze away before it becomes embarrassingly obvious where my thoughts have gone.

For years I've kept that part of myself buried, the woman who once noticed the way a man's hands could make her stomach flutter or how a low laugh could linger in her head long after he was gone. I convinced myself I didn't need any of it, didn't want it. That all my love and energy belonged to my children and my flowers. It was safer that way, easier to manage a quiet life than risk wanting more.

But standing here in the soft morning light, watching them move through my field like they belong there, the edges of my resolve are beginning to crumble. And for the first time in years, I don't want to stop it.

"Mum, can we show Mr. Hudson the secret hideout?" Lorelai's voice snaps me out of my thoughts.

"Secret hideout?" I ask too quickly, clinging to the distraction.

"The one in the old apple tree," Daniel says, pointing toward the far edge of the property.

"It's not really a hideout," I explain to Hudson. "Just a few boards we found in the shed."

"Boards, you say?" His eyes brighten, that unmistakable spark of mischief I'm beginning to recognize. "Sounds like a proper treehouse waiting to happen."

"Oh no." I lift a hand in warning. "No treehouses. Fairy houses are one thing, but—"

"Every kid needs a treehouse," Hudson interrupts, blue eyes gleaming. "Simple platform, maybe a railing for safety. Nothing complicated."

"I don't—"

"I built treehouses for all five of my nieces and nephews," he says, either not hearing or willfully ignoring me. "Not one broken bone between them."

"Not one?" I arch a brow.

"Well, maybe one," he admits, grinning. "But that was because Jackson tried to jump from the treehouse to the roof with an umbrella after watching Mary Poppins."

A laugh bursts out of me before I can stop it, and the sound is so unfamiliar it nearly startles me. "No treehouses," I repeat, trying for stern and failing miserably. "At least not until I've approved proper plans and safety features."

The twins exchange a look with Hudson, far too smug for my liking. I sigh, already defeated. This is exactly how it happens. One minute I'm holding the line, the next I'm watching it blur under the weight of their easy charm. They don't just cross my boundaries. They make me forget why I built them in the first place.

After the twins finish showing off every secret of their hideout, we head back toward the field to load the last of the heaters into the truck. Their chatter fades as it hits them that their new friends are leaving, and something inside me tightens, a small, unexpected pull that feels suspiciously close to disappointment.

"Would you like to stay for lunch?" I hear myself ask. "Nothing fancy, just sandwiches. The twins would love it, and it's the least I can do after all your help."

Three sets of eyes swing toward me, surprise flashing across their faces.

"We'd love to," Leo says, speaking for all of them. His words roll through me, low and steady, and for a heartbeat I forget how to breathe. It's been a long time since attraction felt this simple, this unguarded.

As we all walk back to the house, the twins orbiting the men like excited satellites, I can't shake the thought that I might be opening a door I won't know how to close.

In the kitchen, what should be a simple lunch becomes a full-blown production. Leo slices bread with the precision of a man who finds peace in repetition. Levi layers cheese and vegetables like it's art, pausing to adjust a slice of tomato so the colors line up just right. And Hudson, of course, turns the whole thing into stand-up comedy, holding up "sandwich sculptures" for the twins, pretending to take monstrous bites that make them collapse into fits of laughter.

Levi nods toward the jar in my hand, a hint of pride in his voice. "You're using my honey."

I smile as I whisk. "It's incredible. How many hives do you have?"

"We started with two hives last summer," Leo answers without looking up, his knife moving in steady rhythm. "We've got six now."

I try not to stare at Leo's hands, but it's impossible not to notice them. Broad, capable, rough around the edges. The kind of hands that fix engines and handle livestock, yet somehow manage to slice bread without crushing it. The contrast does something strange to me, a slow curl of heat low in my stomach. I wonder what it would feel like if those hands—

"You have sheep, Mr. Leo?" Lorelai interrupts, tugging on the hem of his shirt to get his attention.

"And cattle," he says, smiling down at her. "Small herd of each. Enough to be self-sufficient."

"Plus Leo's leatherwork," Levi adds, lining up tomato slices like he's running quality control. "And Hudson's carpentry commissions."

"You make a living from your hobbies?" I ask, genuinely surprised. It's one thing to be skilled, but another to sustain yourself on craft alone, especially out here.

"Leo's got quite the reputation," Hudson says proudly. "Custom orders from all over Europe. Had some fancy designer from Milan commission a full set of bags last month."

Color rises in Leo's cheeks above his beard. "It's still just a hobby," he mutters, clearly uncomfortable with the attention.

Before I can say anything to ease him, Lorelai pipes up with perfect, devastating timing. "Mummy has secret hobbies, too," she announces. "She writes science papers about lady parts."

I nearly drop the salad bowl. "Lorelai!" I choke out, my face flushing.

"What? You do," she insists, completely unfazed. "You write them at night when you think we're sleeping. I saw your special notebook you keep in your desk."

Three pairs of male eyes turn toward me. My research, my most private passion, the one thing I keep separate from the rest of my life, laid bare by a six-year-old with no filter.

"I, um..." I set the bowl down before I drop it. "I used to be in academic research. Sometimes I still write papers. It's nothing, really."

"That doesn't sound like nothing," Leo says. "What field?"

I hesitate. This is the part I never share. My work on female sexual response and pleasure was deemed "inappropriate" and "unseemly" by almost all of my acquaintances. I learned to keep it quiet, to publish under a pseudonym, to hide behind my flowers instead of inviting the judgment or, worse, the wrong kind of interest.

But Leo's gaze holds none of that. Patient curiosity and something darker, thoughtful. Levi and Hudson are watching me too, the air between us shifting almost imperceptibly.

"Women's health," I say finally, keeping my tone even. "Specifically, aspects of female physiology that have been overlooked in medical research."

"She means organisms," Lorelai announces. "I heard her talking about it to Auntie Isla on the phone."

If I could crawl into the nearest cabinet and stay there forever, I would. I freeze, waiting for the awkwardness, the laughter, the teasing.

But Hudson smirks and takes another bite of sandwich. "That's real science," he says, tone teasing but admiring. "Glad someone's doing the work."

"Very important work," Levi agrees, eyes locked on me. "My mother always said women's health was ignored by the men who should've known better."

Leo doesn't say a word. But his gaze lingers, his mouth curving just slightly, and the silence between us hums with tension.

"Anyway," I say quickly, desperate to move on. "Should we eat at the table or take advantage of the sunshine and have a picnic outside?"

"Outside!" the twins shout in unison, already sprinting for the door.

Lunch unfolds in blessedly ordinary conversation, bits of island gossip, talk about tractors and soil amendments, the twins firing off endless questions about kangaroos and snakes in Australia. By the time we're wiping crumbs from the blanket, I've almost managed to forget my earlier humiliation.

Almost.

Because a few minutes later, I'm alone with Leo, gathering plates while the others wander toward the apple tree that may or may not become future treehouse territory.

"Your research," he says quietly, his words low and meant only for me. "Is that why you publish under a pseudonym?"

The plates tilt in my hands. "How did you—"

"Levi's a bit of a research hound," he says, gently taking the stack before I can drop them. "When we first moved here, he looked into the neighboring properties, local records, that sort of thing. Found a few papers by a Dr. E. L. Mackenzie on female sexual response patterns that listed this address. Didn't take long to connect the dots."

My stomach drops. They've known. All this time, they've known.

"Why didn't you say anything?" I ask, my voice barely above a whisper.

Leo shrugs, broad shoulders shifting under his shirt. "Figured you had your reasons for keeping it private. Didn't seem like our business."

The quiet respect in his tone catches me off guard. So different from Richard, who treated every secret, every vulnerability, as a thing to dissect or control.

"Thank you," I whisper. "Most people don't really understand what I study or why."

"Seems pretty important to me," Leo says simply. "Half the population's pleasure shouldn't be treated like some unsolvable mystery."

Something loosens in my chest at that, something that has been wound tight for years. No judgment. No smirk. Just understanding. Simple, solid, and entirely unexpected.

"Anyway," Leo says, turning toward the house with the stack of plates balanced in his hands. "Your research is your business. But if you ever want to talk about it, we're good listeners. Especially Levi."

Before I can find words, Hudson's voice rings out from the apple tree. "Leo! Come give us your expert opinion on this branch situation!"

Leo gives me a small nod before heading across the yard, his long strides unhurried. I watch him go, curling my hands into fists so I won't reach for him.

These men are nothing like I expected. Nothing like any man I've known before. They respect my work, adore my children, and somehow make my house feel brighter without demanding anything in return.

The walls I've spent years building around myself are starting to crack, and I'm not sure I want to patch them up. For the first time in longer than I care to admit, I wonder if letting them in might not be such a terrible idea.

One of them. Not all three. That would be ridiculous.

Wouldn't it?

**3**

---

I'm soaking up a rare moment of freedom, strolling through the village and mentally high-fiving myself for getting the twins to school without a single meltdown or a last-minute "Mum, I need seventeen pinecones for science *today*" emergency.

The walk from the school into town is suspiciously calm, the kind of quiet that makes me wonder what fresh chaos will be waiting for me later. The cobblestones glisten with dew, and for once, I get to savor the silence. No farm chores. No tiny humans asking if fairies poop glitter. Just the sound of my boots on wet stone and a to-do list that includes gardening supplies and maybe, if the universe is feeling generous, drinking my coffee while it's still hot.

And then I see it.

Their truck. Parked right in front of Henderson's Hardware.

"Son of a biscuit-eating monkey," I mutter, ducking into the nearest alley like I'm dodging an ex, not three unfairly attractive men who saved my dahlias from frostbite and then had the audacity to headline my dreams last night.

I peek around the corner just as Leo steps out of the store, his broad shoulders filling the doorway, arms stacked with lumber like it weighs nothing. Sunlight catches in his salt-and-pepper beard, and my treacherous brain immediately cues up the memory of his voice in my field—low, steady, full of quiet authority as he talked about microclimate control.

Which should not be sexy. At all. And yet here I am, flushed and fidgety over frost prevention tips like some kind of agricultural groupie.

Hudson follows him out, gesturing animatedly, his t-shirt riding up to reveal a strip of tanned skin above his jeans. I absolutely, definitely do not stare. Nope. Not at all. I'm a mature adult woman who doesn't ogle her neighbors like they're walking advertisements for whatever the male equivalent of Victoria's Secret is. Lumberjack Quarterly? Farmers Gone Wild?

There's no sign of Levi. Maybe he stayed home? The three of them share that truck like some kind of absurdly attractive farmer carpool, and I've spent more time than I care to admit imagining the logistics.

When the truck finally rumbles to life and disappears down the street, I exhale in an exaggerated rush, loud and theatrical, possibly deserving of an Oscar for Best Performance in Avoiding Temptation Before Coffee.

The bell above *Blackbird Books* jingles as I step inside, and the smell hits me: paper, ink, and freshly ground coffee. My happy place. My church. My one-stop shop for escaping real life.

"Morning, Lorna," Moira calls from behind the counter, peering over the rim of her glasses. Her silver curls are piled haphazardly on her head, as always, like she got distracted halfway through doing her hair and decided she looked perfect anyway. "The new botany journals came in yesterday."

"You're a saint," I tell her, already making a beeline for the science section.

We fall into easy chatter as I flip through glossy pages, trading updates on Daniel's rock obsession and Lorelai's fairy village expansion that's now threatening to take over an entire flower bed.

"That girl's got entrepreneurial spirit," Moira laughs. "She'll be running her own empire by twenty."

"If I'm not bankrupt first from the glitter and moss budget," I mutter, turning to an article on hybrid vigor in ornamental plants that sounds way sexier to me than it probably should.

The shop bell jingles again.

"G'day, Moira. Any chance those books I ordered came in?"

My head snaps up so fast I nearly give myself whiplash.

Levi. Standing there looking like some indie-rock-god-turned-farmer in worn jeans and a vintage band t-shirt, dark curls falling across his forehead in that perfectly imperfect way that would take me three hours and fourteen products to achieve.

His eyes find mine immediately, and a flicker stirs in their depths. Recognition. Interest. Heat.

"Lorna," he says, the way he says my name doing illegal things to my internal organs. "Didn't expect to see you in town today."

"Kids are at school," I explain, clutching a book like a shield. "Just picking up a few things."

"Your books arrived yesterday," Moira tells him, already pulling packages from behind the counter. "That one on dahlia cultivation you were so keen on, and the Scottish mythology collection. The one on etymology in poetry is backordered."

I blink at the stack of books Moira's placing on the counter.

"I've been wanting to learn more about your hybridization projects," Levi explains, his dark eyes steady on mine. "And the mythology book's for the twins. They were asking about selkies at dinner the other night."

I swallow hard as my heart executes a full Olympic routine—flip, twist, perfect landing.

"They'll love that," I say, my voice coming out scratchy.

"Look," he says, opening the dahlia book to a marked page. "There's an entire chapter on color stabilization in hybrid varieties. Thought it might help with those sunset tones you mentioned struggling with."

He remembered. Not that I just grow dahlias, but that the exact problem I'd rambled about weeks ago, trying to keep warm hues consistent across generations.

"You remembered that?"

"Of course." He says it like it's obvious. Like anyone would catalog my offhand comments about pigment inheritance. "You lit up when you talked about it. The way your eyes got all focused and bright. It was beautiful."

Heat rushes up my neck. I'm not used to being called beautiful while covered in dirt, prattling on about anthocyanin expression.

Moira wanders off, but not before throwing me a knowing wink that makes my face burn hotter. Wonderful. By noon, the whole village will have me romantically entangled with the Australians.

"Would you like a cup of coffee?" The question escapes before I can stop it. "Moira makes the best, and I could show you a few of my current projects, if you're interested."

Please don't be interested.

"I'd love that," Levi says, smiling, and there it is, that devastating dimple I've apparently been repressing. Or maybe I filed it away in the *things-that-are-too-dangerous-to-think-about* folder, right next to *Leo's forearms* and *the-way-Hudson's-eyes-crinkle-when-he-laughs*.

Fifteen minutes later, we're sitting at a table by the window, sunlight spilling across the wood as Moira sets down two steaming mugs. I'm mid-ramble about hybridization techniques and genetic markers, and Levi listens like I'm telling him a story instead of explaining pollination ratios. He asks questions that make it clear he's actually paying attention, not just humoring me.

"So you're essentially creating entirely new varieties that have never existed before," he says, his long fingers curled around his mug. "That's extraordinary, Lorna."

I look down, embarrassed by how much the words affect me. "It's applied genetics. Nothing special."

"It is special." His voice softens. "You're bringing beauty into the world that wouldn't exist without you. That's art, no matter what anyone calls it."

God. How does he see me so clearly? My ex used to wave off my work as *playing with flowers,* like it was an inconsequential hobby. But Levi speaks as if it's something sacred, like he can see exactly how much it means to me. It feels like he's handed me a compliment wrapped in respect and tied with a bow of understanding. And I have no idea how to hold it without coming apart.

"What about you?" I deflect, taking a sip of coffee to hide my flustered state. "The etymology of poetry, was it?"

Now it's Levi's turn to look slightly embarrassed, a faint color touching his cheeks. "I write a bit. Dabble, really. Nothing published, just a way to process, I suppose."

"Processing what?"

"Life. Loss. New beginnings." He pauses, those expressive eyes meeting mine, and I feel the weight of everything unsaid hanging in the air.

For a fleeting moment I wonder if some of those poems might be about me, about my fields of flowers. But that's absurd. I'm a single mom with under-eye circles that could qualify as geological formations and a wardrobe best described as "clean enough to wear." Hardly the stuff of poetic inspiration.

"Also helps with insomnia," he adds with a self-deprecating smile that makes him look younger, softer. "Better than Hudson's solution of dismantling and rebuilding furniture at three in the morning."

I laugh, the tension breaking. "So that's what those sounds are! I've heard hammering sometimes late at night and wondered."

"Leo threatened to move his workshop to the barn after the third night of sawing," Levi chuckles, the sound low and warm. "Though he's hardly one to talk. He works leather until dawn when he can't sleep."

The image of all three of them awake in the middle of the night, each working through their restlessness in different ways, makes me wonder what keeps them up. What demons they're trying to outwork.

"And you? Where do you write your midnight poetry?"

"Greenhouse," Levi admits, his fingers tracing patterns on the table between us. "We built a small one off the kitchen. Something about plants growing in the darkness, reaching for light they can't see but somehow know is there..." He trails off, looking slightly embarrassed at his own poetic observation.

"I understand completely," I assure him, leaning forward without thinking. "Some of my best hybridization ideas come at two in the morning. There's a calm in those hours, you know? When the world is still and your brain can actually think."

Levi looks at me with an intensity that makes my skin tingle. "What else keeps you up at night, Lorna?"

The question hovers between us, loaded with potential meanings. I should deflect, make a joke about farm finances or twin-related anxieties.

Instead, I answer with unexpected honesty. "Wondering who I might have been, if life had taken different turns."

The confession surprises me as much as it seems to surprise him. His eyes soften, and he reaches across the table, his fingers lightly brushing my wrist in a touch so brief I might have imagined it, except I can still feel it burning on my skin.

"I think about that too," he confesses, his voice barely above a whisper. "The roads not taken. The versions of ourselves we could have been."

We sit there, suspended in this moment of shared vulnerability, and I realize with a jolt that I haven't felt this seen in years. Maybe ever.

The shop bell jingles, slicing through the moment so sharply it might as well be breaking glass. Moira's voice drifts from the front of the shop, warm and teasing. "Levi? Your brother's looking for you."

Brother. The word snaps me back to reality. Right. Levi isn't just Levi. He's part of a trio, a package deal that includes Leo's quiet authority and Hudson's wild, golden energy. Three men. One shared truck. And me, apparently losing my grip on basic sanity.

"I should go," I say, fumbling for my bag with hands that don't seem to want to cooperate. "I still need to stop at Henderson's for supplies."

"We can help with that," Hudson says as he rounds the corner, his grin lighting up his entire face. "Leo's an expert on fertilizers."

"For dahlias?" I ask, one brow raised, even as my pulse betrays me.

"For everything," Hudson replies solemnly, though the sparkle in his eyes ruins the effect. "Man's a walking agricultural encyclopedia. It's deeply unsexy."

"I heard that," Leo's voice rumbles as he appears behind him, and just like that, the room feels smaller. His eyes hold mine, and for a heartbeat it's as if no one else exists. "Henderson's, you said?"

"I need some twine and the special fertilizer blend they carry." I'm acutely aware of how close they're standing.

"Perfect timing," Leo says. "We're heading back there anyway. Forgot the soil amendments for the eastern pasture."

Somehow, without really agreeing to it, I find myself strolling down Cromwell Street with all three of them. Levi walks on my left, quiet and observant, his hands buried in his jacket pockets as if he's cataloging the world in silence. Hudson's on my right, practically buzzing with life, every laugh and gesture bright enough to light the damp gray morning. And Leo stays close behind me, solid and calm, every touch leaving a low hum under my skin, a reminder that I'm still capable of feeling this kind of alive.

At Henderson's, Leo leads me toward the garden section, his hand hovering at my lower back. Not quite touching, but close enough that I can feel the heat of him through my sweater.

"This one's got the right micronutrient balance for your dahlias," he says, hefting a fifty-pound bag like it's nothing. "But I'd mix it with a slow-release nitrogen source for the heavy feeders."

"You know a lot about flower nutrition," I say, impressed while trying very hard not to watch the way his forearms flex.

A flicker of embarrassment passes across his face. "Did some reading. After seeing your setup."

He'd researched dahlia cultivation. For me. The realization sinks in slowly, squeezing my chest tight until I can hardly breathe.

"Are we boring you with plant talk?" Leo asks Hudson, who's now constructing a teetering tower of seed packets instead of helping.

"Riveted," Hudson replies solemnly, not looking up. "Phosphorus uptake rates are my Roman Empire."

Leo rolls his eyes, fondness softening the motion. Watching them together, I can see their quiet, lived-in affection. It stirs an emotion inside me I didn't expect.

"Lunch before we head back?" Levi asks as we finish checking out, his gaze steady on mine. "The bakery makes excellent sandwiches."

Three pairs of eyes turn to me expectantly.

I should say no. I have work waiting, children to pick up, a life that's supposed to be safe and simple.

"I'd like that," I hear myself say instead.

Outside, I reach for one of the fertilizer bags, but Leo takes it before I can get a proper grip. "We'll load everything in the truck," he says, stacking the supplies neatly in the bed.

"I can fit it in my car," I protest weakly, though it's clear the decision's been made without me.

Hudson grins over his shoulder. "And deprive us of the chance to flex our impressive upper body strength? Not a chance."

Levi shuts the tailgate with quiet efficiency. "We'll bring it by after lunch," he adds, meeting my eyes for a beat that feels heavier than it should.

Twenty minutes later, we're tucked into a corner table at the Hebridean Bakehouse, the clouds outside thinning just enough for weak sunlight to filter through the windows, glinting off the steam rising from our mugs. Hudson is mid-story, animated and absolutely full of it.

"It climbed the drainpipe!" he insists, leaning forward so that both his knee and Levi's press against mine. "Marsupials are highly intelligent. That one was basically the Einstein of kangaroos."

"Not that intelligent," Leo rumbles, amusement curling through his voice. "You're thinking of wallabies, not kangaroos."

"They're basically the same thing," Hudson argues, waving a hand like facts are an optional accessory.

Levi sighs, long-suffering. "That's like saying daisies and dahlias are the same because they're both flowers."

"Flower blasphemy," I gasp, clutching my chest in mock outrage.

Their laughter spills across the table, warm and genuine, and something inside me loosens, something I hadn't even realized was wound tight.

"What made you choose dahlias?" Leo asks suddenly, his dark eyes fixed on mine with a focus that makes everything else in the bakery fade into the background.

The question catches me off guard, not because it's unusual, but because there's no small talk in his tone. He actually wants to know.

"They're survivors," I say finally, tracing a bead of condensation down my glass. "Most people don't realize it, but dahlias have this incredible history of resilience. They were first cultivated by the Aztecs, brought to Europe in the late 1700s as botanical specimens. But the Europeans kept losing them to frost. They're beautiful, but fragile."

I pause, my mind flashing back to that freezing night in my own field. "There was a brutal frost in 1805 that wiped out nearly all the collections across Europe. Only a few gardeners had the foresight to store their tubers indoors. Those few survivors became the foundation for every modern dahlia we have now—thousands of varieties, each a little tougher than the last."

When I glance up, all three men are watching me. Leo's gaze is steady, thoughtful. Levi's gaze is soft, almost proud. And Hudson looks uncharacteristically serious.

"I guess I admire that," I say, quieter now. "How something fragile can still find a way to come back stronger."

For a long moment, no one speaks. The silence feels full, meaningful. Like they know I'm not just talking about flowers.

Then Hudson, being Hudson, grins and breaks the spell. "Plus, they're bloody gorgeous. Like you."

The line is so unabashedly bold I can't help laughing. "Smooth, Hudson. Does that actually work on women?"

He leans closer, blue eyes sparkling. "You tell me. Is it working?"

I pretend to think it over. "Hmm. No. But I'll give you points for effort."

"She says while blushing," he teases, clearly pleased with himself. "Ice cream? There's a new place by the harbor that does homemade gelato."

"I should get back to the farm," I say, though I'm already half-standing. My body, it seems, didn't get the memo about boundaries.

"One scoop," Leo says, his voice low and warm enough to melt resolve on contact. "The weather's perfect for a walk by the water."

And that's the real problem. When Leo says things like that, I don't think. I follow.

So we end up walking along the water, gelato cones in hand, the air cool and tasting faintly of salt. Leo keeps pace beside me, his arm brushing mine every so often, each light touch sparking awareness that crackles beneath my skin. On my other side, Levi points out the ornate carvings above old shopfronts, seeing patterns and symmetry where I'd only ever noticed peeling paint. And ahead of us, Hudson walks backward, gesturing wildly as he explains his latest woodworking project, nearly colliding with a lamppost in his enthusiasm.

It feels dangerous, not just the pull between us, but the easy rhythm we've fallen into. How natural it feels to belong here, between them. How simple it would be to let go of caution and fall straight into whatever this is becoming.

"I've been working on something for your dahlias," Hudson says suddenly, pausing to lick a smear of chocolate gelato from his thumb. The motion is slow, deliberate, and my pulse stutters so hard I almost drop my cone. "A specialized pollination kit."

"A what?" I stammer, trying very hard not to stare at his mouth.

Or his hands. Or imagine entirely inappropriate things involving both.

"For your hybridization work," he explains. His gaze flicks to my mouth for the briefest second, long enough to confirm he knows exactly where my mind went. "I built a box with divided compartments, tweezers, labels, vials, brushes, all the tools you'd need. Figured it might make your process easier."

I stop walking. "You made that? For me?"

He gives a casual shrug that can't hide his pride. "Been working on it all week. Should have it finished by tomorrow."

My throat tightens, emotion pressing up before I can swallow it down.

"And I've been looking into irrigation systems for your western field," Leo says, his voice steady and practical, like he's discussing the weather. "You're losing efficiency with your current setup. I've sketched a few alternatives that could cut your water use by at least thirty percent."

"I don't—I mean, that's very—" The words trip over themselves, tangled in disbelief. I can't seem to find the right combination to express how undone I feel by this, by them.

"You don't have to use any of it," Levi says softly, his hand brushing my elbow in quiet reassurance.

"It's not that." I stop in the middle of the path, the harbor breeze lifting a strand of my hair, and for once, I don't look away. "It's just —why? Why spend your time on *my* problems?"

The three of them share a look, quick but loaded, like they've already had this conversation without me.

Leo's the one who finally answers. His gaze meets mine, steady and unflinching. "Because it matters to you," he says quietly. "So it matters to us."

Fuck. The word slips through my mind like an exhale, hot and helpless. I've spent years holding everything together with politeness and control, but that simple sentence cracks my heart wide open.

Before I can say anything, before I can even breathe, Hudson's cone gives way, his gelato splattering across the cobblestones.

"Bloody betrayal," he mutters, staring down at it in mock outrage. The tension dissolves in a burst of laughter, but Leo's words stay with me long after the sound fades.

By the time we finish circling the harbor, the afternoon light has softened to gold. I don't want it to end, this strange, easy rhythm we've found. As we head back toward their truck, I drag my feet like a kid avoiding bedtime.

"I should get home before the twins' bus gets in," I say, pulling out my phone to check the time. "Dinner prep waits for no one."

"We'll drive you," Leo says. It's not a question.

I blink. "Oh, that's nice of you, but really, I don't want to put you out."

"We live next door, Lorna," Levi says, smiling in that patient way that makes me want to trust him with things I shouldn't. "Besides, looks like it might rain."

I glance up at the cloudless blue sky. "Right. The famous Scottish clear-sky rainstorms. Very dangerous."

"Extremely," Hudson agrees, straight-faced. "You could drown in sunlight. Happens all the time."

Before I can argue, we're back at the truck, and Leo is pulling open the passenger door like it's settled.

That's when I notice the issue. Three seats. Four people.

My brain tries to compute, fails spectacularly, and throws up sparks of panic. "Um." I stare at the bench seat like it might suddenly sprout teeth. "I think I'll walk after all."

"Nonsense," Hudson declares, grinning. "We'll make room. Leo drives, Levi gets the window, I'll take the middle, and you can sit on our laps."

My brain short-circuits. My mouth goes dry. Sit. On their laps. Plural. Physical contact with not one, but two men who've been short-circuiting my hormones all day.

"Or I can ride in the truck bed," I suggest, trying to sound reasonable and not like I'm panicking at the thought of touching them.

Leo shakes his head. "Not legal. Not safe."

"It's a five-minute drive," Hudson adds. "We'll be perfect gentlemen."

Levi's eyes meet mine, offering silent reassurance that I can trust them. And that's the thing. I do trust them. I'm not sure I trust myself not to do something embarrassing.

"Okay," I say before I can lose my nerve. "But if either of you complains about my bony butt, I'm walking the rest of the way."

"I don't think that will be a problem," Levi says quietly, and the look in his eyes makes my face flame.

They climb into the truck, and then all three look at me, waiting.

This is fine. Totally normal. Just a friendly neighbor giving me a lap ride. Truck ride. Whatever.

I take a deep breath and clamber in, trying for dignity and landing somewhere between awkward flamingo and malfunctioning scarecrow. There's no graceful way to perch on two men's laps at once. My limbs forget the basic mechanics of movement, and my backside ends up precariously balanced across their thighs.

"Comfy?" Hudson asks, his voice a low tease, breath brushing my ear.

"Like sitting on a throne," I choke out, my whole body stiff as a board while I try to distribute my weight evenly, which is an impossible mission given the situation.

The truck starts to move, and gravity instantly betrays me. I slide a fraction closer, a soft gasp slipping from my lips. Levi's hand comes up instinctively, steadying me with a hand splayed above my hip. The warmth of his touch cuts through my sweater, radiating heat straight to my stomach.

"Relax," he murmurs, voice pitched low enough to hum against my skin. "We've got you."

Easy for him to say. He's not the one trying not to hyperventilate over how solid their thighs feel, or how every inhale brings that mix of soap, woodsmoke, and something purely male.

Leo drives slowly through the narrow streets, careful, but each turn nudges me closer. I grip Hudson's shoulder, the muscle tense and warm beneath my fingers. When we hit a small pothole, I bounce and land more firmly in his lap. The shock of contact steals my breath, the silence thickening until I can hear my own pulse pounding in my ears.

That's when I feel it.

The unmistakable press of him against my ass, solid through the denim.

Oh God.

I go perfectly still, like freezing will somehow make it disappear. I don't dare look at Hudson, don't even breathe too deeply, because every inch of me is suddenly aware of the fact that I can feel him. *All* of him.

Warmth floods my face and races downward, pooling between my legs. My cheeks could light up the entire damn village. My core tightens involuntarily, and I curse every life decision that led me to wearing yoga pants this morning.

Hudson clears his throat but doesn't move. Levi's hand on my hip tightens, almost protective, almost possessive, and Leo keeps his eyes fixed on the road like it might save his soul. The air in the cab crackles, sharp and electric, like the moment before a storm breaks.

Another turn, and gravity betrays me again. I slide, landing more solidly in Hudson's lap. His hands shoot to my waist, steadying me, but the grip he takes sends a shock through my whole body. His fingers dig in enough to make my pulse jump, and suddenly I can't tell if he's holding me still or holding me there.

I bite my lip hard, summoning every distraction I can. Dahlia taxonomy. Fertilizer ratios. Shakespeare's entire damn sonnet collection.

None of it helps.

The rest of the drive passes in a blur of lust and nerves. Every breath sounds too loud in the small cab. Every tiny shift sparks against my skin. By the time Leo turns into my driveway, I'm wound so tight I could probably shatter if anyone so much as blinked at me.

The second the truck stops, I'm moving, more like launching, half climbing and half tripping over Levi in a graceless scramble that would make a baby giraffe look poised.

"Thanks for the ride!" I chirp, way too brightly, my voice shooting up an octave as I fling myself out of the cab. "I'll just—I should—"

Words. Gone. My entire vocabulary has been replaced by static.

"Don't you want your supplies from Henderson's?" Leo asks, and I can hear the smile in his voice, warm and teasing.

Right. The gardening supplies. The whole reason for this little adventure and not, you know, my complete psychological unraveling.

Hudson steps down beside me, boots crunching on the gravel. My gaze drops, snagging on what I shouldn't be noticing. I snap my eyes up, but too late. He's smirking, that infuriating mix of amusement and awareness, and I want the ground to swallow me whole.

"Where should we put these?" he asks, casual in that way that's anything but, his voice pitched low enough to curl under my skin.

"The shed," I say, pointing vaguely toward the back field. "I'll show you."

And God help me, I have no idea if I'm talking about the tools anymore.

Leo and Levi are unloading my purchases with the kind of quiet teamwork that feels almost choreographed. They follow me toward the garden shed, and I become painfully aware that I'm leading three men who just participated in one of the most awkwardly arousing experiences of my entire life.

"You should have a consistent temperature in here," Leo says, rearranging my shelves like he owns the place. "And your irrigation controls are outdated. I could install a smart system that would—"

"My irrigation is fine," I cut in, though even I don't sound convinced.

Leo gives me an amused look, like he can see the exact degree of my bluff. "At least let me show you the designs I've drawn up. No commitment."

"Yes to designs, no to you reorganizing my entire shed," I say, trying to ignore how his nearness makes the air feel thinner. The space is small, and he's... not.

When we step back into the sun, Hudson's at the fence, testing the tension in the wire, and Levi's crouched beside my labeled dahlia beds, studying the tags with that sharp, focused intensity I'm starting to crave aimed at me.

"These naming conventions are fascinating," Levi calls out as we approach. "Scientific and poetic at the same time."

"It's my own system," I say, unable to hide the smile tugging at my mouth. "Latin base with descriptive modifiers for each hybrid."

"Like naming children," he says, his tone thoughtful. "A nod to ancestry, but still uniquely yours."

The comment catches me off guard, and for a split second, I'm wondering what kind of father he'd be before shoving the thought away as fast as it comes.

"Speaking of children," Leo says, glancing at his watch, "isn't the bus due soon?"

"Twenty minutes," I say, surprised he remembered. "You don't have to wait."

"Mind if we do?" Hudson asks, perched on my porch railing, looking perfectly at home. "I promised Daniel I'd show him how to carve a whistle."

"And I brought the mythology book," Levi adds.

"And I still want to show you those irrigation plans," Leo finishes.

They've cornered me neatly, each armed with a harmless excuse. I should tell them to go. I should reclaim the quiet, predictable rhythm of my day.

But I don't.

"Fine," I say, pretending to sound put-upon while warmth unfurls quietly in my chest. "But only until dinner."

The twins' reaction when their bus doors fold open is pure, unfiltered joy. Lorelai spots Hudson first and lets out a squeal that could wake the dead, barreling down the drive until he catches her midair, spinning her in a wide circle that sets both of them laughing. Even Daniel breaks into a run when he sees Levi waiting with the promised book tucked under his arm.

"Mr. Leo! You came back too!" Daniel calls, his voice brighter than I've heard it in weeks.

"Brought some ideas for your mom's irrigation system," Leo replies, crouching slightly to meet him at eye level. "Thought you might help me explain the water pressure calculations."

Daniel practically glows, immediately launching into a rapid-fire analysis that would make my old lab advisor proud.

I linger at the edge of the drive, struck by how easily they all fit together, Hudson letting Lorelai tug him toward her fairy village in progress, Levi and Daniel bent close over a page of mythology, heads almost touching. My chest tightens. Those walls I've spent years building? They don't stand a chance.

Leo turns from the truck, catches me watching, and his expression softens. "You have remarkable children."

"They're pretty amazing," I admit, pride bubbling up. "Daniel reminds me so much of my brother Jack—serious, a little stoic, but secretly the softest heart in the room."

"And Lorelai's all you," Leo says, a hint of amusement in his voice. "Creative. Determined. Sees wonder everywhere she looks."

"They're comfortable with you," I say, the words tangling together in my throat. "All of you. That's... unusual. They don't trust new people easily."

Leo's gaze holds mine, steady and unguarded. "Maybe because they know we're not being kind just to get closer to you. They matter, Lorna. On their own."

Before I can respond, Hudson's voice carries across the yard.

"Leo! Come check out this fairy palace design. I think we're going to build a miniature version with that scrap cedar!"

Leo gives me a small nod before heading toward them, and I'm left standing in the quiet, turning his words over like a stone in my hand. These men aren't just humoring my kids to win points with me. They see Daniel and Lorelai for who they are—curious, creative, entirely themselves. And that, I realize, feels a lot more terrifying than any kind of physical attraction.

The afternoon melts into evening almost without my noticing. One minute we're still in the yard, and the next, Leo's manning my grill like he's been doing it for years. Hudson has the twins setting the table and negotiating over napkin placement, while Levi's rummaging through my sad little spice cabinet and somehow turning my random pantry into a gourmet meal.

Dinner, unsurprisingly, is incredible, and slightly unfair, considering these are the same men who swore my lasagna was the best meal they'd had in ages. Turns out that was pure flattery, because apparently all three could moonlight as chefs. We eat on the back porch while the sun sinks low, painting the sky in soft golds and pinks that stretch across my dahlia field. The kids chatter nonstop, and for once, I'm not the only one listening.

When the guys finally announce they should head home, the twins act as if I've canceled Christmas. After extracting solemn pinky promises from all three men—even Leo, who looks both baffled and secretly charmed—they finally trudge inside for baths.

I stay on the porch, arms wrapped around myself against the cool evening air. "Thanks for dinner," I say, my voice coming out rougher than I expect, like it got snagged on everything I'm feeling.

Levi smiles, that gentle, knowing curve of his lips. "We took over your kitchen and your grill. Pretty sure we should be thanking you."

"Feel free to invade anytime," I blurt, then immediately wish I could swallow the words back. "I mean—the twins obviously loved having you here."

Hudson's grin is pure trouble. "Just the twins?"

The space between us shifts, stretching tight. The light fades, leaving everything wrapped in a golden haze that feels too intimate, too heavy with unspoken things. Three men. One wildly unsteady heartbeat in my chest.

Levi steps forward first, reaching for my hand. His fingers are warm when they close around mine, steady in a way that makes my pulse skip. "Thank you for today," he says, his thumb tracing slow circles over my knuckles. "For sharing your time. Your children. Yourself."

"Of course," I whisper, the rest of my words getting stuck in my throat. When he lets go, the ghost of his touch lingers, heat still pulsing through the spot where his hand had been.

Hudson moves next, all that wild, easy energy condensing into a force that's suddenly, startlingly focused. His hands find my waist, and every drop of blood in my body seems to surge toward that single point of contact, electric and unsteady. "Today was..." he begins, searching my face. His grip tightens slightly. "Really good, Lorna. Really, *really* good."

He steps back before I can form a coherent thought, and I tell myself that's the end of it, that my heartbeat will slow, that the air will settle. But then Leo steps forward, the last of the light spilling around him like a halo.

He doesn't speak at first. Just reaches up, thumb brushing the loose strand of hair that's fallen against my cheek. The calluses on his skin catch slightly, rough against my face, and the tenderness of the gesture nearly undoes me. His hand lingers, tracing a slow line toward the corner of my mouth, and the world narrows to the feel of his touch and the weight of his gaze.

"You had a..." he starts, voice rough, then stops. Whatever he meant to say fades between us, unspoken but heavy.

For a long moment, neither of us moves. The only sound is the rustle of the evening breeze through the dahlias, the faint laughter of my children inside.

Finally, Leo's thumb drifts away, his expression unreadable.

"Saturday," he says quietly. "Two o'clock. We'll go over the irrigation plans."

It isn't a question. And still, I nod, because my voice doesn't trust me enough to speak.

They leave then, climbing into their truck with backward glances and half-smiles that promise things I'm not sure I'm ready for. Their taillights disappear around the bend, and I stand frozen on my porch.

"Mummy, can we have ice cream?" Lorelai calls from inside, breaking the spell.

Right. Mother. Responsible adult. Not a woman whose entire body is humming like a tuning fork after being touched for the first time in years. I take a shaky breath and turn toward the door, pressing my fingers to my cheek where Leo's touch still burns.

Saturday. Two o'clock.

I have no idea what I'm walking into, but for the first time in six years, I'm not sure I want to run away from it.

By the time night settles over the house, the earlier haze of warmth and confusion has given way to the comforting chaos of bedtime. The twins' voices float down the hall, and I find myself smiling despite everything.

"Not a chance, young lady," I say firmly as I tuck the blankets around Lorelai. "Mr. Hudson was being silly. You cannot have a real drawbridge on your fairy house."

"But he said it would work with rope and a pulley system," she protests, her lower lip jutting out.

"Maybe a very small one," I concede, knowing I'll probably regret it. "After he checks with me."

Satisfied with the compromise, Lorelai snuggles deeper into her pillow, her dark curls fanning across the case like a tiny halo. "I like them, Mummy. They make you smile the big smile."

I pause, my hand hovering over the night-light switch. "What big smile?"

"The one that shows your teeth and makes your eyes all

crinkly," she murmurs, already half-asleep. "You don't do that smile very much. But you did it lots today."

I lean down and kiss her forehead, swallowing past the lump in my throat. "Goodnight, sweet pea. Love you to the moon and back."

"And all the stars too," she mumbles, her voice fading as sleep claims her.

In Daniel's room, I find him crouched on his bed, pinning Leo's irrigation diagram to his "science inspiration" bulletin board with the reverence most kids reserve for superheroes.

"They're very smart, aren't they, Mum?" he asks as I help him wriggle into his pajamas.

"They are," I agree. "But so are you. Leo was very impressed with your questions today."

Daniel straightens, pride blooming across his small face. "He said I have an engineer's mind. What does that mean?"

"It means you're good at understanding how things work and fit together," I explain. "It's a special way of seeing the world."

He tilts his head, thinking. "Like how you see flowers?"

A smile tugs at my lips. "Exactly like that."

Silence settles for a moment as he considers it. Then, without looking up, he says, "I think Mr. Levi likes you. He looks at you like Grandpa used to look at Grandma in the old pictures."

My heart gives a startled kick. "That's just being friendly, love."

Daniel shoots me a look far too wise for his six years. "Mr. Hudson and Mr. Leo look at you that way too. But different also."

I clear my throat, aiming for briskness I don't feel. "Time for sleep, young man. Big day tomorrow."

"Are they coming back tomorrow?" he asks hopefully as I tuck the blanket around him.

"I don't know," I hedge. "They have their own farm to run."

"But they like our farm better," Daniel says with unshakable conviction. "Hudson told me so."

I turn off his lamp, grateful for the dark that hides my face. "Goodnight, little man. Sweet dreams."

"Night, Mum. Love you."

"Love you more," I whisper into the quiet, standing there a moment longer, listening to his even breathing. The house finally feels still, but inside me, nothing is still at all.

Later, after checking on seedlings and finishing my nightly chores, I'm restless and unable to settle. I try reading a few journal articles, but the words blur into nonsense. My mind keeps snagging on everything else.

Levi's focused gaze across the bookshop table. Hudson's easy touches that felt anything but easy. Leo's quiet, deliberate observations that told me he'd noticed far more than I meant him to.

That truck ride. God, that truck ride.

By the time I realize I've been staring at the wall for the third time, replaying the moment Leo's fingers brushed the corner of my mouth, I finally admit defeat.

In the bottom drawer of my dresser, beneath stretched-out underwear and single socks that lost their partners long ago, lies a small velvet pouch.

"Oh, what the hell," I mutter, fishing it out.

The silicone vibrator is cool and smooth in my hand. Sleek, discreet, and, most importantly, guaranteed not to ask any questions afterward.

"This is simply physical release," I whisper to no one, sliding beneath the duvet. "Basic human maintenance."

But when I close my eyes and let my body relax, it isn't some invented fantasy that comes to mind.

It's three very real men whose touches I can still feel on my skin.

I imagine Leo's big, capable hands moving over me as if my body is a system he's intent on understanding. His palms are rough from work, his touch precise, mapping every inch with the same focus he gives to irrigation lines and soil moisture. I can almost feel the scrape of his callused fingers brushing over my nipples, sliding down my stomach, parting me with a quiet confidence that leaves me trembling.

"Look how wet you are for me," he murmurs in that low, gravelly voice that vibrates through my chest. "Let me taste you, Lorna."

The imagined words alone make my thighs shake. I thumb the vibrator up a notch, hips arching to chase the pulse of it, and suddenly Levi is there too, watching. Always watching. Those dark, thoughtful eyes taking me apart piece by piece.

"I want to feel you come on my tongue," his voice breathes against the inside of my skull. "Want to fuck you with my fingers while you beg for more."

A sound escapes me—half gasp, half prayer—as fire rushes through my veins. My skin feels too tight, every nerve awake and reaching.

And then Hudson joins them, his teasing grin gone, replaced by a darker, hungrier edge. His hands are everywhere, curious and relentless, learning me by instinct.

"You're going to take all of me," I imagine him saying, voice rough with need. "I'm going to fill you so deep you'll feel me every time you move."

My mind can't hold them separate anymore. The fantasy tangles—Leo's strength anchoring me, Hudson's mouth hot against my breast, Levi's fingers in my hair pulling me higher. Three distinct energies converging into one impossible rhythm, all of them working together, their voices overlapping in a low chorus of want and promise.

I press the vibrator harder, my breath breaking apart into small, desperate sounds. The pleasure builds sharp and bright, coiling tight enough to snap.

"Spread your legs wider," Leo orders, his voice low and rough, full of authority that vibrates straight through me.

"That's it," Hudson growls, the sound close, hungry. "Take it deeper."

"You're magnificent," Levi whispers, the words breaking softly against my ear.

The orgasm hits hard, fast, shattering, a white-hot wave that tears through me with no mercy. My back arches, a muffled cry buried in the pillow as pleasure crashes over me again and again, each pulse sharper than the last.

When it finally ebbs, I collapse against the sheets, chest heaving. "Holy shit," I gasp, half laughing, half stunned. I can't remember the last time it felt like that. Maybe never.

The vibrator slips from my trembling hand, and I switch it off with a clumsy flick. Did I really just come so hard thinking about having three men at the same time? Men who live next door. Men who fix my heaters and read bedtime stories to my children. Who can tell a dahlia variety by sight.

I sit up, wipe down, shove the toy back into its velvet pouch like I can shove the fantasy away with it. Out of sight, out of mind. Except my body doesn't get the memo. My pulse is still uneven, my skin flushed, my thighs damp with the reminder that pretending this isn't happening won't make it stop.

This cannot be a thing. It cannot.

But when I finally drift toward sleep, body still humming with aftershocks, Leo's voice threads through the fog. *Because it matters to you. So it matters to us.*

The words linger, tangled with the memory of Hudson's wicked grin and Levi's quiet, knowing eyes. Before I can stop it, a thought slips in: what if my children are right about the way these men look at me?

It's the kind of thought that hums with danger, that feels like standing barefoot on the edge of something vast and inevitable.

And as sleep pulls me under, I already know the answer to the question I shouldn't even be asking—

which of them I'll dream about tonight.

All three, of course.

**4**

———

When I hear the rumble of that truck, my heart does a traitorous little tap dance against my ribs. Two days since our town encounter and that humiliating, lap-sitting ride home. Two days of pretending I haven't been replaying Hudson's hard body pressed against me, Levi's thumb tracing circles on my hip, Leo's dark eyes watching the whole thing like he already knew how it would end. Two days of failing spectacularly at pretending.

What kind of woman lusts after three men at once? Apparently the kind who hasn't had sex in six years and whose body has officially declared mutiny. My libido didn't just wake up; it kicked down the door, ordered shots, and lit itself on fire. And now it's fixated on not one, not two, but three men who look like they were genetically engineered to ruin my peace.

I wipe my dirt-covered hands on my equally filthy jeans and try to look casual. Just your average hardworking flower farmer. Definitely not a sex-starved woman whose vibrator battery gave up the ghost around midnight. Perfectly normal, fully composed, nothing to see here.

The truck rolls to a stop in a cloud of dust. Then they pile out, a testosterone trifecta that should require a prescription. Warning—side effects may include spontaneous combustion, chronic daydreaming, and loss of basic vocabulary.

Leo carries a massive roll of irrigation tubing over one shoulder, muscles shifting beneath his T-shirt. Hudson follows, juggling tools and components, sunlight catching his tawny hair like he's filming a farm supply commercial. Wanted: effortlessly hot man to handle heavy equipment. Levi brings up the rear, arms full of plans and diagrams, a pencil tucked behind his ear that somehow makes him look like he belongs in a Paris atelier instead of a muddy field.

Sweet mother of pearl. It's going to be a long day.

"G'day," Hudson calls, cheerful as always, that dimple flashing like punctuation at the end of his greeting. "Brought you a present."

"Is it amnesia about the lap incident?" I mutter, mostly to myself.

"What was that?" Levi asks, stepping closer, those sharp eyes taking in way too much.

"Nothing!" I say, my voice hitting an octave only dogs should hear. "Just surprised to see all of you."

Leo adjusts the coil of irrigation tubing on his shoulder. "We talked about improving your system," he says, nodding toward my fields. "Forecast says no rain for a week. Good time to start."

"Today? But I didn't—we didn't—"

"Do you have other plans?" His deep voice slides through me like warm honey and distant thunder.

Yes. Incredibly important plans that definitely don't involve watching him get sweaty digging up my fields. Plans that will not, under any circumstances, lead to me fantasizing about those big hands. Super legitimate plans that—

"No," I blurt. "No other plans."

Fantastic. My mouth, the eternal traitor.

"Perfect." Leo nods, already heading toward the western field where my so-called irrigation system consists of me pointing a hose vaguely at things and hoping for divine intervention.

"We're still good for dinner tonight?" Levi asks as we follow, his voice soft, close enough to make my pulse trip.

Right. Dinner. At their house. The invitation they extended after our meeting in town. Another opportunity for my heart to make poor life choices, and it's happening tonight.

"Of course," I hear myself say, as if my mouth made the decision without consulting the rest of me. "The twins will be home from my sister's around three. We can come over after that."

Hudson grins and slings an arm around my shoulders. "Excellent. Leo's been marinating steaks since yesterday. You'd think the Queen herself was coming."

Leo shoots him a look that could curdle milk, but Hudson just winks, unbothered.

"Do you three ever actually work your own farm?" I ask as we reach the edge of the field.

Leo sets the irrigation tubing down and turns that unwavering focus on me. "We woke up at four, finished morning chores by six," he says in the same calm, no-nonsense tone someone might use to announce the weather. Completely serious. Like that's a normal human schedule and not one that requires dark magic or an intravenous coffee drip.

"Sheep are fed, cows are milked, chicken coop's clean as a whistle," Hudson adds, arranging tools with military precision. "Leo's a bit of a taskmaster in the mornings."

Something about the way he says taskmaster, the curve of his mouth when he does, sends an unwelcome shiver down my spine. I have a sudden, wildly inappropriate mental image of Leo giving me instructions in that same calm, authoritative tone, and my pulse decides to join the party.

"Levi's been up even longer," Leo says, oblivious to my internal combustion. "Found him at his desk writing when I got up."

Levi shrugs, cheeks pinking. "Had an idea I needed to get down before I lost it."

I can't look away from the color rising in his cheeks, that soft pink blooming against his skin. For a second, I forget how to breathe. He might be the most beautiful man I've ever seen, and the worst part is he doesn't even seem to know it.

"Okay then," I say too brightly, clapping my hands together like I'm wrangling toddlers instead of three absurdly competent men. "What's the plan?"

Leo straightens to his full height, and my neck actually aches from looking up at him. The man is absurdly tall, like needs-his-own-zip-code tall.

"Your current system wastes water," he says, gesturing toward the chaotic tangle of hoses and sprinklers I've pieced together over the years. "You're losing pressure at the far end of the field. Distribution's uneven."

I cross my arms, defensive despite myself. "It gets the job done."

"Does it though?" Hudson asks, one brow lifting as he eyes the browning edges of the farthest beds.

"I was going to get to those," I mutter, embarrassed he noticed. He's right, of course. I've known for ages that the western field struggles, but between raising twins alone and keeping the rest of the farm afloat, something always had to give. And this was it.

"Let me show you what we've designed," Levi says, stepping forward. He unrolls the papers across the hood of their truck, and my breath catches. It's my farm—mapped, measured, and color-coded with almost surgical precision. Each bed labeled, every inch accounted for.

"You made this?" I ask, genuinely stunned.

"Leo's design, my drafting," Levi explains, his fingertip gliding along one of the carefully inked lines. "He's been refining this concept for a while."

"A while? How long is 'a while'?"

Leo shifts, rubbing the back of his neck. "Couple months."

"Six months, give or take," Hudson adds with that mischievous grin, earning a sharp glare from Leo. "He started sketching after that drought last fall. I've been collecting parts since then. Levi finished the schematics last week."

Six months. That's how long they've been thinking about this.

About me. Six months ago, I barely managed polite conversation when I passed them in town. And all this time, they've been quietly building a way to save my fields.

"Why?" The word slips out before I can stop it.

Leo looks at me then and the world narrows to that single, steady gaze. "Because we saw you struggling," he says, his voice low and certain. "And we wanted to help."

Holy flaming flamingos. The way he says it hits somewhere deep and fragile, like he's touched a nerve I didn't even know was exposed. Somehow, those words feel more intimate than if he'd backed me against the truck and kissed me breathless.

I swallow hard, my throat suddenly dry. "Well," I manage, clearing it. "Thank you."

Leo nods once, the moment folding neatly back into practicality. He turns to the plans, tracing a thick blue line with his finger. "The main line runs here. Secondary branches to each section. Adjustable valves for flow control depending on plant needs."

As he walks me through the design, I realize just how closely they've studied my farm. They know which beds run dry fastest, which stay soggy after a storm, which experimental plots need the most care. Every line, every valve, every measured distance has purpose. It's not just efficient, it's personal. Like they've memorized my land the way I have.

"This is... impressive," I admit, and the corner of Leo's mouth twitches in what might almost be a smile.

I could swear he murmurs, "That's not the only thing that's impressive," under his breath as he rolls up the plans. Before I can ask if I imagined it, he's already moving. "Hudson, start marking the lines. Levi, give me a hand with the trencher."

The next few hours blur into motion and sunlight and far too many opportunities to embarrass myself. I dig where the machine can't reach, fit connectors, and pretend not to notice how Leo's shirt clings to his back, or how Hudson's forearms flex when he tightens a valve, or how Levi's curls catch the breeze like he's filming a cologne commercial. It's like working inside an aggressively attractive HGTV episode. If they aired this, they'd call it Hot Men and Their Pipes, and I'd personally fund the reruns.

By the time the sun hits its peak, I stand too fast and the world lurches sideways. The ground seems to tilt, and before I can recover, Leo's hand is firm on my elbow, steadying me.

"When did you last drink water?" His voice is low, concerned.

I blink, trying to remember. Coffee counts as hydration, right?

"That's what I thought." He doesn't wait for an answer, just guides me toward the shade of an apple tree. "Sit."

His tone leaves no room for argument. It should annoy me. I'm perfectly capable of getting myself some water, but instead I'm lowering myself to the grass before I've even thought about it.

Leo pulls a water bottle from his back pocket, unscrews the cap, and holds it out. "Drink. All of it."

Our fingers brush as I take it, and the jolt that shoots up my arm nearly makes me drop the bottle. Emotion flickers in his eyes, a flash of awareness, and for a heartbeat we both go completely still.

"I'm fine," I say, voice a little too thin. "Just stood up too fast."

"You're dehydrated," he replies, crossing his arms. "And you didn't eat breakfast."

I blink at him. "How do you even know that?"

"Your hands were shaking when we got here," he says evenly. "Low blood sugar. And you keep licking your lips. Dehydration."

"What are you, the Sherlock Holmes of bodily functions?" I mutter.

He tilts his head, and the faintest smile ghosts across his face. "Drink," he says again, gentler this time.

I take a long sip, then another, suddenly aware of how dry my throat is. His eyes track the movement as I swallow, and something in his expression tightens, something that has nothing to do with dehydration.

Hudson and Levi join us under the tree, bickering good-naturedly about pipe fittings and water pressure. The sound of their laughter filters through the leaves, grounding me just enough that I almost miss what Leo says next.

"Good girl," he murmurs when I finish the last drop of water.

Oh.

Those two words hit me like a spark to dry tinder. Awareness rushes low and deep, pooling where it has absolutely no business pooling. The tone, dark honey and quiet command, slides under my skin and short-circuits my brain. I've spent years craving that particular mix of gentleness and authority, and I didn't even know it until now.

"Better?" he asks, voice low, eyes steady on mine.

I realize I haven't answered, haven't moved, haven't done anything except stare at him and drink his water like he just rewired my nervous system.

"Yes." The word escapes on a breath. I hand the bottle back, carefully avoiding his fingers. "Thank you."

He nods once, turning toward the others. "Lunch break."

"Thank god," Hudson groans, tossing his hat onto the grass. "I was about to start gnawing on the PVC pipes."

"I brought sandwiches," Levi says, heading for the truck. "And some of those lemon cookies Leo made yesterday."

"You brought lunch?" I ask, blinking. "For me too?"

"We always bring food when we won't be home for a meal," Leo replies, like it's the most obvious thing in the world.

"You live next door," I point out, still trying to catch up.

"Leo's a control freak about food," Hudson stage-whispers, earning a light kick from Leo's boot. "He doesn't trust us to feed ourselves. If it were up to me, I'd live on cereal and spite."

"Says the man who once ate nothing but cereal for three days," Leo shoots back, his tone dry but threaded with affection. Then his gaze flicks to me. "Stop panicking. We brought some for you too."

"You didn't need—"

He raises one eyebrow, and I snap my mouth shut before he even has to answer.

Levi returns with a large cooler, which he sets down in the shade. The picnic he unpacks is anything but simple—thick sandwiches on homemade bread, a colorful salad with nuts and berries, containers of fresh fruit, and those promised lemon cookies that look absolutely delicious.

"Is this... normal for you?" I ask as we all settle in with our food. "The cooking, I mean."

Hudson chuckles around a mouthful of sandwich. "Leo stress-cooks," he explains after swallowing. "Levi stress-writes. I stress-build things. Better than therapy, according to our old neighbor Mrs. Flemming."

"But you said you hadn't had a home-cooked meal in a while."

"We were just teasing Leo," Hudson says around a mouthful of sandwich, "but I will say it's different eating a homemade meal at your kitchen table with Daniel and Lorelai. It feels more like a home than our house ever has."

Something in my chest tugs at that, but before I can reply, he's off, animatedly recounting the time he installed an irrigation system on Leo's old ranch that ended with a prized bull parading through the pasture with part of a sprinkler stuck to its horn. Levi laughs so hard he nearly chokes on a cookie, and even Leo's mouth betrays him with the faintest twitch of amusement.

When lunch is over and we start cleaning up, Leo glances at his watch. "We should be able to finish before the twins get home. Main lines are in. Just need to connect the secondaries and test pressure."

The afternoon slips by in an easy rhythm, the sound of running water and soft laughter threading through the heat. It takes shape with startling speed—pipes linking, valves aligning, the chaos of my old setup transforming into a steady, dependable system. For once, the farm feels manageable.

I'm crouched over a secondary line, tightening a fitting, when Leo moves beside me. He lowers himself with that unhurried grace that seems completely at odds with his size, and suddenly he's close enough that I can feel the warmth radiating off him. The scent of leather, sun, and clean sweat hits me all at once, and my fingers slip on the connector.

"Here," he says quietly, reaching out. "Let me show you."

Before I can protest, his hands settle over mine, big and steady and callused. He adjusts my grip, guiding my fingers along the joint until the pieces snap together with a satisfying click.

"Like that," he murmurs, his breath brushing the hair near my ear. "Firm, but not too hard."

I'm fairly certain we've stopped talking about pipes. Desire curls through me, and for a second I forget what air is.

"I think I've got it," I say, my voice catching just a little, betraying more than I want it to.

He doesn't move away immediately. His hands linger for a beat, the air between us thick with unspoken words, before he finally pulls back. "You learn quickly," he says, his voice low enough to make my pulse trip over itself.

When he stands, the warmth he left behind disappears too fast, leaving the air feeling colder than it should. I turn back to the next connection, pretending not to notice the slight tremor in my fingers or the weight of his shadow lingering over me.

Across the field, Hudson and Levi work shoulder to shoulder. Hudson says something that makes Levi laugh, a full, unguarded sound that carries through the still air and catches at a soft place inside me. When I glance at Leo, I see that same sound reflected on his face, quiet pride, deep affection, a tenderness so raw it feels too intimate to witness. I look away before he can see me watching.

By two thirty, we're ready for testing. We gather at the main control panel, moving with the kind of wordless rhythm that comes from hours of shared work.

"It's ready," Leo says at last, straightening from his inspection. His gaze finds mine. "Would you like to do the honors?"

I step forward, keenly aware of three pairs of eyes tracking my every move. Leo is just behind my shoulder, a solid, grounding presence. Hudson shifts restlessly beside him, energy sparking off him like static. Levi watches in silence, his gaze so focused it feels like the brush of fingertips against my skin.

I take a breath and turn the valve. Water rushes through the lines with a low hiss, pressure building in the buried network. For a heartbeat, none of us move. Then the sprinklers sputter to life, spinning in perfect rhythm, flinging droplets that catch the sunlight and drift across the field like a fine, glittering rain.

It's mesmerizing—the soft percussion of water meeting soil, the shimmer of mist hanging in the air, the scent of earth coming alive again.

A small, disbelieving laugh bubbles up. "It works!"

Hudson grins. "Of course it works! We're basically the Avengers of irrigation. Pipes, pressure, precision—saving farms one sprinkler at a time."

"What do you think?" Leo asks quietly, stepping up beside me.

"It's perfect," I breathe, my throat tight. "I don't even know how to thank you."

"You can thank us by coming to dinner tonight," he says, voice low enough that only I can hear. "We're looking forward to it."

There's a flicker in his tone, a softness and uncertainty beneath the command, and it hits me square in the chest. As if he thought I might still back out.

"We'll be there," I promise, and I mean it.

A part of him loosens, subtle but unmistakable, like tension finally giving way. "Good," he says, the single word carrying more warmth than a full paragraph could.

We walk toward the truck together, our strides falling into an easy rhythm. The afternoon air is soft and sun-warmed, the scent of hay and earth rising around us. I steady a box while Leo lifts it into the bed, our hands brushing briefly before he moves to secure the load.

"Six o'clock," he reminds me as he closes the tailgate. "Don't bring anything. We've got it covered."

"Yes, sir," I tease, and his sharp look sends an unexpected shiver through me.

"I mean it, Lorna," he says quietly. "Let someone else carry the load for once."

Something in his tone catches me off guard. The quiet understanding there, the way he sees me, really sees me, leaves me momentarily breathless. I nod.

When their truck finally rolls down the drive, the sound of gravel crunching beneath the tires fades into the steady rhythm of my new irrigation system. I check my watch. Just enough time to shower before the twins get home.

I stand there for a moment, surrounded by the soft hiss of water and the lingering warmth of their presence, wondering when exactly I stopped being in control of this situation.

Or if I ever was.

"It's a CASTLE!" Lorelai shrieks as we pull into the gravel drive of our neighbors' farmhouse, her voice echoing inside the ancient Volvo. Excitement vibrates through her small body, barely contained by the seatbelt.

"It's a farmhouse," Daniel corrects, his tone that of a weary professor addressing a particularly fanciful student. "Castles have moats and towers."

"It could have a secret tower," Lorelai insists, nose smashed against the glass like she might merge with the view. "And a dungeon with a dragon!"

"Dragons aren't real," Daniel sighs, but his gaze lingers on the tall stone chimney, betraying a flicker of doubt.

I can't fault her for the dramatics. The farmhouse does look a little enchanted—two stories of weathered stone with broad windows, a slate roof, and gardens that spill into the open fields beyond. It's sturdy, timeless, and touched with quiet beauty. Probably nothing like the ranch they left behind in Australia, but somehow it fits them perfectly.

"Best behavior, both of you," I warn as I park beside their familiar truck. "No running, no touching anything without permission, and absolutely no negotiations for a pet dragon."

"What if they offer?" Lorelai asks, all earnest innocence and deadly logic.

"Then we'll discuss it," I say solemnly. "After we consult a certified dragonologist and confirm our fire insurance covers scorch marks."

We don't make it halfway up the path before the front door swings open. Hudson stands there with a wooden spoon in one hand and a dish towel slung over his shoulder. My ovaries, unhelpfully, decide to stand and applaud.

"Welcome to the Australian Embassy!" Hudson calls as we reach the porch. "Passports, please."

Lorelai collapses into giggles. "We don't have passports, Mr. Hudson!"

"No passports?" He gasps in mock outrage. "Well then, I suppose I'll have to take payment in hugs, if that's acceptable, of course."

Lorelai nods solemnly, granting permission like a tiny diplomat before launching herself into his open arms with enough force to nearly knock him over. Hudson laughs, catching her easily and spinning once before setting her back on her feet.

Daniel hovers behind me, hesitant as always, but Hudson extends one arm without a word. My son studies him for a beat, then steps in for a quick, awkward hug that still manages to be heartbreakingly sincere.

"Mr. Levi's in the library," Hudson tells him, lowering his voice like he's sharing state secrets. "Said something about a special rock book he's been saving for you."

Daniel's eyes go wide, his usual reserve cracking.

"And Mr. Leo?" I ask, trying for casual and landing somewhere closer to breathless.

"Out back, checking the grill," Hudson says, straightening to his full height. There's laughter tucked into his voice. "He's been fussing over that meal since you said yes. You'd think the Queen was coming to dinner."

Heat climbs up my neck. "I'm sure he'd do the same for anyone."

Hudson's grin deepens, dimple flashing. "Funny, the McCauleys came last month and got shepherd's pie."

Before I can think of a reply that doesn't sound embarrassingly flattered, Levi appears behind him, a leather-bound book tucked under one arm.

"I thought I heard voices," he says in that quiet way of his. "Welcome, Lorna. Daniel, Lorelai." His gaze lands on my son. "I found something you might like—a field guide to Scottish minerals with real samples in the pages."

Daniel's face lights up like sunrise. "Real rocks? In a book?"

"Twenty-four specimens," Levi says, stepping aside to usher us in. "My grandfather gave it to me when I was your age."

"Can I see it?" Daniel asks, looking up at me.

"Of course," I say, my chest tightening a little. "Just be gentle with it."

As we step inside, the farmhouse feels instantly alive, warm, grounded, and unmistakably theirs. The entryway opens into a wide, sunlit living space with exposed beams and polished wood floors that creak in welcome. To the right, a kitchen gleams with hanging copper pots and a butcher-block island big enough to host a holiday meal. To the left, floor-to-ceiling bookshelves flank a stone fireplace where a fire crackles, the scent of woodsmoke curling through the air.

It's the smaller things that catch me, though, the fingerprints of three men sharing one life. Leo's touch is everywhere in the solid craftsmanship—the well-oiled hinges, the precise order of the spice rack. Levi's influence softens it, found in the stacks of books, the wildflowers arranged in hand-thrown pottery, the quiet grace of a man who notices beauty in small places. And then there's Hudson. His energy spills over every surface, from the mis-matched throw pillows to the carved wooden kangaroo on the mantel to the mis-matched handmade furniture. It shouldn't work, this clash of order and chaos, intellect and whimsy. But somehow it does.

"Let me give you the grand tour," Hudson says, gesturing dramatically as he strides deeper into the house. "Levi can take Daniel to the library, and Lorelai might want to check out the surprise in the sunroom."

"Surprise?" Lorelai's head whips toward him so fast I half expect to hear something snap. "What surprise?"

Hudson grins down at her, all mischief and charm. "Can't tell you. That's what makes it a surprise."

She practically vibrates in place, eyes bright as stars. "Can I go see it, Mummy? Please?"

"Of course, but remember—"

"Best behavior, no running, no dragon requests," she recites automatically, already inching toward the sunroom. "Got it."

"I'll keep an eye on her," Hudson assures me, following after her with the patience of a saint. "The surprise isn't breakable, edible, or capable of setting anything on fire."

"That's... oddly specific," I say, not entirely reassured.

"Previous experience," Levi murmurs, a faint smile curving his mouth. "We learned early on that Hudson's surprises require boundaries."

As Hudson and Lorelai vanish into the sunroom (her squeal of delight moments later confirming the surprise is a success), Levi gestures toward a doorway on the far side of the living room.

"The library's this way, if Daniel would like to see the rock book."

My son nods eagerly, his usual reserve giving way to bright curiosity. I trail after them, curious myself to see the space that's captured his attention so completely.

The moment I step inside, my breath catches. Shelves stretch from floor to ceiling, filled with books in every shape and color. The far wall is nothing but windows overlooking a small, tidy garden, sunlight spilling across the worn leather chair by a reading lamp. A small table nearby holds a precarious stack of half-read books and a mug ring that suggests long hours spent here. But it's the details that make it feel alive—pressed flowers marking pages, scraps of handwritten notes tucked between covers, and smooth crystals and curious stones arranged among the volumes like quiet companions.

"This is beautiful," I say, meaning it. Daniel climbs onto the window seat Levi points out, already leaning in to inspect the illustrations.

"My sanctuary," Levi admits, lowering himself beside him with the heavy rock book in his lap. "Though I'm happy to share it."

The softness in his tone, the open ease in his expression, hits me square in the chest. This is clearly his most private space, and he's letting us in without hesitation.

"I'll leave you boys to your rocks," I say, hoping my voice doesn't give away the emotion tightening my throat. "I should probably check on Leo. I mean, dinner. The grill. You know."

Smooth, Lorna. Real smooth. Why not announce, 'I'm off to ogle the hot, grumpy one,' and be done with it?

Levi's smile says he's heard the subtext loud and clear, but he only nods. "The door to the back garden's through the kitchen."

I follow the sound of clattering dishes and quiet music, tracing my way back toward the kitchen. More details catch my eye as I pass—a hand-drawn map of the farm in a simple frame, botanical prints that have Levi written all over them, a coat rack carved from wood into the shape of a tree. Every inch of this house feels intentional and personal, built to be loved.

My own farmhouse is nothing like this. Functional. Efficient. A space designed for survival, not comfort.

The kitchen is another world entirely, a chef's dream of gleaming surfaces and practical elegance. Countertops stretch wide and generous, and a commercial-grade range dominates one wall. But it's not the equipment that gets me. It's the warmth. The open cookbook with splattered, curling pages. The mismatched mugs hanging beneath a cabinet. The child's drawing pinned proudly to the fridge—Lorelai's unmistakable fairy village, complete with glittery wings and flowers taller than houses.

When had she given them that? And why does seeing it there, casual and cherished, make my throat ache?

I push open the back door before the feeling can take root. The patio unfolds before me, stone and wood and soft twilight. String lights crisscross overhead, unlit for now but waiting, promising warmth when night settles in. A wide stone firepit anchors the far end, ringed with Adirondack chairs, and beyond that, the faint outline of gardens and sheds disappearing into shadow.

And then there's Leo.

Standing at the grill like it's an altar, his focus absolute. The low flicker of flame paints his profile in amber light. His dark henley pulls across broad shoulders and tapers down a back that looks far too tempting. His jeans fit in a way that could make a nun reconsider her vows.

I tell myself I'm just admiring his technique, but my mouth goes dry anyway.

"Need help?" I ask, stepping forward.

Leo turns at the sound of my voice. For a heartbeat, a raw emotion flickers across his face, unguarded, almost vulnerable, before the practiced calm returns. "Hello, Lorna."

"Thank you for having us," I say, suddenly aware of how quiet it is out here. "The twins are beside themselves with excitement."

"We've been looking forward to it too." He gestures toward the grill. "Dinner's nearly ready. Another twenty minutes."

I move closer, drawn by the scent of searing meat and herbs. The grill is covered with thick, perfectly marbled steaks and a tray of vegetables glistening with olive oil. "Smells incredible."

"Grass-fed from our own herd," he says, a thread of pride winding through his voice.

"You raised this?" I ask, both impressed and a little intimidated by the scale of their self-sufficiency.

He nods. "We try to produce as much of our own food as possible. Keeps us connected to what we eat."

"I'm the same with vegetables," I admit. "Though much smaller scale. Just enough for the twins and me."

Leo shakes his head, a faint smile tugging at his mouth. "What you do isn't small, Lorna." He adjusts the heat with quiet confidence, his focus so steady it's almost hypnotic. "You're raising twins and running a whole flower farm on your own. That's no minor accomplishment."

The way he says it, steady and matter-of-fact, without even a hint of condescension, knocks a fragile piece loose inside me.

"It's just what needs doing," I say, my instinctive deflection falling flat.

"Doesn't make it any less remarkable." He lowers the grill cover and turns to face me fully. "Your twins are thriving. Your dahlias are earning national attention. You've built something extraordinary, Lorna."

His gaze is steady, almost too much. Beneath it lingers an intensity that hums in the quiet space between us, impossible to ignore.

"I should check on the twins," I blurt, stepping back as if distance might cool the air. "Make sure Lorelai hasn't talked Hudson into building her a fairy mansion that won't fit in our living room."

Leo's mouth twitches, the faintest shadow of a smile. "Too late for that. Plans are already underway."

"You're kidding."

"Hudson's workshop is full of tiny furniture prototypes," he says, and this time his grin is unmistakable. "He's very concerned about proper fairy housing regulations."

"Of course he is." I laugh under my breath, picturing the big Australian man hunched over doll-sized chairs and beds. "You spoil her."

"We spoil them both," Leo corrects gently. "Daniel's getting a custom rack for his rock collection. Levi's designing labels."

"You don't have to do all that," I say, though my voice wavers.

"We want to," Leo says simply. "If it matters to them, it matters to us."

God, those words again. Caring, for them, isn't a performance; it's second nature. And I can feel myself yielding to it, my walls softening one quiet, unguarded moment at a time.

A burst of laughter from inside saves me. Leo tilts his head toward the sound. "We should probably check on that. Hudson's surprises have a history of... escalation."

Inside, the sunroom looks like a fairy-tale construction site. Chairs have been dragged across the floor, sheets draped into peaks and valleys, and strings of fairy lights twinkle across what might be the world's most elaborate blanket fort.

"Mr. Hudson says we can eat dinner in here and then watch a movie!" Lorelai announces, her head popping out of the fort's entrance like a prairie dog on reconnaissance. "It has special cushions and everything!"

I glance at Leo, unsure if this chaos in his pristine home is really okay with him.

"We thought the kids might like a picnic dinner," he explains easily. "We'll eat on the patio. If that's all right with you."

The thought of adult conversation without cutting anyone's meat or wiping up spilled milk feels like a luxury I didn't even know I missed.

"That would be lovely," I say, trying not to sound too eager. "As long as I can keep an eye on them."

"The sunroom doors open right onto the patio," Leo assures me. "They'll be in full view."

Levi appears then, balancing a tray of drinks that look straight out of a craft cocktail bar. "Thought we might enjoy these while dinner finishes," he says, handing me a glass of amber liquid dotted with sprigs of green.

"What is it?" I ask, taking it carefully.

"Whisky sour," he says. "Honey from our bees. Thyme from the garden."

I take a sip and nearly groan. The balance is perfect—sweet, tart, a little wild from the herbs. Warmth unfurls down my throat. "This is incredible."

"Levi's our resident mixologist," Hudson calls, ducking out of the fort with a grin. "Best cocktails this side of Edinburgh."

"Hidden talents," I murmur, watching Levi hand drinks to the others.

"You should see what else those hands can do," Hudson adds, waggling his brows.

Leo chokes on his drink, coughing into his fist, while Hudson adopts an expression of mock innocence. "I meant his pottery, obviously. Mind out of the gutter, Lorna."

The flush that spreads up my neck has nothing to do with the whisky. My mind is already in the gutter, stretching out on a chaise lounge with a drink of its own.

"I'd love to see your pottery sometime," I tell Levi, desperate to redirect.

"After dinner," he promises. "My studio's in one of the outbuildings."

"And I'll show you my workshop," Hudson adds. "Where fairy mansions and rock displays are born."

Leo hesitates before speaking. "And I suppose I can show you the leather shop."

"I'd like that," I say softly, and I mean it.

A trace of tension eases in his face, a small, quiet release that makes my chest tighten. It matters to him, being seen.

"Dinner should be ready in fifteen," Leo says, setting his glass aside. "I'll plate the twins' meals first."

Working beside Leo in his kitchen feels more intimate than it should. He moves with quiet precision, slicing the steak into perfect bite-sized pieces, arranging the vegetables in neat little rainbows. I fall into step beside him, filling no-spill cups with his homemade lemonade, pretending this isn't the most domestic I've felt in years.

"You're good at this," I say, watching as he turns carrot sticks into a crooked smiley face that'll absolutely charm Daniel into eating his veggies.

"I've had practice." His tone is mild, but there's something soft beneath it. "My sister has four kids. I cook when I visit."

Another small glimpse into his life before Scotland, one more puzzle piece I can't stop collecting. Each one gleams with quiet weight, revealing a man who feels more solid, more real, the closer I look.

Hudson bursts through the doorway, grinning like a kid himself. "Fort is officially open for dinner service!" he declares, as if announcing a Michelin-starred event. "Also, projector's up for How to Train Your Dragon."

"You put a projector in the fort?" I ask, half laughing, half impressed.

"Only the best for the twins," he says with a wink. "Besides, we've been dying for an excuse to use it."

With the twins tucked into their blanket fort, plates balanced on their knees and eyes glued to dragons breathing fire across the sheeted walls, the four of us carry our dinners to the patio. The evening air has cooled, threaded with woodsmoke and the faint sweetness of cut grass. Leo lights the firepit, and soon the flames are dancing, wrapping the patio in warmth and golden light.

I sink into one of the Adirondack chairs, my plate warm in my lap. The first bite stops me cold. The steak melts against my tongue, perfectly seared and seasoned. The vegetables taste like summer distilled—earthy, sweet, touched with fire. Even the bread, golden and soft, seems impossibly fresh.

"This is incredible," I admit, half in disbelief. "Where did you learn to cook like this?"

"My mother," Leo says, eyes softening as if the firelight has reached some far corner of him. "She thought feeding people was a kind of love. Said everyone should know how to feed themselves properly."

"Smart woman," I say, tearing off another piece of bread. "My mom's philosophy was takeout and frozen pizza. Preferably in that order."

"What about your dad?" Levi asks, settling into the chair beside me, his posture easy but his gaze attentive.

I laugh. "Hopeless. He tried to make pancakes for my birthday once and nearly burned the kitchen down. After that, he stuck to dinner reservations. His specialty was scrolling through delivery apps."

"Your children are lucky," Leo says quietly, not looking away from the fire. "You're teaching them self-sufficiency. And joy."

The comment catches me off guard. I take a sip of my drink to steady myself. "Thank you," I murmur. "I try."

"Try?" Hudson leans forward, grinning. "You're raising tiny geniuses. Daniel explained photosynthesis to me today like he was lecturing at a university."

"And Lorelai's fairy stories," Levi adds, smiling. "She builds entire worlds. Characters, conflicts, endings. She's a born storyteller."

"They're pretty special," I say softly, pride filling my chest like sunlight.

Leo's gaze meets mine across the firepit. "Wonder where they get that from."

Something secret part of me stirs. The night hums around us, the fire crackles, and I know he means more than neighbors. More than friends.

The conversation flows easily after that, stories spinning out like sparks from the fire. Hudson keeps everyone laughing with tales from Leo's ranch in Australia, like the time an escaped cow wandered into the local schoolyard and refused to leave until bribed with cafeteria sandwiches. Levi's stories are quieter, threaded with warmth, about growing up alongside a twin who saw the world in a completely different way. And Leo offers brief but piercing glimpses of his own past, a childhood spent moving from place to place, the ranch he built from nothing, the fire that took it all.

As the sky deepens to indigo, stars pierce through the darkness, brilliant and sharp in the country air. The fire crackles, throwing shadows that dance across Leo's face. From the sunroom, I can hear the muffled hum of a movie and the occasional shriek of laughter from the twins.

"Wine?" Leo asks, already handing me a glass before I can answer.

"Trying to get me drunk, Robinson?" The words slip out, teasing and reckless. It's strange and wonderful, remembering what it feels like to flirt, like using a muscle I thought had atrophied.

"If that were my goal, I'd have let Levi make you one of his blackberry mojitos," Leo says, a flicker of humor softening his voice. "Two of those and you'd be dancing on the table."

"Bold of you to assume I need alcohol for table dancing," I shoot back, grinning. The fire's warmth, the good food, and the wine have all worked their magic. "I'll have you know I was the table-dancing champion of Edinburgh University, 2005 through 2008."

Hudson nearly chokes on his drink. "Now that's a story I need to hear."

"Absolutely not," I say, laughing. "Some things are better left in the dark corners of university bars."

"I'll trade you," Hudson says, eyes glinting with mischief. "My most embarrassing story for yours."

"Don't encourage him," Leo warns, though there's amusement under the gruffness. "He's been looking for an excuse to tell that one again."

"Now I have to hear it," I insist, curling my legs beneath me. "Spill it, Hudson."

He grins like a man about to commit a crime. "Picture this. Important cattle buyers on the ranch. Me, trying to impress Leo by handling the new stallion, which, in hindsight, was roughly equivalent to trying to impress a lifeguard by juggling sharks."

"Oh, this is going to be good," I murmur.

"Good isn't the word," Levi says, smiling into his glass. "Catastrophic is closer."

Hudson presses on. "So I saddle him up and climb on, expecting this cinematic gallop into the sunset. Except..."

"The horse doesn't move," Levi supplies, clearly familiar with the story. "Just stares at him like he's offended."

"Exactly!" Hudson says, delighted. "And before I can figure out what's wrong, while the buyers are watching, mind you, the horse lies down. Just... folds his legs and takes a nap with me still on top of him."

I laugh so hard my stomach hurts. "No!"

"Oh yes. Full sprawl. Dust cloud. Me sliding off like an idiot. Everyone watching. I wanted the earth to swallow me."

"And what did you do?" I ask Leo, wiping tears from my eyes.

"Walked over, told the horse to get up," Leo says simply, his tone betraying the faintest smile.

Hudson groans. "Whispered something in his ear and boom, up he goes, like magic. Made me look like a total fool."

"Because you were being one," Leo says, voice even. "That horse was trained to respond to certain commands. You didn't know them."

"You could've told me," Hudson complains.

"Then you wouldn't have learned," Leo replies, quiet but firm.

A current passes between them then, a flicker of old trust, the kind that only comes from years of shared work and stubborn loyalty. The kind that feels like home, even from across the fire.

I study them in the firelight, watching the way they tease each other, casual and unguarded, a shorthand born from years of shared history. There's a rhythm to their banter, a kind of wordless fluency that feels older than friendship. Maybe even older than family. Whatever they've lived through together, it's written in every inside joke, every easy smile.

"Your turn," Hudson says, breaking into my thoughts. "Table-dancing story. Fair's fair."

I take a long, bracing sip of wine. "Fine. But this does not leave this firepit."

Three solemn nods. Hudson's expression ruins the effect, mischief practically vibrating off him.

"Second year of university," I start, feeling a flush rise in my cheeks before I've even begun. "End-of-term party. I'd been buried in finals prep for two straight weeks. No sleep. Living on caffeine and self-loathing, and my roommate decided I needed to 'blow off steam.' Her definition of that involved cheap tequila and bad decisions."

"Already promising," Hudson says, grinning.

"So we go to this pub where they have this tradition—if it's your birthday, you stand on the table while everyone sings to you. My roommate, bless her chaotic heart, tells the bartender it's mine. Then she announces I'm a professional dancer who's only shy when sober."

"But it wasn't your birthday," Levi guesses, a smile ghosting across his lips.

"Not even close," I say. "December party, July birthday. But I was too tired and too drunk to argue, so up I went. In heels."

Hudson leans forward. "And then?"

"And then I learned I'm surprisingly coordinated in tight spaces," I admit. "The crowd went wild, the bartender rewarded me with endless free drinks, and before I knew it, it became a thing. People would challenge me to dance on anything flat enough to balance on. Tables, bars, once even a grand piano at a faculty event. Let's just say the Dean of Music still crosses the street when he sees me."

Hudson whistles low. "Lorna MacLeod, table-dancing legend. Who'd have thought our prim, elegant flower farmer had a scandalous past? The quiet ones always do."

"Not quiet enough," I laugh. "They banned me after the piano. My photo's probably still behind the bar. 'Do not serve this woman. Will dance on furniture.'"

Levi chuckles, the sound soft and low. "I would've paid good money to see that."

His eyes meet mine, steady and dark, and something in the air shifts. The laughter fades, replaced by a pulse of awareness that hums beneath the crackle of the fire.

"Maybe someday I'll give a command performance," I say lightly. "After sufficient wine and total darkness. And a signed liability waiver."

"I'd settle for regular dancing," Hudson says suddenly, pushing to his feet. "Music! We need music."

Before anyone can protest, he's gone, returning moments later with a speaker. The soft strum of acoustic guitar drifts into the night, blending with the fire's quiet rhythm.

For a moment, no one speaks. The night holds its breath, wine-warm and firelit, alive with the quiet ache of possibility.

"Dance with me, Lorna," Hudson says, extending a hand. "No tables required."

I hesitate, glancing toward Leo and Levi. Neither looks opposed to the invitation, though a flicker passes through Leo's eyes.

"Go ahead," Leo says. "Hudson's insufferable when he doesn't get his way."

"Completely unbearable," Levi adds, a faint smile tugging at his mouth. "Best to humor him."

I set my wineglass down and slide my hand into Hudson's. His fingers curl around mine, rough and warm, the calluses catching slightly on my skin, a reminder of all the hours he spends shaping things with those hands. The touch sends a jolt through me, electric and low, and before I can protest, he's pulling me to my feet. He leads me to a stretch of patio where the firelight spills in soft gold, turning the stones into a makeshift dance floor. The music drifts around us, slow and tender, the kind of song meant for swaying under open skies.

Hudson wraps one hand around my waist, threading the fingers of the other through mine. There's a gentleness in the way he moves me, surprising for a man who looks built to tear down barns with his bare hands. The heat of his palm seeps through the thin fabric of my dress, branding me with warmth until I'm certain the firelight isn't the only thing making me glow.

"See? Much safer than table dancing," he murmurs, his breath brushing my ear, whisky and cedar and summer air.

"Depends on your definition of safe."

He laughs softly, the sound low enough that I feel it in my chest, a pulse under my ribs. "Fair point. Nothing particularly safe about dancing with you, table or no table."

Something in his tone slips past my guard. There's no practiced charm, no act, only unfiltered honesty and heat. The space between us feels unbearable now. I can feel the restraint in his touch, the way his hand hovers instead of claims, and it makes me ache.

"I don't bite," I murmur, meaning it to sound teasing, but it slips out low and husky instead.

"Pity," he whispers, close enough that the word skims across my skin.

For one reckless heartbeat, I forget we're not alone. My gaze flicks to the firepit. Leo and Levi are still watching us, their expressions darker now. Leo grips the arms of his chair, knuckles white, as if holding himself in place. Levi's face is all tension and quiet want, the firelight painting his cheekbones in gold and shadow, his lips pressed together like he's one breath away from crossing the space between us.

"They don't mind," Hudson says, catching my glance with a knowing half-smile.

"What are you to each other, exactly?" The question burns coming out, unsteady and too honest. "The three of you, I mean. It's an... unusual arrangement."

Hudson's gaze cuts to Leo across the patio, then back to me. "It's complicated. You remember how our mom got sick?"

I nod. He turns me, hand firm at my waist, reeling me in until there's barely a breath between us. Heat bleeds through the thin fabric of my dress, his hand, his chest, his thighs brushing mine with every sway. I can feel a pulse pounding between us, but I can't tell if it's his or mine.

"Leo had excellent private insurance," Hudson says, voice dropping low. "He married her so she could get the best treatment."

"He married your mother." The words barely make it past my throat. "For insurance?"

He nods. "They were close, but it was never romantic. Leo and

I... had something before that. It ended the day he told me he was going to marry her. It wouldn't have been right to keep going."

My lungs feel too tight. "And her cancer?"

"Went into remission for a while." A raw edge cracks through his voice. "Then we lost her anyway. House fire. Middle of the night. She was alone."

The grief hits me like cold water. "Hudson, I'm so sorry."

His smile is small, crooked, barely holding together. "After that, we couldn't stay. Too many ghosts. So we sold the ranch, pooled what we had, and ended up here. Next door to a pretty flower farmer with two kids who build blanket forts and think I'm a super-hero." The grin tries to catch, but the sadness is still there, threaded through every word. "And here we are."

The music shifts to a faster tempo, sultry, the kind of rhythm you feel in your hips. I'm still finding the beat when the air goes electric. Charged. Different.

Levi steps into the firelight so quietly I don't know he's there until his presence registers like a hand on bare skin.

"May I?" His voice is barely above a murmur, but it races over my skin like wildfire.

Hudson's hands leave me slowly, deliberately. He presses a kiss to my cheek that burns—lips, breath, stubble dragging just enough to make me gasp. "She's all yours," he says to Levi. Then his eyes find mine, hot enough to restart the fire. "For now."

Before I can catch my breath, Levi's hands are on me. The shift makes my head spin. Where Hudson was all heat and easy laugh-ter, Levi is control and coiled intention. His touch is cooler, measured, each point of contact feeling deliberate. Like he's mapping me. Learning me. Deciding what he wants and exactly how he's going to take it.

"You dance beautifully."

He keeps a careful distance, but somehow I still feel wrapped in him. His scent hits me, old books and rain, clean linen dried in cold air. It makes me want to bury my face in his neck and breathe him in.

"Thank you." My voice catches, goes soft. "My mother insisted on lessons. Said every proper Scottish girl should know how to dance at ceilidhs."

"Your mother was smart." He turns me and my skirt flares. Fabric whispers against my bare legs, the lightest friction, and I want more. Want his hands where the cotton is. "Though I imagine you'd move beautifully even without lessons. It's in the way you walk, the way you work in your garden. Natural rhythm."

The compliment seeps into me, intimate and disarming. Levi sees what others don't, small patterns, quiet truths, the things you do when you forget someone might be looking. Like the way I move through my garden. Through my life. When I think I'm unwatched.

"I think that's the nicest compliment I've ever gotten." The music softens, and he pulls me closer until the space between us disappears. His heartbeat presses against mine—slow, steady, certain—while mine thrashes like it's trying to claw its way free.

"Merely truth." His hand settles at the small of my back, fingers spreading wider. His pinky grazes the curve of my ass, light enough it could almost be accidental, except for the way his eyes meet mine.

My heart flips in my chest. "You notice a lot."

"Only when it comes to you." His voice drops, resonates in my ribs like a low note held too long. "You're worth noticing."

The shiver that runs through me has nothing to do with the night air. His thumb starts tracing circles above my hip, slow, methodical, winding something tight and hot inside me with each rotation. To be seen like this, not just the mother, not just the farmer, but me, all the parts I thought I'd hidden away, it's like oxygen after holding my breath for years.

"Thank you." The words feel small, insufficient.

Levi's hand tightens at my waist. A soft sound escapes me and I can't disguise it as anything but what it is.

"No thanks needed." His voice is rough velvet.

The melody shifts, a softer tune now, haunting and sweet,

echoing under the starlight. I'm lost in Levi's orbit, drunk on his quiet intensity, so I don't see Leo approach.

But my body knows. Goosebumps rush up my arms. Every hair at the nape of my neck stands on end. My skin registers him before my brain does, like static before lightning.

"May I?" Leo asks, his deep voice rumbling between us like distant thunder, the bass notes of it vibrating in my chest, between my thighs, everywhere.

Levi steps back without hesitation, his fingers trailing along my arm as he releases me, a touch so light yet so deliberate that it leaves a path of tingling awareness in its wake. His eyes meet mine with one last lingering look before he cedes his place.

And then I'm in Leo's arms, and the world tilts on its axis. Where Hudson was playful and Levi graceful, Leo is pure contained power, a force of nature barely harnessed into human form. His hand engulfs mine completely, making me acutely aware of the difference in our sizes, while his other hand spans nearly my entire waist, his thumb easily reaching the bottom of my rib cage. He holds me with quiet confidence, leading without dominating, his large frame moving with surprising elegance. Heat radiates from him like a furnace, his body temperature seemingly higher than normal human levels, burning through my dress until I feel naked against him though layers of fabric separate us.

I'm suddenly, acutely aware that this is the man who married a dying woman to save her life, who put his own desires aside out of principle, who moved across the world to help two grieving sons start over.

"Didn't take you for a dancer," I say, looking up at him. Way up. The man is practically at cloud level.

"I'm full of surprises," Leo replies, the corner of his mouth lifting slightly. "My mother insisted all her kids learn. Said no child of hers would be a wallflower."

"Another wise mother," I observe, relaxing into his lead. "Did you resist?"

"Terribly," Leo admits, executing a perfect turn that somehow brings us closer together, my breasts now pressed against the solid wall of his chest, the friction creating a sweet ache that has me biting the inside of my cheek to stifle a moan. "Until I realized it was actually useful."

"For impressing women?" I tease.

"For understanding bodies," he corrects, his voice dropping lower. "How they move, how they respond, how to read subtle cues."

Oh. Sweet merciful macaroni. My pulse quickens at the implications of his words, blood rushing in my ears, spreading through my chest and climbing up my neck to stain my cheeks. My body responds traitorously, nipples tightening against the thin fabric of my dress, thighs clenching against a sudden rush of wetness.

"You're good at it," I manage, my voice not quite steady. "The reading part."

"You're easy to read," Leo says, his dark eyes never leaving mine, pupils so dilated they've nearly swallowed the iris completely. His hand slides infinitesimally lower on my back, applying just enough pressure to arch me slightly closer, the movement bringing the juncture of my thighs against the solid muscle of his leg. "When you allow yourself to be."

That's the key, isn't it? I've spent so long guarding myself, building walls to my heart, and my children, safe. But tonight, wrapped in firelight and starlight, with the distant sound of the twins laughter from the sunroom, those walls feel paper-thin.

"And what is my body saying now?" I ask, my heart in my throat.

Leo's hand splays slightly wider, possessive in a way that should alarm me but instead makes a primal, hungry need unfurl deep inside. "That you're curious," he says quietly, his lips so close to my ear that his beard tickles my temple, the sensation sending sparks racing down my neck. "That you're confused but intrigued. That you're fighting attraction because you're afraid of complications."

The accuracy of his assessment steals my breath. "That's... perceptive."

"I also see," he continues, his voice dropping even lower, the sound of it like velvet dragged across bare skin, "that you're wondering why you're drawn to all three of us. Why that confuses and excites you at the same time."

A rush of heat floods my face. Is he reading my mind now? If so, I hope he skipped the explicit parts where I wondered what that beard would feel like against my inner thighs, what those large, capable hands could do given free rein over my body. Nope. Not going there.

"It's all right," he murmurs, his lips hovering above the sensitive skin below my ear. "You're allowed to feel whatever you feel, Lorna. There's no wrong answer here."

The song ends, but neither of us moves to break apart. We stand in the firelight, his arms still around me, my hands still resting on his solid frame, our bodies connected from chest to knee, every point of contact sending electric currents through my nerve endings. I'm acutely aware of my own breathing, shallow and quick, and his, deeper but no less affected. Out of the corner of my eye, I catch Hudson and Levi watching us, not with jealousy but with hunger. There's a charge in their faces, a shared anticipation that sends a shiver through me. It isn't competition I see there. It's intent.

"I should check on the twins," I say suddenly, needing space to process the intensity of the moment, to regain control of my treacherous body before I do something truly reckless, like reaching up to tangle my fingers in Leo's hair and pulling his mouth down to mine.

Leo releases me immediately, stepping back with a small nod. "Of course."

I make my way to the sunroom on slightly unsteady legs, feeling three pairs of eyes on my back as I go. Inside, I find both twins sound asleep in their blanket fort, the movie's end credits still rolling. Daniel is curled protectively around his sister, both of them looking peaceful and completely at home.

The sight centers me, reminding me of what matters most.

Whatever I'm feeling, whatever is happening between me and these three men, my children's well-being has to come first. Always.

I turn back to the patio, where they've resumed their seats around the fire. They look up as I approach, questions in their eyes.

"Both asleep," I report, settling back into my chair. "The movie and all that fresh air knocked them out."

"They can stay the night if you'd like," Leo offers. "The fort is comfortable enough, and we have spare toothbrushes."

The offer is tempting, more time in this peaceful setting, more adult conversation, maybe more dancing under the stars. But I'm not ready for that step, for what it might suggest to my children about my relationship with the neighbors.

"Thank you, but I should get them home to their own beds," I decline gently.

"Of course." Leo nods, his expression open, easy. No hint of disappointment. "At least let us show you around before you head out. The workshops we mentioned?"

"I'd like that," I agree, genuinely curious about these spaces that reflect their individual passions.

We start with Hudson's woodshop, a converted outbuilding awash in honeyed light. The air hums with the scent of sawdust and lemon oil, rich and intoxicating, tugging at a place deep and instinctive inside me. I breathe it in, filling my lungs with that warm, masculine aroma. The space is immaculate despite its purpose. Tools hang in perfect order on pegboards, planks of wood are stacked by type and size, and half-finished projects rest neatly on solid workbenches.

"This is where the magic happens," Hudson says, gesturing around like he's giving a royal tour. "Furniture, carvings, custom commissions. Also where I talk to myself and occasionally lose a fight with a hammer."

I laugh softly, drifting through the shop. My fingertips skim the polished edges of his work, tracing the texture of the grain, the small imperfections that make each piece feel alive. My body still hums from our dance earlier, every nerve alert, every breath a little too shallow. A rocking chair gleams in the corner, its inlay so intricate it looks hand-stitched. Nearby, a set of nesting tables with seamless grain lines that must've taken hours of precision. One bench holds tiny chairs and tables, each one perfect down to the carved legs.

"These are beautiful," I say, lifting a miniature armchair light as a bird, the cushions no bigger than my thumbnail.

"Just prototypes," Hudson says with a shrug that fails to hide his pride. The same satisfaction flickers in his eyes that I saw when I trembled under his hands earlier. "The real versions will be better."

"I can't imagine how," I tell him, setting the tiny chair back with care. "They already look perfect."

Next is Levi's pottery studio, a sanctuary of soft light and quiet breath. Sunlight spills through broad windows, catching on the suspended greenery that drips from the ceiling in gentle arcs. The air is thick with humidity and scent—wet clay, mineral glaze, and threading through it all, the unmistakable trace of ink and paper that clings to Levi like a second skin. It hits me all at once, that this space isn't just where he works. It's where he feels. The room seems to pulse with him, every curve of pottery, every brushstroke, an echo of his rhythm.

Clay-dusted worktables sit beneath the windows, pottery wheels waiting mid-spin, tools scattered with effortless precision. Shelves line the walls, crowded with vessels of every shape and glaze, none of them arranged by size or type, but by an order that feels more instinctive, like memory or mood. It's chaos by design, and somehow it fits him perfectly.

"I started all this as therapy," Levi says quietly, lifting a vase with flowing, wave-like ridges that shimmer under the light. "After our mother died."

"They're beautiful," I say, reaching out to touch the rim of a bowl glazed in oceanic blues and greens. It's cool under my fingertips, impossibly smooth. My mind flickers to his hands as he guided me across the dance floor, and my pulse stumbles. I can almost see those same hands coaxing the clay into shape, patient and unhurried, molding it the way he might touch a body he knows too well.

"I'm still learning," he murmurs. The tone isn't modesty, it's something darker, something that curls low in my stomach. His eyes follow my finger as it traces the bowl's edge, and for a heartbeat, I swear he's picturing my hands somewhere else entirely.

Finally, we reach Leo's leather workshop, and the moment the door opens, it hits me. The scent. Thick, rich, and alive. Leather, oil, wax. It's dark and intoxicating, the kind of smell that goes straight to the bloodstream. My body reacts before I can stop it, warmth unfurling low in my belly. It smells like him. Like control and desire and a need I probably shouldn't crave as much as I do.

The room mirrors its owner, precise, deliberate, every detail considered. Hides hang along one wall, some butter-soft and pliant, others still rough, waiting to be tamed. Tools gleam from their places on the racks, organized with surgical precision. The massive worktable at the center is worn smooth from years of use, yet spotless, commanding the space like a stage.

"This is where all those fancy European orders happen?" I ask, turning in a slow circle.

Leo nods, watching me from the doorway. There's a hesitance to him I haven't seen before, a quiet vulnerability beneath all that strength. His gaze follows me, steady, unblinking, predatory. The air thickens with memory, the ghost of his hand on my back, the solid weight of him pressed close.

A half-finished handbag sits on a nearby table, the leather a soft caramel that glows in the light. "May I?" I ask.

"Go ahead," he says, voice even but tight, the muscle in his jaw ticking.

I pick it up, surprised by its perfect weight. The leather yields under my fingers, supple and warm. I smooth my fingers over it, feeling the grain, and somewhere behind me Leo breathes in sharply.

"This is stunning," I murmur. "No wonder you have clients in

Milan. This makes my Tesco purse look like it was assembled by blind raccoons in a bin."

His mouth twitches, almost a smile. The tension drains from his shoulders, replaced by something quieter, more dangerous. My eyes catch on the way his henley strains across his chest, the flex of muscle as he crosses his arms. My pulse stutters.

"We'll have to fix that," he says, holding my gaze.

The air crackles between us, thick with everything we're not saying. For a moment, neither of us moves. There's only charged silence, the scent of leather, and the slow, dizzy realization that whatever this is, it's already gone too deep.

I drop my gaze, and a belt on the nearby rack catches my attention. It's beautiful, practical, the kind of thing that speaks of hours of careful work. I reach out and trail my fingers along its surface. The leather is warm beneath my touch, supple and alive, almost as if it's breathing with me.

"That one's mine," Leo says, his voice suddenly closer, deeper, rough enough to raise goosebumps along my arms. I hadn't heard him move. Somehow this enormous man is standing behind me, silent as a shadow. Heat rolls off his body, the air around him charged. The scent of him fills the room—leather, spice, and something warm and male that does indecent things between my legs.

"It's beautiful," I whisper, running my fingers over the smooth buckle. His breath stirs the hair at my neck and my heart starts to pound. My skin prickles, aware of every inch between us, every inch that could vanish if he took a single step closer.

He studies me in silence, his eyes flicking from my hand on the belt to my face. The look in them makes a part of me unravel.

"Want to see what it can do?" His voice is barely more than a whisper, low and dangerous.

I should say no. I should smile, step away, remember that I'm a mother, that I'm standing in my neighbor's workshop, that this is the sort of moment I'm supposed to avoid.

"Yes." The word escapes before I can stop it, soft and shaky, closer to a moan than an answer.

Leo moves before I can think. In one smooth, effortless motion, he takes the belt from the rack, steps into my space, and suddenly my wrists are caught above my head, secured to a hook in the beam I hadn't even noticed. The leather is soft against my skin, snug but not painful, the perfect balance of restraint and comfort. My pulse jumps. My breath falters. Then he's there, his chest pressed to mine, his body caging me against the wall, heat and muscle and quiet dominance filling every inch of space.

"I don't know what it is about you," he growls, his mouth hovering beside my ear. He drags his nose along my jaw, breathing me in. The sound he makes is deep and rough, a noise that lights a fire low in my stomach.

Holy hot cinnamon rolls.

I can't breathe. Can't think. Can only feel. The hard lines of his body molded to mine, the rough scrape of his beard against my neck, the scent of leather and skin filling my head. Need builds between us, thick and clinging, every breath steeped in it. My heart hammers so hard I can hear it.

"Six years." The words scrape out of me, barely audible. "It's been six years since anyone touched me."

Leo stills. Then his eyes find mine, darker than I've ever seen them, pupils wide and hungry. "That," he says quietly, "is a tragedy I intend to fix."

His mouth hovers a fraction from mine, the air between us charged enough to combust. I can taste the faint burn of whisky on his breath, feel the heat of his lips without contact. My whole body tightens, nipples straining against my bra, thighs pressed together against a pulse I can't ignore. This is the moment, the edge of it. One more breath, one more second, and there'll be no turning back. No pretending I don't want this. No pretending I haven't already given in.

"Leo?" Hudson's voice cuts through the haze. "You might want to—oh."

He stops in the doorway, and for a second I brace for embarrassment, for teasing, for anything that might pull me fully back to earth. But what I see instead sends a different kind of shiver through me. His expression shifts, hunger replacing surprise. His eyes darken as they travel over me, my arms still bound, my body flush against Leo's.

"Well," he says, voice dropping low. "This is interesting. Don't stop on my account. I'll grab some popcorn."

Leo doesn't move. Doesn't even look away. He only turns his head slightly toward Hudson, my wrists still caught above me, my pulse still pounding against the leather. "Hudson."

"Daniel woke up," Hudson says. "He's asking for his mum."

My stomach twists, heat draining as reality crashes back in. What am I doing? Leo's body still cages mine, Hudson's eyes still on me, and for a dizzy second I feel like I've stepped out of my life completely. I'm a mother, not some fever dream of temptation. A responsible woman with a farm and two kids who depend on me, not a heroine about to lose her mind in a leather workshop.

Leo feels the shift in me instantly. He reaches up and releases the belt, the leather sliding away from my skin in a whisper. The ghost of its pressure remains, a hot, invisible imprint I can still feel when he steps back. His eyes are darker now, pupils blown wide, his breath rough.

"I need to go," I manage, my voice catching. "The twins—"

"They're fine," Hudson says, finally pushing off the doorframe, his tone softer now. "Levi's with them."

I nod, not trusting myself to speak. My body feels electrified, oversensitive, like I've been struck by lightning and survived, every nerve ending awakened and now screaming for attention. My legs are unsteady beneath me, my core still throbbing with unfulfilled desire.

I slip past Hudson, trying not to notice how his eyes darken when he catches my scent, or how his hand twitches at his side as if he's restraining himself from touching me.

Levi looks up when I enter, and in that quiet, knowing way of his, I can tell he doesn't need to ask where I've been. The faint curve of his mouth, the desire in his gaze, it's all the confirmation I need. He knows exactly what was happening in Leo's workshop.

"Mummy!" Lorelai mumbles, reaching for me with the uncoordinated movements of a child half-asleep. "We fell asleep in the fairy castle."

"I see that," I say, grateful for the distraction of motherhood. "Time to go home, sweet pea."

Daniel rubs his eyes, sitting up in the nest of pillows. "Did we miss saying goodbye?"

"No," Levi assures him, helping him find his shoes. "We're all here."

At the door, I pause, Lorelai nearly asleep in Leo's arms, Daniel leaning heavily against my leg. "Thank you for tonight," I say. I mean all of it—the dinner, the laughter, the dancing, the quiet moments that felt like more. Even the workshop. "It was lovely."

"Our pleasure," Leo says, his voice low as he shifts Lorelai carefully into my arms.

"We'll walk you to your car," Levi adds, and the three of them fall in step behind me, Hudson scooping up a half-asleep Daniel without a word. My son doesn't even protest, just sighs and curls against his shoulder.

The night air is cool and fragrant, the moon a bright silver coin hanging low over the hills. Once the twins are settled and buckled into their seats, I turn back to them. Under the moonlight, the three men stand shoulder to shoulder, silent and watchful. Their faces are softened by shadow, their bodies outlined in silver, and for a strange, suspended moment, it feels like stepping out of time.

"Goodnight," I whisper. "And thank you again."

Hudson steps forward first, the sound of gravel crunching under his boots grounding the moment. He leans in, the scent of woodsmoke and soap filling my lungs, and presses a kiss to my cheek. The contact is brief, but it burns. "Sleep well, Lorna," he murmurs, his breath warm against my ear. Goosebumps chase down my spine.

Levi follows, his lips brushing my other cheek, lingering long enough to make my knees wobble. "Sweet dreams."

Then Leo steps forward, tall enough to block the moonlight. He doesn't kiss me. Instead, he takes my hand, his fingers enveloping mine, his thumb tracing slow circles over my knuckles. The rasp of his calluses sends a shiver straight through me. "Until next time," he says, voice rough, quiet, certain.

It isn't a goodbye. It's a promise.

He holds my gaze, steady and unflinching, until I have to look away just to remember how to breathe.

I drive away with my fingers trembling on the wheel, the night air cool against my flushed skin. In the rearview mirror, three silhouettes stand in the yard, watching until my taillights disappear down the long, winding drive. The weight of their combined gaze feels like a physical touch, trailing over my skin even as the distance between us grows.

My body still hums. Hands. Lips. Heated glances. The belt around my wrists.

What am I doing? What game am I playing with these men, with my heart, with my children's attachments?

I've never felt anything like this before, this electric pull toward more than one person, this magnetic current that seems to link all four of us together. It defies reason. It defies sense. It shouldn't work. But somehow, impossibly, it does.

I think about Hudson's revelation, the one that changed everything. Leo married Ruby to save her life, even when he and Hudson had feelings for each other. Then they all lived through that terrible loss together. No wonder they share such an unshakable bond. And now I'm part of it, caught in their orbit like a comet drawn too close to the sun.

Even as the questions swirl in my mind, I can't bring myself to regret a single thing about tonight. The laughter, the conversations, the dancing, the joy of being seen and wanted and known by not just one person but three, each in their own way.

For the first time in six years, I want more than survival. More than stability. I want something that breathes. Something wild and untamed and gloriously uncertain. Something that could break me open and still be worth every bruise.

**5**

---

LEO'S POV

I pull up to Lorna's driveway, clutching the steering wheel like it's the only thing holding me together. It's been fourteen days since I had her wrists bound with my belt, felt her body trembling against mine in my workshop. Two weeks of cold showers and restless nights while we tended our separate farms and kept our distance.

Two weeks of thinking about nothing but her.

Hudson and Levi are going crazy too. We've all been respecting her space, letting her process what happened. Letting her make the next move.

But I'm done waiting.

Patience is overrated when it comes to things I want.

And goddamn, do I want Lorna MacLeod.

The dashboard clock reads 7:12 a.m. The twins' school bus left twenty minutes ago. Lorna's alone. Probably in her fields already, despite the lingering chill fogging my truck's windows.

I cut the engine, and the sudden silence slams into me, heavy and absolute. No sound but the distant call of birds and the faint bleating of sheep beyond the ridge. My fingers throb on the steering wheel, the ghost of their grip still biting into my skin. That rush in my veins, the raw, electric surge of it, feels almost feral. The same pulse that used to hit right before I climbed on the back of a wild stallion. Same edge of danger. Same high stakes.

This woman. This maddening, brilliant, gorgeous woman has gotten under my skin in a way I can't shake. The way she touches the soil like it's sacred. The way her voice softens when she talks to her plants, as if they're old friends who've trusted her with their secrets. The steady confidence in her hands when she coaxes life from a seed. Then there's the way she is with her kids. Gentle but firm, laughter tucked in every word, patience where most people would lose their temper.

It stirs something deep in me, something raw and ancient. The part of me that's spent a lifetime searching for something that feels like home.

My dreams are filled with her. Sometimes fragments: the curve of her neck, the sound of her laugh, her hands buried in dirt. Other times so vivid I wake up hard and aching, sheets damp with sweat, her phantom scent still in my nostrils.

Like I'm some horny teenager instead of a man pushing forty.

I push the door open and climb out, boots crunching on the gravel as I follow the narrow path toward her western field. Mist drapes the ground in thin, shifting veils, softening the edges of everything. It reminds me of mornings back on the Queensland range, when the world felt half-formed and waiting. The spring sun fights to break through, sending long, golden streaks across the dew-slick earth, the light catching on every blade of grass like it's been brushed with fire.

And then I see her.

Lorna is kneeling in the grass, wild curls escaping her bun, completely absorbed. She's wearing those chic-looking overalls that make her look like she's playing farmer, but I know better. Mud already stains the knees. Flannel sleeves rolled to her elbows reveal forearms streaked with dirt. Her fingers, bare with no gloves, handle her plants with a gentleness that makes my mouth go dry.

But it's her expression that stops me cold. Pure, unguarded joy.

Tears slip down her cheeks, catching the morning light until they glitter like dew on petals. She's smiling so wide it remakes her face, turns it radiant, almost holy.

I go still, every instinct urging me not to move, not to breathe. It feels like I've walked in on something sacred. A private communion between Lorna and the earth itself, too intimate for anyone else to witness.

Then she looks up, sees me, and that smile, God help me, only grows brighter.

"Leo." Her voice holds a note of wonder that makes my chest ache. "They're blooming. The first seedlings. Come look."

She doesn't ask why I'm here at dawn. Doesn't question how long I've been standing here watching her like some creeper. She invites me into her world with a trust that knocks the air from my lungs.

I close the distance, careful not to disturb the freshly tilled earth. As I crouch beside her, our shoulders brush. Even that minor contact sends electricity sparking through my system like a cattle prod to bare skin.

She doesn't pull away.

"See?" She points to a flower bud beginning to show peach-colored petals.

"These are the experimental crosses, right?" I ask, recognizing the section we'd frantically covered during that midnight frost weeks ago. The beds she'd been most worried about losing. "They made it."

"Not just made it." Her voice trembles as she touches a tiny shoot with a reverence that makes me ache with jealousy. I've never wanted to be a plant so badly in my life. The way her fingertips caress that delicate stem.

Christ.

"They're thriving. And look, here's another one already showing color. It's going to be a deep burgundy, I think."

She stands, her voice brimming with pride and excitement. "I babied them all winter for this exact moment. Pretty soon this field will be covered in flowers nobody else has ever seen." She trails off, a slight blush coloring her cheeks. "Sorry. I'm babbling."

"Don't apologize." I stand, brushing my hands on my jeans. "I like hearing you talk about your work."

I do. The way her eyes brighten when she talks about her flowers, how her mind races ahead of her words, mapping out ideas and experiments makes her magnetic. Every bit of her alive with purpose.

There's a faint smudge of dirt on her cheek. Before I can stop myself, I reach out and wipe it away with my thumb. Her skin is cool from the morning air but warms instantly beneath my touch. She goes still, her gaze lifting to meet mine. The moment stretches, long and weightless, every heartbeat loud in the quiet.

"Lorna," I say, my voice coming out lower, rougher than I mean it to.

She doesn't pull away. Doesn't even blink. Just looks at me with those extraordinary blue-gray eyes that remind me of storm clouds gathering over the outback. Awareness crackles between us, a current of desire that's been building since that first night we showed up to save her flowers.

"I can't stop thinking about you." All my carefully planned words turn to dust. "About that night in my workshop. About how you felt against me. How you sounded. How much you liked it." I drop my hand, giving her space. "It's driving me insane."

Her breath catches, color flooding her cheeks. "Leo—"

"I want to kiss you." The confession slips out before I can stop it, raw and heavy in the quiet between us. "It's all I've thought about for two weeks. The way you'd taste. The way you'd lean into me. Whether you'd let me take the lead or make me earn every inch."

A pulse throbs at the base of her throat like a frightened rabbit. She swallows, her gaze flicking to my mouth before lifting again, eyes wide and bright with a look that reads an awful lot like want. "I've been thinking about it too." The words are barely sound, mostly breath.

"Tell me," I murmur, stepping closer, my voice rough with need. "Tell me what you've been thinking."

Her blush deepens. "I'm analyzing my own physiological responses, if you want the truth. Heart rate elevated. Pupils dilated. Respiratory rate increased." She gives a self-deprecating smile. "Old habits from my research days. When I get nervous, I retreat into data."

Of course she does. Even her anxiety is adorable.

"And are you nervous now?" I ask, though I can see the answer in the slight tremor in her hands.

"Terrified," she admits. "Not of you. Of this. Of how much I want it."

The words cut straight through whatever restraint I had left. This woman, this fierce, brilliant, impossibly guarded woman, has spent six years building walls around her heart, and now she's standing in front of me, admitting she wants this.

Christ, I'm absolutely done for.

"Let me teach you to stop thinking." My voice comes out low, coaxing. I lean in, slow enough to give her every chance to pull away. "Let me show you how to just feel."

Her eyes flutter closed, a silent yes, and I'm gone.

I move slowly, though every instinct screams to take. My thumb traces the curve of her cheekbone, sliding down to the corner of her mouth. Her skin is impossibly soft. She trembles, a sound catching in her throat.

I've imagined this a hundred ways, but none of those fantasies touches the reality of her, warm and real beneath my hands. She smells of soil and morning air, of new life. I tilt closer until my nose brushes hers, breathing her in. Her breath skims my lips, quick and shallow, and the space between us feels electric, unbearable.

Her hands come to my arms, fingers tightening, as if she needs something to hold on to. I can feel her pulse hammering where my fingers rest at her throat. The early sun catches in her chestnut hair, threading it with gold until it glows. For a moment, I forget how to breathe. Her lips are parted, her cheeks flushed, her whole body alive with the same aching need that's unraveling me from the inside out.

She's the most beautiful thing I've ever seen.

When my mouth finally finds hers, it takes everything I have not to lose control. Her lips are soft, a little rough from sun and wind, and they part for me on a quiet gasp. I taste her lower lip, then catch it gently between my teeth, earning a soft, desperate sound that vibrates straight through my chest.

I slide a hand to the back of her neck, fingers threading into the silk of her hair, guiding her to me. She tilts her head, opens for me, and her tongue meets mine with cautious curiosity that quickly burns into hunger.

My other arm wraps around her waist, pulling her close until there's nothing left between us but heat and heartbeat. Her softness molds to me, her chest rising against mine, and I can feel her pulse racing, wild and erratic, a perfect echo of my own.

I promised to teach her how to feel, so I pour everything into the kiss, the wanting, the restraint, the ache that's lived under my skin since that frozen night when I first realized she'd taken root there. I kiss her like a man claiming what's sacred, like I could brand her with my need and rewrite every touch that ever came before mine.

She meets me with fire. Her hands slide up my arms to my shoulders, one curving around the back of my neck, the other fisting in my shirt as if she's afraid I'll let go. As if I could. As if anything short of the world ending could pull me away from her right now.

When we finally break apart, she's breathing as hard as I am. For a moment she bends forward, hands on her knees, dragging in quick gulps of air like she's trying to remember how to breathe normally.

"Holy forking shirtballs," she gasps, and the ridiculous, almost-curse pulls a laugh out of me despite the heat still roaring through my veins. "That was..."

"Just the beginning." I take her hands and help her straighten.

Her legs wobble, and a surge of pride kicks through me. There's nothing quite like watching a woman struggle to stand after your kiss.

Before I can think better of it, I scoop her up. One arm slides behind her back, the other under her knees.

"Leo!" she squeaks, arms flying around my neck. "What are you doing?"

"Taking you inside." I'm already halfway there, striding across the field toward the farmhouse. "Unless you'd rather I kiss you senseless right here in your dahlia beds."

Her fingers tighten in my shirt, and she hides her face against my neck. Her breath is warm on my skin when she whispers, "Inside is good."

I nudge the farmhouse door open with my shoulder, carrying her across the threshold like a bride. The thought sends an unexpected surge of possessiveness through me that hits harder than cheap whiskey on an empty stomach.

The moment we step into the kitchen, a change ripples through her. She slides from my arms, her feet barely touching the floor before she launches herself at me. Her mouth crashes into mine, her hands diving into my hair, nails scraping my scalp, and the growl that rumbles out of me sounds feral.

I back her into the kitchen counter, lift her easily onto it, and step between her thighs. Her legs wrap around my waist, heels digging into my back like she's trying to fuse us together. Her mouth is level with mine now, and I kiss her deep, greedy, my hands gripping her waist like she's the only thing anchoring me.

The press of her against my stomach nearly undoes me. I'm throbbing, hard and aching, and the urge to grind into her, to chase even a second of relief, claws at my control.

"Leo," she gasps when I trail kisses down her neck, finding the sensitive spot below her ear that makes her shiver. "Oh God, Leo."

My name on her lips is the sweetest sound I've ever heard. I want to hear it again, in every possible variation. Breathless with need. Hoarse with pleasure. Screaming in ecstasy until her neighbors file a noise complaint.

Her head tips back, giving me better access to her neck. I take full advantage, tasting her skin with open-mouthed kisses, feeling her pulse flutter beneath my lips like a captive butterfly. Her hands are everywhere, in my hair, on my shoulders, sliding down my biceps.

When I graze my teeth over her pulse point, she makes a sound that's half gasp, half moan, her fingers digging into my arms hard enough to bruise. I soothe the spot with my tongue, then suck lightly, not enough to mark her but enough to make her squirm against me.

"I've dreamed about this," I confess, unable to stop the words. "About how you'd taste. How you'd sound. How you'd feel in my arms."

"Leo." She whispers my name, voice cracking. She pulls back just enough to look into my eyes, her own dark with desire, pupils blown wide. "I never thought... I didn't allow myself to imagine..."

I understand what she's not saying. After six years of being both mother and father to her children, of rebuilding her life from the ashes of her marriage, of protecting her heart from further damage, allowing herself to want this, to want me, is earth-shattering.

"I know." I press my forehead to hers, our breath mingling in the narrow space between us. "I know exactly what this costs you."

The vulnerability in her eyes nearly undoes me. Her hands frame my face, thumbs stroking over my cheekbones with a gentleness that makes my chest ache.

"Kiss me again," she whispers.

I kiss her again, deeper this time, hungrier. Her tongue meets mine without hesitation, all heat and urgency, molten need sparking between our mouths. Her hands roam down my chest, fingertips skimming over my pecs, then lower, tracing the lines of my abs through the thin stretch of my shirt.

When she tugs at the hem, I nearly lose it. I want to strip her bare, lay her out on the counter, and take my time worshipping every inch. But I don't. Not yet.

Instead, I lift her, pivoting to pin her to the fridge. Papers and magnets scatter to the floor, forgotten, as my hands slide down to grab her ass, pulling her higher. She gasps into my mouth, legs tightening around me, hips tilting so her heat presses flush to the ache in my jeans.

"Christ, Lorna," I breathe, voice rough. The friction is exquisite. Torturous. Perfect.

Her fingers fumble at my buttons, impatient and trembling. When she gets the first few undone, her hand slips beneath the fabric, palm pressing flat against my chest. Her touch scorches me, skin to skin, and I swear I feel it echo through my bloodstream. I want her hands all over me. I want her nails clawing at my back. I want her fingers tangled with mine as I sink inside her.

But not like this. Not yet.

Not when I've seen the way Hudson and Levi look at her. Not when I've watched her look right back. Whatever this is, whatever we're building, it's bigger than heat and hunger. It deserves more than ripping clothes off in a moment of reckless want. It deserves more than fast.

This thing between us, between all of us, is something none of us has words for. No blueprint. No map. Just instinct and hope and a whole lot of trust.

With effort that borders on agony, I slow the kiss. Ease it back. Let my forehead rest against hers as I try to catch my breath.

She's wrecked. Flushed cheeks. Kiss-swollen lips. Pupils blown wide with need. Her hair's completely unraveled, loose curls spilling wild around her face, and there's a patch of skin on her neck going pink where my beard scraped her. She looks like sin and salvation wrapped in the same soft skin.

And I want her. God, I want her.

I want to lay her across the kitchen table, spread her thighs, and eat her until she forgets her own name.

But not yet.

Not until we all know exactly where we stand.

Instead, I press my lips to hers one more time, then carefully set her on her feet, keeping my hands on her waist until I'm sure she's steady.

"We should slow down." My voice rough as sandpaper. "There are complications we need to talk about first."

Understanding flickers in her eyes, followed by a flash of what might be disappointment. But she nods, loosening her grip on my shoulders.

"You're right," she agrees. "There's a lot to figure out."

I step back and instantly miss her, like someone ripped off a wool blanket in the dead of winter. The air feels colder without her pressed to me. I turn to the sink and fill the kettle, focusing on the sound of the water, the weight of the metal in my hand, anything to steady the thundering pulse in my neck.

"Let me make you some tea," I say, voice rougher than I mean it to be. I reach for the canister I've seen her use a hundred times, the one that smells like blackberry and vanilla and a sweetness I can't quite name.

She watches me navigate her kitchen with a bemused expression, tucking escaped curls behind her ears in a futile attempt to tame them. "Most men don't pivot from 'take me now' to 'let me steep you some tea' quite so gracefully," she says, the corners of her mouth twitching. There's laughter in her voice, but something softer too, like she's still catching her breath.

"I'm not most men." I find her favorite mug, the one with tiny dahlias printed around the rim. "And this isn't a typical situation."

"No kidding. Pretty sure the *Heartstopper Handbook* doesn't list 'brew tea for your hot neighbor' in the top ten post-makeout moves."

I snort. "The what?"

"The *Heartstopper Handbook*. It's what I call those romance novels my sister-in-law keeps sending me. You know the ones. Shirtless cowboys. Heaving bosoms. Questionable decision-making."

"And what do these handbooks recommend?" I ask, curious despite myself.

She grins, some of her equilibrium returning. "Typically tearing off clothes and banging like screen doors in a hurricane."

I nearly choke, not expecting that level of bluntness from proper little miss won't-say-a-curse-word. "Is that right?"

"So I'm told," she says primly, but there's a mischievous twinkle in her eye I've rarely seen. "I wouldn't know personally. It's been a while since I've had any... screen doors."

Jesus, Mary, and Joseph. This woman is going to be the death of me.

I busy myself with the familiar ritual of tea-making, partly to give myself time to cool down, partly to give her the same. By the time I place the steaming mug in front of her, my pulse has slowed to a more manageable rhythm, though my body is still achingly aware of her every movement.

She wraps her hands around the mug, inhaling the steam. The morning sunlight streaming through the kitchen window gilds her profile, highlighting the elegant slope of her nose, the fullness of her still-swollen lips, the delicate shell of her ear.

"So," she says finally, "about those complications."

Right on cue, there's a knock on her front door. Lorna's eyes widen in panic.

"Those complications are here right on time." I'm chuckling, both frustrated and relieved by the timing.

She sets down her mug, smoothing her hair self-consciously. "They'll know," she whispers. "They'll take one look at me, and know exactly what we've been doing."

"Would that be so terrible?" I ask, genuinely curious.

A blush stains her cheeks. "No, not terrible. Just... complicated."

There's that word again. Complicated. As if anything worth having in this life comes easy. As if the heart-stopping, soul-changing things don't come with warning labels the size of Scotland.

Moments later, Hudson practically bursts through the door, Levi on his heels.

"Morning, Snapdragon!" Hudson calls, then stops abruptly, eyes narrowing as he takes in the scene before him—Lorna with her mussed hair and flushed cheeks, her lips swollen. His gaze flicks to me, something dangerous flashing in those blue eyes. "Well now. What have we here?"

Levi says nothing, but I don't miss how his hands clench briefly at his sides before relaxing. He closes the door behind him, leans against it, his dark eyes unreadable. But there's a tension in his jaw, a slight flare of his nostrils that speaks volumes to those who know him well.

"Leo dropped by to see the plants," Lorna says with as much dignity as possible. "The experimental crosses are starting to bloom."

"Is that what they're calling it these days?" Hudson asks, that dimple appearing as he grins, though it doesn't reach his eyes. "Funny, I didn't know that was a euphemism for 'pinning each other against the refrigerator.'"

Lorna's blush deepens, and her eyes dart to the fallen magnets still scattered on the floor. "Hud—"

"Hudson," I warn, recognizing the edge in his voice. The jealousy. The raw tension that's been building between us for years, that we've never had the guts to talk about. We've never discussed sharing a woman before, never even hinted at it. This is as new to him as it is to me.

Hudson raises his hands in mock surrender, but there's a challenging gleam in his eyes. "Just making an observation. You look thoroughly... examined, doc." His gaze slides appreciatively over Lorna in a way that makes my fingers itch to throttle him. "I'm guessing Leo's agricultural inspection was quite thorough."

Levi clears his throat quietly, drawing Hudson's attention. A silent communication passes between them, some unspoken warning from Levi that makes Hudson's shoulders drop slightly.

"Sorry," he mutters, shoving his hands into his pockets. "That was out of line."

Lorna looks between us, her quick mind clearly catching the undercurrents. The tension crackling between me and Hudson isn't just about her. It's about us too. About boundaries neither of us have ever had to consider before.

"Leo and I were just about to have a conversation about... complications," she says carefully. "I think maybe we all should."

"Definitely," Levi speaks for the first time, his quiet voice drawing everyone's attention.

We glance between each other, no one willing to be the first to speak. The silence presses in, dense and suffocating, like the room itself is holding its breath. Even the clock on the wall sounds deafening, each tick landing like a drumbeat. I swear I can hear Lorna's heart pounding, or maybe it's mine. Maybe it's all of ours. Because none of us has a script for this, whatever *this* is. No rules. No roadmap. Just a cliff edge and the question of who's going to step off it first.

"I think I have feelings for all three of you," Lorna blurts, immediately covering her face with her hands.

We all start talking at once.

"Told you!" Hudson's shout echoes off the walls, his face splitting into a grin.

"Thank fuck," Levi mutters, shoulders sagging in relief.

Relief crashes over me so hard it nearly knocks me flat. My chest heaves, heart hammering like it's trying to break free from my ribs. I kissed her like a man with everything to lose, and if she hadn't wanted this with all of us, I don't know how I would have walked away.

"Fuck," I rasp, dragging a hand over my face as I lean back against the counter. "I think I'm actually having a heart attack."

She peeks at us between her fingers, those wide blue eyes doing nothing to still the feelings she stirred up earlier.

"So... you're happy?" she asks, voice soft, testing the air. Her gaze moves between the three of us, like she's waiting for one of us to flinch. "It's really okay that I like all of you?"

I watch the panic creep in as the words leave her mouth. Her shoulders curl inward. "Oh my God, what am I even saying? Fuck. Three of you? That's not okay. What the hell am I supposed to tell the children?"

I blink. "Lorna MacLeod. You said fuck."

Her eyes go wide. She slaps a hand over her mouth. "Fuck, I did, didn't I?"

The three of us stare like she's just announced she's running for prime minister. Dr. Proper, with her polite little substitutions and endearing non-curses, suddenly dropping F-bombs like they're punctuation.

"Sorry. That—um—that won't happen again," she says, fingertips brushing her lips like she can't quite believe what came out of them.

What I don't say, what I barely stop myself from blurting out, is that I'd give anything to hear her say it again. Bent over the kitchen table. Breathless. Desperate. Filthy. I want to learn every obscene syllable that might tumble from her mouth when my body is pressed to hers, my hands on her skin, my cock buried inside her.

But we're not there. Not even close. Not with the way her eyes keep darting between the three of us like she's trying to solve a complex equation with too many variables. Not when we haven't even begun to figure out what this means for any of us.

We're interrupted by a goat screaming. Loudly.

"Is that your ringtone?" I ask incredulously, nearly jumping out of my skin.

She rolls her eyes, but I don't miss the smile tugging at her lips. "Hi, Isla! Sure. Six weeks?!" Lorna yelps, her face going white as she fumbles with her phone. "The gardens are nowhere near ready for events. Last time I was there, the east terrace was practically a wilderness."

As she listens, her expression cycles through disbelief, alarm, and finally resignation. "No, I understand. But the gardens... yes, I know I'm the only one who can... but my seedlings are blooming, and it's critical timing for—"

Her face falls as she listens to whatever Isla is saying. "How long would I need to stay? A month? Isla, that's impossible. My farm is my livelihood. I can't just—"

She glances over at the three of us, and her expression shifts. A flicker of calculation. Possibility. Her eyes lock with mine for a heartbeat, then flit to Hudson and Levi. I can practically see the gears turning behind those stormy eyes.

"Let me call you back in ten minutes," she says abruptly, ending the call before turning to us, chewing her bottom lip like it might anchor her.

"As you know, my brother Jack runs our family estate on Harris," she says, fingers raking through her already wild hair. "He and Isla, along with their families, have been renovating it, with the hopes of opening for special events to help cover the upkeep. Apparently, an editor from some wedding magazine was touring the Hebrides and fell in love with the place. She wants to feature it, but only if they can shoot an actual wedding there. And the only date that works is six weeks from now."

Levi whistles low. "That's a huge opportunity."

"It is," she says, nodding, though it sounds more like a weight than a win. "But the gardens are a wreck. They were my grandmother's pride and joy, but no one's touched them in years. Isla says they need a full redesign, complete replanting, everything, and apparently I'm the only one they trust to pull it off in time."

Hudson's brow creases. "You'd have to stay there? On Harris?"

"I mean, I *could* drive back and forth, but you know how brutal that drive is. And I hate driving." She exhales hard, dragging both hands down her face, frustration rolling off her in waves. "I'd have to stay for at least a month. But I can't just walk away from the farm right now. These next few weeks are make-or-break for the dahlias. If something goes wrong and I'm not here to catch it, I could lose half my crop, maybe more."

The three of us exchange a look, an entire conversation passing silently between us. Hudson raises his eyebrows in question. Levi gives a small nod. I make the final decision with a slight inclination of my head.

"We'll take care of your farm," I tell her, the words coming out as a statement rather than an offer.

Lorna blinks at me as if I've started speaking in tongues. "What?"

"While you're at the castle. The three of us will manage your farm. Care for your flowers according to the schedule you provide. Maintain the irrigation. Whatever needs doing."

"That's..." She shakes her head, clearly struggling to process. "That's incredibly generous, but you have your own farm to run. Your animals. Your schedules."

"We can work it out," Hudson says, warming to the idea. "Split shifts between our place and yours. The irrigation system Leo designed practically runs itself, and lambing season is nearly done."

"I could manage the hybridization records," Levi offers quietly. "You have a very organized system, which makes it easy."

"And you've seen Leo's planning skills," Hudson adds with a grin. "The man makes military generals look disorganized. He'll have your plants growing on a schedule so tight they'll bloom on command just to avoid his disappointment."

Lorna looks stunned. "You'd really do that? All of you?" Her voice wavers, edged with disbelief, like she's bracing for the catch.

"Of course we would," Hudson says, like it's the most obvious thing in the world. "We're invested in your success, Lorna."

"The twins would love it," she murmurs, half to herself. "They adore the castle. And it'd be good for them to spend time with their cousin."

"Even better," I add, "they get to *live* in a castle for a month. What kid wouldn't lose their mind over that?"

She still looks uncertain, her brow pinched, wheels turning fast. "I'd need to write everything down. Create detailed instructions.

Daily care schedules for each bed. Notes on which hybrids need extra watering or pinching."

"We'll follow it all to the letter," I promise.

"The truck," she says suddenly. "You three share one vehicle. How would you manage both farms?"

"We'll stagger schedules," Hudson answers without hesitation.

"And the nights you have to do late checks on your animals?"

"We'll figure it out," I assure her. "This is important to your family, Lorna. Let us help."

She studies each of us in turn, her gaze pausing on me a fraction longer, like she's hoping I'll flinch or give something away. I hold still, let her look. Let her see there's no bluff in this. No performative kindness. Just the truth. Just us.

Whatever she finds in our faces seems to ease a tension in her. Her shoulders drop a little, like she's been carrying too much for too long and finally set one thing down.

"Okay," she says finally. "If you're sure."

"We're sure," all three of us say, almost in sync.

Lorna blinks, then lets out a surprised laugh. "Do you guys practice that? The whole choreographed response thing?"

"Years of living together," Levi says with a small smile. "You pick up a rhythm."

The double meaning hangs there, quiet but undeniable. Her cheeks flush, and she clears her throat, reaching for her phone.

"I should call Isla. Let her know I'm coming. She'll need to sort something out for the twins' schooling while we're there." She hesitates, her gaze sweeping over us with a softness that wasn't there before. "Thank you. All of you. This means more than I can say."

"Our pleasure," I say, meaning it.

She steps into the living room to make the call, and the second the door clicks shut behind her, Hudson turns to me. His eyes are sharp, his voice low, but there's an edge under it that doesn't pretend to be casual.

"So. You and Lorna, huh?" He folds his arms, muscles tense

beneath the worn fabric of his shirt. "Moving pretty fast there, old man."

"It wasn't planned," I say, keeping my tone level even though my pulse hasn't settled. "I came to check the seedlings. Things escalated."

"I'll bet they did." His mouth tightens. "That's your thing, right? Taking control. Getting ahead of the rest of us before we even know there's a race."

"Hudson," Levi says, stepping between us, voice firm. "Not here. Not now."

"Why not?" Hudson's jaw flexes, but he keeps his voice down. "When *is* the right time? After Leo's staked his claim? After he's already decided how this whole thing is gonna go down without asking anyone else?"

"That's not what I'm doing." I breathe through the burn in my chest, fists curling at my sides before I make myself let go. "You *know* that's not how I operate. Not anymore."

For a second, a flicker crosses his face, hurt, maybe. Regret. Then he exhales through his nose and mutters, "Sorry. I just... I thought we were going to approach this as a team."

"We are," I say. "What just happened, it wasn't some power move. It was a moment. That's all. Nothing's set in stone."

"Nothing except your mouth on hers." Hudson lifts a brow, but the heat is already bleeding from his words.

I hold his gaze. "You can't blame me for reacting when the opportunity was right in front of me. You would've done the same if you'd found her on her knees in the garden, covered in dirt, looking like every dream you've ever had."

"Damn right I would've," Hudson mutters.

Levi rests a hand on Hudson's shoulder, grounding him with that quiet steadiness he always seems to carry. "We all want her," he says simply. "I think we knew it the night she had us over for dinner. But she has to want *us*. All of us. However it works. That's the only way this stands a chance."

"However it works," Hudson echoes, raising an eyebrow. "You

say that like we've done this before. None of us has a clue what we're doing."

"One day at a time," Levi says. His voice is calm but firm. "We talk. To each other. To *her*. We don't assume. We build it together."

Hudson exhales, long and slow, some of the tension bleeding out of his frame. "You're right. I know you're right." He looks over at me, a familiar spark returning to his eyes. "So? Was it at least a good kiss? Worth the wait?"

Despite everything, I can't help the smile tugging at my mouth. "Better than good."

"Bloody hell," Hudson mutters, rubbing a hand over his jaw.

"She analyzes her body's responses when she's nervous," I tell them, a smile tugging at my lips. "Heart rate. Pupil dilation. Even skin temperature. Like she's monitoring her own reactions in real time. It's... kind of adorable."

"Of course she does," Levi says with a soft laugh. "Probably helps her feel in control when the rest of her doesn't."

Hudson grins, full mischief now. "Think she keeps spreadsheets of her orgasms? Logs them with little charts and color-coded tags?"

"Jesus, Hudson," I groan, but the mental image hits like a punch straight to the gut.

"What? You can't tell me the idea of Dr. MacLeod treating her orgasms like a lab study isn't hot as—"

"Focus," Levi cuts in, though he's smiling too. "We've got bigger things to handle. Like the fact that she's leaving for a month."

Hudson straightens, already calculating. "So we're doing this? Running two farms at once? While she plays Lady of the Manor?"

"We've faced worse," I remind him. "Remember the flood during calving season? The bushfire that nearly swallowed the south paddock? This is flowers and dirt. We'll manage."

Levi nods, more serious now. "And when she comes back? What then?"

"We figure it out," I say. "All of us. Together."

"No secrets," Levi adds. "No resentment. We have to be honest, even when it's hard."

"Agreed," Hudson says without hesitation. He extends his hand, palm down, just like we used to before cattle drives and early-morning storm preps. A silent pact.

Levi places his hand on top. I cover them both with mine.

"For Lorna," Hudson says. Simple. Steady.

"For all of us," Levi echoes quietly.

And when our hands fall away, something has shifted. We're no longer circling the idea. We're in it now. All of us.

Lorna comes back a few minutes later, cheeks flushed, eyes shining with a kind of nervous electricity. "It's settled. Isla's over the moon. We leave in two days. That gives me enough time to pack and put together everything for the farm."

"Two days," Hudson echoes, glancing at me and Levi. "We'll be ready."

"I should start making lists," she says, already moving toward the little desk tucked in the corner of the kitchen. It's crammed with spiral notebooks, seed packets, and coffee-stained plant tags. "Daily care schedules, transplanting priorities, watering rotations—"

"Write it all down," I tell her. "We'll follow it to the letter."

She stops, hand resting lightly on the back of the chair, and looks at us like she's seeing ghosts. Or miracles. Like it still doesn't compute that someone might show up for her. No strings. No conditions. Just love, in its simplest form, showing up, staying put, helping carry the weight.

"Thank you," she says softly. "All of you."

"We should head out," Levi says, checking his watch. "The vet's coming to look at the new lambs at nine."

"Right," Hudson mutters, dragging himself toward the door like a man facing a firing squad. "Duty calls. Nature's alarm clocks wait for no man, especially not ones with udders and hungry babies."

As they step outside, Lorna's gaze finds mine again, still threaded with something uncertain, something unfinished.

"We'll talk when you get back," I tell her quietly. "About everything."

Her lips twitch in a tight, almost-smile. "Everything is a lot."

"It is." I take a breath. "But nothing has to be decided right now. Just... take this time at the castle. Figure out what you want. We'll still be here."

She nods, and I can't resist reaching out to tuck a stray curl behind her ear. She leans into the touch, her eyes drifting closed briefly. Before I can think better of it, I dip my head and capture her mouth one more time. This kiss is different from earlier, slower, deeper, filled with promise rather than urgency. A kiss that says I'll still be here when the dust settles.

My hand cradles her jaw, thumb stroking over her cheekbone as our tongues meet, memorizing the feel of her, the taste of her, the small sounds she makes in the back of her throat that go straight to my cock.

"Something to think about," I murmur, voice rough.

"As if I could think of anything else," she admits, opening her eyes to look at me with such naked longing that it takes every ounce of my self-control not to carry her upstairs and spend the rest of the day making sure she never forgets me.

Instead, I step back, putting distance between us. "Don't forget to write everything down. We'll go through the farm routines tomorrow, make sure we understand everything."

She nods, visibly gathering herself. "Tomorrow."

With a final nod, I turn and leave, feeling her eyes on me until I close the door behind me, knowing, with bone-deep certainty, that whatever happens next will change all of us forever.

**6**

———————

LEO'S POV

The next morning breaks bright and clear, a postcard-perfect Scottish spring day that doesn't match the storm still tearing through my chest. I slept worse than I did that time I spent three days chasing a feral bull through the bush. Sheets twisted around my legs, sweat soaking the pillow, dreams fractured and relentless. Every time I closed my eyes, there she was. Her face. Her mouth on mine. That soft, breathy sound she made when I touched her.

By the time I give up on sleep and head downstairs at 5 a.m., I've already plotted out exactly how we'll manage two farms simultaneously, down to fifteen-minute increments.

Hudson finds me at the kitchen table an hour later, surrounded by printouts of Lorna's farm layout, detailed schedules, and task assignments.

"Jesus, Mary, and all the bloody saints, Leo," he says, scrubbing his hands over his face as he stumbles toward the coffee pot. "Did you sleep at all, or have you been color-coding spreadsheets since midnight?"

"Pretty much." I don't look up from where I'm marking irrigation zones in blue, planting zones in green, and maintenance areas in red.

He doesn't respond. Instead, he pours himself coffee and drops into the chair across from me, studying the papers with increasing clarity as the caffeine kicks in.

"This is... comprehensive," he finally says, picking up a schedule that details hourly tasks for the next month.

"That's the point. We can't afford to miss anything. Her livelihood depends on it."

Hudson sips his coffee, regarding me over the rim of his mug. "This is about more than just helping a neighbor, isn't it? More than just a good deed for the pretty lady next door."

I finally meet his eyes. "You know it is."

He nods slowly. "You fell for her that first night, didn't you? When we were all out in that frost?"

"Did you?" I counter.

He smirks. "Hard not to. The way she fought to save those plants. That fierce determination. The way she looked in the moonlight, hair everywhere, dirt on her face, like Mother Nature had decided to lace up her boots and throw hands. Like a warrior goddess ready to punch Jack Frost right in the nuts."

Levi's voice floats in from the doorway, softer but no less certain. "For me it was how she looked at us when we got there. Like it didn't make sense that someone would come only to help. Like she'd forgotten people could be kind without there being strings attached."

Silence settles between the three of us. We're all lost in the same memory. Lorna on her knees in the half-frozen mud, fighting a battle she already knew she was losing. The guarded look in her eyes when we offered to help. The walls she tried to hold up even as they cracked apart.

"And now we're in it," Hudson says, tipping his chair back. "All of us. Head over heels for a prickly flower farmer who might not choose one of us. Or might choose all of us. And none of us have a damn clue what comes next."

"She wants something." I remember the taste of her, the way she'd pressed herself against me like she was trying to crawl inside my skin. "She's just not sure what yet."

"Or who," Levi adds quietly.

Another silence falls, heavier this time. The three of us steal glances at each other, none of us brave enough to name the thing hanging between us. We've never talked about sharing a woman. Never unpacked the mess of feelings between me and Hudson. Never imagined we'd all fall for the same stubborn, brilliant woman next door.

"What if she does choose just one of us?" Hudson asks, voicing the fear that's been lurking in all our minds. "How do we handle that?"

"We talk it out," Levi answers immediately.

"And the ones not chosen?" Hudson challenges. "We—what? Pretend we're fine with it? Act like nothing's changed when we see her at town events or pass her on the road? 'Oh hey, Lorna, don't mind me while I slowly die inside watching you with my brother?'"

"It needs to be all or none," I say, though the thought sends a cold weight settling in my stomach. "I refuse to let this rip the two of you apart. You've already dealt with enough heartache."

The reminder of what we've already endured together, the losses, the grief, the slow, stubborn rebuilding, steadies us. We've faced harder storms than this. We'll survive this one too, if we have to.

"Besides," Hudson says, some of his usual mischief returning, "I don't think it'll come to that. Did you see how she looked at all three of us yesterday? That wasn't a woman trying to choose. That was a woman wanting everything on the whole goddamned menu."

"Hudson," I warn, but there's no heat behind my words.

He grins unrepentantly. "I'm just saying, I've seen that look before. Back in Sydney, when we used to hit the clubs. That's the look of a woman who's just discovered she can have her cake, eat it too, and then get seconds."

"That was different," I interrupt. "That was dancing. Making out. Maybe a little more. It wasn't a relationship."

"No," he agrees, suddenly serious again. "It wasn't. But this is the real deal, isn't it? The forever kind of thing."

The three of us exchange glances, understanding passing between us. Whatever happens with Lorna, it won't be casual for any of us. It's already far beyond that point.

"We should head over there," Levi says, glancing at the clock. "She'll need to go over the plan before she leaves tomorrow."

Ten minutes later, we pull into Lorna's driveway as the school bus rounds the corner with the twins on board. We planned it that way. Today we need to stay focused on practical things: farm instructions, schedules, logistics. The twins are pure delight, but trying to work with them here would feel like holding a serious meeting inside a bouncy castle full of glitter and sugar-high gremlins.

Lorna meets us at the door, already dressed for a day of farm work in worn jeans and a flannel shirt with the sleeves rolled up. Her hair is secured in that practical bun she favors, though a few rebellious curls have already escaped around her face. She looks tired, with faint shadows beneath her eyes suggesting she slept as poorly as I did.

My first instinct is to pull her into my arms, to kiss those shadows away, but the tentative smile she offers reminds me that yesterday was a beginning, not a conclusion. We're still finding our footing on this new terrain. All four of us, stumbling blind through uncharted territory.

"Morning," she says, stepping back to let us in. "Coffee's ready. I've made schedules and instruction packets for each of you."

"Great minds," Hudson says with a grin, holding up my color-coded plans.

A smile tugs at her lips. "Let me guess—Leo's work?"

"Who else?" Hudson rolls his eyes good-naturedly. "The man can't help himself. It's a sickness, really. If there's a twelve-step program for compulsive organizers, he's a prime candidate."

"It's called preparation," I grumble.

"Well, between your schedules and mine, nothing will be overlooked," she says, leading us to her kitchen table where neat stacks of papers await each of us, labeled with our names. "I've divided the farm tasks to try to make it easier. You can change things up if you need to, I just wanted to try to make it as seamless as possible."

I glance down at my packet. It's meticulous, full of detailed notes on the irrigation system, water schedules for each variety, and maintenance checklists. Hudson's stack is all about the physical work—planting depths, harvesting times, diagrams showing proper technique. Levi's covers hybridization records, plant lineages, and observation logs in her tidy handwriting.

"This is incredibly thorough," Levi says, flipping through his pages with genuine appreciation.

"So is Leo's plan," she counters, spreading out the papers I brought. "Let's see what we can do to combine the best of both."

For the next hour, we go over every aspect of her farm. Lorna is a patient teacher, her natural academic tendencies emerging as she explains the science behind each practice. Her whole face lights up when she talks about her experimental hybrids, hands gesturing animatedly as she details the specific care they require.

It's captivating, watching her in her element. So different from the guarded woman who kept us at a distance for months. Like watching a butterfly emerge from its chrysalis, wings still damp but eager to fly.

I can't take my eyes off her. The way she tucks her hair behind her ear when she's focusing. The little furrow between her brows when she's explaining something intricate. The unconscious way she bites her lower lip when she's thinking. Every tiny detail makes me want her more.

After the indoor briefing, she takes us on a walking tour of the farm, pointing out specific beds and their requirements, showing us the emergency supplies, explaining the quirks of equipment that needs "the right touch" to operate properly.

"This mechanism sticks sometimes," she explains, crouching

beside an ancient piece of machinery that looks like it belongs in a museum. "You have to jiggle the handle while pressing this button, or it'll burn out the motor."

"We should replace this." I'm already calculating costs and installation time. "It's a fire hazard."

"It's fine," she insists.

"Lorna." My voice comes out in the tone that used to stop the most stubborn ranch hands mid-argument. "We're replacing it. I'm not letting your greenhouse go up in flames while you're away."

She looks ready to argue, then sighs. "Fine. But nothing fancy. I'm on a tight budget."

"We'll handle it," I tell her, exchanging looks with Hudson and Levi. We've already discussed pooling resources to upgrade certain critical equipment while she's gone, a surprise we plan to implement whether she agrees or not.

Hudson grins behind her back and throws me a thumbs up. Levi gives a small nod, already doing the math in his head. Complicated feelings or not, we're locked in. When it comes to taking care of her, we're all on the same team.

By mid-afternoon, we've covered every inch of her farm, discussed every plant variety, and reviewed every possible emergency scenario from frost to flood. Lorna finally suggests a break, and we settle on her back porch with cold drinks.

"I think that's everything," she says, tugging loose strands of hair back from her face. "Any questions?"

"Just one," Hudson says, leaning forward, elbows on knees. "When would you like us to start staying here? Tonight? Tomorrow after you leave?"

Lorna blinks, clearly caught off-guard. "Staying here?"

"Someone needs to be on-site overnight," I explain. "For security and in case of weather emergencies."

"Right," she says slowly. "I just... I hadn't thought about someone actually sleeping here. In my house."

The thought of sleeping under her roof, surrounded by her things, her scent, her presence even when she's gone makes my heart rate pick up. Like a teenager getting to stay in his crush's room. From the way Hudson shifts in his seat and Levi's eyes darken slightly, they're thinking the same thing.

"It makes the most sense," Levi says gently. "Rather than driving back and forth constantly, especially with only one vehicle."

She nods, processing this new wrinkle. "I suppose you're right. There's a guest room upstairs that you can use. It's small, but it has a double bed."

"Perfect," Hudson says with a grin. "We can rotate, switching every few days to share the truck."

"You've really thought this through," she says, sounding impressed despite herself.

"Leo doesn't do anything halfway," Hudson tells her. "Once he commits, it gets his full focus."

Her gaze catches mine across the porch, and for a heartbeat the air shifts. Her cheeks color, and I know exactly where her mind's gone. Yesterday. The kiss. The heat that still lingers between us.

"I'm starting to see that," she says quietly, holding my gaze a moment longer than necessary. The meaning's unmistakable.

My body reacts before I can stop it, blood rushing south so fast I have to adjust my seat, pretending I'm not already thinking about what it would mean for her to have my full attention again.

Levi clears his throat. "What time do you leave tomorrow?"

"Early," she answers, reluctantly breaking eye contact with me. "Around seven."

"We'll come by at six thirty to see you off," I tell her. "In case you need any help loading up."

"That's not necessary," she protests. "I'm perfectly capable of handling luggage while wrangling two six-year-olds."

"Come on, humor us," Hudson says with that annoyingly charming smile. "Let us be the overly helpful neighbors just this once. No brass bands or rose petals, I swear, though I can't make any promises about Leo. He might show up with a full marching band and a sky writer."

She rolls her eyes, but a smile pulls at the corners of her mouth. "Fine. Six thirty. But I don't need help carrying bags or anything."

"Of course not," Levi agrees solemnly. "We would never suggest the competent Dr. Lorna MacLeod might need assistance with something as simple as luggage."

His deadpan delivery makes her laugh, a genuine sound that transforms her face. The sound ripples through me like music, giving me full-body goosebumps. It's like hearing my favorite song for the first time. I want to hear that laugh every day for the rest of my life. Want to be the cause of it.

"You three are impossible," she says, but there's no bite in it, just that soft, teasing warmth that makes my chest tighten in the best, most dangerous way.

"But growing on you," Hudson suggests with a wink.

"Like a fungal infection," she shoots back, laughing.

As the afternoon stretches into evening, Lorna insists we stay for dinner. "It's the least I can do," she says, already pulling ingredients from her refrigerator. "One last home-cooked meal before I leave you to fend for yourselves."

"We won't starve," I assure her, though the thought of her cooking is admittedly appealing. "I do know how to feed myself and these two yahoos."

"Yes, but you'll be busy with both farms," she points out. "Let me do this."

I recognize the need in her, the urge to provide, to care, to hold on to control in the small ways she still can. It mirrors the same instinct in me, the part that needs to fix what's broken, protect what matters, and make order out of chaos. So I nod and take a seat at the kitchen counter, letting her find her rhythm.

Hudson joins her at the stove, refusing to take no for an answer. Soon they're moving in sync, trading utensils and quiet smiles, their coordination effortless. Levi moves through the background, setting the table with quiet precision, tucking a handful of her garden flowers into a vase like it's second nature.

I watch them all, and my chest tightens, part protectiveness, part ache. The kind that lives in the hollow spaces of a man who's lost too much. I want this. Every day. Lorna in our kitchen. The twins' laughter echoing down the hall. The soft hum of people who feel like home. It's been a long time since I've wanted something this much, and even longer since I've let myself believe it could last.

When the twins return from their after-school playdate, they're ecstatic to find us all there. Daniel immediately shows me his latest rock specimens, while Lorelai drags Hudson to the living room to show him the journal she's making about every kind of fairy.

The scene is so domestic, it catches me off guard. It's too much, too soon, and I need air. I step outside, the cool evening wrapping around me as I inhale the scent of cut grass and woodsmoke, trying to steady the ache building in my chest. The kind that feels dangerously close to hope.

When I finally go back inside, Lorna glances up, her brow creased in question. I shake my head, not trusting myself to answer. As she passes, her fingers brush mine, a fleeting touch, nothing more. But it feels like everything.

Dinner is lively, with the twins chattering excitedly about spending a month at the castle with their cousin.

"Maybe Auntie Isla will let me have my own garden plot," Lorelai says, stabbing a piece of chicken with her fork. "For fairy gardens!"

"That would be wonderful, sweet pea," Lorna says, smoothing a hand over her daughter's wild curls. "What about you, Daniel? What are you looking forward to most?"

Daniel considers the question with his characteristic seriousness. "The geology. Uncle Jack says there are very old rocks on the castle grounds. Rocks that were there when dinosaurs were alive. Maybe even fossils."

"We'll have to start a new collection," Levi says, earning a rare full smile from the boy.

I'm struck again by how natural this feels. The six of us around the table like we've been doing this for years. The way Levi and

Hudson have slipped so easily into relationships with the twins. How right it all seems, even with all its complications.

As the meal winds down, the reality of tomorrow's separation begins to settle over us all. The twins grow quieter, occasionally casting glances between their mother and us, as if trying to understand the subtle currents running beneath adult conversations.

"Will you take care of Mummy's flowers?" Lorelai asks suddenly, her small face unexpectedly solemn. "They're very important. They're her babies, like us."

"We'll take perfect care of them," Hudson promises, reaching over to tuck a curl behind her ear. "Just like we'd take care of you and Daniel if your mum needed us to."

Lorelai studies him for a moment, then nods, apparently satisfied. "Good. Because she loves them almost as much as she loves us."

Lorna blushes. "Lorelai, the flowers are just my job—"

"No, they're not," Daniel interrupts with the kind of unshakable certainty only a child can pull off. "You talk to them when you think we're not listening. And you get sad when they die. That's love."

The room stills. Lorna doesn't say a word, but I see it in her face, the way her expression falters like she's been caught off guard. Not embarrassed. Just exposed.

For a moment, I see her completely. Not only the mother holding it all together, not the farmer with dirt under her nails and a to-do list a mile long. The woman beneath all that. The one who feels so much and has learned, somewhere along the way, to bury that tenderness beneath practicality.

"Your mother loves deeply," I tell the twins. "It's one of her greatest strengths."

A change moves through Lorna's expression, surprise, then a softening that makes her seem years younger. Like no one's ever seen that part of her as anything but a weakness. Her eyes find mine across the table, a flash of raw vulnerability that makes my heart clench. I've seen that expression before, in frightened animals, in people who've been hurt too many times to trust easily. It's the face of someone whose armor has been pierced, not by an attack but by unexpected kindness.

The twins are oblivious to the emotional undercurrents swirling around the adults. Daniel returns to his methodical eating, while Lorelai launches into a detailed explanation of which fairies prefer which flowers, her small hands animated as she illustrates her point.

But Lorna's still looking at me, something different in her gaze now. A question, perhaps. Or the beginning of an answer.

Hudson clears his throat, breaking the spell between us. He raises his water glass in a mock toast. "To Dr. MacLeod, botanist extraordinaire and secret plant whisperer. May all your flowers stand at attention when you speak to them."

"Hudson!" she protests, but she's laughing, color rising in her cheeks.

The rest of dinner passes in comfortable chaos—the twins telling elaborate stories, Hudson making terrible puns, Levi quietly ensuring everyone's plate stays full. It feels natural in a way that should terrify me but doesn't.

After the twins are settled in bed with a story from Levi (who has proven to have an extraordinary gift for bedtime tales), the four of us find ourselves on the back porch nursing a six-pack of local beer. The spring evening is cool but not cold, the sky painted in spectacular strokes of orange and pink as the sun begins its slow descent.

"So," Lorna says finally, curling her legs beneath her in the porch swing. "I guess this is it until I get back."

"We'll still see you off in the morning," Hudson reminds her from where he's perched on the railing like an overgrown bird.

"I know, but that will be rushed. With the twins and luggage and the drive." She takes a sip, then licks her lips. "This feels more like the real goodbye."

"Not goodbye," Levi says quietly from his spot on the steps. "Just... intermission."

She smiles at that. "I like that. Intermission."

I can't stop studying her. The way the dying light catches in her hair, turning it golden. The graceful curve of her neck as she tips her head back to gaze at the sky. The delicate arch of her foot beneath the hem of her jeans.

I want to memorize every detail to keep me company during the long month ahead. A month without her laughter, her scent, her stubborn determination that both frustrates and captivates me.

"I should probably confess something," Lorna says suddenly, her fingers nervously picking at the label on her beer bottle. "I'm not just going to the castle for the gardens. I'm also going to... think. About what happens next."

"With us," I clarify, though it's not really a question.

She nods, not looking up. "Yesterday was... intense. And wonderful. And terrifying." She takes a deep breath. "And complicated, because it's about all of us." She gestures to include Hudson and Levi. "And I don't know what that means, or what it could mean, or what I want it to mean. And then when you throw the twins into the mix..." she trails off, sighing heavily.

"That's okay," Levi says gently. "You don't need to have answers right now."

"But I owe you honesty," she insists. "And the truth is, I'm attracted to all three of you. In different ways, for different reasons. And that's... well, that's not something I ever expected to feel. Or admit out loud." Her cheeks flush deeply. "Dear God, I can't believe I said that. Take me now, sweet merciful death."

Hudson slides from the railing to crouch before her, taking one of her hands in his. "Thank you for being brave enough to say it. That's more honesty than most people manage in a lifetime."

"He's right," I add. "And for what it's worth, the feeling is mutual. From all of us."

Her eyes widen slightly, as if she didn't realize until that moment that we all want her. "All of you? But... I mean—" She shakes her head. "See? Complicated."

"Complicated isn't always bad," Levi observes. "Some of the

most beautiful things in life are complicated. Your hybridization work, for instance. The genetics are incredibly complex, but the results are extraordinary."

A small smile tugs at her lips. "Did you just compare potential relationship dynamics to flower genetics?"

"If the metaphor fits," Levi says with an answering smile.

"There's something you should know," I say, my voice serious enough that all three of them turn to look at me. "We've talked about this. About us, and you, and what it might mean."

Lorna's expression shifts to uncertainty, her hands tightening around her beer bottle.

"We've decided it's all of us, or none of us," I tell her, holding her gaze steadily. "We're a package deal, Lorna."

Her lips part in surprise. "You've actually discussed this?"

Hudson nods, his usual playfulness subdued. "We have. And we're in agreement. You deserve to know what you're considering."

"So... if I only wanted one of you...?" She lets the question hang in the air.

"Then you get none of us," Levi says quietly. "You'll always have us as friends. But romantically, it's all or nothing."

Lorna sits back, visibly processing. "That's... a lot to think about."

"That's what the month is for," I remind her. "To figure out what you want. What we all want." I lean forward slightly. "But know this, Lorna. If you choose all of us, you get all of us. Fully committed. No holding back. No half measures."

She shivers visibly, and I know it's not from the cool evening air.

"You don't have to say anything," I tell her. "Just think about it while you're away. And when you come back, we'll talk. All of us, openly and honestly."

She nods slowly. "Okay. I can do that."

The moment stretches between us, thick with all the words we haven't said. The air feels charged, humming with tension and desire, like the space itself is holding its breath. It isn't only attraction, it's the possibility of a beginning—fragile and wild, capable of changing everything.

It could be extraordinary. Or it could destroy us.

Either way, there's no going back now. Not after yesterday's kiss. Not after tonight's confessions. We've already crossed the line, and all that's left is to see where it leads.

Hudson, never one to let serious moments last too long, suddenly stands. His gaze locks on Lorna with such intensity that she presses back in her chair, her throat working. Without a word, he pulls her to her feet from the swing.

"Something to think about while you're gone," he murmurs, before capturing her mouth with his.

Unlike my somewhat controlled approach yesterday, Hudson kisses her like a man drowning, desperate, hungry, holding nothing back. He cradles her face as he pours everything into the kiss, and I watch as Lorna's initial surprise melts into surrender, her body arching toward his like a flower seeking the sun.

When he finally pulls away, they're both breathing hard. Lorna sways slightly, looking dazed, her lips red and swollen.

"Jesus, Hudson," she whispers.

He grins, that dimple appearing as he steps back. "Just making sure you don't forget about me while you're off playing lady of the manor."

Levi clears his throat and stands, his quiet presence drawing Lorna's attention. "Walk with me a moment?" he asks, offering his hand.

She takes it without hesitation, glancing back at me and Hudson as Levi leads her around the corner of the house, just out of sight. Hudson drops back into the swing with a self-satisfied smirk, and I raise an eyebrow at him.

"Subtle," I comment dryly.

"Effective," he counters.

When Lorna and Levi return minutes later, the change is obvious. Her hair is more disheveled than before, her cheeks flushed, and her eyes bright with an inner fire I've rarely seen. Levi, normally so composed, is slightly rumpled, the faintest hint of a blush on his cheeks.

"Everything okay?" I ask mildly.

"Perfect," Levi answers, his voice huskier than usual.

Lorna giggles, then slaps her hand over her mouth like she can't believe that sound just came out of it.

Hudson grins and squeezes her hand. "Just so you know, I expect a full report from the castle. Secret passageways, ghost stories, the works. And pictures of the suits of armor. Do they have those? Or is it all just plaid and bagpipes?"

Lorna raises an eyebrow, a smile creeping across her face. "I'll take pictures. And it's tartan, not plaid. That's an American thing."

"Tartan, plaid, same difference," Hudson says with a dismissive wave.

"Tell that to a Scotsman and you'll be wearing his kilt as a neck brace," Lorna warns, but she's smiling.

The evening ends naturally after that, with promises to see her off in the morning and assurances that her farm is in good hands. As we prepare to leave, Lorna walks us to the front door, arms wrapped around herself against the cooling night air.

"Thank you," she says simply. "For everything."

Hudson goes first, pulling her into a hug that lifts her briefly off her feet. "Sleep well, Snapdragon," he murmurs, pressing a quick kiss to her forehead before releasing her.

Levi follows, his embrace gentler but no less heartfelt. "Safe travels," he tells her, squeezing her hand once before stepping back.

Then it's my turn. As Levi and Hudson head toward the truck, I close my hand around Lorna's wrist, pulling her back over the threshold.

"Hold on a second," I tell the guys. "Forgot something inside."

Before anyone can question me, I kick the door shut. The lock clicks into place and I press her against the wood, my body caging hers. Unlike yesterday's careful exploration, this time I let her see all of my emotions—the hunger, the possessiveness, the raw need that's been growing since I first saw her across the fence line two years ago.

"Leo?" she says softly, pressing her thumb to my chin and tilting my head until my gaze meets hers.

"My turn," I murmur, voice rough, before capturing her mouth in a kiss that leaves no room for doubt.

I kiss her with my entire being, my hand sliding into her hair while the other anchors at her hip. She makes a sound that nearly undoes me, soft and raw, the kind of sound a man could live off if he were starving. She clutches my shoulders, nails biting through the fabric as she kisses me back with equal fire, matching me breath for breath, need for need.

When I finally pull away, her cheeks are flushed, and her eyes are heavy-lidded with desire. I press my forehead to hers, both of us gasping for air.

"That," I tell her roughly, "is what will be waiting for you when you come back. Along with them. All of us, Lorna. Think about that while you're gone."

She nods, speechless for once, her hands still clutching my shirt like she might fall without the support.

Slowly, reluctantly, I let her go and take a step back. She touches her lips with trembling fingers, breath uneven, pupils blown. She looks completely undone, thoroughly kissed and heart-breakingly beautiful.

"I should go," I say, gesturing to the door where muffled knocking can now be heard. "They're getting impatient."

"Leo," she says softly as I reach for the lock. I turn back, and the vulnerability in her expression nearly undoes me. "I will. Think about it, I mean. About all of you."

I nod once, then unlock the door to find Hudson and Levi waiting with identical knowing expressions.

"Forgot something, huh?" Hudson smirks.

"Shut up," I mutter. "See you in the morning," I tell her. "Six thirty."

She nods. "Six thirty."

As we drive away, I can't help glancing in the rearview mirror. Lorna stands framed in the doorway of her farmhouse, one hand raised in farewell. Like a scene from a movie, her silhouette a perfect snapshot of what we're leaving behind.

"Well," Hudson says into the silence of the truck. "That was..."

"Yeah," Levi agrees quietly.

"It's going to be a long month," Hudson observes, staring out the window at the darkening sky.

I nod, hands tightening on the steering wheel. "It'll be worth it."

As we drive over the hill toward home, it hits me like a punch to the gut. I've never wanted anything this badly in my entire life. Not the ranch in Australia, not success, not even the life we've built here. Whatever this becomes, this messy, beautiful thing between all of us, it's worth every uncomfortable conversation and every moment of doubt.

Hell, some things are just worth the wait. Worth the work. Worth putting everything on the line.

And that stubborn, brilliant, gorgeous woman with dirt under her fingernails and flower petals in her hair? The one who measures her heartbeats when she's nervous and curses like a sailor when she's surprised?

She's worth it all.

7

M other Trucker!"
I swerve as the castle comes into view. I'd forgotten how enormous it is. Judging by the dramatic gasps from the backseat, so have they.

"It's so big," Daniel breathes, his usual calm replaced by wide-eyed awe.

I can't blame him. Even after all these years, the sight of Amhuinnsuidh Castle knocks the air right out of my lungs. It sits between the sea and the hills like it grew there, stone turrets and arched windows rising out of the green, weathered by wind and time yet impossibly proud. I haven't been back in nearly five months, and seeing it now, my childhood home, hits different. The awe remains, but so does something heavier, a weight that knots tight in my chest.

"The castle got BIGGER!" Lorelai shrieks, her voice sharp enough to make me wince. "It's for princesses and dragons and KNIGHTS!"

"And very loud little girls who are about to burst my eardrums," I say, smiling as I steer our little blue Volvo down the winding drive toward home.

Generations of MacLeods have walked these grounds. My siblings and I inherited the estate after our parents died, but Jack, the reluctant duke, has carried the weight of it for most of his life. I was already planning my escape to university, and Isla was too young to shoulder any of it. Now Jack has a growing family, and Isla has moved back with her husbands to help with the restoration. For the first time in years, the castle feels alive again, as if it's finally remembering what it means to be a home.

As we roll into the circular drive, I spot a small welcoming committee on the front steps. A tiny blonde missile breaks formation and barrels down ahead of the adults, moving with the wild, unfiltered joy only toddlers can pull off.

"DEY HERE! DEY HERE!" my niece Summer shrieks, her two-year-old legs pumping at a speed that defies physics.

Before I can shift into park, Jack swoops in, scooping her up before she collides with our bumper. My brother, all six-and-a-half feet of him, looks absurdly soft with his daughter perched on his hip. His tawny hair is tied back in a bun that would look ridiculous on anyone else, but somehow works on him, like a Viking who took a detour through a lumberyard.

"Look who finally decided to grace us with her presence," he calls, grinning like the smug older brother he's always been. "The prodigal plant whisperer returns!"

The twins are practically vibrating beside me, wrestling with their seatbelts in their rush to get out. The second they're free, they tumble onto the gravel like a pair of overexcited puppies.

"Uncle Jack! Summer!" they yell in unison, darting toward him. Summer wriggles in his arms, demanding freedom with all the authority of a toddler dictator.

I climb out and stretch, spine popping in protest after two hours on narrow Highland roads. My whole body aches, not just from the drive but from everything I've been carrying lately. Every muscle seems to hum with leftover memories of what happened at the farm. Three men, too many charged glances, and kisses I can't stop replaying no matter how hard I try.

I shove the thought aside. I'm here for the garden renovations. For family. Not to stand in the shadow of my childhood home daydreaming about my dangerously handsome neighbors like a lovesick teenager.

"There she is!" Isla's voice rings out as she bursts through the castle doorway. Unlike Jack's earthy steadiness, Isla is all fire—vibrant red hair tumbling in perfect waves, freckles scattered across pale skin, and an energy that makes everyone else look like they're moving in slow motion. Behind her, three men trail in her wake, orbiting her like planets around their sun.

Henry, Theo, and Dylan are Isla's husbands. Yes, husbands. Plural. My little sister has never done anything halfway, least of all falling in love. Why settle for one man when you can collect three? The MacLeod family motto should honestly be *Go Big or Go Home.*

"Christ, you look exhausted," Isla announces cheerfully, pulling me into a hug that could crack ribs. She leans back, studying me with narrowed eyes. "You've been working too hard on that farm of yours. Or is it those hot neighbors keeping you up at night?"

I give her a look sharp enough to wilt roses. "Getting everything ready for a month away is a lot of work."

"Well, you're here now," she says, looping her arm through mine and steering me toward the castle. "You can relax while fixing our garden disaster. It's only several acres of neglected horticulture. Easy peasy."

"Some relaxation," I mutter. "Nothing says vacation like sunburn, sore muscles, and impossible deadlines."

"At least you found help for your farm," she teases, lowering her voice as we walk. "Your hot neighbors, right? Leo, Levi, and Hudson? The ones you've been *not-so-subtly* stalking for two years?"

My jaw nearly drops. "I have not been stalking them!"

Isla rolls her eyes. "Please. You've been crushing on those three for over two years now. You're about as subtle as a neon sign. I've considered staging an intervention."

Heat burns across my cheeks. Was I really that transparent? "I haven't been—"

"Yes, you have," she interrupts with a knowing smirk. "Though I never understood why you suddenly stopped mentioning them last year. Like they entered witness protection or something. And now they're watching your farm while you're gone? Spill. The. Tea. Now."

"It's not—they're just—" I stammer, feeling like I'm fifteen and being interrogated about a crush. "It's complicated."

"The best things usually are," she says with a wink. "Don't worry, your secret's safe with me. I won't tell Jack about them. Yet. But you *do* owe me every juicy detail later."

"Thank you," I mutter, because arguing with Isla is pointless and this is the best deal I'm getting.

Behind us, Henry tries and fails to hide a laugh, pretending he didn't overhear every word. Isla's men might look cut from the same tall, dark, and dangerously handsome mold, but that's where the similarities end. Henry, the middle brother, is the sweetest, all dimples and romantic gestures that would make a romance novel hero look lazy. Theo, the oldest, hides a soft heart behind his gruff exterior, like a storm that secretly loves the rain. Dylan, the youngest, doesn't say much, but his eyes miss nothing. Quiet, steady, constantly watching.

"I have something to tell you," Isla says, guilt flashing across her face. "I leave tomorrow morning for the cooking course at Ballymaloe."

"Tomorrow?" I blink. "But I just got here. And the gardens—"

"I know, I know!" She raises her hands in surrender. "I feel absolutely terrible about the timing. The course was booked months ago, non-refundable deposits paid, and then this magazine opportunity fell into our lap..." She grabs my hands. "I can cancel. Seriously. This is more important than some cooking course."

"You will not cancel," I say firmly, squeezing her fingers. "You've been talking about this for ages. It's important to you."

"But you'll be stuck here handling everything alone."

"I won't be alone. Besides, I've been managing a farm single-handedly for six years. I think I can handle some overgrown hedges without having a nervous breakdown."

"Some?" Theo snorts. "Have you seen the west garden yet? It's like Jurassic Park out there. I swear something tried to eat my boot last week."

"My point stands. Isla, go to Ireland. But you have to promise you'll cook for me when you get back."

"Every night for a month," she vows, relief and gratitude softening her features.

We climb the stone steps together, the sound of our footsteps echoing off the walls like old memories. The massive oak doors swing open, and the familiar scent of hearth smoke and lavender polish greets me. For a moment, it feels like stepping back in time, only now laughter spills from the hall instead of silence.

Jack's wife Charlotte, Charlie to everyone but Jack, meets us inside. Her chestnut waves are pulled into a simple ponytail, and she's dressed in worn jeans and a soft blue sweater that matches her eyes. After escaping a marriage so bad it could have been a Lifetime movie, she found an unexpected home with my brother and his two best friends, Cameron and Lachlan.

"The twins' room is right through there," Charlie says after pulling me into a hug that smells like cinnamon and fresh laundry. "Why don't you take some time to settle in while I rescue them from whatever sugar-fueled chaos Jack has unleashed? Last time he watched kids unsupervised, they came back sticky and speaking in tongues."

I laugh, the weight lifting from my shoulders. "That sounds about right."

"Welcome back, Lorna," she says, giving my hand a squeeze before heading off down the hall.

After Charlie leaves, I unpack on autopilot, hanging my plain, practical clothes in the carved mahogany wardrobe. My favorite jeans, soft sweaters, and work shirts look wildly out of place here, like I've stumbled into Downton Abbey in a pair of muddy boots.

I move to the adjoining room where the twins will sleep,

arranging Daniel's rock collection on the windowsill. Lorelai's fairy books and dolls go on the nightstand between the twin beds. I can't help but smile at the thought of how excited they'll be to sleep in a real castle.

A soft knock at the door interrupts my thoughts.

"Come in," I call, expecting Charlie or Isla.

Instead, Jack's broad frame fills the doorway. My brother looks like he stepped out of a Scottish tourism ad in worn jeans and a flannel shirt with the sleeves rolled up, his ducal heritage evident in the confident way he carries himself, like he owns the place. Which, technically, he does.

"The terrible twosome are helping Summer feed the chickens," he says. "Thought you might want to see the gardens while you have a moment of peace. And before you need a stiff drink to cope with what you're about to see."

"That bad?" I ask, already mentally cataloging what supplies I'll need.

Jack's grimace is so severe I'm worried his face might get stuck that way. "Let's just say we've gone from 'neglected' to 'post-apocalyptic' in record time."

"Wonderful," I mutter, trying to breathe through the anxiety clutching at my chest.

We walk in companionable silence through the castle's winding corridors and out a side door that leads directly to what was once our grandmother's pride and joy, the formal gardens.

"Sweet baby Jesus on a pogo stick," I breathe as we round the corner.

Calling it neglected would be generous. The once-meticulously planned landscape resembles a place where Mother Nature declared war and brought reinforcements. The hedges have grown wild and misshapen, flower beds are choked with weeds, and what were once elegant gravel pathways have all but disappeared beneath encroaching grass.

"Told you," Jack says grimly. "The west section is worse. I think something's built a nest in there. Possibly a dragon."

"God, don't tell Lorelai that." I step forward like a general surveying a battlefield, mentally cataloging what can be salvaged and what's already lost. Even with the wreckage around me, a familiar spark flares to life. This is a blank canvas. A chance to build new from the bones of what used to be.

"Six weeks is tight," I murmur, crouching to examine a struggling rose bush nearly strangled by ivy. "But doable. I'll need supplies, labor, and possibly an exorcist."

"All arranged," Jack says, squatting beside me. "Supplies are being delivered tomorrow. Lach's hired a team of local workers who can start Monday, and as for the exorcist..." He grins, nudging my shoulder with his. "That's why we called you, plant whisperer."

I roll my eyes, warmth rising in my cheeks. For all his teasing, Jack has never failed to take me seriously. When I traded research papers for seed trays, he didn't make me feel foolish. He accepted it without question, like he'd known all along I'd find my way back to the dirt.

"Tell me more about this magazine and the wedding."

Jack makes a face. "The editor stumbled across the castle during a tour of the Hebrides. Said it was the most romantic setting she'd ever seen." He gestures to the weed-infested disaster around us. "Obviously she was using her imagination."

"Or hallucinogenics."

"The feature could bring in dozens of bookings," he explains. "Enough to cover maintenance costs for years without dipping into capital. But they need an actual wedding to photograph, and the only date that works is six weeks from now."

"Who's getting married?"

"We're trying to convince Father Calum. He and Tyler were planning to elope, but I told him this would be the perfect full-circle moment."

Father Calum had to leave his church when he and Tyler met, when whatever that thing was between them caught fire and refused to be tamed. For months, they were the center of every whisper on the island, the kind of scandal people pretended to condemn but secretly rooted for. Eventually, the talk died down, because it was obvious they belonged together.

He's the one who married Jack, Charlie, Cam, and Lach here at the castle. And Jack's right, it would be the perfect full-circle moment.

"You better hurry up and convince him. Six weeks isn't much time to pull off a wedding."

Jack grins, unbothered. "I'm confident in our problem-solving abilities. One crisis at a time. We're MacLeods. Last-minute miracles are our specialty."

We continue our tour through what used to be the gardens, though "wilderness" feels more accurate now. The old reflecting pool is nothing but a murky pond thick with algae, its surface broken by the occasional ripple of something best left unidentified. The pergola where we used to have summer lunches is nearly swallowed whole by overgrown vines, only the edge of its roof visible beneath the green tangle. The greenhouse stands at the edge of it all, its brick floor buried in weeds, steel frame streaked with rust, and glass panels cracked and clouded with age.

"I should check on Daniel and Lorelai," I say, needing to focus on anything other than the overwhelming task ahead. "I didn't expect the gardens to be quite this... murderous."

Jack looks thoughtful. "We can hire more help if needed. The magazine feature is worth the investment."

"We'll see what we're dealing with after a full assessment tomorrow. I may surprise myself."

"You always do," Jack says, a tender smile pulling at his lips. "Remember when Grandmother let you design a rose garden when you were twelve? Everyone said it was too ambitious, but you proved them wrong with your stubborn MacLeod genes."

I'd nearly forgotten that childhood triumph, my first real gardening project, approved reluctantly by our grandmother after weeks of persistent lobbying. "She was furious when I tore out all her perennials. I thought she was going to disown me on the spot."

"Until your design won that garden society award. She bragged about her 'prodigy granddaughter' for years afterward. Nearly bored her bridge club to death with pictures."

The memory warms me from the inside out. Our grandmother was formidable, all pearls and sharp opinions, a proper Scottish matriarch through and through. But she saw my love for plants early on and, in her own brisk, no-nonsense way, encouraged it. This renovation feels like a tribute to her. Order pulled from chaos. Beauty coaxed back from neglect.

As we head toward the castle, Jack's phone buzzes. He glances at the screen, frowning. "I have to take this. Roofing company."

"Go ahead," I tell him. "I should track down the twins anyway. Make sure they haven't convinced Summer to lead a chicken rebellion."

Back inside and left to my own devices, I wander through the familiar corridors of my childhood home. Much has changed, with new furnishings, fresh paint, and modern touches meant to tame its age, but the soul of the place endures. The stone walls hum with memory, steeped in centuries of MacLeod triumphs and heartbreaks, ours now folded neatly among them.

I find the children in the kitchen, where Charlie is teaching them how to make bread. All three are covered in flour, looking like tiny ghosts kneading dough with varying degrees of success.

"Look, Mummy!" Lorelai cries when she spots me. "I'm making fairy bread!"

"It's not fairy bread yet," Daniel corrects with the seriousness of a culinary professor. "It needs to rise and bake first. Then we put butter and sprinkles on it. You have to follow the steps."

"That's right," Charlie agrees, wiping flour from her cheek and only succeeding in adding more. "And what do we need for the dough to rise?"

"Yeastie beasties!" Summer announces, her small hands patting her lump of dough with surprising gentleness. "Dey eat sugar and make bubbles!"

"That's exactly right, pumpkin," Charlie praises, dropping a kiss on Summer's blonde curls. "The yeast eats the sugar and releases carbon dioxide, which makes the bubbles that help our bread rise."

Charlie catches my eye and smiles. "Want to join in? We've got plenty of dough. Though I should warn you, bread-making with a toddler is classified as an extreme sport."

"I think I'll leave the baking to the experts. But I'd love to sample the results later. Especially if wine is involved."

"Perfect timing," a deep voice says behind me. I turn to find Cameron, Charlie's leaner husband, his sharp eyes glinting behind dark-rimmed glasses. "We're planning a lakeside cookout tonight. First grill of the season. Men and fire. A sacred ritual throughout the centuries."

"In April? Isn't it a bit cold?"

"That's what I said," Charlie interjects with a long-suffering sigh. "But apparently challenging the elements is some sort of testosterone-ridden ritual I'm not allowed to question. Like watching sports or leaving wet towels on the floor."

"It's the last day of April, which means it's really May," he says, smiling. "We'll have a bonfire to keep warm and Lach's bringing out the good whisky. The kind that makes you think you're invincible after two sips."

"I'm in," I decide impulsively. A night by the fire sounds exactly like what I need. "What can I help with?"

"Just bring your appetite," Charlie says. "These three insist on handling everything. I've learned to let them have their caveman moments."

"I hungry," Summer announces, abandoning her dough to toddle over to Cameron.

"Almost dinner time, little bug," he assures her, scooping her up despite the cloud of flour that follows. "Should we go see if they've got the fire started?"

"Fire! Fire!" Summer agrees enthusiastically, clapping her floury hands together.

"Don't worry," Cameron assures me, noting my expression. "She's not a budding pyromaniac. She just likes to watch the flames from a safe distance. Unlike her father, who nearly burned down the boathouse when he was fourteen."

After Cameron and Summer leave, I help Charlie clean up the twins. The simple rhythm of it, washing small hands, wiping flour from button noses, listening to their excited chatter about bread and fairies and rocks, settles a quiet, steady warmth inside me.

"You're good with them," I observe as Charlie helps Lorelai pull a clean sweater over her head. "Natural."

Charlie's smile softens. "It wasn't always easy. I had no idea what I was doing when Summer was born. I basically Googled 'how to keep a tiny human alive' every day. She's been teaching me ever since."

"I can imagine," I say with a laugh, remembering how lost I'd felt with the twins.

Once the children are scrubbed and presentable, we bundle them into sweaters and head outside. The castle stands on a rocky promontory above a sheltered inlet of clear, glacial water. In summer, it's perfect for swimming, though even then it's cold enough to sting your skin. Tonight, with the April air still edged with winter, only the brave or the foolish would dare.

We cross the wide stretch of grass to the pebbly beach below, where the evening hum of activity has already begun. Jack and Lachlan tend a roaring bonfire that spits sparks into the wind, while Theo and Henry work over a portable grill. Dylan has dragged a semicircle of Adirondack chairs close enough to feel the heat, his expression one of deep satisfaction at the organized chaos.

"The conquering gardener arrives!" Lach calls out, raising a beer in my direction. "Jack says you're plotting a miraculous transformation. Going to turn water into wine next?"

"Don't get ahead of yourself. I haven't done a proper assessment yet. For all I know, there could be actual man-eating plants out there."

The scene feels like something out of a brochure for Scottish family living, the ancient castle rising behind us, the loch spreading silver-blue before us, the fire casting dancing shadows across familiar faces. For a moment, time seems to slip sideways, and I could be sixteen again, sneaking beers with Jack and his friends during summer holidays.

Except now, there are children racing along the shoreline, collecting rocks, and the men who once treated me as Jack's annoying sister are now family.

And I'm not sixteen anymore, I'm a single mother with a farm, responsibilities, and a complicated attraction to three men who are currently tending said farm and probably sleeping in my bed.

As if reading my thoughts, Isla appears at my elbow. "You're thinking about them, aren't you?" she asks quietly.

"Who?" I try for innocence and fail spectacularly.

Isla gives me a look that says she's seeing straight through me. "Your fantasy farmers," she teases. "Don't deny it. You've got that dreamy, faraway expression that only means one thing—you're mentally undressing someone. Or, knowing you, three someones."

"I do not get 'dreamy looks,'" I protest, taking a swig of beer to hide my face. "I'm a serious botanist with serious thoughts about... photosynthesis and soil pH."

"You absolutely do. Right now, you're probably wondering what they're doing, if they've fed the chickens, if they're sitting on your porch watching the sunset... maybe getting all sweaty doing farm chores..."

She's so spot-on I nearly choke on my beer. Because yes, that's exactly where my mind had gone—Leo on my porch swing, his broad frame making it look absurdly small, probably reading one of his old leather-bound books. Hudson on the steps, tinkering with some project, wood shavings gathering around his boots. And Levi, pen in hand, writing in his journal but glancing up now and then to watch the light shift over the fields.

"Your face!" Isla crows triumphantly. "I knew it! You've got it bad. Like, teenager-with-a-boyband-crush bad."

"Shush!" I hiss, glancing around to make sure no one else is within earshot. The others are occupied with food prep and child wrangling, safely out of range. "I'm just concerned about my farm."

"Mmm-hmm," she hums skeptically. "Your farm. Not the farmers. Not their strong, capable hands tending your... soil conditions."

I scoff, but there's no point denying it. Isla knows me too well. "Fine. I'm... thinking about them. But it doesn't matter. It's complicated, it's messy, it's probably a terrible idea. And I don't even know if they're interested in... soil conditions with me."

"The best ideas usually are," she says with uncharacteristic seriousness. "Look at me and my guys. Look at Jack with Charlie, Lach and Cam. Conventional wisdom would say we're all making terrible choices. But I've never been happier."

"It's different."

"Is it though? Love is love, Lorna. Whether it's one person or three. The heart wants what it wants. And sometimes what it wants is a sexy farmer throuple."

"Who said anything about love?" I sputter. "I barely know them. I just think they're hot. And kind. And good with my kids. And surprisingly thoughtful. And—"

Oh God.

Isla's smile widens. "You've been watching them for two years. You know them better than you think. And honey? The way your face lights up when you talk about them, even when you're trying not to? That's not just neighborly appreciation."

Before I can formulate a response, Jack calls everyone to attention. "All right, who's brave enough for a pre-dinner swim? Family tradition says the season isn't officially open until someone takes the plunge! Any volunteers for hypothermia?"

"I'll pass, thanks," Charlie says, wrapping her arms around herself with an exaggerated shiver. "Some traditions deserve to die. Like bloodletting and this particular form of torture."

"Coward," Lach teases, pulling his shirt over his head. "The water's probably a balmy seven degrees by now. Almost tropical."

"Seven degrees? That's practically freezing!"

"Practically, but not actually," Lach winks, kicking off his shoes. "Come on, Lorna. For old times' sake. Remember when we used to race to that rock and back? Before you went all responsible adult on us?"

I do remember. I remember the burn of the cold in my lungs, the way my limbs would go numb almost immediately in that icy water. But a reckless urge stirs at Lach's challenge, a flicker of the girl I used to be, before the failed marriage, before motherhood, before life started feeling like a series of responsibilities instead of adventures.

"You're on," I find myself saying, ignoring the rational part of my brain telling me not to be a complete idiot.

"Same rules as always."

A small crowd gathers along the shoreline as Lach and I ready ourselves. Jack, naturally assuming the role of referee, lays out the rules: swim to the big rock jutting from the water about thirty yards out, touch it, and come back. First one to shore wins. Dylan claims lifeguard duty, lounging like royalty in a rowboat nearby.

"You're both insane!" Charlie shouts from the safety of the sand. "At least make it worth it. Winner gets first pick of steaks!"

"Deal!" Lach and I shout in unison.

I peel off my layers until I'm down to my underwear and bra, the late April air biting at my skin, goosebumps prickling in protest.

"Ready to lose?" Lach teases, bouncing on his toes, a devilish grin on his face.

"In your dreams, Lachlan."

Jack raises an arm like he's officiating the Highland Games. "On my mark. Three, two, one—GO!"

We crash into the water, and regret slams into me, instant and brutal. The cold is a living thing, biting, vicious, stealing the air from my lungs in a single, panicked gasp. It feels like being stabbed by a thousand tiny icicles, and every nerve in my body screams at me to turn back, to crawl toward the fire and sanity.

But pride is louder than pain. Lach's already a body length ahead, his stupidly long limbs cutting clean through the water. I grit my teeth and force my arms to move, the cold burning so deep it almost feels hot.

Then comes that strange clarity, the way everything else falls away. No thoughts, no worries, no garden renovations or irrigation schedules or confusing feelings about three aggravatingly beautiful men. Only cold and breath and motion. Only me and the rhythm of my strokes, and the old MacLeod stubbornness pulsing through my veins.

I reach the rock seconds after Lach, slap my hand against its slick surface, and spin back toward shore. The chill has sunk into my bones now, numbing my fingers, dulling everything except the drive to finish. The twins are jumping and shouting on the beach, their tiny voices carrying over the water like a battle cry.

With one last burst of strength, I dig deep, arms slicing through the freezing water until my fingers hit pebbles and wet sand. I drag myself onto the shore, collapsing in a heap of laughter and shuddering breaths, half-frozen, half-triumphant.

"Winner!" Jack declares, as Charlie immediately wraps a thick towel around my shoulders.

I'm shaking too hard to speak, my teeth chattering like castanets, but the triumph still tastes sweet. Lach emerges a second later, accepting his defeat with a dramatic bow.

"I'm... still... the... fastest." I manage through chattering teeth.

"Only because I let you win," Lach says, the words puffed out between breaths, but the grin tugging at his mouth ruins any attempt at dignity. "What can I say? I'm a gentleman."

"Into dry clothes, both of you," Charlie orders, every inch the worried mother. "As entertaining as it would be to explain why you both have hypothermia to the emergency services, I'd rather not spend the night in A&E."

Twenty minutes later, warmed by dry clothes, the blazing bonfire, and a generous dram of excellent whisky, I'm almost grateful for the swim. The buzzing energy lingers, making me feel alive.

"That was epic," Henry says, passing me a plate loaded with grilled steak, roasted potatoes, and salad. "I can't believe you actually beat Lach. He never loses at anything physical. It's annoying, actually."

"He does to me. Always has."

"Always will," Lach agrees good-naturedly from across the fire, raising his whisky in salute. "Something about those MacLeod genes produces champion swimmers."

"And champion gardeners," Jack adds. "And champion troublemakers."

"That's rich, coming from you. Who nearly burned down the boathouse sneaking a smoke at fourteen and then blamed it on 'spontaneous combustion'? Very convincing." Isla laughs, shaking her head.

"Ancient history," Jack dismisses with a wave of his hand. "And I maintain it was spontaneous combustion. Those sailing magazines were clearly highly flammable."

The conversation drifts as easily as the whisky, childhood memories slipping into newer family stories. The twins and Summer, worn out from the beach and the day's chaos, start to fold into us. Summer's already asleep in Jack's lap, her curls spilling over his arm. Lorelai's curled against my side, warm and heavy. Across the fire, Daniel's fighting a losing battle with sleep, mumbling about rock layers around the loch, his words softening, slurring at the edges.

It's perfect. This easy blend of old and new, the family I was born into and the one we've built. For the first time in a long while, I feel my body unclench, my lungs expanding all the way. The tension I've been hauling around starts to loosen.

Then my phone buzzes in my pocket. I shift Lorelai carefully, her soft weight pressing against me as I check the screen, and my heart pulls an Olympic routine in the space of a single beat.

Leo.

*Just checking in. All is well at both farms. Irrigation system running as planned, animals fed, all secure. Sleep well. – L*

The message is short, practical, totally Leo in its no-nonsense efficiency, and somehow, it still sends a slow, impossible heat spreading through my chest that has nothing to do with the whisky or the bonfire. I stare at the screen, reading those simple lines again and again, like I'm decoding a secret message.

"Everything okay?" Charlie asks, noticing my fixed attention on the phone.

"Fine. Just a message from home."

"Farm check-in?" Jack asks, poking at the fire.

"Mmm-hmm."

Isla catches my eye across the fire, her knowing smirk making it clear she's guessed exactly who texted me. She mimes locking her lips and throwing away the key, a promise of continued discretion that I appreciate more than she knows.

"I should get these two to bed," I say softly. "It's been a long day."

"I'll help," Charlie says, scooping up Daniel, who's gone completely limp, his head resting on Cam's shoulder.

With murmured goodnights and promises to pick up where we left off tomorrow, we head back toward the castle. Charlie carries Daniel, his small hand dangling against her arm, while I shift Lorelai higher against my hip, her breath warm against my neck. By the time we tuck them in, both are deep in sleep, out cold before their heads even touch the pillows.

"They're great kids," Charlie says softly as we tiptoe from their room. "You've done an amazing job with them."

"Thanks. Sometimes I wonder if I'm doing it right."

"All parents wonder that. It's practically a job requirement. But trust me, those two are thriving."

After Charlie heads back to the gathering, I'm too wired to sleep even though my body begs for it. The castle always does this to me. Too many ghosts in the walls, too many memories pressing close. I reach for my phone.

*Thank you for the update. Glad to hear everything's running smoothly. The castle is exactly as I remembered, though the gardens are in worse shape than expected. Give my best to Hudson and Levi – Lorna.*

Simple. Professional. Friendly without crossing any lines. I hit send before I can start second-guessing myself, then crawl into the massive four-poster bed, the sheets cool against my skin and the quiet pressing in from all sides.

Sleep won't come. My mind won't stop spinning, running through garden layouts, repair budgets, and, inevitably, the three men I left behind. I can see Hudson stretched out on my couch, his long legs propped on the coffee table. Levi nosing through my shelves, discovering the romance novels I keep tucked behind the botany texts. Leo at my kitchen table, pen in hand, brow furrowed in that maddening, beautiful way of his.

They shouldn't feel so close. They shouldn't feel like home. Yet the thought of them there, moving through my space, breathing my air, leaving traces of their warmth, settles deep inside me.

When sleep finally comes, it's filled with wild gardens and bonfire laughter, and three pairs of eyes watching me from a distance that feels suddenly, achingly far.

The next morning breaks bright and clear, one of those days that practically begs you to get your hands in the dirt. After a solid breakfast and waving Isla off on her trip to Ireland, Charlie and I head out to the gardens, clipboard in hand and a more detailed plan buzzing in my brain. This time, I'm not just wandering. I'm ready to take it all in—what needs saving, what's too far gone, and what might bloom if given half a chance.

"Any idea if these roses are still hanging on?" I ask, nodding toward a tangle of brambles near the stone wall.

She squints at the mess. "Some of the climbers on the east wall still flower now and then. The rest..." She waves a hand. "Total chaos. It's like Game of Thorns back here."

I huff a laugh. "They've been here as long as I can remember."

"One of the people from the magazine said they reminded her of a fairy tale—ancient roses crawling up ancient walls."

"They might be salvageable. With the right care, they could come back."

Charlie smiles softly. "Jack said your grandmother was protective of them. She'd be proud that you're trying to bring them back."

We fall into a comfortable rhythm, taking notes, flagging beds for clearing, not saying much. It's the kind of silence I don't mind, the kind that feels like breathing room.

My phone vibrates and I barely glance at the screen before my heart does that same stupid leap it did last night. Another message from the farm.

This time it's from Hudson:

*Morning sunshine! Found your coffee stash (the GOOD stuff you hide behind the flour—sneaky!). Leo says that's an invasion of privacy but what he doesn't know won't hurt him. Miss your scowling face already. - H*

I can't help the smile that spreads across my face. Trust Hudson to find my secret coffee reserve within 24 hours. And the casual "miss your scowling face" sends a flutter through my chest that I try desperately to ignore.

"Good news?" Charlie asks, noticing my expression.

"Just an update from my neighbors. Everything's under control."

"Lucky you have such reliable neighbors. Having good help makes such a difference."

"Yes. It was fortunate timing."

I should respond to Hudson's text, but what do I say? That I miss them too? That I woke up this morning with a strange hollow feeling knowing I wouldn't run into any of them today?

Eventually, I settle on: *That coffee is expensive, so enjoy it responsibly. And it's not hidden, it's strategically placed. Garden assessment underway. Situation dire but not hopeless. - Lorna*

I hesitate over the sign-off. Should it be more personal? A joke about my scowling face? An admission that the castle feels strange after so long away? In the end, I keep it simple, then tuck my phone away before I can overthink it further.

"These borders will need complete renovation," I tell Charlie, indicating a stretch of overgrown perennials that have long since lost any sense of design. "But we could salvage some of these heritage varieties and replant them in a more structured arrangement."

"Jack will be thrilled. He tries to pretend he doesn't care about the gardens, but I've caught him looking at old photos of how they used to be. I think he wants to restore your parents' legacy."

The observation catches me off guard. Jack almost never talks about our parents, the ache of losing them still raw after all these years. Knowing he's been quietly wanting to honor their memory adds a new kind of weight to my shoulders. Great. No pressure or anything.

We continue working through the morning, mapping out sections, taking soil samples, and creating lists of plants to order. It's satisfying work, the kind of methodical planning I excel at. But my mind keeps drifting back to my farm, to the three men moving through my daily routines, sleeping under my roof, caring for my plants.

My phone lights up again around noon, and this time it's a photo from Levi, a perfect close-up of one of my dahlia hybrids beginning to unfurl its first bloom, peach-colored petals edged with sunset pink.

*Your "Sunset Symphony" is making its debut. Thought you'd want to see it. The color is holding true. - Levi*

My heart does a full somersault. He remembered the name I'd given that hybrid I'd mentioned once, in passing, over dinner. The fact that he not only remembered but spotted the plant, recognized it, and thought to share it with me... it's too much.

"I need a break," I announce abruptly, suddenly overwhelmed by the confused tangle of emotions in my chest. "I'm going to check on the twins."

Charlie looks up in surprise from where she's measuring a planting bed. "They're fine. Jack took them riding with Summer on the ponies."

"Right. Good." I scramble for another excuse. "I should get some water then. It's getting hot."

It's not, but Charlie lets me get away with the lie. Which is kind of her, considering what I really mean is, *I need to go have an emotional breakdown over a picture of a flower.*

"I'll finish marking this section. Take your time."

I retreat to a stone bench partially hidden by an overgrown lilac, my hands slightly shaking as I type a response to Levi.

*It's beautiful. I wasn't sure the color would hold in the second generation. Could you take measurements? Length of petals, diameter of bloom, color saturation compared to the reference chart in my desk drawer?*

I hit send and then immediately regret it.

*No! Sorry. You don't have to do all that. Just enjoying it is enough. Thank you for sharing this moment. - Lorna*

This particular hybrid has been my obsession for two breeding cycles, my attempt to create a uniquely beautiful flower that could become my farm's signature bloom. And instead of experiencing its first unfurling in person, I'm sitting on a cold stone bench an entire island away.

But Levi made sure I didn't miss it completely. That means a lot to me.

His reply comes through almost immediately.

*Already documented everything in your research journal. Used your color scale and measurement protocols. Will continue daily observations. It's extraordinary, Lorna. Like watching a sunset captured in living form. Your vision brought to life. You should be proud. - Levi*

I press a hand to my chest, right over my sternum, as if I can steady the warmth spreading there. It's been so long since someone really saw me. Not the mother. Not the farmer. But the passion underneath it all. Levi sees the patterns and the poetry. The art inside the science. The quiet obsession that hums beneath my skin.

And that's the problem, isn't it?

All three of them see pieces of me most people never even bother looking for. Leo values the work I put into running the farm. Hudson understands the stubborn spark that keeps me moving when I should probably stop. And Levi? Levi sees the part of me that treats knowledge like a religion, a quiet devotion that drives everything I do.

If it were one of them, maybe I could breathe through it. But it's not. It's all three. And that? That's absolutely, deliciously terrifying.

"You okay over here?" Charlie's voice breaks into my thoughts. She approaches with a concerned expression, two water bottles in hand. "You look a bit overwhelmed."

"I'm processing the enormity of the garden project." I accept the water gratefully. "It's a lot to take in."

Charlie settles beside me on the bench. "You don't have to tackle it alone, you know. We've hired help, and Jack's willing to invest whatever's needed to make this work."

"I know. It's not only the gardens. It's... being back here. So many memories."

That, at least, is honest. The castle carries the ghosts of my childhood, the parents whose absence still stings, the traditions that shaped me, and the expectations I've spent half my life trying to live up to and the other half trying to escape.

"I get it," Charlie says quietly. "My first year here, I used to wander the corridors just to get lost. I needed to find corners that didn't feel so heavy with history and expectation. It's a lot to carry."

She sees right through me, and somehow that feels like relief.

"Exactly. And now I'm the one responsible for restoring a piece of that history."

"You're also creating something new," she says. "That's the magic of gardens, isn't it? They remember the past, but they never stop growing and changing."

My throat tightens. "Thank you."

"Anytime." She bumps her shoulder gently against mine. "That's what family's for."

We finish the assessment by mid-afternoon, our pages crowded with notes, rough sketches, and the first glimmers of a plan. There's a list of plants worth saving, a vision taking shape out of the ruin. By the time we return to the castle, my legs ache and my hands are stained with soil, but the exhaustion hums with quiet satisfaction.

The twins return from their pony adventure dirty, exhilarated, and full of stories about their cousin Summer's fearlessness on horseback.

"She's only TWO and she didn't cry ONCE when Bluebell went fast!" Lorelai exclaims as I help her into the bath. "I was a little scared but I pretended not to be."

"That's very brave. It's okay to be a little scared of new things."

"Mr. Hudson says that too," she informs me seriously. "He says being brave doesn't mean not being scared, it means doing it anyway."

The casual mention of Hudson takes me by surprise. "When did he tell you that?"

"When he was helping me build the fairy houses. I was scared to use the hammer but he showed me how."

I do my best to push aside the ache in my heart at the thought of Hudson patiently showing my daughter how to hammer nails.

"Mr. Levi is writing me a special fairy story," she says, splashing water with her hands. "And Mr. Leo said Daniel can help with the vegetable garden when it's time to plant the beans."

"They've been very kind to you and your brother." I smile, trying to sound casual, though I can't quite hide my surprise. After a day full of adventures and excitement, she's still talking about *them.*

"Mr. Leo said re-lie-bull neighbors are important. What does re-lie-bull mean, Mummy?"

"It means someone you can count on. Someone who does what they say they'll do."

"Like you," she says confidently. "And like them."

"Yes. Like them."

After getting both kids cleaned up and settled with their books before dinner, I finally have a moment to check my phone. There's one more message waiting, this one from all three of them: a photo of my kitchen table buried under farming manuals, hand-drawn maps of the farm, with what looks suspiciously like color-coding.

*Farm strategy session complete. Daily chore rotations established.*

*Seedlings planted according to your schedule. Irrigation zones optimized. Everything running smoothly. Your home is in good hands. Rest easy. - Leo, Hudson & Levi*

The message is short, efficient, completely businesslike, yet the sight of my kitchen table turned into their command center stirs a feeling in me that has nothing to do with business. They're treating the farm with the same care I would, not merely keeping things afloat but fully investing themselves in it.

My thumbs hover over the screen, suddenly unsure how to respond to a group message.

A soft knock at my door interrupts my spiral of overthinking. Jack pokes his head in, still wearing his barn clothes. "Are you decent? Charlie said you finished the assessment."

"Come in. And yes. I have notes, sketches, the works."

Jack settles at the foot of my bed, looking more relaxed than I've seen him since I arrived. "You were always the organized one."

"One of us had to be. You probably still can't find matching socks without help."

"That's why I have three partners," he counters with a grin. "Statistical improvement in sock location."

I laugh despite my tangled emotions. "Smart strategy."

"So what's the verdict on our horticultural disaster zone? Salvageable or should we salt the earth and start over?"

"Dramatic as ever. It's challenging but not impossible. The bones are there, good structure, mature specimens worth saving, and the soil quality is better than I expected. Six weeks is tight, but with the team Lach's hiring and proper planning, we can do it."

Relief washes over Jack's features. "That's... incredible news. Thank you, Lorna. I know it's a lot to ask, especially leaving your farm during planting season."

"What are sisters for if not impossible garden renovations? Besides, my farm's in good hands."

"Your neighbors, right?" Jack asks, and I nod, praying my face doesn't give anything away.

We linger on practicalities for a while, plant budgets, labor schedules, equipment logistics before he heads off to help Charlie with dinner. Once he's gone, I find myself reaching for my phone again, staring at the photo from the farm like it might reveal some secret I've missed.

What am I doing? Sitting here pining over three men I've spent most of the past two years trying not to think about? Can one late-night frost rescue and a few thoughtful messages undo six years of carefully constructed independence?

And yet, the image won't leave me. Them at my kitchen table, heads bent together over planting charts and soil reports. The teasing warmth in Hudson's text when he says he misses my scowl. The way Levi notices the smallest things without me ever having to say it. And Leo, steady and grounded, making it all feel possible.

It's ridiculous. It's dangerous. And still, I can't stop the quiet ache of wanting more.

With a sigh of surrender, I type a response:

*Looks like you have everything under control. Thank you for the updates and for taking such good care of things. The garden project here is massive but doable. The twins are thriving. Pony riding today was apparently life-changing. Castle feels strange after so long away. Different but familiar. Like coming home to a place that isn't quite home anymore.*

I hesitate over the last line, the unexpected vulnerability surprising even me. But something about the distance between us makes honesty easier. I hit send before I can overthink it.

Their response comes faster than I expected, not jointly this time, but from Leo alone.

*Home isn't always a place. Sometimes it's the people. Enjoy your time with your family—we've got everything handled here. The farm, and all of us, will be waiting when you come back.*

How do a few simple words manage to cut straight to the center of everything I've been wrestling with? For six years, home has meant my farm, my kids, my independence. It's safe. Predictable. Entirely mine.

But lately, a new feeling has been taking root beside my dahlias, a fragile, dangerous hope. The idea that home could stretch wider than my fences. That it might include three men who see me, push me, and hold space for me in ways I never expected.

And that terrifies me. What if I let them in, for real this time, and it all unravels? What if I'm not enough for them, or worse, too much? What if my kids open their hearts, only to lose the people they've come to love?

I set the phone on the nightstand and stare at it for a long moment, the screen fading to black, taking his words with it. The quiet of the castle settles around me—thick, ancient, full of memories that whisper from the stones.

Through the open window, the wind carries the scent of the sea and roses from the overgrown gardens below. I close my eyes and try to imagine the farm at this hour: the soft hum of the greenhouse fans, the rhythm of sprinklers, the glow of the porch light over the field. I picture them there, moving through the spaces I built, their laughter threading through the night air.

Maybe home isn't one fixed thing after all. Maybe it's what grows when you stop guarding the edges so carefully.

I turn off the lamp and lie back against the pillow, the darkness settling over me like a quilt. The last thing I see before sleep takes me is the faint reflection of the phone screen, waiting.

**8**

------

I'm wrist-deep in what might technically qualify as soil but is, in reality, more of a "compost heap from hell"—the kind that steams when you turn it and smells faintly of regret—when my phone buzzes in my back pocket. For the fifth time in an hour. Which would be fine, totally fine, if I didn't know exactly who it was. A certain Australian trio has apparently decided that "farm updates" require the frequency and urgency of breaking news alerts. As if I need another photo of Hudson holding a lamb like it's a centerfold, or Levi's daily dissertation on soil pH. Honestly, the only thing I need less than their updates is a third nipple.

"You're going to wear out your phone at this rate," Charlie calls from where she's clearing a mountain of dead vines. "What's so fascinating over there? Stock market crash? Alien invasion? Nudes from your hot neighbors?"

I nearly drop my shovel. "Jesus, Charlie!"

"What? I've seen the tall one. And the slightly less tall one. And the one who looks like sin decided to grow a beard and move to Scotland." She fans herself with her gardening glove, eyes glinting with mischief. "If I had that trio on speed dial, I'd be checking my phone every five seconds, too."

I lob a dirt clod at her with the precision of someone who's made a lifelong hobby out of pelting annoying people with projectiles. She sidesteps it without breaking a sweat, like she's been dodging me her whole life.

"They're sending farm updates," I say, trying for dignity despite being covered head to toe in mud and what might actually be a worm in my hair.

"Mmm-hmm." Her smirk is pure sin. "Educational updates, I'm sure."

I take the high road and ignore her, pulling out my phone to check the new message.

**Leo:** *Hudson tried to reorganize your seed storage alphabetically instead of by planting date. Crisis averted. Though I may have to hide the label maker.*

A snort-laugh explodes out of me before I can stop it. Classic Hudson. Meanwhile, Leo's probably having an aneurysm as his military precision clashes with Hudson's well-meaning chaos.

I've been at the castle for six days, and in that time, I've received no fewer than eight thousand texts. Updates range from chicken mutinies to irrigation flow charts to hourly weather reports annotated with personal commentary. Every message is its own little tether, yanking me back toward home. Toward the farm. Toward the three maddeningly different men who've set up camp in my brain like charming squatters with matching throw pillows, artisanal coffee, and no intention of ever leaving.

**Me:** *Tell Hudson he's banned from my seed cabinet. But he can alphabetize my spice rack if he gets desperate.*

The response comes suspiciously fast.

**Leo:** *He's now threatening to organize your sock drawer. Send help.*

I bite my lip to keep from grinning like I just won free ice cream for life.

"You know what that face means, right?" Charlie's voice startles me.

"What face? This is my regular face."

"That face says you're mentally undressing someone," she insists, jabbing her garden fork at me.

"I do not mentally undress people!"

The lie is so enormous it practically needs its own postal code. Because I absolutely have been mentally undressing Leo Robinson on a regular basis since that night they saved me from the frost. His broad shoulders. Those powerful thighs. Hands that look like they could bend steel but touch plants with heartbreaking gentleness.

And let's not even discuss Hudson's forearms or Levi's long, elegant fingers.

"Right," Charlie drags the word out. "And I'm the Queen of England."

Before I can formulate a suitably cutting response, my wildling daughter comes tearing around the corner of the hedge, curls flying, knees muddy.

"Mummy! Mummy! Uncle Cam found a REAL SKULL in the old wall!"

"A skull." I stare at her. "A human skull?"

"No, silly!" Lorelai rolls her eyes with the exasperation only a six-year-old confronted with parental stupidity can muster. "A sheep skull! With HORNS! Daniel's set up a dig site with flags and everything! Can I help? PLEEEEEASE?"

Charlie laughs at my deer-in-headlights expression. "Don't worry, it's really old. Probably from the 1800s when they were building the retaining walls. They used all sorts of things as filler."

"Of course you can, but no arguing with your brother," I tell Lorelai. "And listen to Uncle Cam's instructions."

"I WILL!" And she's off again, a human tornado wearing light-up sneakers.

"God, to have that energy," Charlie sighs. "I remember when I could run all day without needing ibuprofen and a nap."

"Same," I say. "If you see me running now, assume something with teeth is chasing me."

Charlie laughs, and we linger there a moment longer, the

warmth of shared exhaustion settling between us. But eventually, the to-do list starts tugging at the edges of my mind, and Charlie has to put Summer down for her nap.

I lose myself in the rhythm of it for several more hours. Eventually, the world narrows to dirt and thorns and the quiet satisfaction of bringing a bit of order to the wild. The satisfying rip of invasive roots, the careful pruning of overgrown shrubs, the methodical clearing of choked pathways, it's meditative, the kind of work that hushes the noise in my brain.

I'm so lost in it, hands deep in a particularly stubborn bramble, that I don't register the footsteps behind me until a low voice breaks the silence.

"Your form could use some work."

I nearly jump out of my skin, pitching forward into the very bush I've been fighting. Strong hands catch my waist before I faceplant into a century's worth of thorns.

"Jesus, Mary, and Nessie's ghost!" I yelp, twisting around to find myself nose-to-chest with Leo Robinson.

Leo. Here. At the castle. When he's supposed to be two hours away at my farm. His hands still grip my waist, warm and solid through the thin cotton of my work shirt.

"Sorry," he says, looking about as sorry as a cat who casually knocked your favorite mug off the counter. "Didn't mean to startle you."

My brain chooses this exact moment to pack its bags and head to Tahiti. All I can do is blink up at him, acutely aware of how close he is, how his thumbs rest right above my hip bones, how his dark eyes crinkle slightly at the corners with suppressed amusement.

"What are you doing here?" I finally manage, my voice sounding like I've been inhaling helium.

"Farm report. Thought it might be easier to explain in person."

"You drove two hours to give me a farm update?"

"Among other things," he admits, his hands still not moving from my waist.

I should step back. Give us both a little breathing room. Remind myself that I'm streaked with dirt, hair full of leaves, looking more bog witch than human, and standing in the middle of my brother's estate where anyone could appear at any moment.

Instead, I sway slightly toward him.

"What other things?" I ask.

His expression shifts, the mask slipping just enough to reveal heat lurking beneath.

"I wanted to see you," he says simply. "Is that a problem?"

God, the directness of the man. No games, no pretense. Just raw honesty that hits me like a freight train.

"N-no," I stammer. "Not a problem. Just unexpected."

His gaze drops briefly to my mouth, then back to my eyes. "I can leave if you're too busy."

"Don't you dare." The fierceness in my voice surprises me. "I mean... you drove all this way. The least I can do is give you a tour of the grounds."

Leo's mouth quirks. "A tour sounds perfect."

I step back, immediately missing his hands. "Just let me..." I gesture vaguely at my dirt-encrusted appearance.

"You look fine," he says, his eyes sweeping over me in a way that makes heat pool low in my belly. "Better than fine."

"I look like I've been mud wrestling with a bear."

"It's working for me."

The simple statement, delivered in that low, velvety voice, flips a switch somewhere deep in my brain. Words? Gone. Neurons? Fried. How is anyone supposed to think straight when he's looking at me like I'm the first real meal he's had in weeks and he plans to savor every bite?

"Tour," I say firmly, more to myself than to him. "This way."

I lead him through the winding paths of the castle grounds, pointing out the beds I've cleared and outlining my plans for what's next. Leo listens the way he does everything, with quiet focus and questions that make me feel seen instead of scrutinized. As we walk, I can't help noticing him. The faint brush of his arm against mine. The way he adjusts his stride so we stay in step. The soft, sidelong glances that make it very hard to remember what I was saying about soil drainage.

"The greenhouse is through here," I say, leading him around a crumbling stone wall. "It's one of the few structures still somewhat functional."

The Victorian glasshouse rises at the edge of the formal gardens, its wrought-iron frame still graceful despite the missing panes and the tangle of weeds creeping up the path. Inside, the air turns thick and warm, wrapping around us with the scent of damp soil and stubborn life, as if the place has been quietly breathing all this time, waiting to be found again.

"Beautiful space," Leo says, running his hand along an ancient wooden potting bench. "Good bones."

"My grandmother propagated prize-winning orchids here. I used to help her as a child, before I decided roses were more my speed."

"Like grandmother, like granddaughter," Leo observes. "If what Hudson says is true about all those dahlia society medals."

I blink in surprise. "You talk about me? When I'm not there?"

"Constantly."

The single word, delivered without qualification or explanation, sucks the oxygen from my lungs. Leo isn't a man who wastes words or offers empty compliments. If he says they talk about me constantly, they do.

"All good things, I hope."

"Always," he says, moving closer. "Though we disagree about our favorite aspects of your character."

My pulse kicks into overdrive. "Oh?"

"Hudson thinks your stubbornness is your most endearing quality. Levi would argue it's your mind."

Now he's close enough that I can feel the heat radiating from his body.

"And you?" I whisper.

"I think it's your strength." His voice drops to a register that sucks the air from my lungs. "The way you rebuilt yourself after everything fell apart. How you keep fighting for the life you want, no matter the odds."

His words hit me like an emotional sledgehammer, cracking open parts of me I thought were permanently sealed. "You don't know everything about me," I remind him.

"No," he agrees, reaching up to gently brush a leaf from my hair. "But I want to."

I swallow hard, my body leaning toward him like he's gravity. "This is complicated. You, me, Hudson, Levi. My kids. Our farms."

"Fuck complicated," Leo replies, his thumb tracing the curve of my cheek. "Do you want me to stop touching you?"

"No." The word escapes before my brain can catch it.

A spark flares in his eyes. "Then tell me what you do want, Lorna."

What I want is his mouth on mine. His hands on my body. His weight pressing me into the potting bench behind me. I want to stop thinking about consequences and complications and feel alive again after six years of emotional hibernation.

"Kiss me," I whisper.

I don't have to ask twice.

His mouth finds mine with barely contained hunger, his hands cradling my face, fingertips trembling against my cheekbones like I'm rare and he's afraid to break me. His scent floods my senses. It's nothing like that frantic, adrenaline-laced kiss we shared at the farm. This one is slower, surer, deliberate. A man taking his time to learn me by heart.

I melt into him, fingers curling in the soft cotton of his shirt, the fabric bunching in my fists as I pull him closer. My pulse thunders in my ears, drowning out everything but the catch of his breath. His beard scrapes my skin, a delicious sting that sends electricity racing down my spine. The rough texture contrasts with the surprising softness of his lips, making me gasp into his mouth.

Leo takes advantage, deepening the kiss, and I taste mint and something darker, richer. My knees go liquid. When his hands slide to my waist, strong fingers spanning my ribs and thumbs brushing the sensitive skin just above my hip bones, he lifts me onto the potting bench behind us. The cool wood presses against the backs of my thighs. A sound escapes me that would mortify me if I were capable of coherent thought. But rationality has long since packed its bags and fled the country.

The height difference disappears. My legs wrap around his hips without permission, denim against denim, dragging him close. The heat of him radiates through the layers between us, making my breath catch and my fingers dig into his shoulders where I can feel the bunch and flex of muscle beneath my fingers.

"Lorna," he growls against my throat, the vibration of his voice buzzing through my skin where his mouth is doing things that will certainly leave marks. Each press of his lips sparks a slow burn deep in my core, and the gentle scrape of his teeth makes my pulse jump wildly.

His large hands slip beneath my t-shirt, fingers rough against my sensitive skin as they slide up my ribcage with agonizing slowness. I can barely breathe, my chest tight with anticipation. When his thumbs finally brush the undersides of my breasts through the thin lace of my bra, electricity shoots through me. I arch into his touch, my back bowing off the bench, a moan escaping that would make me blush if I could think straight.

"Please," I whisper against his jaw, tasting salt on his skin, though I'm not entirely sure what I'm asking for. More? Everything? My fingers tangle in his hair, soft and thick.

Leo seems to understand anyway. His mouth returns to mine, hot and demanding, as his hands start to...

"Hey there!" Jack's voice shatters the moment like a sledgehammer through glass. "Sorry to interrupt the garden tour, but dinner is ready and the twins are asking for—oh. OH."

Cold air rushes between us as I jerk away from Leo with the speed of someone who's just realized they're sitting on a hornets' nest. My skin still burns where he touched me. Only his quick reflexes, his arm banding around my waist, keeps me from landing in an undignified heap on the greenhouse floor. My legs shake as my feet find the ground.

My brother stands frozen in the doorway, backlit by the fading daylight, his expression cycling through surprise, understanding, and brotherly outrage faster than I can blink.

"I was going to invite our guest to stay for dinner," he says stiffly, his voice dripping with forced politeness. "Though it seems he's already found something to... snack on."

Heat floods my cheeks. "Oh my God, Jack," I groan, mortification burning through me like wildfire. "Please stop talking."

But Jack only crosses his arms, fixing Leo with what I recognize as his lord-of-the-manor stare. "Dinner will be ready in fifteen minutes. That should give you both time to straighten yourselves." He winks, so casually it knocks the air right out of me, and a startled laugh slips free before I can stop it. Then he turns, striding down the gravel path, each step fading into the hum of the garden until all that's left is the echo of that damn wink still fluttering in my chest.

"I'm so sorry," I whisper, unable to look Leo in the eye as I try to tame my hopelessly mussed hair. "He's not usually so..."

"Protective?" Leo supplies, reaching out to brush a leaf from my shoulder. "It's what I'd expect. What I'd do if it were my sister."

"Still. It's embarrassing."

"Getting caught in general? Or getting caught by your brother specifically?" Leo asks quietly, a hint of amusement in his voice.

The question makes me groan. "Have you ever had your little brother walk in on you? It's mortifying. I'm thirty-two years old and Jack just made me feel like I'm sixteen again, sneaking around behind the bleachers."

"Can't say I have that particular experience," Leo admits with a grin.

"Well, now I have to sit through dinner knowing he's going to be making pointed comments all evening. Maybe Charlie too if Jack tells her." I gesture helplessly. "Family dinners are about to get very awkward."

Leo chuckles, understanding in his eyes. "I'm pretty sure they'll get over it. Besides, from what I've seen of Jack, he'll probably enjoy teasing you about it more than being actually upset."

"Oh, he definitely will. Which is almost worse." I smooth down my shirt, trying to restore some dignity. "We should probably go in. Before Charlie sends out a search party or something equally dramatic."

"One thing first." Leo steps close again. Before I can react, he brushes his thumb across my lower lip, then shows me the smudge of dirt he's removed. "Evidence."

I laugh despite myself. "My hero. Saving me from the horror of appearing at dinner looking like I've been making out in a greenhouse. Which I absolutely have not been doing."

Dinner is... interesting, in the way that watching two predators circle each other while you're tied to a chair between them is interesting.

Jack has arranged what I can only describe as a strategic seating plan worthy of a military operation, placing himself directly across from Leo with Lach and Cam flanking him like medieval knights prepared for battle. The twins bracket me like tiny bodyguards, with Charlie completing our end of the table.

"So," Jack begins, fixing Leo with his duke stare, the one that makes grown men apologize for crimes they haven't committed. "Lorna tells me you're helping with her farm while she's here."

"Along with Hudson and Levi," Leo replies evenly. "It's the neighborly thing to do."

The way he emphasizes neighborly causes Jack's eyebrows to rise. My pulse kicks up a notch. "Neighborly, hm?"

"Jack," I warn, my foot connecting with his shin hard enough to make him flinch.

"What?" my brother says, all wide-eyed innocence that wouldn't fool a toddler. "I'm making conversation."

Leo appears entirely unfazed, calmly spreading butter on a slice of bread. The scrape of his knife against the crust fills the suddenly silent room. "We started as neighbors. We're becoming friends."

"Friends," Jack repeats, the word dripping skepticism like honey laced with arsenic. "I see."

"Mummy, is Mr. Hudson coming to visit too?" Lorelai asks, thankfully interrupting before I commit fratricide with a butter knife. "And Mr. Levi? I want to show them the fairy houses we could build in the castle garden!"

Leo smiles, a real, full smile that transforms his usually guarded face. My heart stumbles in my chest. "I'm sure they'd love to see your plans. Maybe next time."

"Next time," Jack echoes, and I can practically hear the gears grinding in his head, calculating, assessing, planning his next move.

"If that's all right with you," Leo says, meeting Jack's gaze directly. The testosterone in the room is thick enough to choke on. "The truck schedule means we have to take turns. Levi will probably come next, then Hudson."

"Truck schedule?" Charlie asks, genuine curiosity threading through her voice as she passes the potatoes.

"We share one vehicle between the three of us," Leo explains, his fingers absently turning his water glass. "Makes logistics challenging sometimes, but we manage."

"Interesting," Jack says, in a tone that suggests he finds it about as interesting as a tax audit.

I shoot him a glare that could wilt every dahlia in my greenhouse. My brother merely smiles back, bland as unseasoned porridge.

"So you three aren't related?" Lach asks, joining the subtle interrogation with the finesse of a sledgehammer.

"Hudson and Levi are brothers," Leo answers, his jaw tightening almost imperceptibly. "I'm not related by blood, but we're family."

Something in the way he says family silences even Jack for a moment.

"Are you going to marry my mum?" Daniel asks suddenly, his little face solemn and intent, eyes fixed on Leo with that fearless, unblinking scrutiny only children possess when they decide to go straight for the jugular.

Water goes down the wrong pipe and I choke hard enough to see stars. "Daniel!"

"What?" my son asks, genuinely puzzled by my near-death experience. "You kissed him. In the greenhouse. I saw."

If the floor could open up and swallow me whole, I would send it a thank-you card written in my own blood. Every adult eye at the table swivels toward me. Lach's grin nearly takes up his entire face, Charlie's lips twitch with barely suppressed laughter, and Jack looks like Christmas came early, wrapped in a bow of sisterly mortification.

"Sometimes grown-ups kiss without getting married," Leo answers calmly, saving me. "Right now, your mum and I are still getting to know each other."

Daniel considers this. "But you like her. A lot. I can tell."

"Yes," Leo says simply, his eyes finding mine across the table. The look sends heat racing through my veins. "I like her a lot."

"Good," my son decides, returning to his meal as though he hasn't just publicly dissected my love life. "She likes you too. She gets all weird when you text her."

Sweet saints and soggy biscuits. I'm going to die. Right here at this dinner table, face first in the mashed potatoes.

"Weird how?" Leo asks, and I can hear the smile in his voice even though I'm studiously examining my plate like it holds the secrets of the universe.

"She stares at her phone forever," Daniel reports with the enthusiasm of a town crier. "And sometimes she smiles at it like it told a joke. But phones can't tell jokes."

Leo catches my eye across the table, a glint of warmth flickering in those caramel-brown eyes that are usually all discipline and restraint. "I'll take that as a compliment," he says, voice low enough to make it feel like it's meant only for me.

The table falls into that easy kind of quiet that only happens when everyone's full and content, silverware resting on plates, the air thick with roasted herbs and the ghost of laughter that clings to everything like wood smoke. My shoulders finally unhitch from somewhere near my ears.

As dusk bleeds purple and orange across the sky like spilled wine, Leo shifts in his chair, the wood creaking beneath him. "I need to head back."

"You're welcome to stay for the night," Jack offers, surprising me so thoroughly I nearly drop my wine glass. "We have plenty of room."

Leo shakes his head, already pushing back from the table. "Thank you, but I need to be back for morning milking. Levi and Hudson are handling evening chores, but they'll be spread thin with both farms."

"Another time, then," my brother says, with a look that promises future interrogation sessions that would make the Spanish Inquisition look friendly.

I walk Leo to his truck, my skin prickling with awareness of watching eyes from every blessed window in the castle. The gravel crunches under our feet, each step echoing in the evening quiet.

"I'm sorry about my family," I say, wrapping my arms around myself against the evening chill. "Especially Jack. He's always been overprotective."

"Don't apologize." Leo leans against the driver's side door, solid and sure in the fading light. "It's good that they care about you so much."

"Still. The questions were a bit much."

Leo reaches out, tucking a strand of hair behind my ear. The gesture is so tender it cracks open a place in my chest, warm and terrifying. His thumb lingers against my cheekbone for a heartbeat. "If our positions were reversed, I'd have asked the same things. Probably more directly."

I laugh, the sound shaky. "That's true. You're not exactly known for beating around the bush."

"Life's too short for games."

We stand there, the air between us practically vibrating with everything we're not saying. My fingers itch to grab his shirt, to pull him down for another kiss that would fog up every window in the castle. But I can feel Jack's stare burning a hole between my shoulder blades.

"Levi will probably drive up sometime next week," Leo says finally, his voice rougher than usual. "If that's all right with you."

The thought of seeing Levi has my heart flip-flopping in my chest. "Of course. And Hudson too, when he can make it?"

Leo nods, and I see in his eyes that he understands what I'm really asking, that I want to see all of them, that this impossible thing between us includes them all. "We'll take turns. The truck makes coordinating visits interesting, but we'll make it work."

"I should let you go. It's a long drive."

Before he opens the truck door, his knuckles graze my cheek, the touch so light I might have imagined it if not for the trail of fire it leaves behind. "Sweet dreams, Lorna."

The words roll off his tongue like aged whisky, part wish, part command, part promise that has me pressing my thighs together. As I watch his taillights disappear into the gloaming, red eyes blinking out in the darkness, I feel fundamentally altered. Like he's left fingerprints on a part of me deeper than skin.

Holy cannoli. I'm in so much trouble.

Later that evening, after the twins are tucked into bed with Uncle Lach's elaborate castle ghost stories still echoing in their dreams, Jack corners me in the library. The fire crackles in the hearth, casting dancing shadows across leather-bound spines.

"So," he says, settling into the leather armchair across from mine with a creak of old wood and older secrets. "Three of them, huh?"

The wine glass nearly slips through my fingers. "Excuse me?"

"Leo mentioned 'taking turns' with the truck. Then there was Lorelai asking about the other two visiting. Plus that look on your face when Daniel asked if Leo was going to marry you." My brother's expression softens, the Duke mask slipping to reveal just Jack, my annoying brother who used to steal my Halloween candy. "I'm not judging, Lorna. I'm just trying to understand."

I sink deeper into my chair, the leather sighing beneath me. The wine tastes sharp on my tongue, or maybe that's just panic. "If it makes you feel better, I don't understand it either."

"Try me," Jack encourages, gesturing around us at the castle where he lives with three partners like it's the most natural thing in the world. "I might have some relevant experience in the non-traditional relationship department."

"It's different."

"Is it though?"

The question hangs between us like smoke from the fire. No. Yes. Maybe. I honestly don't know.

"I haven't been with anyone since Richard," I admit, the words scraping my throat raw. "Six years of nothing. Not even a date. And then this frost warning happened, and they showed up with supplies at two in the morning, and suddenly they were part of my life. All three of them."

"And you have feelings for all three?" Jack's voice is gentle, probing like fingers checking for broken bones.

My cheeks burn hot enough to rival the fire. "Different feelings for each of them. Leo is... steady. Protective. Makes me feel safe but also challenged. Hudson brings out a playfulness I thought Richard had killed. And Levi sees parts of me I've kept locked away for years."

"And they know about each other? About what's developing?"

I nod, my stomach churning like I've swallowed a live eel.

Jack is quiet for a moment, swirling the amber liquid in his glass. The firelight catches in the whisky, turning it to liquid gold. "I had a similar conversation with Leo this afternoon. While you were getting the twins ready for dinner."

My head snaps up so fast my neck cracks. "You did what?"

"Relax. It wasn't an interrogation. Well, not entirely." His lips twitch. "I only wanted to understand his intentions toward my sister."

"And?" The word comes out strangled.

"And I was impressed," Jack says simply, surprising me for the second time tonight. "He didn't minimize the complexity of the situation. Didn't try to gloss over the challenges. He also made it very clear that all three of them are committed to making sure you and the twins are happy and supported, whatever that looks like."

Something warm and dangerous unfurls in my chest. "They're good men, Jack."

"I believe they are. But that doesn't mean this won't be complicated. Especially with kids involved."

"I know." The weight of it presses against my ribs. "Believe me, that's what keeps me up at night. That and the mental image of explaining this to their school teachers."

Jack leans forward, firelight catching the serious set of his jaw. "Just promise me one thing, Lorna. Promise you'll be honest with yourself about what you need. What makes you happy. After everything with Richard, you deserve that much."

Tears prick at my eyes, hot and sudden. I blink them back, but one escapes anyway, tracking down my cheek like a traitor. "When did you get so wise, little brother?"

"Probably around the time I entered into a relationship with three people," he says, his smile crooked and knowing. "Nothing teaches wisdom quite like having your heart split into multiple pieces and discovering it somehow works better that way."

The truth of it sits between us, heavy as the ancient books surrounding us, and twice as full of possibility.

I think about what Jack said later, lying in the enormous four-poster bed. *Heart split into multiple pieces.* Is that what's happening to me? Or is my heart, long dormant, simply expanding to accommodate more love than I'd previously thought possible?

My phone buzzes on the nightstand. A message from Leo.

**Leo:** *Home safe. Farm secure. Your dahlias send their regards.*

Simple. Practical. Quintessentially Leo. Yet it makes me smile in the darkness.

Before I can respond, another message appears.

**Leo:** *Hudson wants me to tell you he misses your orneriness. Levi says the sunset tonight reminded him of your special dahlia. I miss the feel of you in my arms. Sleep well, Lorna.*

And I do.

**9**

———

There's nothing quite like the crunch of gravel under tires to make a woman's heart attempt an Olympic routine. Especially when said woman is elbow-deep in dirt, wearing her most tragic pair of overalls, and rocking a hairstyle that could double as a bird sanctuary.

I go still, trowel suspended midair, as the low rumble of a truck winds its way up the castle drive. My blood surges before my brain can issue a single rational thought. It's been seven days since Leo left, seven days of pretending I'm not checking my phone every hour for messages that are definitely *not* about irrigation schedules, no matter what my smug sister-in-law says.

But this isn't Leo's driving. The truck takes the curves carefully, with that steady, measured precision that could only belong to one person.

Levi.

"Someone's here!" Charlie calls from the far end of the terrace garden, her voice carrying that singsong mix of amusement and mischief. "Wonder who it could possibly be?"

"Shut it," I mutter, frantically tucking stray curls back into my bun while brushing dirt from my cheeks. Both attempts are disasters.

The truck rounds the final bend, sunlight glinting off the windshield. It slows, then eases to a stop, and my heart decides to do the same. The driver's door swings open.

Levi steps out, all faded denim and soft henley sleeves pushed up to his elbows. His dark curls catch the light, longer than I remember, and there's a quality to him that feels both wildly out of place and completely at home here, like a poet who traded his pen for a pair of work boots. Too beautiful for my peace of mind.

He's reaching into the cab and hasn't seen me yet. Which means I have about fifteen seconds to decide whether to a) hide behind the nearest hedge, b) pretend I'm too busy pulling these godforsaken weeds to notice his arrival, or c) act like a functional adult woman who isn't having heart palpitations over a man carrying what appears to be my hybridization journal.

"Aren't you going to say hello?" Charlie stage-whispers from somewhere behind me, clearly reveling in my emotional collapse. "Or are you planning to stare at him until he bursts into flames?"

"I hate you," I reply sweetly, wiping dirt from my hands onto my already mud-caked overalls. "With the fire of a thousand suns."

"You'll thank me later," she sings, backing away with all the subtlety of a cartoon villain. "I'll just check on those things that definitely need checking. Very far away. But not *too* far to eavesdrop."

"Traitor," I mutter, though she's already gone.

Levi finally turns and sees me. The change is instant and almost dizzying. His whole face lights up, those big ocean eyes sparkling bright. His smile starts small, tugging at one corner of his mouth, then spreads until it's bright enough to challenge the Highland sun.

A faint flush rises from his collar, painting his cheeks, and his posture shifts, shoulders squaring, chest lifting, as though seeing me recharges him. He takes a small, instinctive step forward, the movement so natural it's like his body's following a pull he doesn't bother to question. The journal in his hand nearly slips before he catches it, fingers tightening around the worn leather.

"Lorna," he says, my name leaving his lips on a breath that feels more like a confession than a greeting.

I straighten, brushing off my hands. "Levi. This is—I didn't expect you."

A blatant lie. I've been expecting someone—*any* of them—every day since Leo left. Watching the drive. Jumping at every engine that passed. Much to Charlie's eternal amusement.

He hesitates long enough to set the journal gently on the hood of the truck, then closes the distance between us in a few long, deliberate strides that send my heartbeat skittering into chaos.

"I couldn't stay away," he says, stopping just shy of touching me. "I've been thinking about you. Every minute."

I have to lock my knees to keep them from giving out. This isn't the steady, soft-spoken Levi I know. There's a new spark in his eyes, focused and deliberate, like he's finally decided to stop holding back.

"You've got dirt on your cheek," he murmurs, his voice low as he lifts his hand. When his knuckle skims my cheek, electricity runs through me, spreading fast and reckless, until every nerve is on fire.

He doesn't pull back. The scent of ink and paper wrap around me as his fingers linger, tracing the line of my cheekbone, slow enough to make my pulse trip over itself. My eyes flutter shut and I lean into his touch.

"Lorna," he breathes, my name caught somewhere between a prayer and a plea.

"Yes," I whisper, unsure if he even asked a question. It doesn't matter. My body already knows the answer, every heartbeat spelling it out against my ribs.

When his lips touch mine, a small, helpless sound slips out of me, somewhere between a sigh and a whimper. The kiss isn't what I expected. It isn't gentle or cautious. It's hungry, rough around the edges, all fire and feeling. His mouth moves against mine like he's been waiting years for this moment, his hands sliding into my hair, anchoring me.

I grip his shoulders, dirt-streaked fingers surely ruining his shirt, but I can't make myself care. Not when his tongue teases the edge of my lips, not when he groans deep in his chest as I part for him.

He tastes like cinnamon gum and a heat that's all his own, and the combination makes my head spin. I'm dizzy from the taste, from the way his body presses against mine, from the quiet urgency threaded through every touch.

When we finally pull apart, we're both panting. My heart hammers in my chest, and his pupils are blown wide, dark and wanting. A flutter of pride sparks in me, small but fierce, at the sight of Levi Robinson looking anything but composed.

"I, uh, brought a few things from the farm," he says, his voice rough. He clears his throat and takes a small step back, as if he needs the space to pull himself together.

I nod, words stuck somewhere behind my sternum. My lips are still swollen, tingling with the memory of his mouth. My pulse stutters in my throat, and the taste of cinnamon still lingers on my tongue.

He reaches into the truck again, muscles flexing, and lifts out a small flat of plants, each one nestled secure for the journey. "And a few roses Leo propagated. He thought you might want them."

My chest twists painfully at the sight of them, tender new growth, each leaf delicate and perfect.

"Also," Levi says, reaching for something else, "Leo sent these." He holds up a pair of gardening gloves, leather so smooth it looks like butter, stitched and reinforced exactly where my hands always crack and bleed.

"He made them," Levi says quietly, watching my face. "Said your old ones were on their last legs."

I take them with trembling fingers, the leather warm from sitting in the truck, from being held in Levi's hands. Each stitch is precise, patient, perfect. I can see Leo at his workbench, those careful hands creating these just for me.

"And Hudson added these," Levi continues, producing my favorite gardening tools. The handles gleam, replaced with smooth, custom-carved wood that fits my grip like they were molded for my hands alone. "He said they'd be easier on your wrists."

My throat burns. "I don't know what to say."

Levi smiles, that small, devastating smile that makes my knees forget their primary function. "You could start by showing me those famous castle gardens I've heard so much about." His voice drops an octave, rough as tree bark. "Though if I'm being honest, gardening wasn't exactly what I had in mind when I drove over here today."

Oh. Oh my.

My brain short-circuits. Every coherent thought scatters like startled birds, and for a second I forget what words are. I stand there, heartbeat tripping over itself, trying to remember how to breathe.

I pull in a deep breath, steady enough to pass for casual. "They're a disaster zone," I say, tucking the journal beneath my arm. "My grandmother's probably rolling in her grave at the current state of affairs."

"I'm sure they're not that bad," he says, ever the diplomat, right before his hand finds the small of my back.

The touch is casual. Friendly. Innocent. It should mean nothing.

But my body doesn't get the memo. It fires anyway, desire sparking along my nerve endings.

Twenty minutes later, Levi stands in the middle of what used to be the formal rose garden, eyebrows practically in orbit.

"Okay," he concedes, "they're that bad."

I laugh, full and unguarded for the first time in what feels like weeks. "Told you. It's like Mother Nature declared war and brought backup. I've managed to clear about a third, but the rest—" I wave a hand toward the chaos.

Levi crouches beside a half-choked rose bush, fingers brushing a bloom that's still trying to unfurl against all odds.

"It's a metaphor," he murmurs. "Beauty clawing its way out of the mess. Life fighting through the chaos, refusing to give up even in forgotten places."

And this is why Levi is dangerous. Because he doesn't just see weeds and wreckage. He sees hope. Poetry. A future where most people only see ruin.

"That's a very kind way of saying it looks like crap," I tease, brushing hair out of my face.

He glances up, sunlight catching in his eyes, turning them into a wild mix of blue and gold with a shadowed depth at the center. Impossible to pin down. Like him.

"It looks like potential."

And the way he says it makes it clear he's not talking about the roses.

We spend the next two hours wandering the grounds while Levi listens, never interrupting or offering quick fixes.

Where Leo would've rattled off practical solutions and Hudson would already be halfway through building a trellis, Levi lets the silence breathe. He asks questions that make me look closer, think deeper, dream bigger. He doesn't impose. He invites.

And if his fingers brush mine now and then, if his shoulder lingers near mine when I point out crumbling archways and sun-warmed stone, if his gaze dips to my lips like he's weighing a risk he might just take—well. I'm not exactly stopping him.

It's nearly noon when Jack appears, all long strides and brotherly authority, cutting across the lawn like a man on a mission. He stops a few feet away, hands on hips, and levels me with a look.

"You need a break," he announces. "Charlie says you've been out here since dawn. Again."

I open my mouth to argue, but he raises a brow and keeps going.

"The gardens'll still be a mess tomorrow," he says, softer now. "And your guest didn't drive two hours to help you add more things to your to-do list."

Levi steps in smoothly, like he's been waiting for the cue. "Actually, I was hoping to steal Lorna away for lunch, if that's all right." He glances at me. "There's a spot on the coast I found last time I was here. Thought it might be good for a picnic."

Jack nods. "Charlie already has the picnic basket ready for you." At my startled look, he shrugs, all innocence.

"Did everyone know you were coming except me?" I ask Levi as Jack strolls away, far too pleased with himself.

Levi's smile unfolds slowly, a quiet thing that feels like he's letting me glimpse a thought he hasn't quite put into words. "I called ahead to make sure you'd be free," he says, then adds with a hint of shy pride, "I wanted to surprise you."

And just like that, my stomach flips, tightening and fluttering in the space of a heartbeat. I'm thirty-four, a mother, supposedly immune to this kind of nonsense, and yet here I am, blushing like a teenager because a man wants to take me on a picnic.

Forty minutes later, we're bumping along a narrow track in Levi's truck, the suspension groaning with each pothole. Gravel pops under the tires like tiny firecrackers as the coastline reveals itself. I've swapped into jeans that aren't decorated with mysterious stains and a sweater that actually remembers what shape I'm supposed to be. My hair, on the other hand, has declared independence and formed its own sovereign nation of curls. But Levi doesn't seem to mind. His gaze keeps sliding over, catching on the loose strands whipping around my face from the half-open window.

"How are the twins?" he asks, steadying the wheel with one hand as the truck lurches over a rut that probably has its own postcode.

"Thriving," I say, warmth spreading through my chest. "Daniel's launched a rock classification project with Cam. Very serious business. Color-coded labels, spreadsheets, the whole nine yards. I'm half expecting him to request a peer review."

"And Lorelai?"

I can't stop the grin that takes over my face. "She's been teaching Summer how to do 'fairy garden installations.' Which is basically glitter terrorism with a side of strategic cookie placement on every available surface."

Levi laughs, rich and unguarded, the sound filling the cab and making my stomach flip. "Hudson's going to be devastated he missed the fairy construction boom."

"She's saving some top-secret assignments for him, I'm sure." I hesitate, fingers playing with the hem of my sweater. "She asks about all of you every day."

His eyes find mine, and the look in them knocks the air clean out of my lungs. "We think about her every day, too. About all three of you."

Silence settles between us, easy and familiar, the kind that doesn't need filling. Not Leo's charged quiet, heavy with unspoken thoughts and that edge of restraint. Not Hudson's restless one, all coiled motion and barely contained energy. Levi's silence drifts between us like morning mist. The kind that says, *I see you. I'm here. Take your time.*

We crest a hill, and my gasp escapes before I can catch it. Rolling green headlands tumble down to a pale crescent of sand, waves folding onto shore in lazy, hypnotic rhythm. The Atlantic stretches beyond, endless and impossibly blue, as though someone spilled the entire sky into the sea.

"Holy Highland cow," I whisper.

"I thought you might like it," Levi says, pulling into a small clearing tucked behind a sand dune. "I did some digging for remote beaches in the hopes of finding one you haven't been to yet."

Of course he did.

These men will be the absolute death of me. And I'm starting to think I might die happy.

Levi retrieves the picnic hamper and a thick blanket from the truck bed. We make our way down a winding path, the grass brushing our calves, wildflowers nodding in the wind. It's one of those rare, perfect Highland days—sunlight spilling golden, the breeze lazy and almost warm, the air scented with salt and faintly sweet.

The beach is deserted, as if the universe preserved this moment especially for us. Levi spreads the blanket in a sheltered hollow where the dunes curl protectively around us, softening the wind to a hush. We unpack the hamper, and Charlie has well and truly outdone herself—still-warm bread that steams when we break it open, tangy local cheeses, delicate slices of smoked salmon, charred vegetables laced with herbs, and a flask of what turns out to be whisky-spiked hot chocolate.

"So," I say once we've eased into the quiet rhythm of eating, our legs stretched out and brushing. "How are things at the farm? No polite summaries. I want the real version."

Levi's expression softens. "Good," he says slowly. "The irrigation's running perfectly. Leo checks it constantly. Hudson's been busy building the fairy houses we promised Lorelai. And I've been keeping an eye on your dahlias."

He reaches into his pocket, pulls out his phone. "Actually, I've got something to show you."

He shifts closer, his thigh pressing solid against mine, and begins scrolling through photos. The images are stunning—petals glowing in golden hour light, droplets caught on leaves like glass pearls, color shifts so subtle I wouldn't have noticed them otherwise.

"These are incredible," I say, eyes still on the screen. "You've got an eye."

"They're easy subjects," he replies, one corner of his mouth pulling up. "Your dahlias practically flirt with the camera."

Our eyes lock, and I feel that gravitational pull again. Somehow, we've closed the distance, our shoulders touching now. Levi's gaze drops to my mouth, lingering there. I hold perfectly still, waiting.

But he only smiles, almost to himself, and turns back to the phone. Keeps talking. Keeps not kissing me.

The restraint is maddening. Delicious. More intoxicating than any whisky. Because it means he's not in a rush. He wants me, but he wants the moment more. The anticipation. The slow, maddening burn.

I can't stop watching his hands, those clever, steady fingers swiping across the screen. All I can think about is how they'd feel against my skin.

We finish the meal, the food vanishing without either of us noticing. The conversation turns to stories from the farm and the castle. Levi tells me about the sheep that escaped and led Hudson on a chase worthy of slapstick comedy, three fields and a full face-plant into a bog. I counter with tales of the twins and their cousin, including the now-infamous incident involving a rogue chicken, a mud puddle, and Lach's beloved wellington boots.

We're laughing, loose and warm from the sun and the food and a feeling neither of us is ready to define. But it's there. Thick in the air between us.

As the afternoon stretches golden around us, the sun low on the horizon, Levi reaches into the picnic hamper and pulls out a worn leather notebook. His fingers linger on the edges for a moment, almost as if he's bracing himself.

"I brought something else," he says, his voice hesitant. "I wrote some poems. About your gardens. About the way they looked in the moonlight that first night we met."

My heart does that stupid fluttery thing again. "You wrote poetry about my flowers?"

He nods, a faint blush rising in his cheeks, eyes fixed on the notebook like it's suddenly the most fascinating thing in the world. "Would you like to hear one?"

"Please," I whisper, not sure I've ever wanted anything more.

Levi opens the notebook carefully, his fingers brushing over the pages with hesitation, as though releasing what's written might cost him something. When he starts to read, his voice shifts, dropping lower, softer, threaded with something that feels dangerously intimate. It's a rhythm that pulls me under, gentle and soothing, but charged with a quiet intensity I feel in my bones.

He paints pictures with language, describing frost-kissed petals shivering beneath the weight of winter's breath, roots pushing stubbornly through the soil to prove they belong, and blooms rising, steady and defiant, in the face of impossible odds.

But it's not only the flowers. As he reads, I realize he's written about me, too. About the cold I've endured, the quiet strength of a woman who keeps going no matter what. About a beauty that refuses to fade, a resilience forged in the middle of unbearable things. And at the center of it all, the courage to keep blooming even when the world feels like it's pressing in from every side.

When he finishes, silence settles between us, not empty, but dense with everything he's just given me. I blink rapidly, trying to hold back the sting of tears.

"That was—" The words catch in my throat, tangled in all the things I can't quite say. He doesn't just see me; he studies me, reading the story in the curve of my mouth and the dirt beneath my nails. For one dizzying second, I swear he can see every hidden piece of me—the hopeful, the hurting, the parts I've kept buried to survive.

"I see you, Lorna," he says softly. "We all do."

The simplicity of it catches me off guard, lodging somewhere deep inside my chest and holding tight. Because this is what I've been starved for. To be seen. Not only as a mother, or a farmer, or someone who traded her dreams for a more practical career. But as me. The chaos and contradictions. The pieces I've kept tucked away from the world, and maybe, even more painfully, from myself.

"Would you tell me more about your research?" Levi asks, his voice low but clear over the rhythm of the waves below. "You looked embarrassed when the twins mentioned it at dinner that first night, but I'd really love to hear about it. From you this time."

Blood rushes to my face so fast it's dizzying. God, that dinner. "Please tell me you didn't actually read the papers."

"Yes. All of them," he says, turning to face me fully. "That paper on the autonomic nervous system was brilliant. I want to know that part of you, Lorna. Would you share that with me?"

I pick at a thread on my sweater, my heart hammering. "Most people find it strange. The scientist who gave it all up for her kids and flower farming. Like I'm made of parts that don't fit together."

"They're not contradictory at all." He says it with quiet certainty, like it's self-evident. "They're two facets of the same brilliant mind. Both require patience. Precision. A deep understanding of how things work, how they respond when given the right conditions."

"You really want to hear about my work?" The question comes out small, quiet.

"I want to hear about all of it," he says. "The theory, the passion behind it, what drives you to keep writing even when you have to hide behind a pseudonym." His eyes darken a fraction. "Besides, understanding the theory can be quite helpful in practice."

Oh. *Oh.* Heat floods through me like I've been set on fire from the inside out.

"Useful in *practice*?" I manage, my voice climbing an octave.

"Mmm." His gaze stays locked on mine, steady and impossible to look away from. "Theory is important. But I've always believed in hands-on application. Wouldn't you agree, Dr. Mackenzie?"

Sweet baby Jesus in a basket. The way he says my title, dripping with suggestion, sends electricity racing down my spine. Suddenly I'm vividly picturing those poet's hands applying very specific theories to very specific places on my very cooperative body.

The afternoon sun spills gold across the beach, casting everything in that too-perfect glow that makes you wish time would stop. We talk. Really talk. About my research, about his poetry, about the odd, magical overlap between art and science. He reads me more of his poems, ones about flowers, yes, but also about his childhood on the ranch, about losing his mother, about grief and memory and the quiet beauty of a Scottish winter.

I tell him everything I've never said aloud, not to Jack, not even to Isla. About the academic dismissal. How Richard's colleagues treated my work like a punchline. How I started publishing under a different name because it felt safer than trying to defend myself. How I miss it. How I still want it. Even now.

"You should start again," Levi says, and there's no hesitation in his voice, only quiet certainty. "The world needs your perspective. Your voice."

For a moment, I can't speak. The idea catches in my throat, too delicate to examine. No one's said anything that honest to me in years, maybe ever. It stirs a part of me I thought I'd buried beneath layers of practicality and exhaustion, a part that's still restless and hungry and remembers what it felt like to chase knowledge.

The day exhales around us, the sun sinking low, painting the sky in wild oranges, electric pinks, and streaks of gold.

But we stay. Neither of us moves to leave, as though we're trying to preserve this beautiful little bubble we've built. This space where the air feels easier to breathe. Where the words don't need permission to come out.

"We should probably head back," I say finally, reluctant to shatter the stillness. "The kids will be waiting for me."

Levi nods and begins to pack up with the same unspoken gentleness that seems woven into him. Every motion is careful, measured, like he's putting the moment itself away for safekeeping. As we climb the hill toward the truck, he reaches for my hand without thinking, and I meet him halfway. Our fingers fit together easily, like we've been doing this for years.

At the crest of the path, we stop to look back. The beach below glows faintly in the last of the light, a stretch of silvered sand and darkening waves.

"Look," Levi says, gently tugging my attention upward. "Venus is rising."

I follow his gaze to a bright pinpoint hovering near the horizon, achingly aware of how close he's standing. Close enough that I can smell the hot chocolate on his breath, feel the heat radiating from his body in the cooling air.

"It's the symbol of love and beauty in most cultures," he says, and his voice slips into that low, lyrical cadence that makes my skin prickle with want.

I turn to him then, caught by the roughness threading through his tone. The last of the daylight traces the curve of his cheek, the line of his jaw, the hollow of his throat. He's beautiful, not in the way that stops traffic, but in the way that stops time. Not like Leo, whose presence commands every room. Not like Hudson, who vibrates with chaotic energy. But deeper. Quieter. Like still water that hides dangerous currents underneath.

My fingers itch to touch him. Have been itching all day, every time he's brushed past me, every accidental contact that felt anything but accidental.

"Levi," I say, his name coming out breathless, desperate.

He steps closer, and my heart slams against my ribs. His hand rises slowly, giving me time to pull away, but instead I lean into it as he tucks a curl behind my ear. His fingertips linger against my cheek, and I can feel the slight tremor in them. He's been holding back too. All day. All these hours of careful distance when what we both wanted was this.

"I need to kiss you again, Lorna," he says, his voice frayed at the edges. "I've been thinking about it every second since this morning. May I?"

"God, yes," I whisper, the words torn from somewhere deep. "I've been going mad all day, Levi. Every time you looked at me, every time you didn't touch me—"

He silences my confession with his mouth, and it's nothing like this morning. There's no urgency now, no edge of surprise. It's slow and consuming, the kind of connection that feels practiced, as if he's spent all day imagining exactly how he wants to taste me. His lips are soft but unrelenting, coaxing mine open until I'm pliant beneath him. When his tongue meets mine, a sound slips out that I'll probably regret later, but right now I don't care.

He tastes like salt air and hot chocolate and a deeper note I can't quite name, something smoky and rich, threaded with desire. His hands cradle my face as if I'm precious, but his mouth tells a different story. It's hungry, consuming, making up for every moment we've held back today.

My fingers twist in his shirt, pulling him closer, and he lets out a low sound that rumbles through me. The kiss deepens, and time slips away. There's only his mouth on mine, his thumb tracing my jaw, his body anchoring me against the chill of evening.

When we finally break apart, we're both gasping, lungs greedy for air that suddenly feels too thin. The stars crowd the sky above us, silent witnesses to the ruin of our restraint. Levi leans in, his forehead resting against mine, eyes still closed, chest rising and falling in ragged rhythm.

"I haven't been able to think straight since I got out of the truck this morning," he says, voice rough. "Every second since has been torture, Lorna."

A shaky laugh slips out of me before I can stop it. "You hid it well. I thought I was the only one losing my mind, wanting you to kiss me again."

"I was hanging on by threads," he admits. "Every time you smiled, every time you tucked your hair back, every time you said my name. Fuck, Lorna, you're killing me."

"Good," I whisper, brushing my lips against his. "That only seems fair."

～

The drive back to the castle is quiet in the best way, no rush to fill the silence, just the hum of the engine and the weight of Levi's hand wrapped around mine on the seat between us.

Every so often, he lifts my fingers to his mouth, brushing his lips over my knuckles as if he can't bear to not touch me. Each one sends a shiver down my spine, sparks settling low and deep.

By the time we pull into the castle drive, the windows glow with light, soft squares of gold spilling across the lawn. I can see Jack's silhouette pacing in the great hall, probably halfway to launching a search party.

Levi puts the truck in park but doesn't move to get out. Instead, he turns to me, the dashboard lights casting a gentle glow across his face.

"I should tell you something," he says, his thumb drawing lazy circles on the back of my hand.

My heart hiccups. Here comes the catch. The twist. The thing that ruins everything before it really begins.

"Leo, Hudson, and I talked about coming to see you," Levi says, voice careful but edged with emotion he's not bothering to hide. "You told us you needed space, and we've been trying to respect that. But if that's still what you want, you have to say it, because it turns out we're completely incapable of staying away."

Relief loosens the tight knot in my chest, and I sink back against the seat. "I know I said I came here to think, but the only thing I've managed to think about is what I want to do with each of you when I see you again."

Levi's mouth curves, eyes catching the light. "Good. It's only fair," he says, echoing my words from earlier.

I glance toward the castle, sighing. "I should go in. The twins will be waiting."

He nods and releases my hand, slow and reluctant. "I should head back too. Early milking tomorrow. My turn to suffer."

We both climb out of the truck and meet at the front, the castle's golden light spilling across the gravel until everything feels touched by the gods. For a moment, the air hums with that strange in-between stillness that belongs to dusk.

And Levi? He looks unreal in it. Like he's stepped out of some half-remembered story, a figure made of warmth and quiet conviction. Like a poem whispered to the dark and finally answered.

I must hesitate, linger just a little too long, because he steps closer, his hands finding my waist with a tenderness that steals my breath. "I've dreamed of this," he murmurs. "Of us. All of us."

Then he kisses me. His mouth fits over mine, warm and hungry, and the world goes quiet except for the sound of us breathing. My fingers dig into his shoulders, pulling him closer, trying to keep him there, to make it last.

When he finally pulls back, my lips are swollen, my pulse wild. He presses his mouth to my forehead, the brush of it tender enough to break me.

"Until next time," he says, voice rough.

"Until next time," I whisper, the words catching on the taste of him still on my tongue.

I watch his truck disappear down the long drive, taillights glowing red in the dark. Only when the last bit of light vanishes do I turn toward the castle, still tingling, still full of him.

As I reach the door, I realize something strange is happening to my face. I'm smiling. Not the polite, public version I've worn like armor for the last six years. No, this one's wide. A little ridiculous. And terrifyingly, beautifully full of hope.

Jack is waiting in the entrance hall, arms crossed, eyebrows raised in a silent question.

"Not a word," I warn, but there's no heat behind it.

"Wasn't gonna say anything," he says innocently, falling into step beside me as I head toward the family wing. "But if I were saying something, it might be about how you look right now."

"And how do I look?" I ask, even though I already know. The answer is in the ache in my lips and the fizz in my bloodstream.

Jack studies me for a moment, his expression softening in a way that makes my chest sting. "Like someone who's remembering what life is all about."

"Maybe I am," I say, voice barely above a whisper.

Jack nods. Squeezes my shoulder. "Good," he says, simple and final. "It's about damn time."

Later, after the twins are asleep, Daniel buried in his rocks and Lorelai mumbling about fairy kingdoms, I sit by the window with the night pressed close around the castle.

The journal Levi gave me rests in my lap, the leather warm from my hands. Inside, tucked between two blank pages, is a single sheet of thick paper covered in his handwriting. A poem.

*The petals tremble,*
*    caught between the pull of moonlight*
*    and the weight of soil,*
*    fragile skin holding a secret*
*    it was never meant to keep.*
*    This garden is no sanctuary.*
*    It's a battlefield—*
*    roots clawing through time,*
*    thorns marked with the memory of every wound*
*    no one else saw.*
*    And still,*
*    the roses rise.*
*    Unbroken.*
*    Unforgiven.*
*    Carrying the quiet promise*
*    that they will bloom again.*
*    The soil is the body of the world,*
*    soft, giving,*
*    split open by hunger,*
*    by want,*
*    by the ache of holding on too long.*
*    Yet from the fracture,*
*    something survives.*
*    Something wild.*
*    Starved.*
*    Relentless.*
*    It drives the roots deeper,*
*    reaching for what waits beneath the hurt.*
*    You—*
*    you are storm and stillness,*

*the moon pulling the tide,*
*the pulse under the skin of the earth.*
*You are fire that never dies,*
*burning low,*
*building slow heat in hidden places.*
*You bloom not because you are untouched,*
*but because you have been broken,*
*bleeding,*
*and still choose to rise.*
*And in that rise,*
*that stubborn, defiant reach toward light,*
*is the truth.*
*You were never meant to shrink.*
*Not for the world.*
*Not for the dark.*
*You grow because you are both the garden*
*and the wild thing*
*that refuses to be tamed.*
*—Levi Walker*

**10**

―――――

I've always been a planner. Lists upon lists. Everything color-coded and neatly stacked in the Notes app like tiny digital soldiers ready for battle. I'm the kind of woman who has backup plans for her backup plans. So the fact that my brain has devolved into one endless loop of emotional static is supremely irritating. Two and a half weeks into the castle garden renovation, and my entire mental state can be summed up in one word: waiting.

I haven't heard from any of them in three days.

Not that I'm counting.

Except, of course, I am. Because the last message had been from Hudson, something about a supply run to Inverness, and then nothing. No texts. No calls. Just silence loud enough to rattle around my head every time I check my phone. Which, for the record, is roughly every twenty seconds.

Like a lovesick teenager with a new crush.

Or, more accurately, three of them.

"You're doing it again," Charlie says, watching me try to dig a hole for the fourth time in the same spot. Her knowing smile has become increasingly insufferable with each passing day.

"Doing what?" I snap, jamming the shovel into unyielding earth with more force than necessary.

"That thing where you check your phone, sigh dramatically when there's nothing, then pretend you weren't checking."

"I wasn't checking," I lie, for possibly the fiftieth time today. "I was making sure the weather forecast hasn't changed."

Charlie's eyebrow arches so high it practically leaves her forehead. "The weather forecast that needs checking six times per hour."

I open my mouth to deliver what I'm sure would have been a spectacularly cutting comeback, when the unmistakable sound of tires on gravel sends my heart into immediate cardiac arrest. My head snaps up so fast I'm surprised it doesn't detach completely.

The castle entrance is blocked from view by the ancient yew hedge we've spent the last three days wrestling into submission, but I'd recognize the rumble of that truck anywhere.

My pulse kicks into overdrive. My insides turn to liquid fire.

Charlie grins, all cat-with-cream satisfaction. "Sounds like the weather forecast just arrived."

I resist the urge to chuck my trowel at her head, but only barely.

"Go," she says, taking the shovel from my white-knuckled grip. "I'll finish this section."

I try for dignified indifference but abandon it halfway through. "Are you sure? Because I can—"

A happy shriek cuts through the air, Lorelai's specific pitch of pure joy that I'd recognize anywhere. It's followed by deeper laughter, rich and warm as summer honey.

Hudson.

Any pretense of cool detachment evaporates. I'm moving before I consciously decide to, nearly tripping over a wheelbarrow in my haste to round the hedge. So much for dignity. So much for playing it cool. So much for—

The sight that greets me stops me dead in my tracks.

Hudson Walker stands in the middle of the castle lawn, but he's not alone. Strapped to his back is my son, arms wrapped around his neck like a koala, whooping with delight. Perched on one broad shoulder is my daughter, her wild curls whipping about as Hudson spins in circles. Clinging to his leg like a determined barnacle is little Summer, her blonde head thrown back in helpless giggles.

"Higher!" Lorelai demands, fearless as always. "I want to touch the SKY!"

"Your wish is my command, princess." He bounces on his toes to make all three children squeal with delight. "Though if you actually touch the sky, I think your mum might have something to say about it."

I don't know why I'm frozen. Why I can't move or speak or do anything but stare. It's not like I haven't seen him with my children before. He's been building fairy houses with Lorelai. Helping Daniel with his rock collection. But here, against the backdrop of the ancient castle, with my children's joy echoing off stone walls that have witnessed centuries, it feels different. Monumental.

And then Hudson glances up and sees me.

His smile, that devastating, dimpled smile that should come with a government warning label, falters. Something flashes in his eyes, something heated and hungry that makes my stomach drop like I've flung myself off a cliff.

Then just as quickly, the playful grin slides back into place.

"Well, if it isn't the enchanted gardener herself!" he calls, adjusting his stance to better accommodate his giggling cargo. "I was introducing myself to the local wildlife. They seem friendly enough, though this one"—he bounces Summer gently—" has quite the grip for such a tiny person."

Summer's response is to grip his leg tighter and declare, "MINE!" with the possessive certainty that only toddlers can muster.

I force my feet to move, crossing the lawn with what I hope passes for casual friendliness rather than the electric awareness humming through my veins.

"I see you've made a new friend," I say, choking back a laugh as Summer squeezes tighter, her face turning red and her little nose wrinkling. "Though I'm not sure Jack will appreciate his daughter claiming you as personal property."

"I've been claimed by worse," Hudson winks, and holy heck, that wink should be illegal in at least twelve countries. "Besides, I come bearing gifts for the young lords and ladies of the realm."

As if on cue, Daniel's head pops up over Hudson's shoulder. "He brought us TREASURE, Mum! Real stuff, not baby toys."

"The finest treasures this side of the Hebrides," Hudson confirms solemnly. "Though I may need to be relieved of my current duties to retrieve them."

"Down, down!" Summer commands, finally releasing her death grip on his leg.

With impressive dexterity for a man currently serving as a human jungle gym, Hudson lowers all three kids to the ground without breaking a sweat. Lorelai immediately reclaims him, wrapping herself around his arm and swinging like she's training for the uneven bars.

"Easy there, monkey," I warn, though she's already giggling too hard to listen.

"It's all good," Hudson says, lifting her higher. Her giggles bubble up again, bright and wild. "I lift heavier things than this little pixie every day."

He straightens and grins at the kids. "Race you to the truck!"

They take off across the grass in a blur of limbs and laughter, Summer's shorter legs churning like she's running for Olympic gold. Hudson doesn't move right away. His gaze lingers on me, steady and intense, and the air between us evaporates.

"You look good, Lorna," he says, voice low enough to make my pulse trip. "Really good."

I become painfully aware of what I must look like. Mud-streaked jeans, an ancient flannel rolled at the sleeves, hair barely clinging to what was once a bun and has now collapsed into a full-blown disaster. There's probably dirt on my face. Definitely some under my nails.

"I look like a swamp creature," I mutter.

"Yeah," Hudson says, pupils flaring as they make a slow, unhurried pass from my face to my boots and back again, pausing in places that make my stomach twist. "It's definitely working for me."

Words scatter in my head before I can grab a single one. The kids' voices call from the driveway, saving me from whatever embarrassing noise was about to leave my mouth. Hudson's grin turns wicked.

"Coming!" he calls, but his eyes stay on me for one more charged second. "We'll finish this conversation later."

Then he jogs away, and I'm left standing there with my heart racing, my face flushed, and the undeniable sense that I've just been completely undone by a man who smells faintly of sunshine and mischief.

Later turns out to be several hours away, because Hudson Walker, it seems, has appointed himself Official Entertainer to the castle children. I catch glimpses of them throughout the afternoon —building an elaborate fort from old blankets and garden stakes, staging what appears to be a dramatic reenactment of a pirate invasion complete with Hudson playing all the villainous roles, and finally, a treasure hunt that takes them all over the grounds.

I try to focus on the gardens. Really, I do. But it's nearly impossible when Hudson's laughter keeps floating across the lawn, when I keep catching sight of him with grass in his hair and my children hanging off him like he's their personal climbing frame.

"You know," Charlie says as we plant the last of the rose bushes, "you could go join them."

I straighten, pressing a fist to my aching lower back. "I have work to do."

"The gardens won't disappear if you take an afternoon off," she points out reasonably. "Besides, you've been working non-stop since you got here."

"Because there's a deadline," I remind her. "The magazine shoot—"

"—is still weeks away," she interrupts. "And we're ahead of schedule. Jack said so last night."

I sigh, glancing toward where Hudson is now teaching all three children what appears to be some kind of elaborate war dance. His movements are wild, unreserved, completely lacking in self-consciousness. He's like a force of nature, this man, chaotic, exuberant, impossible to ignore.

"Go," Charlie says firmly. "I'll watch the kids."

For once, I don't argue.

As I approach, Hudson spots me and says something to the children that sends them scattering in different directions, giggling madly. His expression shifts, the playful energy becoming more focused, more intentional.

"Where are they going?" I ask, nodding toward the retreating children.

"On a mission," Hudson says, taking a step closer. "Very important garden business. Specifically, finding the perfect sticks for fairy wands."

"And how long will this mission take?" I find myself asking.

Hudson's eyes darken, that dimple appearing as his lips curve into a slow smile. "Long enough."

"Long enough for what, exactly?"

Instead of answering, Hudson closes the distance between us, reaching out to curl a lock of hair around his finger. The simple touch shouldn't affect me the way it does, shouldn't send electricity sparking down my spine.

"I missed you," he says, direct and devastating in his honesty. "I've been thinking about you. About this."

And then he's kissing me, right there in the middle of the gardens where anyone could see. Unlike Leo's controlled passion or Levi's poetic tenderness, Hudson kisses like he does everything else, with reckless abandon, holding nothing back. He frames my face, his body pressing close as his mouth claims mine with infectious enthusiasm.

I should pull away. I should remember we're in full view of the castle, that my brother or Charlie or, worse, the twins could round the corner any second. Instead, I find myself melting into him, my hands gripping his shirt, pulling him closer.

When we finally part, both breathless, Hudson's eyes are bright with the gleam of someone hatching a plan.

"Come with me," he says, taking my hand.

"Where are we going?" I ask, but I'm already following, helpless against the pull of his energy.

"Somewhere we can be alone for more than thirty seconds," he says over his shoulder, tugging me toward a part of the grounds I know well, the massive hedge maze that's been a fixture of the castle gardens for generations.

"The maze? Really?" I smirk even as I let him lead me through the intricate entrance. "That's a bit cliché, don't you think?"

Hudson stops so suddenly I nearly crash into his back. He turns, pulling me against him in one smooth motion. "Maybe," he concedes, his voice dropping to that register that makes my knees weak. "But I've been thinking about getting you alone since I drove through those gates three hours ago."

"Three hours is a long time," I rasp.

"Tell me about it," he murmurs. "Do you have any idea how hard it was playing with those kids when all I could think about was how their mom looked standing in the sunshine with dirt on her cheek and fire in her eyes?"

I swallow hard, caught in his gaze like a moth drawn to flame. "Hudson..."

"Race you to the center," he says suddenly, stepping back with a challenging grin. "Unless you're scared."

The abrupt shift gives me whiplash, but the competitive spark in his eyes ignites the fight in me. "Scared? Please."

"Then go," he says, eyes dancing. "Unless you need a head start?"

I narrow my eyes at him. "I grew up here, remember? I could navigate this maze blindfolded."

"Prove it," he challenges, taking another deliberate step back.

Without another word, I turn and sprint down the path on the left, heart pounding with the thrill of the chase. Behind me, I hear Hudson laugh, that full-bodied sound of pure joy, before his footsteps echo mine, gaining quickly with his longer stride.

I know this maze like the back of my hand, every twist and turn, every dead end, every shortcut. But what I'd forgotten was how the adrenaline of being pursued could make those familiar paths seem new again, how the sound of Hudson's footsteps closing in could scramble my brain.

I cut right, then left, then right again, following the shortcut I discovered as a teenager. The center of the maze is just ahead, a circular clearing with an ancient stone bench and a weathered fountain. I'm almost there, only a few more steps—

Strong arms wrap around my waist from behind, lifting me clear off the ground. I shriek, half laughter, half surprise, as Hudson spins me in a circle.

"Cheater!" I accuse. "You can't just—"

Whatever I was about to say is lost as Hudson sets me on my feet and turns me to face him in one smooth motion. The playfulness in his eyes has become darker, hungrier.

"Can't what?" he challenges, backing me up until I feel the cool stone of the fountain pressing into my back. "Can't want you so badly I can't think straight? Can't dream about you every night since we last saw each other? Can't follow you into this maze with very specific ideas about what I want to do when I catch you?"

Any response I might have made evaporates as his body presses against mine, solid and warm and thrumming with barely contained energy. His hands bracket my face, thumbs brushing over my cheekbones with surprising gentleness that contrasts with the intensity in his eyes.

"Last chance to tell me to stop," he murmurs, his lips hovering above mine.

Instead of answering, I pull him down to me, claiming his mouth with a desperation that stuns us both. Hudson responds instantly, a growl rumbling up from his chest as his hands slide into my hair, cradling my head as he deepens the kiss.

There's nothing careful about it, nothing restrained or measured. It's messy and urgent and perfect, his mouth hot and insistent against mine, his body pinning me in place in a way that should make me feel trapped but instead makes me feel anchored. Safe, even as I'm falling.

"God, Lorna," he breathes against my mouth, his hands seemingly unable to stay still, sliding down my sides, over my hips, behind my thighs. "You have no idea how many times I've thought about this."

In one smooth motion, he lifts me onto the lip of the fountain, palms cupping the backs of my thighs, and I instinctively wrap my legs around his waist. The position brings his hardness directly against my center, and even through layers of denim, the contact makes my insides light up like fireworks.

"Hudson," I gasp, my head falling back as he trails hot, open-mouthed kisses down my throat. "We can't—not here—"

"I know," he murmurs against my collarbone. "I just need—can I just touch you? Please?"

The raw need in his voice undoes me. I nod, unable to form words as his hands slide beneath my shirt, fingers mapping the skin of my lower back, my ribs, inching higher with teasing deliberation.

His touch is electric, setting off a chain reaction along my nerve endings. When his thumbs finally brush the undersides of my breasts, I arch into him with a moan I barely recognize as my own.

"Beautiful," he whispers, reverent and awed, as he cups me through the thin cotton of my bra. "So goddamn stunning."

I should be embarrassed by how responsive I am, how quickly he's reduced me to trembling need with only his hands and mouth. But there's no room for embarrassment, not when he's looking at me like I'm everything he's ever wanted.

Hudson rolls his hips until I'm gasping his name, nails digging into his shoulders. He captures the sound with his mouth, kissing me deeper, harder, his tongue tangling with mine in a rhythm that mimics what our bodies are desperate for.

I'm lost in sensation, in the feel of him against me, around me, when a stone shifts beneath Hudson's foot. The sudden movement throws him slightly off balance, and we stumble sideways, nearly tipping the fountain over.

"Shit," Hudson chuckles against my mouth, adjusting his stance to keep us both upright. "Sorry—not exactly the smooth move I was going for."

The near fall breaks the spell just enough for reality to come crashing back. We're in a hedge maze at my brother's castle, in broad daylight, with three children somewhere nearby on a scavenger hunt that could end at any moment.

"We should probably..." I trail off, reluctantly unwinding my legs from his waist.

Hudson sets me gently on my feet but doesn't step away. "Yeah, probably."

Neither of us moves. His forehead drops to rest against mine, our breathing gradually slowing.

"I can't seem to keep my hands off you," he confesses, brushing his nose against mine in a gesture so tender it makes my chest ache. "It's becoming a problem."

"Is it?" I ask, my lips twitching.

"Mmm," he murmurs, brushing a kiss against the corner of my mouth. "Dangerous condition, really. Symptoms include complete loss of focus, obsessive thoughts about how soft your skin is, and recurring fantasies about getting you alone. Might need immediate treatment."

"Sounds terminal," I tease, playing with the hair at the nape of his neck.

"Completely," he agrees solemnly. "Only known cure is more of you."

Before I can respond, a familiar voice calls from somewhere in the maze, distant but getting closer.

"Mummy! Mr. Hudson! Where ARE you?"

We jolt apart like teenagers caught making out behind the gym, both of us scrambling to put ourselves back together. I tug at my shirt, he smooths his hair, and the air between us hums with leftover heat. Hudson's mouth curves, somewhere between a grimace and a grin, as he drags a hand through his already-messy hair, looking entirely too pleased with himself for a man interrupted mid-makeout.

"Bad timing," he mutters, adjusting himself in his jeans with a rueful grimace that makes me bite back a laugh. "To be continued?"

"To be continued," I confirm, cupping his face and running my thumb over his full bottom lip.

"MUMMY!" Lorelai's voice is closer now, the impatience in it growing with each repetition.

"Coming, sweetheart!" I call back, taking a deep breath to steady myself.

Hudson grips my hand before I can move past him, bringing it to his lips for a kiss that's surprisingly sweet given what we were doing only moments ago. "I meant what I said," he murmurs against my knuckles. "About missing you. About thinking about you."

"I missed you too," I admit, the words tumbling out before I can stop them. "All three of you."

His smile spreads slowly, lazy and satisfied, like I've given him exactly what he wanted. "Good to know."

By the time Lorelai finds us, we've relocated to the stone bench, sitting at a perfectly respectable distance. Still, the air between us hums with leftover heat, the kind that could probably ignite the hedges if it had half a chance.

"There you are!" my daughter declares, hands on hips in a posture so like mine it's almost comical. "We've been looking EVERYWHERE!"

"Sorry, monkey," Hudson says, his expression transforming into one of exaggerated contrition. "Your mum was showing me the middle of the maze. Did you find good fairy wand materials?"

Just like that, Lorelai's indignation vanishes, replaced by bubbling excitement as she launches into a detailed inventory of their findings. I watch them interact, struck again by how naturally

Hudson relates to her, how he listens with genuine interest to her rambling explanations.

As we wind our way out of the maze, Hudson's hand brushes mine. It's barely anything, skin against skin for the briefest heartbeat, but it feels like a promise, one that hums along my nerve endings long after his fingers slip away. The afternoon light stretches across the lawn, honey-gold and lazy, and for once, I don't try to plan or analyze or overthink. I let myself exist in it. Let myself feel.

Another hour slips by in a blur of laughter and fairy-wand chaos. Daniel's wand has enough feathers to qualify as a small bird, and Hudson, bless him, is acting like he's just engineered a NASA prototype instead of a stick covered in glue and sparkles. By the time I glance at my watch, reality comes crashing back in. Dinner's creeping up fast. Charlie had mentioned Jack wanted to do some kind of "proper sit-down meal" since we have a guest, which means I probably shouldn't show up looking like I rolled in craft supplies and lost the fight.

"I should go get cleaned up for dinner," I tell Hudson. He's crouched beside Daniel, carefully looping twine around the base of the wand. "Apparently Jack's going all out tonight."

He glances up, and when our eyes meet, my stomach flips. "Mind if I grab my bag from the truck? I should probably get cleaned up too."

There's something in his tone that isn't innocent, a low undercurrent that catches on my skin and lingers. My breath hitches before I can stop it.

"Sure," I manage, aiming for casual but landing squarely in breathless territory. "I'll show you where you can leave your stuff."

I tell Charlie we're heading in to clean up, pretending not to notice the smirk tugging at her mouth. She raises a brow, clearly onto me, and says, "Go on. I'll finish up with the kids and get them cleaned up for dinner." Her tone is all casual sweetness, but the glint in her eyes screams *I see you, Lorna MacLeod.*

Hudson retrieves a battered duffel from his truck, and we fall into step, walking in that easy kind of silence that somehow feels anything but. The air between us hums with the memory of his mouth on mine in the maze, the taste of him still lingering at the edges of my thoughts.

"Your room's actually in the east wing," I say as we climb the main staircase, grateful for the distraction. "But you can drop your bag in mine for now if you want."

Hudson's mouth curves into that slow, devastating smile that should come with a warning label. "Lead the way."

My room sits at the far end of the family wing, the same one I had as a teenager. It's been updated since then, but it still smells faintly of lilac and old books and memories. I push open the door, and awareness hits me all at once. The bed. Hudson. The quiet click of the door closing behind us. Suddenly the room feels smaller, the air heavier, like it's holding its breath right along with me.

"Bathroom's through there," I choke out, nodding toward the en suite. "I'm going to, uh," I gesture helplessly at my dirt-streaked clothes.

Hudson sets his bag on a chair, his gaze steady and unreadable. "Don't let me stop you."

My cheeks burn, but recklessness stirs inside me, fanning the embers that ignited when he kissed me in the maze. Without breaking eye contact, I walk toward the bathroom and leave the door cracked behind me, a silent invitation I don't quite have the nerve to say out loud.

The shower roars to life, filling the quiet with steam and water and my racing heartbeat. I strip quickly, step under the spray, and let the heat sink into me. It feels good, cleansing and grounding, but it doesn't do a thing to cool the ache humming under my skin.

"Hudson?" I call out, surprised by the steadiness in my voice. "Could you hand me the shampoo? I forgot to grab it."

For a moment, there's silence, and I wonder if he didn't hear me, or worse, if he understood perfectly and chose not to take the bait. Then I hear footsteps, and the bathroom door pushes wider.

Hudson stands there, hesitating at the threshold. He's removed his boots and shirt, standing in only his jeans, and sweet mother of maple syrup, all that lean muscle and tanned skin nearly short-circuits my brain.

"The shampoo?" he asks, his voice cracking.

I gesture vaguely toward the counter, not even trying to hide behind the glass door. "Right there."

His eyes darken as they travel over me, lingering on the water streaming down my body.

"Lorna," he says, my name scraping rough from his throat, question and warning tangled together like barbed wire.

My pulse hammers so hard I can feel it in my fingertips, in my throat, behind my eyes. "Are you coming in or not?"

The words come out breathless, reckless. Bolder than I've been in six years. Maybe ever.

Hudson doesn't hesitate. His jeans hit the floor, then he's grabbing the shampoo and stepping into the shower, boxer briefs clinging to his hips, leaving absolutely nothing to the imagination. His abs are cut deep. The V of his hips sharp enough to make me stare, a trail of hair disappearing into the waistband like it's leading somewhere I already know I want to go.

The heat wraps around us like a living thing, thick and suffocating and electric. We stand frozen in a moment that stretches like taffy, not touching, barely breathing, just watching each other through the rising fog. Water streams down his chest, catching on every ridge of muscle, and I'm burning up from the inside out.

"Turn around," he says, voice so low I feel it in my bones. The bottle clicks open, sharp in the silence. "Let me wash your hair for you."

I turn. Slowly. Deliberately. Show him the vulnerable curve of my neck, the wet fall of my hair, the way my hands shake as they press against the tile.

His fingers slide into my hair and I nearly collapse. They're warm, steady, sure, but there's a tremor in them that matches the earthquake in my chest. The first pass of his fingers against my scalp pulls a sound from me I didn't know I could make. He works the lather through with devastating focus, like my hair is precious, like this moment matters.

"Does that feel good?" he murmurs.

"Yes." It comes out broken, shattered. I'm coming apart under his hands and he's barely touched me.

He rinses me with excruciating slowness, water sliding over my skin as he follows its path, down my shoulders, across my back, his fingers gliding over slick curves with a care that splits me wide open. Every pass ignites a fresh line of fire. My breathing turns ragged, unsteady, pulled from someplace deep and aching.

"You have no idea," he says, voice wrecked now, raw, "how fucking incredible you are."

His lips find the curve where my shoulder meets my neck, and my vision whites out at the edges. I can feel him behind me, the solid wall of his chest inches from my back, the evidence of what this is doing to him pressed against me.

I turn in his arms because I have to see him, need to know if this is wrecking him the way it's wrecking me. Water runs down his face, his chest, his abs—and those boxer briefs? They're nearly see-through now, clinging to the thick shape of him in a way that makes my mouth water and my thighs clench.

"Your turn," I say, my voice barely more than a whisper.

Hudson ducks his head, and the trust in that gesture, this strong, chaotic man making himself vulnerable for me, nearly brings me to my knees. His eyes flutter closed as I work the shampoo into his hair, lips parting on a soft exhale that shoots straight to my core. I memorize him like this, water-beaded lashes, the strong arch of his throat, the way his whole body leans into me like a plant seeking sun.

When I rinse him, my hands don't stop. Can't stop. They map the geography of his shoulders, the solid breadth of his chest where his heart pounds rabbit-quick under my palm. Down the ladder of his ribs, across the taut plane of his stomach that jumps under my fingers. Each touch pulls his breathing tighter, rougher. A muscle in his jaw flexes.

"Lorna." My name is gravel in his mouth when my fingers brush the waistband of those useless briefs. "If you keep touching me like that, we're going to be very late for dinner."

I should care. Jack is waiting. The kids are waiting. Instead, I rise on my toes, grip his shoulders for balance, and crush my mouth to his.

The kiss detonates like a bomb. Gentle for exactly one second before Hudson makes a desperate sound and then his tongue is sliding against mine and I'm drowning. He tastes like mint and rain and pure need. His hands find my waist, fingertips digging in, then slide lower to grip my hips, hauling me against him. There's almost nothing between us, only soaked cotton and the hard length of him, and the pressure alone pulls a sound from deep in my chest.

"You're driving me insane," he groans, his hand sliding up to cup my breast, thumb dragging over the peak until my vision goes white at the edges. "Since that first day—watching you fight that frost like you could bend the world to your will. You haven't left my head. Not for a goddamn second."

"We're going to be late for dinner," I rasp, even as I arch into him, shameless and needy. "We should probably stop."

"Probably," he agrees, but his mouth is already tracking down my throat, teeth grazing my collarbone. His other hand slides down my spine, pressing me impossibly closer. "Any minute now."

Neither of us stops. His mouth trails down my neck, finding the place where my pulse flutters beneath thin skin, sucking just hard enough to draw a sound from me. Then harder, until I know he's leaving a mark, until my knees give out and I'm gripping his shoulders to keep from sliding down the wall.

"Hudson," I whisper, the word trembling out of me like a confession.

His teeth catch on my collarbone, a sharp, electric sting that sends pleasure shooting through every nerve. He soothes it with his tongue, then does it again, like he's experimenting, seeing what makes me gasp, what makes me shiver. His mouth drifts across my shoulder, and every touch sparks a new ache I didn't know I could feel. His thumbs graze the undersides of my breasts, then retreat. Return. Vanish. Return. Each teasing pass more unbearable than the last, until I'm making small, desperate sounds I can't control.

One hand slides down my spine, fingertips tracing each vertebra like he's counting them, like he's memorizing the architecture of me. The other cups my breast fully, finally, and when his thumb circles the peak, I cry out loud enough that I'm grateful for the sound of running water. My back arches, pressing into him, shameless and desperate.

"That's it," he encourages. "Let me hear you."

His mouth moves lower, unhurried, every kiss slicker, hungrier, like he's losing his grip but still fighting to savor it. By the time his breath grazes my breast, my lungs have forgotten their job entirely. He looks up once, eyes gone dark and heavy, and then his lips are on me.

The first touch is almost nothing, a whisper of warmth that sends a tremor straight through me. Then his tongue traces the edge of my nipple in slow, deliberate circles until it tightens under his mouth. My fingers tangle in his hair, holding him there, desperate for more.

When he finally takes me into his mouth, everything in me clenches. His tongue moves in slow, maddening flicks, alternating gentle licks and pressure until I'm trembling. Then he nips and the world blurs out, my vision sparking white at the edges. A raw, broken sound spills from my throat as my nails drag down his shoulders, marking him.

He groans against my skin, the vibration sinking straight through me, and I arch into him helplessly. The thought of him wearing my marks tomorrow, of anyone seeing them and knowing exactly what he did to me, sends a rush of molten desire low in my belly, sharp and consuming.

"Please," I gasp, though I'm not sure what I'm begging for. More. Everything. Him.

Hudson's touch slides lower, across my stomach, and my muscles jump under his touch. He stops short of where I'm aching for him, his fingers splayed across my hip instead, holding me steady as his mouth continues its exploration. The denial makes me want to sob. Or scream. Or possibly climb him like a tree.

"So beautiful," he breathes against my skin. "The way you respond, the sounds you make—fuck, Lorna, you're perfect."

His other hand tangles in my hair, tugging gently to tilt my head back, exposing my throat. He kisses me there, right over my racing pulse, and I swear I'm going to come apart just from this, just from his mouth and hands and the solid heat of him pressed against me.

My hands map him in return, the bunch and flex of his shoulders, the rigid line of his spine, the dimples at the base of his spine that make him groan when I trace them. When I drag my nails lightly down his back, he makes a sound that's almost feral, his hips jerking forward, pressing the hard length of him against my stomach.

"Lorna," he warns, or maybe begs, I can't tell anymore. His control is fraying, I can feel it in the tremor of his hands, the harsh rasp of his breathing.

"I know," I gasp. "I know, but—"

But I can't stop. My hands explore his shoulders, his back, the solid heat of him beneath my fingers. I pull him closer until our bodies align completely. My leg hooks around his hip, pulling him tighter, and the new angle sends pressure exactly where I need it. The sound that escapes us is shared, low and raw and full of hunger, as if we've both been starving for this.

"Fuck." His forehead drops to my shoulder. His whole body is taut, vibrating with restraint. "We have to—dinner—your brother—"

"I know," I whimper, even as I rock against him, chasing the friction that's making stars explode behind my eyelids. "Fuck—one more minute—please—"

But it's Hudson who finally tears himself away, and the loss of his warmth makes me actually whine out loud. He presses his forehead to mine, his hands coming up to frame my face like he needs to hold me steady, or maybe hold himself steady. We're both panting like we've run marathons, like we've been drowning and just broke the surface. His fingers shake against my jaw, thumbs stroking my cheekbones with a tenderness that's at complete odds with the hunger still burning in his eyes.

"If we don't stop now," Hudson says, voice wrecked, "I'm going to take you against this wall, and your brother will definitely know why we're late."

The mental image of Hudson lifting me, pressing me against the tile, my legs wrapped around his waist makes me clench around nothing, empty and aching.

"Would that be so bad?" I ask, only half-joking.

Hudson chuckles. "Your brother owns a sword, Lorna. Multiple swords."

"Good point," I concede, though every cell in my body is screaming in protest.

"Later," he promises, voice shredded. His eyes are black with want, making my insides liquefy. "After dinner. When we don't have to rush. When I can take my time learning exactly what makes you fall apart."

"Later," I agree, though it comes out more like a whimper.

By the time we make it downstairs, my hair is still damp and Hudson's cheeks are still pink. There's no hiding it. One glance at us and anyone with a brain will know exactly what we've been doing. But I can't bring myself to care. Not when he keeps brushing his hand against mine, not when he looks at me like that.

Dinner at the castle that night hums with noise and laughter. Hudson sits in the center of it all, a glass of wine in hand, his grin wide and wicked. He claims it's "from a local vineyard," but the gleam in his eye says otherwise. He's in full performance mode, telling stories that have everyone, from Jack to Lachlan, bent double with laughter.

Hudson in a crowd is its own kind of magic. Where Leo commands a room through quiet authority and Levi captivates with his stillness, Hudson shines. He sparkles. Every word, every gesture, every offhand joke feels electric. The air around him seems charged, and everyone leans closer without realizing it.

Even Jack, who was slow to warm to Leo, is completely taken in. He's hanging on Hudson's every word as he describes, in vivid detail, the day their truck got trapped between a stubborn kangaroo and what Hudson insists was "the most aggressive wombat in the Southern Hemisphere." The table dissolves into laughter, and Hudson looks so pleased with himself I can't help smiling too.

"So there I am," Hudson says, gesturing with his wine glass, "kangaroo blocking the road, wombat gnawing my boot, Leo leaning out the window with that straight face of his, saying, 'You really have a way with animals.'"

The table erupts, and I find myself studying Hudson's face in the candlelight. The way his expressions shift keeps pulling my attention back to him. The crinkles at the corners of his eyes, the dimple that appears when his smile reaches full strength. I don't realize I'm staring until he feels it, his gaze meeting mine.

Instead of looking away, I hold his gaze, laughter fading until it's just him and me and the light flickering between us. His smile lingers, quieter now, and desire weaves her web in the space separating us. A private spark, familiar and dangerous, the kind that makes my pulse stumble and my heart feel a little too full.

"Mr. Hudson is going to teach me how to build a REAL fairy house," Lorelai announces to the table at large, breaking the moment. "With a working door and everything!"

"Is he now?" I ask, tearing my gaze from Hudson. "And where exactly is this fairy house going to be located?"

"Under the big tree by the garden," Lorelai explains as if it should be obvious. "We made a map today. Daniel helped."

Daniel, who's been quietly absorbed in his food, looks up at the mention of his name. "I made a scientific survey," he confirms seriously. "With proper measurements and everything."

"Very impressive," Jack nods, lips twitching. "I'm sure the local fairy population will be properly accommodated."

"They WILL," Lorelai insists, oblivious to the adult amusement. "Mr. Hudson said he could stay extra days to finish them all!"

My eyes snap to Hudson, who has the grace to look slightly sheepish at this announcement. "Sorry," he mouths across the table. "She's very persuasive."

"You're welcome to stay as long as you want," Jack says, his gaze flicking between Hudson and me with barely disguised curiosity.

The words hang heavy in the air, a simple offer that carries too many possibilities. Hudson staying. Overnight. Here at the castle. The thought sends a slow throb of desire through me, the kind that refuses to fade.

"That's very kind," Hudson says, his tone even though his eyes, when they find mine, tell a different story. There's a spark there, quiet but unmistakable. "If it's not an imposition."

"Not at all," Charlie adds, far too quick to reassure, her expression so angelic it might as well be a warning. "The more help with the kids and the gardens, the better."

Jack grins, raising his glass in triumph. "Then it's settled. To fairy houses and extra hands."

The toast feels harmless on the surface, but when Hudson's knee brushes mine beneath the table, the words take on a whole new meaning.

The rest of dinner passes in a blur of good food, better wine, and conversation that flows as easily as the bottle Jack opens after the first is emptied. The children are sent off to get ready for bed, with Hudson extracting solemn promises to start fairy house construction the next day.

As the evening drifts toward its end, I can barely pretend to pay attention. My focus keeps slipping, drawn again and again to Hudson. The way his fingers tap absently against his glass. The curve of his mouth when he hides a smile. The quiet confidence in the way he takes up space without trying to. Every small movement tugs at my attention until I feel restless under my own skin. The anticipation builds slow and relentless, pooling low in my stomach, making it hard to breathe evenly, let alone think straight.

When Charlie finally stands and stretches, relief floods me. "I think it's time to call it a night," she says, far too casually. "Lach, would you help Jack with those boxes in the library? And Lorna, will you show Hudson his room?" The look she gives me is anything but innocent.

"Of course," I whisper, my voice barely audible.

Within minutes, the others have drifted off, leaving the room quiet and warm, the candlelight flickering low.

"So," Hudson says, standing with that easy grace that wrecks me. "About showing me to my room."

"Follow me," I say, trying, and failing, not to sound breathless. My hands feel useless at my sides, and I tuck one into my pocket as I turn toward the stairs. "It's upstairs."

We climb the grand staircase side by side, not touching but close enough that I can feel the heat radiating from him, smell the faint scent of the shampoo that clings to his skin. The guest wing is on the opposite side from the family quarters, a deliberate choice that feels significant in this moment.

Each step up the stairs winds the tension tighter until it's a living thing inside me. By the time we reach the hallway to his room, my pulse is a drumbeat in my ears.

"Here we are." I push open the door, the scent of old wood and furniture polish drifting out. "Bathroom's through there, fresh towels on the—"

The words die when his hand closes around my wrist. He tugs gently, drawing me into the room. The door closes behind us with a click that echoes through my body. Suddenly, the quiet stretches wide and heavy.

"Hudson—" I start, though I have no idea what I mean to say.

His voice drops low, roughened by something I've only heard hints of before. "Come here," he murmurs. The teasing ease from dinner is gone, replaced by a quiet intensity that gobbles up the air between us. "Please."

I go willingly, stepping into the circle of his arms like I've done it a million times before. His hands settle on my waist, warm and steady, as he studies my face in the soft lamplight.

"I've been wanting to do this all night," he murmurs. He skims his fingers along the side of my face, tracing the curve of my jaw, the fragile line of my throat. "Watching you laugh, seeing you with your family—you're incredible, Lorna. Do you know that?"

The sincerity in his tone hits harder than any flirtation could. It knocks the air right out of me. "I'm just me," I manage, my voice barely above a whisper. "Nothing special."

"See, that's where you're wrong." His thumb ghosts over my bottom lip. "You are special. Extraordinary. And I've been waiting all night to show you exactly how much I mean that."

My mouth parts on an unsteady inhale. "Hudson, I—we're in my brother's house. The twins—"

"Are sound asleep," he finishes, his tone soft but firm, his hand sliding around to the small of my back. The warmth of his hand burns through the fabric of my shirt as he draws me in until every inch of him is pressed against me. "And your brother," he adds, his breath ghosting over my lips, "seemed very intent on giving us privacy."

Every thought, every hesitation dissolves under the weight of his nearness. His scent wraps around me, and I can't think of a single reason not to close the gap.

He's right. The knowing looks from Charlie, Jack's transparent machinations with the seating arrangements, the way everyone conveniently dispersed at the exact same moment, it wasn't subtle.

"Still," I hesitate, years of careful walls trembling under the force of his gaze. "It's complicated."

"Life usually is," Hudson agrees, his expression softening. "But this? This doesn't have to be. Not tonight."

And just like that, every wall I've built caves in. The space between us vanishes, and I rise onto my toes, drawn to him like it's inevitable, like gravity's been conspiring to pull us together from the moment we met. My hands find his shoulders, then the back of his neck, and when our mouths finally meet, it's not careful or tentative. It's a collision years in the making, gentle for a heartbeat before heat floods through both of us.

Hudson groans into the kiss, the sound vibrating through me. His hands slide down my sides, anchoring me, claiming me, before settling on my hips. Then he's lifting me, effortless, and I gasp against his mouth as my legs wrap around his waist.

He backs me toward the wall beside the massive four-poster bed, his movements sure and hungry, until my spine meets wood and the world tilts. His hips find mine again, grinding in a rhythm so perfect and filthy I could come from it alone.

"You have no idea how long I've wanted this," he murmurs against my throat, the scrape of his stubble leaving a slow burn in its wake. "How long I've been wondering what you taste like. What sounds you'd make if I touched you just right."

His words add to the molten ache building between my legs. "Hudson," I gasp as his hands slip beneath my shirt, callused fingers skating over the sensitive skin of my ribcage. "Please."

I'm not sure what I'm asking for, only that I need more, more of his hands, his mouth, the solid weight of him against me.

He seems to understand anyway. He sets me on my feet and steps back, just enough to unbutton my flannel and slide it over my shoulders. The cool air against my heated skin makes me shiver, a reaction that intensifies as Hudson's gaze travels over me, dark and hungry.

"Holy hell, Lorna," he breathes as his touch settles on my waist, thumbs brushing the undersides of my cotton-clad breasts. "You're fucking perfect."

I should feel self-conscious. My body carries the marks of two children, of time, of a life fully lived. But the naked admiration in his eyes makes it impossible. Instead, I feel powerful, grounded, confident in a way I haven't felt in years.

I reach for the hem of his shirt, holding my breath as I tug it up with trembling fingers. Hudson stands perfectly still, raising his arms to help as I pull the fabric over his head. When the shirt finally comes off, my thoughts scatter. He's all golden skin and lean muscle, every inch of him unfairly perfect. I want to press my face to his chest, breathe him in, taste the heat of his skin, follow every line with my tongue until I've memorized him.

"You're not so bad yourself," I murmur, my fingertip circling his nipple before gliding lower, tracing the curve of his ribs, the hard planes of his abs, then following the faint trail of dark hair that disappears beneath his waistband.

Hudson swallows hard as my fingers skim the line of his belt. "Lorna," he warns, his voice strained. "If you keep touching me like that, this is going to be over embarrassingly fast."

"Maybe I want it to be," I say. "Maybe I want to see what happens when you lose control." It's all I can think about, if I'm being honest.

His eyes darken, pupils blown wide. "Careful what you wish for," he murmurs. "I've been on the edge since that shower." His expression shifts and then he's sweeping me into his arms and carrying me the few steps to the bed. He lowers himself over me, his weight settling just enough to make me feel surrounded, claimed. Propped on his elbows, he cages me in, every heartbeat syncing with mine.

"I need to taste you, Lorna," he says, voice catching on my name. His lips brush my collarbone, feather-light, reverent. "Everywhere. Every inch. Will you let me?"

I can only nod, my throat too tight for words, as his mouth begins its slow, worshipful descent.

He takes his time. God, he takes forever. Exploring the geography of my body like he's a cartographer mapping uncharted land. His lips trail over my collarbones with devastating tenderness. He pauses at the curve of my breasts, his breath hot and uneven against the skin above my bra, and my pulse stumbles. Then lower, his mouth marking a path down my ribs, my waist.

When he reaches the faint silver lines on my lower belly, the stretch marks I've hated for six years, proof of everything my body went through, I tense. My hands fly down to cover them, shame flooding through me hot and sharp.

Hudson catches my wrists, pinning them gently at my sides. "Don't," he whispers, and his voice cracks. "These are beautiful." And then he presses his lips to each mark. "Gorgeous," he breathes against my skin, and I feel the word more than hear it. "Every. Single. Inch."

My chest tightens, heart pressing hard against its confines like it's outgrown the space entirely. Tears burn behind my eyes, hot and sudden. It's been so long since anyone touched me like this. Like I matter. Like my body exists to be cherished instead of tolerated. Like the parts of me I've learned to hide are exactly what makes me desirable.

Hudson's fingers tremble as they find the button of my jeans. He gazes up at me, tenderness beneath the raw devotion.

"Please," he whispers. Only that. *Please.* As if I could say no.

I lift my hips in answer, and he makes a sound like I've saved his life.

He peels the denim down my legs with excruciating slowness, like I might disappear if he moves too fast. When he pulls back to look at me, sprawled out in my plain cotton bra and underwear, nothing special, nothing sexy, his whole body shudders.

"Fuck," he rasps, voice wrecked. His thumb traces the inside of my thigh, and I feel it everywhere. "I don't think you understand, Lorna. You don't know what you do to me. How many nights I've laid awake thinking about this. About you."

The confession hangs between us, vulnerable and raw.

His fingers hook into my underwear, and he pauses, eyes finding mine. Asking without words. Always asking.

"Yes," I breathe. "Hudson, please."

He removes them slowly, like he's unveiling something sacred. When he settles between my thighs, his hands are shaking so hard he has to grip my hips to steady them.

"If you want me to stop," he says, voice barely a whisper, "tell me now. Otherwise, I'm not stopping until you come on my tongue."

The first graze of his mouth makes me sob. Not only from the pleasure, but from the tenderness of it.

"You're the sweetest thing," he murmurs against me, and the vibration makes my back arch. "God, Lorna, you're everything."

He takes his time, learning what makes me gasp, what makes me moan. His tongue moves in devastating patterns while he holds me steady, thumbs stroking my hip bones in soothing circles even as he takes me apart with his mouth.

"That's it, baby," he encourages when my breathing goes ragged. "Let go. Let me catch you."

The tenderness in his voice, the quiet promise that he'll catch me when I break, is what finally undoes me. Pleasure crashes through me so fast it feels like my body forgets how to exist. My back arches, my fingers clutch at the sheets, at his hair, at anything that might keep me tethered to the world. My cry splits the air, rough and helpless. "Hudson! Fuck!"

He groans against me, the sound raw and wrecked, vibrating straight through me until I'm splintering apart under his mouth. Then his whole body goes rigid, muscles drawn tight like a bowstring. His hips jerk against the mattress once, twice, and the sound that tears from him is somewhere between a prayer and a surrender, like he's dying, or maybe being reborn.

He's coming. Just from this. From me. From the taste of my body and the sound of my voice. The realization hits with such force my chest aches. It's too much and not enough all at once, this impossible, dizzying tenderness that feels less like pleasure and more like falling in love.

When the aftershocks fade, when we can both breathe again, he's still there between my thighs, pressing gentle kisses to my trembling skin.

"Hudson?" I whisper, reaching for him.

He lifts his head slowly. "I'm sorry," he rasps. "I couldn't—you were so— fuck, Lorna, I've never—"

"Come here," I whisper, tugging at his shoulders.

He crawls up my body, pressing kisses to my stomach, my ribs, my throat. When he finally reaches my mouth, the kiss is different. Soft. Tender. Too big for words.

"I didn't even touch you," I say against his lips, awed.

"You didn't have to." He cups my face with one trembling hand. "You wreck me just by existing, Lorna. Just by being you."

The words settle in my chest, slipping into the hollows Richard left behind. Hudson presses his forehead to mine and we stay like that, tangled and breathless, skin cooling, as if the broken parts of us are learning how to fit together.

"You're extraordinary," he whispers. "Every single part of you."

And for the first time in six years, I believe it.

He kisses me again and then murmurs something about cleaning up. When he disappears into the bathroom, I stay where I am, sheets tangled around my hips, skin still thrumming, staring up at the ceiling while my heartbeat stumbles toward normal.

He came from touching me. From giving. No ego, no shame, just that raw, unguarded need that stripped us both bare. The intimacy of it settles heavy in my chest, sharp and sweet.

This man. These men. They're going to undo me completely, piece by piece, until I don't recognize who I was before them. And the terrifying, beautiful truth is, I want them to.

I think I already love them for it.

**11**

———————

About a week after Hudson departed, leaving me with memories that still make my cheeks burn and my thighs clench, I'm elbow-deep in the walled garden, watching twilight paint the ancient stones in shades of amber and gold. The garden renovation is moving at a pace that's surprised even Jack, who's taken to strutting around like he's personally responsible for my horticultural miracles.

"You're obsessed," Charlie announces, appearing at my side with two steaming mugs. She hands me one, the scent of whisky-laced coffee curling in the cool evening air. "It's nearly eight. The workmen left hours ago."

"Just a few more beds," I promise, accepting the mug gratefully. My back aches and my fingernails are permanently soil-stained, but there's a satisfaction humming under my skin that feels better than anything I've experienced in years. "These primroses are temperamental little divas demanding perfect placement."

The truth is, I can't stop. This garden, neglected for so long, choked with weeds and wild with overgrowth, feels like a metaphor I'm too superstitious to voice aloud. With every root I untangle, every bed I reclaim from nature's greedy grip, something inside me unfurls alongside the tender new growth. Something I'd buried so deeply I'd forgotten it was there.

Charlie settles beside me on the stone bench, steam rising from her mug as she studies my face in the fading light. "It's not only the garden pulling late hours, is it?" Her voice is kind, free from judgment. "It's what's waiting at home."

Home. My farm. The three men who've been methodically dismantling my defenses with text messages and whispered promises and hands that touch me like they're mapping undiscovered land.

"Maybe," I admit, the confession easier in this twilight hour. "It's all happening so fast. Everything feels..." I pause, searching for the right word. "Possible."

"And that scares you," Charlie says. Not a question.

"Terrifies me," I correct, the laugh that follows sounding brittle. "I just got my life in order, Charlie. My farm's finally profitable. The twins are thriving. And now I want to risk it all for what? Three men who might decide tomorrow that they don't want the complication of a ready-made family?"

Charlie's silent for a moment, swirling her coffee thoughtfully. "Would it help if I told you I had the exact same fear? That I looked at Jack and Lach and Cam and thought, 'This is too good to be true. I'm going to wake up tomorrow and all of this will vanish like smoke.'"

"Did it go away?" I ask. "The fear?"

"No," she admits with brutal honesty. "But it got quieter. And the happiness got louder."

I absorb this, turning the mug in my hands. The night air is cool enough to raise goosebumps on my arms, but I don't move. Not yet. There's peace in this garden that I've come to crave, a stillness that allows me to hear my own thoughts.

"Jack thinks you should stay another week," Charlie says, breaking the silence. "The magazine editor called. They're thrilled with the progress photos. Apparently roses are all the rage for forest-themed weddings this year."

I roll my eyes, though secretly, I'm pleased. "Roses aren't trendy. They're classic."

"Tell that to the bridal magazines," Charlie laughs, bumping my shoulder companionably. "But seriously, what do you think? The twins are loving it here, especially with Lach teaching them to ride ponies. We'd all be happy to have you stay longer."

The offer is tempting. Another week of this. Working with my hands, sleeping in a room untouched by memories of loneliness, watching my children's faces light up with castle adventures.

Another week away from whatever complicated reality awaits me at the farm.

"I need to think about it," I say finally, right as the distant crunch of tires on gravel reaches us. Charlie's head turns toward the sound, her eyebrow lifting.

"Expecting someone?" she asks innocently, though the mischief dancing in her eyes gives her away.

"No," I say, suddenly very interested in the dirt under my fingernails. "Are you?"

"Me? No." Charlie rises, gathering both our mugs with suspicious efficiency. "But I think Jack mentioned something about a farm supply delivery. From Lewis. Or was it Australia?"

I throw a clump of soil at her retreating back, which she dodges gracefully, her laughter floating back to me on the night breeze.

"You're welcome!" she calls, disappearing around the hedge just as the sound of a truck door closing echoes across the grounds.

My heart ricochets off my ribs like it's trying to escape. There's no mistaking that engine. The particular way it purrs, then growls as it navigates the castle's winding approach. No confusing those footsteps either. Steady and measured, each one landing with purpose.

Leo.

I don't move from the bench, fear and anticipation warring in my chest as those footsteps grow closer. Part of me wants to hide. Part of me wants to run toward the sound, throw myself into his arms like a character in one of Charlie's romance novels.

Instead, I wait, heart thundering, as he rounds the corner of the walled garden and stops dead, silhouetted in the silvery glow of the rising moon. His powerful frame is outlined in ethereal light, transforming him into something almost mythical.

For a moment, neither of us speaks. The world narrows to this stone-walled garden, this shadowed corner where time seems to have stopped.

"Lorna," he says finally, my name a graveled rumble that sends shivers down my spine. "Charlie said I'd find you here."

I stand, wiping my hands ineffectively on my already dirt-streaked jeans. "Leo. I wasn't expecting you."

Not true. I've been expecting him every day since Hudson left, jumping at the sound of tires on gravel, checking my phone like it might spontaneously produce a text if I stare at it long enough.

Leo takes a step forward, then another, closing the distance between us with unhurried confidence. Even in the moonlight, I can see his eyes tracking over me, taking in the messy bun, the smudges of dirt, the too-large flannel I'd thrown on when the evening cooled.

"I brought a farm update," he says, voice deliberately neutral though warmth flickers in his eyes. "Thought you might appreciate the in-person version."

"You drove all that way for a farm update?" I ask. "You could have texted."

"I could have," he agrees, stopping a few feet away. Close enough that I can smell him. That unique combination of leather and cedar and something indefinably Leo that makes my pulse skip. "Or I could see the progress on this garden that's had you too busy to answer my texts for the past two days."

Guilt flushes hot across my cheeks. I'd seen his messages, but after what happened with Hudson, I needed space. Time to process the hurricane of emotions threatening to sweep away all my carefully constructed defenses.

"I've been busy," I say, gesturing to the garden. "The magazine shoot's been moved up. We're scrambling to finish in time."

"It's looking good," Leo says, but he's not talking about the garden. His eyes are fixed on me, dark and intent. "Really good."

The air between us feels charged, a live wire of tension stretching taut. I take an involuntary step backward, spine bumping against the ancient stone wall.

A week without them has given me too much time to think. Too much space for doubt to creep in like morning fog. Each passing day brought more questions. Was I fooling myself? Could anything sustainable possibly grow from this strange, four-cornered connection?

"How's the farm?" I ask, desperate to redirect to safer ground. "Are the dahlias behaving themselves?"

Leo watches my retreat with patient understanding. "The farm's thriving. The irrigation system's working perfectly. Hudson figured out that chicken problem. Turns out she was broody, sitting on a nest she'd hidden under the shed. Levi's been documenting those special hybrids. He says the color stabilization is impressive."

I nod, swallowing down the lump in my throat. "Would you like to see what I've been working on?" I offer, gesturing to the garden. "Since you drove all this way?"

Leo's mouth quirks in that almost-smile that never fails to make my stomach flip. "Lead the way."

I guide him through the garden, pointing out the newly planted beds, the intricate pathways we've unearthed, the archways that now support climbing roses rescued from decades of neglect. As I talk, my nervousness gradually fades, replaced by genuine enthusiasm.

"This will be the ceremony site," I explain, leading him to the center where an ancient gazebo stands, newly restored and gleaming like a pearl under the café lights.

Leo moves past me to examine the structure, running his hand along the weathered stone with the same reverence I've seen him touch my dahlias. "Beautiful workmanship," he says quietly. "They don't build like this anymore."

"Jack had to bring in a specialist from Edinburgh for the restoration. It's been here since the late 1700s."

Leo turns back to me, moonlight casting his features in silver and shadow. "Thank you for showing me," he says simply. "This place suits you."

"The garden?" I ask, confused.

"The castle," he clarifies, moving closer. "The grounds. All of it. There's a rightness to you here. Like you belong."

Something in his words catches me off-guard, bringing an unexpected sting to my eyes. I turn away, not wanting him to see.

"I don't know why I left," I say, voice carefully controlled. "Jack's the one who stayed, who shouldered the responsibility. I ran away first chance I got."

Leo's hand settles on my shoulder, warm and steady. "And built something of your own," he says, turning me gently to face him, his thumb brushing over my cheek. "There's no shame in that."

"You have dirt," he murmurs, the corner of his mouth lifting. "Right here."

His thumb lingers, stroking across my skin in a caress that has nothing to do with removing dirt and everything to do with the way his pupils have expanded, black eclipsing brown.

"Leo," I whisper, breathless.

He doesn't respond with words. Instead, his head dips, lips brushing mine with exquisite gentleness. A question, not a demand. A spark ignites in my veins, and I press forward, eliminating the space between us, my mouth seeking his with a hunger that should embarrass me.

It doesn't.

Leo responds instantly, one hand sliding into my hair while the other settles at my waist, drawing me flush with the solid wall of his chest. The kiss deepens, his tongue teasing the seam of my lips until I open for him with a soft sound of surrender.

This isn't like our other kisses. This is heat and command and barely leashed control. Leo kisses like he's waging war, strategic and devastating, claiming territory with each sweep of his tongue, with each nip of his teeth on my lower lip. The taste of him floods my mouth, dark and intoxicating.

I lose myself in it, in him, gripping his shoulders as if I might float away without his anchoring weight. When he finally pulls back, we're both breathing hard, his forehead resting against mine in the moonlight. His ragged exhale ghosts hot across my lips.

"I missed you," he says roughly, the admission scraped from somewhere deep and vulnerable.

"I missed you too," I confess, the truth easier to voice in darkness, with stars scattered overhead like silent witnesses.

His eyes search mine, looking for doubt or hesitation. Finding none, he captures my lips again, this kiss harder, hungrier. His hands move restlessly now, skimming down my sides, over my hips, curving around to pull me closer until there's no space left between us. Heat radiates from his body, seeping through my clothes.

The evidence of his desire presses against my stomach, hot and hard even through layers of denim, and liquid heat pools between my thighs in response. When his mouth leaves mine to trail fire down my neck, I gasp, head falling back to give him better access.

"We should stop," I croak, though my body screams in protest, every nerve ending alive and begging. "Anyone could—"

"Everyone's in bed," Leo murmurs. The vibration of his voice travels straight through my skin. "Charlie made sure of it."

The realization that this meeting isn't accidental, that Charlie, and possibly Jack, orchestrated this midnight rendezvous, should probably concern me. Instead, a wild, reckless freedom surges through my veins, hot and insistent.

Leo must feel the change in me, the moment my last resistance crumbles, because his grip tightens, his mouth growing more insistent. His touch slides lower, cupping my ass and lifting me slightly until I'm on my tiptoes, pressed fully against the hard length of him.

"Tell me what you want, Lorna," he demands.

What I want is everything. His hands on my skin. His weight over me. His mouth everywhere at once. The cool night air forgotten, replaced by the furnace heat of his body.

"You," I whisper. "I want you."

In one smooth motion, he backs me against the gazebo, lifting me until I'm perched on the wide ledge, my legs falling open to accommodate his broad frame between them. The ancient stone is cold on my thighs, a sharp contrast to the heat of him.

His lips crash back to mine, hungrier now, more demanding. His hands slide beneath my flannel, palms skimming over the sensitive skin of my waist, my ribs, leaving trails of fire in their wake until his thumbs brush the undersides of my breasts through the thin cotton of my bra.

I press into his touch, desperate for more, and he obliges, cupping me fully, thumbs circling over rapidly hardening peaks. Each touch sends sparks of pleasure racing through me, building a need so intense it borders on pain.

"Leo," I gasp as his mouth trails fire down my throat. "Please."

"Please what?" he asks, voice like gravel on my skin, the roughness of it making me clench. "Tell me what you need."

The demand unlocks something in me, something I've kept buried for so long I'd forgotten it existed. In that moment, with moonlight spilling over us like liquid silver and the scent of night-blooming jasmine thick in the air, I want to surrender. To place myself in his capable hands and let him take control.

"I need..." I struggle to voice the desire that burns through me like wildfire, incinerating my carefully constructed walls. "I need you in control."

Leo goes utterly still, his hands freezing. For one terrible moment, I fear I've said too much, revealed a part of myself that will send him running. Then his gaze meets mine, and the hunger I see there makes my pulse hammer so hard I can feel it in my fingertips.

"Say it again," he commands.

I swallow hard, heart hammering, feeling the thunder of it in my throat. "I want you to take control," I whisper, the admission setting me free even as it makes me feel unbearably vulnerable. "Please."

The only movement is the subtle flare of his pupils as understanding dawns, not judgment, but recognition. He presses his thumb against my lower lip.

"Open," he commands, voice dropped to a register so low it reverberates in my bones, vibrates in my chest.

I part my lips, taking his thumb into the wet heat of my mouth. The taste of him explodes across my tongue, salt and leather and man, earthy and masculine as he pushes deeper. A groan rumbles from his chest, so deep I feel it vibrate through my body where we're pressed together, feel it in my core.

"Good girl," he murmurs.

The endearment crashes through me like a lightning strike, every nerve ending lighting up at once, white-hot and electric. Liquid heat floods between my thighs, my core clenching with such sudden ferocity that I have to bite back a sob. Leo's eyes track the way my pupils dilate, how my breathing fractures into desperate little pants, how my thighs tighten around his hips.

"Fuck," he groans, almost to himself. "Look at you, falling apart just from those two words."

His thumb withdraws, slick with my saliva, leaving a glistening trail as he traces my swollen bottom lip. "What else makes you wet, Lorna?" he asks. His free hand cups my breast through my shirt, the weight of it possessive, the heat of his hand burning through the fabric. His thumb finds my nipple, already pebbled and aching. "This?"

My back arches, offering myself up to him, pressing my breast more firmly into his palm. "Yes," I pant.

"And this?" He wraps his hand around my throat, his fingers covering my thundering pulse, fingers long enough to nearly encircle my neck completely. The pressure is exquisite, not enough to restrict breathing, but enough to remind me of his strength, of how easily he could hold me down.

The effect is instantaneous and devastating. My pussy floods with such sudden arousal I can feel the slickness coating my inner thighs, hot and liquid. A broken moan tears from somewhere deep in my chest. My hands fly to his wrist, not to pull away but to hold him there, to keep that delicious weight against my thundering pulse, to feel the strength coiled in his forearm.

"Leo," I whimper, his name a prayer and a plea, the sound broken and needy.

His lips curl into a smile that's pure sin. "I knew it," he says, voice dropping to a growl that I feel in my cunt. "The woman who controls everything, her farm, her flowers, her entire life, wants someone to make her surrender. To take that control away so she can finally let go." His thumb strokes over my pulse point, feeling it race beneath his touch, feeling the rapid flutter of my life force under his fingers. "Isn't that right, Lorna?"

The truth of it breaks me wide open, walls I've built over years of self-reliance, of being both mother and father, of carrying the weight of my entire world alone crumbling like ancient stone. To be seen so completely by this man who somehow understands the darkest, most secret parts of me... it's terrifying. Exhilarating.

"Yes," I admit, voice hardly more than a whisper, threadbare with need. "Please, Leo."

His grip tightens fractionally, making the world narrow to the points where his skin touches mine. "Do you trust me, Lorna?" His gaze pins me in place, demanding absolute honesty.

"Yes." The word falls from my lips without hesitation. And I do, trust this man with the gentle hands and careful strength, with the callused fingers that handle my delicate flowers like spun glass. This man who saved my blooms, who looks at my children like they're precious, who sees me, *really* sees me beneath all the armor I wear.

"Then beg for it," he growls, voice thick with restraint, with the effort of holding himself back.

The demand should infuriate me. Instead, it unlocks a primal force inside me, wild and hungry, caged for far too long.

"Please," I whisper, letting him see every ounce of my hunger, letting it pour out of me uncensored. "Please take me. Control me. Make me yours, Leo. I need, I need your hands on me, your mouth, everything. I'm so empty, so fucking empty without you inside me."

Something snaps in his expression, the last thread of his legendary control finally breaking, fraying and splitting apart. He kisses me, all teeth and tongue and bruising pressure that steals the air from my lungs. There's nothing gentle about it. This is possession, pure and animal. One hand remains firm around my throat, thumb pressing into my pulse point as the other shoves between us, wrestling with the button of my jeans.

The drag of his hand over my stomach as he yanks at the denim makes me gasp against his mouth, the scrape of rough skin on sensitive flesh electric. I'm dimly aware that we're outside, that anyone could walk into the garden and discover us like this. I should care. Should demand we move somewhere private. Instead, I find myself arching into him, spreading my legs shamelessly wide, begging with my body for what I'm too far gone to ask for with words.

Leo's hand finally slips beneath the waistband of my jeans, fingers instantly finding the soaked cotton of my underwear. "Fuck," he groans. "You're drenched."

His fingertips trace the outline of my pussy through the thin fabric, mapping my folds, learning every curve and valley. When he reaches the apex, where my clit throbs desperately for attention, he pauses. The bastard actually pauses, looking down at me with dark satisfaction, drinking in my desperation.

"This cunt," he says, pressing hard enough to make me whimper, "is fucking soaked for me. Tell me who it belongs to, Lorna."

"You," I groan, hips bucking into his hand, chasing the friction. "It's yours, Leo. Please—"

"Please what?" He's relentless, the pressure of his fingers increasing just enough to drag a desperate sound from my throat, raw and broken, but not enough to give me what I need. Not nearly enough.

"Please," I beg, beyond shame now, beyond anything but the aching need. "Make me come, Leo."

His grip on my throat tightens fractionally, sending sparks of pleasure straight to my core as he begins to stroke me through the cotton, finding a rhythm that has me trembling in seconds. The friction of the fabric adds another layer of sensation. "Like this?"

"Yes," I sob, chasing the building pleasure like my life depends on it. "God, yes, like that, don't stop, please don't stop."

His mouth drops to my neck, hot and wet, teeth scraping over the sensitive skin beneath my ear. "I can feel how close you are," he murmurs, his breath hot against my damp skin. "You're going to come for me, aren't you? Right here in this garden, with nothing but my hand on your throat and my fingers on your pussy."

The filthy words in that deep, commanding voice hit me harder than any touch ever could. Heat floods low in my belly, spreading until it's all I can feel, white-hot and consuming. Every muscle tightens, tension winding tighter and tighter, until I'm trembling on the edge of release, caught between wanting to fall and fearing how hard I'll break when I do.

"That's it," he urges, increasing the pace. "Let me see how gorgeous you are when you come."

The band of tension inside me snaps, pleasure exploding outward from my core in waves so intense they border on pain, obliterating everything but sensation. My body bows as a cry tears from my throat, his name, broken and desperate. Colors burst behind my eyelids, fireworks in the darkness, my fingers digging into his shoulders as I ride out the most intense orgasm of my life.

He works me through it relentlessly, drawing out every last aftershock, every tremor, coaxing more from my body than I thought possible until I'm boneless and gasping in his arms. Only then does his grip on my throat gentle, his hand sliding up to cradle my jaw with surprising tenderness, the contrast making my chest ache.

"So fucking beautiful," he whispers, his voice filled with awe as he presses his forehead to mine. "You have no idea what you do to me, Lorna. No fucking idea."

I slump against him, legs trembling like a newborn foal, breath coming in ragged pants that sound loud in the quiet of the garden. His arm wraps around my waist, taking my weight easily as he holds me to the solid wall of his chest. I can feel his heart thundering beneath my cheek, matching the wild rhythm of my own.

His lips brush my temple in a kiss so gentle, so at odds with the intensity of what just happened, that tears prick at my eyes, hot and unexpected. "I've got you," he murmurs, and I believe him. For the first time in years, I surrender completely to the feeling of being held, being supported, letting someone else carry the weight.

I should feel embarrassed. Should be mortified that I had an orgasm outdoors, in the garden of my childhood home, fully clothed with the stars watching overhead. Instead, I feel powerful. Seen. Accepted in a way I've never experienced before, like he's looked past every defense and loved what he found there.

Leo's own desire is evident, pressing insistently against my thigh, thick and hard, but when I reach for him, he captures my wrist with gentle firmness.

"Not here," he says, his voice strained but controlled, fighting for restraint. "Not like this."

"Then where?" I ask, surprised by the boldness in my own voice, by the hunger still burning beneath my skin. "Because I need more of you. All of you."

Heat flares between us.

"Your bedroom," he says, the words half-request, half-command, rough with need. "Now."

Without waiting for a response, he lifts me from the ledge, setting me on my feet, his touch lingering at my waist. I sway slightly, the world still tilted and spinning, and he steadies me with an arm around my waist.

"Can you walk?" he asks, concerned.

"If I say no, will you carry me?" I challenge, surprising myself with the playfulness in my tone, with how light I feel despite everything.

Leo's eyes darken further, pupils blown wide, his arm tightening around me. "Always," he says simply, the promise in his voice making my stomach flip. "Just tell me where to go."

The image of Leo carrying me through the castle corridors is suddenly all I can think about. The fantasy consumes me, makes my skin flush hot.

"East wing," I hear myself say, voice breathless. "Third door on the left."

Leo doesn't hesitate. In one smooth motion, he bends and sweeps me into his arms, cradling me against his chest like I weigh nothing at all. The shift in gravity makes me gasp, clutching at his shoulders. I've never been a petite woman, but in Leo's arms, I feel delicate. Protected.

"Hold on," he says, already moving toward the castle with sure, steady strides.

I nod, not trusting my voice, and bury my face against his neck. His pulse beats strong beneath my lips. I can feel the rise and fall of his chest, the controlled power in every step.

The journey to my room passes in a blur of moonlit corridors and whispered directions. My fingers trace idle patterns on his shoulder, feeling the heat of him through his shirt. By some miracle, we encounter no one, the castle sleeping peacefully around us.

Leo shoulders open my bedroom door and kicks it closed behind us, the solid thud of wood meeting frame echoing in the quiet. The playfulness from the garden fades, replaced by something deeper, more significant. This isn't only about physical release anymore. This is about trust, and surrender, and things I'm not brave enough to name yet. The weight of it makes my skin feel too tight.

Leo sets me on my feet beside the massive four-poster bed. In the soft lamplight, his expression is equal parts hunger and hesitation, vulnerability flickering in his dark eyes.

"We can stop," he says, and the effort it takes to get the words out is written all over his face, his jaw tight, breath uneven. "If you've changed your mind."

The offer, quiet but absolute, cuts through the haze of heat between us. It isn't hesitation. It's respect. Even with his pulse pounding against mine, with the hard press of him still lingering at my hip, he'd walk away if I asked. No protest, no persuasion. Just stop. The certainty of that, the trust he offers without words, unravels me in a different way.

This man, all control and quiet strength, would break himself before he ever broke me. And somehow, that's what makes me want him even more.

In answer, I reach for the buttons of my flannel, undoing them one by one with trembling fingers until the shirt falls open, revealing the simple cotton bra beneath. Cool air kisses my exposed skin, raising goosebumps that ripple across my chest and arms. Leo's gaze tracks the movement, his throat working as I let the fabric slide from my shoulders to pool on the floor in a whisper of cotton.

"Does this look like I want to stop?" I ask softly.

He half groans, half growls, the sound vibrating through the space between us and settling low in my belly. "Say it," he demands, fists held at his sides like he's physically restraining himself, knuckles white with the effort, tendons standing out in his forearms. "Tell me what you want, Lorna."

The directness of his gaze, the raw need in his voice, strips away any remaining hesitation. "I want you," I say simply, the truth of it resonating in my bones, humming through my blood. "All of you. I want to feel you inside me, around me. I want to stop thinking and just feel."

Leo closes the distance between us in one stride, hands framing my face as his mouth claims mine in a kiss that leaves no doubt about his intentions. His palms are hot against my cheeks, the roughness of them sending sparks across my skin. This isn't gentle or questioning. This is possession, pure and simple, his tongue claiming my mouth with devastating thoroughness, stealing my breath and my thoughts.

"I know what you need," he murmurs, the words vibrating into me, fingers sliding into my hair to tug my head back, exposing my throat. The pull on my scalp sends pleasure-pain racing down my spine, liquid and electric.

"Tell me," I gasp as his teeth graze the sensitive juncture of neck and shoulder, scraping hard enough to make me shudder, hard enough that I'll feel the ghost of it tomorrow.

"You need someone to take the weight from your shoulders," he says, working the button of my jeans. "Someone to make the decisions. Someone to make you feel safe enough to let go."

The zipper follows, the rasp of metal teeth loud in the quiet room. Leo hooks his thumbs into the waistband and slowly pushes the denim down my hips, taking my underwear with it in one smooth motion. The fabric drags over sensitive skin, making me shiver. I step out of the puddle of fabric, toeing off my boots in the process, the thud of them hitting the floor marking my surrender, until I'm left in only my bra, exposed to his hungry gaze.

"So fucking beautiful," he breathes, hands settling on my hips possessively his touch branding me. "Every inch of you."

His touch is fire on my skin, hands rough against my soft flesh, creating a friction that makes me tremble with need. When his mouth returns to mine, I surrender to it completely, melting into him, letting him walk me backward until my legs hit the edge of the bed. The mattress gives behind my knees, soft and yielding.

Leo follows me down, his weight pressing me into the mattress in a way that makes me feel protected, surrounded by his heat and strength and the masculine scent of him. The solid mass of him covers me, grounds me, makes the rest of the world disappear. His hands seem to be everywhere at once, in my hair, on my breasts, skimming down my sides to grip my thighs with enough pressure to leave marks.

But it's not enough. I need his skin on mine, need to feel the furnace heat of him, need to touch and taste and claim him the way he's claiming me.

"Off," I demand, tugging at his shirt with impatient fingers, frustrated by the barrier of cotton between us. "I want to feel you."

For a moment, I fear I've broken whatever spell we're under with my demand, shattered the fragile magic. Then Leo smiles, a slow, predatory curve of lips that makes my heart stutter and restart, racing.

"Since you asked so nicely," he says, sitting back on his heels to pull his shirt over his head in one smooth motion, muscles rippling beneath skin.

The sight of him empties my lungs completely. Broad shoulders taper to a powerful chest dusted with dark hair that narrows to a trail disappearing beneath his belt. Muscle shifts beneath dark skin as he reaches for that belt, watching my face as he slowly unbuckles it, his gaze tracking every hitch in my breathing.

The soft rasp of leather sliding through the loops sends a shiver straight down my spine. Leo's gaze catches the reaction, and something shifts in his eyes—darkens, deepens, heat sparking in their depths. He gathers my wrists easily in one hand, lifting them above my head. With his other hand, he winds the belt around them, the leather still warm from his body. When he knots it, the hold feels unyielding yet inexplicably safe, as if he's tethering me not to restraint, but to trust.

"Tell me if it's too tight," he says, checking with careful fingers, his touch gentle on the delicate skin of my inner wrists where my pulse flutters wildly. "Or if you want me to stop. Just say the word and it's done."

"It's perfect," I assure him, testing the bonds with a slight tug, feeling the leather hold firm, the smooth grain soft against my skin. "Don't stop."

Leo's smile is pure male satisfaction, predatory and possessive and utterly devastating. "Wasn't planning to."

With my wrists pinned above my head, everything sharpens. Every nerve ending, every breath, every inch of skin he touches becomes hypersensitive, alive. He doesn't rush. Leo moves like he's got all the time in the world, dragging his fingertips over my sides, my hips, the soft dip between my ribs, pausing like he's bookmarking every reaction, cataloging every hitch in my breathing.

When he finally reaches my chest, he doesn't go for the clasp right away. Instead, his fingers trace the edge of my bra, slowly, maddeningly, drawing lazy shapes into the fabric. Watching me. Watching the way I arch toward him, the way my nipples peak beneath the thin barrier.

"Please," I whisper, barely a sound.

He answers with action, undoing the clasp, peeling the cotton back and letting the bra slip off. Cool air hits my skin, making me gasp. For a long beat, he just looks. And I let him. His expression is reverent, quiet awe in the way his eyes take me in, dark and hungry with something softer underneath.

The moment his lips close around one nipple, heat explodes through me, white and blinding. He palms the other breast, then pinches.

My back bows off the bed, chasing sensation, the silk sheets sliding cool beneath my overheated skin. His mouth is relentless, tongue and teeth and the slow pull of suction that steals all coherent thought. He switches sides without warning, giving the other breast the same focused attention, his tongue circling and flicking until I'm whimpering.

I moan, broken and pleading, not quite sure what I'm asking for. But he knows.

When he finally starts to move again, I think I might sob with relief. He kisses his way down my body. Open-mouthed and hungry. His lips move over my ribs, my stomach, the sharp curve of my hip. I'm gasping by the time he parts my thighs, his big hands guiding them open, the heat of his palms searing my inner thighs.

And then he's there. Between my legs. Right where I need him, every exhale ghosting over my center.

The first drag of his tongue knocks the air straight out of my lungs. He groans, the vibration making my thighs twitch around his shoulders and my core clench desperately.

Leo eats me like I'm the best meal of his life, slow and deliberate, every flick of his tongue impossibly precise. It's not rushed or greedy. It's something else entirely.

He's methodical. Focused. Quietly lethal in the way he learns me. He pays attention to everything, how I jerk when his tongue circles a certain way, how I moan when he sucks harder, how my whole body trembles when he slides a finger inside me, the stretch and burn of intrusion, curling it until I see stars bursting behind my eyelids.

"Fuck," I choke out, my voice wrecked, raw. My hips buck helplessly, chasing him, chasing release.

And Leo just keeps going. Pushing me higher, deeper, until I'm nearly levitating off the bed.

"Leo," I gasp, tugging uselessly at my bonds, the leather biting into my wrists. "I need, I can't—"

"Let go," he commands, adding a second finger to the first, stretching me in a way that treads the exquisite line between pleasure and pain. The fullness, the pressure, the way his fingers curl and stroke. "Come for me, Lorna. Now."

His lips close around my clit, sucking firmly as his fingers pump steadily inside me, and I shatter. The orgasm rips through me with such force that I cry out, back bowing off the bed, thighs clamping around his head as waves of ecstasy crash over me, drowning me in sensation. My vision whites out, every muscle locking tight.

Leo guides me through it, gentling his touch as I come down, pressing soft kisses to the inside of my trembling thighs. When he finally raises his head, the satisfaction in his eyes nearly undoes me all over again.

"Beautiful," he says again, crawling up my body to press a kiss to my mouth that tastes of me. "Absolutely fucking beautiful."

I can feel him hard against my thigh, still constrained by his jeans. With renewed purpose, I tug at my bonds, the leather creaking.

"Please," I whisper. "I need to feel you."

Leo understands. He reaches up to untie my wrists, massaging each one gently before pressing a kiss to the marks left by the belt, red impressions on pale skin.

"Better?" he asks, watching my face with genuine concern, his thumbs stroking the tender flesh.

"Yes," I assure him, already reaching for the button of his jeans, fingers clumsy with need. "But it would be even better if these were gone."

A low chuckle rumbles from his chest, the sound vibrating through me. "Demanding woman," he says, but there's only affection in his voice as he helps me push the denim down his powerful thighs, the muscles flexing beneath my touch.

When he's finally, gloriously naked, I take a moment to look at him. He's all lean muscle and controlled power. Scars scatter across his torso, pale lines against dark skin. And currently, very impressively aroused, his cock thick and flushed and beading at the tip.

"See something you like?" he asks, the teasing tone in direct opposition to the tension in his jaw.

"Very much," I admit, reaching out to wrap my fingers around his cock. The broken sound he makes as I stroke him sends a fresh wave of heat through me, liquid and insistent. He's hot and hard and silky smooth, pulsing in my hand. "But I'd like it even more inside me."

Leo's eyes slam shut, his breathing ragged as he fights for control, his abs tensing. When he opens them again, the heat in his gaze nearly burns me alive.

"Soon," he promises, voice strained. "But not yet. I need to savor this thing between us, Lorna."

Before I can protest, he's rolling onto his back, pulling me on top of him in one smooth motion. My knees bracket his hips, my core pressed to the hard length of him in a way that makes us both groan, the slide of wet heat against rigid flesh obscene and perfect.

"Like this," he says, large hands settling on my hips to guide me into a slow, torturous rocking motion.

The friction is exquisite, the hard ridge of him sliding between my pussy lips, dragging across my clit with every pass. But it's not enough. I need him inside me, need to feel the stretch and burn of him filling me completely.

"Leo," I plead, trying to position myself to take him in, my body aching and empty. "Please."

His grip tightens, preventing me from getting what I want, fingers digging into soft flesh. "Not yet," he says, voice strained but determined.

One hand leaves my hip, sliding between our bodies to circle my clit, his fingers slick with my arousal. "That's it," he encourages as my movements grow more frantic, chasing the building pressure. "Take what you need."

I'm beyond words now, reduced to sensation and instinct as I chase my release. Leo watches me, his own control visibly fraying as I slide over his length with increasing urgency, my breasts swaying with each movement, his cock slick and throbbing beneath me.

Just when I think I can't take any more, when I'm teetering on the edge of oblivion, Leo's hand slides from my hip to the small of my back. His fingers trail lower, teasing the cleft of my ass before circling that forbidden entrance with gentle but insistent pressure.

"Trust me," he murmurs again, watching my face for any sign of hesitation.

I nod, too far gone to form words, and am rewarded with a finger pressing slowly, carefully inside as his other hand continues its relentless rhythm against my clit. The pressure, the fullness, the wrongness that feels so right.

The contrasting sensations merge into a state that borders on transcendent. My nerve endings fire in chaotic symphony, pleasure spiraling outward from two points of perfect intensity. I come with a sharp cry, my entire body convulsing as wave after wave of ecstasy crashes through me, my inner muscles clenching rhythmically around nothing. Leo guides me through it, his hips rising to meet my frantic movements, his own control finally shattering.

With a guttural sound that might be my name, he follows me into oblivion, his release pulsing hot between us, painting his stomach with cum. I collapse against the bed, snug to his side, boneless and panting, my heart racing as we both struggle to catch our breath.

For long moments, we simply lie there, the room thick with the smell of sex and sweat and satisfaction, the world slowly reassembling itself around us. His fingers stroke lazily up and down my back, gentle, soothing touches that gradually bring me back to myself.

"Was that okay?" he asks finally, voice rough with lingering desire and something else, concern, maybe, or tenderness.

I lift my head, meeting his gaze with a smile I know must look ridiculously sated. "More than okay," I assure him. "Perfect."

The tension in his shoulders eases, and he presses a soft kiss to my forehead, his lips warm and gentle. "Let me clean you up," he says, shifting to roll me gently onto my back.

He disappears into the bathroom, and I hear the soft rush of running water. He returns holding a warm washcloth. There's something disarmingly intimate about the way he wipes my skin with slow, careful strokes, the heat of the cloth soothing, almost tender.

When he's done, he tosses the cloth in the general direction of the bathroom and slides back into bed, the mattress dipping under his weight, pulling me against his side like he's done it a thousand times before. I settle into the crook of his arm, my head finding a natural resting place on his chest, over the steady beat of his heart.

"That was..."

"Yeah," he agrees, seemingly as unable to find the right words as I am. "It was."

Silence settles around us, comfortable rather than awkward. Leo's fingers trace abstract patterns on my shoulder, occasionally drifting up to play with my hair.

"I like this," he says eventually, voice low and thoughtful.

"Seeing you here, in this bed. Hearing you talk about the garden. Watching you with your family."

I prop myself up on one elbow to study his face, surprise blooming in my chest. "You do?"

"Is that so hard to believe? That I'd want to know all of you? Not just the flower farmer, but the woman who grew up in a castle. The sister. The daughter."

I swallow hard, my heart in my throat. "No one's ever..." I start, then stop, unsure how to explain. "Richard, my ex, he was only interested in the parts of me that were useful to him. The academic who made him look good at faculty functions. The wife who could host dinner parties. Later, the mother of his children, though he wanted as little to do with them as possible."

Leo's expression darkens, a muscle ticking in his jaw. "He sounds like an asshole."

A surprised laugh escapes me. "He was. Is. Definitely an asshole."

He cradles my cheek, his touch achingly gentle. "He didn't deserve you. Any part of you."

Something warm unfurls in my chest, spreading through me like sunlight after a long winter, melting ice I didn't know I'd been carrying. "Then the three of you came along, wanting to know every single part of me," I whisper, turning my face to press a kiss to his palm, tasting salt and skin. "It's nice. More than nice."

We fall silent again, content to simply exist in this moment, this space where the walls between us have crumbled to dust. Leo's heartbeat beneath my ear is strong and steady, his breathing gradually deepening as exhaustion claims him, his chest rising and falling beneath my cheek.

I should feel strange. Like the gravity of what just happened should be catching up to me by now, sparking panic, second guesses, some internal scramble to make sense of it.

But I don't.

I feel steady. Sated. Like my body understands what this is, even if my mind hasn't caught up yet. The usual post-intimacy spiral doesn't come. No what does this mean, no where do we go from here, no what the hell am I doing.

Instead, I let myself drift. I'm warm. I'm safe. And for once, I'm not trying to run or fix or figure anything out. The weight of him beside me, the smell of his skin, the sound of his breathing slowing into sleep.

The last thing I remember before my eyes drift closed is the weight of Leo's arm tightening around my waist, anchoring me to him like he couldn't bear to let go, even in his dreams.

**12**

———

Morning arrives like a slow confession. Soft golden light slipping through curtains I definitely meant to close but never did, too tangled up in Leo to care.

I wake in pieces. First the warmth behind me, solid and radiating heat. Then the steady weight of an arm slung around my waist, heavy and possessive. The quiet puff of breath at my neck. The soreness radiating through my hips and thighs, delicious and unmistakable, a deep ache that throbs with every small shift.

Leo.

It floods back. His mouth between my legs, hot and demanding. His hands everywhere, fingers mapping every curve. The way he looked at me like I was sacred and sinful and precious. The way I asked. The way he listened. The way he gave.

He shifts behind me, his body a furnace against my back, lips brushing the curve of my neck.

"Morning," he rasps, voice thick with sleep, rough as gravel. "You're thinking too loudly."

A laugh slips out before I can stop it. "Sorry. Habit."

He hums low, the sound melting straight through me. "Want me to help with that? Pull you out of your head for a bit?"

His hand drifts from my waist to my hipbone, thumb tracing slow circles that inch closer, each one lighting a trail of fire across my skin.

Someone knocks on the door.

We both freeze. My heart slams against my ribs as I imagine Daniel or Lorelai on the other side, asking if they can eat ice cream for breakfast or if I've seen the sock their dinosaur swallowed.

"Lorna?" Charlie's voice filters through the door, bright and knowing. "You up? I've got coffee. Jack's about to take the kids riding."

Relief floods me, cool and sweet. "Just a sec!" My voice cracks.

The bed shakes with Leo's silent laughter, his face buried in my shoulder. "Cockblocked by caffeine," he murmurs, pressing one last kiss to my skin, lips lingering.

We dress like we're on a timer, bumping into each other, still buzzed on whatever last night was. His fingers brush mine as he helps button up my shirt. The air still smells like sex and sleep, intimate and private. When we're marginally presentable, I open the door.

Charlie stands there with two steaming mugs and a smirk that would normally make me want to throw something at her head. The scent of rich, dark coffee wafts between us.

Today, though? I just take the coffee. And smile.

"Morning, lovebirds," she chirps, thrusting mugs at us, the ceramic warm in my hands. "Sleep well?"

Leo answers before I've located my voice. "Best night's sleep I've had in years."

Charlie's grin turns wicked. "I'll bet."

I narrow my eyes. "Was there something you needed, or is this just caffeine delivery with a side of smug?"

She laughs, bright and unrepentant. "Jack's taking the twins and Summer to meet the new foal, then giving them lessons on the ponies. They'll be out most of the morning. I figured you two might want breakfast on the beach. There's a hamper waiting downstairs."

The shift from teasing to tenderness catches me off guard. "That's really kind of you. Thank you."

Her expression softens, genuine beneath the mischief. "You deserve to be happy, Lorna. So does he."

The words land with quiet weight, settling in my chest. She doesn't wait for a response, only offers a small smile and disappears down the hallway, her footsteps fading on ancient stone.

Leo lifts his mug, steam curling between us. "She's solid. They all are."

I nod, throat tight. "Yeah. They really are."

We find the hamper in the kitchen, where Lachlan is leaning on the counter with a mug the size of his face. He offers Leo a slow fist bump, mutters something unintelligible, and shuffles out, still half-asleep.

The walk down to the cove is quiet, comfortable. Leo carries the basket in one hand, reaches for mine with the other, threading our fingers together.

The path winds through the dunes, gravel crunching beneath our shoes, each step releasing the earthy smell of crushed stone. The air smells clean, like salt and wildflowers. Bluebells and butter-cups dot the edges, swaying with each small gust of wind.

The beach reveals itself slowly. Pale sand, smooth and untouched, still cool in the morning shade. The sea, a soft blend of turquoise and green, curling gently into the shore with a rhythmic hush. The sky is wide and cloudless, the morning sun warming my skin, turning everything golden.

Leo spreads the blanket with an easy sweep, then lowers himself onto it, muscles flexing. He pats the spot beside him, gazing up with that soft, crooked smile that makes my chest ache. I sink down next to him as he pulls the hamper between us, the wicker creaking softly.

Inside is a loaf of crusty bread, still warm. A round of soft cheese, pale and creamy. A small container of dark, glossy berries that glisten like jewels. And nestled beside the napkins, a chilled bottle of champagne and orange juice, condensation beading on the glass.

I blink. "She packed champagne?"

Leo grins, eyes crinkling. "Breakfast of champions. She doesn't do things halfway."

"Apparently not," I laugh, extracting two flutes from the hamper, the crystal catching the light. "Though I'm beginning to suspect my entire family has been conspiring to get me laid."

"If so, I'll have to send them a thank you note."

We eat in comfortable silence. The only sounds are gulls calling overhead, their cries sharp and wild, and the soft lap of waves. The sun climbs steadily, warming the backs of our necks, lighting the champagne bottle like glass touched by fire. The bread is chewy and perfect, the cheese sharp and soft, the berries bursting with sweetness.

But the questions are still there. Circling.

"Can I ask you something?" I say finally, turning toward him.

Leo's eyes flick toward me. I catch the subtle shift, shoulders drawing in slightly, bracing. "Of course."

"It's about you and Hudson."

The smallest pause. Then a nod. "Go on."

"Hudson mentioned that the two of you were together. Before his mom got sick."

Leo meets my gaze without flinching. "We were. It was never official, no labels or anything. But yeah. We were something."

I hesitate. "Are you still?"

"No." No hesitation. "Not since I married Ruby."

I nod slowly. "You still care about him." It's not a question.

Leo exhales, a smile tugging at his lips, wistful, a little worn. "Is it that obvious?"

"Only to someone who's been paying attention. The way you look at him sometimes. How your voice softens when you talk about him."

He's quiet, then gives a small nod. "I never stopped. Even when I had to let him go. Even when I married Ruby, which was never about romance. It was about making sure she had what she needed —that Levi and Hudson had what they needed."

I try to picture it. Leo carrying that weight. Protecting all three of them. Making sacrifices that carved him open in ways he doesn't talk about.

"Then why haven't you—" I trail off, not sure how to ask. "Now that things are different?"

His eyes go to the horizon, tracking the line where sea meets sky. "Fear. I think we're both afraid. Of undoing the balance we've managed to build. Of what it would do to Levi. Of opening the door to something we might not know how to navigate anymore."

I nod. For a moment, we just sit there, watching the tide creep closer, the water darkening the sand.

"I get it," I say softly. "Fear's been sitting in the passenger seat of my life for years."

He turns to look at me, something unspoken in his eyes, vulnerable and raw.

"Still," I murmur, "life's too damn short for fear. Too short to keep pretending we don't want what we want."

Leo searches my face. "And what do you truly want, Lorna?"

The question hangs between us, deceptively simple yet impossibly complex.

"I'm still figuring that out," I admit. "But I know I want to stop running from possibilities just because they scare me. Stop denying myself joy because it doesn't fit some predetermined mold."

His expression shifts, understanding, perhaps, or recognition. "That's brave."

I laugh, the sound catching on emotion. "I don't feel brave. Most days, I feel like I'm one minor crisis away from a complete breakdown."

"That's exactly what makes you brave." He leans in, brushes a strand of hair from my face, his fingers lingering. "You keep showing up. Even when it's hard. Even when you're scared. You built something out of the wreckage, for your kids, for yourself, and you never stopped."

My throat tightens, emotion pressing hot behind my eyes. I blink fast, pushing the tears back. I don't want to cry today, not with the sea glittering like scattered diamonds and the sun warm on my skin.

The rest of the morning unfolds in quiet pieces. We walk the curve of the shoreline, pausing to collect shells with intricate swirls for Lorelai, smooth flat stones Daniel will declare perfect for his collection. The tide laps at our feet, icy and playful, and we laugh when it sneaks higher than expected, soaking our hems.

Sometime between laughter and silence, Leo laces our fingers together again. His grip is warm, solid, and when he tugs me gently toward the outcropping of rock at the far edge of the cove, I go without hesitation.

He turns to me, eyes dark with something deeper than desire. Something that sees all the way through me, past the armor, down to the tender, vulnerable core.

And then he kisses me.

It starts slow. Intentional. He cradles my face, thumbs brushing along my cheeks like he's grounding both of us, anchoring us to this moment.

This isn't just a kiss. It's a study. A confession. A promise written in breath and touch.

My whole body tilts toward him, drawn like gravity. I slide my hands under his shirt, palms pressing against the heat of his back, and he shudders beneath my touch. His skin is smooth and alive, muscles flexing under my fingers, his heartbeat thundering. I tug on his bottom lip with my teeth, and he fractures, the last thread of control snapping.

His mouth grows hungrier, his grip tighter, fingers digging into my flesh. One hand twists in my shirt as his tongue sweeps past my lips, claiming and tasting, stealing the air from my lungs.

I kiss him back with everything I have. My nails scrape lightly over his shoulders, and his hips jerk forward, a groan catching low in his throat, rough and desperate.

He breaks the kiss with a groan, foreheads pressed, gaze locked on mine. His pupils are blown wide, swallowing the brown.

"I didn't want it to be like this," he says, voice rough and ragged. "I wanted to take my time with you. I meant to."

His hand slides up my back, curls around the nape of my neck. His thumb strokes there, tender and possessive, the touch making me shiver.

"But every time I'm near you, I forget how to slow down. You undo me, Lorna. Completely."

I don't answer. Instead, I kiss him again. Harder this time. My fingers twist in his shirt, dragging him closer, and he lifts me like I weigh no more than air. I wrap my legs around his waist and feel the hard press of him through his jeans as he pins me against the rock. He drags his tongue along my jaw, down my neck, and I'm moaning before I can stop myself, the sound raw and needy.

"I need you," he whispers, words fraying at the edges. "God, Lorna. I need you right now."

There's no space left between us. Just heat and hands and the frantic rhythm of breathing that can't quite catch up. He pulls at my clothes with desperate fingers, urgent, fumbling with buttons and fabric.

His mouth is everywhere. At my throat, my collarbone, the sensitive place below my ear. My head falls back against the rock. The sun is hot on my face, the stone warm at my back, and Leo's looking at me like he's unraveling, coming apart at the seams.

He stills, lips brushing the shell of my ear, his breath hot and uneven. "I need to taste you."

The words crack me wide open.

Before I can even think, he's on his knees in the sand. His fingers hook into my waistband, and in one fluid, unhesitating motion, he pulls my jeans and underwear down. The denim scrapes over my thighs, rough against sensitive skin, before pooling around my ankles.

The salt air hits me a heartbeat before he does. Then his tongue is on me, one slow, devastating lick up my center that sends my hips jerking and my thoughts scattering.

He tugs my pants off one ankle before sliding his hands up my legs. One grips my hip, the other curls beneath my thigh, guiding it up until my leg rests over his shoulder.

Leo holds me there, one hand firm at my hip, the other bracing my thigh open. Then his lips are on me again.

My head thumps softly against the stone. My fingers search for something to hold, finding only the grit of rock until one tangles in his hair. It's thick and soft between my fingers, grounding me as everything else dissolves into heat, salt, and the steady rhythm of his tongue.

He groans into me, the sound vibrating through every nerve, resonating in my bones.

I can't think. Can't breathe. My whole body strains toward him, and he shifts closer, locking me in place, dragging me closer to the edge with every flick of his tongue, every pull of his lips.

I bite my lip hard, stifling a cry, tasting copper. The water crashes gently somewhere behind us, but it feels far away, muted and distant. All I know is him. His mouth. The sharp, beautiful ache building inside me, coiling tighter and tighter.

I come fast. Helplessly. One hand clenched in his hair, the other clutching the stone, knuckles white. My body shudders as pleasure rips through me, sharp and bright and unbearable, whiting out my vision. He doesn't stop, not even as I cry out, his name torn from my throat, not even as my thighs shake.

He holds me steady. Devours me through the aftershocks, prolonging every tremor.

Only then does he lower my foot to the ground, slowly, carefully.

He looks wrecked. Flushed, panting, lips wet and swollen, eyes glazed with satisfaction. Like he's just taken something that was always meant to be his. Like he'll never be the same.

My heart's still pounding, my legs trembling like a newborn

colt, my whole body humming with residual pleasure. I should feel undone.

But I don't. I feel feral.

His expression, that smug tilt of his mouth, the fire still flickering behind his eyes, should irritate me. Instead, it fuels me.

I push him back with both hands to his chest until he stumbles into a seated position on a nearby log. He barely has time to blink before I drop to my knees between his legs.

His eyes go wide. "Lorna—" he starts, but the rest never makes it out.

Because I'm already there, fingers moving to the fly of his jeans. The zipper cuts through the quiet, sharp and indecent, the metallic scrape loud enough to make my pulse stumble. He tenses as I slip my hand inside, past the waistband of his briefs, and wrap my fingers around him.

He's hot and heavy in my hand, velvet over steel, and the low, broken sound he makes is nothing short of obscene. Half curse, half prayer, all mine.

And then I lean in, tongue flicking over the tip, tasting salt and musk before I slide my mouth around him, taking him slow and deep.

He wraps my hair around his fist, anchoring me, grounding himself. His thighs flex beneath my grip as I take him deeper, tongue swirling, cheeks hollowing, the stretch making my jaw ache.

He tries to hold still. He fails.

"Fuck," he breathes, voice shattered, hips twitching as I swallow him deeper, taking him to the back of my throat.

"Lorna," he grits out, warning layered under desperation, his voice breaking. "If you don't stop—"

But I don't stop.

I want to see him fall apart. I want to feel it, to own this moment of his surrender.

So I suck harder. Take him deeper. Swallow around him like I've got all the time in the world, like this is all I want to be doing today, tomorrow and every day after that. And maybe it is.

He breaks.

His hips jerk, control splintering as a ragged sound rips from his throat. His fingers tighten in my hair, guiding me, holding me there while he tries and fails to keep his voice steady. "Fuck—you're good at this. Just like that. Don't stop." His breath stutters, hips thrusting once, twice, lost to the rhythm of it. Then his whole body goes taut, trembling as he breaks, my name spilling from him in a rough, desperate groan. He comes hot and thick on my tongue, every pulse of him raw and helpless, every sound a confession he can't take back.

I don't move. I hold him there, swallowing until the last tremor fades from his body and the tension drains into a loose, shaky sprawl. I trace him with my tongue, slow and thorough, licking him clean until he flinches from the sensitivity. Only then do I pull back, resting my cheek against his thigh, catching my breath in the quiet between us.

When I finally look up at him, he's staring at me like I just wrecked the laws of gravity, like I've fundamentally altered his understanding of the universe.

"Christ," he mutters, voice raw. He reaches for me, tugging me gently to my feet with unsteady hands. "You're going to kill me."

I smile, practically glowing, feeling powerful and sated. "But what a way to go."

He kisses me like he already wants more, like he'll never get enough.

We straighten our clothes, smoothing hair and refastening buttons, both still flushed and panting, grinning like fools. My fingers fumble with my zipper. His hands shake slightly as he tucks in his shirt. When we finally step out of our rock sanctuary, the beach is still quiet, peaceful and unchanged.

The only witness is a single seagull eyeing us with what feels like judgment.

"Shut up," I mutter as we pass. "Nobody made you sit there and watch."

Leo's laugh bursts out, bright and unrestrained, carrying over the water until it mingles with the sound of the waves. The sheer joy of it is like sunlight breaking through clouds, filling my chest until it aches in the best way. I want to bottle that sound, keep it somewhere safe, pull it out whenever the world feels dull and colorless.

We pack up what's left of the picnic, brushing crumbs from the blanket, shaking out sand. The walk back up the narrow path is quiet, thoughtful. My legs are still unsteady, and it has nothing to do with the climb. It's him, the memory of what just happened still thrumming through me, alive beneath my skin like an aftershock.

At the top of the hill, right before the castle comes into view, Leo stops. Turns.

"I don't want to go," he says.

The simplicity of it guts me.

"I know," I whisper, tracing the edge of his jaw, the rough bristle of his beard, the heat of his skin. "I don't want you to go either."

Leo leans into my touch, turning his head to press a kiss to my palm, his lips soft and warm. His eyes never leave mine.

"I'll be back," he promises. "Or Hudson will. Or Levi. We'll figure it out. Take turns. Whatever you need for as long as you need it."

My heart squeezes. I don't mean to say it. But it comes anyway.

"And if I want all of you?"

The question hangs there. Raw. Exposed. Terrifying.

"Then you'll have all of us," he says. No hesitation. "Whatever that looks like. Whatever you need it to be. We'll make it work, Lorna. Together."

I nod because speech feels impossible, my throat too tight for words.

He leans in and kisses me again. "Until next time," he murmurs.

"Until next time," I echo, stepping back even though I don't want to, even though every cell in my body protests.

I watch him walk away, his stride purposeful, shoulders squared against the morning light, backlit and golden. He doesn't look back.

He doesn't need to. And I don't move until he disappears behind the castle wall, until the last glimpse of him fades.

Only then do I let myself feel it. The thing that's been quietly growing since the three of them walked into my world with dirt on their boots and heaters in their hands.

I'm falling for them. All of them. Not identically. But entirely. And for the first time since that frosty April morning, that doesn't feel like a disaster waiting to happen. It feels like the beginning of something worth fighting for.

**13**

———

LEVI'S POV

The gravel crunches under the tires as I take the final curve, and there it is.

Amhuinnsuidh Castle rises from the landscape like something out of a fever dream. The kind of place that begs to be written about. Turrets catching the light, walls weathered by centuries, the whole thing perched between hills and sea like it's daring you not to fall in love with it.

I'm already composing lines in my head. *Stone bones weathered by centuries/Salt air clinging to every curve/The wind never softens, only learns her shape.*

My notebook's in my back pocket, same as always. I'll write it down later. After.

The truck rolls to a stop and I kill the engine, sitting there for a beat while my heart does this complicated thing it's been doing for three weeks. Three weeks of texting. Three weeks of wanting. Three weeks since her lips were against mine, since she melted into me and made that soft sound that's been haunting my dreams ever since.

Three weeks of being stuck at home, writing increasingly

desperate poetry about the curve of her neck and the sound of her laugh.

The rational part of my brain knows we're taking turns. Knows this is practical, necessary even. The irrational part, the part that's been scribbling her name in margins and lying awake at two a.m. imagining the weight of her against me, doesn't care about logistics.

I round the hood of the truck, and that's when I see her.

She comes flying around the stone wall like she's been shot from a cannon, cheeks pink and breathing hard, tank top plastered to her skin, hair escaping from that messy bun she always wears when she's working.

And she's running. Running straight toward me.

My heart stops. Then restarts, slamming against my ribs.

She crashes into me at full speed, and I catch her, arms wrapping around her waist as her momentum carries us both back a step. Her hands are in my hair, on my face, everywhere at once, and then her mouth is on mine and I'm drowning in her.

The kiss is desperate. Hungry. Three weeks of longing compressed into this single moment. She tastes like salt and heat and home, and I can't get enough, can't get close enough. My hand traces the line of her spine, pulling her against me, feeling every curve, every breath.

She makes that sound again, that soft, needy whimper that's been playing on repeat in my head, and something inside me snaps. I deepen the kiss, tongue sliding against hers, one hand tangling in her hair while the other grips her hip hard enough to leave marks.

"Levi," she moans against my mouth, not pulling away, just breathing my name like a prayer.

"Missed you," I manage between kisses, my voice rough and wrecked. "God, Lorna, I missed you so much."

"I know," she says, kissing me again, harder. "I know, I missed you too."

Her hands are under my shirt now, palms hot against my skin, and I shudder at the contact. She's touching me like she's been starving for it, like three weeks apart has been as unbearable for her as it has been for me.

I walk her backward until she hits the side of the truck, pressing her against the warm metal, caging her in with my body. She arches into me, one leg hooking around my hip, pulling me closer, and the friction makes us both groan.

"We should—" she starts, but I kiss the words away, biting gently at her lower lip.

"Should what?" I murmur against her mouth. "Stop? Because I've been writing poetry about this moment for three weeks, and I'm not ready to stop yet."

She laughs, breathless and bright, and it's the most perfect sound. "Poetry about this?"

"Among other things." My lips trail down her jaw to her throat, tasting salt and earth and her. "Your neck. Your hands. The way you look when you're concentrating. The sound you make when—"

She cuts me off with another kiss, this one slower, deeper, full of promise. When we finally break apart, we're both panting, foreheads pressed together, hearts racing in tandem.

"I wasn't expecting you for a few days," she says, her fingers still tangled in my hair, playing with the curls at my nape.

"I couldn't wait," I admit, the truth easy and raw. "I was going insane at home, counting days, writing terrible lovesick poetry."

"Terrible?" She pulls back to look at me, eyes sparkling with amusement and heat.

"The worst," I say, grinning despite myself. "Full of metaphors about roses and thorns and how you're like a wildflower bending in the wind but never breaking."

Her expression softens, tenderness flickering in her eyes. "That doesn't sound terrible."

"It's embarrassing," I counter, but I'm smiling now, feeling lighter than I have in weeks. "I have an entire notebook filled with verses about you. Leo found one and threatened to read it to Hudson if I didn't come."

She laughs again, the sound warming something deep in my chest. "So he sent you."

"He didn't have to send me." I cup her face, thumbs stroking her flushed cheeks. "I've been dying to come. I thought I should wait my turn, be patient. But patience is overrated."

"I'm glad you came," she whispers, eyes searching mine. "I've been thinking about you. About what happens next."

"And what do you want to happen next?" I ask, voice dropping lower, heat pooling in my gut.

She pulls me down for another kiss, this one full of intention. "I want you to help me finish this garden," she murmurs against my lips. "And then I want you to take me somewhere private and show me what else you've been writing poetry about."

Desire slams through me.

"And then I desperately want to go home, but I need to stay a couple more weeks," she says, pulling back to look at me properly. "I need to stay through the wedding. To make sure everything's perfect."

The disappointment is sharp, immediate. "Two more weeks."

"Is that okay?" Her expression shifts, uncertain now. "I know you've been managing both farms—"

"If you need to stay, then stay." I kiss her forehead, her temple, the corner of her mouth. "But I'm not waiting three more weeks to see you again."

"No?" She's smiling now, soft and warm and everything I've been dreaming about.

"No." I kiss her again. "Being away from you is the worst kind of torture. The farm feels empty without you. My *life* feels empty without you. I'm falling for you, Lorna. Hard."

Her eyes go wide. "Levi..."

"I know it's messy," I say quickly. "I know we haven't figured out how this is all going to work yet. But I'm here. And I want you, Lorna. All of you. In this lifetime and the next."

She kisses me again, fierce and possessive, and I feel the answer in the press of her lips, the grip of her hands in my hair.

"Show me what needs doing in the garden," I say when we finally break apart, both pink-cheeked and panting, hearts still racing. "And then later, when we're alone, I'll help with your lady garden."

A sharp laugh bursts from her, bright and unexpected. "My lady garden? Are you offering to trim the bushes, Levi?"

Blood rushes to my face. "That sounded significantly better in my head," I admit, but I can't bring myself to regret it. Not when I just made her laugh like that.

"Deal," she says, eyes sparkling, her lips twitching with suppressed laughter.

But neither of us moves. We stand there, wrapped around each other beside the truck, stealing kisses in the Scottish sunlight like we have all the time in the world.

Eventually, reluctantly, we break apart. Work calls. The garden won't restore itself, no matter how much I'd rather spend the day doing this. Doing her.

She leads me around the stone wall, pointing out what she's been working on, her hand finding mine as we walk. I grab more tools from the shed, shouldering bags of mulch while she explains her vision for the space. And then we begin.

By noon, we've found a rhythm, and I remember why being next to her feels right.

She directs and I follow, matching her pace, slipping into sync like we've done this a hundred times before. It's easy. Natural. The kind of partnership that doesn't need discussion.

I shed my button-down within the first fifteen minutes, down to the undershirt that's now plastered to my chest. The heat makes everything feel liquid and slow, and I can feel her watching me when she thinks I'm not paying attention. The way her gaze snags on my shoulders. The flush creeping up her neck that has nothing to do with the temperature.

I'm not above using it to my advantage.

"You can look as long as you want," I say without turning around, unable to keep the grin out of my voice.

"You're in my way." Too fast. Too flustered. The breathiness in her tone sends heat racing down my spine.

I straighten slowly, deliberately, and turn to face her. The world seems to narrow, the garden fading until there's only her. Sunlight threads through her hair, turning escaped curls to copper and gold. There's a smudge of dirt across her cheekbone, and sweat traces a path down her throat that I want to follow with my lips.

"What?" she asks, her voice wavering.

I move toward her, crossing the space between us with slow, measured steps. Each one deliberate. "You're covered in dirt," I say, my voice coming out rough. "Your hair's falling out of that bun."

Another step. The air between us sparks with tension.

"And you've got sweat running down your neck."

I'm close now. Close enough to see gold threaded through the blue of her eyes. Close enough to watch her pupils dilate, her chest moving faster with each passing second.

"And you're the most beautiful thing I've ever seen."

"Levi..." she breathes, her lips parting as her head tilts back, eyes finding mine with a mix of desire and something that feels dangerously close to surrender.

"I'm not done." I reach out, finally giving in to the urge, and brush my thumb across the dirt on her cheek. Her skin is hot beneath my touch, flushed from sun and exertion. "You're strong, Lorna. Stronger than anyone I know. You're out here in this wild jungle, turning chaos into order, into beauty, and you make it look effortless. Like you could bend the world to your will if you wanted to."

"It's just gardening," she whispers, but she's swaying toward me now, drawn by the same gravity pulling me to her.

"Nothing you do is just anything." My hand slides from her cheek to cup her jaw, thumb stroking along her jawline. "You walk into a space and it transforms. You touch things and they grow. That's not ordinary, Lorna. That's alchemy."

I lean in slowly, giving her a chance to pull away if she wants.
She doesn't.

When my lips finally brush hers, it's coming home and catching fire at the same time. The first touch is soft, exploratory, tasting salt and heat and her. Then my hand slides into her hair, fingers tangling in the damp curls at the base of her neck, angling her head so I can kiss her deeper, claim her more completely.

She melts into me with a sound that's half-sigh, half-whimper, and I feel her surrender in the way her body goes liquid against mine, in the way her lips part for me without hesitation. Her hands fist in my shirt, pulling me closer, desperate, and I can taste the summer heat on her lips, feel the rapid flutter of her pulse beneath my thumb where it rests against her throat.

I kiss her with everything I haven't said yet. With every unfinished poem scattered across my notebooks. With every sleepless night spent thinking about this moment, about her mouth, about the way she tastes. My free hand is at her waist, fingers spreading across the bare skin where her tank top has ridden up, and she's burning hot beneath my touch, all smooth skin and racing heartbeat.

The world disappears. There's no garden, no castle, no overbearing heat. Just her mouth moving against mine, her body pressed along the length of me, the taste of her flooding my senses until I'm drowning in it.

When we finally break apart, we're both gasping for air. Her eyes are still closed, lashes dark against flushed cheeks. My thumb traces the curve of her jaw, feeling her pulse hammering wildly beneath delicate skin.

"Levi," she whispers, my name barely audible, a prayer or a question or maybe both. Her fingers are still twisted in my shirt, holding on like I'm the only solid thing in a spinning world.

"Yeah," I breathe back, my voice wrecked and raw, because I don't trust myself with actual words right now. My heart is still trying to break through my ribs, and every nerve ending is singing with the feel of her.

She opens her eyes slowly, and the blue-gray depths are molten, darkened with desire. Her lips are swollen from kissing, slightly parted as she tries to catch her breath, and it takes everything in me not to kiss her again.

"I want to show you something," I say, the words spilling out before I've even decided what exactly I'm offering, only that I need a distraction before I do something reckless, like make love to her right here in the dirt.

She blinks at me, dazed. "You want to show me something?"

"I stumbled on it when I was grabbing those tools earlier," I explain. "That overgrown area by the old wall we haven't touched yet. I caught a glimpse of stone through the ivy. A flash of white. Thought it was a dead tree at first, but..."

I trail off, already moving, and she follows without question. We leave the neat rows behind and push into the wilder parts of the garden, where time has reclaimed everything. Ivy coils thick as rope around crumbling brick. Brambles stretch defiant and dense.

"It's in here," I tell her, tugging on gloves. My eyes scan the tangle of green until I spot it again. That glimpse of pale stone.

We work side by side, cutting back vines and twisting stems. The sun presses down relentlessly, and within minutes we're both dripping sweat again, breathing hard, arms brushing as we move in tandem.

"There." I still, lifting a gloved hand to point through the opening we've carved. "Look."

She steps closer, and I watch her face as she tries to make sense of what we're seeing. At first it's only texture. Moss, dirt, stone. But then the light shifts.

"Oh my god," she whispers, pulse visible in her throat. "Is that a statue?"

"Only one way to know for sure." I pull my knife from my belt.

The next twenty minutes pass in near silence, broken only by the rasp of tools and the faint sound of us working side by side. We work carefully, methodically, revealing her inch by inch. First a wing, then an arm, then the curve of a face so serene it makes my chest ache.

She's life-sized, standing on a pedestal, carved from white

marble gone creamy with age. An angel. Time has weathered her, softened her edges, but she's still breathtaking. Her head tilts skyward, listening for something divine, something only she can hear.

"She's incredible," Lorna whispers, reaching up to trace the curve of a wing, her fingers reverent against the cool stone.

"She's been waiting," I say quietly, unable to look away from the statue. From this beautiful, forgotten thing we've uncovered. "All these years. Just waiting for someone to find her again. Like you."

When I finally glance at Lorna, she's already looking at me, and my mouth goes dry.

"Lorna." Her name comes out rougher than I mean it to, heavy enough that it scrapes my throat on the way out. It costs me something to say it without closing the distance.

"Levi?"

I move before I can think better of it. Her exhale shudders, the air between us gone heavy and hot. Sweat slides from the back of my neck down between my shoulder blades as the warmth of her body reaches mine. I cradle her face in my hands, thumbs brushing over the delicate curves of her cheeks, and every inhale seems to tangle with mine, shallow and uneven.

"I've been losing my mind," I murmur, voice low and unsteady. "Lying awake at night, wondering if you ever think about me the way I think about you."

"How do you think about me?" she whispers.

My fingers slip into her hair, twining through the soft strands. "I think about your laugh. The way you bite your lip when you're focused. How your eyes light up when you talk about flowers or weather patterns or whatever obsession's claimed you that week."

My voice drops lower, rougher. "I think about my mouth between your thighs." My thumbs trace the edge of her lower lip, watching her breathe go shallow. "How you'd taste. How you'd move. What sounds you'd make if I held you open and took my time, if I used every part of me to learn what makes you fall apart."

Her eyes flash. "Then why don't you find out?"

The words land like a match in dry grass. In a heartbeat, I've got her pinned against the marble pedestal. Her back arches, a sharp sound escaping as the cold surface meets her skin. The contrast only makes the warmth between us burn hotter, every inch of air charged, waiting to ignite. My body is wound tight, each inhale a confession, as I press in close and brace my arms on either side of her hips.

"Because once I start," I say, voice low and hungry, "I won't want to stop."

Her pulse flutters visibly in her throat. She meets my gaze head-on, unflinching.

"Then don't stop, Levi."

My control shatters.

One second we're breathing the same air, the next my mouth is on hers. Urgent, hungry, undoing me completely. She melts into me with a sound that goes straight to my core, half gasp, half moan, all heat.

I kiss her with absolute attention, devastating precision. My hands cradle her face, anchoring her while my mouth moves over hers with mounting desperation. When her lips part, I groan. A low, wrecked sound. And deepen the kiss, my tongue sliding against hers in a rhythm that makes my knees weak.

"God, Lorna," I murmur against her mouth, barely pulling back enough to speak. My hands drag down to her waist, gripping tight, hauling her closer until there's no space left between us. "You taste like salvation."

A breathless laugh escapes her. "Pretty words for a man who's currently got me pressed against a stone angel."

"Maybe that's the point." I trail kisses along her jaw, down to the sensitive spot below her ear. "The saints are watching, and I'm about to defile one of their own."

She sucks in a sharp breath. "Is that what this is? A desecration?"

"Absolutely." My teeth scrape along her pulse point, drawing a shuddering gasp. "That angel has a front-row seat to my downfall."

Her fingers tighten in my hair. "And if I'm the one pulling you down?"

"Then we fall together, and I'll make you beg for mercy while I worship you the whole way down."

"I don't beg," she whispers.

I smile against her skin. "Maybe not yet. But you will." My hands skim up her sides, fingers splaying wide, thumbs brushing beneath her breasts through the thin cotton of her tank. "Because I have plans for you, Dr. MacLeod. Detailed, comprehensive plans that involve charting every inch of your skin with my mouth."

The way she reacts to the title, the sharp intake of breath and the sudden flare of heat in her eyes, doesn't escape me. I file the information away for later.

"Here?" she manages, voice rough and unsteady. "In the garden?"

I claim her mouth before she can say more, pouring everything I feel into the kiss. "Everywhere," I whisper against her lips.

After that, she's lost to it, thoughtless and weightless, meeting me with the same desperate need that's been building between us for weeks.

"Summer!" Charlie's voice slices through the heat, sharp and startling, the sound of a mother in hot pursuit of a toddler on a mission of destruction.

We break apart like a pair of guilty teenagers, breathless, cheeks warm, hands still suspended in the space where the other used to be.

"Later," I murmur, holding her gaze, my pulse stumbling over itself.

The rest of the afternoon is its own kind of torture.

Beautiful. Exquisite. Unrelenting.

Every time our hands brush, a spark races up my arm. When her gaze finds mine, heat floods my veins and sinks low, a problem I can't solve without embarrassing myself. It's a constant, throbbing reminder of everything I can't have, at least, not yet.

I can't stop watching her. The way her throat works when she drinks. How she stretches, back arching, completely unaware she's killing me. The little sounds she makes when she's focused, soft huffs of concentration that make me think about every other sound I want to pull from her.

When the heat gets impossible, I peel off my shirt, the fabric clinging to my skin before it finally gives. I grab a bottle of water and pour it over my head, the shock of cold stealing the air from my lungs as it runs down my chest and over the lines of my stomach. For a second, all I care about is not cooking alive.

Then I look up.

She freezes a few feet away, shears dangling useless in her hand, eyes locked on me. Her lips part, and a flush rises from her throat, spreading slow and unmistakable. The shears slip from her fingers and hit the ground with a dull thud.

"I should, um, get more water," she manages, voice breaking halfway through. She turns too fast, nearly tangling herself in the thorns as she disappears behind the roses.

I watch her go, fighting the stupid grin that tugs at my mouth. It wins anyway. For a while, I stand there like an idiot, dripping water onto the grass. Eventually, I pull my shirt back on and force myself to focus on something, anything, that isn't the way she looked at me.

By the time the sun starts its slow descent, we're both wrecked. Heat-drunk and filthy, muscles aching from work and nerves fried from hours of dancing around this thing between us.

"I need a shower," she announces, packing up tools. "Desperately."

"So do I," I say, and it comes out loaded with about fifteen different meanings that all end with both of us wet and bare and tangled together.

We climb the stairs in charged silence, shoulders brushing once, twice, like magnets doing everything they can not to collide. The air thickens with afternoon heat and all the things we haven't said.

At her door, she stops. Opens it. Looks back.

"Come in."

My throat tightens. "Thank you."

The room is all stone and sunlight, gold pouring through the tall windows and pooling across the floor. But I barely notice any of it. All I can see is her—soft skin, damp curls, that impossible calm that makes the whole world go quiet. The air between us hums, charged and trembling, waiting for someone to move first.

"Would you like to go first?" I ask, even though I already know she won't.

She shakes her head, voice barely above a whisper. "You go."

I strip slowly, deliberately, letting each piece of clothing fall to the floor. My shirt. My jeans. Until I'm bare and already half-hard just from the weight of her gaze on my skin. I head for the bathroom, leaving the door cracked open behind me.

The tile is ice-cold under my feet, shocking against overheated skin. The water comes out scalding, needles of heat that make me hiss as they hit my shoulders, my back. I let it burn, let it turn my skin pink and tender, washing away dirt and sweat but doing nothing for the ache sitting low in my gut, heavy and insistent.

I take my time. Working soap over my chest, my arms, until I'm slick with heat and lather, suds sliding down my stomach. My hand wraps around my cock, the thought of her watching from the other room turning everything sharp and urgent.

I move slow. Just enough pressure to feel it building. My other hand braced against the wet tile, water streaming down my back. I imagine her eyes tracking every stroke, every movement of my fist, and my breath comes faster.

Then I glance toward the door.

She's there.

Sitting on the edge of the bed, one hand gripping the sheets, the other lost between her thighs. The magazine beside her has slid forgotten to the floor. Her tank top is pushed up, exposing flushed skin. Her chest rises and falls too fast, lips parted, eyes fixed on me through the steam like she's memorizing every detail.

Holy fuck.

I grip harder without meaning to, my hips twitching forward, a groan tearing from my throat and echoing off the tile. The sight of her watching me, touching herself while she watches, wrecks whatever control I had left. My rhythm falters. It takes everything I have to unclench my fist, to move away, to rinse the soap from my skin and gather the pieces of myself.

When I step out, towel hanging low on my hips, water still beading on my shoulders and dripping down my chest, she's still there. Flushed, glassy-eyed, beautiful and completely undone.

We meet in the doorway. The air between us crackles.

I catch her wrist as she tries to slip past me and bring her hand to my mouth. Her fingers are slick, her taste exploding on my tongue, salt and musk and arousal. I lick each finger clean, holding her gaze while she trembles and makes these small, desperate sounds in her throat.

Then I let her go with a soft slap to her ass that makes her jump.

"Your turn," I murmur, voice wrecked.

She doesn't close the door, either.

I sit on the edge of the bed, every nerve tuned to the sound of the shower. I can almost see her there: the tilt of her head, the way she braces a hand against the tile.

When she steps out again, skin pink, hair dripping, wrapped in white terrycloth, I have to look away to remember how to breathe. The towel clings to her, soft against the pink bloom of her freshly scrubbed skin.

On the bed beside me is the lounge set I bought her in Stromness. I'd gone into town for greenhouse hardware and wandered past a narrow shop between the bakery and the bookstore. The window was full of soft things, folded in careful stacks, linen and silk in beautiful pastel colors. I saw the set and thought of her immediately. The color matched her eyes, that impossible shade between blue, purple, and gray—the sea before rain. I told myself it was practical, a gift she could wear after long days in the fields. But the truth is, I wanted her to have it because it felt like her: soft, unexpected, indulgent. Something that would cling to her skin and make her think of me every time she put it on.

"It's the same color as your eyes when you smile," I tell her, my voice hoarse.

Her lips part, that small, devastating smile tugging at the corner. "Thank you."

She takes it back to the bathroom, and I wait, heart pounding in my throat until she steps out again. The sight of her in it empties my head. The fabric skims her body like it was made for her, clinging where she's still warm from the shower. All soft curves and warm skin, her hair damp against her neck, her eyes lifted to mine like she has no idea what she's doing to me.

Then Lorelai's voice cuts through the air from downstairs.

"Mummy! What's taking you so long? Come downstairs!"

"Coming, monkey!" Lorna calls.

"She sounds impatient," I say, chuckling.

"Lorelai's always impatient," she says, squeezing my hand as she passes me.

I stop her before she reaches the door, my fingers closing around her wrist. She turns, surprise flickering in her eyes, lips parted on an unspoken question, and then I pull her against me. Hard. Her body collides with mine, still damp and warm from the shower, and my hand cups her jaw while the other tangles in her hair, gripping tight enough to make her gasp.

Then I kiss her like it's the only language I know.

It's not careful. It's not sweet. It's everything I've been holding back since that frozen night in April. Desperate. Hungry. A confession made with my mouth instead of words, my tongue sliding against hers while my fingers tighten in her hair.

She melts into me, makes this broken sound against my lips that nearly destroys me. Her hands find my chest, nails scraping lightly over still-damp skin, and I groan into her mouth, deepening the kiss until we're both dizzy with it.

When I finally break away, we're both panting, foreheads pressed together.

"Figured I wouldn't get another chance for a while," I say, voice raw. "Had to make it count."

She stares at me, lips swollen and glistening, eyes gone dark. Her chest rises and falls rapidly, breasts pressing against me with each breath. "We'll finish this later," she promises, and it sounds like a vow.

And then she's gone, slipping from my grip and heading down the stairs, leaving me standing in the doorway with my pulse still racing, my cock hard beneath the towel, and every inch of me aching for more.

**14**

———————

Levi follows me down the hall, our steps in sync. At the edge of the family room, we pause together, listening. Laughter. Tiny footsteps. Daniel's soft voice and Lorelai's giggle tangled with the rustle of pages and the murmur of wind through the open window. He listens like he's tuning into his favorite radio station, like the voices of my children are sacred.

"They've been asking about you," I say quietly.

His throat works. "Yeah?"

"Every day."

When we step into the doorway, Daniel glances up first. The change in his face is immediate, like watching clouds part for the sun. "Levi!" He scrambles off the couch, the book in his lap tumbling to the floor.

Lorelai sits up from where she's been arranging flowers on the rug. "You came back!" She's on her feet in an instant, a little chain of clover blossoms still clutched in one hand.

"'Course I did." Levi moves into the room, and Daniel crashes into him at full speed. He catches the boy easily, one arm wrapping around his small shoulders as he crouches down to their height. "Told you I would, didn't I?"

Lorelai arrives half a second later, pressing into his other side. She reaches up, serious and determined, and tucks a purple clover bloom behind his ear.

"You were gone so long," Daniel mumbles into his shirt.

"I know, buddy. I'm sorry."

"Are you staying?" Lorelai asks, her hand resting on his arm like she's making sure he's real.

"For a bit."

"Good! I want to tell you about how Daniel fell off his pony yesterday."

"Lorelai—" Daniel's voice is muffled against Levi's shirt.

"Well, you did!" she says, giving him a dirty look.

"What about you, fairy girl? Did you fall off your pony?"

"I don't want to talk about that," she grumbles, folding her arms over her chest.

I bite back the smile tugging at my mouth and take her hand, guiding her down beside her flowers. Together we press the petals flat between sheets of paper, sliding them into the pages of one of my old gardening books. Her small fingers mimic mine, her brow furrowed in concentration. When I rest my hand over hers, she relaxes instantly, nestling into me like a kitten curling into sun-warmed stone.

Daniel's wedged up beside Levi on the couch now, his head tucked under Levi's arm. Levi opens the heavy book of Scottish folklore that was left on the coffee table, his voice low and rough-edged, wrapping around the words like smoke curling in a hearth.

Lorelai keeps glancing over her shoulder at him, the flowers forgotten in her lap. "Tell us about the angel," she says when the selkie story ends, her eyes wide and bright. "Aunt Charlie said you found one today."

"We had to cut her out of the vines," Levi says, his voice soft, threaded with that quiet wonder the kids love. "She's beautiful and has giant wings."

"Like fairies?" Lorelai asks, already halfway lost to the idea, her fingers twisting a daisy stem.

"Similar," Levi says. "But bigger. Stronger. Do you know what they say about angels?" His voice drops just a little, enough to pull them closer. "That sometimes they help lost things find their way home."

Daniel tilts his head, frowning in that serious way of his. "Was *she* lost?"

"I think she was hidden," Levi says after a beat. His gaze drifts toward the garden through the open door, where the evening light catches on the trees. "Waiting. For someone to notice her again."

There's a pause, the kind that stretches long enough to catch on an unspoken truth beneath it. He doesn't look at me this time, but I feel the weight of it anyway, like a hand hovering above my skin.

*Waiting for someone to notice her again.*

My hand pauses over the open book of pressed flowers. My breath stalls. Lorelai leans into my side, like she can feel it too, the quiet shift between us, subtle as the sway of wild grass.

Before I can say anything, Daniel pipes up, tugging the conversation into safer territory. "We ate dinner with Summer! Outside! There were tiny sandwiches and little cakes and everything."

Lorelai nods, suddenly animated. "Uncle Theo made the tea, Uncle Henry made cucumber sandwiches, and Uncle Dylan did the strawberry cakes. It was like a tea party for fairies!"

Levi smiles, eyes flicking toward me again. "Sounds like you've got some talented uncles."

"They're the best," Lorelai says seriously, placing one last violet in the crease of the book and pressing it flat with her fingers. "We didn't like the crusts, but Sorcha loved them."

Not even an hour later, both kids are drooping. Heads heavy, words slurring, energy long gone. We fall into a quiet rhythm, shepherding them through baths and toothbrush battles, Levi naturally stepping in with Daniel while I wrangle Lorelai into pajamas.

It's seamless in a way that startles me. Like we've done this before. Like we do this every night.

"Mr. Levi," Lorelai murmurs as I pull the blankets up around her shoulders, her lashes beginning to brush her cheeks, "are you staying here tonight?"

"Yes, sweetheart," he answers, looking over at her from where he's crouched beside Daniel's bed, helping him organize his rock collection one last time.

"Good," she says on a sigh, her voice fading. "Mummy smiles more when you're here."

Warmth flares in my chest, rising to my cheeks. But Levi doesn't miss a beat. He just smiles and walks over to us, smoothing her hair back with a gentleness that undoes me.

"Sweet dreams, little one."

The house settles into its familiar quiet once the kids are down. These walls have held a lifetime of bedtime stories and whispered secrets, but tonight the silence feels different. Expectant.

Charlie, Jack, Cam, and Lach have pulled their magic disappearing act, the coordinated kind where they all remember urgent things they forgot to do at the same time, leaving behind the kind of pointed absence that screams "go have sex" without actually saying it.

Subtle as a neon sign.

Which leaves me standing in the kitchen with Levi, and the space feels both too big and not nearly big enough.

"Are you hungry?" The words tumble out too fast, desperate, and I'm already moving toward the fridge because standing still feels dangerous.

"Starving."

The word lands low in my stomach. He's not talking about food. The way he says it makes my pulse kick hard against my throat.

I yank open the fridge, the blast of cold air doing nothing to cool the heat crawling up my spine. Charlie's pasta sauce. I grab it with hands that shake just enough to make the glass jar rattle on the shelf. Tomatoes slow-cooked with basil. It should smell like comfort, like Sunday dinners and safety.

All I can smell is him.

Clean cotton and skin. Warm, masculine, and far too intoxicating to be legal. The scent of him fills the kitchen, displacing the air in my lungs. I can taste it on my tongue, soap and salt and a darker note that makes my teeth ache.

The jar hits the counter harder than I mean it to. I reach for the pot rack, but he's there. Right there. So close his body radiates heat against my back, thick and suffocating and not nearly close enough. His breath ghosts across the nape of my neck, stirring the fine hairs there, and goosebumps cascade down my spine like dominoes.

I need to move. Need to breathe. Need to—

My hand freezes mid-reach for the cabinet. If I shift even an inch, I'll touch him. Skin to skin. And I know, bone-deep certain, that I won't survive it. That whatever fragile control I'm clinging to will shatter like spun glass.

His fingers find my hip.

Not a grab. Barely a touch. Just the whisper of his fingertips through the thin fabric of my shorts, but it burns. White-hot and electric, the sensation rockets through me, stealing the air from my lungs. A soft, broken sound slips out before I can stop it, and I feel him react. Feel the way his chest expands on a sharp inhale, the way his whole body goes taut.

He steps closer, his chest grazing my back, the faintest touch, yet every nerve ending in my body sparks to life. He's everywhere. The weight of him. The smell of him drowning out everything else until the world narrows to his body surrounding mine, his breath at my ear, the thundering of my heart so loud he must hear it.

His arm slides around me, caging my body between the counter and his. His fingers close over mine on the pot handle, and the contact burns straight through me. Callused fingertips. Broad palm. The rough drag of his skin against mine.

Time fractures.

Then he lifts the pot from my trembling hand and steps away.

The cold air rushes in where his body was, and the world tilts back into focus. Too sudden. Too intense. My hands grip the counter edge, knuckles white, holding myself upright because my knees have turned to water.

Levi moves to the stove, filling a pot with water. He's giving me space. Distance. Room to collect the pieces of myself he just scattered across this kitchen floor.

But there's intention in the way he's doing it. Purpose. Like he's planning something that requires me functional. Fed. Ready.

The thought sparks deep in my gut, a slow, insistent ache.

He glances back at me, catching my stare, and a shadow flickers in his expression. "You're going to need your strength," he says quietly. "For later."

The promise in those words nearly buckles my knees again.

We fall into a rhythm like we've done this a hundred times. I slice the bread, pretending my hands aren't shaking, pretending my pulse isn't a metronome gone wild.

He stirs the sauce, slow and focused, like he's unaware of what he's doing to me. But I can't stop watching. The way his forearms flex with every turn of the spoon, muscles shifting beneath tanned skin. The veins that trail down to his hands, prominent and masculine. Hands that know exactly how to hold. How to grip. How to coax pleasure. The kind of hands that could wreck a person with gentleness or ruin them with purpose.

And his ass. Jesus. Perfectly framed in those damned pants, tight enough to make my brain short-circuit.

And I'm over here slicing bread like it's a meditation practice, trying not to whimper over carbohydrates and gluteus maximus.

The salt shaker becomes a moment. He doesn't pass it. He offers it. Slow. Purposeful. His fingers brush mine, lingering, the touch intimate. Like he's tracing a map he plans to follow later, memorizing the landscape of my knuckles, the ridges of my hand. My skin flares under the contact, sensation blooming outward in waves that pulse through my nerves, and I have to bite the inside of my cheek to keep from making a sound.

By the time the water starts to boil, I'm gone. Fully and completely undone. My skin feels too tight for my body, stretched thin over raw nerves. Every synapse is firing his name in Morse code.

He still doesn't say a word.

He stays close. He stirs the pot like this isn't witchcraft. Like he's not cooking me from the inside out.

Then he moves.

His hands are at my waist, steady and warm, fingers spreading across my hip with enough pressure to make me feel claimed without actually holding me captive. He nudges me back. One step. Then another. Until the edge of the counter presses into my lower back.

He stops a hairsbreadth away. Not touching, but close enough that my body can't tell the difference, close enough that I can feel the heat radiating off his chest like standing too near a fire. The energy rolling off him is a living thing, dense, suffocating, intoxicating. My heart hammers so hard I can feel it in my throat, behind my eyes, between my thighs. My knees threaten complete rebellion.

He stands there. Still. Watching. Like he knows he doesn't have to touch me to wreck me. Like the anticipation alone will do the work.

He holds my gaze, dark and searching, pupils blown wide. Like he's asking without asking. Like he's reading me, sifting through my defenses, trying to find the part that will tell him if this is okay, if I want this as badly as he does.

He doesn't need to look that hard.

"Lorna."

My name in his mouth breaks the last of my restraint. His chest rises and falls with controlled breaths. A muscle ticks in his jaw. And those eyes, God, those eyes promise things I've dreamed about.

Then he's kissing me, and the world tilts sideways.

It starts soft. Careful. His lips brush mine, a whisper of contact that feels more like a question than a kiss. Like he's giving me an out. But I don't. I lean in. I take.

His mouth opens over mine, warm and searching. My bottom

lip catches between his teeth and he tugs, his tongue following, coaxing mine into a rhythm that feels inevitable.

I make a noise, half whimper, half sigh, and suddenly his hands are on me. One sliding up under my shirt, fingers splayed over the bare skin of my stomach. The other holding my hip, pulling me tighter until our bodies lock together.

He lets out a low sound into my mouth, a raw vibration that runs down my spine. Every kiss now is hungrier, wetter, messier. Less careful.

Grabbing his shirt in both hands, I kiss him harder. He presses me tighter to the counter. His hips roll with mine. We kiss like we're starving, like we've both been waiting our entire lives for this.

God, I need him.

The water hisses loud behind us, boiling over with a violent sizzle. We break apart gasping, and Levi curses softly, spinning toward the stove. He grabs the pot, jerking it off the burner as water cascades over the sides, steam erupting in a hot cloud.

"Shit," he mutters, turning off the burner, but his other hand is still on me, fingers gripping my hip like he can't quite let go.

He wraps his arms around me, our breaths collide, rough and uneven, until they fall into the same rhythm. My lips are swollen, my skin feels like it's been plugged into an electrical socket and someone just cranked the voltage.

"We should eat," I whisper, though food is the last thing on my mind.

He leans back, his mouth tilting into a smile. "Yeah," he says, but his hand doesn't move from where it's anchored at my waist. His thumb keeps tracing slow, lazy circles on my hip like he's spelling out everything he's not saying. And his eyes are locked on my mouth like it'll kill him to look away.

He leans in again, voice low and devastating. "I hope you mean you. Because I could feast on you for hours."

My whole body clenches. Desire surges fast and wild, licking up my spine, stealing the air from my lungs.

For a moment, we stand there, frozen in the aftermath of his words, the promise of them hanging heavy between us.

Then reality crashes back. The stove. The food. The pretense of normalcy we're both clinging to by our fingernails.

We move quickly, working around the mess of boiled-over water on the stove. Drain the pasta in rushed, jerky movements. Stir in the sauce with hands that aren't quite steady. We plate the food carefully, like each brush of elbow or hand isn't just another match striking a box soaked in gasoline.

We sit side by side at the table, bowls in front of us, pretending we're not both about to crawl out of our skin. We eat slowly, each bite stretched out between glances that burn and words that catch in our throats.

When I reach for the wine, our hands meet and hold. When he passes the bread, his thumb drags across my palm, and I have to bite back a sound.

The air feels heavy, alive, as if the world has gone still, waiting for the spark that will set it off.

By the time our bowls are empty, he leans back. One hand drifts to my thigh, squeezing tight.

"I can't stop thinking about having you spread out on the greenhouse floor," he says, voice rough. "What do you say?"

It's not a question.

I nod, wordless. I push up from the stool, unsteady, breath caught somewhere between my lungs and my throat.

His eyes track every movement. Hungry. Possessive.

At the doorway, I pause. Turn back.

He hasn't moved. Still sitting there, watching me with barely leashed restraint. Like he's giving me this last chance to change my mind. Like he's terrified I will.

I turn toward the greenhouse.

The sound of his stool hitting the floor tells me everything I need to know.

. . .

The greenhouse holds onto the day's heat, thick and heavy, like the air hasn't quite remembered how to exhale. It smells of soil and damp leaves, sweetness threaded through the humidity, maybe jasmine, maybe just the quiet kind of magic that happens when daylight gives in to night.

We spread blankets across the stone floor between clay pots and seed trays, forgotten gloves and rusting trowels, all of it softened by moonlight. The old glass panels overhead are streaked with dew, letting through fractured beams of silver light.

"This is nice," I say, settling cross-legged on the blanket. "Peaceful."

"Mmm." Levi's not looking at the night sky or the greenhouse walls. He's looking at me. His gaze lingers on my face, quiet and focused. "I've been thinking. About what you said earlier. About staying another two weeks."

I tug at a loose thread on the blanket, trying to keep it light. "Regretting your decision to help me with the farm?"

"No." His voice is sure. Steady. "The opposite. I'm glad you're staying. It gives us time to figure this out."

My breath catches, chest tight. "What kind of 'this' are we figuring out?"

He shifts closer, knee brushing mine. I feel it everywhere.

"*This*," he says. "You. Me. Leo. Hudson. What I feel for you... it's not simple. It doesn't fit into neat little categories. And it's not only me. All three of us feel it."

My heart thuds so loud I'm afraid he'll hear it. "So what exactly do you feel?"

He doesn't hesitate. "Everything." Then his voice drops, soft and raw. "Love. Lust. This ridiculous, consuming need to take care of you. I think about you constantly. About the way you sound. The way you taste. About everything we haven't done, and everything I want to do with you."

I swallow hard as the tension between us shifts, deepens, grows teeth.

"I know this isn't easy," he goes on. "I never saw myself in a relationship like this. But with you, somehow it just fits. When Leo comes back from seeing you and he's smiling again, like you poured sunlight straight into his chest... I don't feel threatened. I feel lucky that I get to be part of that."

His voice drops to a near whisper. "And Hudson. When he talks about you, when he talks about the twins... there's this light in him. This hope. He hasn't had that in a long time."

The ache behind my eyes comes fast and hot. My throat tightens.

He reaches for me, fingers curving around my jaw, thumb tracing my cheek with unbearable gentleness. "Tell me you feel it too. Not only the pull, not only the wanting. All of it. Because I need to know I'm not the only one losing my mind over this."

I nod, swallowing hard past the tightness in my throat. "I do. I feel it. And it terrifies me."

"Thank god," he chokes out, his entire body shuddering with relief.

"What happens now?"

Levi lowers his forehead to mine, his voice rough around the edges. "Now I kiss you."

And he does.

His mouth meets mine, soft at first, careful. A question more than a claim. But when I answer, when I press back with that small, aching yes, everything shifts. The pressure deepens. He takes my mouth, tasting and learning, memorizing the shape of my lips against his. This isn't the hungry, half-wild kiss from earlier. This is slower. More dangerous.

My fingers tangle in the damp curls at the nape of his neck and tug, just enough to make him groan, the sound vibrating through both our bodies.

He pulls me into him, backing me toward the weathered potting bench until the wood presses into my lower back. Our bodies fit together, chest to hips, thigh to thigh, heat bleeding through fabric, and still it's not enough. His mouth moves over mine, then drifts along my jaw, slow and unhurried, his stubble rasping along my skin. The scent of earth and growing things surrounds us, humid greenhouse air thick and warm.

"Lorna," he whispers, voice wrecked and raw. His hands slip down my sides, curling around my waist like he's holding on for dear life, fingers digging into soft flesh. "You're driving me completely fucking insane."

"Likewise," I gasp, tipping my head as his lips trace the line of my throat, his tongue flicking at the fluttering pulse beneath my skin.

He kisses me again, and all traces of restraint go up in smoke. There's no hesitation now, no thought of timing or consequence. His fingers tangle in my hair, guiding my mouth to his, and he kisses me like he's been starving for this, like I'm the only air he'll ever need. He slips his hands beneath my shirt and my brain short-circuits, every thought scattering like sparks.

"I want you," he rasps, mouth brushing mine. "I want you so much it hurts."

"Then have me," I whisper. No fear. No filter. Just fire racing through my veins.

In one fluid motion, Levi lifts me onto the potting bench. The wood is rough and solid beneath my thighs, anchoring me when nothing else feels steady. He steps between my legs and pulls me to the edge until our bodies are aligned. Even through fabric, the hard length of him slots against me, warmth seeping through, and the thin barrier does nothing to soften the impact. It's want and the sharp, sweet ache of restraint, all of it crackling to life where our bodies meet.

My legs wrap around his hips instinctively, pulling him closer, and he exhales sharply, his fingers digging into my thighs hard enough to leave marks.

"Fuck, Lorna," he moans, head tipping back as I move my hips, slow and testing, learning what he likes.

I lean in, pressing soft, open-mouthed kisses along the sharp line of his jaw, tasting sweat and skin and the warm, earthy scent that's become unmistakably him. I trail lower, lips brushing the hollow of his throat, feeling his pulse hammer beneath my lips.

"Yes, please," I murmur against his pulse, the words vibrating through him.

He laughs, but it catches halfway through, unraveling into a low sound when I find the spot beneath his ear and suck gently, marking him. His hands flex at my hips, grip tightening, anchoring me to him. Then he starts to move me. Slow, steady pressure. Guiding me into a rhythm that's exploratory at first, but it builds, deeper, filthier, with every roll of my hips, every broken exhale between us, every place where our bodies grind together. Tools rattle on hooks behind us. Glass panes fog over.

His hands slide up my back, under my shirt, palms skating over bare skin, leaving trails of fire. When his thumbs brush the undersides of my breasts, I gasp, arching into him, chasing more, needing more.

But then he stills. One hand cups my face, thumb stroking my flushed cheek, the other gentling my hips with firm pressure.

"Wait," he says, voice frayed and desperate. "Wait, before this goes any further, I need to say something."

I blink, dazed, my vision blurred at the edges. "What?"

"I desperately want to make love to you, Lorna," he says, the words rough and honest. "But Leo and Hudson would kill me if I took this all the way without talking to them first. Not because they'd be mad at you, they wouldn't, but because the three of us promised we'd do this right. Together. No secrets. No one getting left behind."

His words don't feel like rejection. They feel like truth. Like steadiness anchoring me in the storm.

"Then don't take it all the way, Levi," I say, surprised at how steady my voice is despite the trembling in my limbs. My hands flatten against his chest, feeling the frantic pace of his heartbeat beneath my palms, wild and racing. "Take it as far as you can."

The look he gives me in that moment is molten, scorching.

"Those are dangerous words, Dr. MacLeod," he says, voice dropping into a different register.

I smile, slow and wicked, feeling powerful despite being undone. "I'm a dangerous woman."

His grin tilts and he picks me up off the bench and lays me on the blanket, a growl curling out of him as he crawls over me. His mouth crashes into mine, no hesitation this time, and I melt for him, under him, around him.

What follows is the sweetest, slowest kind of ruin. Levi traces every inch of me like he's learning a language with his hands, fingers sketching patterns on my skin that feel like poetry. His mouth drifts to the curve of my throat, the hollow of my collarbone, the soft swell above my bra, each kiss a vow pressed into flesh.

By the time he peels my shirt over my head and drops it somewhere behind us, he exhales like I've stolen the breath from his lungs. The greenhouse air clings to my skin, heavy and humid, as if the whole room has moved in closer to watch.

"Jesus," he whispers, voice hoarse and reverent. "You're so fucking beautiful."

His hands skate across my bare skin with a tenderness that threatens to undo me entirely, and his mouth follows, leaving traces of him wherever he lingers, tongue tasting salt and skin.

When he finally closes his mouth around one nipple, I arch into him with a strangled sound, a raw, broken sound spilling from my throat. His tongue circles and flicks, his teeth scraping until I'm writhing beneath him.

He takes his time, switching sides, lavishing me with attention until I'm trembling, every nerve ending lit up and singing, every wordless cry a plea I can't control.

"Please," I gasp, fingers tangling in his hair, holding him to me.

He gazes at me with heavy-lidded eyes. "Please what? Tell me what you want, Lorna."

"You," I breathe. No hesitation. No hiding. "All of you. As much as you can give me."

He moans, the sound torn from somewhere deep and desperate. "Fuck it," he mutters, already fumbling with the button on my jeans.

"Leo and Hudson will understand," he says, even as his eyes betray him. That flicker of conflict cutting through the hunger.

"No." I cup his face, grounding us both. My thumbs stroke along the sharp cut of his cheekbones. "We don't have to have sex, Levi. There are plenty of other things we can do."

His gaze snaps to mine, raw and unguarded. "I want to," he says, voice shredded and aching. "God, I want you so much it fucking hurts." He slides his nose along mine. "But I want it to matter more than that. I want this to be right. For you. For me. For all of us."

That choice, that painful, beautiful choice, splinters something soft inside me. I lean in, brushing my lips over his, tasting myself there.

"Then let's compromise," I murmur against his mouth. "There are plenty of ways to get each other off."

His hunger doesn't fade. It sharpens, hones to a razor's edge. "I can do that," he says, voice low. "I can definitely do that."

He undresses me slowly, his mouth tracing the path his hands leave behind. Each inch of skin he uncovers gets its share of attention. The scrape of his stubble along my stomach makes my breath hitch. When he drags my jeans down, he lingers at the inside of my thigh, then my knee, then my ankle.

When there's nothing left between us, the blanket rough beneath my back and the scent of earth heavy in the air, he pauses. Looks at me like he's seeing something he can't quite believe. My pulse stumbles, the world shrinking to the space between us. His chest rises and falls hard before he exhales, as if the sight of me has stolen the air from his lungs.

"Fuck," he mutters. His hands drag over my breasts, thumbs circling peaked nipples, down my ribs, gripping my hips like he's anchoring himself to reality. "You're so goddamned beautiful."

His touch changes, rougher now, stripped of patience. His hand moves between my thighs, fingers pressing into me, and I sob, my hips lifting for more. I'm soaked, pulsing, so ready it's almost painful. He drags his fingers through the slick, slow at first, then firmer, testing.

His growl is pure satisfaction, masculine and possessive. "God, Lorna. You're fucking soaked."

I try to respond, but my brain is static and sparks, thoughts dissolving into sensation.

He watches every twitch of my body like he's addicted to the way I unravel. Fingers working my clit in tight, controlled circles, drawing out the pleasure until it's so sharp it borders on pain.

And when I'm close, right there, hips jerking, body trembling on the edge of release, he stops.

I cry out, frustrated and needy, but he doesn't flinch. Doesn't give in.

His voice is low and rough as gravel. "Not yet. I need to taste you first."

He moves down my body, worship made flesh. Over the soft curve of my stomach, lips gentle against hypersensitive skin. Lower, to the sharp edge of my hips. His mouth lingers on the stretch marks scattered across my lower belly, silver lines etched deep. He doesn't flinch or glance past them. He kisses each one like it matters, like it's sacred—proof of life, of survival, of everything my body has gone through. "So fucking beautiful," he murmurs, and whatever I'd been holding onto gives way.

He keeps going, mouth tracing a path down the inside of my thighs, the heat of him ghosting over sensitive skin, his hands steady and sure, spreading me open. I'm trembling, anticipation coiling tight in my belly.

He starts softly, barely a brush, then deepens it. Greedy. Starved. Claiming. His tongue follows, sliding through me with a filthy kind of hunger, lapping at my entrance before dragging up to circle my clit. He groans, the sound vibrating through his mouth and straight into my spine, making me arch off the blanket.

His fingers come next, pressing inside me without hesitation, stretching me open, curling until I see stars. His mouth never lets up, tongue flicking and dragging, lips sealing around my clit and sucking with a rhythm that makes my whole body pulse in time.

He watches me as he wrecks me, his eyes locked on mine over the plane of my stomach. He adjusts every time I gasp, every time I twitch, chasing every tremor.

I don't last long.

The orgasm crashes over me hard, pleasure detonating at my core and radiating outward in waves. My thighs clamp around his head, my fingers clenching in his hair as I sob his name, the sound echoing off glass and stone. My whole body seizes, wave after wave ripping through me, white-hot and consuming.

He eases me down gently, fingers slowing, tongue softening until the sharp edge of pleasure melts into trembling aftershocks. He presses kisses to the inside of my thighs, my belly, each one a benediction, a promise.

"Fucking stunning," he breathes as he crawls back up my body, pulling me into him as he settles beside me, his arm solid and warm around my waist.

I'm boneless. Wrung out. But I can feel the thick press of him against my hip, and I want to give him the same release, want to watch him come apart the way I just did.

"My turn," I say, reaching for the waistband of his jeans, my voice shaky.

"You don't have to," he starts, swallowing hard, trying to be noble.

I cut him off with a kiss, slow at first, coaxing, then deeper, needier, tasting myself on his tongue. My fingers fumble at the button of his jeans, not from nerves but from urgency, from the desperate need to touch him.

"I want to," I whisper. "I need your cock in my mouth, Levi. I need to taste you."

The look he gives me is enough to make me wet all over again, raw hunger and disbelief and pure male satisfaction.

"In that case," he says, lifting his hips to help me, voice gone low and wrecked, "I'm all yours."

Getting him naked is a revelation. He's leaner than Leo, less muscular than Hudson, but there's a whipcord strength in his frame that calls to me. Moonlight pours through the glass above us, painting his skin in silver and shadow. He's achingly beautiful.

"My turn to look," I murmur, skimming my hands over his chest, down the flat plane of his stomach, across the sharp cut of his hips. He shivers beneath my hands.

When I wrap my hand around his cock, he hisses, hips jerking reflexively. He's thick and hot and hard, already slick at the tip.

"Lorna," he groans as I begin to stroke him, slow and steady. "Fuck, that feels..."

"Good?" I ask, all mock innocence, twisting my wrist on the upstroke.

"Incredible," he pants, head falling back. "Your hands... God, your hands are magic."

I lean down to pepper kisses across his chest, his throat, anywhere I can reach while keeping that same rhythm going.

When I take him into my mouth, he chokes on a sound that's half gasp, half plea. His grip in my hair tightens instantly, not rough, but desperate.

He's hot and heavy on my tongue, thick and smooth, every inch of him pulsing with heat. I suck gently, then drag my tongue along the underside. The taste of him floods my mouth. I moan softly, the sound vibrating through him, and he curses through his teeth.

"Jesus, Lorna," he rasps. "You feel... fuck... you feel so good."

I take him deeper, slowly, until I feel the pressure of him at the back of my throat, then pull back and suck again. My hand joins in, working around the base, twisting, stroking, matching the rhythm of my mouth.

His control is crumbling by the second. Every flick of my tongue, every slip and drag, makes him groan louder, deeper. His abs contract under my free hand, a trembling ripple of effort as he tries to hold back.

I flatten my tongue and let him slide across it again, teasing the sensitive spot beneath the head. He bucks hard, cursing like he's in pain.

"Fuck. Don't stop," he begs. "Please don't stop."

I don't.

I keep going. Mouth and hand working together, fast and messy and relentless, until the taste of him thickens, until the tension in his body hits a fever pitch.

God. If I'd known it could feel like this, I would've written my dissertation on blowjobs. I had no idea going down on someone could be this hot, this intimate, this addictive. I didn't know giving could feel so much like receiving. Like power and surrender all tangled together.

And then he's coming.

He chokes out my name like it's being dragged from the depths of his soul. His hold tightens, hips stuttering, body seizing with every wave. I swallow him down, gaze locked on his face, watching it twist with pleasure so raw and beautiful it brings tears to my eyes.

When he finally stops, his muscles relax, his hand falls from my hair, drifting tenderly across my cheek.

His voice is wrecked, shaky and quiet. "You just... holy shit. You ruined me."

I crawl up his body, lips tingling, heart thudding hard behind my ribs. I press a kiss to the corner of his mouth and whisper against his jaw.

"Good."

"Jesus," he pants. "That was..."

"Yeah," I whisper, pressing my lips to his collarbone. "It really was."

We lie there for a while, our bodies tangled, the air thick with the scent of sex and dirt and moonlight. All I can hear is the steady beat of Levi's heart beneath my cheek.

Eventually, though, reality starts to edge its way back in.

"We should go inside," I say reluctantly. "The twins might wake up and wonder where I am."

"I know," he says softly, but neither of us moves. His hand strokes slow circles across my back.

"I'd sleep out here with you," I admit. "Under the stars. But..."

"But you're a good mother," he finishes, kissing the top of my head. "And they need to know where to find you."

The way he says it, so simple, so accepting, makes my throat tighten. No guilt. No resentment. Just quiet understanding.

We wrap ourselves in the blankets, still barefoot and a little wild, and make our way back across the moonlit lawn. The castle rises ahead of us, ancient and silent, its stone walls bathed in silver light. At the side door, we pause. Neither of us says it, but we both feel it, crossing this threshold changes something.

"No regrets?" Levi asks quietly.

"None," I say, meeting his gaze without hesitation. "You?"

His smile is a little sad. "Only that we waited so long."

The walk to my room feels both endless and too damn short. Every step thrums with the echo of Levi's hands, the weight of him on my tongue, the way my body aches in that delicious, used-up kind of way. I pause at the door, nerves flickering under my skin.

"Stay with me tonight?" I ask. Barely a whisper.

His gaze softens, desire giving way to tenderness. "Are you sure? The twins..."

"They won't come looking unless there's trouble," I say. "And even then, they knock. Please, Levi. I'm not ready to let you go yet."

Emotion flits across his face, relief, maybe. Or something deeper.

He steps closer, lifts his hands to cradle my face, his thumbs brushing over my cheekbones.

"I was hoping you'd say that," he says, voice little more than a breath. "Because there's nowhere I'd rather be than here. With you. I want to fall asleep with your skin against mine and wake up with your name on my lips. I want all of it, if you'll let me."

I smile up at him. "I want it all, too, Levi. I have for a long time, I just didn't let myself believe it could be this good."

We move without speaking, the bedroom door clicking shut behind us, closing out the rest of the world.

"I need to wash the greenhouse off," I murmur, reaching for the shower controls. "Join me?"

His only answer is to let the blanket fall.

For a long beat, we just stand there. Lit by the soft overhead glow, streaked with moonlight from the window. Naked and marked up by sweat, by dirt, by each other. His gaze drags down my body, and I do the same to him. No shame. No hiding.

We walk into the bathroom hand in hand, starting the water and stepping under it together.

It hits my skin like a second wave of him, all warmth, steadiness, and a kind of sweetness that makes me want to stay here forever, suspended in it. But it's his hands, slick with soap, that undo me. Not rushed this time. No wild hunger. Just slow, deliberate care, every touch a promise I feel down to my bones.

His fingers trace over my arms, my shoulders, the slope of my stomach. Mapping me. When I reach for the shampoo, he intercepts my hand.

"Let me," he says.

I nod and drop my arms to my sides, closing my eyes as his fingers work through my hair. I melt beneath his hands as he massages my scalp, then smooths conditioner through the length of my hair.

"Your turn," I whisper when he's finished, and I take my time with him, learning the shape of his skull beneath my hands, the way his curls cling to my fingers when wet. Washing him turns into touching him. Touching turns into more.

His hands skim down my sides, over the curves of my hips, and then we're pressed together beneath the stream of water, mouths colliding.

"I thought we were cleaning up," I whisper, breathless, as his mouth trails wet kisses down my throat.

"We are," he murmurs. "Very, very thoroughly."

When he pushes his fingers inside me again, the sensation is almost overwhelming. I'm still sensitive, nerves buzzing, but he's patient, so gentle it feels like worship. He works me open slowly, steadily, drawing soft gasps from my mouth, my hands scrambling for purchase on his shoulders.

"God, I love those little sounds you make." His thumb finds the perfect spot, making my knees tremble. "I could spend hours watching you fall apart for me."

"Hours?" I echo, barely able to speak.

"Days," he corrects, pushing a second finger inside, stretching me with aching care. "Weeks. However long you'll let me."

He pulls his fingers from me with a broken sound. I whimper at the loss, but then he's guiding me gently, turning me to face the wall.

"Lean forward," he murmurs, his hands tightening on my hips as he pulls my ass back toward him.

My forehead meets the slick tile, cool and grounding amid the rush rolling through me. And then I feel him. God. I feel him, his cock pressing between my thighs, sliding through the slick ache of me. Not inside. Just riding the seam of me. The head nudging up along my clit with each slow, torturous thrust.

A broken sound slips from my throat, hips pushing back instinctively.

His hand moves around to my front, keeping him snug to me, making sure I feel the full length of him. He thrusts along my pussy in tight, controlled strokes, and it's too much and not enough. Each drag of him over my clit is a lightning strike, pulling sounds from my throat I didn't know I was capable of making.

"Shhh." He presses his lips to my shoulder. "I've got you."

His mouth drifts along the curve of my neck, each kiss wet and deliberate, searing hotter than it should. He pauses beneath my ear, then finds the place between my neck and shoulder and bites, not hard, just enough to pull a sound from my throat.

"Fuck, Levi—" I can't finish the sentence.

He groans, grinding harder against me, the thick head of his cock dragging over my clit in slow, devastating strokes. His other hand cups my breast, thumb flicking across my nipple until I'm arching into him, chasing every scrap of friction like it's the one thing keeping me upright.

I brace myself on the wall, forehead still pressed to the tile, water rushing down around us. My skin is slick. My legs are shaking. I'm unraveling by the second.

He catches my hand, brings it down between us, pressing my fingers to his cock. "Take what you need, Petal," he says, rough and hungry.

I do. I press him harder to me, rocking my clit over the head of his cock with frantic, messy rhythm. Wild with it. Desperate.

"Good girl," he growls. "Now come for me."

When I do, it hits like a wave breaking. He bites down on that spot he's already marked, growling into my skin as I shatter under him. I cry out as my body seizes, my thighs clamping around him. My hips stutter, caught in the current of it.

But he doesn't stop. He keeps grinding into me, cock slick with both of us, chasing his own edge while I whimper and shake.

Then he breaks.

His whole body goes tight behind me, a guttural sound ripped from his throat as he thrusts once, twice, and comes hard, hips locked to mine, cock pulsing where I'm wet and aching. The rush of it is hot, thick, slicking my thighs. He stays there, pressed to my back, forehead dropping to my neck, breath ragged, fingers clutching my hips like he doesn't want to let go.

He turns me to face him, eyes dark and wild, and drags his thumb through the mess between my thighs. He brings it to my lips, smearing his cum across them before crashing his mouth to mine.

"You're gonna ruin me."

I smile against his mouth, still breathless, still trembling, and tangle my fingers in his damp hair, tugging him closer until there's no space left between us.

"Right back at you," I whisper.

We finish our shower in silence, but it's not awkward, it's full.

Full of lingering touches and stolen kisses and that grounded, sacred kind of closeness that needs no words.

By the time we crawl into bed, exhaustion has settled into my bones. Levi pulls me in like we've been doing this for a lifetime. My cheek finds its place over his heart, the steady beat a rhythm I didn't know I'd been craving.

"Thank you," he murmurs.

I tilt my head, drowsy but curious. "For what?"

"For trusting me. For letting me in. For being brave enough to want this, even when it scares you."

I shift enough to see him. His face is soft in the dim light, all the edges gone. No armor. No walls.

"Thank you," I whisper, "for seeing me, for understanding the parts that don't make sense. The messy ones. The ones I usually keep hidden."

His gaze doesn't waver. "And I love every single one of those parts," he says, voice thick with it.

The word hangs there. Love.

Not a declaration, not exactly. But it vibrates between us like something inevitable.

"Sleep," he whispers, pressing a kiss to my hair. "I'm not going anywhere."

And for once, I believe it. I don't spiral. Don't brace for the fall. I just let go, sinking into the comfort of him, wrapped in the rare, staggering peace of being held by someone who loves me.

## 15

LEO'S POV

The phone buzzes against my thigh while I'm elbow-deep in the milking shed, and I almost ignore it. Hudson's been sending hourly updates about the ram, swears the bastard's developed a personality disorder, and I don't have the bandwidth for another sheep saga before coffee.

Unease twists deep in my gut, keen enough to make me reach for it anyway. Maybe it's the silence. Lorna's been quiet for two days, which isn't like her. She's been religious about check-ins, sending grainy photos of sunrises over flower beds and triumphant little updates on taming decades of neglect into something beautiful.

Her name lights up the screen, but it's not a text.

It's a voicemail. Three minutes old.

I press play, expecting her usual blend of grit and barely contained chaos to fill the barn.

What comes through the speaker makes my stomach drop straight to the straw-covered floor.

"I can't breathe, Charlie, I can't. They're coming two weeks early!"

Her voice breaks on the word, high and thin like a snapped wire.

"Nothing's ready, nothing's—" She cuts herself off with a sharp inhale, her tone hardening. "The roses look like shit, the herb garden's a mess, and she's going to take one look and cancel the shoot, and it'll be my fault because I was too fucking stubborn to—"

A loud crash cuts through the audio, metal on tile, or something worse. Then her breath hitches, ragged and broken. Muffled sobs follow, quiet and unguarded.

"I can't do this. I can't fix it in time. Jack's going to lose the booking, and I'll have ruined everything because I thought I could..."

A wet, choked sound.

"I just can't. I just... I can't."

My grip on the phone tightens until the case creaks. In the years I've known Lorna, I've never heard her like that. Not frantic. Not fragile. Not like she's being torn apart piece by piece. I'm already moving, boots pounding across the barn floor.

"Levi!" I shout. I scan the stalls until I spot him at the far end, rinsing out the milking lines.

He glances up, frowns at my tone. "What—"

"Lorna needs help," I say, already pulling off my gloves. "Hudson and I are going. Hold down the fort until we get back."

"How bad?"

"Full-blown meltdown. The magazine's showing up early, and she's losing it. We're gonna go kidnap her if we have to."

Levi nods once, no hesitation. "I'll finish here and cover as long as I need to."

"Appreciate you."

Then I'm out the barn door, sprinting toward the house.

"Hudson!" I bellow as I hit the steps. "We're leaving. Now."

He appears in the kitchen doorway, towel slung over his shoulder, hair still damp from the shower. One look at my face and the post-breakfast ease vanishes.

"What happened?"

I hold up the phone. "Lorna's having a breakdown."

That's all it takes. He drops the towel and pulls on a pair of pants that were hanging over the back of a chair.

We're on the road in under three minutes, Hudson behind the wheel, one hand clenching the gearshift while I stab at my phone. Straight to voicemail. Again. The knot in my chest draws tighter.

"Talk," Hudson says, taking the curves too fast. "What exactly did she say?"

I replay the message, Lorna's voice raw and unraveling. Hudson listens without a word, his jaw rigid. When it ends, his foot presses harder on the gas.

"Jesus. Sounds like she's barely holding it together." His grip on the steering wheel goes white. "A woman who has two wildlings for kids probably has a very dramatic definition of 'disaster.'"

The image should make me laugh. It doesn't. Not with her words still echoing in my head, panicked and breaking.

She's ours now. Whether she knows it or not.

Even if we have to drag her home to prove it.

The castle rises out of the morning mist like a fever dream, all turrets and stone and impossible angles. Hudson doesn't head for the front entrance. He takes the gravel service road around back, straight to the heart of the gardens.

We see her before the truck's even parked.

Lorna's a blur of motion in the mist, crouched deep over a flower bed in mud-caked jeans and a hoodie two sizes too big. She's moving fast, frantic, like she's trying to outrun her own panic. Her hands fly from plant to plant, jagged and unsteady, and there's a wild edge to the way she yanks weeds that makes my gut twist.

She doesn't notice us until the sound of the truck doors closing makes her jump. Then she spins, eyes wide and dark in her pale face.

"What are you doing here?" she asks, but there's no heat behind it. Only bone-deep exhaustion.

"You butt-dialed us," Hudson says, already walking toward her. "Sounded like you were on the verge of setting the whole place on fire."

Color floods her face. "I didn't mean to—God, I'm sorry."

"It's fine," I say, crossing the space between us. Up close, it's worse than I thought. Her hands tremble, nails torn and packed with dirt. Shadows bloom under her eyes, not the kind from missed sleep, but from holding too much for too long. From breaking quietly. "What matters is you need help."

"The magazine's coming tomorrow to check that we're ready," she says, her chin wobbling halfway through the sentence. "Everything has to be perfect. Look at this place—"

I do.

Maybe through her eyes it's a battlefield.

What I see is stunning. The pathways are clean. The stonework's been scrubbed. The flower beds are thoughtful, layered, curated with an artist's eye. It's not a disaster; it's a miracle. I know how her brain works—perfection or failure, no in-between. When I take it in again, I notice the mulch that still needs spreading, the clover creeping into the herb beds, the corner near the greenhouse that's a touch sparse.

"So we fix it," Hudson says, rolling up his sleeves and squinting toward the nearest wheelbarrow. "What's on the list?"

She blinks at us like we've both lost our minds. Like the two of us showing up uninvited with nothing except time and muscle and love to offer isn't just unlikely, it's impossible.

"I'm sure you have your own chaos to tame back home—"

"Levi's got it," I say. Firm. Final. "Talk, Lorna. What needs doing?"

Her mouth opens, then closes. She exhales through her nose.

"Mulch. The rose beds and the beds along the rock wall. The pathway edges need a clean trim. Deadheading along the trellises. Weeding the herb garden. That whole section—" She gestures toward the greenhouse, exasperation bleeding into despair. "Everything died. I need to replant it. It looks empty and bare and—"

"Done," I say, cutting her off before she spirals.

We work for hours, falling into a rhythm that feels instinctive.

No talking, only tools and breath and bodies moving in sync. I take the heavy stuff—wheelbarrows of mulch, thick roots that need pulling, beds that need trimming back.

Hudson handles the detail work, crouched close with that laser focus of his, trimming hedge lines like it's a meditation. There's an unwavering steadiness about the way he works, hands sure, movements quiet and exact. It's how he is with animals, too. Calm. Patient. Tuned into what the rest of us miss.

Lorna moves through the chaos as if she owns it. The panic from earlier is gone, burned off by motion and momentum. Now she's locked in, calling out tasks without missing a beat. Her hoodie's been shed, sleeves rolled up, skin kissed pink by the sun and streaked with dirt. There's a pencil behind one ear, smudges on her cheek, and her shirt clings in places from sweat. She's fucking breathtaking. Not polished or untouchable, beautiful like fire, all heat and motion and impossible to turn away from.

The work is satisfying in that way only hard labor can be, but there's something else moving between us. A quiet thrum that hums louder with every passing hour.

It's in the way our hands brush when passing tools. In the glances that linger a second too long when we're crouched side by side. In the careful choreography of moving around each other in tight spaces, trying not to touch but never quite managing it.

We've worked together plenty of times before, but this? This is different.

This feels like foreplay disguised as manual labor.

Around noon, Charlie shows up with a paper bag full of sandwiches. She takes one look at our dirt-streaked faces, catches the charge in the air, and backs away with a smirk that practically shouts, *Oh, I see what this is.*

"You're going to work yourself into the ground," Hudson says a while later, dropping onto the stone bench beside Lorna. He's flushed and sweat-damp, forearms streaked with dirt, his gaze soft when he looks at her.

"I'll rest when it's done," she replies, already glaring at the next unfinished corner like it personally offended her.

"You need to rest now, Lorna." I step in, standing in front of her, voice flat and immovable. "Five minutes. Sit. Eat something. Drink some damn water."

She opens her mouth to argue, but I level her with a look. She shuts it, takes the sandwich Hudson offers, and bites down, jaw tense, eyes scanning the garden as though sheer will alone might hold it together.

"It's going to be beautiful," I tell her, settling on the low wall across from them.

"You don't know that," she grumbles.

"I do."

"You don't know what she's expecting. What she's comparing it to."

"We know *you*," Hudson says, brushing a streak of dirt from her sleeve. His hand lingers, warm and solid, long enough to say the rest without words. "And you don't do anything halfway."

She doesn't answer, but something shifts, the angle of her shoulders, the way her jaw unclenches. Not quite softening. More like a crack in the armor. An exhale. A gate left ajar.

Just enough to let us in. Just enough to keep going.

The afternoon blurs into a series of stolen touches and quiet collisions. My hand brushes over hers when we both reach for the same trowel, and neither of us pulls away. Hudson's fingers trail across her back when he walks past. We crowd around beds to assess spacing, our bodies slotting together like we've been doing this for years. No one speaks it aloud, but the electricity is there, crackling beneath the surface.

By the time the sun slips toward the horizon, the transformation is staggering. The gardens look unreal. The paths wind neatly through the space, beds sculpted and blooming as if pulled from a dream. Color flows in deliberate waves. The air smells of damp earth and fresh lavender.

"Holy shit," Lorna says, standing dead center in the middle of it all, cheeks streaked with dirt and eyes wide with awe. "We actually did it."

"We did." Hudson slings an arm around her shoulders, tugging her in. "And it's fucking spectacular."

I move to her other side, the warmth of her pressed between us lighting up my insides. I take in what she made. It's more than a garden. It's proof. Of what she's capable of.

"The magazine people are going to lose their minds," I say. "In the best possible way."

Lorna steps into us without pause, slipping between Hudson and me like she's done it a thousand times. Like her body knows exactly where it fits. And it does, right there, shoulder brushing his, hip pressed to mine, solid and steady.

We stand that way for a while, not speaking, not moving. The sun paints everything in honeyed light, and the air smells of crushed grass, skin, and the first hint of summer. It's quiet, but not empty, filled with a kind of tired that feels earned. Full of her. Of us.

Then she exhales, a sound that's almost a laugh. "I need a shower. I'm pretty sure I've got half the garden in my bra."

"We all need showers," Hudson says, voice light enough to pass for casual, but there's a rasp beneath it. His hand flexes on Lorna's shoulder, then his gaze flicks to mine, sharp with mischief. "Question is, do we take them separately... or together?"

He smirks, casual, as if just tossing out a line to make us laugh. But the moment shifts anyway. The air thickens, warmer now, charged, the split second before a storm hits.

Lorna doesn't laugh. She doesn't roll her eyes or toss it back with some dry remark. "Together," she says.

And in that instant, it's no longer a joke.

The walk back to the house stretches and snaps. None of us speaks. There's no need. The silence between us is thick, heavy with everything we haven't said yet, a silence that buzzes in your bones.

In the entrance hall, we run straight into Jack.

He takes in our mud-streaked clothes, flushed faces, and the hum of tension clinging to us like static. His brows lift. Then, with the subtlety of a man who's both seen too much and wants absolutely no part of it, he turns on his heel and vanishes down the opposite hallway.

Twenty minutes later, after sitting Lorna down in the kitchen to eat before we head up to shower, I find Jack in his study. He has one elbow braced against the windowsill, watching the courtyard below as if it might give him answers he can't get from anyone else.

"How bad was she today?" he asks without turning.

I drop into the chair across from his desk. "Bad. Panic attack level bad."

Jack's jaw clenches. He finally looks at me, eyes shadowed with concern. "I've been offering help for weeks. When the contract was up with the previous crew, I told her we could hire another."

"Let me guess—she turned it down flat."

"Said it'd take longer to explain her vision than just doing it herself." He rubs a hand over his face, frustrated. "Swore every detail was already in her head. That bringing anyone else in would mess it up."

"Sounds about right." I sigh. "She's so used to surviving on her own, she doesn't know how to stop. Even when she's drowning."

Jack doesn't argue, only stares out over the landscape like it might tell him what he could have done differently.

"She needs rest," I say after a beat. "Real rest. I'm thinking about taking her home tomorrow."

He nods slowly. "Good. She's done such a spectacular job. It's far beyond what I thought she would be able to accomplish."

"She's an amazing woman," I agree.

From outside, laughter spills in through the open windows, bright and wild, unmistakably Daniel and Lorelai. Jack glances toward the sound, and his expression softens.

"Those two have been a damn delight," he says, shaking his head with a smile. "First few riding lessons were chaos. Daniel fell off twice, and Lorelai tried to make her pony jump a puddle like it was the Grand National. But they're naturals. Smart. Brave. Funny as hell."

I glance out the window at them, cheeks flushed, arms flailing, joy pouring off them in waves. God, I fucking miss them.

Jack leans back in his chair, watching me. "Take her home, make sure she rests. I'll keep the kids here," he continues. "They can finish their riding lessons. Lach's got a whole program for them to go through. They're learning to groom, muck out, jump. They're loving it so far."

"You're sure?"

"Summer's not quite so hard to manage with them around," he says, winking. "Plus, the castle feels different with them here. Like it's waking up again. There's laughter in the bones of it."

I nod. "She'll rest easier knowing they're here and taken care of."

"And when she's ready," Jack says, "she can come back and let us take care of her for once. Maybe a barbecue. Some swimming. We'll get her to really let her hair down."

As if summoned by the weight of our conversation, small feet thunder up the stairs. A second later, Daniel and Lorelai burst into the study, still in their muddy riding gear, cheeks flushed with joy and chaos.

"Uncle Jack!" Lorelai launches herself at his chair. "Sorscha likes me best! She tried to eat my hair three times!"

"That doesn't mean she likes you the best," Daniel grumbles with the solemnity only a six-year-old can muster. "She tries to eat everyone's hair. It's because you smell like the carrots we fed her."

"Do not!"

"Do too."

"Oi!" Jack cuts in before the sibling war escalates. "What's the rule about mud in the house?"

They freeze. "Boots off at the door," they recite in unison.

"And where are your boots now?"

Silence.

"On our feet," Lorelai says, her tone suddenly very small.

"On the carpet," Daniel adds with a wince.

Jack tries for a scowl but only manages a twitch of the lips. "Right then. Go clean up the mess, scrub yourselves spotless, and then we can make some hot chocolate."

They bolt for the door, bickering forgotten in the rush to earn more pony time.

But Daniel stops in the doorway, his words quieter now, more serious. "Mr. Leo, Mr. Hudson? Are you here to bring us home?"

The question lands like a pin drop in the room. Jack glances at me, and I give him the barest nod.

"Daniel," he says carefully, "your mum might need to go home for a little rest. But you two... how would you feel about staying here a while longer? For a proper riding summer school?"

Their faces light up like it's Christmas morning.

"Really?" Lorelai breathes, eyes wide.

"For how long?" Daniel asks, a line of worry between his brows.

"A couple weeks, maybe. If your mum agrees."

"She'll agree," Lorelai says with unwavering confidence. "She wants us to learn new things. And she likes it when we're not asking her questions every five minutes."

Jack barks out a laugh. "Fair enough. Now off you go, before Auntie Charlie sees the state of you and has my head."

They thunder down the hall, already debating what color brushes they'll use tomorrow and whether Sorscha wants her hair braided.

Jack exhales and sinks into his chair. "I'll talk to Lorna in the morning. Frame it like the twins are doing me a favor by keeping Summer entertained."

"She'll see right through that."

"Probably. But she'll also see how happy they are." His tone softens. "They've changed since you lot showed up. More settled. Daniel's started talking about the future. What he wants to be when he grows up. He never used to do that."

My heart rises into my throat as I push to my feet. "I should get back. Before Lorna comes looking and thinks we've been conspiring."

At the door, Jack calls my name. I turn, heart still thudding from everything that just happened.

"Whatever this is between the four of you—I know it's messy. Complicated. But I haven't seen my sister this happy in a long time. Don't fuck it up."

I hold his gaze. "Wasn't planning on it."

"Good." His mouth twitches. "Because if you do, I'll feed you to the sheep."

I grin. "Understood. Death by sheep. Got it."

I'm still grinning as I take the stairs two at a time, the sound of running water tugging me down the hall like a tether. The bathroom door is cracked enough for steam to curl out into the bedroom, thick and fragrant.

"Where the hell have you been?" Hudson calls over the hiss of the shower. "Lorna was two minutes from launching a full-scale search and rescue."

"Had to check on something," I say, already stripping off my shirt. "Miss me?"

"Desperately," Lorna answers, her voice thick with laughter, all lazy warmth. "Now get in here before the hot water runs out."

I don't waste a second. My clothes hit the floor in a trail behind me, and I step into the humid air. Lorna stands with her back to Hudson, her body a study in tension and surrender. Water traces her curves as his fingers work shampoo into her hair. Her head rests against his shoulder, eyes half-shut, lips parted, the barest sound catching in her throat.

"Perfect timing," she murmurs without opening her eyes. "Hudson was telling me about the Great Sheep Crisis."

"There is no crisis," I mutter, stepping in behind her, one hand sliding over the curve of her hip. I press in, anchoring her between us, and feel her melt into me. "The ram's just a dick."

"A dick who chased Levi up a tree," Hudson says, his grin audible. "Twice."

Lorna hums, body soft and boneless now, slick, flushed skin pressed between ours. "Poor Levi," she says, though she doesn't sound the least bit sorry.

I grab the soap and work it into a lather, gliding it over her shoulders, down her arms. She shudders, head tipping forward to give me better access.

It's a slow unraveling after that, touch and motion, skin and breath, the quiet rhythm of care. Fingers gliding across tired muscles, finding the places that make her sigh. Hudson kisses along her neck, slow and open-mouthed, while I sink to my knees, my lips tracing the edge of her hip. Her fingers tangle in both our hair, holding on as if she needs the grounding. She gasps. Groans. Whispers our names until they're the only words she has left.

By the time we make it to the bed, wet and breathless and half-laughing, we're past the point of thought. Every nerve raw. Each inhale shallow.

There's only skin. Want. Heat thrumming beneath the surface.

But the second Lorna's head hits the pillow, she's out. Not fading. Not fighting it. Just gone. One heartbeat she's murmuring softly, and the next her breathing steadies, lips parted, lashes casting long shadows on cheeks still flushed.

Hudson and I freeze.

The heat between us folds in on itself, quiet and clean, replaced by something that doesn't burn at all.

"She's done," Hudson murmurs.

"Completely," I say, adjusting her carefully, easing her more fully against my chest. I brush damp strands of hair from her face. "She ran herself into the ground."

Hudson lowers himself to her other side. The mattress shifts beneath his weight as he tucks in close, his arm curling around her waist. His hand finds mine across the space between us, resting lightly on my side.

It should feel strange. Too much. Too intimate.

But it doesn't.

It feels inevitable.

"She was terrified this morning," he says, barely audible. "Shaking. I've never seen her like that."

"She doesn't let herself fall apart in front of people." My hand moves over her back, slow and steady. "Spent too many years learning she couldn't afford to."

Hudson exhales hard, the sound sharp, almost a growl. "Well, she's not alone anymore."

There's a steel edge to him. Protective. Uncompromising. A vow wrapped in quiet fury.

I look at her, peaceful now, her body slack between ours, and then at him. His expression is softer than I've seen in years.

"How did we get here?" I ask quietly. "Three months ago she barely waved when she passed us on the road."

"Now you'd drop everything for her." He doesn't smile, but it's there in his tone. "Drive two hours on a whim because she butt-dialed you."

"Wouldn't you?"

"In a heartbeat." He swallows. "And that scares the hell out of me."

Silence settles in around us, not awkward or empty, but full. Her breathing is the only sound in the room, soft and steady, anchoring us.

"Leo," he says, quieter now.

"Yeah?"

"When she comes back home and we finally stop pretending we don't know what this is…" His words catch. His fingers press firmer into my side, not grasping, just holding on. "I need you to know. I never stopped. Even when I was supposed to. Even when it wrecked me to walk away."

I know the words he's not saying: *I never stopped loving you.* I press my hand flat to my sternum, trying to hold myself together, trying to quiet the sharp ache cracking through me.

Because I know.

I've always known.

What it cost him to walk away. What it cost both of us to let it go. I thought marrying Ruby meant sealing that part of myself away forever. I thought time and distance would dull it.

But he's always been there. In the corner of every memory that mattered.

"I never stopped either," I say, my voice breaking. "Even when I tried."

# 16

I wake slowly, like surfacing through warm honey. Heat comes first, low and steady, pressed into every inch of me. Then the rise and fall of Leo's chest beneath my cheek. Finally, the hand draped across my waist, fingers spread wide and hot where they rest against my ribs.

Hudson.

I stay still and let it settle. My legs tangled with theirs, my body bracketed by two men who smell like salt and sleep and something distinctly them. Morning light filters through the curtains, hazy and gold. For a heartbeat, maybe more, I don't move. I don't think. I just feel.

Then Leo shifts.

The hard press of him nudges against my hip, thick and obvious beneath his boxers. My breath hitches, quick and quiet, but Hudson hears it. I know he does. His own breathing changes, heavier now, a rough exhale against the back of my neck that sends goosebumps skimming down my spine.

I shift without meaning to. Only a little. And suddenly I feel everything.

Hudson's cock, hard against my lower back. Leo, thick against my thigh. The slow rise of hunger curling under my skin, deep and undeniable.

Mine. Theirs. All of it, waiting.

"Morning," Leo says, voice low and ruined with sleep. The sound of it vibrates straight through his chest, down to where I'm already aching. His hand slides up my spine, fingers tangling in my hair.

"Good morning," I whisper, and when I tip my head back to look at him, I nearly forget how to breathe.

His eyes are half-lidded, pupils blown wide, the kind of look that tells me exactly what he's been dreaming about. And it wasn't sweet. It was filthy.

Hudson shifts behind me, his nose nuzzling the spot where my neck meets my shoulder, and when he speaks, it's a warm brush of lips against skin. "Sleep well?"

I nod, barely, my breath catching as he slips a hand beneath the hem of my sleep shirt, fingers splaying wide against my bare stomach.

The corner of Leo's mouth tips up, making my pulse skip. "Good," he says. "Because we've been lying here for the last hour, watching you sleep." He dips closer, mouth brushing the corner of mine. "Thinking about all the things we want to do to you."

My body snaps tight, loosens, then coils again. "What kind of things?" I ask, my words barely more than sound.

Leo's eyes darken. "The kind that'll have you screaming our names loud enough to wake ghosts in these walls."

Blood rushes to my cheeks. And lower. So much lower.

Hudson laughs softly, his lips still against my skin. "Careful." His hand slides lower, grazing the edge of my panties. "You're going to give her ideas."

"That's the plan," Leo says, not breaking eye contact. "Question is, what's she going to do about them?"

I roll onto my side, facing Leo, bringing our bodies flush. Hudson presses in behind me, pinning me between them, and suddenly I'm all sensation: warm skin and slow friction and the quiet kind of desperation that starts in the chest and spreads.

Leo cups my cheek, thumb brushing slowly over my bottom lip like he's already imagining it parted around him. "Tell me what you want, Lorna."

"You," I say, the word tumbling from my mouth. "Both of you." I don't think I've ever wanted anything more in my entire life.

A flicker passes through Leo's eyes. The desire is still there, but it deepens, rooted now, threaded with more than want, with meaning. Behind me, Hudson goes still, his palm flat against my stomach, holding me steady.

"Lorna," Leo says, quiet and careful, as if the next words might break the air between us. "If we do this, if we go all the way, I want it to be right."

His thumb brushes the skin below my ribcage, grounding me.

"Not rushed," he continues. "Not stolen. No missing pieces."

My throat tightens. "Levi?"

Hudson nods. "He should be here." His voice is so soft it barely clears the air between us.

"You're right," I whisper. And I mean it, even if my body aches at the thought of waiting. This isn't just about the three of us tangled in heat and hunger. It's about all of us. Trust. Balance. A solid foundation for our future.

But then Leo shifts and his hand trails up, fingers sliding from my collarbone to the center of my chest where my heart pounds like a war drum.

"That doesn't mean we can't still take care of you," he says, voice roughened by the very control he's clinging to.

"How?" I ask, breathless. "Show me."

And they do.

God, they do.

What follows is worship in the language of hands and mouths. A liturgy written on skin, spoken in broken moans and whispered names. A sacrament of pleasure, wordless and wild and holy in its own way.

Leo drags open-mouthed kisses down the column of my throat, teeth catching just enough to make my toes curl. Hudson traces shapes on my back, swirls and lines that make my spine arch and my pulse stumble.

"Fuck. Me," Hudson groans. His hand slides over my ribs, cupping my breast. His thumb circles my nipple until it peaks, and I swear the air leaves the room.

Then Leo dips down, his mouth finding the other nipple, hot and wet and slow, and that's it. My brain shorts out.

The contrast of textures, the rough drag of Hudson's fingers, the slick pull of Leo's mouth, it sparks down every nerve ending like I've been rewired to respond only to them.

They work together in sync, switching off, teasing, exploring.

My body starts to tremble, and the sounds leaving my mouth aren't even words anymore. Just soft, broken things that spill out between gasps.

"Please," I whimper, arching into Leo as his hand skims lower, fingers dipping beneath the waistband of my underwear. "I need..."

"We know what you need," Leo murmurs, his voice so wrecked it makes my stomach flip. "Let us give it to you."

He parts my thighs, and a low, guttural sound tears out of him. Behind me, Hudson groans, his hips grinding the curve of my ass like he can't help himself. The hard line of him presses into me, thick and insistent through too many layers.

"Christ, Lorna," Leo breathes, his voice cracked open. "You're drenched."

I really am. Drenched, trembling, already on edge and somehow still unraveling. I've never felt like this before. Not just wet. Not just ready. Seen. Known. Like my body's been waiting for this exact touch my entire life.

Hudson's mouth moves to my throat, open and hot, dragging a long, slow kiss across the curve where my neck meets my shoulder. I tilt my head, offering more, greedy for it, and he hums against my skin like he's thanking me for it.

His hand spans my hip, grounding me as Leo works me open.

I'm barely holding on when I feel Hudson shift behind me, his fingers slipping between my cheeks, spreading me open. He dips his hand lower, stealing some of the slick Leo's coaxed from me, and drags it back, circling the tight ring of muscle at my back entrance with the same quiet focus that makes me want to crawl out of my skin.

The first brush of his finger there makes my breath stutter. It's too much and not enough, a different kind of sensation that sparks heat low in my belly. He doesn't push, just circles, slow and steady, getting me used to the touch. I tense, then melt, the contrast of his gentleness and Leo's intensity pulling a broken sound from my throat.

Hudson leans in, lips at my ear. "You're doing so well, baby," he murmurs, voice rough and full of want. "Let me make you feel even better."

I nod without thinking, body already yielding. And when his fingertip presses in, it's a shock of pleasure that wrestles me right to the edge.

"Be a good girl and come for us," Leo murmurs, the heel of his palm grinding into my clit with devastating precision.

The effect is immediate.

I come hard, my spine arching, muscles clenching around both of their fingers like I can't bear to let them go. Heat surges through my limbs, white-hot and relentless, like my skin's been lit from the inside. The tension snaps all at once, then keeps snapping, wave after wave ripping through me until sound breaks from my throat unbidden. Their names spill from my lips like prayer, like plea, like they're the only anchor keeping me tethered to earth.

The rhythm of their hands doesn't stop. Hudson's mouth lingers at my neck, open and hot, anchoring me while my world narrows to nothing but their bodies, their touch, the raw sounds spilling from my lips.

When it's finally over, I collapse onto Leo's chest, everything gone loose and shaking. My breath stutters. My thighs tremble. My heart hammers like it's trying to punch its way out of me. His arms close around me instantly, holding me tight.

"What about both of you?" I ask, reaching for where they're pressed hard against me.

Hudson catches my hand, brings it to his lips, and presses a kiss to the center of my palm.

"Later," he says. "When we can do this right."

An hour later, we're dressed, barely presentable, and padding barefoot through the castle halls, my hair still damp from the world's quickest shower, my body sore in the best way. Sunlight spills in through the tall windows, casting warm stripes across the stone floor, and I breathe in the smell of coffee and bacon before we even reach the stairs.

From the kitchen, I hear them. Those familiar voices, high-pitched and full of sugar-spiked excitement.

"Mummy!" Lorelai launches at me like a missile the moment I step through the doorway. She barrels into my legs with the entire force of her six-year-old body, her curls wild and her cheeks flushed. "Uncle Jack says you're going home today, but we can stay for proper summer riding school!"

Daniel hovers at my side, quieter but just as bright-eyed. "Can we, Mum? Please? I want to learn how to jump like the Olympic horses."

"I'm going home, am I?" I look over at Jack, eyebrow raised.

He practically glowers at me. "I was going to give Leo time to convince you, but after thinking about it more, I'm going to have to put my foot down and insist."

"Insist?" My voice goes dangerously quiet.

"Yes, insist." He leans forward, elbows on his desk. "Look at yourself, Lorna. You're running on fumes. You've worked yourself ragged for weeks. You're done here. The garden's perfect. The kids want to stay for riding. And you need rest—actual rest. Without stress from the magazine and a break from the kids."

"I can decide when I need rest."

"Can you? Because from where I'm sitting, you'd work yourself into the ground before admitting you need help." His expression softens slightly. "Go home. Let them take care of you. The kids will be fine—better than fine. And you'll come back in a few days actually human again instead of whatever sleep-deprived garden zombie you've been channeling."

I look at Daniel and Lorelai, their faces so hopeful it makes my chest ache. Then at Leo and Hudson, standing quiet and steady like they've been waiting for me to catch up to what everyone else already knows.

I'm exhausted. Bone-deep, soul-tired exhausted. And the thought of the farm, of space and quiet and hands that want to take care of me instead of needing things from me, makes something tight in my chest finally loosen.

"Fine," I say, and it comes out sharper than I mean it to. Then, softer: "Fine. But I'm agreeing because *I* want to, not because I'm being managed like some kind of project."

Jack grins. "Noted."

"Can we stay, Mummy?" Lorelai asks, tugging on my hand.

I crouch to their level, pressing a kiss into Lorelai's forehead as she wriggles with excitement. "Well," I say slowly, "if Uncle Jack doesn't mind having two wildcats terrorizing the ponies for a little while longer..."

"We'll be good," Daniel says, solemn and straight-backed. "And we'll practice our maths and reading every day."

I look at the twins, really study them, and it hits me how settled they are. Happy. Safe.

"All right," I say, and their faces explode into twin beams of joy. "You can stay. But I want daily check-ins. And you have to listen to what Uncle Jack and Aunt Charlie tell you. No arguments."

"We will!" they chorus, practically vibrating with delight.

"And I'll come back and check on you in a few days," I add, my voice catching.

"Well, what are you waiting for?" Jack says, making a shooing motion with his hands. "Get."

I flip him off when the kids aren't looking, but can't keep the smile from my face.

The goodbyes are harder than I want to admit. Lorelai clings to me like a baby koala, her little hands sticky with syrup as she whispers sweet nothings in my ear.

Daniel hugs me tighter than he ever has, his small body fierce and certain. "I hope you really relax," he whispers. "Promise me, Mum."

"I promise." Tears prick behind my eyes. I kiss the top of his head, then Lorelai's. "Be good," I say, voice wobbling. "I love you to the moon and back."

"And all the stars too," they say together, giving me one last hug.

Outside, the air is already warming, the truck packed and waiting. Jack walks us out, the usual gruffness of his voice softened into something quieter.

"Take care of her," he says to Leo and Hudson. "She needs to rest. Really rest."

Leo nods, his hand sliding to the small of my back. "We've got her."

The drive starts quiet. Not tense, more of that rare, heavy calm that settles after a day that wrings you out. Outside, the landscape unfurls in ribbons of green and gold, hills rolling like slow waves under a pale blue sky. I sit in the middle seat, tucked between Leo and Hudson, their warmth wrapping around me until I can't tell where I end and they begin. Our fingers rest loosely tangled in my lap, a quiet promise in the way they hold on, like none of us are ready to let go.

"You're thinking too loudly," Hudson says after twenty minutes, voice low, teasing. He doesn't look over, only slides his hand to my thigh, thumb tracing idle circles through the denim.

"Processing," I murmur. "Yesterday was... a lot."

Leo glances at me then, that steady, grounding look of his. "You were incredible," he says simply. No humor, no edge, only quiet truth. "The gardens looked unreal. Those magazine people are going to lose their minds."

"In the best way," Hudson adds, flashing a grin that feels like sunlight after rain. "Jack's going to be fending off wedding inquiries for months."

A laugh slips out before I can stop it. "I hope so. He deserves it. They all do."

We stop in Stornoway for breakfast, a small café tucked by the harbor, its windows fogged from the morning chill. The place smells like butter and coffee, the kind of cozy that sinks straight into your bones. Chipped teacups, sun-faded menus, a radio humming something old and familiar. Outside, the water shimmers silver and gold whenever the light catches it, and for the first time in weeks, I feel my shoulders loosen. The knot in my chest finally loosens.

When the server sets down our coffees, Leo reaches into his jacket pocket, pulls out a slim silver flask, unscrews the cap, and pours a quick splash into my cup.

I blink at him. "Are you trying to drug me?"

He doesn't even flinch. "Just a splash. Doctor's orders."

"I don't remember asking for a prescription," I mutter, but I take a sip anyway. The heat hits instantly: burning and smooth, with that telltale whisky bite that blooms low in my stomach and loosens everything tangled and tight.

"Preventative medicine," Hudson says, stealing a piece of bacon off my plate. "For panic. Or rage. Or whatever it was that almost made you torch the castle."

"I wasn't having a panic attack," I lie. Badly.

They both give me matching looks: raised brows, unimpressed, and I cave with a groan.

"Fine. Maybe I was spiraling a little."

Leo arches a brow. "Lorna, you sounded like you were five seconds away from salting the earth and declaring yourself Queen of the Ashes."

I wince. "I may have been... slightly dramatic."

Hudson snorts. "Slightly. Just like the Titanic was slightly damp."

I throw a piece of toast at him. He catches it mid-air and pops it into his mouth.

"You're both the worst," I mutter, but the smile is already tugging at my lips.

"Yeah, but you love it."

I roll my eyes, but they're right, and we all know it.

The rest of breakfast drifts by in that easy, golden way, the kind that makes you forget what it's like to feel rushed. Laughter, shared bites, the clink of cups against saucers. When we finally pile back into the truck, the sun's higher, the air softer, and the warmth in my chest feels a lot like contentment.

By the time we get back to the farm, I'm dozy and soft from the whisky and their quiet affection. The fields spread out before us, green and thick and impossibly alive.

"God, I missed this place," I whisper as Leo kills the engine.

"It missed you right back," Hudson says, hopping out of the truck. He turns, hooks an arm around my waist, and pulls me across the seat and out his door. "C'mon," He grins. "Let's go see your babies."

The moment we hit the fields, the rest of the world disappears. The stalks are tall, thick with buds, their heads heavy with color that hasn't quite broken free. I move between them like I'm walking through a dream: brushing fingers across leaves, checking stems, touching the soil. Everything looks strong. Steady. Thriving.

"They're perfect." I pause beside a plant where deep purple peeks through the green. "They'll bloom any day now."

"Levi's been out here every morning," Leo says from behind me. "Taking pictures. Making notes in your journals."

I swear my heart grows three sizes. "He didn't have to do that."

"He wanted to." Leo steps beside me, threading his fingers through mine.

"Thank you," I say, knowing words aren't enough but wanting to say them anyway. "For everything. For showing up. For helping. For..." I trail off, helpless against the wave of feeling. "For seeing me."

Leo's eyes soften. He reaches up and tucks a piece of hair behind my ear, grazing my cheek on the way down.

"Always." He presses a soft kiss to my forehead, then turns toward the barn. I watch him go, still feeling the ghost of his touch on my cheek.

～

I spend the rest of the afternoon in the fields, my hands sunk deep in soil, my body humming with a kind of quiet joy that feels older than language. I move row by row, reacquainting myself with each plant like an old friend: checking leaves, lifting stems, breathing in that sharp, green perfume.

There's something religious about it. The way the dirt clings to my skin, the sun warming the back of my neck, the sweat pooling at the base of my spine. I lose track of time out there, let the rhythm of the work carry me somewhere soft and real. Somewhere I almost forgot I belonged.

By the time the sky starts turning gold, I'm filthy and exhausted and completely at peace. My knees ache, my nails are wrecked, but my heart feels like it's beating in the exact right place.

I take a long shower, letting the hot water wash away the grime and the last remnants of tension. Clean clothes. Damp hair. And then I head downstairs with a different kind of energy humming under my skin.

I can't remember the last time I wanted to cook like this.

I'd taken steaks out of the freezer earlier, thick, well-marbled cuts I've been saving. Potatoes go into the oven to roast slow and lazy while I toss a salad with mint and parsley from the garden, the scent bright and sharp as I tear the leaves with my fingers. Nothing fancy. Just good food, made with love, for the men who've spent six weeks taking care of my farm.

The scent of rosemary and sizzling meat fills the kitchen. That's what brings him in.

I feel him before I see him, that subtle shift in the air that says

Levi's nearby. I turn, and sure enough, there he is. Hair a mess, sunglasses dangling from his shirt, wearing an expression that's equal parts sin and sunshine. And just like that, my brain short-circuits into a reel of very bad ideas.

"Hey," he says, voice rough.

"Hey yourself."

He crosses the kitchen in three long strides, and suddenly I'm wrapped in him, solid and warm and smelling like earth and work and home. His hand cups my face, thumb brushing my cheeks as he searches my eyes.

"You look better," he murmurs.

"I feel better."

"Good." Then he kisses me. Not gentle. Not tentative. Deep and claiming, making up for every day we've been apart. His other hand slips to the small of my back, pulling me flush to him, and I melt into it with a sound that's half relief, half hunger.

When we finally pull apart, I'm breathless and flushed, my fingers tangled in his shirt.

"I missed you," I whisper near his lips.

"Missed you too." He tilts my chin up, eyes searching mine. "Leo said yesterday was... a lot."

"It was," I admit, my hands flattening against his chest. "But I'm here now. And I'm better."

His thumb traces my jaw, tender and possessive all at once. "I'm so happy you're home."

"Yeah," I whisper. "Me, too."

Within minutes, Leo and Hudson appear, drawn by scent, instinct, or that magnetic pull that seems to hum between us now. They slip into the rhythm of the kitchen like they've always belonged here. Leo grabs plates without being asked. Hudson sets out cutlery, humming under his breath. Levi uncorks the wine, pouring with the kind of quiet reverence that turns it into something sacred.

"We're eating out on the porch," I tell them. "It's too pretty an evening to waste indoors."

The deck overlooks the fields, the light spilling across the rows in molten gold. Beyond them, the hills stand guard. Leo builds a fire in the stone pit while Hudson sets the table. When we finally sit, the air is thick with woodsmoke, the clink of cutlery and the sound of home.

"To taking care of each other," I say, lifting my glass and meeting each of their eyes in turn. "In all the ways that matter."

We eat slowly, savoring everything, the food, the company, the quiet rhythm we've found again. The conversation drifts from the farm to the twins to the gardens. The sun sinks behind the hills, smearing the sky in rose and lavender. The fire pops beside us, little bursts of sound marking the easy flow of laughter.

Time smears at the edges. It feels like an evening that could last forever. But the light begins to fade, the air cools, and everything tilts.

"We need to talk," Leo says, and the tone of his voice makes my stomach drop. Not dramatically, just that quiet, sinking feeling that tells you something's about to change.

My hands freeze halfway to my glass. "Okay."

Levi exhales, running his fingers through his hair. "We know this isn't... conventional. It's not what any of us pictured."

"But it's what we want," Hudson says softly.

Leo's gaze locks onto mine, steady and unflinching. "Do you want this, Lorna? All of it, the messy, complicated, the beautiful? Are you really in this with us, for real? Because if you're not, we have to stop now. I can't risk the twins getting caught in the middle."

"The twins?" My voice comes out small.

"They're already attached." Leo's throat works as he swallows. "And if you wake up one day and decide you want something simpler, something easier, then they're the ones who'll pay for it. And I can't..." He stops, the words fraying at the edges. "I can't be the reason they lose this."

God. Of course I've thought about this, turned it over in my head until it kept me up at night, but hearing that they have too? It guts me.

"I'm in," I say, and the words feel like the most honest thing I've ever spoken. "Not just here for now. Not just curious. Committed. To this. To all three of you."

"Thank fuck," Hudson mutters.

"Even if it's messy?" Levi asks.

"Especially then," I say, a smile tugging through the ache in my throat. "I'm done with easy. Done with safe. Done pretending fear is a good enough reason to keep my heart locked away."

Hudson grins. "Good. Because this is about to get really messy."

"And very, very hot," Leo adds, his voice dropping low and rough enough to scrape over every nerve ending I have. It skitters down my spine, leaving a trail of heat in its wake.

My pulse trips. The air between us hums, too charged, too heavy to ignore.

"So what happens now?" I ask, though the answer is already thrumming beneath my skin.

Leo stands, extending his hand toward me.

"Now I take you upstairs and we stop pretending we don't know exactly what we want."

My heart trips as I lace my fingers with his, breath catching somewhere between a laugh and a curse. "What about—?"

He squeezes my hand, gaze unwavering. "Hudson and Levi will stay down here," he says. "We've already talked about what comes next. We don't want to rush this. Each of us wants to really be with you one-on-one before anything happens with all of us together." He swallows, voice rough. "But only if that's what you want too."

"Yes," I whisper, desire burning low in my belly. "That's exactly what I want."

I glance at the other two. Levi's smiling, that quiet, steady kind of smile that says *go on*. Hudson, naturally, is giving me that exaggerated eyebrow waggle that belongs in a rom-com blooper reel. The laugh slips out before I can stop it. I blow them both a kiss and turn toward the door, heart pounding as I step inside.

Leo follows me inside, his presence a weight at my back, solid, scorching, overwhelming in the best way. In the kitchen, I barely make it two steps before he's there, crowding me against the counter.

"I've wanted you for so fucking long," he growls near my ear, voice dark and frayed at the edges. His grip tightens on my hips, drawing me in until our bodies align. "Every night I've thought about it. How you'll feel when I finally sink into you. Slow at first, just to hear those little sounds you make. Then hard enough to make you forget everything but my name."

"You have me," I whisper, tilting my head to bare my throat. "I'm yours, Leo. I've been yours."

That's all it takes.

His control shatters like glass. One heartbeat we're talking, the next, I'm lifted onto the counter, thighs parted around his hips, his mouth crashing into mine with a desperation that ignites every nerve in my body. His hands everywhere at once, tangled in my hair, sliding down my spine, gripping my hips like he's terrified I might disappear if he doesn't hold on tight enough.

"Upstairs," he says against my mouth. "I want you in a proper bed. I'm not doing this rushed or half-dressed on a countertop. I want all of you. Spread out."

He doesn't wait for a yes. He doesn't need it. I'm already saying it with the way I wrap myself around him.

He carries me up the stairs like I weigh nothing, and the ease of it, the careful way he holds me, nearly undoes me.

When we reach my room, he sets me down beside the bed, his hands slipping beneath the hem of my shirt, his voice rough when he asks, "I want this to be perfect for you, Lorna. Tell me exactly what you want."

The question slices right through me. I don't hesitate.

"I want you to take control," I say. "I want to stop thinking about everything but you."

His eyes go dark. Not with lust alone. With possession. "Are you sure?"

"Yes."

"Because once I start, I'm not stopping. I'm going to ruin you for anyone else. I'm going to mark you."

"Do it," I whisper, fingers already tugging at his shirt. "Leo, please."

And then I'm his.

He strips me slowly, his mouth following his hands. Collarbone. Hip. The soft curve beneath my breast. By the time I'm bare, I'm trembling, wound so tight I can barely breathe.

He steps back, his gaze raking over my skin.

"Fuck," he groans, voice raw. "Look at you."

When he finally joins me on the bed, there's a pause, just long enough to make butterflies explode in my stomach. And then it's skin on skin and everything inside me combusts. He's nothing but muscle and soft skin as he lowers over me. He leans in, chest to chest, and the scrape of his chest hair against my nipples makes me jerk, hips lifting instinctively, a raw little sound tearing out of me before I can stop it. His thighs bracket mine, holding me in place, grounding me. And his hands, God, his hands, cradle my face like I'm the most precious thing in the world.

I close my eyes, just for a second, because the closeness is too much. Too good. Too real.

"Open your eyes, Lorna," he says.

So I do. And it feels like free-falling straight into him.

His touch drifts down between us until he finds me swollen and wet, throbbing with need. The sound he makes is low and wrecked, like it claws its way out of his chest before reaching his throat.

"You're so fucking wet," he rasps, pressing his forehead to mine. "Fuck, Lorna."

He eases two fingers inside, working me open with a pace slow enough to make me whimper. He moves with maddening control, curling and stroking until another wave of slickness spills free and my hips lift to meet him.

His mouth follows, grazing down my throat, over the swell of my breast, his tongue dragging over my nipple before he sucks it deep. Heat shoots straight through my core. My back arches off the bed, a gasp tearing from my throat. I'm shaking now, wound so tight every nerve ending feels like it's on fire, my hips chasing friction, chasing him.

And then, finally, I feel the thick, blunt press of him nudging against my entrance.

My lungs lock, muscles taut with anticipation.

He reaches down and drags himself along my slit with a low curse that sounds like surrender. "Look at me," he says, voice rough as gravel.

I force my eyes open. Meet his gaze. The intensity there steals the air from my chest.

The first inch sinks in, slow enough to steal the air from my lungs. My body clenches, caught between wanting and surrender, the fullness already dizzying. A sound slips out of me, somewhere between a gasp and a plea.

"Fuck," he groans, and I feel the tremor run through him. "Do you have any idea how many times I've imagined what this would feel like?"

He pushes deeper, and the pressure is dizzying, pleasure edged with the sweetest burn. Then he stills. Just holds there, letting me adjust, letting me feel every impossible inch. I clench around him, trying to pull him deeper, the fullness making my eyes water.

"Christ, Lorna." His voice shreds down my spine, wrecked. "You're gripping me like a fucking vice."

My nails bite into his shoulders, my legs locking high around his hips like I'm trying to fuse us together.

"I need more," I gasp, the words snagging in my throat. "Need you to fuck me, Leo. Hard. Deep. All of it."

His groan is filthy, feral. It vibrates against my throat as he leans in, grinding deeper. "Yeah? You want this cock to ruin you, baby? Want me to stretch this pretty little cunt until you can't even remember your own name?"

"Yes." It's a whimper and a challenge. "Please. Leo."

He shifts, pushes in another thick inch, then another, dragging it out like he's savoring my unraveling. His eyes are locked on my face, hungry and possessive, like every twitch, every moan is another notch in his belt.

"Look at you. Taking every inch like you were made for this cock. Like this pussy's been waiting for me to fill it."

A moan claws out of me, loud and broken. "Then do it," I whisper, arching into him, nails raking down his back. "Don't make me beg, Leo. Just *fuck me.*"

That's all it takes.

He drives the rest of the way in, and the sound that rips from us is pure sin. The stretch is exquisite, the weight of him filling me until I'm trembling. My body clenches around him on instinct, pleasure cresting so sharp it borders on pain.

We freeze there, breathing each other in. Skin slick, hearts pounding as if we've survived something, or started something we might not survive at all.

It doesn't feel like sex. It feels like a claim, a mark burned deep.

"Jesus fuck," he groans. "I didn't know it could feel this good."

And I believe him, because I've never felt anything like this either.

"You're mine," he growls, voice shaking. "Say it."

"Yours," I gasp, legs wrapping around him. "All yours. Only yours."

"Good fucking girl." His rhythm starts slow, each thrust driving deeper, claiming more. I can't think, can't speak, can't do anything but feel.

His hands grip my hips like he owns them, like he's claiming every inch of me with every brutal, perfect thrust. He drops his weight just enough to grind his pubic bone against my clit, and the friction sparks a sharp, desperate whine from deep in my chest.

"Fuck, that's it," he pants, mouth dragging over my throat, open and filthy. His teeth catch beneath my jaw before he bites down, not hard enough to mark, but enough to send a lightning bolt straight through me. My body clenches around him in response, instinctive, desperate, begging for more.

He braces his elbows on either side of my head, caging me in. His hands cup my face, thumbs tracing slow circles across my cheeks, impossibly gentle beside the rough rhythm of our bodies colliding. The contrast is dizzying. His care and his control. His hunger and my unraveling.

Every thrust drives me higher. The rhythm is brutal, perfect, a relentless press and grind that has me drowning in it, in him. He fits so deep I swear I can feel him in my throat, but it's the friction that unravels me. The constant drag of his cock over the swollen, aching spot just inside, and the way his pelvis grinds hard into mine at the end of each thrust, rubbing my clit with every stroke. Not directly. Not gentle. Just pressure. Dense and maddening and *exactly* what I need.

The sensation builds sharp and tight between my legs, white-hot and insistent. My cunt pulses around him, overworked and overwhelmed, the burn turning to heat turning to something unbearable. It's too much and not enough, every nerve ending screaming for release, for relief, for more.

I'm soaked, every inch of me slick with sweat and want. The filthy rhythm of our bodies meeting only drags me closer to the edge. Deep inside, my muscles flutter and tighten with each thrust, pleading for release, desperate to fall apart while he's still buried inside me.

"That's it," he grits out, hips snapping forward with more force, grinding his pubic bone into me until sparks dance behind my eyelids. "It feels good, doesn't it baby? Having my cock inside you?"

"Leo—" It's a sob, a plea, a warning. I can't get enough air. The air feels too thick, too hot, and I can't tell where his body ends and mine begins.

He lifts his head, eyes catching mine, pinning me there. His pupils are blown wide, his jaw tight, mouth swollen and wrecked from all the places he's been. "God, you're gorgeous," he rasps. "Let go for me, beautiful. Let me see you fall apart."

And I do.

It rips through me, hot and endless. My body clenches around him, thighs locking, spine bowing tight as I come apart beneath him. The world narrows to the way he holds me, fills me, fucks me through every last wave.

His name tears from my throat like it's the only word I've ever known.

And still, he doesn't look away. His eyes stay locked on mine, wild and burning and wrecked.

"God, Lorna. Fuck."

He drives deep and holds, hips pressed flush to mine, arms shaking from the effort to stay grounded. His gaze stays fixed on me for one final, shattered second. Then he breaks.

His forehead drops to mine. A groan tears out of him as he comes, cock twitching inside me, his whole body trembling with it. The sound pulls another wave from me. My walls flutter around him, and it hits us again, sharp and consuming.

We stay still, caught in the aftershock. Our breathing evens into something raw and quiet. His weight holds me there, skin slick against mine. My fingers remain tangled in his hair. He stays deep inside me, as if he belongs there, as if any movement would shatter the fragile thing we've just pieced together.

There's no space between us. Not an inch. Not a thought. Only him.

Eventually, he eases out of me with a quiet groan, then shifts, rolling onto his back and pulling me with him. My body follows without thought, pliant and aching, every nerve still humming. He settles me on his chest, one arm banded around my waist, the other sliding up to cradle the back of my head like he can't bear the idea of space between us.

He traces the length of my spine, slow and soothing, over skin that still feels too sensitive. His lips brush my temple. He doesn't speak right away.

Then, quietly, almost shy, he asks, "Was that what you needed?"

I lift my head and meet his eyes. He looks undone in the soft light. Skin glowing with sweat. Mouth swollen. Curls mussed from my hands. Heart wide open.

"That was perfect," I murmur, my voice barely more than a breath. "Absolutely perfect."

His arms tighten. I sink into him, muscles loose, thoughts quiet.

Sleep pulls at me from the edges, heavy and sweet, and I don't fight it. Not with him wrapped around me. Not with his heartbeat steady against my cheek and his hand still buried in my hair.

This isn't the aftermath of something reckless.

It's the start of something real.

**17**

---

The stack of mail on my kitchen counter has been taunting me since I got back. Bills, seed catalogs, the usual detritus of adult life that accumulates when you're too blissed out on good sex and even better company to care about mundane responsibilities.

I'm still floating on cloud nine from last night with Leo, my body humming with the kind of satisfaction that comes from being thoroughly, completely claimed. The memory of his touch, his mouth, the way he whispered filthy words against my skin makes me shiver even now, alone in my kitchen with nothing but tea and correspondence for company while I wait for the guys to finish with their evening chores.

I flip through the envelopes absently, tossing junk mail into the bin, setting aside what looks important. Then I freeze, my breath catching as I stare at the elegant letterhead in my hands.

My pulse kicks in my throat as I tear open the envelope, fingers trembling slightly. The letter is printed on heavy cream paper, official and intimidating.

*Dr. E. L. Mackenzie,*

*We are pleased to invite you to present as keynote speaker at the 15th*

*Annual European Women's Health Conference in Copenhagen this October. Your groundbreaking research on female physiological response patterns has garnered significant attention in our community...*

I sink into a kitchen chair, reading the same paragraph three times before the words actually penetrate. They want me to give a keynote. A full-hour presentation, followed by Q&A. On the main stage, in front of hundreds of researchers, doctors, and academics.

On my own research.

My *secret*, pseudonymous research.

*—we believe your insights into the neurological and physiological mechanisms of female sexual response could revolutionize how we approach women's health and pleasure...*

My phone is in my hand before I consciously decide to reach for it, fingers flying over the keyboard.

**Me:** *Can you come over? Got some news today. Not bad, just—I need to talk to someone.*

The response comes back immediately.

**Levi:** *On my way.*

Five minutes later, he's standing in my kitchen doorway, hair windblown, as if he'd run the whole way, eyes creased with concern. "What's wrong? Are you okay?"

I wordlessly hand him the letter, watching his face as he reads. His expression shifts from worry to surprise to a quiet, fierce pride.

"Lorna," he breathes, looking up at me. "This is incredible. Do you understand what this means?"

"It means they want me to stand in front of hundreds of people and talk about..." I gesture helplessly. "You know. Female orgasms. In explicit detail. On a stage. With microphones. And probably cameras."

"It means they recognize you as a leading expert in your field," Levi says firmly. "It means your work matters. That you could influence how an entire generation of medical professionals approaches women's health."

I slump back in my chair, overwhelmed. "I can't do this, Levi. I'm a flower farmer now. A mother. I'm not a keynote speaker."

He sets the letter down and crouches in front of my chair, taking my hands in his. "You're Dr. Lorna MacLeod, brilliant researcher and the woman who's spent years studying something that affects half the population. You're exactly who should be giving this talk."

"But what if I mess it up? What if they ask questions I can't answer? What if…"

"What if you don't go," he interrupts gently, "and spend the rest of your life wondering what might have happened if you'd been brave enough to try?"

The words cut straight through my spiral of anxiety to the truth underneath. "You think I should do it."

"I think you should put together a presentation and practice giving it to us. See how it feels." His eyes hold mine. "Do you miss it? The research? The academic world?"

The question catches me off guard, mostly because I've been trying not to think about the answer. "Yes," I admit quietly. "I miss feeling like my mind matters for something other than remembering which flowers go where."

"Then it's pretty simple, isn't it?" Levi stands, pulling me up with him. "Come on. Let's go outside. Clear your head."

The evening air wraps around us like silk, soft and still carrying the day's fading warmth. Jasmine drifts in from somewhere behind the garden wall. And beneath it all, there's the faintest trace of loch water curling in from the distance, clean and mineral and cool.

Above us, the sky has settled into that impossible shade of electric blue that only exists for a breath. The moment after the sun disappears, before the dark fully arrives. That sliver of time when everything feels suspended.

"Give me one second," Levi murmurs, ducking back inside.

He returns with a thick wool blanket and spreads it over the slope behind my farmhouse. We lie down side by side, limbs not quite touching but close enough to feel the pull. The sky opens above us, vast and endless, scattered with stars just beginning to show, shy and trembling.

"You know what I love about astronomy?" Levi asks, his voice quiet, as if he's afraid to disturb the night.

I turn toward him. "What?"

"How small it makes everything else feel. All the things we let keep us up at night, the fear, the self-doubt, the stories we tell ourselves about why we're not enough." He lifts his arm, gesturing up at the Milky Way as it threads itself across the sky, a soft river of fractured light. "There are billions of stars. Billions of galaxies. And here we are, terrified to speak up. To try."

His profile is haloed in moonlight, sharp jaw, dark lashes, the soft curve of his mouth.

"Are you trying to make me feel better or worse?"

His laugh is low and velvety, wrapping around me like another blanket. "Better. Because if we're small, then so are our fears. So is failure. But the things we do, the good we put out there, the moments we choose to try anyway, they echo. Sometimes further than we know."

I think about his words as the sky deepens into black velvet. The moon's only a sliver, a quiet suggestion of light. Orion's belt gleams sharp above us, the North Star steady, Cassiopeia barely a whisper on the horizon.

"It's beautiful," I breathe, the words slipping out with the last of my tension.

"*You're* beautiful," Levi murmurs, rolling toward me on the blanket, propped on one elbow. His touch drifts over my cheek, featherlight. "And brilliant. And brave. Even when you forget."

There's no defense against that kind of honesty. Not when his voice roughens like that, low and certain. Not when it slides beneath my skin and burns hot in my chest.

"We need to talk about the conference," I say, partly because I need to anchor myself in something academic, and partly because I love hearing him talk. "I don't even know where to start. What would I say? Like, specifically."

"You tell me," he says, his hand coming to rest on my hip, a warm weight through my clothes. "Pretend I'm your audience. What's the most important thing you want them to know?"

A blush rises before I can stop it. "Like... in detail?"

"Yes, Lorna." His mouth quirks slightly. "In detail. This is science, not porn. There's a difference."

But there's a spark in his voice, playful, edged with challenge.

I inhale slowly, finding that familiar switch inside me, the one that turns nerves into composure, thoughts into sentences. The voice I use when I'm writing, presenting, lecturing. "Most people think the female orgasm is binary. Clitoral or vaginal, like we've all been handed a multiple-choice test with only two answers. But it's so much more intricate than that."

"Go on." His voice is softer now. Encouraging. But I catch it, that hitch in his breath, the subtle tension in the way his thumb strokes a small, tight circle at my waist.

"There are at least seven types," I continue, voice steadier than I feel. "Clitoral. Vaginal. Cervical. A-spot. U-spot. Blended. There's a spectrum of pleasure most people don't even realize exists."

He nods, gaze steady, unreadable, focused entirely on me.

"The G-spot isn't a myth, despite what some frustrating publications have claimed. It's actually part of a larger structure. The clitoral network includes the clitoris, the urethra, and the anterior vaginal wall. It's all erectile tissue. It's all interconnected."

His hand anchors at my hip for a heartbeat, and I swear I feel it through every nerve ending.

"What else?" he asks. Voice a little rougher now.

"The nerve clusters involved are fascinating," I say, shifting slightly on the blanket. The movement brings me closer to him, my thigh brushing his. I pretend it's accidental. It's not. "Pudendal, pelvic, hypogastric. They respond differently depending on the type of stimulation. We've seen entirely different brain activity during clitoral orgasm versus cervical. And don't even get me started on blended responses—the whole other hemisphere lights up."

"Tell me more."

"Hormones. Oxytocin. Prolactin. Endorphins." I'm getting flushed now, animated in that way I get when I talk about this stuff with people who actually listen. "The release varies with type and intensity. But more than that, it's the psychological impact. Women who understand their anatomy—who advocate for their needs—report significantly higher satisfaction. Emotional, physical, relational. It makes a huge difference."

There's a pause.

And then, in a voice so low it barely registers. "You are absolutely fucking brilliant."

It's not only the words that lodge in my throat; it's the way he says them. "You're not saying that because I'm talking about orgasms, are you?"

His laugh is quiet, but it ripples through me like a current. "No," he says. "But it definitely doesn't hurt."

The way he looks at me then, eyes full of pride and heat and something terrifyingly close to tenderness—I know this moment's already carved itself into memory.

"Did that... did talking about orgasms turn you on?" I ask, teasing, even though I can barely get the words out.

Mischief sparks in his eyes. "Did it turn *you* on?" he counters, his voice gone rough around the edges. His hand slides from my hip, knuckles grazing under the hem of my sweater until his fingers find the waistband of my jeans. "Because I think maybe it did."

It did turn me on. The way he listened. The way he looked at me as if I were the smartest woman alive. The way he didn't flinch when I said "blended orgasm" but leaned in, curious, like I'd just handed him the secret to the universe.

"Maybe," I whisper.

"I think I'd like to find out," he murmurs, fingers already working open the button of my jeans. The zipper hums down, loud in the quiet, teeth rasping through the dark. Cool air brushes my skin as he slips beneath the fabric, skin to skin, and finds me.

He drags in a sharp inhale. "Jesus, Lorna. You're soaked."

I gasp at the contact, hips lifting instinctively toward his touch.

Above us, the stars seem to throb in time with my heartbeat, the vast universe suddenly contained in this moment, this blanket, this man's hands on my body. "Levi..."

"Should we do some research?" he asks. "Prove that the G-spot is real once and for all?"

I nod, but it's not really an answer. It's surrender. "Prove it," I breathe, already unraveling beneath his touch.

And he does.

He eases my jeans down inch by inch, denim snagging on my thighs before slipping lower, his skin grazing mine, heat and chill tangling together. His mouth follows the path, languid, teasing, lips brushing my hipbone, tongue flicking over the hollow just below it. Each exhale hits my stomach in a warm shiver. The night air rushes in to fill the space he leaves, cool and biting where his hands have traced fire. My pulse stumbles. The stars blur.

When he slides his fingers inside me, I'm already trembling. He's focused, intent, working deeper until he presses against that firm, ridged spot tucked high inside. The sound that slips out is half gasp, half plea. My back lifts off the blanket, hips chasing the pressure, desperate for more. Every nerve sparks to life, sharp and hungry.

"There," Levi murmurs, lips grazing fragile skin as his fingers curl again, more deliberate this time. "Found it."

A moan tears out of my throat. It's not quiet. It's not delicate or graceful or anything I could package into a soundbite. It's raw. Shattering. The kind of pleasure that starts in my chest and rushes outward, breaking open everything I've been trying so hard to hold together.

I can't speak. Can't think. I can only move, hips chasing his hand, head tipping back into the night. The sensations layer like poetry, the cool press of grass under my hand, the solid weight of his body braced beside mine, the sky stretching infinitely above us. And Levi, his hands, his breath, the exquisite pressure of his fingers coaxing me apart piece by piece.

When his thumb presses against my clit, the angle and pressure exactly right, pleasure detonates through me. I cry out, the sound tearing free and vanishing into the night.

"Perfect," he breathes, coaxing me through the aftershocks with slow, steady strokes. "Absolutely fucking perfect."

Before my pulse can settle, he's already peeling off our clothes. His movements urgent, hungry, a little unsteady like he's been holding back for too long. My shirt first, then his. Jeans kicked away in the dark. And then there's skin. Heat. The press of his body against mine, solid and overwhelming.

He reaches for his phone in the pocket of his discarded jeans and, after a beat, soft music begins to drift between us. A slow, aching melody.

Levi kisses me with intent, tender at first, then deeper, searching, as if he's trying to uncover every place I've ever hidden. When he finally draws back, just enough to meet my gaze, his voice is rough with need. "I want to make love to you under the stars," he says. "I want the universe to know you're mine."

And then he's pushing inside me, slow, deep, and all-consuming, and I forget how to breathe. The stretch, the heat, the rightness of being filled by someone I trust so completely. There's nothing careful in the way we come together. Only need. Only us.

I wrap my legs around his waist and pull him in, the way I've been aching to for what feels like forever. He moves inside me, each thrust measured, as though he's etching a vow into my skin. Above us, the stars spin and blur, ancient and watchful, and for the first time, I don't feel small beneath them.

I feel infinite.

Starlight spills across his face, catching on his cheekbones, jaw, the stubborn curve of his mouth. I trace each line with my fingertips, learning him by touch and breath, as if I could keep him this way, etched beneath my skin.

"I love your mind," he rasps, punctuating each word with a slow roll of his hips. "I love the way you light up when you talk about your research. I love how you see the world. How you see me."

And I'm undone. Not by his hands or his mouth or the way he's moving inside me, but by his words. By the fact that he sees every messy, brilliant, scared part of me and still wants this. Still wants me.

I bury my face in his neck, breathing him in, warm skin, salt, summer grass, pressing my mouth to the hollow of his throat.

"God," he groans. "I know I probably shouldn't say this with my cock inside you." He laughs then, low and breathless, the sound rough with disbelief. "Christ, listen to me. I sound insane. But I think I'm in love with you."

A laugh catches in my throat, shaky and wet. "Me too, Levi," I whisper. The words feel huge, dangerous, true. "So fucking much."

We move as one, bodies meeting and parting in a rhythm older than time. His exhales ghost my neck, his grip tightens on my hips, and the world collapses to the space between us. It feels sacred, etched into our bones. When I come, it's with his name on my lips and tears slipping hot down my cheeks, from the unbearable, beautiful weight of it all, the stars wheeling above, the wind whispering through the leaves, and the man inside me who sees every part of me and still chooses to stay.

Levi follows a breath later, burying himself deep as his release tears free in a sound that echoes into the night, carried on the same breeze that stirs the tall grass and ripples across the loch. The world feels impossibly still in the aftermath, a quiet buzz lingering under my skin.

He gathers me close, both of us trembling, breathless, the night still thrumming around us. The blanket beneath us is warm and tangled, carrying the scent of grass and skin. He pulls a corner over our cooling bodies and folds me against his chest, holding me as if he could keep the night itself from touching me.

"Thank you," I whisper against the curve of his collarbone, lips brushing salt and skin.

"For what?"

"For seeing me," I say, throat tight. "For believing in me. For reminding me who I am underneath all the chaos and fear."

His arms tighten around me. "You're extraordinary, Lorna. You always have been. Don't let the world make you forget."

Eventually, the air turns cool. Goosebumps rise on my skin despite the blanket. Levi sits up, gathering our scattered clothes without a word. But when I reach for my boots, he stops me with a shake of his head.

"Let me," he murmurs, and then he's lifting me, effortless.

The change from the open field to the glow of my farmhouse feels startling in the best way. He carries me up the narrow stairs, holding me close, and lays me on the bed with a care that makes my chest ache.

He presses a kiss to my forehead. "Stay here."

He disappears into the bathroom and returns with a warm washcloth.

"You don't have to..." I start.

But he cuts me off with a look. "I want to. Let me take care of you."

When he's finished, he climbs into bed beside me, pulling me to his chest. His fingers thread through my hair, and his voice drops low.

"You're going to be incredible at that conference," he says against my temple. "All those women who've been taught their bodies are wrong, or shameful, or broken, you're going to help them reclaim something that should've been theirs all along."

His voice is steady, certain, like he can see the future and it's already written.

"Sleep, beautiful," he murmurs, his fingers still moving through my hair. "Dream about changing the world."

When I wake the next morning, the other side of the bed is empty but still warm. Voices float up from the kitchen, overlapping with clinking dishes and the unmistakable sound of Leo having a very serious discussion about the best way to cook bacon.

I tug on Levi's shirt from the night before, bare-legged, hair a wild mess, and make my way downstairs.

The sight nearly knocks my feet out from under me.

Leo at the stove, sleeves rolled up, working three pans at once with the easy confidence of someone who knows exactly what he's doing. Hudson at the counter whisking pancake batter, flour dusting his forearms and a smear of it across his jaw. Levi at the table with his laptop open, coffee steaming beside him, reading glasses perched on his nose.

My kitchen. My space. Filled with them.

They're talking, low voices, easy laughter, the kind of comfortable rhythm that comes from years of friendship. The coffee's already brewed. The table's set. There's a vase of wildflowers I didn't pick sitting in the center.

It's so...domestic. So utterly *them*. Like they've always been here. Like they belong.

A fault line opens in my chest.

I've spent so long doing everything alone, managing the farm, raising the kids, holding it all together with white-knuckled determination. And here they are, in my kitchen at dawn, making me breakfast as if it's the most natural thing in the world.

Leo glances up and catches me staring. His face softens. "Morning, sweetheart. Sleep okay?"

I can't speak. Can barely breathe around the knot in my throat.

"There she is." Hudson sets down his whisk and comes to me, pulling me into a hug that smells of sugar and sunshine. "The brilliant keynote speaker herself."

"We're making breakfast," Leo says from the stove, flipping something that sizzles. "You're going to need your brain firing on all cylinders today."

"And once you're fed," Levi adds, eyes lifting from his screen, "we're getting to work. I pulled all your published papers last night, sorted by topic, citation strength, and relevance to the keynote themes. Built you an outline to start from."

I stare at him. At the neat stacks of printouts beside his laptop. At the color-coded tabs.

"You did what?"

"You're not doing this alone," he says simply, as if it's obvious.

My throat goes tight. I've prepared every lecture, every paper, every presentation by myself for years. Late nights at the kitchen table with cold coffee and the weight of doubt pressing on my shoulders. Nobody to bounce ideas off. Nobody to tell me it was good enough.

And here's Levi, who spent hours organizing my entire body of work while I slept.

"You're all completely mad," I manage, and my voice comes out rough.

"Mad about you," Hudson says, grinning as he releases me and darts back to rescue a pancake before Leo can shove him away from the stove.

Leo catches my attention over Hudson's shoulder. His expression is soft, knowing. Like he can see exactly what this means to me.

And he probably can.

An hour later, belly full of Leo's perfectly crisp bacon and Hudson's lopsided but shockingly delicious pancakes, I'm seated at my kitchen table. Levi slides his laptop in front of me, open to a blank document.

I crack my knuckles. Take a breath. And start to type.

*"Female Sexual Response: Beyond the Myths"*

*Dr. Lorna MacLeod*

My fingers hover for a moment. Then I add one more line:

*Supported by the unwavering love and encouragement of Leo Robinson, Hudson Walker, and Levi Walker.*

# 18

The guys head back to their farm after breakfast, each of them kissing me goodbye with the kind of lingering promise that makes it hard to let go. They've got their own work waiting for them, things they've been putting off for too long and can no longer wait.

I don't mind. I've got my own work to do.

I spend the day in the dahlia field, moving methodically through the rows with my notebook and stakes. Each plant gets assessed, labeled, notes taken on bloom size and color intensity. The ones showing signs of stress get extra fertilizer. Weeds get pulled. It's the kind of quiet, focused work that lets my mind drift while staying busy.

By late afternoon, my back aches and my knees protest every time I stand, but the field looks immaculate. Organized. Under control.

The house is too quiet when I finally make it inside. I reheat last night's steak and potatoes and eat standing at the counter, scrolling through my conference notes on my phone. The guys have their own chaos tonight—Leo texted earlier about a fence break, then again about a burst pipe in the barn.

Just me. The hum of the refrigerator. The settling sounds of an old house.

I should be used to this. I was alone for years before they came into my life. But now the silence feels different. Heavier. A piece of me is missing.

I finish my dinner, rinse the plate, and head upstairs with my chamomile tea and the stack of research papers I've been meaning to review.

The text comes as I'm settling into bed.

**Hudson:** *Come over. I want to show you what I've been working on.*

I stare at the message, a low burn pooling in my belly at the casual command in those words. It's nearly nine o'clock, the sun painting the sky in amber and rose, but his tone, even through text, makes me reach for my boots without hesitation.

**Me:** *On my way.*

The walk across the fields to their farmhouse takes about ten minutes, long enough for my pulse to pick up, for curiosity to edge into anticipation. Long enough to wonder what Hudson Walker wants to show me at this hour, when the day's work is done and the night feels like an open invitation.

I expect him to answer the front door, maybe lead me to the kitchen for a late dinner or the living room for wine and conversation. Instead, he's waiting by the side gate, silhouetted against the dying light, arms crossed like he's nervous.

"Hey," he says, that crooked smile spreading across his face as I approach. "Thanks for coming."

"What's up?" I ask as he takes my wrist and leads me not toward the house, but around it, toward the workshop.

"There's something I've been wanting to do with you," he says, voice quiet with an edge of vulnerability that makes my chest tighten.

The door is painted sage green, its surface softened and scarred by years of Highland wind and rain. Hudson pauses at the latch, shoulders tense, a flicker of uncertainty crossing his face. For the first time, he looks younger. Unsure. Almost boyish in his hesitation.

"I don't usually work in here with anyone," he admits, not quite meeting my eyes. "It's... mine, you know? The one place that's for me."

The significance of the invitation settles over me. "Are you sure you want me here?"

He looks at me then, really looks, and whatever he sees in my face makes his shoulders relax. "I'm sure," he says, lifting the latch.

The door swings open, and I step back into Hudson's world. The smell hits me—fresh-cut cedar and Hudson himself, that intoxicating combination of sawdust and citrus that clings to his skin. Beeswax threads through it, mixed with the faint metallic tang of well-oiled tools and the lingering sweetness of wood shavings. It's masculine and earthy and utterly intoxicating.

The string lights hanging from the exposed beams overhead cast everything in honeyed light, transforming the space from utilitarian to magical.

"God, I forgot how magical it felt in here," I breathe, taking it all in again with new eyes.

The workshop is meticulous chaos. Tools hang in neat rows along the walls, chisels and planes and saws I couldn't name if my life depended on it, all gleaming and well cared for. Half-finished projects occupy every surface. A rocking chair with one arm completed, its mate still rough-hewn; a jewelry box with intricate dovetail joints that speak of hours of patient work; bowls in various stages of becoming, some still blocky and raw, others smooth as silk.

In the center of it all sits a workbench made of thick, honey-colored wood, its surface scarred from years of labor but polished to a golden gleam. Tonight, it's been cleared completely, an altar waiting for an offering.

"This is incredible," I say, trailing my fingers along the edge of the bench. The wood is warm to the touch, smooth as silk. "How long have you been—"

"Since I was sixteen," Hudson says, moving to flip on another light. "Started with a pocket knife and a piece of driftwood. Drove my mum mad, leaving shavings all over her kitchen table."

There's something different about him here, a quiet confidence that only exists in his own space. He moves with ease, shoulders relaxed, sure as he adjusts tools and straightens already-straight lines. This is where he feels most himself. Where the playful facade drops away to reveal a steadier kind of presence, grounded and unguarded.

"I come here when I can't sleep," he admits. "When the house feels too big or too small or when my brain won't shut up. There's a peace in working with wood that quiets everything else."

My throat tightens at the vulnerability in his voice. "Thank you," I say quietly. "For letting me be here with you."

He turns, the last of the gold light catching in his hair, softening the hard lines of his face. "You make beautiful things," he says, voice low. "Living things. But they don't stay. They grow, they fade. Thought maybe you'd want to try your hand at something that lasts." He runs his fingers over the wood in front of him. "Something you can hold years from now and remember exactly where you were when you made it."

He moves to a shelf and pulls down a block of pale wood, smooth and solid. "Birch," he says, offering it out. The weight surprises me. It's denser than it looks.

"Feel like making a bowl?"

"I don't know how."

His mouth curves, just barely. "I'll teach you." His thumb drags over my knuckles, rough skin catching mine. "You trust me?"

The question lands deep, heavy with everything unsaid.

I meet his eyes, that steady blue that never lets me hide. "Always."

Hudson's smile could light the whole island. He moves to the lathe, examining the machine with obvious affection. "This old girl's been with me for ten years. Temperamental, but she'll treat you right if you respect her."

He secures the wood block, checking and rechecking before turning to his wall of tools. He picks out a chisel and passes it to me.

"The trick," he says, moving behind me, "is to let the wood tell you what it wants to be. Don't force it. Guide it."

His chest presses against my back, solid and steady. The air thickens. He covers my grip on the chisel, and suddenly I can't remember how to breathe properly.

"Relax," he murmurs against my ear, and the word reverberates through me. "Let me guide you."

He reaches around to start the lathe. The block begins to spin, slowly at first, then faster, until it becomes a blur. The vibration travels up through the machine, the bench, into my arms.

"Now." His voice drops. "Touch the blade to the wood. Gently."

He guides me forward. The chisel makes contact with a quiet rasp, and pale shavings curl away in delicate ribbons.

"That's it," he breathes, and there's something in his tone that makes butterflies riot in my belly. "Perfect."

His jaw grazes my cheek as he leans in to adjust the angle, stubble rasping against my skin. A shiver runs through me. I feel him go still for half a heartbeat, but he doesn't pull back. Instead, he presses closer, his thighs bracketing mine, solid and unyielding.

"You okay?" His voice is gravelly now.

I manage a nod because words are impossible. I'm drowning in sensation—the scent of cedar and sawdust, his hand steady on my hip, the way his breath fans across my neck.

We work in silence for a while, his touch steady over mine, coaxing the wood into submission. Every pass of the blade feels like it carves open a hidden place inside me. The vibration of the lathe travels through my palms, up my arms, settling deep in my belly like a tuning fork struck against bone.

Slowly, impossibly, a shape begins to emerge from the spinning block. A curve here, a hollow there. The birth of a quiet kind of beauty.

"Look at that," Hudson says, wonder softening his voice. "You're making a bowl that didn't exist an hour ago. Creating beauty from a plain old block of wood."

I glance down at where we're joined, at the way his strength dwarfs mine, callused, impossibly gentle. A touch that knows how to coax and shape and transform.

The wood shavings keep falling like snow, and I lose myself in the rhythm of it, the steady whir of the lathe, the whisper of blade against wood, the solid certainty of Hudson behind me.

"You're tense," he observes after a while. "Breathe, love."

Love. The word lands somewhere under my ribs and unfolds, dangerous and heady.

"I don't want to mess it up," I whisper.

"You can't," he says simply. "Wood forgives mistakes. It incorporates them. Makes them part of the story."

The way he says it, like he's talking about more than just wood-working, makes my eyes sting.

"There," Hudson says, easing me away from the spinning wood. "Let's see what we've made."

He switches off the lathe, and as the motion slows, the shape resolves into a form I finally recognize. A bowl. Small, imperfect, undeniably ours. The grain of the birch swirls through it like captured water, and the rim, slightly uneven, has an organic beauty that could never be mistaken for anything mass-produced.

"Hudson," I breathe. "It's beautiful! I can't believe we actually made this."

"*You* made this," he corrects, lifting the bowl with reverence. He turns it slowly in the honeyed light, and the smile he gives me is brighter than the string lights. "This is yours, Lorna. You shaped this."

He sets it into my grasp, and I'm struck by the living weight of it, how real it feels. I trace the rim, stunned that it exists at all. When I look up, his gaze is so intense something in my chest clenches.

His eyes drop to my mouth. Stay there. The air shifts, charged and waiting. Sawdust floats through the air, the scent of fresh-cut birch filling the space between us.

"I've wanted you here with me for so long," he murmurs, reaching up to frame my face. His thumbs trace my cheekbones, and I lean into it like I've been waiting my whole life for this. "In this space. Creating together."

"Why?" I ask, needing to hear the words.

"Because this is where I'm most myself," he says, nothing but raw honesty in his voice. "Where I'm not trying to be charming or funny or anything but me. And I wanted you to see that. To see the real me."

I set the bowl carefully on the workbench and step closer, closing the last sliver of space.

"Thank you," I say, my hands resting on his chest, feeling the strong, steady beat beneath. "For trusting me with this."

His expression shifts. His jaw tightens. His eyes go dark. He dips his head deliberately, giving me every chance to pull back.

I don't.

When his lips meet mine, it's different than before. Deeper. Purposeful. As though he's pouring everything he hasn't found the words for into this one kiss.

I part my lips and he groans, sliding his hand into my hair, gripping tight. The other hand drops to my hip, hooking into my waistband.

The kiss turns hungry. His tongue sweeps against mine, and I forget how to think. My world narrows to his mouth and the solid weight of him pressing me back against the workbench.

He breaks away long enough to curse under his breath, then he's gripping my hips, lifting. In one smooth motion, I'm on the workbench, weathered wood solid beneath my thighs, and he's stepping between my legs.

"Christ, look at you," he breathes, his palms sweeping over my thighs and hips, then up my waist.

His mouth crashes into mine again, ravenous now, every trace of restraint burned away. I drown in the taste of him, in the way he trembles just slightly as he skims the hem of my shirt, asking without words if I want it as badly as he does.

"Please, Hudson," I whisper against his lips.

He pulls my shirt over my head and tosses it aside without looking. The air is cool against my skin, carrying the scent of night, but his gaze is pure heat. It moves over me, lingering on my shoulders, my collarbone, the curve of my breasts, and the desire in his eyes lights a slow burn between my thighs.

His touch glides over me with something close to reverence, tracing the slope of my shoulders, sweeping down my ribs, brushing the sensitive skin just beneath my bra. He reaches behind me to unhook it, and my breath catches. The clasp gives way, and when the fabric slips down my arms, the sound he makes is one I want to bottle, to keep for the quiet nights when I need to remember how it feels to be wanted like this.

"So fucking perfect," he murmurs, his mouth drifting over my throat, down to the hollow between my breasts. "Every fucking inch of you." He lowers his head, lips sealing around one tight peak, and the shock of it makes me gasp, clutching at his shoulders.

My jeans are next. He pops the button, slides the denim down my legs, and lets it pool at my feet. His hands follow the path back up, his fingers catching on the lace at my hips.

"Lift," he murmurs, and I do, letting him strip away the last barrier between us.

For a moment he looks at me, his breathing harsh, before he drops to his knees.

The first touch of his mouth makes my spine arch off the bench. His tongue drags through me, unhurried and searching, savoring the taste. A broken sound tears from my throat.

"Already soaked for me," he groans against my thigh, his mouth returning to me. His tongue moves over my clit, circling, teasing, driving me out of my mind. "Fuck, you taste good."

Words tangle in my throat. My breath staggers. I pull his head closer as he works me with his mouth, alternating between broad strokes and focused attention that makes my thighs shake.

When he slides two fingers inside me, the combination nearly undoes me. The stretch, the curl, the relentless pressure of his tongue, it's too much and not enough. I bite the base of my thumb, trying to keep back the god-awful sounds climbing up my throat.

"Don't you dare hold back," he growls against me, the vibration shooting straight through my core. "I want to hear every fucking sound."

The pleasure builds until it's blinding, until thoughts scatter and my breath goes ragged, until I can't do anything but feel. My body goes taut, every nerve ending firing, and when he curls just right while sucking hard on my clit, I shatter. His name rips from my throat as I come, waves of fire crashing through me while he works me through it, drawing out every trembling aftershock.

When I finally go limp, breath coming in ragged bursts, he presses slow kisses along my inner thighs, up to my hip, then higher until his mouth meets mine.

When he pulls back, I'm trembling so hard he has to steady me, his arms locking around my waist to keep me upright. My pulse crashes in my ears, and the world blurs at the edges, soft and shimmering.

"Look at me," he orders, voice scraped raw.

I lift my gaze. He's staring at me like I'm a miracle he doesn't quite deserve, and it makes emotion well up so fast I feel like I'm suffocating on it.

He strips off his clothes, and I can't help the shaky breath that stumbles from my lips. Broad shoulders, tanned skin, a trail of dark hair arrowing down his abdomen to where he's thick and hard, the head of his cock flushed.

"Please," I whisper, reaching for him. "I need you inside me, Hudson."

A low, broken sound tears out of him. "Fuck."

He kicks the last of his clothes away and steps in close, framing my face as he leans down and kisses me, deep and claiming, stealing every shaky breath I have left. Then he draws back, dragging the tip of his cock through the slick, swollen heat of me, his jaw clenched so tight I half expect it to crack.

"Tell me you want this," he rasps, voice breaking. "Tell me you want me."

"I want you," I breathe. "God, Hudson. I've never wanted anything more."

His eyes close for a moment, jaw clenched tight, holding himself back by sheer force of will. When they open again, the darkness there sends a steady pulse spiraling through me.

He pushes inside, one slow, deliberate thrust, and the stretch rips a sound from me I don't recognize. I gasp, clutching at his shoulders as he sinks deeper, filling me until it feels like he's carved into my very bones.

"Fuck," he groans, forehead dropping to mine, his whole body trembling. "You feel incredible."

He holds still, giving me time to adjust, his grip on my hips almost bruising. When I shift, rolling my hips in silent plea, a broken laugh escapes him.

"Greedy little thing," he murmurs against my mouth, and starts to move.

The rhythm is measured, filthy, each deep thrust grinding against that spot inside me that makes my eyes roll back and my mouth fall open. He knows exactly what he's doing, how to angle his hips, how to drag it out until I'm shaking. He slips his hand down, rubbing tight circles, slick and ruthless.

The combination wrecks me. That thick stretch inside, the grinding against my clit, the obscene wet sounds between us, I'm spiraling fast, panting his name like it's the only word I remember.

"Fuck, look at you," he growls, voice frayed. "Split open around me, taking every fucking inch."

His words wrap around me, sinking into every raw, open place. His pace quickens, the workbench creaking beneath us, and his hand slides over my ass.

My whole body goes taut.

"Is this okay?" His voice cracks on the question.

"Yes," I gasp. "Please."

He pushes in, so goddamn careful, like he's trying not to break me, like he doesn't realize I'm already broken. The stretch, the pressure, the unbearable fullness of it sends me flying. I come with a cry I can't hold back, loud and wrecked, echoing off the walls as my body clamps down around him.

It doesn't stop, wave after wave crashing through me, shaking me apart. He follows with a ragged groan, my name torn from his throat as he spills inside me.

We stay locked together, pressed close, both of us shaking and breathless.

When he finally pulls out, the loss makes me whimper. He steadies himself against the bench, pressing a kiss to my temple.

"You wreck me," he whispers, voice destroyed.

He lifts me without a word, cradling me against his chest as he carries me to a stool draped with a heavy blanket. He settles me down gently, tucking the soft wool around my bare shoulders.

"Stay there," he murmurs, brushing hair from my cheek. "Let me clean you up."

I can only nod, throat too tight to speak. He moves around the workshop, collecting a clean rag and a bottle of water, his body still gloriously bare.

He kneels between my legs and wipes me gently, his touch achingly tender. When he finishes, he lifts my wrist to his mouth, pressing a kiss to my pulse point.

"You okay?" he asks, searching my face.

"More than okay," I manage, voice hoarse. "That was..."

"Yeah," he says, a crooked smile tugging at his mouth. "It was."

The moment stretches between us, golden and languid. He kisses me one more time, helping me dress again, lingering at every button, every zip. Like he can't bear the thought of not touching me, even for a second. When I'm fully clothed, he tugs me back into his arms, holding me close as our heartbeats slow.

"I've been thinking," he says, a little wry, a little hopeful. "About what it would be like if all three of us were with you like this."

Heat flares in my cheeks, sharp and unmistakable. It's not

embarrassment. It's want. A tentative, glimmering curiosity I've been mulling over for weeks.

"I... I've thought about it," I admit, voice low. "About what it would be like. With all of you."

"And?" He fingers stroke along my jaw, so tender it makes my throat ache.

"And it terrifies me," I whisper, "and it thrills me at the same time."

Hudson smiles, a promise etched into the curve of his mouth. "That's exactly how it should feel."

The walk back feels dreamlike, my body still pulsing with the imprint of him. He keeps hold of me the whole way, his thumb brushing over my knuckles in a steady, absent caress. The night air is cool against my flushed skin, carrying the smell of rain-damp earth and the faint trace of sawdust clinging to my clothes.

When we reach my front step, he turns to face me, cradling my face like he can't quite let me go yet. The porch light halos him in gold, turning his eyes to aquamarine.

"Tonight was perfect," he says, sweeping my hair away from my forehead.

I swallow around the tightness in my throat. "Yeah. It was."

"Sleep well, Snapdragon," he murmurs, pressing one last kiss to my forehead before he turns and walks back down the path. I stand there for a long moment, watching him go, feeling like the world has tilted enough to let in something good.

## 19

———————

The house is too quiet.

I press my palm against the kitchen counter, the cool granite grounding me. Without the kids, the silence feels wrong. No steady stream of Daniel's questions. None of Lorelai's bright laughter echoing down the hallway. Just the tick of the wall clock and my own breathing.

Coffee. I need coffee.

I open the tin, stare into its empty bottom, and groan. Of course. The universe clearly hates me. I grab the kettle, fill it with cold water, and flick it on. The quiet hum steadies me. Tea it is. I drop a bag into the mug, pour the water, and watch the steam rise. Warmth seeps into my hands as I stand at the sink, the kitchen still and soft around me.

Outside, through the foggy glass, Leo moves across the far paddock, checking fences with that sure, steady stride. Hudson emerges from their barn, gesturing wildly at something, probably explaining some overcomplicated fix that'll take twice as long as the simple solution. Even from here I can see him grinning. Levi's nearby with his ever-present notebook, head tilted as he studies something, the way light hits the dew, probably, or the pattern of clouds.

Something cinches behind my ribs.

I force myself away from the window and sit at the table, years of documentation spread before me. Journals crammed with interview transcripts, sketches of physiological patterns, notes scrawled in margins when thoughts came too fast for organization. Years of research on female sexuality, and now I need to distill it into forty-five minutes that won't bore an auditorium full of scientists to tears.

I open my journal. My handwriting looks manic in the morning light, cramped, urgent, the script of someone terrified of losing a single thought.

Focus, Lorna.

My phone buzzes. Isla's name flashes across the screen.

**Isla:** *How are the twins? Missing you yet?*

**Me:** *Having the time of their lives!*

**Isla:** *And YOU? Alone with your guys?*

**Me:** *They're giving me space to work.*

**Isla:** *Boring.*

**Me:** *ISLA.*

**Isla:** *What? If I had three gorgeous men next door, I wouldn't want space.*

**Me:** *You DO have three gorgeous men.*

**Isla:** *Oh right. Better go get on that. Literally.*

I set the phone down, but her words linger.

She's not wrong. Having space feels strange after weeks of constant togetherness. I've gotten used to Leo showing up with coffee. Hudson stealing bites of my lunch while explaining his latest project. Levi reading poetry aloud while I work, his voice a steady backdrop.

The quiet should feel productive. Instead it just feels empty.

A soft knock sounds at the back door, three gentle taps I'd know anywhere. Leo stands on the porch, a travel mug in hand, steam curling through the cool morning air between his fingers.

"Coffee?" His voice carries that gravelly, just-woken rasp.

The mug is still warm from his hands when he passes it to me, his fingertips grazing my knuckles.

"Thank you." I inhale the rich aroma. Darker than what I usually make, with notes of chocolate and something smoky. "What have the three of you been up to?" I ask, stepping onto the porch where morning air kisses my heated cheeks.

"Hudson's working on a new pasture," he says, eyes skimming my face. "Levi's been correlating herd health with weather patterns."

"And you?"

"I've been watching you," he says, voice dipping low enough to make my breath hitch. "Making sure you eat. Sleep. Don't disappear into that brilliant head of yours."

My heart kicks against my ribs.

Before I can answer, Hudson's voice crackles through the radio on Leo's belt. "Leo! I need a second opinion on fence post spacing!"

Leo sighs. "Duty calls." His hand comes up to cup my jaw, thumb brushing over my bottom lip. "We're cooking tonight. Dinner. Six o'clock."

He leans in, his breath warm against my cheek, lips so close I can taste the hint of coffee on them. "And if you're good," he murmurs, voice rough with promise, "maybe you'll get dessert."

He wraps one of my curls around his finger, tugging lightly. Then he leans in and kisses me, unhurried, lingering, the kind of kiss that hums through my whole body. When he finally pulls back, he gives me one last look before turning toward their farm.

I make myself go back inside, back to my notes, but the words won't stay still. They blur and shift until I give up pretending and glance again toward their property. With a sigh, I open my laptop and start a new document. *Female Sexual Response Patterns: A Comprehensive Analysis.* For the next two hours, I transcribe years of handwritten observations, sorting data into neat columns of response types, arousal patterns, and orgasmic variations. The analytical part of my mind stirs, stretches, and finally starts to breathe again.

My first real breakthrough is accidental—a survey participant describing multiple distinct types of climax, each with different physiological markers. The discovery stuns me, clear proof that female sexual response is far more complex than medical literature suggests.

As I compile the data, new patterns emerge, ones I'd missed in the day-to-day rush. Some response types stay consistent across demographics, while others create completely unexpected variations.

Another knock interrupts my thoughts, softer this time, less demand, more question.

When I open the door, late-morning light spills in around Levi, outlining him in gold. He's squinting against the sun, a plate balanced in his hands and covered with a tea towel.

"Hi." My voice comes out in a squeak.

"I made scones," he says, and his gaze travels over me slowly, deliberately, like he's taking inventory. "They're still warm."

The smell hits me first. Butter and vanilla and something so sweet my mouth waters. I lift the towel, revealing perfect golden triangles studded with currants.

"These look incredible."

"Hudson's nervous about cooking tonight," Levi says, stepping past the threshold.

"Nervous? Hudson?" I bite into a scone, and the flavors explode over my tongue—sweet, buttery, tart. "Hudson doesn't get nervous, he gets excited."

Levi's mouth curves. "Different expressions of the same thing." His gaze holds mine. "He wants to impress you. They both do."

"Both?"

"Leo's been planning tonight's menu for three days. Making lists, rearranging the pantry, arguing with Hudson about spice ratios." He's close now, close enough I can see the flecks of gold in his eyes. "Don't even get me started on the wine debate."

A smile tugs at my lips. "What about you? Are you nervous too?"

He doesn't answer right away. Just studies me with that focused intensity that makes my skin prickle. Then he leans in, head tilting like he's deciding whether or not to ruin me.

"Eager," he murmurs, voice low and threaded with want. "I'm very eager."

The word settles between us, heavy and electric.

"I should..." I start, but the sentence falls apart as his hand comes up to cradle my jaw. His thumb brushes the corner of my mouth, and my thoughts scatter completely.

And then he kisses me.

It isn't soft. It isn't polite. It's claiming, a hungry crush of his mouth against mine that obliterates thought. I taste currants and butter and him as his hand grips my hip, pulling me flush against him.

He pulls back just enough to speak, his forehead still resting against mine. "I can't stop thinking about your mouth," he says, voice low. "Or the sounds you make when you come."

My pulse kicks hard, heat climbing fast.

"If you keep looking at me like that," he murmurs, "dinner's not happening."

Heat floods through me. "Levi—"

He kisses me again, slower this time but no less intense, then pulls back with visible effort. His thumb drags across my bottom lip.

"Six o'clock," he says, and his smile is wicked. "Don't be late."

"I won't," I whisper.

Then he's gone, leaving me with a racing pulse and the plate of scones I'm no longer hungry for.


By four, I've wrangled my data into something resembling order, but my brain feels like overcooked porridge. I save the file, shut the laptop, and admit defeat. A shower seems less like self-care and more like damage control. The hot water beats against my shoulders, loosening knots I didn't even know I had, steam curling around me until the world blurs. I stay too long, because it's the first time all day I don't have to think.

My closet isn't exactly inspiring, just rows of farm clothes, all practicality and no charm. After some digging, I find soft jeans that actually fit and a navy sweater that feels comfortable but still put-together. I study my reflection for a beat, then nod. Good enough.

At ten to six, I head out, crossing the field that separates our farms. The air carries that unmistakable scent of wood smoke and the rich scent of garlic, herbs, and roasting meat. My stomach twists with hunger, but it's not just food I'm craving.

Their farmhouse glows against the deepening dusk, windows spilling golden light across the fields. I knock, my pulse beating in my throat. Footsteps cross the floor, and then the door swings open.

Leo fills the frame in dark jeans and a white button-down, sleeves rolled high on his forearms. The fabric pulls across his chest with each slow breath.

I force a steady exhale, dragging my gaze up from his body to his eyes.

"Lorna." My name in his mouth comes out low, weighted. "Perfect timing."

Before I can answer, his hand slips around my waist, pulling me in. Heat sears through my sweater where his palm settles, and then his mouth is on mine. My lips part on a startled breath as he deepens the kiss, thumb tracing my jaw like he's learning me by touch alone.

When he pulls back, it's only far enough to breathe.

"Hi," I whisper.

His mouth curves, slow and devastating. His thumb drags over my bottom lip, swollen from his kiss. "Hi." He exhales. "Come inside."

Warmth and the scent of roasting meat wrap around me as I step inside. "Something smells incredible."

"Hudson's been obsessed with perfecting the lamb all afternoon. Levi made bread from scratch. I handled vegetables and referee duty." Leo's hand stays at the small of my back, steering me toward the kitchen like he's not ready to let go.

The kitchen is a beautiful kind of chaos. Hudson's at the stove, stirring a saucepan and taste testing with exaggerated concentration. His hair's a wreck, and there's flour streaked across his shirt like war paint. Levi sits at the island, slicing bread with careful precision, a contrast to Hudson's whirlwind energy.

"Lorna!" Hudson's grin splits his face. "Perfect timing. We need a tie-breaker on the rosemary situation."

"I'm not qualified to settle culinary disputes," I say, but Leo's already easing me onto a stool.

"Taste this." Hudson materializes in front of me with a spoon. "Too much rosemary?"

I open my mouth, and flavor floods in, lamb and wine and herbs, rich and decadent. My eyes flutter closed. "Oh my god. Hudson, that's perfect."

His grin is pure satisfaction. "See? I told you the rosemary was perfect."

"I said it was adequate," Leo says, calm as ever.

"Adequate?" Hudson throws his hands up. "You hear that, Lorna? Genius underappreciated."

"Wine?" Leo asks, already reaching for a bottle.

"Please."

He pours, and the glass he hands me is smooth and cool in my palm. The wine's warmth blooms on my tongue as I take a slow sip and watch them, taking in Hudson's easy showmanship, Levi's quiet focus, and Leo's steady command of the room.

A small ache opens under my sternum. It's not jealousy exactly, but a kind of longing. The way they move together feels earned, like trust built through a thousand shared dinners and late nights.

"Tell me about your research," Levi says, glancing up from his task. "How did today go?"

"Better than I expected." I take another sip. "I've been so focused on hiding the work that I didn't realize how much data I'd already gathered. Once I started organizing it, it told an entire story."

"What kind of story?" Hudson asks without looking up, his spoon swirling through the gravy.

"About how women's bodies are capable of so much more than medical literature gives them credit for." The words come easier than they usually do. "Most people think female orgasm is a simple process, but it's incredibly layered. Different types of stimulation trigger distinct physiological patterns. Emotional context changes everything—anticipation, safety, trust. Even duration alters the body's rhythm."

I stop, catching myself mid-ramble. "Sorry. I get carried away."

"Don't," Leo says, his tone low and certain. "It's fascinating. Keep going."

But Hudson breaks the spell with a triumphant clatter of the spoon. "Dinner's ready," he declares, switching off the burner with a grin. "Let's eat outside. Leo built a fire."

Outside, their back porch has been transformed. String lights crisscross overhead, candles flickering beneath them, casting everything in warm gold. The fire crackles in the stone pit, sending sparks drifting into the blue-gray light of evening. The table is set with mismatched dishes that somehow look perfect together.

The food is extraordinary. The lamb falls apart at the touch of my fork, so tender I barely need to chew. Levi's bread has a crackling crust that gives way to a soft, pillowy interior. Leo's roasted vegetables glisten with olive oil and herbs, caramelized at the edges.

"This is incredible," I say, closing my eyes as I savor another bite.

Hudson leans back in his chair, watching me with an expression that sends warmth creeping up my neck. "We're glad you like it, Snapdragon."

Hours slip by in laughter and low voices. We talk about bad TV, favorite childhood meals, what we wanted to be when we grew up. The wine leaves me loose and warm, the night soft around us.

"I should probably head home," I say eventually, though I don't move.

"Should you?" Levi asks, his eyes reflecting firelight. "It's a beautiful night. The fire's still going."

"And you've been drinking," Hudson adds, lips twitching. "Safer to stay awhile, given the treacherous ten-minute walk across flat ground."

I laugh, but he's not wrong. Not about the wine, anyway. Though sitting here with three men who make my pulse stumble feels like the real danger.

"I don't want to impose."

"You're not." Leo's voice cuts through the crackling of the fire. "You're exactly where you should be."

*Where I should be.* The words sink into me, filling all the empty spaces.

"Lorna." Leo's voice pulls me to him. "There's something we want to ask you."

My pulse stutters. "What kind of something?"

"We want to make you come," Leo says, voice low enough that it slides right under my skin. "All of us. Together." His gaze doesn't waver. "Not sex. Not tonight. I don't want a drop of alcohol in your system for that." He pauses, the firelight catching in his beard, throwing his face into shadow and gold. "But there are other ways we can make you feel good. Ways we can show you how much you mean to us."

"Tonight?" My voice is a ghost.

"Only if you want."

I stare into the fire, the heat licking my skin, my pulse kicking harder with every breath. "I definitely want to, but I'm scared," I admit.

"Of what?" Hudson murmurs.

"Of not being enough. Of ruining it. Of doing something wrong."

"Lorna." Leo's voice sharpens. "Look at me."

I drag my gaze to his. His eyes are steady, dark, and burning.

"You're enough," he says, each word slow and certain. "More than enough."

The air shifts. Desire curls low in my stomach, spreading until it's hard to tell if it's from the wine or the way they're all leaning in, drawn tight around me like gravity.

"Okay," I whisper, the word catching on a breath that doesn't quite make it out.

The word hangs there, bright and buzzing in the quiet. Leo stands first, reaching for me with a hand that looks steady but feels anything but when his fingers brush mine.

"Come inside," he says, and the words rumble through me, settling low in my belly.

I slide my hand into his, his palm radiating heat straight into my bones. The world tilts, and before I can catch myself, Hudson locks his arm around my waist.

"Easy," he murmurs against my ear, breath hot enough to raise goosebumps. "I've got you."

His arm stays around me as he steers me deeper inside, each step pulling us further into the dark.

The bedroom is all shadows and dark wood, heavy furniture and darker bedding. The air is thick with cedar and clean linen and something distinctly masculine—leather and soap and skin.

"Lorna." Levi's voice, close enough to feel. When I turn, he's right there, eyes catching what little light filters through the window. Dark. Searching. "Are you sure?"

My voice won't work. So I reach for him instead, fingers curling into his collar, tugging him down until we're almost touching. The first brush of contact is soft, questioning.

I part my lips in answer.

He makes a raw, broken sound and kisses me like he's been dying of thirst and I'm the first drop of water. His hands slide into my hair, fingers gripping just enough to make my scalp tingle.

Hudson crowds behind me, solid and hot, pressing close

enough that I feel his heartbeat through my spine. His arms wrap around me, one hand flattening low over my stomach, fingertips grazing the waistband of my jeans. He finds that spot just below my ear, dragging his tongue over it slow and wet, and my knees nearly give out.

"God, Lorna," Hudson breathes against my pulse, his voice barely more than a rasp. "You have no idea what you do to me. I'm already so fucking hard, and I haven't even kissed you yet."

Leo's hands slip under my sweater, unhurried, hands warm against my skin. His thumbs trace slow circles at my hips, small, teasing movements that pull heat from deep inside me. I lift my arms in silent surrender, and he pulls the sweater up and over my head. The air hits my skin, cool against the fever he's built, and goosebumps rise in a rush. He inhales sharply, something raw sparking behind his eyes as he takes me in.

"Gorgeous," he murmurs, voice gone gravelly. His look drags over me in a slow, lingering sweep. It feels like he's mapping me, each curve, each freckle, each place I turn pink under his attention.

Hudson and Levi move in together, and suddenly there are hands everywhere. Reverent but hungry, deliberate but barely controlled. Fingers hook under my bra straps, dragging them down my shoulders with agonizing slowness. The backs of knuckles graze my collarbone and I shiver, goosebumps spreading across my chest.

Levi's mouth moves to the hollow of my throat, hot and open, and the slick heat of his tongue against that sensitive dip makes my knees buckle.

Hudson's breath is warm against my neck, his fingers finding the clasp of my bra. He pauses, just for a second, his knuckles pressed against my spine, and then I hear the soft snick of it coming undone. The fabric loosens, slides forward, and the deliberate brush of his hand along the side of my breast as he pulls it away sends electricity straight through me.

The sound that tears from my throat is unrecognizable. Raw. Desperate.

Hudson groans behind me, the vibration rumbling through his chest into my back. I feel it in my bones.

Then Leo's hands are at my jeans, fingers working the button, the faint graze of his skin against my stomach sending sparks racing under my skin. The zipper's rasp cuts through the quiet, tooth by metal tooth, and his thumbs hook into the waistband. He eases the denim down, hands tracing the curve of my thighs, the rough heat of his touch making my muscles tense and tremble.

Levi's hand locks onto my hip, fingers pressing into bare skin, steadying me as I step out of the denim.

Now I'm standing between three fully clothed men wearing nothing but black lace that suddenly feels insubstantial, phantom-thin, like it might disintegrate under the heat of their attention. The weight of their stares lands on my skin with actual pressure. Leo's eyes drag down my body, achingly slow, and I feel it like fingers tracing my collarbones, my ribs, the curve of my waist. Levi's grip tightens on my hip, just enough that I feel each individual fingertip pressing into flesh. Hudson hasn't moved, but his gaze burns tracks across my shoulders, down my sternum, lingers on my breasts until the air itself feels too warm.

My skin prickles and tightens everywhere at once, hypersensitive, like I've been stripped of a protective layer. My nipples harden until they ache, peaks straining against lace that's suddenly rough, abrading with each shallow breath I take. Heat pools low in my belly, a molten weight, then spills lower between my legs. The pulse there grows stronger, more demanding, until I have to lock my knees to keep from shifting my weight, from pressing my thighs together to ease the building pressure that's quickly becoming unbearable.

By the time they lower me onto the bed, I'm trembling all over, from my hands to my thighs to the muscles low in my belly. The duvet is cool cotton against my overheated skin, and the contrast rips a gasp from me, my back arching off the mattress. My heartbeat pounds so hard it's everywhere at once, in my throat, my fingertips, the pulsing ache between my legs.

I'm shaking, caught between need and surrender, between the sharp edge of wanting and the fear of how much I already do.

"Please," I whisper, my voice wrecked and unfamiliar.

"Please what?" Hudson's voice is gentle, but his eyes are black, pupils swallowing the blue until there's nothing left but hunger.

"Touch me." It comes out breathless, broken.

Then three sets of hands are on me. Three different ways of pulling me apart until I can't tell where one sensation ends and the next begins, until I'm drowning in them.

Leo takes my mouth first, kissing me hard and deep and slow, like he needs to catalog the taste of me. His hand slides up to cup my jaw, thumb stroking while his tongue drags against mine.

Hudson's fingers slide through the slick heat gathered between my thighs with a confidence that makes me moan. His other hand grips my hip hard enough to bruise, holding me still when I try to grind against him.

"God, Lorna." His breath is hot against my hip, words vibrating through me. "So fucking wet for us already."

My breathing fractures into broken gasps. Levi follows, kissing down my collarbone, the center of my chest, his tongue tracing the upper swell of my breast. When his mouth closes around my nipple, the wet heat and suction send lightning straight through my core.

"Please," I hear myself beg. "I need more." My hips roll helplessly into Hudson's hand, chasing friction, chasing relief. "I need all of you."

Hudson's laugh is dark, almost wicked. He pushes two fingers inside me, making my vision blur. "You have us, sweetheart. We're not going anywhere."

I reach for them without thought, gripping Leo's shirt in my fists, sliding up Hudson's forearm to feel the flex of muscle as he works me, tangling my fingers in Levi's hair as his tongue circles my nipple in maddening spirals.

"More," I gasp. "God, please, let me touch you—"

"No." Leo's tone is soft but immovable. His palm presses flat over my racing heart. "Tonight isn't about us. It's about you. Every fucking second of it."

"But..."

"Shh." Hudson drags his mouth along my jaw, open and hot, teeth grazing just enough to make me shiver. "You've done enough," he murmurs, voice thick and low. "Tonight, you just take."

Levi lifts his head then, eyes soft in a way that undoes me completely. "We'll give," he says, his breath ghosting over my skin, "until you can't take any more." Then he sucks my nipple deep into wet heat.

I lose control of my body. My hips buck. My hands scramble for purchase against sheets, skin, anything solid. I can feel all three of them pressed against me, the hard length of them through their clothes, but their focus is entirely on me.

"God, look at you." Hudson groans as he slowly pulls his fingers from me. He drags the mess upward, spreading it over my clit in a slow, lazy stroke that makes my whole body jolt. "So fucking pretty when you're falling apart for us."

Leo's hand slides up my chest, fingers closing gently around my throat. Not squeezing, just holding, possessive and claiming. He kisses me until my lungs burn and I'm dizzy from lack of air.

"Don't you dare close your eyes," he commands.

"Please." It comes out like a sob. "Please, I can't..."

"You can." Levi's hand settles low on my belly, grounding me in my body. His breath ghosts over my wet nipple, making me shudder. "Come for us, Lorna."

I don't have a choice. My body locks up tight, every muscle seizing as pleasure rips through me. Sharp and violent and so intense it borders on pain. My vision whites out. My ears ring.

And they don't stop. Hands keep moving, mouths keep working, drawing it out until I'm sobbing, shaking, completely wrecked.

When I finally go limp, there's a blur of movement. Bodies shifting, trading places. And then Leo is settling between my spread thighs, his broad shoulders forcing my legs wider, his big hands gripping the tender skin of my inner thighs.

"Look at you. You're fucking drenched, Lorna." His thumbs spread me open, exposing me completely to his gaze. "You want more?"

I try to answer but all that comes out is a choked, desperate sound.

"Words," he growls.

"Yes." I gasp it out. "God, yes, please..."

"Good girl."

His mouth is on me before I can draw another breath. Hot and wet and relentless. He licks a slow path up my center, the flat of his tongue dragging through every sensitive fold before flicking against my clit just once. Then his lips seal over it and he sucks hard while pushing two thick fingers deep inside me.

"Fuck." Hudson's groan comes from somewhere above me. "I can hear how wet you are, baby."

The obscene sound of Leo's fingers working me fills the room, slick and rhythmic, and heat floods my face even as my hips tip shamelessly toward his mouth.

I try to lift my head but Levi is there, hand cupping my cheek, turning me toward him. His kiss is soft, coaxing, his tongue sliding against mine in slow, drugging strokes.

"You're going to come again," he whispers when he pulls back, still so close I feel each word. "Don't fight it. Give us what we want, Petal."

Leo's fingers curl deep, finding that spot that has its own gravity, pulling everything in me toward it. He seals over my clit, tongue flicking in quick, merciless passes. I'm panting, helpless against the pull. My thighs tremble violently, every muscle quivering as he keeps me suspended right there, wound impossibly tight.

"God, you taste so fucking sweet," Leo mutters against my slick flesh, the vibration of his words sending fresh shockwaves through me.

Hudson closes his mouth over my breast, hot and wet, sucking the tight peak deep. His teeth scrape just enough to make pain and pleasure blur together. His other hand finds my neglected breast, rolling the nipple between his fingers, pinching, tugging, sending sensation cascading through my nervous system.

"Such a perfect handful," he growls, lifting his head to bite at the sensitive underside. "Bet I could make you come just from playing with these."

"Fuck." It tears out of me, desperate and pleading. "Please, please, I can't..."

"We know." Levi grips my hair, tilting my head so I have to look at him as he hovers over me. "You're taking it so well, sweetheart. Leo's fingers buried deep, his mouth working that pretty clit." His eyes are dark, pupils blown. "You're going to come for us again. We want to hear you scream."

I clench hard around Leo's fingers and he groans into me, the vibration pushing me closer to the edge. He sucks harder, fingers pumping faster, and the pleasure building low in my spine is too much, too bright, too overwhelming.

"That's it," Hudson growls against my breast. "Come on, love. Show us how gorgeous you are when you break."

I shatter.

Pleasure tears me open from the inside out, so intense I can't breathe, can't think, can't do anything but shake and sob and cling to them. Leo doesn't stop. His tongue gentles but keeps moving, drawing it out until I'm boneless and trembling, until aftershocks ripple through me with every breath.

When the world finally stops spinning, when I can remember how to breathe again, I collapse against the mattress. Completely undone. Their hands are still on me, holding, anchoring, claiming me as theirs.

Leo shifts up my body, settling his weight over me. I feel the hard, thick length of him straining against his jeans, pressing into my hip. All that restraint. All that control he's kept locked down while he made me fall apart. He kisses me slow and deep, letting me taste myself on his tongue.

Hudson settles beside me, his hand spanning my belly, thumb

stroking lazy circles over my skin. Levi presses against my other side, his fingers threading through mine.

"Sleep," Leo murmurs against my temple, his breath warm in my hair. "We'll be right here when you wake up." He kisses my forehead, then shifts to Hudson's far side, close enough that I still feel his warmth.

Hudson pulls the blanket over us, wrapping me in warmth and the solid weight of their bodies.

My heart feels cracked wide open. Exposed in a way that should terrify me but doesn't. Because for the first time in years, I'm not alone with the vulnerability. They're holding all the broken, raw pieces of me like they're something precious.

I let go. The fear, the doubt, every last scrap of loneliness I've carried like armor.

I drift into darkness surrounded by them—Leo's steady breathing, Hudson's hand warm on my stomach, Levi's fingers laced with mine. Their scent filling my lungs. Their heat soaking into my bones.

This. This is where I belong.

## 20

The knock is soft, barely there, but it lands in perfect sync with the kettle's whistle. A quiet signal that Leo knows me too well.

His shape fills the window. Broad shoulders, that familiar stillness. His usual travel mug steams in one hand, but there's a change today. A tension in his spine. His other hand cradles a small, neatly wrapped box.

"Morning, beautiful," he says when I open the door, and the gravel in his voice sends heat pooling low in my belly.

"You caught me right before my second cup." Our fingers brush as he passes me the mug, awareness skittering over my skin. The coffee is perfect. Strong and dark with a kiss of cream.

He steps inside and the entry seems to shrink, the air tightening between us. The latch clicks, and his scent fills the space, coffee and cedar soap and that deep leather warmth I've learned to crave. Every nerve sparks at once, remembering, wanting.

My eyes drop to the package in his hand. "What's the occasion?"

He settles into his usual chair, long legs folding into the space beneath the table. "A conversation," he says, setting the box down between us. "And a gift."

My name is scrawled across the brown paper in his careful handwriting.

I set my mug down and reach for it. The paper is worn at the edges, handled repeatedly. Maybe second-guessed. Maybe passed from hand to hand while he worked up the nerve to bring it here. My fingers hesitate on the tape.

I set it down and take another sip of coffee, trembling slightly. I wipe my palms on my sleep shorts, hyperaware of the heat trapped between my thighs, the cotton suddenly too thin.

"Lorna." His voice cuts through my spiraling thoughts. "Open it."

I peel back the paper, stretching out the moment. Inside is a sleek black box. Clean lines. Expensive.

I lift the lid.

Everything inside me goes quiet. And loud.

Three silver plugs rest in velvet, graduated in size, gleaming and flawless. Tucked beneath them, a small remote and what I quickly realize are vibrating panties.

My thighs press together automatically, an instinctive attempt to contain the fire surging through me. It doesn't help.

"Fucking hell, Leo." His name scrapes out of my throat, barely formed. "A girl could use a little warning."

He doesn't smile. Doesn't look away. Holds my gaze with raw hunger, eyes so dark my stomach drops.

"We need to talk about what you want," he says. "About what we want. How this is going to work."

I set the box down carefully, my heartbeat thundering in my ears, pulsing under my skin.

"What exactly are you asking me?" The words come out rough.

His eyes don't waver. "You know what I'm asking."

And I do. God help me, I do.

I've been thinking about it for weeks. Lying awake at night, imagining their hands on me, imagining being so full I can't think straight.

"I want to be stretched," I whisper, the admission tearing out of me. "Used. I want to feel so much I can't think about anything else. I want the surrender."

Leo's pupils blow wide, his control fracturing at the edges. "Fuck, Lorna."

He moves closer, near enough that I feel the heat radiating off him. "If you want to be with all three of us at the same time, we need to prepare you properly. Make sure your body can take everything we want to give."

The words send fire spiraling through my core. "You've thought about this," I say, eyes flicking back to the box. "Planned it."

He nods, voice rough. "Of course we have."

The image of three grown men sitting around discussing how to fill all of my holes slams into my mind. They've been planning this. Preparing.

"We want to give you everything," he says, tilting my chin up so I have no choice but to meet his gaze. "Every stretch, every inch. You'll be so full you won't be able to think about anything but us."

"I don't need logistics," I murmur. "I need you to wreck me."

His smile is wicked. Devastating. "We will. Completely."

"So what do we do first?" The words come out steady despite the pulse pounding between my thighs.

The shift in him is subtle but seismic. His pupils dilate further. His breath catches. When he looks at me, it's as if he's seeing what he's only dared to imagine until this moment.

"First," he says, "you're going to make us dinner."

My eyebrows shoot up. "Make you dinner?"

He nods. "All three of us will be here tonight. But before that..." His hand trails down my bare arm, a scorching path. "I'm going to put the smallest one inside you. And you're going to wear these," he lifts the panties, "while you cook for us."

"Leo..."

His thumb grazes my bottom lip, silencing me. "We go at your pace. Always. But make no mistake, Lorna." He leans in, breath warm on my skin. "When you're ready, we're going to take you apart piece by piece. And put you back together completely ours."

Jesus Christ.

Every part of me trembles, blood rushing in every direction at once. Terror and lust twist together into something incandescent. Alive.

I'm nodding before I can second-guess myself. "Okay."

"Okay?" His voice drops even lower, rougher. His thumb presses slightly into my bottom lip.

"Yes." I meet his eyes, holding nothing back. "I want everything you said. I want to be filled until I can't take anymore."

The smile that spreads across his face is pure sin. "Good girl."

Leo pushes his chair back and reaches for me, his hand wrapping around my wrist. One gentle tug, and I'm out of my seat, falling easily into his lap. His kiss meets me halfway, deep and hungry, tasting of coffee and something darker. When he finally pulls back, I'm breathless, my lips tingling, my pulse racing.

"Bedroom," he says. "Now."

My pulse jumps. I move because there's nothing else I can do, following him down the hall, the air between us thick enough to taste. He doesn't look back to see if I'm coming. He doesn't have to. I feel the pull of him everywhere.

The moment we cross the threshold, he stops. Turns. His eyes drag over me, slow and hungry, and my knees threaten to give out.

"Strip for me." Not a request. A command. "Slowly."

My hands shake as I reach for the hem of my shirt, but I obey. The fabric whispers over my skin as I pull it off, and Leo's eyes track every movement. When I hook my thumbs in my shorts, he makes a low sound of approval.

"Exquisite," he murmurs as the last piece hits the floor. "So fucking gorgeous."

He guides me to the bed with gentle pressure, positioning me exactly where he wants me. "On your stomach. Knees under you. I want to see that beautiful ass."

Heat floods my cheeks, but I do as he says. The position makes me feel exposed, vulnerable, but his voice softens the embarrassment until it feels like worship.

Leo's hands settle on my hips, thumbs stroking the curve where my ass meets my thighs. "So beautiful," he murmurs, and there's genuine awe in his voice. "This gorgeous ass has been driving me crazy for years."

He spreads me open. The air hits me, and everything tightens instinctively. My hips twitch. Warmth rises to my cheeks and settles low in my belly.

"Easy," Leo murmurs. He presses a kiss to the small of my back, and the softness undoes me. "I've got you, baby."

His mouth finds me, not where I expect, but higher. His lips brush the curve of my ass, then his tongue follows, warm and wet, tracing lazy paths across my skin.

"Leo," I gasp, unsure what I'm asking for.

"Relax," he breathes against me, the word scorching. "Mouth first. Fingers. Plug. Patience."

He kisses lower, spiraling inward until his lips ghost over a place no one's ever kissed. The sound that escapes me is half surprise, half disbelief.

His groan rumbles against my skin. "God, Lorna. Don't hold back. Let me hear you."

When his tongue finally slides over me, I break.

The wet heat of him is overwhelming, every nerve lighting up at once. My brain can't keep up, can't make sense of pleasure this sharp. My fingers twist in the sheets as the world tilts and contracts around the relentless drag of his tongue. It shouldn't feel this good, but it does. It's ruinous, consuming, and I'm gone before I can even try to stop it.

"That's it," he growls, his grip tightening on my thighs as though he needs me to stay exactly here, open and trembling beneath him. "Fuck, the way you move, Lorna. You're driving me insane. Look at you, begging without a word."

His tongue keeps working me open. Circling gently, pressing in with shallow, teasing dips that leave me panting. He takes his time. Lets me squirm. Every swipe makes my hips jerk. Every pass ratchets my need higher until I'm delirious.

His hands hold me wide, fingers stroking grounding circles over my hips. Reminding me I'm safe.

He presses another kiss there, softer this time. "This ass is going to take everything I give it, isn't it?"

"Yes." The word tears from my throat, rough and desperate. I'd beg if he asked me to.

When he pulls back, a broken sound escapes me. The loss hits hard, like waking too soon from a perfect dream.

Then I feel the cool slide of lube on his fingers, the slick drag over heated skin.

"Now," he says, voice thick with want. "We move to the next step."

The first press of his finger is careful. Deliberate. A measured invasion that makes everything tighten, and melt.

I inhale sharply, the stretch unfamiliar and electric. Nerve endings snap awake, pleasure and pressure braided so tightly I can't tell where one ends and the other begins.

He doesn't rush. Eases in, giving me time to adjust, to breathe, to want.

And God, I want. I want this, him, so badly every part of me leans into it. Everything softening, my body offering itself to him.

Leo groans as though he can feel the shift. "That's it. Let me in. Let me show you how good this can feel."

He works me open with infinite patience. One finger at first, then another. Skillful and devastating. Scissoring gently. Twisting. Testing. His praise comes in a steady stream as he kisses along the dip of my spine, the curve of my hip, every bit of skin within reach.

"You're doing so well," he whispers. "So fucking well. Look at you, opening up so beautifully for me."

I believe him. Not because the words feel as though they're sunlight in the deepest parts of me, but because I feel it in my bones.

I was made for this. For him. For them.

When the tip of the plug touches me, I flinch.

It's cold. Shockingly so. Metal kissed by air and lube, pressing into fire. A sound catches in my throat as he begins to push, the chill giving way to deeper sensation.

It's small, I know that. But it feels impossibly large as it starts to enter me.

The pressure is steady, relentless. Everything resists, clenches reflexively. Little by little, I begin to open around it. I feel every fraction of movement as it glides deeper, the smooth metal unforgiving. It stretches me wider than I'm used to, dragging a startled, broken sound from my throat.

My fingers curl into the sheets. Thighs tense. My mouth parts on a gasp that turns into a moan as he eases past that tight ring of muscle.

I clench around it without meaning to, and the sensation leaves me reeling. It's strange and overwhelming, so much fuller than I imagined. The weight of it sits deep, an intimate pressure that doesn't go away. I feel it when I breathe. When I shift. When I so much as think about him behind me, watching me take it.

"Gorgeous," Leo says, pressing a kiss to my hip. "Absolutely stunning. How does that feel?"

"Full," I manage, voice shaky. "But good. Really good."

He helps me roll onto my back, the shift making the cool weight press deeper, a steady pressure that sends a ripple of sensation straight up my spine. I choke on a whimper, my muscles fluttering around the fullness.

He holds up the panties.

"Lift your hips for me."

I nod, cheeks burning, and brace my hands beside me as I tilt up. His fingers skim my thighs, guiding the lace into place. My hips jerk as he adjusts them, fitting them against my clit. He pulls the remote from his back pocket and holds it up—a promise. A warning. The look in his eyes says both.

"This stays with me."

His thumb brushes the dial but doesn't turn it. Everything in me stills, aching for it. Dreading it. Craving it.

"You're going to wear them all day," he says. "Cook dinner in this. Go through your day knowing I'm the one in control."

He steps back and drags his gaze down my body. Possessive. As though he's burning the sight into memory.

"You can get dressed," he says, voice low and absolute. "But remember, every step you take, every breath you draw belongs to me until dinner."

My lips part before I can stop them. "When will you—"

That smile. Wicked. Devastating. Pure sin. "The moment the door closes behind me."

He pulls me to my feet, backing me into the wall, his body a mass of heat and muscle. The air disappears between us.

His mouth claims mine. Not sweet. Not soft. A kiss that tastes like dominance and want. I melt into it, into him, my fingers clutching his shirt, my knees giving way beneath me.

"Don't you dare come until I say so," he growls against my lips, the words sliding down my spine like smoke and iron.

When he finally steps back, I'm panting and shaking, spine pressed to the wall like it's the only thing holding me up.

At the door, he pauses, remote in hand, eyes dark and glinting with promise.

"This is just the beginning, beautiful."

And then he's gone.

The second the door clicks shut behind him, the panties ignite.

The vibration slams into me, sudden and merciless. Low, deep, perfectly placed. My knees buckle and I slide down the wall, gasping. The plug shifts with the movement, dragging pressure across nerves I didn't know existed.

Oh God.

A whimper tears from my throat, high and breathless. My chest heaves as wave after wave rolls through me, building, backing off, hitting even harder. It's relentless. Strategic. As though he's mapped out exactly how to break me without laying another finger on my skin.

I swear I can hear him laughing all the way back to his house.

The hours that follow are quiet hell.

I try to go about my day. Get dressed. Prep for dinner. But every task becomes a battle between my body and my will. The vibrations are unpredictable. Sometimes they're barely there, a faint hum that keeps me strung tight. Other times they spike hard and fast, deep enough to knock the air from my lungs.

Getting ready is almost impossible.

My hands shake as I try to do my hair. I jab myself in the scalp twice before giving up and twisting it into a messy bun. The vibe kicks up as I start my mascara, and I have to grip the edge of the sink to stay upright.

I reach for my makeup bag and it hits. Hard.

A choked sound claws up my throat. I brace both hands on the vanity, my body going rigid, thighs clenching. My hips rock forward before I can stop myself, nearly grinding into the counter.

*Don't you dare come.*

I freeze. Swallow hard. Stay still until the pulse fades and my legs stop shaking.

By afternoon, I'm pacing the kitchen, caged and restless. Flushed, aching. The plug feels heavier, as though my body is molding around it. As if it belongs there. As though I need it there.

Cooking is a mess. My hands won't stop shaking. I drop the spoon repeatedly. Nearly slice my finger open. When the toy pulses as I'm stirring the sauce, I grip the edge of the stove and squeeze my eyes shut, hips twitching forward, chasing friction I'm not allowed to have.

I'm soaked. Desperate. Every nerve ending screams for a release I'm forbidden. My thighs are slick. My core throbs. And still, he hasn't turned it all the way up.

When I hear the crunch of tires in the driveway, their truck rolling to a stop, I nearly sob with relief.

The sun is low, spilling honey-colored light through the

windows. I stand frozen in the kitchen, breathing shallow, heart thundering.

They're here.

Leo, Hudson, and Levi move in easy sync as they step through the door, all T-shirts and worn jeans, sun in their hair, a trace of sweat at their temples. They look relaxed, smiling and laughing, but the air around them hums with something sharper, a current just beneath the surface. The atmosphere shifts the moment they step inside. It grows thicker, charged, almost too heavy to breathe.

My knees nearly give out. Because I know the game is over, and what comes next isn't mercy. It's the reward. Or the reckoning.

"How are you feeling?" Levi asks gently, eyes scanning my face as though he already knows the answer.

"Desperate," I whisper.

Hudson's grin is downright wicked. "Good."

Leo pulls the remote from his pocket and turns it up.

The jolt makes me cry out, half gasp, half moan. My body folds forward on instinct, clutching the back of a chair for balance. The spike is sharp, devastating, fading to a wicked pulse. I'm dripping. Trembling.

"Dinner first," Leo says, calm as ever. "We take care of our girl after."

Dinner is exquisite, drawn-out torture.

I try to focus. On finishing touches, plating, passing wine. But Leo keeps the vibrations randomized. Sometimes a whisper-soft tease that leaves me aching. Sometimes a sharp flicker that nearly makes me sob. I spill the salt. Drop my fork. Lose the thread of conversation over and over.

Hudson and Levi don't take their eyes off me.

Hudson rests his hand on my thigh beneath the table, fingers curling just enough to shift the plug inside me. I nearly choke on my wine.

"You're doing so good, Snapdragon," he murmurs, lips brushing my ear. His fingers slide higher, finding the edge of the lace. "Fuck, Lorna. You're soaked."

Between the nickname and his fingers dipping between my legs, I'm completely wrecked.

"Open," he commands, holding his glistening fingers to my lips. "Taste how ready you are for us."

I part my lips without thinking, sucking his fingers clean. Hudson groans low in his throat.

He leans in and kisses me, his tongue sweeping into my mouth. I moan into it, shivering as his heat sinks into my bones. He doesn't rush. He devours. He makes me feel owned.

When he finally pulls back, his words brush over my ear. "You taste incredible. I'm going to bury my face between your legs tonight and drink every drop."

I whimper, already on the brink.

Across the table, Levi reaches casually for the remote in Leo's hand.

"May I?" His tone is polite, but there's nothing gentle in his eyes. They're dark with mischief. Hunger.

Leo hands it over.

A second later, the vibrator kicks to life. Hard. The intensity spikes so fast I see white. My spine arches. My hands fly to the edge of the table, gripping it as though it might keep me from floating off the planet.

My mouth drops open on a soundless scream.

"Breathe," Levi murmurs, holding my gaze as his thumb works the dial as though he's playing a symphony on my nerves. "Breathe through it, love. You're so beautiful when you're close."

The vibrations pulse in erratic waves. Build and retreat, build and retreat. I chase each one, a drowning woman clawing at the surface, but it always pulls back before I can break through.

"Please," I whisper, the word barely audible.

Hudson's hand slips beneath the tablecloth, trailing over the curve of my ass, lower. Tracing the plug through the soaked lace.

He hums low in his throat. "Look at you. Sitting there so sweet, trying to act normal, while you've got a plug stretching your ass and a toy buzzing on your clit. You love it, don't you?"

Before I can answer, before I can even breathe, his palm lands on my ass. Not hard, but firm. The jolt of sensation punches through me, fast and brutal, and I nearly come right there at the table.

"Careful," Leo warns, his voice rough. "She's not allowed to come yet."

"That was for being so fucking stunning," Hudson replies, grinning, though his touch gentles. Stroking the spot he smacked, apologetic.

By the time dinner ends, I'm unraveling. My thighs are a mess. I've forgotten how to speak in full sentences. Can barely breathe.

When I stand to clear the table, I nearly drop the first plate. Because Levi turns the dial.

"Oops," he says, utterly unrepentant. "You look so pretty, I can't help myself."

Leo finally reaches over and clicks the toy off.

The silence it leaves inside me is deafening. But it's not relief. It's hunger. Everything is a live wire, strung too tight, buzzing with denied pleasure.

"It's time," Leo says, his voice cutting through the tension with brutal command. Rough. Final. "Bedroom. Now."


We move to my bedroom together, not walking so much as surrendering. Each step up the stairs is a silent vow, each movement along the hallway thick with anticipation. By the time we reach the door, it doesn't feel as though this is a room anymore. It's a sanctuary. A place for worship. A place for ruin.

Inside, the only light comes from the bedside lamp, its amber glow turning everything soft and golden. Shadows climb the ceiling. Everything feels sacred. Electric. Inevitable.

Leo undresses me with devastating patience. Each button, each strap, each inch of damp fabric peeled away is its own ceremony.

He kneels to slide my panties down, and the reverence in his touch makes me shiver.

The plug shifts as he lifts me onto the bed, sending a shock of pleasure straight through me. My thighs tighten instinctively. I press my cheek to the cool sheets, breath shuddering as tremors ripple through me.

Hudson's hand settles on my lower back. "Jesus," he mutters, eyes locked on me. "You really wore that thing all day?" His thumb brushes the base of the plug, and I jerk. "Bet you fucking loved it."

I can't answer. Can barely breathe. Leo's between my thighs, fingers locked on my hips, but instead of touching me where I'm aching, he pulls me up onto my hands and knees.

"I need to see you," Leo says, voice rough, full of fire. "See how ready you are."

Hudson joins him at the edge of the bed, and together they spread me open. The way they're looking at me undoes me completely. As though they've been starving for this. For me. As if seeing me plugged, trembling, split open is the best damn thing they've ever seen.

"Fuck," Hudson mutters, giving the base of the plug a teasing pull. The sensation rips a whimper from me. "Look at you. This thing's kept you ready all day, hasn't it? I bet you've been wet since the moment he put it in."

Leo strokes a thumb down the curve of my ass, right where the plug disappears inside. "You've done so well, baby. You think you're ready for more?"

"Yes," I breathe, glancing back at them over my shoulder. I'd agree to anything right now if it meant they'd let me come.

"Hold her open," Leo says.

Hudson doesn't hesitate. His hands replace Leo's, spreading me open. Then Leo's mouth finds me, his tongue tracing the edge of the plug in slow, deliberate circles. A cry tears from me, muffled against the sheets as my arms shake and every muscle pulls tight.

Levi moves behind me, one hand threading through my hair,

grounding me. "Breathe, sweetheart," he murmurs. "You're doing so fucking good."

"Please," I gasp, the word barely there. "Please, I need..."

"What do you need, Petal?" Levi asks, voice low, rough around the edges.

He's not on the sidelines anymore. He's moving behind me, taking Leo's place. Palms skimming my hips, knees sinking into the mattress. I feel the heat of his body as he settles in close, the rasp of his breathing at the base of my spine.

"More," I gasp, shaking. "Please."

Hudson's hand lingers on my back for one last second before sliding away, giving Levi space.

"You want us to open you up?" Hudson says, voice grinding. "Stretch this tight little hole until it can take a cock?"

"Yes," I sob. "Yes. God, please."

Levi grips the back of my neck, and he leans in close, his mouth right at my ear.

"Look at you," he murmurs. "Begging. Trembling. So fucking ready."

His hand moves lower, sliding between my thighs, fingers dragging through the mess they've made of me. He strokes over my clit once, and I jerk, muffling my cry with my heel of my hand. He grips the plug with his other hand, twisting, easing it free with steady pressure. The loss makes me whimper, everything clenching around nothing.

Two of his fingers slide into me before I can catch my breath. "So wet," he groans, the sound rough, almost pained. "All this for us?"

I nod into the mattress, legs shaking.

He fucks me with his fingers, curling them perfectly until I'm gasping. His mouth is there, slick and filthy and relentless. He licks up through my folds, then higher, tongue teasing around my rim. I choke out a sob, twisting under him, but he doesn't stop. One hand keeps my hips in place, the other still working my pussy open while his tongue circles my ass.

"You taste so fucking good," he groans into me.

"Levi..." I sob. "I'm... I'm gonna..."

"No, you're not," he says, pulling back enough to speak. "Not yet."

He grabs the next plug from the nightstand. It's bigger. Thicker. My stomach clenches at the sight of it.

"You ready?" he asks.

"Yes," I whisper, the word barely a breath. "Please."

He coats it with lube and presses it into me, steady and sure, and the stretch hits instantly. My fingers clutch the sheets as tremors roll through me. I'm shaking, panting, on the edge of tears from how full I already feel.

"That's it," Levi groans. "You're doing so well for us."

The burn teeters on the edge of too much, but I don't fight it. I breathe through it, sinking deeper.

When the plug finally settles inside me, a sob breaks free, my whole body trembling.

Behind me, Hudson curses softly. "Jesus. Look at her."

"She's stunning," Leo murmurs, his hand gliding down the curve of my back. "So fucking gorgeous."

He moves, gripping my hips, flipping me onto my back as though he can't wait one more second to be inside me. Then he's over me, knees bracketing my thighs, cock in hand, lining up at my entrance.

The anticipation is brutal. Everything is coiled so tight I might snap.

"Eyes on me," he orders. His fingers catch my chin, forcing me to meet his gaze. "I want to see your face when I slide into this sweet little pussy with that plug stretching your ass wide."

Hudson closes in on one side, Levi on the other, their hands gripping mine, holding me steady.

Leo thrusts forward and a cry rips from me as my nails bite into their arms, my thighs trembling beneath him. It's too much. It's not nearly enough. The pressure of the plug from behind makes everything sharper.

"Oh my God," I sob, legs trembling, clinging to whoever I can grab. "Leo..."

"Fuck, that's it," he groans, driving in deep. "You feel that? Feel how deep I am? That plug's right there, pressing into me every time I fuck into you."

I nod frantically, too strung out to speak. Every thrust is a collision. His cock driving into the plug, the stretch inside me doubled, tripled, twisted into devastation.

Hudson moves closer, one hand settling on Leo's back. When their eyes meet, God. It's not fire. It's memory. Years of wanting and not touching. Of holding back.

Leo shudders under the contact, as though Hudson's touch is undoing him as much as being buried inside me.

"Fuck," Hudson rasps, eyes fixed on where Leo's buried deep inside me, his voice breaking open. "Look at her. Taking you so damn well. Like her pussy was made for your cock." His gaze lifts to mine, darker now, voice dropping to a growl. "Feels good, doesn't it, love? You love it—being stretched, filled, fucked just right."

"I... I..." The words fall apart, fracturing under the pressure.

Leo's rhythm is deep and ruthless, each thrust making the plug shift inside me, pressing hard into a spot that turns me inside out.

"You're close, aren't you," Leo mutters, his mouth brushing my jaw. "I can feel it. This tight little cunt's gripping me as though it doesn't wanna let go."

"God," I gasp, blinking through the blur. "Please, I want..."

"Do you want all of us?" Hudson murmurs, his lips brushing my ear. "You want to be filled everywhere? To be used the way that greedy little body of yours craves?"

I whimper, everything locking up as Leo pushes in deep and stays there, grinding into me.

"Yes," I sob, raw and desperate.

"I know what you need, Petal," Levi says, standing beside the bed. His tone roughens as he strokes a thumb over my lower lip, his other hand already working his belt buckle.

The metallic clink of his belt, the rasp of his zipper. Every sound makes my pulse spike. He frees himself, and I watch through hazy eyes as he wraps his hand around his length, stroking once, twice. His breathing is already uneven, his gaze locked on my face.

"Open your mouth for me," he says.

I do, eager and shaking, and he steps closer, one knee on the mattress for leverage.

He guides himself to my lips. The head of his cock is already slick with precum. I open wider, and he slides in. So slow. Giving me time to adjust, to taste, to feel the weight of him on my tongue.

Heavy. Hot silk. Iron underneath.

My lips stretch around him, the taste of him flooding every part of me that isn't already being fucked or filled. Salt and skin and Levi.

He groans, his hand sliding to the back of my head. Not to push. Just to hold. Like he's grounding both of us with that one touch.

"God," he breathes, voice wrecked. "Your mouth, Lorna. It's fucking heaven."

I feel like I'm nowhere and everywhere at once.

Leo's still driving into me, the plug shifting with every thrust. Levi's fucking my mouth, his fingers under my jaw as though he's holding something fragile. Hudson's hands are roaming, pinching my nipples, dragging across my hips, whispering things so filthy I can't even process them.

"Jesus," Leo groans, voice gone hoarse. "Look at her. Mouth stuffed, cunt dripping, ass stretched. You fucking love this, don't you? Taking everything we give you."

The words hit with the force of a spark to dry tinder, catching fast. Heat coils low, twisting tight. Leo's thrusts sync with Levi's movements in my mouth, every shift of his hips driving the plug tighter into that sweet, devastating spot inside me. My hips buck on instinct, and a helpless moan escapes around Levi's cock.

"You're stunning," Hudson murmurs at my neck, words burning. "So fucking gorgeous when you let us use you. You love it, don't you, baby? Letting us take what we want?"

I moan and Levi groans above me. "You never cease to amaze

me," he whispers, cupping my cheek, thumb brushing my jaw. "Such beauty in your surrender. This... this is what you were made for."

Hudson's hand lands on Leo's hip, a fleeting touch, just skin to skin, and Leo shudders. His rhythm falters. Their eyes lock above me, and something raw and wordless passes between them.

Hudson strips off his shirt, tossing it aside. His hands go to his belt, movements quick and efficient, and I watch through half-lidded eyes as he sheds his jeans and boxer briefs in one motion. He's already hard, cock heavy and flushed, and the sight of him bare and ready makes my mouth water.

"Switch with me, Hudson," Leo says, voice ragged.

Hudson doesn't pause. He moves into position as Leo pulls out, leaving me empty for half a second before Hudson sinks into me with one hard, confident thrust that knocks the air from my lungs.

"Fuck, you're tight," Hudson groans, already moving. Faster. Rougher. "That plug's got you clenching so goddamn hard."

I whimper around Leo as he replaces Levi at my mouth, his cock on my tongue. I taste salt, skin, and the sharp edge of his need. I open wider, needing all of it, needing him.

Hudson's pace is brutal, each thrust hitting deep, pushing the plug tighter inside me until I'm a mess of sound and sensation. I sob around Leo, nerves on fire, brain short-circuiting.

"That's it," Hudson pants. "Taking it so fucking well. Such a good fucking girl."

Levi moves to my side, brushing the hair from my damp forehead, his touch gentle amid the chaos of what they're doing to me. "God, look at you," he says, his voice ragged. "Mouth full, body stretched. You love the taste of him, don't you? Love having your throat fucked while he pounds into you?"

Leo's hand slides between my legs, fingers finding my swollen clit. He circles it once, twice, the pressure perfect and maddening, and I moan around the cock in my mouth.

Hudson's hand slides over his, not replacing but joining. For a heartbeat they move together, fingers perfectly aligned, pressing against my most sensitive spot. The shared rhythm pulls a broken sound from me, and from Leo.

Leo freezes. His hips jerk forward in my mouth, his groan breaking open around our names. His length pulses on my tongue, and I feel him shaking, fighting for control. Hudson's hand stays over his for one more second, squeezing gently before sliding away.

The moment stretches between them, heavy and electric.

Leo pulls out before he comes and I gasp as though I've been drowning. My lips are wet, swollen, slick with spit and salt.

"Levi," I manage, voice ragged as I turn toward him. "Please... please..."

"I've got you," he murmurs, and he's between my thighs, his hand sliding under my knee to open me wider.

Hudson shifts up, cock hard and slick. He brushes it across my lips, and I can taste myself on him. Sharp and familiar. I part my lips, take him in, and he groans as if it physically hurts to be inside me.

Levi pushes in.

Deep. As if every inch is a vow.

As though he's offering me up at the altar of this moment. Of us.

His hips roll in grinding circles, working the plug inside me with every thrust until I can't tell where the pressure ends and the pleasure begins. I cry out around Hudson's cock, my whole body unraveling.

"Fucking exquisite," Levi groans, his grip on my thigh tightening as he holds me open. "You were made to be worshipped like this."

Above me, Hudson's breathing falters. One hand threads into my hair, the other cups my jaw. "Look at her," he mutters, voice unraveling. "Wrecked. Still begging."

Leo's hands move over me like he knows exactly what I need. When his fingers graze my clit, the jolt slices straight through me.

It's too much.

"Come," Leo growls, the command rough and absolute. "Come on his cock while Hudson fucks your pretty mouth."

His fingers don't ease up. No hesitation. No mercy.

I shatter.

The orgasm crashes through me like a tsunami, every muscle locking tight around Levi, the plug amplifying each pulse until I scream around Hudson, the sound lost to his body, to the sheer, consuming bliss tearing through me.

"Fuck, yes," Hudson groans, voice raw and shaking. "That's our girl."

I can't stop. Can't breathe. I'm sobbing around him, mouth still working, still desperate, as Levi curses, hips stuttering. He spills inside me with a raw, guttural sound, half growl, half broken prayer, his hips grinding deep as he rides it out, my body clenching hard around him, wringing him dry.

Seconds later, Hudson shudders, a wrecked moan ripping from his chest as he throbs on my tongue. I take him deeper, desperate, swallowing him down as though it's a sacrament. Levi moves aside, and Leo slides into me, his girth stretching me open all over again. I cry out, voice raw and shaking, nerves oversensitive but still begging.

He gives me a few strokes, deep and unhurried, anchoring me to the moment. He stills, buried to the hilt, his body trembling. But he doesn't come. Instead, his hand slides up to cup my jaw, forcing my gaze to his.

"One more," he says.

"I can't," I whisper, breath hitching. "I can't."

"Yes," he says, firmer. "You can. Give me one more, sweetheart."

He pulls out, and I gasp at the sudden emptiness. He shifts, sliding his knees under my thighs and settling back on his haunches. He draws my ass up into his lap, positioning me so I'm open and stretched and already gasping by the time he pulls me onto his cock.

Hudson moves fast, dropping to his knees beside my hips. He buries his face between my spread thighs, right where my body is stretched around Leo's cock. His breathing ghosts over my clit before he seals his lips around it.

The first pull nearly has my soul leaving my body, a shock that rips through me and arches my spine off the bed. A broken sound tears from my throat. He doesn't ease up, working me harder, licking and sucking, his tongue flicking in rapid passes that make my thighs shake violently.

"Fuck," Leo chokes out above me, his whole body going rigid.

Hudson hums into my clit in response, the vibration devastating, and doubles his efforts. His tongue works faster, more insistent, and I feel Leo's cock throb inside me, responding to every lick, every pull of Hudson's mouth over my swollen flesh.

"Jesus Christ," Leo groans, his voice wrecked. "She's clenching so fucking hard. Keep going. Make her come on my cock."

One more thrust and the world splinters. Blinding pleasure explodes through me, crashing through every nerve ending, flooding my veins until I stop being a person and become sensation. I sob, chest heaving, mouth open in a scream I can't voice as Leo grinds deep, thrusting into my pulses while Hudson drags me tighter into his mouth, eating me alive.

Only when I'm soaked and trembling, shattered from the inside out, does Leo slam deep with a hoarse curse. His rhythm turns feral, desperate, every thrust rougher than the last. He's chasing the end, and I give it to him without hesitation, every part of me open, wrecked, his to ruin.

He buries his face in my neck, breathing hot and ragged over my skin. "You feel so fucking good," he groans, voice breaking. "I'm gonna fill you up, sweetheart. Gonna come so deep you taste it."

And he does. Hips locking, body shuddering, his mouth still pressed to my throat as he spills inside me with a sound that borders on a sob. Raw and broken. Worship and possession all tangled up in one ruined breath.

We collapse together, a heap of slick skin and unsteady breaths. The plug's still inside me, muscles still clenching, a living reminder of everything they gave me. Everything we became.

Leo presses his mouth to my hair. "How do you feel?"

I blink through the haze. "Good," I whisper. "Really fucking good."

"Thank God," Hudson murmurs, smoothing my hair back from my face, looking at me with awe.

They remove the plug slowly, every breath a wordless check-in. Leo's hands are steady as he eases it free, his mouth pressing soft kisses to my hips while I tremble through the sudden emptiness.

Then come the washcloths, the warm water, the murmured praise that sounds closer to prayer. The same hands that wrecked me minutes ago now move with aching care, tracing over my skin as if I'm something sacred.

"You were stunning," Levi says, pressing a kiss to my bare shoulder. "Absolute heaven. Every inch of you."

"You did so good, sweetheart," Leo adds, his thumb dragging over my bottom lip. "The way you took everything we gave you. You're goddamned amazing."

Hudson huffs a quiet laugh, voice still ragged. "Fucking legend," he mutters, brushing a hand through my hair. "Never seen anything like you."

The aftercare binds us tighter than the sex did. Leo holds the water glass to my lips. Hudson massages my aching legs, working out the tremor. Levi reads to me, voice soft and rich, and it makes me feel cared for. Kept.

I fall asleep wrapped in them. Arms around my waist, lips in my hair, skin to skin. Sore. Sated. Safe. My mind quiet and at peace.

I'm theirs. They're mine. And everything else can wait until morning.

**21**

───────

## HUDSON'S POV

The morning sun burns my shoulders as I kneel between Lorna's dahlia rows, wooden stakes scattered around me like pick-up sticks. My hands move automatically. Measure, mark, drive the stake carefully beside the tuber without piercing it. But my mind keeps drifting back to last night. To the way Lorna felt between us, the sounds she made, the way Leo's eyes met mine over her trembling body.

Fuck me sideways.

My heart jams up into my throat just thinking about it. This thing between us is a freight train with no brakes, picking up speed whether we're ready or not. And the terrifying part? I don't want to stop it. None of us do. Hell, I'd probably throw myself on the tracks just to feel that rush again.

I shake my head, grinning despite myself. "Get it together, you absolute numpty," I mutter.

"Hudson." Lorna's voice cuts through my scattered thoughts, and I glance up to see her watching me with amusement. She's three rows over, dirt streaking her cheek, hair escaping its bun. Even disheveled and sweaty, she's the most stunning thing I've ever seen. Makes me want to mess her up even more, preferably without her clothes on. "You're staking those too close to the tubers."

I check my work and groan. I've been driving stakes with a hand that won't stop shaking. The wood's jammed barely an inch from the stem when it should be nowhere near that close.

"Well, shit." I pull the stake out, soil crumbling around the hole. "Sorry, Snapdragon. My head's elsewhere. Specifically thinking about how you looked last night when you…"

"Hudson!" Her cheeks flush pink, and I grin wider.

"What? Being honest."

She stands, brushing dirt from her knees, and walks over with that fluid grace that drives me fucking wild.

"Want to talk about it?"

Do I? Last night was everything I've wanted for months. Lorna beneath us, Leo's touch on my skin again, the four of us falling apart together as if this was always meant to be. But here in daylight with dirt under my fingernails, the intensity of what we've started is slightly terrifying.

It feels like a black hole. Bigger than all of us, pulling us together whether we can handle it or not.

"It's complicated," I say finally, driving another stake with fingers that won't quite steady. "But when has anything worthwhile ever been simple? That'd be too bloody easy." I flash her a crooked smile.

Lorna stands beside me, close enough that I can smell her soap and the faint sweetness of flowers that always clings to her clothes. Close enough that my skin prickles with awareness, with a craving that never seems to fade.

"The best things never are," she says.

"Leo and I…" I start, stop, not sure how to explain the tangle of history and lust and terror that keeps my stomach in knots. "I know you understand there's history there. But it's more than you probably realize."

"I figured." Lorna's tone is gentle, no judgment or jealousy. "The way you two are around each other... it's love. Complicated, maybe, but still there."

I laugh, and there's genuine humor in it. "Love. That's one word for it. Could also call it a clusterfuck, a train wreck, or my personal favorite: emotional Russian roulette with extra bullets."

She waits, giving me time to find the words. My pulse pounds in my throat, but she doesn't rush me. She just stands there, steady, letting the silence bloom between us. That's one of the things I love most about her—she never pushes. She just holds the space open, like a gate I can walk through when I'm ready.

"Leo and I were together for almost two years before Mom got sick," I say finally, the words feeling like pulling splinters from my chest. "Not just fooling around. *Together*. Planning a future, talking about forever, the whole domestic bliss package complete with matching tea towels." My hand trembles as I run it through my hair. "I was in love with him. Stupid, head-over-heels, would-have-followed-him-to-the-bloody-moon-if-he'd-asked in love."

"What changed?"

"Everything." The word tastes bitter on my tongue, but I chase it with a smile because that's what I do. "After Mom got sick, after everything went to absolute hell, it all fell apart. We never talked about what we were to each other anymore. We existed in the same space without addressing what we'd lost." I pause, then add with a wicked grin, "Though to be fair, it's hard to have a heart-to-heart when you're both pretending you don't want to bend each other over the nearest flat surface."

Lorna chokes on a laugh. "Hudson!"

"What? I'm being honest here. Do you want the sanitized version or the truth? Because the truth involves a lot more sexual frustration and a lot less noble suffering."

I tie off another stem, the motion giving my fingers something to do while my throat works around words that still hurt to say. "And there's you, and last night, and the way we finally touched each other again... it felt like finding solid ground and realizing it was quicksand."

"Is that good or bad?"

"Terrifying." I laugh shakily, my pulse quickening. "Because what if I mess this up? What if I can't be what he needs, what you need? What if this thing between us burns too hot and destroys everything?" I gesture between us with my free hand. "I mean, let's be brutally honest here. My track record with delicate situations is about as good as two bulls in a china shop. Usually I build things to fix my problems, but you can't exactly nail together a relationship and call it good."

"Hudson." But she's laughing, and that sound makes everything worth it.

Lorna's hand finds mine where it's clenched around the twine, her touch steady while my heart trips over itself. "And what if it's everything you've ever dreamed of? What if you stop borrowing trouble and let yourself fall?"

The word *fall* makes my stomach flip, because that's exactly what this feels like. A free fall with no safety net, no control, no way to stop even if I wanted to. And I don't want to. That's the scariest part.

"How the hell are you real?" I ask, staring at this woman who somehow unties every knot in my chest with just a few words. "Seriously, did someone custom order you? Because I need to know where to send the thank-you note."

Her smile makes butterflies riot in my stomach. "I ask myself the same thing about all of you." She smiles, tucking a loose strand of hair behind her ear, and bends back to the work.

"Flatterer." I grin, feeling some of the tension ease from my shoulders. "Keep talking that way and I might start believing you. Dangerous territory, love. My ego's barely contained as it is."

We work in silence for a while, but my head is anything but quiet. I feel her in every cell. The way she bites her lip when she's concentrating, the soft grunt when a stake sinks home, the way her shirt clings to the curve of her back in this thick, humid air. Every time she leans close, I have to hold myself back. I keep imagining pressing her into the dirt and pulling sounds from her that would echo off the hills.

It's madness. Gorgeous, brutal madness. Cliff-diving with no idea what's at the bottom. Pure adrenaline. And I keep leaping, because the rush? Worth every damn second.

"I need more stakes," Lorna says, wiping sweat from her forehead with the back of her hand. The gesture makes her shirt ride up, revealing a strip of skin that has my mouth going dry and my brain short-circuiting. "Think you could make some for me? These store-bought ones are so flimsy they probably won't last the season."

"Of course. How many do you need?"

"Couple dozen should do it."

"Right. Operation Stake Production, coming right up." I lean in and brush a kiss on her cheek, already mentally cataloging which wood would work best.

My workshop feels cool after the heat of the fields, dust motes dancing in shafts of sunlight that slice through windows I really should clean one of these days. The familiar smell of wood and varnish settles my chest. This is my domain, where my grip knows exactly what to do without my brain getting in the way. Where I can fix things instead of worrying about breaking them.

But Lorna changes everything just by being here. She follows me inside, her fingertips trailing over tools and half-finished projects with the same reverence she gives her flowers. I try to focus on the wood, on the work, but all I can think about is those careful hands moving over my things.

"This is incredible, Hudson." She stops at my workbench, where a partially carved music box sits waiting. "You built this?"

"Yeah." I pick out a piece of cedar, my fingers skimming the grain as I try to ignore the way she's looking at me, like I'm something remarkable instead of just a bloke who spends too much time buried in sawdust and wood shavings.

She traces the delicate roses I've carved into the lid, each petal detailed enough to look real. "It's gorgeous. Who's it for?"

Heat floods my cheeks. "You, actually. I was gonna give it to you for your birthday, but—" I shrug, suddenly feeling exposed. "Seemed too forward before last night. Didn't want to come across as some lovesick puppy."

"Hudson." There's a note of disbelief in her voice, and when I glance up, she's staring at me as if I've handed her the moon. "You made this for me?"

"The song's from that first night we had dinner. You were humming it when you pulled the lasagna out of the oven. It sounded like a lullaby. I've been trying to recreate it in the mechanism ever since." I rub my jaw. "Turns out mechanical music boxes are a bit more complicated than regular furniture. Who knew?"

The look on her face makes my cock jump. I have to turn away before I do reckless things. Like sweep all my tools onto the floor and fuck her right there on the workbench. Again.

"Help me with the stakes?" I ask, before she can say anything else. "You can sand these smooth while I cut more." I pass her a sanding block, trying to ignore the way her fingertips brush mine and send sparks shooting up my arm.

We work side by side, the tension winding tighter with every glance that lasts a beat too long, every satisfied hum she lets out when she moves to the next piece. My skin feels too small, as though I've been plugged straight into an outlet, every nerve twitching under the surface.

By the time an hour's passed, I'm ready to crawl out of my skin. She's humming again, that same old Scottish tune, and between that and the scrape of sandpaper, the delicate clench of her teeth on her bottom lip, and the way she keeps stretching to reach for another stake—Yeah. I'm one breath away from losing my goddamn mind.

"Hudson," she whispers, and there's a quality in her tone that makes me look up.

I cross the small space between us like a man in a dream, my heart hammering so hard I'm sure she can hear it. She touches my face, mapping the stubble on my jaw, and I lean into the contact like a starving man.

"I love watching you work," she says, the words making my knees weak.

God, when she looks at me that way. "Lorna…"

She kisses me before I can finish the thought, sweet at first, deeper when I groan and pull her closer.

This is what I've been craving all morning. Her mouth on mine, her body pressed to me, the taste of her on my tongue. I slide my hands around her waist, thumbs stroking over the strip of skin where her shirt has ridden up. She's perfect, and I want to memorize every inch of her.

"We should go back to the field," she murmurs into my lips, but her fingers are tangling in my hair, holding me close.

"Should we?" I ask, already knowing the answer by the way her breath hitches when I kiss her neck.

"The stakes…"

"Can wait." I lift her onto my workbench, stepping between her thighs. "The truth is I've been thinking about you all morning. About the way you looked last night, the sounds you made when you came." I roll my hips into her, showing her exactly what she's doing to me. "And from the way you're watching me right now, you've been thinking about it too."

"Someone's impatient," she laughs, but her legs wrap around my waist, pulling me closer.

"Someone's been going fucking crazy all morning," I correct. I kiss her again, deeper this time, and she responds with a hunger that matches my own. But part of me wants more than kissing in my dusty workshop.

"Not here," I rasp into her mouth, dragging myself back an inch. "Come with me." I help her down from the workbench, my hands lingering on her waist.

"Where?" she asks, but she's following me outside.

"Trust me?"

Her smile is answer enough.

The dahlia field feels like a cathedral. Sunlight filtering through petals like stained glass, every row a living aisle that leads straight into the sky. The blooms are massive, coral and cream and blushing peach, their heads bobbing gently in the breeze.

I stop between two rows where the flowers grow thick and tall enough to create a hidden alcove.

"Here?" Lorna asks, her voice low, that edge of excitement slamming straight into my chest.

"Here." I drop the blanket I grabbed from the shop to the ground, already reaching for her. "I want to make love to you surrounded by your flowers."

"Someone could see," she says, but she's already tugging at the hem of her shirt.

"Let them." I help her pull it over her head, and hell, the way the sunlight hits her skin. Golden and glowing and dusted with freckles. It undoes me. "Let them see how beautiful you are."

She reaches for my shirt and I let her strip it off, her palms sliding over my chest, mapping the muscle and scars with gentle pressure. When she reaches for my belt, I catch her wrists.

"Not yet," I murmur, pressing a kiss to the throb of her pulse, feeling it jump under my mouth. "My turn first."

I guide her hands back to her sides, and reach for the button of her jeans. "Let me strip you down right here and make love to you in your field, so every time you walk these rows, you remember exactly how it feels to come with me buried deep inside you."

Her mouth falls open, and I realize this is what she craves. The raw honesty. The claiming. The kind of need that strips you bare and makes you grateful for it.

I guide her down onto the blanket and take my time undressing her, slow and steady, like I have forever. No rush. Just reverence and the aching sweetness of watching her unravel one breath at a time.

I kiss as I go, tongue tracing sun-warmed skin that tastes of salt and summer.

"So damn stunning," I murmur against the hollow of her throat, dragging my mouth lower. Her fingers find my hair, clinging, trying to ground herself, but her shallow gasps tell me she's already gone.

By the time she's bare beneath me, she's trembling, eyes glazed, nipples hard in the open air. "Please," she whispers.

"Please what?" My voice is rough, already frayed as I strip down. I kick off my boots, shove my jeans and briefs aside in one motion. Her gaze follows every movement, hunger darkening her eyes.

"I need you," she groans. "Inside me. I need—"

"I've got you, baby." I press her down beneath me, every inch of skin burning where it meets hers. I line myself up, slide through her slick heat, and bite back a curse.

The first thrust steals the air from my lungs, everything tightening to a single, blinding point of pleasure.

She grips me hard, pulling me deeper, her body taking me in like it's been waiting for this. Like I was always meant to be here, buried inside her in a field of flowers on this tiny island.

I don't move. Not yet. I stay still, fighting for air and control, trying not to fall apart too soon.

"Fuck," I gasp into her neck. "Lorna, you... God, you feel incredible."

I let the rightness of her around me sink into my bones. Let myself feel every inch of where we're joined, the way she's stretched around me, the flutter of her muscles as she adjusts to my size.

"Look at you," I groan, finally starting to move. I draw out inch by inch, the tension twisting tighter, then drive back in until I'm buried to the hilt. The drag of it, the friction, sends sparks up my spine. "That sweet, tight little cunt taking everything I give it."

"God, Hudson," she gasps, her body arching beneath mine, nails scoring down my back. The way my name breaks on her lips unravels me from the inside out. "I love—"

My heart stutters. My rhythm falters. Everything in me goes still except for the thunder of my pulse.

"Say it," I bite out, barely holding on. "Say it so I know I'm not the only one that's absolutely fucked."

"I love you," she sobs, the words hitting me like a punch to the sternum. "God, I love you so much..."

Everything cracks wide open in my chest. The wall I've kept around my heart since Leo, since Mom, since everything fell apart. It shatters. And instead of terrifying me, it feels like relief.

"I love you, too," I rasp, my voice breaking around it, my eyes stinging. "So damn much it scares the fuck out of me." I drive into her harder, deeper, pouring everything I feel into it. Every fear, every hope, every broken piece of me that she's somehow made whole again. "I love you, Lorna. I love watching you think through things, that little furrow between your brows when you're working out a problem. I love how you built this whole damn field from nothing. I love the way you see people, really see them. And God, I love the way you surrender to me."

I brace on one arm and slide my other hand between us, rubbing circles into her clit just the way she likes.

"Come for me," I growl against her throat. "Strangle my cock right here in your garden. Let the flowers watch while I fuck every thought out of your head."

She breaks with a cry, body locking up beneath me. Her pussy clenches around me, pulsing hard. I come with her, emptying everything I have into the woman I never saw coming and can't imagine life without.

We collapse together, her body soft beneath mine. I shift just enough to keep from crushing her but can't bring myself to let go, to pull away.

We stay like that, tangled in the fading light, her head-on my chest, my fingers drifting through her hair. The sun warms our cooling skin, a bee hums somewhere close, and a single petal falls, landing gently on her shoulder.

"We have to do that again sometime," I murmur into her hair, a smile tugging at my lips.

She lets out a breathless laugh. "God, I love you."

"I love you, too." The words come easier now, no fear behind them. "Always will, Snapdragon."

We dress slowly, dragging the moment out as long as we can. Shirts half-buttoned, kisses stolen in between. She's glowing, flushed and gorgeous, her hair wild with bits of grass caught in the strands. Before I can reach for my boots, she plucks a massive coral dahlia from a nearby plant and tucks it behind my ear with a satisfied smile.

"There," she says. "Perfect."

I laugh, pulling her close for another kiss. "Think Leo and Levi will be suspicious?"

"Baby, they're going to take one look at us and know exactly what we've been doing."

The thought of facing Leo makes my stomach clench with familiar anxiety, but it's different this time. Less fear, more anticipation. Whatever's between us, it's time to face it head on.

"Hey," Lorna says, reading my face the way she always does. "Talk to him. Whatever's between you two isn't going anywhere until you face it."

She's right. She usually is. After everything we've shared, after hearing her say she loves me, I feel like I can face anything.

Even Leo Robinson and the tangle of what we used to be.

I help her gather the scattered stakes, our fingers brushing, stealing touches like teenagers. The sun hangs low, turning the world gold and amber, and I realize this moment, this woman, this love, is going to change everything.

For the first time in my life, the thought doesn't scare me.

I find Leo in his workshop that evening, the scent of leather and oil wrapping around me the way it always does. Worn-in, unmistakably him. God, I used to live for that smell. For any excuse to be in his workshop back in Australia, watching his hands coax an exquisite work of art out of hide and thread, pretending I cared about the craft when really, I just wanted to be close. Wanted him to look at me the way I looked at him when he wasn't paying attention.

He looks up when I step through the doorway, his gaze catching on me and holding. His expression barely changes, but something sparks behind his eyes, a mix of recognition and heat that tightens low in my stomach.

"Hudson." His tone is low, neutral in that careful Leo way, but I catch the way his eyes snag on my mouth. "How was your day?"

"Good." I lean on his workbench, trying to act as though my heart isn't trying to climb out of my chest. "Helped Lorna with her dahlias."

"I can see that."

There's an edge in his voice. Barely-there tension. Sharp underneath the calm. It sets my nerves jangling, makes the air between us feel electric and dangerous. I hate it. I hate how much I still want him after all this time.

The silence drags out, thick with all the things we've been too polite or too scared to say.

I break first.

"Are you happy?" The words come out faster than I mean them to, like ripping off a bandage. "With Lorna. With all of this. Us."

Leo sets the leather aside. Steady even though I can feel the storm starting behind his eyes.

"Are you?"

"I'm terrified," I admit, the truth spilling out before I can swallow it down. "That I'll mess this up. That we'll mess it up again. That I'll wake up one day and you'll be gone because I wasn't enough."

"We're fine, Hudson." His tone goes flat, controlled. The walls slamming back up so fast I nearly get whiplash. "Everything's fine."

"Bullshit." The word comes out harsher than I intended, echoing off the workshop walls. "You can't even meet my eyes properly anymore. We dance around each other as though we're strangers who shared a bed once and regretted it in the morning."

"We are what we need to be."

"What the hell does that even mean?" I push off the workbench, frustration boiling over. My hands shake so I shove them in my pockets. "God, you're still doing it. Still hiding behind those carefully constructed walls as if they'll protect you from actually feeling anything."

He picks up his tools again, focuses on the leather as if it holds the secrets of the bloody universe. "I'm working, Hudson."

"No, you're running. Same as you always do when things get real." I take a step toward him, and he goes rigid. Every muscle in his body locks down. "I came here to talk to you, Leo. Actually talk. I can't take any more of this surface-level bullshit."

"There's nothing to talk about."

The dismissal nearly knocks my legs out from under me. All that hope I'd been carrying around, all the careful courage I'd built up after being with Lorna in the field, after finally feeling as if maybe, just maybe we could have this. It crumbles.

"Right." I turn toward the door, anger and hurt warring in my chest, making it hard to function. "Sorry I bothered you."

I make it three steps before his fingers wrap around my wrist.

"Don't."

The word is rough, desperate enough to stop me cold. Before I can react, he's on me, walking me back until my shoulders hit the wall. His body cages mine, hands braced beside my head, and my pulse spikes hard enough to steal the air from my lungs.

"Don't what?" I whisper, the words shaky and thin.

His eyes are wild, that careful control finally cracking down the middle. "Don't walk away from me."

"You told me there was nothing to talk about."

His expression breaks. "I can't do this," he says, barely audible. "I can't pretend anymore."

"Then don't." My voice shakes.

"You don't understand." His voice is low, unsteady, each word dragging against the next. "Every time I look at you, I remember what I threw away. What I was too scared to fight for. What I let slip through my fingers because I was a coward."

My heart hammers in my ribs. "Leo..."

"I've regretted it every goddamn fucking day. Watching you pull yourself back together after I broke you. Watching you smile again, laugh again, be whole again. And when I see you with Lorna, when I see you open and happy and brave enough to love her the way you used to love me..." His voice cracks. "I think about everything I could have again if I wasn't so goddamned scared."

My chest aches so badly it feels as though my ribs might crack. "What are you saying?"

"I'm saying I still love you." He frames my face, thumbs brushing my cheekbones with devastating gentleness. "Always have. It never stopped. Not for a single second. Not when we fell apart. Not when I pushed you away. Not through any of the years we spent trying to ignore our feelings." His eyes search mine, vulnerable in a way I haven't seen since before everything went to hell. "And I want this. Us. All of us. Together. More than I've wanted anything in my entire life."

The room tilts. My body can't seem to decide between freezing and collapsing.

"Leo..."

"I know it's messy. I know I don't get to snap my fingers and fix what I broke. But I can't keep pretending I don't want you. That I don't ache for you every single day." His body presses closer, pinning me to the wall with his heat, his solidity, his presence. "I want to earn back your trust. I want to be the man you believed in, even when I didn't deserve it. Even when I was too broken to believe in myself."

I can't breathe. Can't think. He's always done this to me. Melted my logic into liquid and turned it into pure, desperate desire.

"You're sure?" I whisper, needing to hear it again. Needing to know he means it. "You want all of this? The mess, the history, the complicated tangle of us? You want me?"

He lifts a hand slowly, as if he's worried he'll scare me off, and brushes dahlia petals from my hair. They fall between us like confetti. "I want you. Not the easy parts. Not only the sunshine and flowers and nights in Lorna's bed. I want the parts we buried. The parts that still hurt when we touch them. The anger and the grief and the love that never died no matter how hard we tried to kill it." His thumb traces my jaw. "I want *us*, Hudson."

My fingers twist in the front of his shirt, dragging him close until our mouths collide. Words stopped being enough a long time ago. Maybe they never were.

The kiss is desperate, years of longing condensed into a single breath. His hand slides into my hair, holding me close like he's afraid I'll vanish if he lets go.

"I love you, too," I murmur into his lips when we finally break apart. "Always have. Even when I hated you for making me love you. Even when loving you felt like drowning."

He kisses me again, and it's like finding solid ground after years of free fall. Finally being allowed to want him again without shame or fear or the weight of everything we lost.

When we break apart, we're both breathing hard, foreheads pressed together.

"So where does this leave us?" I ask, still clutching his shirt like it's the only thing keeping me upright.

"Together." The certainty in his voice eases the tightness in my chest. "All four of us. The way it should've been from the start. The way it was always meant to be."

I smile, feeling lighter than I have in years. "Mom would have wanted this, you know. She always said love was the only thing worth fighting for."

"She was right." Leo's thumb traces a tear over my cheek. "About a lot of things."

"Including the fact that you're too stubborn for your own good?"

He laughs. "Especially that."

"Come on," I say finally, reluctantly pulling back. "Let's go find our girl and Levi and tell them we figured our shit out."

Leo huffs out a laugh, shaking his head. "Think she already knows?"

"Probably knew before we did." I run a hand through my hair, dislodging more dahlia petals. "She's been waiting for us to stop being such stubborn bastards and talk to each other."

We walk back toward the house, close enough for our arms to brush but never quite touching. Old habits die hard.

Through the kitchen window, I spot Lorna and Levi moving together, cooking in that easy rhythm they've found, bodies swaying around each other like they've been doing it for years.

"You ready for this?" Leo asks.

I glance at him, this man who's put me through hell and back, who I'd follow into hell again without question. Who I love despite everything. Because of everything.

"Ready as I'll ever be."

"Good," he says, and pushes open the screen door. "Because there's no going back."

Lorna looks up when we step inside, her eyes softening when she sees us standing close, the air between us finally calm.

"About time," she says, a knowing smile curving her lips.

And just like that, everything falls into place.

## 22



The leather's cool when I first touch it, but it picks up the heat of my skin fast, warming under my hands. I flatten the strip to the workbench, feel the grain under my fingers, the faint give of a perfect hide. I cut clean, following the lines I sketched in the dead of night when sleep wouldn't come.

These have to be perfect. Snug but not tight. Buckles that slide easily but never slip. I've remade them twice already, and I'll do it again if I have to. I don't half-ass things meant for her.

My hands work on instinct, which means my mind's free to wander where I don't want it to. To Hudson's mouth on mine last night, the fire of it, the way it cracked open what I'd kept locked up for years. To Lorna grinning at us when we told her. To the sudden, sharp understanding that the walls I built weren't as solid as I thought.

Fuck.

I force myself to lean into the rhythm of the work. Thread sliding, leather creaking, the occasional tap of metal on wood. One thing at a time. Finish the cuff. Breathe. Deal with the rest later.

The knock is hesitant, barely audible.

I glance up, and there she is.

Framed in the doorway. Hair piled into a messy knot, wisps catching the morning light. Two steaming mugs in her grip. Those worn jeans cling to her hips in a way that drags my eyes down before I can stop them. Her mouth curves, teasing, and when I meet her eyes, there's no question in them. Only quiet fire.

"Morning," she says, voice low and raspy. "Brought you this."

I drop the tools without thinking. "Get in here."

She crosses the room, carrying the scent of coffee and that soap she loves. Earthy and herbal, like sun-warmed dirt after rain.

"I heard you're shearing sheep today," she says, setting her mug at the edge of my bench, careful not to spill. "I could use a break from my presentation. Thought maybe you could use an extra pair of hands."

Our fingers brush as I take the coffee. Her skin is silk under mine. There's already dirt under her nails from the garden.

"It's filthy work," I warn, watching her over the rim of the mug. "You'll sweat through everything you're wearing."

"Perfect." A smile touches her mouth. "Exactly what I need to clear my head."

"What are you making?" she asks, leaning in.

I set my coffee aside and lift the cuffs. No point in hiding them. "These."

Her eyes widen, a flush crawling up her neck and into her cheeks. "Oh."

"Come here," I say, the wobble in my voice betraying me. "I need to make sure they fit."

She hesitates for only a beat before stepping into my space, offering her wrists. I slide the cuffs on, buckle them carefully, feeling the tremor under her skin. Her pale skin looks almost fragile against the dark leather, and it makes me want to map her veins with my tongue.

"How do they feel?"

"Good." The word is barely a whisper. Her pulse flutters at her throat. "Snug, but nothing's pinching."

I test the give of the leather, fingertips grazing her skin, and desire licks up my spine. The next move isn't even conscious. I walk her back, press her to the workshop wall, lift her bound wrists over her head, and pin them there.

Her eyes go wide and dark. "Fothermucker—"

I kiss her before she can finish, laughing into her lips. She tastes like coffee and honey, and the sound she makes shoots straight to my cock.

"Christ, Lorna," I mutter, my free hand gripping her waist, holding her to the wall. Fire radiates through her jeans, into my skin, into my blood. "You have no idea what you do to me."

"I think we all have a pretty good idea," Levi's voice drawls from the doorway, full of amusement.

I don't let her go, just turn my head to find Levi and Hudson in the doorway, both in faded jeans, sweat-damp shirts, and wearing matching wicked grins.

"Don't stop on our account," Hudson says as they close in. "We came to let you know the sheep are ready whenever you two are done."

Levi slips under my arm, his mouth brushing Lorna's neck. "Morning," he murmurs into her skin, lips ghosting along the curve of her shoulder. She shivers, and his grin widens.

"Started without us?" Hudson's voice is playful, but his eyes are heated. He trails kisses along her jaw, finding the spot beneath her ear that makes her melt. Her weight sags between us.

"You're all menaces," she manages between shaky laughter. "I came out here to work, not to be pinned to a wall."

"Multitasking," I tell her, finally releasing her wrists. The leather leaves faint marks on her skin that make me ache to follow them with my lips. "We're very good at it."

"Extremely," Hudson says, stealing a quick kiss before stepping back. "But sheep wait for no one." He swats her ass lightly, grinning. "Meet you in the barn in five?"

"We'll be there," I promise.

"Don't be late," Levi adds with a wink, already heading out. "Or we'll start brainstorming creative punishments."

They vanish as fast as they arrived, leaving behind air thick with tension.

Lorna sags back, cheeks pink, chest rising and falling rapidly. The cuffs are still on her wrists.

I step back into her space, my hands dragging up her sides. "Think we can make good use of five minutes?"

Her pupils dilate. "Leo—"

"Maybe you should take those jeans off," I murmur in her ear, my fingers already working her button free. "Let me take the edge off before we go deal with the sheep."

She gasps as I slide my hand into her jeans, finding her already soaking wet.

"Five minutes," she gasps, her bound wrists twisting in my shirt, pulling me closer.

"More than enough time," I promise, dropping to my knees and dragging her jeans down with me.

Some things are worth being late for.

The snip of the shears cuts through the thick air, steady as a heartbeat. The ewe under my grip gives a weak bleat, shifting but not really resisting. She's resigned to it.

"Easy, girl. Almost done."

Sweat slides down my spine, stinging as it finds the scrape on my back from earlier in the day. The barn's a furnace, the heat trapped beneath the high rafters and thickened by the press of wool and bodies. The air reeks of lanolin, hay, and that raw, animal tang of life.

Lorna moves through the pens with her sleeves rolled up and hair coming loose, sorting through fleeces with a sharp eye. She's fast for a beginner, separating them by length and quality the way Levi showed her, her concentration fierce. Levi works beside her, examining each piece, making notes about quality and condition.

Somewhere amidst the sweat and noise, the four of us find a

rhythm, moving together like we've been doing this for years instead of hours.

"You're good with them," Lorna says, watching as I flip an ewe onto her haunches. There's a streak of dirt across her cheek, and her eyes, more green than hazel in the low light, stay fixed on me. "The way you calm them down."

I shrug, uncomfortable with the compliment. "Practice. This type of work teaches you patience."

"Learn to take a compliment, old man," Hudson huffs, pushing the next sheep forward.

My retort dies in my throat when my eyes catch on him, his shirt plastered to his chest, every muscle drawn tight beneath the sweat. My breath stumbles. I force my gaze back to the ewe, fingers tightening around the shears. But last night's kiss won't let go; it flares hot and alive every time I look at him.

A bleat, sharp with panic, cuts through my spiraling thoughts.

"Something's wrong," Hudson says, already moving toward the sound.

We find the culprit tucked in the corner, sides heaving, eyes rolling white with pain. My gut drops.

"Damn it." I drop to my knees, running my hands over her side. "She's in labor. Late, by the look of her, and it's not going well."

Lorna drops to her knees beside me, worry etched across her dirt-streaked face. "Is she going to be okay?"

"I don't know. She's worn out, too weak to finish on her own. We'll have to help her."

"Tell me what you need," Hudson says, moving closer.

"Clean water. Towels. The OB lube. And someone to keep her steady."

They move fast. Levi disappears toward the house, returning within minutes with arms full of supplies. Clean towels, a bucket of soapy water, and a small first aid kit I hadn't even thought to ask for.

"Anything else?" he asks, kneeling beside me and laying out the supplies while Hudson returns with the lube.

"Stay close. If there are complications..." I trail off, not wanting to voice the possibilities.

Hudson shifts the ewe into place, guiding her onto her side. Lorna kneels at her head, murmuring softly until the trembling eases. Her fingers trace over the ewe's face, slow and soothing. Levi crouches by her flank, one hand feeling the rhythm of her breath, the other holding a stack of clean towels.

I slick my arm with the gel, taking a deep inhale to steady my nerves. "I'm going to have to go in and turn the lamb," I warn, glancing at them all. "It's going to hurt her, but it's the only way."

Lorna nods, her grip firm on the ewe's head. "We've got her," she says, and somehow, I believe her.

The world shrinks to the ewe's body and the slick, fragile limbs under my hand. I move carefully, every cell focused, trying not to hurt her, trying not to lose the life curled inside. The barn fades. No creak of rafters, no flies buzzing in the sunbeams. Only the ewe's ragged breathing, the faint suck of my arm moving through lubricant, and the sound of Lorna's low voice murmuring encouragement.

"Come on, little one," I mutter, coaxing as my fingers find the twisted limb. A tiny hoof slides under my touch, slick and impossibly small. I guide it gently, twisting my wrist to align it with the other leg.

"There," I whisper when I feel the lamb slip into proper position. "She's ready."

Nature takes over. Minutes later, the ewe's body heaves, and the barn fills with the wet, miraculous sound of new life arriving. A slick, shivering lamb tumbles onto the straw.

"It's a girl," Hudson says, grinning as he clears her nose and mouth.

Levi immediately wraps the newborn in a clean, dry towel and rubs her briskly. "Strong heartbeat," he murmurs, checking her carefully. "Good color. She's perfect."

The mother's instincts kick in the second Levi sets the baby on the ground. She noses her, licking her clean while the lamb wobbles, legs quivering. My chest tightens in that old familiar way, the quiet awe that comes with watching life start fresh, raw, and real.

I look up and catch Lorna staring at me.

"What?" I ask, suddenly aware of the straw on my knees, the sweat plastering my shirt to my skin.

She shakes her head, smiling. "That was incredible."

I grunt and wipe off my hands, trying to shake off the flush creeping up my neck. "I just did what needed doing."

"No," she says, her voice cutting through the quiet, steady enough to root me in place. "You didn't just help. You knew what to do, every step." She meets my eyes. "It was beautiful to watch."

I can't hold her gaze for long, not with that kind of admiration in her eyes. I busy myself with the straw, clearing away the mess. But her words slip past my defenses, lighting up places I'd almost forgotten could feel alive.

Finishing the shearing takes another hour, and by the end of it, the sun's bleeding low across the fields, painting everything in gold and shadow. My arms throb. My shirt is stiff with sweat and God knows what else. It's that bone-deep exhaustion that tastes of victory, the kind you only earn when the day wrings you out dry.

"I'm starving," Lorna says, dragging the back of her wrist across her forehead and smearing a line of dirt that somehow makes her look even better. "Levi and I will handle dinner. You two finish up here."

She heads toward the house, Levi following to raid the garden for dinner. Then it's just Hudson and me, the barn settling into a thick, quiet hum. The shuffle of sheep fades to background noise. What's left is the heat under my skin and him.

Hudson strips off his shirt, dragging the hem over sweat-slick abs before tossing it aside. His skin catches the dying light, golden, dirty, too perfect for his own good.

He catches me staring and grins, slow and knowing. "What? You planning to keep looking, or are you gonna do something about it?" His voice drops low, rough with challenge.

I don't think. I pull my own shirt off, the cooling air licking across my skin. His gaze follows the movement, lingers a fraction too long. My pulse kicks hard.

"Damn," he says, voice soft but wicked. His head tilts, eyes dragging over me. "I almost forgot the quiet one came with all that."

I step closer, until I can smell him—salt, sweat, hay, sun. The air tightens between us, humming with everything we're pretending not to want.

We don't speak. We don't need to. The next move is inevitable.

He closes the distance, and then his mouth crashes into mine, no hesitation, no testing the waters, just raw hunger. His hands find my hips, grip tightening until I swear he'll leave marks, and he drives me backward until my shoulders hit the barn wall. The wood digs into my back, but it's a distant discomfort, blurred by the heat of his body pressed against mine.

He grinds against me once, hard enough to steal my breath, and I feel exactly how far he's gone. The friction rips a sound from my throat, something between a gasp and a grunt. My fingers clutch at his shoulders, his neck, pulling him closer even though he's already all over me.

He pulls back just long enough to breathe, lips red, eyes blown wide. A crooked grin curves his mouth. "We should get inside before we end up fucking right here in the barn."

Before I can answer, his mouth crashes into mine again, harder, hungrier, like he's daring himself to ignore his own warning. His teeth catch my lip, the sting sharp. When he finally drags back, we're both gasping, foreheads pressed together, balanced on that knife-edge between need and control.

My pulse pounds, every beat a challenge to keep going. I don't want to stop. But we do. Somehow. We finish the chores in silence, tension simmering in every glance, every brush of skin.

By the time we make it home, the air is thick with the smell of roasted chicken and warm spices. Lorna's managed to turn a handful of leftovers into something that smells like a feast.

We wash up at the sink, trading space and elbow bumps, the water running brown before it clears. The sting of soap on raw skin feels almost good after the long day, grounding in its own way. By the time we sit, plates steaming between us, the tension has softened into something easy and familiar.

"How'd you make lettuce taste this good?" Hudson asks around a mouthful, lips slick with vinaigrette.

"Secret's in the dressing," Lorna says, sliding into the chair beside him. "And it doesn't hurt that everything was growing this morning."

I watch her instead of my plate. The way she leans back, content, a small smile tugging at her mouth. She looks like she belongs here, in this kitchen that's been hollow for years. The woman who shows up at my workshop with coffee at dawn. Who murmurs to anxious sheep until they settle. Who's slipped into the rhythm of our days so seamlessly I can't remember what the silence felt like before her laughter filled it.

"The lamb seemed strong when we closed them in for the night," Hudson says to nobody in particular, loading his fork with the perfect bite. "The mother's taken to her well."

"I've found that they usually do, if you don't interfere too much," I reply. "Nature knows what it's doing."

"Unlike us," Hudson grins, raising his beer bottle in a mock toast. "We're stumbling through, hoping for the best."

"Speak for yourself," Lorna laughs. "Some of us have plans."

"And some of us," Levi says with a pointed look at Hudson, "prefer organized stumbling to no plan at all."

The easy banter flows between us, and I realize this is what I've been missing. The end-of-day satisfaction, good food, people who know your rhythms and accept your rough edges. People who've seen you at your worst and still pull up a chair. Who know the parts of you that are hard to love and love you anyway.

"Thank you, Lorna," I say, quieter than I mean to. "For today. For everything."

Her gaze meets mine across the table, steady, a little knowing. "You're welcome."

After dinner, we drift to the porch with sweating beer bottles and full stomachs. The air is humid, heavy with the scent of cut grass and the distant metallic tang of rain. Lorna curls into Hudson's side on the porch swing, his arm draped over her shoulders, her bare feet tucked up beneath her. I take the rocking chair across from them, Levi settling into the other chair beside me, long legs stretched out, bottle dangling from his fingers.

We drift into comfortable silence, the kind that only comes when nobody feels the need to fill it. Lorna sinks a little deeper into Hudson's side, his thumb brushing idly along her upper arm.

In the dim porch light, I can see how exhaustion has mellowed her, how content she looks folded into him. And a hard, certain weight settles in my chest—she belongs here. With us.

"Stay," I say, letting the word carry the weight I mean it to. Not a question. An invitation.

Her gaze flicks between us, surprise melting into warmth. Hudson's touch stills on her arm, and when our eyes meet, there's no question there. Only agreement. He's been thinking it too, waiting for one of us to be brave enough to ask.

"Stay," he repeats, softer this time. "Tonight."

The word hums between us, heavy with everything it doesn't say.

Lorna's eyes flick between us before she nods. "Okay. I'll stay."

Heat surges low in my gut. I rise, reach for her hand. "Good," I murmur. "Come on."

Our shower's big enough for four, if you don't mind getting close. Real close.

The water scalds my back, pounding the knots from my

muscles one by one. Steam blurs the glass, or maybe that's Lorna. Her head's tipped back, wet hair plastered to her skin, the dark strands tracing down her spine. Water runs in silver trails over her collarbones, her chest, her stomach. My hands find her shoulders, thumbs pressing slow circles until she sighs.

"Better?" I rasp, my voice shot to hell.

"Much," she breathes, voice rough and low. She arches into me, her ass grazing my cock just enough to turn my vision dark at the edges.

Hudson moves in behind her, heat rolling off him in waves. His hands trail up her sides, fingers sliding under mine, the lightest brush that still pulls a shiver from her. Skin against skin—dark brown, tan, cream—and Lorna caught between us, trembling, her pulse fluttering wild against her throat.

The glass door opens, and Levi steps in, grinning sheepishly. "Room for one more?"

She laughs and reaches for him. Hudson moves over, and Levi slides in behind her, letting the spray hit his shoulders as his grip curves over her hips. He glides one hand over her stomach, his mouth brushing that tender spot under her ear.

We're a living circuit. Her at the center, sparking off all of us, every nerve in our bodies strung tight.

"Look at me."

She does, and everything inside me tilts. Water clings to her lashes, runs down her cheek, gathers at her lips. My mouth aches to chase every drop. Christ, she's beautiful, not polished, not practiced. Wild. Alive. The kind of beautiful that wrecks you just by existing.

I kiss her hard. Hudson's hands roam her body, tracing every line, while Levi's palms find her breasts, his teeth skimming her shoulder. She gasps into my mouth, caught between us, every touch pulling another sound from her throat, every movement a spark feeding the fire we've been circling all day.

Hudson's gaze meets mine over her shoulder. Pure need. I don't even speak. I lean in, press my forehead to his for an instant, steam curling between us, the promise of what comes next sparking through my veins.

"Bedroom," he growls, voice ragged, water dripping off his jaw. The command vibrates through me, low and electric, and Lorna shivers.

We wash fast, barely patient enough to rinse the soap away. The water cuts off and we're toweling off in a rush, still dripping as we stumble into the hallway.

Levi lingers by the door, pulling on a pair of sweats, watching us with fire in his eyes and a crooked grin. "Go ahead without me," he says, voice rough but teasing. "I'll be back in a few. I want to check on the lamb and her mama first."

Lorna blows him a kiss as I reach for the plug waiting on the nightstand. The next size up. Lorna's gaze snaps to it, her pupils swallowing all that blue. What flickers across her face isn't fear. It's hunger.

"Ready for this?" My voice is a low rasp, and my heart feels like it's trying to tear out of my chest.

"I... I think so." Her words hitch, fragile and breaking. "Talk me through it?"

"Every step," I promise, crawling between her thighs, voice scraping low. "We'll go easy."

I start with my mouth. Her skin is still damp from the shower, and I follow a bead of water down the inside of her thigh with my tongue. Her taste is salt and fire, laced with the sweetness of surrender. I kiss higher, closer, my exhalation ghosting over slick folds, until she's squirming, until her fingers claw at the sheets.

"God, Lorna," I mutter into her skin, and she whimpers, hips arching toward my mouth. Each sound she makes lights me up, tightens the coil low in my gut, and I'm already half-feral with need.

I flip her gently, and guide her onto her knees. Her face sinks into the mattress, wet hair spilling in dark ribbons over her shoulders. She arches instinctively, parting her thighs.

The sight nearly undoes me. Her ass is perfect, round, flushed from the shower. I grip her hips, thumbs pressing into the dip where thigh meets ass, and I spread her wider. She lets out a shivery whimper into the sheets, and the new angle makes my cock jerk hard. Because I can see it all. Her pussy is pink and open, dripping for us, the tight ring of her ass pulsing faintly.

I lean in, close enough to smell her. Skin, musk, that wet sweetness that's all her. I spread her open with my tongue, tasting her, and she jerks, a strangled sound catching in her throat. I circle higher, tracing slow patterns around the tight ring of muscle that still makes her tense every time. Her hips twitch, a soft plea buried in the movement. I hold her steady, fingers digging into her hips, and take my time—gentle licks that test her edges, teasing flicks over her slick folds, the slow, filthy drag of my tongue that makes her shudder and push back for more.

She whines, high and broken, her hips rocking. The bed creaks under the rhythm her body can't control. I give her enough to keep her right there. Quivering, leaking, that wet heat coating my tongue. Until she's shaking apart under my mouth.

By the time I finally pull back to grab the plug, arousal is dripping down the inside of her thighs. Her hair is a mess around her face, gasps ragged and uneven, her body swaying between collapse and chasing more.

I drag the tip of the plug through her folds, slicking it with her before circling her entrance. She's fluttering. So fucking ready my cock aches to sink into her and feel that tight, desperate squeeze for myself. The first push in has her crying out, her back bowing so hard it looks like she might snap in half. Tendons strain in her throat as her mouth drops open in a silent scream, her body swallowing it inch by inch. I can see her clench around the toy, see the pulse of every tremor inside her. My vision swims for a second. She's trembling, open, and so goddamn needy. And I can barely keep my grip steady.

"How's that feel?" My voice is shredded, raw from holding back.

"Full." The word stumbles out on a gasp, her eyelids fluttering shut. "So full. But... God, it's good. So good."

Her body tightens around the toy as I give it a slow twist, and I watch, helplessly transfixed, as the widest part sinks past that tight ring of muscle. The way she flutters around it is mesmerizing, every pulse drawing me closer to the edge. My thumbs part her, tracing the stretched rim, feeling the twitch and flutter as her body adjusts. She's trembling, slick and hot beneath my hands. A drop of her arousal slips down, darkening the sheets. The sound that rips out of me is raw, guttural, my cock kicking hard in response.

Hudson lies back and pulls her onto his chest, guiding her until her knees slide wide around his hips. The sight knocks the breath from me. Her flushed skin against his, his hands firm on her thighs, the curve of her ass framed just for me. My cock throbs, leaking, the want so sharp it hurts, like someone punched the air out of me.

"Ready?" Hudson's voice is steady, but his whole body's drawn tight, every muscle straining to hold back.

She nods, eyes gone unfocused. Her lips part, a sound slipping free as he presses forward, sliding into her slowly, inch by inch.

The sounds they make nearly undo me. Her sharp gasp. His low, broken groan as her body opens around him. My vision tunnels to where they meet, her slick folds clinging to him, glistening as he slides deeper, her body fluttering between surrender and need.

Hudson's jaw tightens, a bead of sweat slipping down his temple as he holds himself back, fingers biting into her hips to keep her still. But she moves anyway, rocking against him, chasing more with a desperate rhythm. Her back arches, breasts lifting with each slow grind, hair spilling wild over her shoulders.

And his face—Christ. Awe and hunger tangled together. Eyes half-lidded, mouth open on a forgotten breath, like he's seeing something holy for the first time and can't quite believe it.

It's raw. Beautiful. So perfect it hurts to look at.

"Leo." My name tears out of her, ragged and pleading, her hand groping blindly behind her for me. "Please."

I don't know what she's asking for, only that I can't stay still. I move in behind her, chest to her trembling back, the heat of her skin searing through me. My cock slides between her thigh and

Hudson's shaft, catching on the slickness of her arousal. A sound breaks from my throat, rough and hungry. My hands grip her hips, shaking, pulse crashing in my ears. I thrust once, then again, the friction so good it borders on pain.

"More, Leo," she begs. "I want you both inside me." She looks back at me, eyes dark and glazed, half delirious with need.

Fuck. The thought of her pussy snug around both our cocks has my balls drawing up. "Are you sure?" I ask, voice shredded, even as every muscle screams to move.

"I can take it," she promises. And whatever I've been holding back, fear, restraint, the last thin edge of control, disintegrates.

I grip my cock and press forward, slow at first, the head nudging against where he already fills her. The resistance makes my pulse stumble. I push harder, groaning when the tip slips past, the friction white-hot. Her body clenches, adjusting to us both, and I have to fight not to lose control right there.

The stretch is unreal, wet and pulsing around me, every inch a battle between restraint and the need to drive in harder. Hudson's thick inside her, unyielding, our cocks pressing together, slick and grinding through the molten heat of her body.

"Fuck," Hudson whimpers, flexing, pushing himself as deep as he'll go.

My vision blacks out at the edges, jaw locking as every nerve fires at once.

The rough, broken sound Hudson makes tears right through me. His eyes catch mine over her shoulder, wild and wide, pupils blown black with need. Sweat shines along his temple, his ribs lifting hard with every ragged breath.

"Leo. Jesus Christ." My name cracks apart in his throat.

His hand burns against my thigh, her body hot and trembling around us. It's too much. It's everything. My own voice is raw when I manage, "I know," because there's nothing else. Just this. Her tight, wet heat around both of us, Hudson's fingers digging into my skin, the three of us tangled and moving as one.

I grip her ass, spreading her open, watching as I push in the last few inches. There's no space left, only heat and the slick grind of our cocks sliding together inside her. It's filthy. It's perfect. It's the kind of feeling that ruins you for anything else.

"You okay, sweetheart?" I manage, barely trusting my own voice.

"Yes," she sobs, voice breaking as her hips start to roll in earnest, greedy and desperate. She takes us both, deeper with every grind, her pussy spasming around us. "Please—"

We move together, finding a rhythm as her body yields, drawing us in. Every thrust sends sparks racing up my spine. Friction everywhere. Inside her, between us. Our cocks sliding through her slick core, a sensation so intense my lungs can't keep up.

"Look at you taking us both," I groan, my gaze locked on the way her body takes us. Her slick, stretched pussy clutches around both our cocks, glistening, every twitch and flutter visible from where I'm driving into her from behind. "Fuck, this perfect little cunt was made for it."

All I can see is the arch of her back, the damp strands of hair stuck to her neck, the way her body ripples with every movement. Hudson's eyes lift over her shoulder to meet mine again, and before I can second-guess it, I lean in and take Hudson's mouth. His lips part for me instantly, and the taste is dizzying. Familiar but new, coming home and jumping off a cliff at the same time. The kiss is messy, hungry, perfect. All the years of wanting him back, of regret and restless need, pour out in a rush. His tongue slides over mine and a raw groan breaks free from my throat. I don't care. I can't hold any of it back anymore.

Lorna watches us, her pupils blown wide. I feel her clench around both of us, tight as a fist.

"Oh fuck," she gasps, voice wrecked. Pure sin.

"You like that?" My lips are still brushing Hudson's when I speak, our exhalations mingling. "Watching us kiss while we're buried inside you?"

"Yes," she whimpers, desperate, trembling. "Please don't stop—"

"Not fucking stopping," I grind out, thrusting deeper, our cocks sliding together inside her slick, pulsing heat. My hips hit her ass hard, the sound filthy and perfect. "You feel that, sweetheart? Both of us inside you, splitting you open. We're gonna fill you up, make you take every drop."

Her whole body bows, a wild, broken cry tearing out of her as her pussy clamps down on us. The squeeze is unreal, pulsing and milking, and it rips me open from the inside out.

"Fuck. Fuck!" Hudson's hips jerk beneath us as he comes, his whole body shaking. The sound that rips out of him is half growl, half surrender.

Her body clamps around us at the same time, a sharp cry tearing from her throat as she shatters. She's trembling between us, tight and pulsing, drawing us deeper with every spasm. It's too much. Wet and slick and burning hot, both our cocks still locked inside her as she milks us for everything we have.

Pleasure tears through me until everything blurs, stars bursting behind my eyelids. My whole body shakes, every pulse spilling into her and over Hudson's cock, the heat of it endless.

We keep moving through it, chasing every aftershock while her body quivers around us. It's raw, animal, so intense it borders on pain. And I know I'm finished. Nothing in this life will ever touch this.

We fall in a heap of sweat and skin, breaths ragged, the air heavy with sex. My heart is still stumbling in my chest when the door creaks open.

Levi stands there, framed in the doorway, eyes gone black with hunger, the front of his pants straining against the evidence of exactly what he's just seen.

"My turn?" His voice is low, strained with the effort of holding back.

Lorna's head turns toward him, her flushed face lighting with fresh, impossible hunger. Her voice is shattered.

"Please, Levi."

What happens next blindsides me.

Levi. The quiet one. The calm one. He changes in an instant.

Commanding. Fierce. His voice drops to a growl that makes Lorna whimper and has my spent cock twitching back to life.

"That's my good girl," Levi growls, stalking toward her. He grips her chin, thumb pressing into her lower lip, tipping her face up. "You let them fuck each other inside you, didn't you? Let their cocks stretch that greedy little pussy wide open. Did you like that?" He nips her lip. "Two cocks and you still want more?"

The words ignite the air, gasoline on open flame. Lorna whines, the sound scraping through me until I can barely breathe. My blood pounds, every muscle drawn tight as Levi takes hold of her hips and drags her toward him. Her slick body slides over the sheets, slow and helpless, until her head hangs off the edge, hair spilling in a dark, tangled halo, lips parted, chest rising in quick, shallow breaths.

Levi grips the base of his cock and guides it to her mouth. The second her lips close around him, his jaw goes rigid, a low, guttural sound tearing from his throat, filthy and primal.

"That's it," he murmurs, his hand circling her neck. She moans around him, throat working, spit catching at the corner of her mouth before it drips down.

"Take it all, baby," he grits out, voice gone hoarse.

I can't look away. Her body's arched, trembling, the curve of her throat flexing as Levi feeds her more, and her moan vibrates down his length.

Hudson reaches over without a word, wrapping his fingers around my cock, and then we're both jerking each other in an uneven rhythm while we watch Levi use her mouth. Desire snarls low in my gut at the way Hudson gasps, his knuckles brushing my balls as he works me over.

Levi's gaze cuts to us, dark and sharp. He eases his cock from her mouth, letting spit and precum trail down her cheek. "Turn around," he orders, voice rough. "Knees to your chest. Let them see what they've done to you."

Lorna moves fast, curling in on herself, trembling as she pulls her knees tight. Her thighs glisten, our cum sliding down in pearly streaks.

Levi kneels between her legs, keeping a firm grip on her thigh as he drags his thumb through the mess we've left. A thick streak clings to his skin, and he pushes it back into her slowly.

"Feel that?" he growls, his voice a low rumble that vibrates through the air. "I'm putting their cum back where it belongs. Because you're ours, Lorna."

She gasps, her body tightening around the intrusion. He works his thumb deeper until she's squirming and whining against the sheets.

"Good girl," he mutters, lining himself up and sliding inside her in one wet thrust. The sound is obscene. He groans, hips rolling, driving our cum deeper with every stroke.

Hudson grunts beside me, his fist working my cock in rhythm with Levi's thrusts. My own grip matches his pace, the coil tightening low and savage in my gut. The bed rocks, slick sounds filling the air, her cries blurring with our groans.

Levi's control frays, a harsh sound breaking from his chest. He lifts his thumb, slick with our cum, and presses it to her lips.

"Clean it," he commands.

She opens for him without hesitation, lips closing around his thumb, tongue swirling over the mess he's given her. Levi curses low, eyes locked on her mouth as he thrusts into her, deeper, rougher. Her body bows, trembling hard, and then she's coming, tight and pulsing around him, her cry muffled against his hand.

The sight wrecks me. Whatever control I had left snaps clean in two. I groan with Hudson, both of us spilling together, our fists working in time until thick ropes of cum stripe our stomachs and the sheets.

Levi's hips jerk once, twice, before he buries himself deep, emptying into her with a sound that's half snarl, half surrender. For a moment, everything stops. Only the slick sound of him easing out, the heavy scent of sex in the air, and the sight of her slick, trembling body.

We collapse in a tangle of limbs and sweat, nothing left but the wild thud of our hearts. For a long moment, all I can do is pull her closer. Lorna's skin is damp against my chest, her hair plastered to my shoulder, her breath soft and steady against my throat. Her lashes flutter once, twice, before she melts into that heavy, boneless calm that tells me she feels safe, sated, and we did our job right.

I press a kiss to her temple, then ease away, careful not to disturb her. She murmurs something quiet, half-asleep, as I wash off and grab a few clean cloths. I toss one to Hudson and kneel beside her, wiping the slick from her thighs, tracing the inside of her knees. When I ease the plug free, she exhales a small sound, and I whisper against her skin, "Good girl. You did so well." Her lips curve in her sleep, the tiniest smile.

Hudson catches my eye, and for a second we just look at each other, sharing a tired, wordless smile that says everything. Levi doesn't speak either; he just slides closer, curling around her back, his hand resting on her hip, thumb drawing slow circles against her skin.

By the time I climb back into bed, Hudson's already there, Lorna tucked against his chest, her leg thrown over his hip. I slide in behind him, my body fitting to his back. Hudson's arm rests over her, his face slack with a peace I haven't seen in years. Maybe ever. Levi's already half-asleep on her other side, his breath slow and steady against her neck.

I let my eyes close, sinking into the quiet. The warmth of them surrounds me, their weight grounding me, steadying something that's been restless for as long as I can remember.

This. This is it. Home.

**23**

———

The sound of tires on gravel makes me drop the dish towel and rush to the window. My pulse hammers as Jack's car pulls into the driveway.

They're home. My babies are home.

The car doors slam and I hear them. Daniel's measured tone explaining something to Charlie, Lorelai's bright squeal floating through the evening air. Relief rushes through me so fast my knees almost give out.

I'm out the door before I can think, bare feet hitting the gravel.

"Mummy!" Lorelai launches herself at my legs, all tangled hair and grass-stained knees. Her small arms wrap around my thighs and I'm so grateful for her solid weight because I might float away otherwise.

"We missed you so much." Her voice is muffled against my jeans. "Uncle Jack has a secret room behind the library with old books that smells like dust and magic! And Aunt Charlie taught me to make flower crowns from roses and lavender, and there was a wedding, a *real* wedding, Mummy, and Sorscha let me brush her mane and it was so soft, softer than my hair even, and I showed Summer how to braid it with ribbons—"

"Breathe, fairy girl." I scoop her up, laughter spilling out of me. She smells like dirt and adventure, castle stone and Highland air. "I missed you too. It felt empty here without you."

Daniel approaches with more reserve, but his expression is radiant. He's clutching a box to his chest as if it contains the crown jewels.

"Mum, I collected seventeen new specimens," he says with the gravity of someone announcing a scientific breakthrough. "Uncle Cam helped me identify the geological formations. Did you know Harris has some of the oldest rock in Europe? Over two billion years old! And Uncle Lach showed me the tide pools where I found this piece of serpentine. It's metamorphic, which means it was formed under lots of pressure."

"I didn't know that!" I keep one hand on his shoulder, needing to touch them both. "Tell me everything."

As I hold them close, their voices tumble over each other. Stories full of scraped knees and wildflowers, who won what, who fell in the creek. All of it laced with breathless excitement to tell the neighbors. My gaze drifts to the farmhouse where I know they're out there. Watching. Waiting.

"Are Mr. Leo and Mr. Hudson and Mr. Levi still helping with the farm?" Daniel's tone is light, but the way he asks, like he's bracing for disappointment, makes something twist behind my ribs.

"Yes, sweetheart," I say quietly. "They are."

"Good." Lorelai's relief is instant and fierce. She wriggles down from my hip and starts digging through her backpack with single-minded determination. "I made them pictures."

She holds them out one by one like precious offerings. "This one's for Mr. Levi because he loves stories, and this one's for Mr. Hudson because he's funny, and this one's for Mr. Leo because he's big and safe."

Big and safe.

The words knock the air from my lungs.

When did Leo become the protector in her world? When did Hudson shift from neighbor to the man who makes all of us laugh until we ache? When did Levi turn into the one who tucks them in with stories about dragons and magic? They're getting used to having them around. Folding them into the rhythm of our days as though it's always been this way.

And somewhere along the line, I did too.

"Those are beautiful, love. I'm sure they'll treasure them."

Jack and Charlie approach, silhouettes in the last stretch of golden sunlight.

"How were they?" I ask, smoothing Lorelai's hair where it's gone wild around her temple.

"A delight," Charlie says, and there's affection in her voice, real and full, that makes my eyes sting. "Truly. Summer's going to miss her cousins terribly."

"We taught her to skip stones," Daniel says, puffed up with pride. "She's really very good. I showed her the best way to throw it so it skips a lot. You have to tilt it a little, this way."

"And I showed her how to make fairy houses," Lorelai cuts in, practically vibrating. "Proper ones. With tiny doors and windows made of shiny stones. She said they were enchanted. We left out honey cakes for the fairies every night and they were gone by morning!"

Daniel gives her a look that's half-fond, half-factual. "The ants probably got them."

"Fairy ants," Lorelai says solemnly.

God, I missed this. I missed them. The chaos and the chatter. Sticky fingers and made-up magic.

"Would you two like to stay for dinner?" I ask Jack and Charlie. "There's a roast in the oven."

Jack glances at Charlie, then back at me, wincing.

"We'd love to," he says, and I can tell he means it, "but Lach's on dinner duty tonight. He'll kill us if we're late."

"Of course. Next time, then."

After our goodbyes, I stand with the twins watching taillights disappear down the drive.

"Mummy," Lorelai says, tugging my shirt. "Can we go next door? I want to give them their pictures."

"After dinner, sweetie. Let's get you two fed first."

Dinner is wonderful chaos, the kind that fills every corner of the house. The twins talk over each other, words and half-finished sentences bouncing off the walls. Daniel's more confident these days, slipping in words such as sedimentary and compression as though he's testing them out. Lorelai's stories have turned into performances, every sentence a painting, every gesture big and wild.

But even in the thick of it, I catch them glancing out the windows. Again and again. Toward the glow spilling from the farmhouse next door.

They're trying to be polite. But they're practically vibrating.

"Mummy?" Daniel asks, voice careful, trying not to sound too eager. "Can we go? I want to show Mr. Levi the new preservation technique Uncle Cam showed me."

"And I want to give them their pictures," Lorelai chimes in, practically bouncing out of her chair. "I made them so pretty. I even used glitter glue!"

I can't hold back the grin that tugs at my lips. "All right. But not for long. Baths and bed after. Deal?"

"Deal!" they shout together, already diving for their treasures, Daniel snatching up his fossil case, Lorelai hugging her stack of drawings to her chest like they're priceless.

We walk across the field together, the grass cool against our ankles, damp where the day's heat still clings to the earth. The air smells of damp soil and green things settling for the evening, sweet and loamy, touched with the faint smoke of someone's far-off fire.

Hudson opens the door, and the second he sees the twins, his whole face lights up.

"Well, look what the wind blew in! How are my favorite fairy and my favorite scientist?"

"Mr. Hudson!" Lorelai squeals, launching herself at his legs. He scoops her up, spinning her around until she shrieks with delight.

"We brought you presents," Daniel says, all serious business.

"Presents?" Hudson's eyes go wide. "I love presents. Come on in. Everyone's in the kitchen."

The house smells like them. Leather, wood, ink. Familiar. Lived-in. Leo and Levi are still cleaning up from dinner, but the second we step inside, they look up. And there it is. That unfiltered happiness you can't fake.

"Daniel, Lorelai," Leo says, his voice all gravel and gentleness. "How was the castle?"

"Brilliant," Daniel says, already unzipping his little case. Everything inside is neat, each fossil labeled in his careful, slightly wobbly handwriting. "Look what I found. Mr. Levi, this one's for you." He holds out a small stone, the fossil faint but clear, a fern frond frozen in its surface, every vein delicate as lace. "Uncle Cam said it's from the old peat beds by the loch. Millions of years old."

Levi takes it as though Daniel handed him a crown. He holds it up to the light and whistles low. "This is incredible, buddy. I can see every leaf. Thank you. This is going in my collection."

Meanwhile, Lorelai is passing out her drawings with the gravity of a museum curator.

"This one's for you, Mr. Leo," she says solemnly, holding up a crayon drawing of a man with big arms standing next to smaller stick figures. "Because you protect us."

Leo's expression softens as he takes it, something quiet and raw passing over his face, the kind of emotion that catches in my chest and makes it hard to breathe.

"This one's for Mr. Hudson because you make Mummy laugh." A swirl of yellow scribbles surrounded by hearts.

"And this one's for Mr. Levi because you tell the best stories." That drawing's a riot of blues and stars and what might be a dragon wearing a top hat.

"These are beautiful, fairy girl," Hudson says, holding his drawing as though it's precious. "I'm gonna frame this and hang it next to my tools so I can see it every single day."

"Really?" Lorelai's eyes go huge.

"Really. It's the best thing anyone's ever made for me."

The way he says it, meaning every word, makes my heart squeeze. This isn't pretend. It's not kindness dressed up as affection. It's family. Quiet and true, winding its way around us before I even had the sense to see it coming.

"Can we all go to the garden?" Lorelai asks, already tugging at Hudson's hand. "I want to see if the fairy houses are still there."

"Of course," Hudson says, and they're off.

We spend an hour wandering the garden, the twins chattering while the men trail behind them, listening like every word is gospel. Leo kneels beside Daniel in the dirt, massive hands surprisingly careful as he sifts through the soil.

"Feel this," he says, scooping a handful and holding it out. "Good soil sticks together, but crumbles when you poke it."

Daniel nods thoughtfully, testing a clump for himself before scribbling a note in his little notebook. "And the earthworms make it better," he adds, voice steady with the confidence of someone who remembers everything.

A few feet away, Hudson crouches beside Lorelai, who's staring wide-eyed at a dinner-plate dahlia. Her fingertips trace the petals as if they're made of spun sugar. "It's bigger than my head," she says, awed.

"That's because your mum's a flower witch," Hudson tells her, giving me a wink. "She sweet-talks plants into outgrowing their own potential."

Lorelai beams as if he's confirmed her long-held theory.

Levi walks beside us, journal in hand, reading scraps of poetry in that low, thoughtful voice I love. The kids hang on every word.

When Lorelai giggles or Daniel nods, serious as a scholar, Levi's mouth curves, unguarded and real.

I watch them move through the space I built with my own hands, these three men I've somehow fallen hopelessly in love with. Teaching my children like it's the most natural thing in the world. Like it's a gift.

Daniel keeps stealing glances at Leo, like he's trying to decide if he's real. Lorelai nearly tumbles into the dahlias when Hudson uses one of his ridiculous flower voices, laughing so hard she can't stand. And both of them look at Levi as if he holds every secret worth knowing.

"We should head back," I say finally, though I don't really want to. The sky's gone dusky, and Lorelai's yawning even as she insists she's not tired. *"One more fairy house, Mummy."* I brush hair from her face. "I know two little ones who need baths and bedtime stories."

"Come on, fairy girl," Hudson says, scooping her up with easy strength. "Let's get you home."

She melts into his chest without a second thought, small arms looping around his neck as if she was made to fit there. The trust in it, the ease, makes my pulse trip.

They walk us back across the field, a constellation of bodies drifting through the dark, lit by the moon and the golden spill of light from the kitchen windows. Daniel's hand slips naturally into Leo's. Levi trails behind, cradling the collection basket like it carries prize possessions.

The twins murmur about their discoveries. Daniel, half-asleep, explaining rock types in slurred, earnest science-speak. Lorelai whispering which fairy houses need renovations. It's a lullaby, steady, and everything feels right with them here.

This is what we are, I think, watching Hudson shift Lorelai so she can tuck her head more comfortably into his shoulder. Not the kind you're born into, but the kind you build. The kind that chooses you back.

At my front door, there's an awkward moment where no one seems sure how to say goodbye.

"Thank you," I say quietly, meaning it for so much more than tonight. "For welcoming them back, for listening to their stories."

"Thank you for sharing them with us," Leo says simply.

Hudson transfers Lorelai to my arms, kisses my cheek, and I watch them walk away.

After the twins are bathed and tucked in, I linger by their window, staring across the dark field at the farmhouse next door. The lights glow warm through the trees, too far and too close all at once. The loneliness hits hard—fifty yards might as well be fifty miles.

Before I can change my mind, I grab the baby monitor, clip it to my waistband, and slip outside.

They're on the porch when I reach the edge of the light, bottles in hand, voices low and easy beneath the hum of crickets.

"Lorna?" Levi looks up as I approach. "Everything all right?"

"Yes. No. Maybe." I take a shaky inhale. "Would the three of you come over? Have a bonfire, toast some marshmallows? The twins are asleep, and I..." I trail off, not sure how to explain the loneliness clawing at my chest.

"You don't want to be alone," Hudson finishes gently.

"No. Not anymore."

Twenty minutes later, a fire crackles in the pit at the edge of my backyard, throwing sparks into the dark like tiny, ecstatic fireflies. The baby monitor sits on the porch railing, volume turned up, its green light steady.

"Here," I say, passing out roasting sticks. "Just a heads up, only one of these is actually decent."

"We'll share," Hudson says, his grin pure mischief. "I'm excellent at sharing."

"Are you?" Leo's voice drips with dry amusement.

I sink into the circle beside them, the scent of woodsmoke and caramelized sugar curling sweet and sticky in the air. They take their time, turning the marshmallows carefully.

"Perfect," Hudson announces, lifting his stick triumphantly.

"Let me," I murmur, leaning in until our thighs touch, friction bleeding through denim. I slide the marshmallow from the stick, my fingertips brushing his lips as I bring it to his mouth. He opens without hesitation. His tongue grazes my skin, slick and deliberate.

My pulse snags in my throat.

"Mmm," he hums, desire roughening the sound. "Sweet."

"My turn," Levi says, low and smooth as satin.

He holds his marshmallow in the flame until it's perfectly blistered, then pulls it back, blowing on it. I reach out, slide it off his stick, and lift it toward his mouth. His lips close around the marshmallow, his mouth brushing my fingers. He lingers, a small kiss pressed to my skin, a flick of tongue catching the sugar. His breath ghosts over my knuckles, and my stomach flips hard.

"Thank you," he whispers, not breaking eye contact.

Leo's next. His marshmallow is textbook golden brown. No scorch. No impatience. I hold it out, expecting him to bite. To play the same game. But instead, he leans in and takes one of my fingers into his mouth with it. His tongue sweeps over the sticky sugar, thorough, and I swear the ground tilts.

"Leo," I gasp, like his name is all I have left to hold on to.

He doesn't speak. Watches me as he lets my finger slip free, eyes dark and steady, still tasting me.

"Your turn," Hudson says, the words noticeably rougher.

He's already got another marshmallow waiting, the tip of his stick still glowing faintly red. When he offers it, I lean in without thinking. So does he. Our mouths meet over the sugar, hesitant for a heartbeat, like we're both pretending this is still just a game. Then the fuse catches. The taste of burnt sugar and smoke disappears into the heat of his mouth, the kiss deepening until I can't tell where breath ends and hunger begins.

It's wild. Consuming. The kind of kiss that leaves the world tilting.

"Messy," Levi says, voice low, almost approving.

"Very messy," Leo adds, reaching out. His thumb skims the corner of my mouth, dragging a streak of marshmallow across my skin. He holds my gaze as he lifts it to his lips, tongue curling around the sugar, slow and deliberate.

Jesus.

We don't stop.

It becomes a rhythm. Them feeding me, kissing me, touching me. A spiral of sugar and sin. Time folds in on itself. All I know is the firelight. Their mouths. The dizzy rush of being tasted and wanted and surrounded.

When I finally catch a glimpse of our reflection in the kitchen window, hair mussed, marshmallow smeared, eyes glassy with sugar and lust, my shoulders shake.

"We're a disaster," I say, voice breathless.

"The best kind," Hudson says, stealing one more kiss before I can object.

"Come on," I say, untangling from their bodies. "Let's get cleaned up before we attract every ant in Scotland."


Inside, we crowd into the bathroom. Four adults in a space barely big enough for two. It should feel cramped, awkward. But it doesn't. It feels close. Intimate. Bodies brushing, tension pooling in every inch of air we share.

Hudson stands behind me at the sink, his chest flush to my back, working a stubborn blob of marshmallow from my hair. I feel his exhale on the top of my head, the careful concentration in the way he sifts through the strands.

"Better?" he murmurs near my ear, his voice rough with desire that curls down my spine.

"Much," I whisper, even though I'm not sure I'm talking about the marshmallow.

At my side, Levi offers me his sugar-coated hands. I lather soap between us, our skin tangling and sliding. His eyes don't waver, locked on mine as if he's cataloging every flicker of thought.

"You have beautiful hands," I say, not even sure where the words come from, only that they're true.

And unhelpfully, my brain supplies the memory of those fingers inside me. Sensation crawls up my neck before I can stop it. I drop my gaze, cheeks flushed, but I feel the ghost of his smile anyway. He knows exactly what I'm remembering.

Leo appears beside me, holding a damp washcloth. "Turn around," he says quietly.

I do.

He starts with my forehead, slow and careful, tracing the cloth down my skin. Cheekbone. Jaw. The corner of my mouth. His thumb pauses at my lips, eyes gone dark as he watches me breathe him in.

Then he kisses me. Deep and quiet, his hand framing my face like I'm the most precious thing in the world.

By the time the last bit of sugar and laughter is gone, exhaustion settles over us like a heavy blanket. No one says a word as we drift to my room, the silence warm, full of things that don't need to be spoken.

The bed that always feels too big for me feels impossibly small for four. Sheets rustle, bodies shift, the air thick with warmth and the kind of peace that hums just beneath the skin.

"What about the twins?" Levi asks after a moment, his voice quiet in the dark. "If they wake up and find us all here…"

"Then they'll find you here," I whisper. "It's time they understood this isn't temporary anymore."

"You're right," Leo says, his arm tightening around my waist.

"Tell me a story," I whisper to Levi, my words thick with sleep.

He shifts, finding my hand in the dark. "What kind of story?"

"One with a happy ending."

He's quiet for a beat. I can almost feel him sifting through thoughts, shaping words in the dark. He begins, his voice low and textured and a little rough.

"Once upon a time," he says, "there was a woman who grew flowers in a place where nothing was meant to bloom. People said it was too cold. Too rocky. Too lonely. But she didn't listen. She had magic in her touch and stubborn hope in her heart, and everything she nurtured thrived.

"One day, three travelers stumbled into her garden. They were lost, each in their own way. Carrying scars they didn't show and baggage they didn't speak of. But when they saw her flowers, her beauty, her wild love, they stopped running.

"The woman didn't trust them at first. She'd learned the hard way that love could vanish. That people left. That promises broke. But the travelers stayed. They weeded and watered and watched the seasons turn beside her. They didn't ask her to bloom for them. They made space for her to grow.

"And steadily, she opened. Let them in. Let them love her the way she'd loved the life she had made for herself. Fiercely. Tenderly. Without condition.

"And together..." His voice catches, and I feel the curve of his smile on my neck. "They built what could weather anything. A home. A future. A garden that bloomed in every season, even the cold ones."

Silence stretches, full.

"And they lived..." he murmurs, already slipping toward sleep.

"Happily ever after?" I whisper.

"Happily ever after," he echoes, pressing a kiss to the curve of my shoulder, his mouth lingering on skin.

I drift, wrapped in their presence. Hudson's hand on my thigh. Leo's exhale ruffling my hair. Levi's voice still hanging in the air. For the first time in years, the future doesn't feel frightening. It feels certain. A path lined with flowers. Lit by stars.

And this?

This is the beginning.

**24**

---

LEVI'S POV

The morning light cuts through Lorna's kitchen window like molten honey, pooling in golden squares across the table where her research papers lie in neat stacks. Each page is a testament to the brilliant chaos of her mind. Steam rises from the coffee mug between my fingers, dark and bitter, mingling with the earthy scent that clings to her, soil and green things made flesh.

The twins left for school an hour ago, and the house holds that particular quiet of their absence. The two of us alone.

She stands at the stove, mug cupped in both hands, and the morning light threads through the loose strands escaping her messy bun. My fingers itch to sketch the curve of her neck, the way shadows pool in the hollow of her throat.

Christ. I'll never get used to her. It's as if my body only remembers how to exist when she's near.

"The seedlings are ready for evaluation," she says without turning, her voice quiet but edged with that unmistakable tone. The one that means her mind is already racing ahead, mapping, sorting, turning disorder into order.

"Can I help?" The words come out rougher than I mean them

to, betraying how much I need to be part of whatever she has planned.

She leads me outside, and I watch her slip her bare feet into a pair of Wellington boots two sizes too big. The sight of her in pajama pants and an oversized sweater tugs at something deep in me. Tenderness rises, sharp and certain. This is Lorna unfiltered, fierce and soft all at once, real enough to make my chest ache.

The morning air greets us like a shock of cold water. Crisp, biting, alive. Dew clings to everything, the scent of wet soil and new growth thick in the air. My breath fogs in front of me as I kneel beside her in the dirt, close enough that her warmth seeps through my shirt and settles in my bones.

"Here," she says quietly, her hands gentle as she examines each delicate stem. "These are from the cross I did last fall. Look at the leaf formation. See how the serration is more pronounced than either parent?" She pulls out her phone, flipping to pictures of the seed parents, bringing the plants' lineage to life.

I open my journal, charcoal moving across paper as I try to capture what she sees. But I'm distracted by the way she bites her lower lip when concentrating, the way her fingertips stroke over leaves as if she's reading love letters written in chlorophyll. The concentration on her face is captivating, a quiet communion with the sacred.

"Tell me what you see." My hand shakes slightly as I sketch, and I force myself to focus on the page instead of how badly I ache to push my hands under her sweater and feel her bare skin.

"This one," she brushes a fingertip over the seedling, gently cradling the stem, "looks as though it'll have the burgundy under-tones I was hoping for. But look at this growth. It's going to be massive. The bud size alone suggests the blooms could hit twenty centimeters across."

Her excitement radiates in waves: raw, infectious, impossible to ignore. I sketch frantically, trying to capture not only the plant but the fire in her eyes, the way wonder lights up her face. But my touch betrays me, trembling with every quiet hum of satisfaction that slips from her lips.

"And this one?" I ask, indicating a smaller seedling, my shoulder nudging hers as I lean in.

"Oh, this beauty." Her voice drops to that husky tone that goes straight to my cock, and I bite back a groan. "Compact growth, but look at the bud formation already showing. This is going to bloom early and often. Disease resistant, weather hardy. Perfect for cutting gardens."

I jot her words alongside my sketches, creating what feels less like a record and more like worship. Part tribute, part proof of how much I admire the way she throws herself into this work with unapologetic devotion.

"You're making this look stunning," she says, leaning over to see my work.

"It is." I turn to face her, near enough to see the ribbons of blue in her eyes, to feel her exhalation brush over my lips. The air between us crackles. "Everything you do floors me, Lorna. Your research, your garden, the way you find potential where others only see the ordinary. You're art in its highest form."

Color rushes to her cheeks, and she ducks her head with that shy gesture that makes me ache to lift her chin and kiss her senseless.

"Levi," she starts, but her voice catches.

"We should finish documenting these," I say, stepping back before my impulse to strip her bare right here in the dahlia field becomes impossible to resist. "Afterwards, we can work on your presentation."


Back inside, Lorna spreads her research across the kitchen table, like a fortune teller arranging tarot cards. The papers rustle beneath her touch, and I find myself mesmerized by the fluid grace of her movements as she turns chaos into clarity.

I brew fresh coffee, letting the ritual steady me, but underneath, my skin buzzes with the weight of her. Every time she reaches for a page, a jolt runs through me. Static under my skin, sharp and aching.

"Have you looked up the other speakers?" I ask, settling beside her near enough that our thighs brush.

"No, I've been too nervous." She takes a sip of coffee, and my eyes follow the movement of her throat as she swallows. When she pulls the tie from her hair, it tumbles loose around her shoulders, catching the morning light. A drop of coffee glistens on her upper lip, small and perfect, and I have to fight the urge to lean in, to taste it, to taste her.

What the hell is wrong with me? I've kissed her a hundred times, had her in my arms, in my bed, and still one look, one breath, one goddamn drop of coffee is enough to undo me. She's everywhere. Under my skin, in my blood, taking up space I didn't even know was empty.

"What if they ask a question I can't answer? What if my research isn't rigorous enough?"

Her voice climbs with each word, panic threading through. It guts me. She says it as though she actually believes it. As if she doesn't know she's the smartest person in every room she walks into. My fingers tighten around the mug, knuckles whitening with the effort it takes not to pull her into my lap and kiss it all away. Every hesitation, every lie she's ever been told about her own brilliance.

"Your research is groundbreaking, Lorna. Let me show you."

I pull out my laptop, and she leans in, warm against my side, as I navigate to the conference page.

"Dr. Tashia Murphy from Johns Hopkins," I say, voice thick as I try to stay focused. "She's published extensively on female arousal disorders. Dr. James Liu from Stanford, specialist in sexual dysfunction. Dr. Priya Patel from Cambridge, researching neural pathways in sexual response."

"They're all so accomplished." Her breath warms my neck, slightly sweet from the coffee. I lock my jaw to keep from reacting.

"Look at their publication lists." I pull theirs up, scrolling through them. "Now look at yours. Eighteen peer-reviewed studies. Your work on multiple orgasm types has been cited over three hundred times. That paper on arousal patterns? It's required reading in most grad programs."

She goes still beside me. Her spine straightens, as if the world inside her snapped into alignment. Watching her recognize her own brilliance is addictive. It coils tension low in my belly, stirs depths I can't name. Pride, hunger, reverence.

The wonder in her voice when she whispers, "I had no idea," makes my throat go tight.

There's disbelief there, yes, but also awe. The flare of self-recognition. It's achingly real. It's fucking devastating.

"Because you've been hiding from it." I turn toward her, needing her to see what I see. Our faces are inches apart. Her exhalation on my lips, the flecks of midnight blue in her irises. "These people requested you because you're doing work no one else is brave enough to do. You're not only studying sexual response. You're redefining it."

She glances back at the screen, and I watch it happen. Confidence catches in her, a spark to dry wood. Small, sudden, controlled. Her shoulders square. Her chin lifts. It's not only stunning. It's arousing.

"Help me practice?" Her voice threads with nerves but holds firm underneath.

"Always." And it's not about the presentation. It's a vow.

Whatever she needs, whoever she becomes, I'm hers.


We spend the next two hours sharpening her presentation, and watching Lorna in full academic mode feels comparable to watching a storm form in real time. Precise, electric, impossible to look away from. Her mind slices through complexity as though it's nothing, every sentence crisp, every gesture instinctive. She doesn't explain, she commands, shaping the air with her movements, her whole body moving in rhythm with the argument she's building, the way her voice lowers when she hits a breakthrough, the excitement building in her eyes. I can't look away. This isn't practice. It's foreplay. Her brilliance peels me open, strips me bare, without ever laying a touch on me.

"So you're saying the traditional medical model of female orgasm is fundamentally flawed?" I ask, the question barely masking the raw need creeping into my voice. I'm staring at her neck, aching to sink my teeth into the curve of her throat, right where her pulse flutters beneath her skin.

"Not flawed, incomplete." Her eyes spark. "We've been looking at female sexuality through a male lens, as though it's some straight line from arousal to orgasm. But it's not. There are multiple climax pathways, different intensity levels, way more variation than anyone's bothered to study properly."

The word climax leaves her lips with enough tenderness to make me think about her climaxing. Heat surges; my jeans go tight, and I shift.

"Go on," I say, my voice hoarse.

"If women understand their own bodies," she murmurs, holding my gaze, "they can ask for what they crave. Explore without shame. Experience pleasure as a right, not a reward."

"I don't think I can take any more, Petal. You have no idea what this does to me." I reach up, my thumb brushing over her bottom lip, feeling the tremor of her breath against my skin. "Hearing you talk like that."

She blinks, startled. "What?"

I reach up and tuck a strand of hair behind her ear. "Show me, Lorna. Teach me."

A small sound tumbles out of her throat. "Levi…"

"Show me what you've learned," I murmur. "Show me how you've mapped yourself. Where to touch, how hard, how soft. I want to know everything." I take her hand, her pulse fluttering against my touch. "I need to feel it."

"That's not how research works," she whispers.

"Says who?" I murmur, leaning in, lips brushing the shell of her ear. "Applied research. Practical trials. Direct observation. I'm right here, Lorna. Perfect subject."

She exhales. Shaky, uneven. Her pupils are so wide they've nearly swallowed the blue.

"You're serious." Not a question. Stunned realization.

"Dead serious." My cock strains. My mind finally goes still, focusing on nothing but her.

She swallows hard, and when she speaks, there's a tremor of nervous laughter in her voice. "Can I put it in the presentation?"

I nearly laugh. Nearly. But the need coiling through me is too sharp, too immediate. "You can do whatever you want, Lorna." I nudge my mouth lower, skimming her throat, feeling her pulse jump beneath my lips. "Be my teacher, and I'll show you how fast I learn."

She stands, glancing back once before heading for the stairs. I follow without thinking. By the time we reach the bedroom, she's tugging her sweater over her head, and I'm already unbuttoning my shirt. Clothes hit the floor in quiet thuds, breath quick and uneven between us.

The crystal hanging in her window throws slivers of color across the room, soft rainbows that shift over her body as she moves. She's sprawled on the bed, bare and flushed, her skin alive with light. Every breath I take feels too shallow.

My hands shake as I trace the slope of her waist, the freckles scattered across her shoulders. The moment feels suspended, fragile and infinite. I lower my mouth to her skin, follow the line of her neck, her shoulder, the small rise of her chest. I taste salt, warmth, sunlight. Each breath she takes pulls me closer, until I'm sure I'll never want to stop learning her this way.

"Tell me what to do," I murmur, settling beside her, everything in me pulled so tight I might snap. "Walk me through your research."

She exhales, a little laugh hiding behind it, and I feel her trying to stay composed. Professional. But her body's already giving her away. Goosebumps rising under my touch, nipples tightening.

"The largest category, forty-three percent, respond best to consistent pressure combined with varied rhythm." She swallows hard. "Gradual buildup tends to work better than steady stimulation. The body needs time to..."

I drag my hand lower, slow enough to feel the shiver run through her, the way her muscles tighten, then soften beneath my touch. My fingers trace the hollow below her hipbone, finding the place where her skin turns warm and velvet, flushed with heat and wanting.

"This way?" I ask, pressing enough to make her arch.

She gasps. "Yes, but not quite." Her hand finds mine. Guides me. "Lighter at first." Her voice shakes, but her grip doesn't. "The nerve endings need time to sensitize. If you go too direct too soon, it overloads the receptors."

I do exactly what she tells me. Not because I have to, but because watching her body respond to her own direction is addictive. Every breath she draws is short and shaky, every shift of her hips a search for more. More pressure. More contact. More of me. And, God, I ache to give her everything.

"What else?" My voice is hoarse.

"Thirty-one percent require multiple types of stimulation at once." The words fracture when my touch slides over her clit. She jolts, hips tipping into my palm. She's so wet my skin glides over hers, her desire clinging to me, marking me.

"The combination," her words stutter as I circle her, "creates feedback loops. Fuck, Levi." She whimpers, muscles tensing. "It multiplies sensation."

"Exponentially?" I murmur as I sink two fingers into her. No resistance, only a slick, hungry pull that swallows me whole.

Her mouth falls open around a gasp so tender and wrecked it almost takes me down with it.

"The input and response become non-linear." Her voice trembles as I work her clit and stroke inside her at the same time. "One plus one equals five instead of two."

My cock throbs hard enough I can barely think. She's shaking, stretched open, dripping around my touch, still talking about neural pathways as though she's defending a thesis. And it's perfect, because her mind doesn't dull her pleasure, it feeds it. Every shiver is sharpened by years of knowing exactly what works.

"What about you?" I rasp. "What works best for you?"

Her eyes burn into mine. "Your cock."

That's all I need. My belt's undone in seconds, zipper down, cock in my grasp. She's already there, grabbing for me, pulling me between her thighs. So desperate she doesn't give me time to undress. Guides me to her, open and ready.

"Deep pressure." Air catches in her throat. I start to push in, and her breath snags, her eyes rolling back. "With external stimulation. And, Christ..."

"And what?" I grind out, forcing myself to keep the pace controlled, even as electricity licks up my spine and sweat beads at the back of my neck. My hand slides between us, circling her clit.

"Dirty talk." Her face flushes deep red. "My research shows auditory stimulation activates alternate neural pathways. And when I interview subjects about fantasy..."

"Tell me." I growl, my voice dragging rough across her skin. "Tell me what you want to hear."

She whimpers, nails digging into my shoulders. "Tell me I'm brilliant. Tell me my mind turns you on as much as my body."

I nearly come right there. That raw, desperate honesty. My hips jerk forward before I can stop them, deeper, harder, all control shredded by the way she begs to be seen. Known.

"You're fucking brilliant." I growl into her throat, tasting sweat and skin and the pulse pounding wild beneath my tongue. "Watching you talk about your research made me so hard I couldn't think straight. I need to wreck you with it. Make you come using every method you've ever studied. Make you prove it."

"Fuck," she cries, back arching as if her body's trying to chase what's out of reach. "Yes, that's... research shows that intellectual arousal increases physical response by..."

"By how much?" I grunt, tension coiling low as she trembles beneath me, clenching so tight I can barely function. I lower my head, take her nipple between my teeth, and bite hard enough to drag a gasp from her throat.

"Thirty-seven percent increase in intensity and duration of... oh God—"

She doesn't finish the sentence.

She can't.

She comes apart under me, the sound she makes caught between a sob and a scream. Her body clamps down, shuddering through an orgasm so intense it appears to rewrite her from the inside out.

Watching her come this way, because of everything she's learned, everything she's taught me, nearly wrecks me. Every instinct screams to let go, to lose myself in her, but I hold the line. I need all of it. Every gasp, every twitch, every shiver that ripples through her as she unravels. My cock aches, air saws in and out, but I stay right there, drinking her in as though I'll never get another chance.

The aftershocks roll through her, one by one, until her breathing hitches, then evens. Her eyes find mine again. Bright, dangerous, already plotting.

"My turn to conduct research," she murmurs.

"Lorna..."

"Shh."

She wraps her hand around me, and I jerk in her grasp, already slick with need. She watches me like she's gathering evidence, eyes sharp and intent, curiosity burning into hunger until I can't tell where study ends and desire begins.

"I want to test the relationship between enthusiasm and technique." Her mouth is on me, devouring, and I forget how to function.

"Fuck," I groan, my fist twisting in the sheets as her tongue moves in slow, relentless circles that turn my vision to static.

She hums around me, and the sound vibrates all the way down into my balls, drawing them up tight.

"Interesting." Her mouth is still full of me. Smiling. Wicked. Brilliant.

She takes her time, eyes locked on mine as if she's studying the exact effect of every movement, every flick of her tongue. She curls her hold tight around the base of my cock, the pressure making my lungs seize, and drags her tongue in a teasing pass along the underside of the head until my hips jerk.

"Fuck," I rasp, my head tipping back as my throat works around a groan. "Are you trying to kill me?"

Her smile is pure destruction. "Not before I document your response."

She takes the head into her mouth, sucking hard before dragging her tongue around the crown.

I watch her take me in, the slow stretch of her lips, the wet pull of her mouth, the quick flick of her eyes as she tracks every change in my face. My thighs tense, muscles straining with the effort to stay still, to keep from pushing deeper, from showing her what would happen if I let go completely.

She sinks lower, controlled and steady, until the suction tightens and her lips seal around me. Her fingers keeps pace at the base, twisting enough to make me twitch, tuned perfectly to the throb under my skin.

"Jesus Christ, Lorna," I gasp, barely hearing my own voice over the wet, obscene rhythm of her taking me down. It's too much. Too good. And she's into it. Hungry for it. As if the mess she's making of me turns her on.

She pulls back, lips wet, eyes blazing.

"Your heart rate spiked."

I bark out a laugh. "No shit."

She laughs, low and pleased, and takes me again. Even deeper this time.

Her nose brushes my pelvis. I feel her swallow. Feel her tongue flatten along the underside of my cock while she holds me there, throat fluttering tight around the head, breath shallow. The pressure of it punches straight through me, lighting up every nerve from the base of my spine to the backs of my knees.

I'm going to come.

It builds sharp and fast. Low tension coiling tight in my gut, climbing with nowhere to go but out. I grab her face, palms bracketing her jaw, thumbs pressed to the wet stretch of her cheeks. My hips tremble. I'm barely holding still, barely sane.

She meets my eyes and holds them, mouth full of me, pupils blown wide. Daring me. Begging for it.

"Lorna, fuck, I'm..." My voice cracks apart.

I come hard, hips jerking forward, buried deep in her throat. Release tears through me in hot, shuddering bursts, and she takes it all, swallowing greedily, like she's been waiting for this. Like she needs it.

My body goes rigid, vision narrowing to flashes of light as wave after wave hits, each one dragged out by the way she keeps going. Still sucking, still watching me with that sharp, focused hunger while I lose every ounce of control.

When I finally catch my breath, she's still kneeling between my legs, licking her lips with quiet satisfaction, the look of someone who just aced the test and knew she would all along.

She meets my eyes with a smug smile. "Hypothesis confirmed."

I pull her against me and we collapse together, the sheets tangled around our legs, her thigh slung over mine, one arm curved across my chest.

I trace my fingers along her bare shoulder, aimless, gathering courage.

"I want to support your work." My voice comes out quiet. "If you go back to academia, if you present again, publish under your real name, I want to be part of it. I want to stand beside you."

She meets my eyes, studies me with that sharp, searching gaze. "What do you mean?"

I swallow. "Research assistant. Editor. Whatever you need." I shift onto my side, tracing her cheekbone. "I can help you organize data, prep presentations, tear apart your drafts. I'm good with language. Good at turning complicated ideas into clarity."

She opens her mouth to say something, but I shake my head. Not yet.

"I know what your research is about. I know how this might sound. But I'm not playing." My voice roughens, pulled from somewhere deeper than I usually let her see. "I'd fly with you to Vienna. Carry your laptop through customs in Edinburgh. Sit in hotel lobbies and proofread your slides while you practice. Wherever your mind goes, I'm already following."

Her eyes glass over with tears she doesn't blink away. And for one sharp second, my stomach flips, wondering if I pushed too far.

"You'd really do that?" she whispers.

I nod. "Yeah. I would. Because your work matters, Lorna. It could change everything for so many women. And if I can help you reach more people, if I can stand beside you while you do it, yes. In a heartbeat."

She's quiet. Not pulling away. Thinking.

Her touch trails across my chest in loose, unconscious circles while her mind spins through the fears, the press coverage, the what-ifs and worst-case scenarios.

"I don't know if I'm ready to come out from behind the pseudonym. To have my personal life dissected."

"You don't have to be." I catch her hand and press it flat over my hammering heart. "You don't have to decide anything tonight. But when you are, if you are, I'll be right here."

She studies me for a long moment, exhales low and quiet, and the last of the tension drains from the space between us.

"Research assistant, huh?" There's the glint of a smile in her voice.

"Very committed to the work." I try to keep a straight face.

Her laugh breaks open the room. "God, I love you," she says, almost too quiet to catch. She blinks, startled at herself, as though she wasn't planning to say it. But she doesn't take it back. "I love your mind. I love the way you believe in me when I can't. The way you see beauty in what I thought was broken."

My chest tightens. Misses a beat. Then restarts, thudding back into rhythm as if it's finally figured out what its purpose is. "I love you, too."

She tucks her head into the space between my neck and shoulder, her hand resting over my heart. I hold her close and let the quiet take over. Her breathing evens, soft and steady, rising and falling with mine. The silence says everything words never could.

# 25

My heart pulls tight as I lean against the kitchen doorframe, the scent of coffee and damp earth wrapping around me. Outside, sunlight spills over the garden, glinting off leaves and tools, warming everything it touches. The twins are out there, laughing, sleeves pushed up, dirt streaked on their arms as they work beside the three men who've somehow become the steady center of our lives.

"Mummy, look!" Lorelai shouts, voice bright as copper pennies. "We're making tents for the flowers!"

"It's shade cloth, not tents," Daniel declares, arms crossed in tiny foreman fashion. "The flowers will probably grow way better."

"And they'll be happy," Lorelai adds matter-of-factly, because in her universe, joy is the only metric that matters.

I leave them to finish and slip back inside, wiping my hands on my jeans. Anticipation hums through me, tangled with nerves that won't quiet. In a few minutes, I'll be standing in front of them, running through the presentation I've spent years keeping hidden —research buried under pseudonyms, embargoes, and the kind of silence that comes from being told to stay small.

It's not the words I'm nervous about.

It's being seen.

"Ready for your practice run?" Levi's voice cuts through my thoughts.

Before I can answer, Daniel barrels inside, a streak of dirt across his forehead. "Can we help with your speech too?"

My stomach drops. I love my children, but no seven-year-old should ever hear the phrase *clitoral stimulation response pattern*.

Thankfully, Hudson steps in at just the right moment. "Actually," he says, tone easy and conspiratorial, "I've got a mission for you two. How would you feel about helping me with the final sketches for the treehouse?"

I could kiss him. The relief that floods my body is so profound it feels as though I'm coming up for air.

"Really?" Lorelai gasps, eyes round.

"Really," Hudson confirms. "But it'll require serious planning. Structural evaluations. Height-to-width ratios. Safety assessments. Very technical stuff."

Daniel straightens as though someone appointed him master planner. "We have to see how big the trees are! And make sure it won't fall down. It'll need to be really, really big!"

Hudson manages not to laugh. "Exactly. Why don't we head upstairs and start sketching some ideas?"

The kids vanish in a blur of pounding feet and excited shouts, voices echoing down the hallway until silence folds in around us.

Leo and Levi settle into the couch for a private viewing of my soul. Backs straight. Eyes bright. Pens at the ready. And their seriousness doesn't rattle me. It steadies me. Anchors me.

This is it.

No aliases. No hedging. No waiting for permission.

"The traditional medical model of female orgasm," I begin, voice even, spine tall, "is fundamentally incomplete. It's based more on assumption than actual data."

My hands move automatically, scrolling through slides I've built and rebuilt. This isn't a jumble of journal scribbles or a fever-dream hypothesis. This is the sharpened tip of every late night, every whispered test, every time I asked myself if I was crazy for wanting more.

"This is the foundation everything else has been built on," I say, gaining confidence. "And it's wrong."

For the next forty-five minutes, I trace the gaps in the data, the blind spots no one bothered to illuminate. I speak of erasure, of the arrogance of simplification, of how we've taken what's vast and intimate and flattened it into a one-size-fits-all model that fails most women.

"This research," I say, my voice lower, more intimate, "could change the way we treat dysfunction. The way we teach pleasure. The way partners interact with each other. It's not about theory. It's about being seen. Being known."

Leo's tone cuts through the quiet, raw and taut. "And if women understand themselves better?"

The way he asks it. It isn't clinical. It's personal.

"They stop apologizing," I say, barely breathing. "They stop shrinking. They stop waiting to be figured out. They start asking. Feeling. Claiming what they want."

There's a beat of silence. Levi exhales as though he's been holding it in since my first word.

"Bloody hell," he murmurs, his voice gone rough. His eyes catch the light, bright with something fierce and certain. "You're going to change the world."

For a moment, the words hang between us, quiet and heavy. My throat tightens, but the smile comes anyway. "One woman at a time."

The thud of feet on the stairs breaks the spell, the sound of laughter spilling closer. Hudson appears first, the twins close behind, bright and breathless with treehouse dreams. They scatter colored pencils and paper across the coffee table, already arguing over rope bridges, lookout towers, and whether a zip line is strictly necessary.

It's absolute chaos. It's perfect.

"We should start thinking about travel arrangements," Leo says, standing to help gather my papers.

My pulse flutters. "We?"

He doesn't elaborate. Watches me, waiting for the realization to click into place.

"You don't think we're letting you go alone, do you?" Hudson grins, bumping my shoulder with his. "Moral support, beautiful. Plus, I've always wanted to see Vienna."

My gaze flicks between them. "All of you?" My voice rises with every word, caught between disbelief and the sharp, swelling edge of hope.

"If you want us there," Levi says quietly, and something flickers between him and the others, quick and wordless, enough to make my pulse stumble.

Silence stretches, not awkward but weighted. Another glance passes among them, subtle and charged, like a secret moving from one to the next while I try to catch up.

"I..." My throat tightens, the yes rising sharp and bright. "Yes. I want you there."

The air thickens, charged and waiting, the kind of stillness that settles before a storm when even the wind holds its breath. Whatever they're keeping to themselves hums in the space between us, alive and insistent, crawling beneath my skin until I can almost taste it.

"What aren't you telling me?" I ask, narrowing my eyes.

Leo only smiles, that infuriating, intoxicating smile that turns my spine to water and sends a pulse curling low in my belly.

"Nothing you need to worry about right this moment," he says, gripping my face as he pulls me into a kiss. And even though I know he's trying to distract me, I sink into it anyway.

The mysterious glances don't stop, even as we drift into dinner prep. I try to ignore them, pressing down the itch of curiosity and focusing instead on the symphony unfolding around me. We've decided on homemade pizza. Not because it's easy, but because the kids love every messy step of it. There's an elemental quality in the way their hands disappear into flour and dough, in the way the kitchen fills with the scent of yeast and olive oil and the rising pitch of laughter.

Hudson ties on an apron with exaggerated flair, posing in celebrity chef fashion while Daniel recites pizza dough measurements as though he's delivering a lab report. "Three cups flour, one cup water, one packet yeast, two tablespoons olive oil, one teaspoon salt, one teaspoon sugar," he announces. Lorelai, already climbing onto her step stool, rolls her eyes and calls him a show-off, but the grin tugging at her lips gives her away.

I take a seat at the kitchen table and pretend to focus on my conference notes, but my eyes keep drifting. Leo's crouched beside Daniel, explaining yeast activation. Across the counter, Hudson shows Lorelai how to scoop flour without sending it into the air in a powder bomb.

"The water has to be right," Leo says, guiding Daniel's index finger under the tap. "Too hot and it kills the yeast. Too cold and it takes a while to work."

"Goldilocks," Lorelai says, right before Hudson dabs a pinch of flour on her nose. She squeals with delight, rubbing at it with flour-coated fingers and making it worse.

Levi appears at my elbow with a glass of wine. "How are the final tweaks coming?" he asks.

"Good," I lie, even though I haven't finished a single edit. "But I keep getting distracted by—" I gesture toward the flour-covered chaos unfolding around us.

"Look, Mummy!" Lorelai holds up her hands, proudly coated in a sticky paste of flour and water. "I'm helping!"

"I can see that, love." I shove my notes aside and join the others at the counter, pulled into the whirlwind of dough and toppings and chaos. Daniel kneads with the focused determination of a scientist on the verge of discovery, and my chest aches with love so sharp it almost hurts.

My children are thriving. They're not just safe. They're loved. And not only by me.

"The gluten needs to develop properly," Daniel mutters as he presses his fists into the dough, "or the crust'll be too thick."

Meanwhile, Lorelai has appointed herself Chief Tomato Sauce Taster. Every few minutes, Levi dips a spoon, blows on it, and offers it to her. "Needs more oregano," she announces, though I'm fairly certain she has no idea what oregano even tastes like.

"The fairy girl has spoken," Levi says, saluting with the spoon before adding more.

When the dough is divided and rolled, Leo claps and declares it's pizza construction time. Daniel places each topping with mathematical precision, building tiny grids of mozzarella and evenly spaced pepperoni. Lorelai goes the other way entirely, turning her dough into an abstract collage of vegetables she insists is a flower garden.

Hudson tosses his dough high, the circle spinning through the air before landing neatly back in his hands. "It's all in the wrist," he says, grinning as Lorelai gasps and bounces on her toes, already demanding a turn. Leo mutters "show-off" under his breath, but the corner of his mouth gives him away.

Levi and I end up shoulder to shoulder, building our pizza together. Our hands brush as we reach for basil. He adds mushrooms where I've layered cheese. I tuck fresh oregano into the curve of his sauce pattern. We work in quiet sync, the kind that only comes when you've let someone all the way in.

The oven timer dings. Daniel's pizza comes out first, perfectly round with toppings arranged in careful symmetry, the cheese bubbling in neat golden circles. Lorelai's follows, a glorious mess of color and chaos, but the pride in her eyes makes it beautiful.

"Masterpieces, both of them," Hudson announces, and their beaming faces make my heart squeeze.

We eat as though we haven't eaten in days. Gooey slices disappear faster than we can cool them, passed hand to hand across the table between bursts of laughter and exaggerated groans of satisfaction. Someone drops a pepperoni in their lap. Someone else tries to convince me that cheese on the floor can still be eaten if it's "mostly clean."

When the last crust has been claimed and Lorelai is visibly wearing more tomato sauce than she consumed, I push back from the table. "Bath time for the grubby pizza makers."

"Do we have to?" she groans on instinct, already sliding off her chair with the dramatic resignation of a child who knows full well that Mum always wins.

"Yes," I say, scooping her up. "You're both coated in flour, sauce, and at least two substances I refuse to investigate further."

Leo and Hudson volunteer for cleanup duty, and Levi follows me upstairs for the bedtime gauntlet. The bathroom becomes a splash zone in seconds. Both kids insist on cramming into the tub, a pair of unruly otters, limbs flailing, bubbles foaming as though we've triggered a science experiment that's one beaker away from combustion.

By the time they're clean, pruney, and wriggling into pajamas, sleep is already tugging at the corners of their eyes. We pile into Daniel's room for story time, the four of us squeezed together on his too-narrow bed in a human game of Tetris.

Levi tells a story about brave little flowers who weather storms and frost by sticking close, their roots entwined beneath the soil, whispering strength to each other. It's part fable, part fantasy, and a quiet masterclass in survival.

Daniel's eyes droop first, his head heavy on my shoulder. Lorelai fights it longer, determined not to miss a single word, but eventually she surrenders too, curling into Levi's side with a satisfied sigh.

～

The house is quiet, the kind of stillness that only comes after the kids are asleep. We end up in my room without speaking, drawn there by habit, by gravity. The floors creak, the air thickens, the quiet shifts from ordinary to charged.

Leo sits on the edge of the bed, the mattress dipping under his weight. The scent of cedar and leather clings to him, curling through the room until it settles low in my stomach.

"I have something to ask you," he says, his voice rough.

My stomach flips, a wild rush of butterflies erupting all at once. "What?"

He looks up at me through his lashes, and the heat in his gaze goes straight to the base of my spine. My knees press together, thighs tightening around a pulse I can't quiet. "How do you feel about taking the next step?" he asks, voice low. "No more prep. Just us."

Oh. Oh God.

My lips part. My throat goes dry.

"No more plugs," Hudson says, kneeling on the bed behind Leo, his hands settling over Leo's shoulders. His hands look massive where they rest, and the intimacy of it makes my core tighten. "Just us."

My face flushes, rising from my chest to my cheeks in a flood of arousal so visceral I feel it in my nipples, already pebbled, aching under the thin fabric of my tank top. I feel it slide down my spine. In the hungry ache building low in my belly.

"I'm ready," I say, my words trembling.

"You're sure?" Levi's voice is lower, quieter, but it threads through me. He appears beside me, steady and silent, smelling of clean skin and the sea and some wild thing that doesn't belong to anyone. His hand glides over the small of my back, and I lean into him without thinking.

"We'll go at your pace," he says, voice barely more than a murmur near my cheek. "You say stop, we stop."

"I'm sure." This time, the words are solid. Strong.

Levi tugs my shirt over my head, his knuckles grazing my ribs as if even the drag of fabric is foreplay. His fingertips skim the curve of my breast, teasing me until goosebumps race across my skin. I'm already arching into him when Hudson steps behind me, the heat of his chest a brand against my back. His mouth is hot on my neck, the scrape of his teeth at the slope of my shoulder so sharp it's almost painful.

Leo is slower. His hands trail down my ribs, pushing beneath the swell of my breasts to lift and weigh them. My nipples tighten even further, desperate for his mouth. My knees threaten to buckle.

"Look at you," Levi murmurs, low and smug, brushing his lips over my cheek. "Fucking trembling already."

Every part of me is touched, kissed, claimed. Hudson drops to his knees, his stubble scraping the tender skin of my inner thighs. The first stroke of his tongue rips a sound from my throat, my head tipping back against Levi's chest. My legs fall open on instinct, hips rocking toward his mouth, my voice dissolving into whimpers and pleas I can't hold back.

"You're dripping for us," Hudson growls. "Sweet little cunt can't stop begging."

Leo grips the back of Hudson's neck and drags him up, kissing him hard enough to steal the air from both of them. Hudson groans, the sound breaking when Leo deepens it, tongue sliding in to taste what's left of me on his lips. He pulls back just far enough to breathe, eyes dark and wild. "Christ," he rasps. "You taste like her. Sweet and fucking filthy."

Levi's hand slides between my thighs with light, teasing strokes before adding the pressure I need. Exactly as I taught him. He sinks one finger inside me, then another, curling them deep until I'm gasping.

"So tight," he murmurs against my ear, voice dark and rough enough to scrape. "So fucking perfect." His teeth graze my skin, his breath hot. "You're going to take every one of us tonight, aren't you? Greedy little thing."

"Yes." The word punches out of me. "God, yes."

They move me as though I weigh nothing, passing me between

them like it's second nature. Levi lies flat on the mattress, and I'm guided down onto him, my spine pressed to his chest. His cock is already hard between my cheeks, but he doesn't rush. One arm tightens around my ribs while the other reaches over to the bedside table, grabbing the bottle of lube.

"Relax for me, Doctor MacLeod. I'm about to teach you the eighth way to orgasm, and I expect you to take notes," he murmurs, kissing the corner of my jaw as he flips off the cap. The sound of lube being pumped fills the air, and then his touch is back between my cheeks, spreading them carefully.

I shudder when his first finger pushes in, then another, the glide effortless. Deep strokes that make me gasp, that leave me panting, aching, clenching around nothing as he withdraws. The stretch burns when he replaces his touch with the blunt head of his cock, but it's the kind of burn I crave. Deep and overwhelming. He presses enough to make my body hitch, to make my thighs tremble.

He leans in, his mouth hot at my ear as his cock presses harder. "You feel that? That slick, aching hole? That's mine. And you're going to take each filthy inch, aren't you, my clever girl?"

He presses in slow, inch by inch, and my whole body arches with the stretch. The lube helps, but the fullness still steals my breath. Every nerve sparks at once, sharp and bright, until I can't tell where the ache ends and the pleasure begins. Beneath me, Levi shudders, a low sound catching in his throat as his arms tighten around me when he finally sinks all the way in.

"Jesus fuck, Lorna," he groans as I pulse around him. "You feel so goddamned good."

Before I can find the words, Hudson is there, kneeling between my legs, his cock thick and flushed, his fingers wrapped around the base as he stares down at me as though I'm the answer to everything.

"Ready?" he asks, voice rough.

"Yes." I can't stop shaking. "Please, Hudson."

He pushes in, and a cry breaks from my throat. Each inch drives me tighter onto Levi's cock, splitting me open until I'm shaking, caught between them, nowhere to run, nothing untouched.

Hudson shudders, hands braced on either side of me. "Fuck, Snapdragon. You enjoying being filled with two cocks?"

I can only moan as they hold still inside me, giving me time to adjust.

The bed shifts under Leo's weight. I can't see him directly, only the ripple of movement as he positions himself behind Hudson, but I can see Hudson's face. Can see the second Leo presses his fingers between his cheeks. Hudson's head jerks, his eyes fluttering shut, a groan punching from his chest as though he's already halfway undone. His lips part on a broken sound as Leo opens him with brutal purpose, and I swear I can feel it too. Every twitch of Hudson's hips, every ragged exhale.

Leo's hand slides around to grip his throat. Not tight, not cruel, enough to make Hudson's mouth fall open wider, his expression wrecked.

"Has your ass missed me?" Leo growls, voice low and rough with need. "Because I've been thinking about fucking you since the second you walked into my workshop the other day."

Hudson's eyes lock on mine, and I see everything in them. Need. Surrender. Lust so sharp it borders on pain.

Leo presses deeper, and Hudson's whole body shudders. "You feel that?" Leo murmurs against his neck, voice dark, fingers still working him open. "That stretch? That's just my fingers, baby. Wait until you feel my cock."

I can't look away. Hudson's wrecked face, Leo's low voice, the slick push and pull of his fingers, it's raw, obscene, fucking beautiful. Heat floods me so fast I forget to breathe. This isn't a fantasy anymore. It's happening, and I'm undone just watching.

Leo glances up, catches my stare. "You like watching, sweetheart?" A wicked smile pulls at his lips. He slides off the bed, grabs the floor mirror from the corner, and drags it closer. "Tell me when it's right."

I raise my hand when the mirror catches it all—Hudson's cock buried between my thighs, the tremor in his shoulders, the slick slide of our bodies. Leo's mouth finds mine, hungry and claiming, stealing the breath from my chest. When he pulls back, his eyes stay locked on mine as he climbs onto the bed again, taking his place behind Hudson.

Leo strokes himself once, twice, the slide so slick the sound alone makes my stomach clench. One hand grips Hudson's hip, the other holding the base of his cock steady, and he pushes in. Hudson jolts, his whole body seizing above me, a broken sound tearing from his throat as Leo fills him in one long, deep thrust. His hips stutter, and it forces him deeper into me, which drives me harder onto Levi.

The chain reaction is blinding.

Each of Leo's thrusts slams Hudson deeper, drives me harder onto Levi, until I'm nothing but friction and pressure, caught under the weight of them. I can't think. I'm trapped between the three of them, stretched to my breaking point, my body wrung out and soaked with sweat and slick and tears.

I'm nothing but nerve endings. Each inch of me is claimed. My skin drips. My thighs quake. My mouth opens but nothing comes out except strangled moans, wrecked whimpers that don't sound human.

Levi's voice is a rasp at my spine, his touch digging bruises into my hips as he fucks up into me from below. "You feel it, don't you? How you fit around us. You were made to take a cock in both holes, made to be stretched and filled until all you know is us inside you."

Hudson's trying to brace himself, trying to keep rhythm, but he looks as though he's seconds from shattering. "Fuck," he gasps, his voice breaking. "This feels too good. I can't hold it."

Leo snarls behind him and grabs his shoulders, snapping his hips forward with long, brutal thrusts that rock us all. He's panting hard, teeth bared, muscles tight. "Don't fucking hold it," he growls, voice pitched as though he's barely holding himself together. "Let go. Let her feel you lose it. Let her feel both of us break you."

Over Hudson's shoulder, Leo's gaze locks with mine. Hot and sharp, feral with pleasure. And he doesn't look away. He fucks harder, his cock slamming into Hudson, forcing him deeper inside me, forcing me harder down on Levi. His body hitches, catches, and I see it start. The unraveling. His jaw slackens, eyes burning into mine as his hips snap forward one last time, burying himself to the hilt, and he groans low and raw, eyes rolling, lips parting around a wordless cry that drags me down with him.

That look, that sound, splits me open.

My orgasm detonates under my skin. Every muscle locks, jerks, shakes uncontrollably as I scream, the sound torn straight from my chest. My pussy clamps down around Hudson, my ass spasms around Levi, and my whole body bucks between them, wild and helpless, lost in it.

Hudson follows with a broken sob, hips grinding as he spills inside me, his cock twitching as he collapses forward, mouth pressed to my neck. He's shaking. Whimpering. His arms cage me in as though he's afraid I'll disappear if he lets go.

Levi breaks on a ragged sound near my shoulder, his thrusts stuttering, teeth scraping skin as he grinds into me one last time and comes hard, hot pulses filling me so deep I feel it everywhere. He murmurs something that isn't words, a sound caught between worship and delirium, like his body's trying to speak a language his mouth can't remember.

Leo's still watching me as he finishes. His arm winds around Hudson's stomach, holding him steady as his hips jerk one last time. The way he looks at me, marking me with his pleasure, claiming me even from across another man's body. It hits harder than anything. A punch to the heart. In my cunt, in my spine, in the air between us.

And we collapse. A wrecked tangle of limbs and sweat and bodies and cum. The sheets soaked. My thighs are shaking. My lips are numb. I can feel Levi's cum leaking from me, Hudson still deep inside, Leo pressed to Hudson's back, all of them wrapped around me as though I'm the glue holding them together.

No one says anything at first. We only exist.

Eventually I blink through the haze, lungs still fighting for air, and manage the only words that make sense.

"Fucking perfect."

Because it is. Every breathless, messy, filthy second of it. Too much and just enough.

## 26

---

### HUDON'S POV

Right, let's see what we're working with," I mutter, dragging my fingers along the rough bark of the oak tree that's about to be the center of Daniel and Lorelai's childhood memories. The texture scrapes at my skin, years of Highland storms etched into every groove.

Daniel materializes at my elbow, notebook clutched to his chest. A pair of fake glasses is slipping down his nose, the lenses smeared with fingerprints. He's been shadowing me all morning, a pint-sized engineer, firing off questions with the focus of a kid who has no idea he's not an adult.

"The trunk circumference is forty-seven inches," he reports, winding his measuring tape back into a coil. "That should support a platform up to eight feet square, as long as we distribute the weight evenly."

I blink. Grin so hard it makes my cheeks hurt. "Bloody hell, you're clever. Remind me to hire you for all my future builds."

His whole face lights up, chest puffed with pride.

"Mr. Hudson!"

Her voice carries across the garden. Musical, bright, unruly, impossible to ignore. Lorelai charges barefoot through the grass, fairy wings strapped to her back, flower petals stuck in her curls, and two perfect grass stains marring both knees. She's chaos incarnate, an explosion of whimsy and dirt, and I wouldn't change a single thing.

"Can we have a rope ladder?" she demands, flinging herself at my legs with zero warning and absolute faith that I'll catch her. "And a slide? And a secret compartment for treasure?"

Her arms wrap around my thighs, small and sure, and I swear my heart grows too big for my chest. A few months ago, the idea of being responsible for kids would've sent me running for the nearest border. Now I can't imagine who I'd be without Daniel's quiet precision or Lorelai's wild, relentless joy.

"All excellent suggestions, fairy girl," I say, scooping her into my arms. "But I need more information. What kind of treasure are we hiding?"

"Important treasure," she says solemnly, eyes wide with meaning. "Pretty rocks. Flower petals. And biscuits."

I nod, pretending to scribble serious notes in my sketchbook, though my vision's a little blurry around the edges. "Understood. Biscuit compartments. Got it."

We build for the next hour. On paper, in our heads, with measuring tapes and blunt pencils and hearts too full to hold. Daniel checks angles, while Lorelai campaigns for rainbow paint and a chandelier made of fairy lights. Both are equally serious in their suggestions. Both are equally heard.

"We need to make sure it's safe," Daniel says after a while, brow furrowed as he double-checks a measurement in my sketch. He glances over at Lorelai, the way he always does, and adds, "But also fun."

God. This boy. This little protector in cartoon socks and blue-light glasses.

"Agreed," I murmur, voice rough, because I'm not sure I could speak clearly if I tried.

"Will you teach us how to build it?" Lorelai asks, her voice rising with hope.

"'Course I will. Can't have you two growing up without knowing how to swing a hammer properly." I wink at her, wiping a smudge of dirt from her cheek. "Besides, the best treehouses are built by the people who are going to use them."

Daniel straightens, shoulders squaring, a soldier accepting orders. "We'll be proper builders."

"The best builders," I agree, because it's absolutely true.

The sound of footsteps makes my skin prickle with awareness before I even turn around. Lorna approaches with a tray of fresh lemonade, condensation beading on the glasses, and that particular smile she gets when she's watching me with her children.

"How's the planning going?" she asks, settling on the grass beside our architectural chaos. Her scent mixes with earth and growing things, and I have to resist the urge to bury my face in her neck and breathe her in.

"Brilliantly," I say, accepting the cold glass she offers. "We're designing a masterpiece. Isn't that right, team?"

"It's going to have secret compartments and rainbow paint and maybe a telescope for stargazing," Lorelai announces, throwing herself into her mother's lap with complete abandon.

"And properly sized beams to make it safe," Daniel adds, because he wouldn't want anyone to think we're being frivolous.

Lorna's laugh bubbles up, light and fizzy as champagne, and it knocks the breath clean out of me. I watch her with the kids—the effortless affection, the way love hums through every small touch—and something settles deep in my chest. This isn't just attraction, not even love. It's the unshakable truth that I want to spend the rest of my life protecting this joy, building something solid and lasting with the three people who've become everything.

I don't just want this family. I need them.

"Where are Leo and Levi?" Lorna asks, gently picking blades of grass from Lorelai's hair.

"Took the truck to Harris for a sheep delivery. They won't be back until late."

I hesitate, say it before I can talk myself out of it. "We need to talk tonight. About the future. How we make this permanent." My ribs feel too small for what's inside them.

She nods. No surprise, no flinch. Steady, as though she's been waiting for me to say it.

"Okay."

The word lands soft but heavy, reverberating through the quiet until it settles somewhere under my skin. For a long moment neither of us moves, the air thick with everything we don't need to say. Then she smiles and the tightness in my chest unravels until I can finally breathe again.

The rest of the afternoon blurs into heat and sawdust, my skin scraped raw from the weight of lumber and the rhythm of work. Daniel and Lorelai stay close, firing off questions faster than I can answer, each one carving a little deeper, tugging me further into the life I never knew I needed.

Daniel approaches each lesson with scientific curiosity, asking thoughtful questions about load-bearing joints and weather resistance while sweat beads on his forehead from concentration. Lorelai treats construction as an elaborate game, but her enthusiasm makes up for any lack of technical skill.

"No, fairy girl, hammer like this, not sideways," I laugh, repositioning her grip for what feels like the hundredth time. Her hands are damp with sweat and determination, and the trust she places in my guidance makes it hard to swallow. "Otherwise you'll be nursing sore thumbs instead of building treehouses."

"But sideways is more fun," she protests, though she adjusts her technique, her tongue poking out the corner of her mouth in concentration.

"Fun doesn't count for much if you nail yourself to the board."

We start on the platform frame, laying out treated lumber on the grass to check measurements before hauling anything up into the tree. The work is methodical, soothing, the kind of project that requires enough concentration to quiet the restless energy that's been building under my skin for days.

The sun climbs higher, turning the air thick and humid. Sweat runs down my spine, soaking through my shirt, but the burn in my muscles feels good.

"Mr. Hudson," Daniel says during a water break, his voice careful in that way it gets when he's thinking hard. Condensation trails from his glass, dripping onto his shoes as he fidgets. "Are you going to stay? With us, I mean?"

The hope and fear tangled in his face knock something loose in my chest, making my hand tremble.

"Yeah, mate," I say quietly, crouching down to meet his serious gaze. "I'm staying. We all are."

His smile is so blinding I find myself blinking back tears. "Good," he says simply. "Mummy's happier when you're here. And Lorelai loves your jokes, even the bad ones."

"*Especially* the bad ones," Lorelai chimes in from her perch on a sawbench.

"What about you?" I ask Daniel, needing to hear it. "Do you want us around?"

He considers it with the gravity the question deserves, his little brow furrowed in thought. "Yes. It's nice having grown-ups who listen to my ideas and don't say I'm too serious. And you actually know how to build things right."

"Well," I say, voice thick. "I guess we'd better build you a tree-house worthy of the best architects in Scotland."

Daniel nods solemnly, then does something that absolutely destroys me. He steps forward and wraps his arms around my waist in a quick, fierce hug before pulling back, cheeks pink with embarrassment.

"Thanks, Mr. Hudson," he says quietly.

I ruffle his hair, not trusting my voice. "Anytime, mate. Anytime."

.  .  .

By evening, we've got the platform frame assembled and ready for installation tomorrow. The kids are covered in sawdust, their hair sticky with sweat and their clothes streaked with dirt. They chatter excitedly about the next phase of construction over dinner, their voices weaving together.

"And we'll add the walls, and the roof, and the secret compartments," Lorelai recites, ticking off each step on crumb-covered fingertips.

"Don't forget the rope ladder," Daniel says between bites.

"Never forget the rope ladder," I agree solemnly. "What kind of treehouse would it be without proper climbing equipment?"

Lorna watches the exchange with that smile that wrecks my composure. When she offers to handle bath time so I can finish cleaning up the construction mess, disappointment hits before I can hide it. Christ. When did I start wanting to be there for bath time? When did tucking Daniel and Lorelai into bed turn into the thing I look forward to most?

After the kids finally crash, worn out from a day of building and laughter, Lorna and I end up on the back porch. The night hums around us, cicadas and the faint creak of cooling wood, the air thick with sawdust and something quieter that's been building all day.

"So," she says, settling beside me on the old wooden bench, the heat of her thigh pressing into mine. "The future."

"The future," I hedge, taking a long pull of beer while I gather thoughts that feel too big for words. "I've been thinking about practicalities," I say finally, my heart in my throat.

She turns toward me, moonlight threading through her hair, and I can see every flicker of hope and fear etched across her face. "What kind of practicalities?" she asks, voice barely more than a breath.

My pulse quickens as I launch into ideas that have been building in my head for weeks. "The farms, for starters. It doesn't make sense to keep running two separate operations when we could combine resources, share equipment, coordinate schedules."

I gesture toward the fields that stretch between our properties, silver-touched grass swaying in the evening breeze.

"That's a big step," she says quietly.

"It is." I reach for her, skin damp from the humid evening air.

She rests her head on my shoulder, her brilliant mind working through implications and possibilities.

"The children would love it," she says at last, her voice soft but certain. "All that space to run and dream and build their little worlds."

"What about you? Would you love it?"

Her smile is sunrise breaking over water. "I think I already do. Love it, I mean. Love the idea of building something together instead of existing in neighboring farms."

"Thank fuck" I say, grinning before I can stop myself. "Because I've been thinking about field rotation, irrigation upgrades, maybe even turning the dahlia plots into a full commercial operation."

"Commercial?" Her eyebrows rise, and I catch the sharp intake that means I've surprised her. "You think there's a market for that?"

"Snapdragon, you could sell those blooms to florists in Edinburgh, Glasgow, London." The words tumble out faster, passion making my voice rough. "The colors you're producing, the size and quality. It's art, not agriculture. And then there are the tubers—the opportunities are endless."

Color rises in her cheeks, unmissable in the moonlight. I want to kiss her, but we've got more to settle first.

"And the kids," I say, because this is the part that matters most. "I know I'm not their father, but I want to be involved. School events. Bedtime stories. Teaching them how to use a power drill without losing fingers."

"Hudson." Her voice catches, thick with feeling. "They already think of you as family. All of you. Daniel asked me yesterday if you were going to adopt them."

The words stop me cold. My pulse kicks hard, erratic.

"What did you tell him?"

"That adoption's complicated. But love isn't. That you and Leo and Levi care about them as much as I do. And that's what matters."

Christ. This woman.

"I care so much," I say, the words dragging up from somewhere deep. "More than I thought I ever could. They're extraordinary, Lorna. You've raised two of the best humans I've ever met."

She reaches over, sliding her hand into mine. "*We're* raising them now." Her voice is low, but the impact is anything but.

We. The word lands and keeps sinking, threading through the cracks in me until it finds where it belongs.

"I want to build them a playground," I blurt, the idea tumbling out. "Not only the treehouse. It'll have swings. A climbing wall. Maybe even a little workshop where they can learn to use tools, build things with their own hands."

She looks at me for a beat, nods. "You want to give them the childhood you never had."

It's not a question. She already knows.

Growing up bouncing from place to place, chasing work, never rooted anywhere long enough to hang a picture. I want more for them. I want permanence. Dirt under their nails from the same patch of earth, year after year.

"Maybe," I say. "Is that selfish?"

"It's perfect." She leans in, pressing her lips to my cheek.

"Come on," I say, pulling her up, needing an outlet for all this restless energy. "Let's build a fire. It's the right kind of night for it."

Twenty minutes later, the fire pit's roaring, flames licking into the sky and painting her face in gold. The second the word *marsh-mallow* slips out, the kids appear like summoned spirits tumbling out of bed in their pajamas, hair wild, bare feet slapping the porch. That uncanny sixth sense children have for sugar kicks in at full power, and the night bursts back to life.

"We saw the fire," Lorelai announces, climbing into my lap without invitation. Her body is solid, pressed to my chest, smelling of soap and toothpaste. "Can we have some marshmal-lows, too?"

"Did you?" I ask, wrapping my arm around her. "What makes you think there are marshmallows involved?"

"Because you always have marshmallows when there's a fire," Daniel says logically, sitting beside Lorna.

The kid's not wrong. I may have developed a reputation for being prepared, mostly because watching their faces light up is better than any drug.

"Well," I say, reaching for the bag I brought out earlier. "Good thing I'm predictable."

We spend the next hour stuffing our faces with sticky sweetness, sugar coating our mouths while sparks dance toward stars. The kids offer increasingly elaborate suggestions for treehouse modifications while Lorna and I exchange amused glances over their heads.

"And we could add a zip line to the barn," Lorelai says around a mouthful of charred sugar.

"Absolutely not," Lorna says firmly, but she's smiling as she wipes Lorelai's face clean.

"A small zip line?" Daniel suggests hopefully, because he never gives up on a good idea.

"No zip lines until you're at least twelve," I say, "but we could discuss a pole to slide down."

The compromise works. We spend a few more minutes huddled over napkins, sketching by firelight, the paper tearing under my pen. Their voices bubble with plans. Secret passages, dragon traps, a snack vault. And I'm grinning so hard my face aches.

When Lorelai starts yawning into my shoulder, her weight growing heavier as exhaustion wins over excitement, I know it's time for the second bedtime routine of the evening.

"Right, you two," Lorna says, reading the same signs. "Back to bed."

"But the fire's still going," Lorelai protests weakly, her voice thick with sleep.

"We can make another one tomorrow," I promise, lifting her as I stand. She wraps her arms around my neck, and tucks her face to my shoulder with a sleepy sigh. "But you need proper sleep if you want to swing hammers without falling over."

Daniel takes my free hand as we walk back into the house, and the simple gesture of trust nearly brings me to my knees. These kids have me wrapped around their little fingers and I wouldn't have it any other way.

After we've wrangled them through teeth-brushing, one more story, another glass of water, and a promise that construction starts again at sunrise, Lorna and I drift back outside. The fire's burned low, embers glowing in the dark like a heartbeat that refuses to fade.

"Alone at last," I murmur, pulling her closer until I can feel her radiating through my clothes.

"For a bit," she laughs, the sound bright in the cricket-song darkness. "Give them ten minutes and they'll remember something vital they forgot to tell us."

The house stays quiet, the kind of deep, content silence that only comes after a long day well spent. We sit in it together, wrapped in the scent of wood smoke and night-blooming flowers, the air soft and alive around us.

"Thank you," she says suddenly, voice low but fierce.

"For what?"

"For seeing them." She turns to look at me, firelight catching in her eyes. "Really seeing them. Not putting up with them because they come as part of the package. For wanting to build them tree-houses. Teach them things. Show up for them."

There's an edge in her voice. Quiet, but sharp. Old hurt underneath.

I nod, throat tight. "Thank you for letting me. For trusting me with the best parts of your world."

She shifts in my arms, her gaze dark and focused, charged with intensity that sends lightning straight through me. My skin prickles, pulse rising before she even speaks.

"Make love to me, Hudson," she says quietly.

I glance back toward the house, where the glow from the

kitchen windows means little feet could show up at any second. "Not here," I murmur. "Come with me."

I take her hand and lead her away from the coals, past the chairs and half-eaten marshmallows, into the garden. The air is cooler here, tinged with ash and soil and the scent of new life.

We walk in silence through the rows of dahlias, the blooms tall and lush around us, petals open to the sky. Moonlight makes everything feel closer. More alive. The air hums with her presence.

I stop when we're deep enough in the flowers that the house is a distant glow, far enough that we have privacy but close enough to hear if the kids call out.

"If we keep ending up out here," I say, stopping in the middle of the row where the tallest blooms brush our shoulders, "we're gonna need to put a bed in the field."

"Hudson—"

I reach for her, bury my hands in her hair, and kiss her. She comes to me without hesitation. Her grip curling in my shirt, pulling me close until our bodies press tight, heartbeat to heartbeat.

"I love you," I whisper at her lips, the words scraping out raw. "You. The kids. This life. All of it."

She exhales, hitching. "Show me how much," she says, sucking at my bottom lip.

I take my time undressing her, slowly easing away each layer. She doesn't rush me. She just watches, chest rising and falling, eyes dark and wide as the moon paints her skin in silver.

"Christ," I whisper, sinking to my knees beside her. The ground is still holding the day's heat, cradling her. "You're the most beautiful thing I've ever seen."

She smiles, small and a little uncertain, then reaches for me. I catch her by the arms and guide her into my lap. She comes easily, knees sinking into the earth on either side of my hips, the warmth of her body fitting against mine. Her hands settle on my shoulders, searching for steadiness, and I realize she's trembling.

"I've got you," I murmur, my hold claiming her hips.

I take my time, tracing her like a map I never want to stop exploring. The curve of her waist, the soft rise of her breasts, the sharp intake of breath when I find the place that makes her tremble. She's already wet when my fingers slip lower, and the sound she makes nearly wrecks me.

"You're soaking wet," I growl against her throat.

She moves against my hand, breath catching, every small sound winding me tighter. I can feel her building, muscles trembling, so close I can taste it in the air. Then I pull back, just enough to make her whimper.

"Not yet," I whisper, my mouth at her ear. "I want to feel you come around my cock."

"Please, Hudson," she gasps, voice breaking open, and the need in it nearly unravels the little bit of control I have left.

I guide her up, my hands firm on her hips, feeling the tremor in her thighs as she hovers above me. The head of my cock brushes her, and she gasps, the sound half shock, half need. I hold her steady, thumb stroking her skin as I ease her down. The first slide of her heat grips me tight, and my breath falters. She takes me slow, inch by inch, every pulse of her body drawing me deeper until she's seated fully, chest to chest, heart hammering against mine. For a moment we just stay like that, shaking, breathing the same ragged air, stunned by how perfectly we fit.

For a heartbeat, nothing moves. We just breathe, skin to skin, learning this new gravity, the weight, the heat, the impossible closeness that feels like it might undo us both.

"Move," I tell her, voice rough. "Ride me, baby. Show me how much you need this."

She does, and it's the most beautiful thing I've ever seen.

Afterward, we don't move. Our skin is slick, our lips swollen, her thigh draped over mine. My hand rests at her hip, thumb tracing slow circles against her skin.

"We're absolutely filthy," Lorna says, dragging her fingers through my hair. Dirt. Petals. Sweat. The mess we made of each other. She smiles anyway, flushed and glowing, utterly unbothered.

"And I know exactly how to fix that." I'm already grinning as I push up onto my feet.

I lead her to the garden hose coiled beside the shed, the metal cool against my fingers as I twist the nozzle until it sprays a fine mist. Moonlight catches the droplets, scattering silver over her skin until she seems to shimmer.

I lift the hose higher, letting the water fall in a soft arc over her shoulders, down her spine, tracing the curve of her hips. She tips her head back and laughs, loud and bright, and the sound stops my breath. Drops cling to her lashes, her hair streams dark and wet down her back. She looks like a garden nymph come to life, all wild grace and glimmering skin, the kind of beauty that could make gods lose their minds.

She takes the hose from my hand. "Your turn," she says, biting her lip.

The first sweep of cool water runs down my chest in shivering lines, but it's her hand that steals my breath. She follows the droplets with her fingers, tracing me as if touch itself is a kind of prayer. She doesn't speak, doesn't hurry, just moves with quiet purpose, like she's blessing every inch of me.

Somewhere between her laughter and my unsteady breathing, something shifts. We start to move, to spin, the hose forgotten but still spraying around us. We're dancing under it, slipping on the wet grass, clutching at each other, laughing too hard to care. The air is thick with the scent of water, earth, and her skin—sweet, wild, and new.

By the time we stumble back toward the house, we're dripping and barefoot and wrecked with joy.

On the porch, I press her against the front door, tilt her chin up, and kiss her. She tastes like marshmallows and summer and something that feels dangerously close to home. Her lips are cool from the water, warm beneath, and the contrast hits deep, dragging a sound from me I don't bother to hold back.

"That was—" she starts, falters, words catching somewhere between her mouth and mine.

"Magic," I finish for her, because it was. All of it. I brush a kiss to her lips. "Go inside before you freeze."

She hesitates. "What about you?"

"I'm running home," I say, stepping back. "I need a change of clothes."

She laughs. "You're going to run across the field naked?"

"Wouldn't be the first time," I grin, already backing away from the porch. "Besides, it's dark. Who's going to see?"

"The sheep," she calls after me as I break into a run, and her laughter follows me across the field like a benediction.

I run through the dark, a grin tearing across my face, night air biting at my skin, every stride thrumming with a kind of life I didn't know I'd been missing.

Tomorrow I'll wake up and finish the treehouse. I'll show Daniel how to set a joist, watch Lorelai sprinkle glitter where it absolutely doesn't belong. I'll help Lorna with the dahlias, steal kisses when the kids aren't looking, and fall asleep to the sound of all of them breathing under the same roof.

And the day after that, I'll do it again.

**27**

---

A FEW WEEKS LATER

The midnight-blue silk clings to my body like a second skin, mapping every curve with unapologetic precision. In the mirror, I watch myself transform into who I've always been on the inside. The woman staring back doesn't shrink. Doesn't apologize. Doesn't hide.

Behind me, Leo adjusts his tie with fingers that aren't quite steady. He catches my eye in the reflection, and something in his gaze sends a thrill through me that has nothing to do with nerves. Pride. Awe. Hunger.

Hudson stops pacing mid-stride when I turn around. Just stops. Stares. His mouth opens like he's going to say something clever, but the words die unspoken.

Levi rises slowly from the chair, his eyes tracking over me like I'm art in a museum he's been waiting his whole life to see. "Christ, Lorna," he breathes.

"You look..." Hudson finally finds his voice. "You look like you could rewrite history."

"That's the plan." My voice comes out steady. Strong. Absolutely certain.

Leo crosses to me, and gently cups my face between his hands.

"They're going to see what we've always seen," he says quietly, fiercely. "That you're extraordinary."

The certainty clicks into place inside me, rising from my own bones, my own years of relentless work. Every late night. Every buried finding. Every year I spent in careful silence has led to this moment.

I'm Dr. Lorna MacLeod. For years, I hid behind a pseudonym, too afraid of what people would think of the work I loved. But today, I get to step into the light and claim it, all of it, under my own name.

The nervousness I expected never materializes. Instead, there's only clarity. Purpose. Power.

"Ready, beautiful?" Hudson asks, offering his arm. I take it without hesitation, my heels clicking against marble with the rhythm of inevitability. "Let's go change the world."

The convention center hums like a living thing—polished marble, glass, and the relentless murmur of ambition. Everywhere I look, scientists and physicians orbit one another, their conversations sparking like static, theories colliding hard enough to rewrite the rules of medicine. My pulse thrums in time with it all, sharp and wild. It isn't fear anymore. It's hunger, pure and electric, curling low in my stomach.

Backstage, Levi leans close. "Show them," he murmurs at my ear. "Show them who you really are."

Beyond the curtain, the murmur swells, hundreds of brilliant minds, a living tide of intellect and expectation. The air hums with potential, the kind that could break you or make you. I smooth the silk over my stomach, grounding myself in the touch

"Dr. MacLeod?" the stage assistant says, voice cutting through the hum. "You're on."

I turn for one last look at them. Leo's jaw is clenched, eyes molten with pride and something fiercer. Hudson's grin is steady, all faith and fire. Levi's gaze locks on mine, a single nod anchoring me. I breathe once, then let go.

"Go claim it," Leo says. Not a wish. A command.

I blow them a kiss and step into the wings just as the announcer says my name. The roar of applause comes first, then the swell of hundreds rising to meet me, then the lights. They crash over me like water. A baptism. Blinding. Absolute. For a second, I can't breathe.

And they're there. Front row, exactly where they promised. Leo, eyes dark and fierce, every muscle in his body tuned to my presence. Hudson, grinning so wide it feels like sunlight breaking through the storm. Levi, tears streaking down his cheeks, no attempt to hide them.

The world falls away until it's just us—them, me, the light—and for the first time in my life, I don't shrink from the brilliance. I step into it.

"Six years ago," I begin, and my voice doesn't waver, doesn't apologize, doesn't hide, "I thought my career was over. Today, I'm here to show you why it was just beginning."

Silence drops like a curtain. Hundreds of faces, all turned toward me. Waiting.

"Everything we think we know about female orgasm is incomplete. My research identifies seven distinct physiological patterns. Seven different ways women experience pleasure that our current medical model ignores completely."

I click to the first slide, and the data speaks for itself. Neural pathways lighting up in different configurations. Hormonal cascades following unique timelines. Response patterns so distinct they might as well be different languages.

"This isn't theory. This is years of rigorous data collection, peer review, and clinical observation. This is proof that we've been getting it wrong. And here's how we fix it."

The questions start almost immediately. Hands shooting up. Voices calling out. Not skepticism. Excitement. Recognition. The kind of energy that happens when people realize they're watching their field crack open and reshape itself.

For forty-five minutes, I hold my own. Every question, I answer. Every challenge, I meet. Every doubt, I dismantle with data so solid it could be carved from stone.

When I deliver the final slide, outlining the implications for treatment, for education, for the millions of women who've been told their bodies are broken when really we've been asking the wrong questions, the room erupts.

Not polite academic applause.

A standing ovation that shakes the floor.

I let my gaze sweep across them. Hundreds of the brightest minds in sexual health, on their feet, for me. For my work. For research I conducted in secret, published under a pseudonym, protected like contraband because I was terrified of losing everything.

But I haven't lost anything.

I've won.


The reception after is a blur of clinking glasses and business cards that keep piling in my hand. Johns Hopkins wants joint studies. Stanford wants to dive into methodology. Cambridge floats co-authorship on a piece that could rewrite clinical guidelines across three continents. Each offer hits my chest in a drumbeat of possibility.

Universities. Positions. Open doors. After years of knocking on walls that never even cracked. But even as I nod and smile, even as my hands fill with names and futures, I can feel them.

My men.

They hover just beyond the edge of conversation, close enough that I can feel them, far enough to pretend restraint. Never intruding, but always there, tethered to me, magnets testing the strength of their pull. Their champagne flutes catch the light, glittering and harmless, nothing compared to the hunger in their eyes.

They watch me like men who already know they'll get what they want. Like I'm both the altar and the sin, something to be worshipped and ruined in the same breath.

"Excuse me," I say, smiling tightly at the cluster of researchers hovering nearby. "I need a moment."

I move through the crowd, heels striking marble in a rhythm that matches my pulse. The air hums with chatter and clinking glass, but all I hear is the rush of my own heartbeat.

"Well?" Hudson says when I reach them, voice rough with pride. "How's it feel to be one of the most brilliant women in Europe?"

"I don't know about that," I manage, laughter catching on the edge of a breath that feels too big for my chest. "But right now? I feel incredible."

Leo's eyes soften. "We're so proud of you. Up there—Christ, Lorna. You were magnificent."

"Absolutely incredible," Levi adds, reverence threading through every syllable. "You didn't just give a lecture. You claimed the room."

Their words pour through me, warm and heavy, but it's the look in their eyes that ignites everything. I step closer, the space between us thick with heat and the scent of them—cologne, skin, something unmistakably theirs. "I think this calls for a proper celebration."

The glance they trade crackles through the air, sharp enough to raise goosebumps along my arms.

"Let us at least wine and dine you first. We're going to London for dinner," Leo says, like it's the most natural thing in the world.

My heart stutters. "London? Tonight?"

His smile curves, slow and dangerous. "Tonight."

Before I can protest, they've swept me into motion—bags collected, car waiting, a private plane courtesy of Lach. The whole thing feels like being caught in a current I don't want to escape. By the time the sun dips below the horizon, we're in Soho, lights flickering to life as they lead me to dinner.

The restaurant glitters above the Thames like a jewel box

caught between water and sky. Windows shimmer with reflected city light, white linens glow in the hush of candlelight, and everything feels impossibly private. The maître d' leads us to a corner table overlooking the skyline, where London stretches out in gold and glass, pulsing with life beneath us.

"Champagne," Leo says, his hand firm at the small of my back. The silk of my dress might as well not exist. "Your best."

When the waiter disappears, something in the air changes. Hudson's foot nudges mine beneath the table. Heat climbs up my leg, pooling low before I can stop it. Across from me, Levi's fingers brush my wrist, tracing light circles over skin so thin he must feel the wild pulse beneath it.

When the champagne arrives, Leo raises his glass. "To new beginnings," he says, eyes on me. "And to the woman who was born to change the world."

We toast. The bubbles fizz against my tongue, bright and electric.

"I still can't believe the offers," I say, my voice unsteady with the rush of it all. "Stanford wants me for a semester. Cambridge is floating a guest seminar. Hopkins wants to co-author research that could change international standards."

Levi leans closer, his tone soft but steady. "What do *you* want, Petal?"

"Everything." The word lands between us, fierce and certain. "The research. The platform. The chance to rewrite how medicine treats women. But also the farm. The kids. The three of you."

Leo doesn't even hesitate. "Then you'll have it," he says simply, his gaze locked on mine. "We'll make it work."

No doubt. No hesitation. Just faith so absolute it guts me.

The food is exquisite. Caviar cool and briny, citrus sorbet sharp and clean, lamb that melts on my tongue. But I barely taste a thing.

Leo's thigh presses against mine under the table, his hand sliding higher beneath the linen. Hudson tops off my wine, his fingers brushing my knuckles just long enough to make my pulse skip. Levi reaches for the bread, his arm grazing mine, and somehow that fleeting touch feels seismic.

They aren't subtle. They're intentional. A symphony of suggestion, turning dinner into foreplay one small movement at a time.

By the time the waiter appears again, my skin is humming.

"Dessert?" he asks.

"No," Leo says, eyes never leaving mine. "Just the check."

The taxi ride is exquisite torture. I'm wedged between Hudson and Levi, their heat crowding out the air. Hudson's thumb drags over the back of my neck, a slow stroke that sends shivers racing down my spine. Levi threads his fingers through mine, his grip steady, his thumb brushing my skin in a way that only makes my pulse stumble harder.

Across from us, Leo watches. Silent. Focused. Starving.

"Where are we going?" My voice sounds too soft, too breathless.

"Somewhere we can dance," Leo says. "Somewhere you can forget everything but us."

Bass thrums through the walls, through the floor, through my chest. The club is all flickering lights and moving bodies, sound and sweat and lust colliding in the dark.

Hudson pulls me into the crowd first, hands settling low at my waist. "You owned that room today," he murmurs against my ear. "Fuck, Lorna."

We move together until the song bleeds into the next, then the next. Levi cuts in, slipping behind me. "You're incandescent," he says at my throat. "As if you've been waiting your whole life to burn this bright."

I lose track of time. One song blurs into five, then ten. We move through each other in rhythm—Hudson's raw hunger, Levi's focused touch, Leo's dark pull. Drinks appear in my hand and vanish without notice. The room spins with heat, bodies, and bass that won't let up.

Then Leo pulls me close and everything else disappears. His thigh presses between mine. "You have no idea how proud I am."

The three of them surround me, Hudson pressed to my back, Levi's hand on my side, Leo claiming my mouth. The music pounds. The lights blur. My dress clings to my skin, damp with sweat.

Time dissolves into sweat and sensation and the endless thrum of music.

"We should get some air," I finally manage, breathless and dizzy.

"Good idea," Leo says, voice thick. "Come on."

He guides us to Westminster Bridge, the cool night air a shock after the heat of the club. The Thames glitters beneath us, Big Ben keeping watch.

"Photos," he says. "To commemorate the night."

They crowd close as Leo lines up the shot. Hudson's arm around my waist, his hand finding bare skin. Levi's thumb drawing circles on my thigh. Leo's fingers digging into silk at my hip, possession and promise.

"One more," Leo murmurs, and pulls me into a kiss. Hungry. Claiming.

We walk along the Thames after, Leo's arm around my waist, Hudson's fingers laced with mine, Levi's hand on my hip.

Leo pulls me into a shadowed doorway, mouth crashing against mine, all heat and hunger. His hands find their way beneath my dress, roaming higher.

"Someone could see," I gasp when his fingers slip between my thighs and discover just how wet I am.

"I won't let that happen," Hudson says, positioning himself to block the view.

Levi watches, jaw tight. "Not here. You deserve more than a doorway."

Leo takes a shuddering breath and steps back. "Hotel. Now."

.   .   .

Lach had worked his magic again, so by the time we arrive, our room is ready, our bags already waiting. The elevator ride up is silent, thick with anticipation. The four of us vibrate with desire that's not civilized, not polite. It's animal. Primal. Pressed tight under the skin.

The penthouse doors open with a soft chime, and we spill inside. London unfurls beneath us through floor-to-ceiling glass, a glittering sprawl of gold and glitter. But I don't see the city.

I see them.

The men who stripped away every defense I ever built and taught me I never needed them at all.

Hudson steps closer, taking my hand. "Tonight, you're in control. After you took that conference room apart, we need to see what else Dr. MacLeod can command."

The words strike low. Fire curls in my belly, a fuse catching flame.

Six years of hiding. Shrinking. Surviving.

That ends here.

My chin lifts. My spine straightens. And the sharp, hungry thing inside me, the one I've kept caged and quiet for so long, finally opens its mouth.

"Undress," I say, low and dirty. "I want all three of you naked and hard."

Leo's eyes go dark, pupils swallowing the brown, leaving only a rim of gold. His jaw ticks. No theatrics. No smirk. Quiet, brutal control as he reaches for his tie.

One motion, and it's loose. His shirt. Button by button, it opens under the pull of his hands. Each inch of skin revealed feels earned. Dark. Smooth. Dangerous. His forearms flex, veins rising, tendons tight.

I can't look away. My mouth goes dry, heart thudding between my chest and my throat.

"Enjoying the view?" The words come out rough, frayed velvet.

"Very much," I whisper, heat clawing up my throat.

Hudson strips like the room's on fire.

His jacket's gone in a blink. Buttons don't stand a chance. He yanks his shirt over his head, hair a wild halo, grin deadlier than sin. His body is all motion: long lines, sun-warmed skin, a constellation of freckles.

He catches my gaze and laughs. "Some of us don't have Leo's patience." His belt's already unbuckled, the leather hissing as it slides free. "Not when there are better things to do."

Levi undresses like it's a religion. Deliberate. Reverent. Every button opened with purpose, every piece of clothing folded before it's set aside. He doesn't rush. Doesn't perform. He strips himself bare with the same quiet intensity he brings to everything.

When his shirt comes off, the moonlight spills over him, pale skin, lean muscle, every line caught between strength and grace. He looks sculpted from something softer than marble, but just as enduring.

That control. That intentional pace. It does something to me that all Hudson's wildness and Leo's power can't touch.

"You're staring," he says, words cracked.

"For good reason."

I meet Hudson's gaze, and my lips curve. "On your knees."

His eyes flare as he sinks to the floor with the kind of grace that makes submission look powerful. Spine straight. Thighs wide. Palms up, resting on thick, powerful legs.

I inhale, let it out.

"Leo," I say, my voice cracking on his name. "I want to watch Hudson take you in his mouth. And I want to guide him."

The silence stretches. One second too long. Leo's exhale stutters. His cock twitches. His fists curl tight.

For a moment, I think I've pushed too far.

"Christ, Lorna," Leo groans, raw. "Yes. Fuck, yes."

Hudson crawls to Leo and presses a kiss to the base of his cock, dragging his tongue up the length. He pauses at the head, tongue flicking out to taste the leaking precum, lips parting around the tip.

Leo swears, sharp and low. His stomach flexes.

Jesus, this is so fucking hot.

I drop to my knees behind Hudson, curling my hand around the nape of his neck. His skin burns under my hand, muscles strung taut.

"Good," I whisper, mouth close to his ear. "Take him slowly."

Hudson groans, the sound vibrating into my touch. His lips stretch wider as he opens for Leo, inch by thick, trembling inch. His throat works, adjusting. I feel every twitch of muscle under my hand.

Leo moans above us, raw and unfiltered. His hips twitch forward, his body unable to stop chasing Hudson's mouth. His abs ripple. His fists stay clenched at his sides, shaking with restraint.

"Look at me, Leo," I say.

He does. And the fire in his eyes nearly incinerates me.

"Let him take care of you."

"Fuck," he rasps. "You're going to undo me."

"And you're going to let me."

He looms over us, chest heaving, jaw locked tight as if he's one breath from losing control. I press closer, my thighs flush to Hudson's back, the heat of him searing through me. My fingers tighten in his hair as he starts to move, taking Leo deeper with every pass of his mouth.

His mouth slides along the length, lips slick, tongue tracing the underside. He pulls back to breathe, a strand of saliva catching at the corner of his mouth before he sinks down again, deeper this time, until his nose grazes the base and Leo's breath breaks apart above him.

"Show me," I murmur, barely breathing. "Show me how you make him lose control."

Hudson moans around Leo's cock, the sound thick and obscene. He pulls back to speak, eyes dark with mischief and hunger.

"With pleasure, beautiful."

He devours him.

He opens wide and takes Leo all the way in, throat flexing, spit slicking everything. His hands slide up Leo's thighs, grip firm and greedy, digging into muscle. Leo growls, the sound low and animal, his hips jerking forward before he catches himself.

"Jesus," Leo mutters, strangled. "I missed that mouth. Fuck."

I guide him with a slow pull through his hair, setting the pace. He follows easily, moving with lazy precision, sucking and swirling, moaning softly into every descent, each sound vibrating through Leo and straight into me.

The sounds fill the room, wet and filthy. Leo's gasps go jagged. The pulse between my legs throbs in time with every stroke of Hudson's tongue.

I uncurl Leo's fingers and wrap them around the back of Hudson's head. "Show him," I whisper, voice rough. "Show him what you like."

He reaches down, sliding into Hudson's hair beside my grip. Our fingers brush. And we're doing it together. Guiding him, feeding him, worshipping through him.

Leo's hips start to move. Tiny, shallow thrusts. Controlled, but barely. The need rolling off him is feral.

"He's always been good at this," Leo says, guttural. "Even in the beginning he knew how to break me. Every time."

I can hear it in his voice. This isn't casual. It's carved in. Lust, yes. But love, too. History, need, want, forgiveness. All of it tangled up and spilling from his lips.

Leo's cock glistens with spit as Hudson pulls back, dragging in a breath before sinking down again, deeper this time. His throat works around him, muscles flexing, a low sound caught in his chest. One hand curls around the base, the other cups Leo's balls, tugging just enough to make him groan. My pulse stumbles, heat coiling low, my thighs pressing together in desperate need for relief.

Leo groans, louder this time, the sound rough and broken. "Fuck," he gasps, his fingers tangling in Hudson's hair as he thrusts deeper into the wet heat of his mouth.

Hudson moans, low and muffled, the sound reverberating through Leo's body. His hips jerk, muscles tightening, head tipping back in surrender. For a heartbeat I think he's going to come then his eyes snap open and lock on mine.

"Enough," Leo growls, yanking back with a curse. "My turn."

The air changes. It crackles. Hums with electricity.

Leo catches my chin, tilting my face up until his gaze burns through me. His thumb presses into the hinge of my jaw, a sharp sting that steals my breath and roots me exactly where he wants me.

"I want to see my favorite mouths on me at the same time."

Desire slams low in my belly, so sharp I have to bite my lip to hold in the sound. I move next to Hudson, our shoulders brushing. He turns to me with that cocky half-smile, lips slick, eyes blown wide.

"Think you can keep up, beautiful?" he rasps, the tease crumbling under the wreck of his tone.

I smirk anyway. "Try not to embarrass yourself."

Leo steps closer, cock flushed, gleaming. We reach for him together. My fingers curl around the base while Hudson licks a long stripe up the side. Then there's no more talking, only motion.

Our mouths trade off, one taking him deep, the other kissing, licking, tasting every inch. His groans echo off the windows, sharp and unguarded. His hands tangle in our hair, pulling tight when we do something he likes. Which is often.

"Fuck, yes. Exactly," Leo grits out, hips rolling forward. "You two. Christ."

Hudson moans around him, the sound vibrating through me in an aftershock. I lean in and lick where his lips meet Leo's skin, and Leo shouts, thighs going taut, whole body trembling.

"You like watching us share you?" I whisper, dragging my mouth down his thigh, tasting sweat and skin and salt. "You like our mouths taking turns ruining you?"

"Fucking perfect," he gasps, rhythm lost. "Both of you."

And we are. Wreckage and reverence. Tongues and teeth. Desire and history.

Leo was made to be worshipped, and we were born to kneel for him.

His praise burns under my skin, ignites a boldness. I watch the way Hudson moves. Memorize the cadence, the pressure, the tilt of his head. I mimic it, take it deeper. A moan slips out when Leo's fingers tighten in my hair. The ache low in my belly turns sharp. Hungry.

Before we can wreck him completely, Leo hauls us up, one arm locked around each of us.

"Your turn to get undressed, Lorna," Leo rasps.

They're already moving before the words settle. No hesitation, no question. Levi steps behind me, fingers brushing the zipper.

"May I?" he asks, voice steady. Always the gentleman. Even now.

"Please," I breathe, lifting my arms, already giving in.

The zipper glides down, and my dress pools at my feet, silk sighing across my skin. The air is cool, a shock against the heat building inside me. I should feel bare. Instead, I feel powerful. Seen. Treasured.

"Magnificent," Levi murmurs, tracing my spine. "Something the masters dreamed about but never quite captured."

Hudson moves next, his touch rougher, grounding. "Nothing hanging in a museum ever looked like this," he mutters against my shoulder. "And if it did, I'd steal it."

Leo's fingers trail over the lace I chose for tonight—midnight blue, sheer, almost nonexistent. His hand settles over my heart.

"You wore this for us?" he asks, voice gone soft.

"For me," I say, meeting his eyes. "But I hoped you'd like it."

Hudson lets out a low whistle, half groan. "Like it? Baby, you're killing us."

"Then stop staring," I tell them, pulse hammering. "And do something about it."

That's all the permission they need.

Hudson unhooks my bra in one effortless motion, the clasp snapping open beneath his fingers. He slides the straps down my shoulders, knuckles brushing my skin, slow enough to make me shiver, then lets the lace fall away.

Levi drops to his knees in front of me, eyes fixed on mine as his fingers slip under the lace at my hips. He eases my panties down inch by inch, never breaking eye contact. When they reach my ankles, he lifts each foot free carefully.

I'm left standing before them, completely bare, skin flushed, every nerve tuned to them.

Leo climbs onto the bed, pulling me with him. His hands bracket my hips, guiding me until I'm straddling him. Heat rolls between us, his cock thick and hard against my thigh, a silent promise of what's coming.

"Hudson. Levi," his voice is tight. "Make her ready for us."

A soft click breaks the silence, followed by the wet sound of lube being squeezed into Hudson's palm. It gleams on his fingers as he steps closer, eyes locked on mine, focus dark and deliberate. He rubs his hands together, warming it, then moves behind me, knees bracketing mine, his body solid and close.

"You ready, gorgeous?"

"Yes," I whisper, bracing myself with a hand on Leo's chest. "Please."

He starts carefully. One slick finger, gentle, teasing, circling my back entrance with maddening patience. The pressure sends a jolt through me, every muscle going taut. But Levi's there to distract me. Lips on my jaw. Lower, dragging across the slope of my shoulder. One hand glides over my stomach. The other cradles my breast, thumb flicking my nipple until I arch helplessly into his touch.

"Relax," Hudson murmurs. "Breath for me, baby."

The first push makes me gasp. My hips jerk forward, straight over Leo's cock. His shaft slips over my slit, the crown dragging across my clit, blunt and unforgiving. Lightning arcs through me. I roll my hips again, greedier, chasing it.

I cry out, and Levi's answering groan vibrates over my breast, his tongue circling my nipple with punishing precision.

"Good girl," Leo growls, his grip tightening at my waist. "Rub yourself on me. That's it. Use my cock."

Hudson works deeper. One finger becomes two. The sting flares bright and sweet, offset by the unbearable pleasure of grinding on Leo's cock. Every pass over my clit blurs pain into ecstasy.

Levi doesn't stop. His teeth scrape, his tongue soothes. "Look at you," he murmurs. "Fucking yourself on his cock while your ass opens up for Hudson. You love it, don't you?"

I moan, incoherent. My thighs shake with every push back, every drag forward. Slick and fire and rhythm. It's all building, high and fast and reckless.

Hudson adds a third finger, and I cry out, full to the brim, hips bucking harder over Leo's cock. The head slips over my clit again and my vision shatters.

"There it is," Hudson murmurs, dark and smug. "Sweet little spot. You feel that?"

Leo's watching everything. Every tremble. Every grind.

"How does it feel?" he rasps.

"Full," I pant, words splintering on a moan. "And good. So good."

My rhythm goes to hell. Chaotic, desperate. Levi works my breast, Hudson stretches me wide, Leo's cock drags over my clit again and again. I'm soaked. Shaking. Gone. Every inch of me undone, fire and pressure and praise tearing through me.

When he can't wait a second longer, Leo catches me, guiding me over him with steady hands. His cock nudges my entrance, thick and already too much. Behind me, Hudson presses in close, his chest flush to my back. Levi moves to my front, his hand over my sternum, anchoring me.

"Slowly, sweetheart" Leo grits, his jaw clenched. "Take every inch."

And I do.

Inch by inch. One trembling exhale at a time.

The stretch drags fire through my core. Too much. Too deep. And still, I take it. My muscles seize around the intrusion, gripping on instinct, and, gradually, they release. I sink down more, thighs trembling, every nerve ending burning.

I bottom out with a gasp, seated fully on Leo. The pressure is everywhere. Around him, beneath me, curled inside my ribs. My pulse hammers at the base of my skull.

Leo groans like I've gutted him. "Christ, Lorna," he growls, both hands locked around my hips. "You feel so bloody good."

He's trembling beneath me, trying not to move, cock twitching inside me.

I'm still adjusting, still clawing my way back to air, when I feel Hudson behind me. Thick. Already slicked. His cock presses to that tight ring of muscle, the head nudging right at the edge of everything.

I freeze.

He pushes.

The stretch is heaven and hell. My whole body jerks. A gasped moan punches out of me. I grab Leo's chest, nails dragging down damp skin, spine arching as the head of Hudson's cock begins to breach me.

"Oh god," I whisper. It's not a prayer. It's surrender.

"Easy," Leo murmurs. His thumb strokes low, circling over my clit. "Relax and let him in."

Hudson leans forward, his chest flush to my back as he sinks deeper. The pressure climbs. The burn sharpens. My jaw drops, eyes unfocused, clutching Leo's shoulders.

Levi squeezes my thigh. "That's it," he murmurs, rough with awe. "You're doing so well."

And I am. I take every inch.

I'm full. Brutally full. My body stretched to the edge of what it can hold. I can't move. Can't think. I'm nothing but sensation, flickering and overloaded.

A shiver rolls through me. My walls flutter around them. I press both hands flat to Leo's chest, for balance, for control. For reality.

"You're perfect. So fucking perfect," Hudson groans behind me, low and guttural. "So goddamned tight," he grits out, voice breaking.

They stay still. Both of them holding back, barely breathing, giving me time to adjust. I can feel their restraint, the tension vibrating through every muscle. I can feel them. Deep inside me, wrapped around me, surrounding me.

And then I move.

Just a subtle roll of my hips, but it detonates pleasure through me, sharp and blinding, every nerve sparking to life at once.

Another roll. Another sharp spike. I find the rhythm without thinking, body rocking between them as if I've been waiting my whole life to move this way.

Leo groans, the sound deep and rough. He catches my hands, guiding them down his stomach, over the hard planes of muscle until our fingers reach where we're joined, where I'm open and slick around him. His voice drops. "That's it. Touch yourself."

I do.

Two shallow rolls. One deep grind. Over and over. Every motion lights me up from the inside. Hudson matches me perfectly. Leo presses up from beneath. Levi watches from inches away, his hand at my cheek, his thumb brushing under my jaw as if I'm the most precious thing he's ever seen.

My hips stutter. My thighs shake. The stretch burns and aches and builds a pressure inside me that feels terrifyingly close to breaking.

Leo feels it. I see it in his eyes. He pushes my hand aside and presses down on my clit.

"Come for us, Lorna," he says. His voice is hoarse, demanding.

That's all it takes.

Pleasure slams into me, wild and brutal. I scream, body convulsing, muscles clenching around them tight. My body locks, my head falls back, and I sob through it, every part of me trembling, pulsing, fracturing.

Hudson's thrusts go erratic. He growls low in my ear, cock jerking deep as he comes, hips locked to mine. Leo follows seconds later, arms cinched around my waist, hips grinding up as he spills inside me.

I collapse forward, the stretch still unbearable, still perfect. My skin is slick, my body humming, my heart a wild drumbeat in my chest.

The pleasure keeps echoing, shaking through me long after they've stopped moving.

And still. Levi. Steady. Watching. His cock flushed and thick, glistening at the tip. He doesn't move right away. Just stands there, fist tight around his cock, looking at me as if I'm the altar, and he's spent his whole life waiting to worship.

Barely a whisper. "Come here."

He gathers me up from the tangle of limbs and sweat like I weigh nothing. He lays me back, positioning me at the edge of the bed, my hips tilted, thighs pinned open against the mattress so he can take in every inch of me.

I try to close my knees on instinct. But he presses harder, keeping me open.

"Bear down," he murmurs.

I contract my muscles, pushing down until I can feel their cum dripping out of me in syrupy pulses, sliding over swollen skin, wetting the sheets beneath me.

Levi doesn't look away. He watches it drip.

"Jesus," he whispers. "Look at you. Fuck. Look at what they did to you."

His thumbs slide in low, dragging through the slick. He glides them up my pussy lips, trapping my clit between them.

I whimper, hips jerking.

"Sensitive, huh? Poor thing." His tone goes darker. "They destroyed you. And I'm gonna keep you this way. Leaking. Shaking. Wide open and wet."

"Hudson," he says, "clean her up."

I barely register the words before Hudson's mouth is on me. His tongue dragging a slick, unhurried line from my ass to my clit. I cry out, my whole body jerking. His lips close around the mess still leaking out of me, and he sucks, groaning like he's getting off on the taste.

It's obscene.

He pulls back with a gasp, mouth wet, face flushed and wrecked. He looks ready to crawl right back between my thighs if given half a chance.

But Levi's already there.

He stands between my legs, one fist wrapping around his cock as he spreads my thighs with the other hand. He drags the slick head through my folds. Filthy. Painting himself in the mess they left behind.

He doesn't thrust. Doesn't rush. Just watches me squirm while he strokes himself through my wetness, taking his time.

"Jesus, you're soaked," he groans. "Still dripping from them, and your pussy's begging for more."

Then he drives in. One deep, punishing thrust that knocks the air from my lungs. My back arches, muscles locking tight around him. He holds there, buried to the hilt, hips rigid, making me feel every inch, every ounce of him.

When he pulls out, he drags the slick head through my folds. Each pass hits my clit and my hips jerk, chasing the pressure he refuses to give.

I whimper, desperate.

He doesn't stop. Just keeps stroking himself against me, filthy and controlled, as if watching me unravel is its own reward.

"Please," I beg, voice wrecked. "Levi..."

He answers with another thrust, sharp and punishing. Then another. Each stroke deeper, rougher, until I'm clutching at the sheets, caught between pleasure and surrender. His hands clamp around my waist, holding me there, dragging me up to meet him again and again.

He's everywhere. Breathe hot on my skin, sweat dripping from his temple, muscles straining. "You were made for this," he grits out. "To be filled, again and again, and again."

I try to speak, to warn him how close I am, but all that comes out is a broken sound.

My body locks around him, pulsing, desperate to keep him, but he pulls out mid-release, still throbbing with what he's holding back. His hand closes tight around the base of his cock, muscles straining.

"Fuck," he rasps, chest heaving. "Open up. Let me see."

I know exactly what he wants. I bear down, trembling, giving him the view he asked for.

A rough, broken sound tears out of him. "Jesus Christ. That's it. Fuck."

Another stroke and his cum splashes across my skin, catching on my clit, dripping down between my folds. It's messy and wet and filthy. And he watches all of it, eyes dark, jaw clenched.

He leans over me, one arm planted by my head, the other sliding down between my trembling thighs. His face is so close I can taste his exhalation.

"Look at me," he demands as he slides through the mess between my thighs. He gathers it on his finger. Pushes it back in.

"You're not done," he says, destroyed. "Not till you come with my cum inside you."

I moan. My hips grind down, chasing more. He pushes deeper.

"Jesus, you're breathtaking," he murmurs.

I'm trembling. My body clamps down hard, greedy for him. Each thrust knocks the air out of me.

"Come for me, Petal. One more time," he whispers near my cheek.

Pleasure explodes through me. My spine arches violently, pussy squeezing as I come apart. I scream his name, the sound raw and shattered, while his cum spills around his touch and he keeps pumping, wringing every last pulse from me.

Even after I'm done he doesn't move. Stays there, still buried, chest heavy above mine. I'm still clenching. Still twitching.

Then he's kissing me.

His tongue slides past my lips and I moan into it, helpless. The kiss is deep and messy and unrestrained, like he's trying to taste the remnants of the sounds I made when I came. When he finally pulls back, he rests his forehead against mine, breath unsteady, hands trembling where they cradle my face.

Leo disappears into the bathroom and returns with a warm cloth. He kneels between my legs, and I flinch when the heat touches me, nerves still raw, but his hands stay steady, patient. He wipes me clean with slow, careful strokes, the warmth seeping into me until my body starts to come back online.

Hudson slides in behind me, fitting himself to my back. One arm drapes around my waist, his leg sliding between my thighs, holding me together when everything in me threatens to unravel.

Levi reaches through the tangle of sheets and finds my hand. I exhale, trembling, and let go. We settle into the mess of it, damp skin, twisted blankets, pillows half on the floor. Three heartbeats falling into rhythm with mine.

London glows beyond the window, a blur of gold and motion, but in here everything is quiet. Three heartbeats move in sync with mine, and the peace that settles over us feels deep, certain, as constant as the tide.

# 28

LEO'S POV

The ring box sits heavy in my pocket, pressing into my hip through worn denim. I haven't been able to stop touching it since I picked it up from the jeweler this morning.

Two weeks since Vienna, since watching Lorna stand before Europe's brightest minds and claim her place with a confidence that nearly dropped me to my knees. Two weeks of waking in that custom California king delivered while we were gone, her head resting on my chest, my hand tangled in her hair, and the quiet certainty that I'll never get used to it.

Time to stop pretending this is temporary. Time to man up and claim what's ours.

"You're gonna wear a hole in that box," Hudson says from the doorway. He tries for casual, but the strain cuts through every word. As he passes, his hand skims my shoulder, a reminder that he's here. That we're in this together.

Behind him, Levi grips a folder of documents, and he's strung out worse than I am. The tension between us hums sharp and restless, ready to snap.

The morning air should cool me. Instead, heat gathers at my

temples, my palms slick. My chest kicks so violently I swear I can feel it in my toes. Each inhale comes short and sharp.

"We need to talk to the twins first," I say, voice rough. "Before we even think about proposing. They need to be on board."

Because that's the real test. Not marrying the woman who's become the center of our universe, but stepping into the role of fathers. Those kids have already carried more than they should. They don't need more adults promising forever and disappearing when it gets hard.

"Jack should be dropping them off any second," Levi says, checking his phone for the hundredth time.

"What if she says no?" I ask, the words sticking in my throat.

The question hangs in the air.

"She won't," Hudson says, but I hear the thread of doubt underneath. He's wondering the same thing.

"You don't know that." I grip the edge of the counter hard enough my knuckles go white. "Marriage. Legal adoption. Three husbands. It's a lot to ask. Maybe too much."

"She chose us," Levi says quietly. "She keeps choosing us. Every day."

"Choosing to be together is different from choosing forever." Fear climbs my throat. "What if we're asking for more than she wants to give? What if she's happy with how things are and we're about to fuck it all up?"

Hudson crosses to me, grips my shoulder. "Then we deal with it. But I don't think that's what happens. I think she's been waiting for us to ask."

"You sound awfully confident for someone whose hands have been sweating since breakfast."

"Terrified," he admits. "But that doesn't mean I'm wrong."

Levi joins us, completing the circle. "We ask the kids first. If they say yes, we'll be sure at least half the family wants this. And Lorna..." He pauses, choosing his words carefully. "Lorna doesn't do anything halfway. When she's in, she's all in."

"Okay," I say. "Let's fucking do this." I straighten my shoulders, tuck the ring box deeper and start preparing.

Daniel and Lorelai burst through the door looking as though they lost a fight with a glitter bomb. It's in their hair, their clothes, even stuck to their eyelashes. They're jittery with leftover excitement, all wide eyes and too-big grins. But underneath it, I see the flicker. They sense that something's different.

"Mr. Leo!" Lorelai launches herself at my legs with her usual force. All flying hair and dirty knees and that sweet kid smell of bubble gum and sunshine. Her small arms wrap around my thighs tight enough to cut off circulation. "You look funny. Are you sick? I can make you some fairy medicine!"

"I'm not sick, fairy girl." I scoop her up, settling her on my hip. "Just thinking about important things."

"What kind of important things?" Daniel asks, blinking in that owlish way he has when he's trying to figure something out. "Rocks? Or feelings?"

Leave it to Daniel to see straight through the chaos to the heart of it.

"The feelings kind," I admit, sitting down. "Actually, we wanted to talk to you both. About all of us."

Hudson meets my gaze from across the room. His hands won't stay still, flexing and clenching. Levi joins me on the couch.

"Are you going away?" Lorelai's voice goes small, scared. Her arms locking around my neck hard enough to choke. "Because our daddy went away and didn't come back, and I don't want you to go away too."

Christ.

"No, Lorelai. We're never going away." I shift her weight, make sure she can see my face. "Actually, we want to talk about staying. Forever."

"Forever?" Daniel's eyes go wide, and I can see him working through what that means. "You want to live here, with us, for real?"

"More than that." Hudson settles on the couch, and Daniel immediately gravitates toward him. "We want to marry your mum.

And if you're okay with it, if you want us, we want to adopt you properly. Become your real dads."

The silence that follows feels eternal. My ribs tighten; my pulse is loud enough they must hear it. What if they say no? What if we've misread everything?

"YES!" Lorelai shrieks, loud enough to make my ears ring. "Yes yes yes yes! Can we help plan the wedding? Can I wear a princess dress? Can we have cake? No—three cakes! Because there's three of you!"

Relief floods through me, turning my muscles to liquid. But beneath it, I'm still holding my breath, waiting for Daniel.

Careful, deliberate Daniel, who guards his trust like something breakable, too valuable to hand out lightly.

"You really want to be our daddies?" he asks, voice so small I almost miss it. "Real daddies? The kind who come to school and help with homework and don't go away?"

My throat tightens. That's it. Every quiet hope he's ever hidden, right there in one breath.

Levi slides off the couch onto his knees, meeting Daniel's gaze. "Yes, Daniel. All of it. We want to be here for science projects. Bedtime stories. Every concert, every scraped knee, every weird little rock you bring home. If you'll have us."

Daniel studies us like he's fitting together a complicated equation only he can see. The silence stretches, then his face breaks open in a grin so bright it fills the room.

"I'd like that very much," he says, formal as ever, before launching himself into Levi's arms with more emotion than I've ever seen from him.

"We've never had proper daddies before," he mumbles into Levi's shoulder. "Only Mummy doing everything and pretending it doesn't make her tired."

Bloody hell. My chest cracks wide open.

Not anymore. Never again.

From this moment on, these kids have four parents who would burn the world down to keep them safe.

"Will you both help us propose?" Hudson asks, looking between the kids. "We want to make it a family thing instead of a grown-ups only thing."

"Yes!" Lorelai shrieks, bouncing in my arms. "I know! I'll draw a picture! A picture of our new family! All six of us together with the house and the flowers and maybe a dragon because dragons are cool!"

"And I'll make a list," Daniel adds, because of course he will. "All the reasons why Mum should say yes. Good reasons."

"That sounds perfect," I say, not even trying to hide the smile pulling at my lips.

The next two hours are barely controlled chaos. The kind that smells of wax shavings and sounds like dozens of crayons hitting the floor.

Daniel writes with surgical precision, tongue sticking out, brow furrowed. Every letter is a labor of love, as though the list might get rejected if his penmanship isn't perfect. Across the table, Lorelai attacks her paper with every crayon she owns clenched in her fist, scribbling with the ferocity of someone trying to invent a new color.

I hover. Help when needed. But mostly, I watch.

"See, this is you, Mr. Leo," Lorelai explains, pointing to the biggest brown figure in her drawing. "You're the biggest because you keep everyone safe. And this is Mr. Hudson with his tools, and Mr. Levi with his books, and Mummy in her garden with all the flowers, and me and Daniel right in the middle where we belong."

The drawing's all stick figures and lopsided buildings, flowers that look more like an explosion than a bloom, and what might be a sun or possibly a very happy potato in the corner. It's absolutely perfect.

"It's beautiful, fairy girl," I manage around the lump in my throat.

Daniel pulls out his list, edges creased from being folded and refolded. His handwriting is painstakingly neat, each letter shaped with precision and concentration.

"Reasons Mum should say yes," he reads seriously. "One: We can all live together. Two: You help with things and Mummy doesn't have to do everything. Three: You can watch us when Mummy needs to work."

Hudson watches him with sparkling eyes, fighting back a smile.

"And four." His voice goes quieter. "We love you. And Mummy smiles more when you're here, and Lorelai doesn't have bad dreams anymore, and I like having grown-ups who think rocks are cool."

Jesus. It's like he carved open my chest and stuffed his little list inside.

"We love you too," I manage, throat tight. "More than you know."

"So when are we proposing?" Lorelai asks, practically vibrating. "Tonight? Tomorrow? Right this second? Can we have a party after? Can we invite everyone? Can I be the flower girl? Can Summer be a flower girl too?"

"Tonight," I decide, the word feeling as though I'm stepping off a cliff. "After dinner. That gives us time to make it special."


The afternoon drags. Hudson's buzzing out of his skin, and Lorelai's right there with him. She's "helping" in the workshop, which mostly means offering him the wrong tools and asking if he's nervous about a hundred times. He's cleaned the space twice already and comes back the third time with sawdust in his hair, eyes bright with nerves he can't burn off.

I try to keep busy too. Daniel's planted at my workbench, carefully organizing my leather tools by size while I pretend to check stock I know by heart. He lines up the awls and hammers in perfect order, his tongue sticking out in concentration.

"Mr. Leo," Daniel says without looking up, "you're shaking."

"Noticed that, did you?"

"You're nervous about asking Mum to marry you."

"That obvious?"

He finally looks up at me, all earnest focus. "It's okay to be nervous about important things," he says, as if it's the most obvious truth in the world. "That's how you know they matter."

This kid.

Outside the workshop, Levi's voice drifts in, steady, patient, rehearsing. He's reading his proposal speech to Lorelai, who's clearly traded Hudson's sawdust and noise for Levi's drama and charm. She's his most devoted audience, offering notes, probably convincing him to rewrite the ending for the tenth time.

"That part's good!" Lorelai declares. "But you should say she's beautiful as a fairy queen, not only beautiful."

We head back to the house a little before Lorna's due home. The twins are practically vibrating with excitement. Lorelai keeps rehearsing her "surprised face" in the hallway mirror, gasping dramatically every few seconds. Daniel's posted himself by the window, issuing quiet status reports like a tiny secret agent.

"She's here!" Daniel shouts.

My chest seizes and my knees nearly collapse beneath me.

"False alarm," he says a beat later, completely unfazed. "Just the newspaper guy."

Ten minutes later: "Delivery truck, not Mummy."

Twenty after that: "Mr. Henderson's orange cat. The one that poops in Mum's garden."

Hudson lets out a laugh that shakes some of the tightness off my shoulders. "Glad to know we've got surveillance covered."

"It's a good thing it's not a school day," Daniel agrees, not moving from his post.

Finally, when the sun turns everything outside to gold, Daniel's voice cracks with excitement. "She's here! She's here! Mummy's home!"

My heartbeat stumbles, tripping over itself. This is it.

Lorna steps inside wearing faded jeans and that blue sweater that makes her eyes look stormy. Her hair's coming loose, makeup slightly smudged as though she rubbed her eyes during the drive home.

Her gaze sweeps over us.

"What's going on?" she asks, setting her bag down carefully. "You all look as though you're plotting. Should I be worried?"

"We are!" Lorelai blurts, unable to hold it in. Her whole body bounces. "We're planning the best thing ever! Now, Daniel! Give her the picture!"

Daniel steps forward, his face so serious it makes my chest tight. "Mummy, we've been thinking about our family. About how it's grown and changed and gotten better."

"Better?" Lorna's voice goes quiet. She takes Lorelai's masterpiece from Daniel's careful grip, and her eyes fill with tears. "This is..." she starts, stops, voice too thick to continue. Her hand comes up to cover her mouth.

"Us," Lorelai says simply. "Our family. The way it's supposed to be."

"We want Leo, Hudson, and Levi to stay here forever," Daniel says, his voice wobbling as he tries to hold it together.

"We want to marry you," I say, stepping forward and pulling out the ring box. I'm shaking but my voice doesn't waver. "You've let us into your life. Trusted us with your children. You're the strongest woman I've ever known, Lorna. And somehow you make us all better by letting us love you."

Hudson moves to my side. "I'm not sure how the legal part works, but I know *this* works. *We* work. We want to be their dads and your husbands and wake up in that too-big bed every morning knowing we're exactly where we belong."

Levi steps in, completing the circle around her. His voice is quiet but steady, every word deliberate. "I've been trying to write this for days. Lorelai kept telling me I needed to say you're beautiful as a fairy queen, and she's right, you are. But you're also the bravest person I've ever met. You let three broken men into your life when you had every reason to keep us out. You trusted us with Daniel and Lorelai when trust didn't come easy." He pauses, composing himself. "We want forever, Lorna. Let us be the fathers your children deserve and the husbands you deserve. Let us spend the rest of our lives proving we're worthy of what you've given us."

Lorna sucks in a harsh breath. She looks between us. Three men standing steady, two children practically vibrating with hope. "All of you want this? You've really thought it through?"

"More than anything in this world." My voice cracks on the words. I drop to one knee and fumble the ring box open, my hands shaking so hard I almost lose it.

Hudson and Levi sink down beside me without a word. Inside the box, the platinum bands catch the light, each one set with stones that trace the map of our lives. Diamonds for April, when the twins were born. Emerald for me. Sapphire for Levi. Citrine for Hudson.

"Marry us, Lorna," I say, the words thick in my throat. "Let us be their dads. Let us be your husbands."

The silence stretches tight. My heart forgets how to beat. Even the kids hold still, locked in place.

Lorelai can't take it anymore. She barrels into her mother's legs, clinging hard, and Daniel joins her a moment later. Lorna bends over them, tears running down her face as she pulls them close.

"Yes," she whispers, the word so quiet I almost miss it. "Yes! Always yes. How could the answer be anything else?"

The kids erupt. Lorelai shrieks with joy, hopping up and down while still glued to her mother's side. Daniel's smile stretches so wide it looks ready to split his face.

My fingers tremble as I slide the first ring onto Lorna's finger. Hudson follows, his touch brushing mine as we work together, clumsy with emotion. Then Levi adds the final band. Three rings catch the light between us, a constellation of birthstones glinting in their settings, a map of everything we've built, and everyone we've become.

"Group hug!" Lorelai declares.

We crash together in the middle of the living room, all six of us tangled in one breathless knot. Daniel's small fists clutch my shirt. Lorelai's laugh rings bright against my ear. Lorna trembles in my arms, her tears soaking through my shirt. Hudson leans in, his forehead pressed to my shoulder. Levi's hand settles at the back of my neck, holding me there, anchoring me in the center of everything we just became—our family, our future, our forever.

It takes three bedtime stories, two glasses of water, seventeen wedding promises, and Lorelai making us swear on the fairy queen that she can wear a purple dress before the twins finally crash. We tiptoe out of their room like we're disarming a bomb, and the second the door clicks shut, everything I've been holding in all day threatens to spill over.

Engaged. We're engaged. The word feels too big for my chest, too good to be real.

We gather in the living room, still a little dazed. Hudson pulls out a bottle of champagne, and I reach for the fifteen-year Macallan I've been saving since the day we moved here. My hands tremble as I pour the whisky, and Hudson's no steadier with the champagne.

Lorna sits on the couch, quiet, eyes shining as she turns the rings on her finger, watching the light catch on them like she still doesn't quite trust they're real.

The cork pops and all four of us jump before laughter takes over, wild and breathless.

"Christ," Hudson exhales, offering Lorna the first glass. "We did it. We actually did it."

"I'm so happy you said yes," Levi says, settling beside her, awe in his voice, like he still can't quite believe it's real.

"Of course I said yes," Lorna says, laughing through fresh tears. "How could I say anything else?"

We stand there for a moment, letting it all sink in. Hudson lifts his glass, and his eyes sweep over all of us. Bright. Wet. Full of everything we don't have words for.

"To forever," he says.

"To family," Levi adds, his voice breaking on the word.

I raise my glass, and the whisky catches the lamplight, turning gold. "To us," I manage around the lump in my throat. "To the life we're building. To the kids upstairs who trust us to get this right. To Lorna, who sees who we are and loves us anyway."

Lorna lifts her glass, eyes bright. "To the three men who found a chaotic dahlia farmer with two kids and too much baggage, and still said, *yes, that's exactly what we want.*"

We drink. The whisky burns, the champagne fizzes, but none of it comes close to the warmth that floods my chest when Lorna steps into our circle and pulls us in, holding us like she never plans to let go.

"I love that you included the kids' birthstones," she says, admiring the rings.

"They're the center of everything," Hudson answers simply. "Without them, we're four adults fumbling around. With them, we're a family."

Levi pulls out his phone, connects it to the speaker, and scrolls for a moment until the room fills with the low crackle of static. Then it clears, and Etta James spills through the air, smooth and timeless. None of us say a word. We just move toward each other, finding the center of the room, where the hardwood turns into an impromptu dance floor and the night begins to slow.

Lorna fits perfectly in our arms, her laughter bright as we pass her between us. First, she's against my chest, warm and soft, her breath catching against my neck. Then Hudson takes her, drawing her close before dipping her low just to make her laugh again. Levi steps in next, slower, gentler, his movements unhurried, guiding her with the quiet confidence that always steadies the rest of us.

Then *At Last* begins to play.


By the time we make our way upstairs, we're drunk on more than whisky. We're intoxicated by the weight of what we did. The permanence of it. The stairs creak and groan beneath our weight, four adults trying to be quiet and failing, stifling laughter like teenagers sneaking in after curfew.

The bed swallows us whole. Lorna settles into the center and we arrange ourselves around her. My arm across her waist. Hudson's fingers in her hair, his other finding mine in the dark, lacing tight. Levi tucked close on her other side, all of us connected.

Sleep pulls at her almost immediately.

"I love you," she whispers, words thick and drowsy. "All of you. More than I knew was possible."

"Love you too," I murmur near her neck, pulling her in. "Always."

"Forever," Hudson says, his thumb stroking over my knuckles.

"And ever," Levi echoes through a yawn.

I should sleep. We all should. But I can't let go just yet. Every breath feels amplified, every heartbeat loud in the quiet. I can feel her shifting beside me, the warmth of her hand resting over my heart, the cool press of her rings against my skin. Three bands. Three promises.

We're done running. Done being afraid. Done pretending this is anything less than forever.

Soon we'll start planning a wedding that somehow includes two overexcited kids and enough flowers to fill a botanical garden. We'll talk to lawyers about adoption papers, decide whose name goes where, make official what's already been true in our hearts for months. At some point, we'll have to face the world, explain this life to people who might never understand, protect our kids from questions they shouldn't have to answer, navigate laws that were never written for us.

But not tonight.

Tonight, in the quiet hum of the house, with her rings pressed against my skin and the steady rhythm of the people I love breathing around me, I let it all settle in. The peace we've earned. The certainty we've built. The home we chose together. Whatever waits ahead, we'll face it together.

# 29

This spade might as well weigh a thousand pounds. Every thrust into the soil jolts up my arms, rattles my teeth, makes my shoulders burn as if I've been hauling bricks instead of tubers. Dirt clings to everything—boots, jeans, sweat-slick skin. It's packed beneath my fingernails in a way I'll be scrubbing at for days, maybe weeks. But the dahlias won't dig themselves, and winter's coming whether I'm ready or not.

The October air bites at my cheeks, sharp and cold, but sweat still slides down my spine, soaking through my shirt until it sticks. Every inhale scrapes, metallic and raw, tasting of blood and pennies and the rot-sweet stink of dying leaves. Three rows over, Leo grunts as his spade slams into something solid, the dull thunk cracking through the quiet.

My back is two seconds from quitting. I straighten, and everything pops and cracks under pressure. The relief is instant and indecent. I actually groan.

I swipe at my cheek with the back of my hand, grinding in more mud, but I'm too far gone to care. My bun surrendered hours ago, hair hanging in damp ropes that stick to my neck and smell of earth and sweat.

"Fucking hell." Hudson's voice carries across the rows, wrecked and ragged. "Remind me again why we're destroying our backs for deformed potatoes?"

I open my mouth to answer, but thunder rolls in first, low and distant at the edge of the hills. It builds fast, closing in until it rattles through my chest. A raindrop hits my forehead, sharp and cold on flushed skin.

Then the sky cracks open.

Rain slams down, pounding so hard it hammers every thought clean out of my head. My shirt soaks through in seconds, plastered cold and heavy. I dive for the nearest tuber clumps, boots skidding through mud that grips at my ankles. Water streams down my neck, cold enough to steal my lungs.

"Get them to the barn!" My voice tears through the storm, but the guys are already moving, Hudson hauling crates, Leo and Levi scrambling to save what we've unearthed.

Chaos swallows everything. Rain pours from my hair, blinding me as it sheets over the armful of tubers pressed to my chest. Every step's a battle—boots squelching, socks soaked, mud slicking out from under me. By the time we stumble into the barn, I'm shaking so hard my bones rattle. Cold, yes, but also that wild exhilaration that comes from outrunning disaster by seconds. Next year's blooms are safe. My teeth chatter, but I'm grinning wildly.

"Look at us." My voice trembles as I shove wet hair out of my face. "We look like we've been mud wrestling."

Hudson smirks, flicking a glob of mud that hits my cheek with a wet splat. "Speak for yourself. I look ruggedly handsome."

He's mud-soaked, grinning, and my heart feels as if it's trying to crawl out of my chest. Surrounded by earth and sweat and rain, by three men who smell of safety and home, gratitude rushes through me so fierce it almost hurts. I've stumbled into everything I never even dreamed of.

We stagger inside in a tangle of limbs and laughter, tracking mud across the back porch. The kitchen door bangs shut behind us, sealing out the storm's roar and leaving us in sudden, dripping quiet. Someone's boot squeaks on the tile. Water pools beneath us, spreading in murky circles as we stand there catching our breath, still grinning foolishly.

We're peeling off our sodden jackets when the doorbell rings.

We all freeze.

"Did anyone—" I start.

"Not me," Hudson says.

The bell rings again, more insistent.

I look down at myself. Soaked through. Covered in mud. Hair plastered to my skull. "I can't answer the door like this."

"We all look as though we've been grave robbing," Levi points out.

The bell rings a third time, followed by knocking.

"Coming!" I call, grabbing a tea towel to at least wipe my face. I crack the door open, trying to hide my mud-covered body behind it.

Mrs. Henderson, the other half of Henderson's Hardware, stands on my porch holding an enormous white bakery box, grinning with triumph.

"Were you out digging up the dahlias in this weather? You're going to catch a cold!"

"Mrs. Henderson, what—"

"The whole village is talking!" she announces, bustling past me and heading straight for the kitchen. "It's been two weeks since the rings, and not a word from any of you."

Oh God. They know. Everyone knows.

The guys appear in the kitchen doorway, still dripping, looking guilty.

Mrs. Henderson sets the box on the table. "Had to strong-arm the bakery into making samples. Can't have you going to Inverness for wedding cake when we've got perfectly good bakers here!"

She opens the box, revealing six enormous slices of cake. Victoria sponge with jam and cream. Lemon drizzle glistening with icing. Chocolate fudge so dark it's almost black. Carrot cake thick with cream cheese frosting. Coffee and walnut with buttercream swirls. And a generous wedge of sticky toffee pudding cake, dark and luscious.

"The baker says she'll do any flavor you want, any design. Margaret from the flower shop wants to do your arrangements—says she owes you for helping with her garden last spring. Tom the butcher's already planning a menu, and don't even get me started on what the distillery wants to contribute."

I sink into a chair, overwhelmed. "Everyone wants to help?"

"Help?" Mrs. Henderson snorts. "Dear girl, we've been watching you four dance around each other for months. The way you look at each other, the way those men dote on your children, the way you've built this beautiful and strange and absolutely perfect life. We take care of our own here, don't you worry about that."

Her eyes soften. "Even the unconventional ones. Especially the unconventional ones. Love is love, and anyone with eyes can see you four have more of it than most people find in a lifetime."

My throat closes up entirely.

"Right," she says briskly, pretending not to notice I'm about to cry, "you'll taste these when you've cleaned up. The bakery needs to know which flavors you want at least three months before the ceremony. And for heaven's sake, put together a proper list. The whole village wants to help, but we need to know what you actually need."

She heads for the door, pauses. "Oh, and Lorna? About bloody time."

The door closes behind her, leaving us all staring at each other, dumbfounded.

"The whole village knows," I say faintly.

"The whole village is happy for us," Leo corrects, moving to stand behind my chair. He squeezes my shoulders.

"We can talk later. Right this moment, I need that chocolate cake, which means scrubbing off this mud first," Hudson says.

Before I can react, his arm hooks behind my knees and suddenly I'm over his shoulder, weightless. I shriek, fists thumping his slick, muddy back, but it only makes him smack my ass.

"Since the kids are with Isla this weekend, you can be as loud as you want," he growls, kicking the bathroom door shut behind us. "And I want you to be really fucking loud, Lorna."

Fire sparks low and steady, cutting through the chill clinging to my rain-soaked skin. My pulse trips, need curling in my stomach at the rough promise in his voice.

He sets me down gently. But I barely register the floor beneath me before he's tugging at my shirt. He works it off inch by agonizing inch, the fabric dragging across my stomach, my breasts until cold air bites and goosebumps rise in waves.

My leggings are worse, soaked through, clinging to me like a second skin, but he doesn't hesitate. He crouches low, his hold firm on my hips, grounding me as he works the fabric down slowly, his knuckles grazing tender skin, tracing over curves made sharper by the cold.

When he reaches my knees, he pauses.

And leans in.

His mouth brushes the inside of my thigh, barely a whisper at first. His nose nuzzles higher, right at the apex, where I'm throbbing. He doesn't kiss. Doesn't lick. Holds there, face buried as if he needs the scent of me to survive. My fingers sink into his hair. My knees nearly go.

He exhales, rough and uneven, tugging the last of the soaked fabric down my legs. When the contact finally breaks, the air feels too cold, my skin still humming with the heat he left behind.

His clothes are next. The fabric clings to muscle, making him look larger, sharper at the edges.

I reach for his shirt, my fingers cold and clumsy against the buttons. He stays perfectly still, watching me with his shoulders tight, jaw locked, and breath uneven. The denim clings, resisting, but I manage the button and the zipper, working it down over his hips. His cock is already hard beneath the soaked fabric of his briefs. He steps out of the jeans land kicks them aside, eyes fixed on mine, daring me to look away.

I hook my fingers into the waistband and pull his boxers down. The wet fabric clings for a moment before giving way, and his cock springs free, flushed and heavy. For a heartbeat, I can only stare, heat curling low and sharp in my belly.

He catches me before I can move, pulling me upright as he turns on the water. Steam fills the air, curling between us, and then we're under the spray. Scalding water crashes over my shoulders, washing away mud in dark, spiraling streams.

A moan breaks from me, raw and unguarded, pulled out by the shock of heat pounding into sore, spent muscles.

Hudson stiffens beside me. "Christ, Lorna," he says, voice rough. "You can't make sounds like that."

But I can't help it. Another sound escapes, softer this time, and he snaps.

He spins me around and cages me to the tile, framing my face as his mouth takes mine. The kiss is fierce and hungry, all teeth and tongue and desperation. I grab at his shoulders, nails biting into his skin as he devours me.

"God, you feel good," he mutters, his hand sliding between my legs.

The first brush of his fingers jolts me, my shoulders hitting the wall. I'm still shivering from the storm, but his touch burns through me, heat spreading fast enough that my knees threaten to give out. When he pushes two fingers inside, I cry out, my forehead dropping against his chest as he works me open, each stroke pulling gasps from somewhere deep in my lungs.

His fingers curl, finding the perfect angle. My thighs clamp around his wrist, hips rocking into his hand, chasing every bit of friction he'll give. He bites my shoulder, voice breaking against my skin, like watching me fall apart might break him too.

"Hudson," I rasp, gripping his wrist, not sure if I'm trying to pull him closer or hold myself together. "Please, I—"

"Shh." His mouth finds mine again, swallowing the plea. His free hand threads through my fingers and pins them above my head.

My body locks, shatters in bright, vicious shards that won't stop coming. I gasp, but the sound dies in his mouth, swallowed by the kiss, by the crush of water and the solid weight of him holding me upright while I fall apart. He doesn't let go. Wraps around me, grounding, his mouth at my temple murmuring words I can't hear.

When I can finally move again, I reach for him, clumsy and hungry.

"Later," he says, catching my wrists. He brings each hand to his mouth, kissing the center. "This was only for you. To warm you up."

We take turns with the soap, scrubbing mud from each other's skin, fingers slipping over muscle and rain-chilled flesh. Dirt swirls at our feet, the remnants of a day spent elbow-deep in dahlia beds. He's methodical about it, starting with my arms, working down, hands steady. I mirror him, dragging suds across his chest, over the ridges of muscle still tight from digging.

His hair drips as he tips his head forward, and I rake my fingers through it, washing away grit and soil. He does the same for me, gentle at the nape of my neck, his touch unhurried.

"Come on," he says at last, his voice still rough-edged from holding himself back. "The others are probably wondering if we drowned in here."

He helps me out of the shower, steadying my elbow when I sway. The towel he wraps around me carries his scent—woodsmoke and clean soap, something earthy that makes my chest loosen. He takes another and works it through my hair, blotting instead of rubbing, fingers gentle against my scalp. The care in it steadies me more than anything else could.

By the time we emerge in clean clothes, skin still warm and scrubbed pink, Leo and Levi are hovering near the kitchen island, eyeing the cake slices like they're planning a heist.

"Let's eat it in bed," Hudson says, grabbing plates. "Cake tastes better under a duvet. Scientific fact."

So that's how four grown adults end up in bed eating cake. Still damp from showers, tangled in blankets, passing around forks like it's the most natural thing in the world. Chocolate and buttercream, someone's thumb swiping icing from my lower lip, Leo's quiet laugh when Hudson tries to steal the last bite. It's messy and sweet and the kind of easy that makes my chest ache.

Eventually, the plates sit empty on the nightstand. Someone sighs. No one moves to leave.

Levi trails a hand down my arm. "You up for a surprise?"

I look between them. "What kind of surprise?"

"The kind you'll enjoy," Leo says, voice dropping low.

"Yes." It comes out quick, almost breathless. "Whatever it is, yes."

Levi stands and takes my hand, drawing me toward the headboard. He slides aside a wooden cap I've never paid attention to, revealing a metal ring built into the bedpost. I touch the polished steel, pulse already climbing.

"You want to tie me up."

"To start." Hudson's grin goes sharp.

Heat rushes through me, settling low. They move around me. Leo behind, Levi to my left, Hudson closing in from the right. Leo catches my wrists, bringing them together behind my back.

"Tell me what you want," he says, voice rough and commanding. "We need to hear it."

"I want—" The words stick in my throat, my face burning. "I want you to tie me up. Use me however you want."

Hudson's breath hitches. "Christ, Lorna."

Leo moves first, slipping his hand under my sweater. His rough palm drags up my stomach, taking the fabric with it, slow and unhurried. Cool air hits my skin as my breasts are exposed, nipples tightening, a shiver blooming across my chest.

Hudson's breath scorches my ear. "I bet you're already wet for us."

Levi kneels, gripping the waistband of my leggings. He drags them down, over my hips, past the slickness between my thighs, until I'm trembling with each inch of exposure. "Christ, Lorna. You're soaked."

I'm shivering, the ache between my legs nearly unbearable. "Please," I whisper.

They guide me back until the mattress catches behind my knees. Leo pushes me down, stretching me across the sheets. Hudson climbs up beside me, the bed dipping.

Leather cuffs slide around my wrists. Levi lifts my arm, fastening it to the ring, while Leo secures the other. I test them and they hold fast, keeping me exactly where they want me.

"Look at you," Leo murmurs, settling between my thighs. His gaze locks on mine, dark and hungry. "Laid out for us. Dripping. So ready to fall apart."

The first stroke of his tongue makes me scream. My back arcs off the bed, wrists yanking at the restraints as fire shoots through every nerve.

"God, the sounds you make." Hudson's voice rumbles against my throat. "I could listen to you scream for us all night."

Levi's hands roam up my ribs, thumbs brushing the undersides of my breasts. My nipples ache as sensation builds and stacks.

"Tell me how it feels," Leo says, his words muffled. His tongue circles, drags, until I'm whimpering.

"Your tongue—" The words shatter on a cry, my body convulsing. "Right there, don't stop, please—"

He lifts his head, breath hot. "Don't stop what? Use your words."

My throat closes, body straining. "Your mouth. Don't stop. Make me come. Please—"

He seals his lips around my clit and sucks hard. White light bursts behind my eyes as Levi mouths at my nipple, as Hudson's teeth catch my earlobe. The three of them at once and everything short-circuits.

The orgasm tears through me. My body seizes, muscles locking, lungs gasping for air as pleasure rips me open.

"Too much," I gasp, pulling uselessly. "It's—"

"You can take it." Hudson's fingers slide inside while Leo's tongue keeps working. "You're going to come for us again. Until we decide you've had enough."

The words shatter me. My second orgasm hits harder, reality blurring until nothing exists but them breaking me apart.

They take turns after that. Hudson's mouth replacing Leo's, then Levi's, each bringing different pressure, different words, pushing me higher until I lose count of how many times I shatter.

By the time they ease back, I'm undone. Wrists aching. Thighs quivering. I can only lie there, chest heaving, completely wrecked.

"You okay, love?" Leo's voice cuts through the haze as he works the cuffs loose, rubbing circulation back into my wrists.

I manage a nod, and a shaky laugh slips out. The room tilts, my body humming, but underneath the exhaustion something sharper stirs. I lick my lips, meet their eyes. "My turn."

The command in my voice makes all three freeze.

"Lorna—" Leo starts, but I cut him off, kissing him hard enough to taste myself.

"No talking," I murmur against his mouth, teeth grazing. "I want you ruined for me."

I start with Hudson, sliding between his thighs and taking him deep. His head tips back, fingers tangling in my hair. I bring him close, so close his hips jerk, then I pull back, watching his face twist.

"Please," he finally breaks, voice cracking. "Christ, Lorna—"

"Please what?" I pull back, watching him struggle. "Use your words."

"Let me come," he begs, honest and desperate.

I lick him slowly, root to tip, then pull away with a wicked smile. "Not yet."

Levi's next. Sweet Levi who breaks so beautifully. I use every trick he ever whispered in my ear until his poet's composure shatters into stammered curses. His cock twitches on my tongue, fingers tight in my hair.

"God, I need to—" His voice wavers.

"You can't," I murmur. "Not until I say."

When I pull back, he's trembling, skin gleaming with sweat, eyes glassy. Right on the precipice.

Leo last, because his control runs deepest. But I know his weaknesses, where to use teeth, tongue, pressure, until he's quaking beneath me.

"Jesus," he rasps when I've denied him the fourth time. "Lorna, I need—"

"I know what you need." I nip at his pulse. "But first tell me how it feels, watching me take control."

"Fucking perfect," he groans, hips jerking.

I smile, still holding him back. "Good. Because I'm not done."

Heat courses through me. "Sit," I order, pointing to the bed.

They do. Three broad bodies lined up, legs spread, cocks heavy.

I start with Hudson, climbing into his lap to grind against him. His fingers twist in the sheets because I haven't given him permission to touch.

"Fuck," he mutters, hips bucking.

I roll my hips slower, teasing us both. My legs shake from holding back.

I leave him twitching and do the same to Levi.

"Please," he whispers. "Please let me—"

I cut him off with my mouth, taking what I need. His hands stay clenched at his sides. Obedient. Such a good boy.

Last is Leo. I climb into his lap, grinding over the thick length of him, watching his jaw flex, his breath catch. Before I can react he grabs my wrists, spins me so my back hits his chest, pinning both wrists in one hand.

"Cross your legs," he orders, voice low.

My thighs squeeze together and he drives between them, thick and hard. Each thrust sends him grinding over my clit, the friction stealing my breath.

"Fuck," I gasp, head falling back, hips bucking. The pressure, the slide, being held immobile, it's too much.

His teeth scrape my ear. "Hope you had your fun, sweetheart. I'm in control now." He nods toward the headboard. "Levi, lie down."

Leo's grip is firm at my waist as he lifts me, turns me, places me on Levi's lap, my back to his chest. His fingers slide between my ass cheeks, slick with lube, spreading me open.

The stretch makes me gasp, body tightening, but Levi steadies my hips and guides me down.

"Easy," Levi murmurs, voice wrecked but tender. "We've got you."

Leo's fingers stay at my ass, working me open as Levi's cock fills me. The drag is relentless, deep, scraping places that make everything blur. By the time I'm fully seated, spine flush to his chest, I'm trembling, displayed for them.

Leo's voice cuts through the haze. "Hudson, fuck her."

Hudson kneels between my legs, eyes wild, hands shoving my thighs back until I'm spread wide.

The first push into my pussy knocks the air from my lungs. He opens me, merciless, every inch dragging fire. Levi stays thick and unmoving beneath me, the double intrusion brutal, obscene. My nails dig into Hudson's shoulders, hips twitching between escape and surrender.

A sob tears from my throat. I'm gasping, stretched to breaking, every nerve firing.

Leo crouches beside Hudson, watching him drive into me. "Look at you. Stuffed full. You were made for this, Lorna."

He lowers his head and seals his mouth around my clit, sucking hard enough to rip a scream loose. His tongue flicks, circles, devours.

And then moves lower.

His tongue drags along Hudson's shaft as it moves in and out of me, licking where we're joined. He catches my swollen flesh with each thrust, mouth working both of us at once. Filthy. Obscene.

"Fuck," Hudson chokes out, eyes locked on where we're joined.

When I think I'll break, Leo pulls back, moving to kneel beside Hudson. He grips my thighs, pushing my knees toward my chest until I'm nearly folded in half. The crown of his cock presses at my entrance where Hudson already fills me. My gasp catches on a sob.

"You're so full, baby," Leo growls, rubbing the head of his cock alongside Hudson's. "But you're gonna take more."

I whimper, trembling.

"You'll be dripping for days, sore every time you sit, throat raw from screaming our names. And you'll beg for it, won't you?"

He pushes. Inch by inch. The burn is white-hot, forcing me wider than I thought possible. Everything tunnels, darkness edging my vision.

"Jesus Christ," Hudson grits out, his cock tight against Leo's.

Words fail. There's nothing but sensation. Levi beneath me, Hudson and Leo buried impossibly deep, my body held open, used. Leo drags his mouth along my throat, teeth scraping. "You're ours. Every hole, every scream, every drop. It all belongs to us."

The words hit harder than the thrusts. My muscles clamp down as they drive into me together, brutal and blinding. Leo presses the heel of his hand to my clit, rubbing tight circles. The pressure is merciless, dragging me higher than I've ever gone before. I sob their names, the sounds raw, shredded.

Levi's hands find mine, threading our fingers together. "Come for us, Petal."

My scream echoes off the walls as the orgasm tears through me. Violent. Endless. My body convulses around them, clenching hard, pulling them deeper.

Levi sobs my name into my shoulder, voice broken, spilling inside me. Hudson buries his face in my neck, roaring as he lets go. Leo's grip bruises as he drives deep and stays there, cursing low as he empties himself.

When the last spasms fade, I'm limp, strung out. Leo pulls out first, mouth brushing praise into my skin. Hudson follows, kissing my temple. Levi holds on longest, still buried deep, before finally lifting me as he slides free. The emptiness steals my breath, cum slipping down my thighs.

He gathers me into his arms and carries me to the bathroom, voice low at my ear the entire time—*You were perfect. Such a good girl for us.* When he sets me on the toilet and crouches to brush damp hair from my face, something in my chest cracks. The intimacy of him staying there while I pee, undoes me more than anything that came before.

After, he cleans me with a warm washcloth, careful strokes that make me shiver. My legs buckle the moment I try to stand, and he catches me with a smug smile before carrying me back to bed.

Hudson pulls me back against his chest while Levi curls into my front, fingers brushing hair from my eyes. Leo slides in behind him, arm reaching over to rest heavy and warm at my waist.

"I love you," I whisper into the tangle of limbs. "All of you. So much it scares me sometimes."

"Don't be scared, Snapdragon." Hudson's voice rumbles against my back. "We're here."

"Always," Levi murmurs, lips brushing my collarbone.

"Forever," Leo adds, thumb stroking lazy circles on my ribs.

Rain patters against the glass, softer now. Tomorrow will bring wedding planning, lists, figuring out how to marry four people with an entire Scottish village as accomplices. But tonight, wrapped in them, I let myself simply be. Safe. Loved. Accepted, not only by these three men, but by a community that sees us and celebrates it.

"Best cake tasting ever," Hudson mumbles sleepily.

"We should send Mrs. Henderson flowers."

"She'd prefer dahlia tubers," Leo says. "Woman's been eyeing your Bishop of Llandaff for years."

"Done. A whole box."

My eyes drift shut, their limbs tangled with mine, breath warm on my skin. Sleep pulls at me with gentle insistence, and this time, I don't fight it.

**30**

***

## 11 MONTHS LATER

September light has a quality nothing else matches.

It pours through my window, sharp and golden, catching on the rings stacked on my left hand before I'm fully awake. Three bands. Three promises. One impossible day that's about to become real.

I'm getting married.

The thought punches through the last fog of sleep and my heart kicks into a sprint. Not panic. I've spent months waiting for panic that never came. Just a huge, rib-cracking awareness that everything is about to change.

Today I marry three men in the field I planted with my bare hands.

My pulse thrums under my skin, alive with nerves and excitement and this wild, soaring certainty that I'm exactly where I'm meant to be. No cold feet. No what-ifs. Just roots spreading deep, anchoring me to this moment, this choice, these men who somehow became my whole world.

Outside, the dahlias stand ready. We worked until dusk yesterday, the four of us orbiting each other in that instinctive way we've developed, adjusting every last detail. Every bloom is flawless, faces lifted to the morning sun.

My phone buzzes on the nightstand, screen glowing with three messages. I already know who they're from before I swipe them open, but the smile creeps in anyway.

**Hudson:** Can't sleep. Been up since 4. Fuck, I can't wait to marry you.

**Levi:** The sunrise is the color of your dahlias. Everything reminds me of you. Hours feel eternal. I'm not being poetic. I'm being literal.

**Leo:** Eat breakfast. Actual food. Not just coffee. You'll need the energy. For the ceremony. And after.

I start typing a reply. *I'll eat when I damn well feel like—*

The bedroom door bursts open.

"No," Isla announces, marching in and snatching the phone from my grip. Charlie's behind her with Summer on her hip, and Penelope brings up the rear carrying enough coffee to caffeinate a small village.

I blink at them. "Good morning?"

"No phones." Isla tucks my phone into her back pocket. "No texting the grooms. No sneaking out for a pre-wedding quickie. You're mine until the ceremony."

"I'm thirty-five years old. I think I can manage."

"Can you?" Charlie sets Summer down, and she immediately launches herself at my bed. "Because I have specific instructions from Leo to make sure you eat. And from Hudson to make sure you don't get distracted by your flowers. And from Levi—"

"Let me guess, make sure I don't overthink?"

"Actually he said 'remind her she's magnificent and this is exactly what they've been waiting their entire lives for.'" Charlie settles on the edge of my bed. "Which, not gonna lie, made me tear up a little."

"Auntie Lorna!" Summer shrieks, patting my face with sticky hands. "You get married today and become a princess!"

I catch her, pulling her into my lap. She smells like soap and syrup. "That's right, baby girl. Today's the day."

Penelope hands me a massive mug of coffee. "Drink. Isla's not joking about the takeover. We've got six hours and a schedule that would make a military operation look relaxed."

The coffee is exactly what I need, strong enough to strip paint, with enough cream to make it bearable. I wrap my hands around the mug, letting the heat ground me. "You didn't have to do all this."

"Yeah, we did." Isla's already in my closet doing God knows what. "You spent your entire life taking care of me. It's my turn."

I blink back tears before she can see how much her words mean to me. "Where are the twins?"

"With Jack and his crew. Making flower crowns and probably eating their weight in pastries. Daniel's been up since dawn asking about every single detail of the ceremony, and Lorelai's composed three different songs about love."

"Sweet Jesus." I'm grinning. "That sounds about right."

"They're amazing," Penelope says, settling cross-legged at the foot of my bed. "Both of them. So excited they're practically vibrating."

"All right." I change the subject before I start crying. "What's first?"

Isla emerges from my closet holding my robe. "Shower. Breakfast—and yes, you're eating actual food, not only caffeine. Hair and makeup. Then you put on your dress and marry your Aussies."

"Sounds perfect."

"You better get moving," she says, pulling back the covers and shooing me toward the bathroom.

The shower helps. Hot water sluices away the last traces of sleep, steam filling my lungs until breathing feels easier. I reach for the honey soap Hudson bought me, the expensive one that leaves my skin slick and soft. He'd handed it over with that filthy little grin,

voice low as he said he couldn't wait to smell it on me later, preferably while I was still wet.

By the time I emerge in my favorite robe, voices have multiplied
downstairs.

Penelope's at the stove, flipping pancakes with athletic precision. Spatula in one hand, phone pinned to her ear, not missing a
beat.

Her five husbands orbit her in perfect rhythm. Archer pours
juice with military precision, lining up each glass in formation.
Spencer arranges butter, jam, and honey with the quiet intensity of
a sommelier curating a tasting flight. Liam weaves between them,
plates in one hand, dishtowel in the other. Jamie and Sammy are
locked in a heated debate about optimal syrup temperature.

"Mummy!"

Lorelai bursts out from under the table, flower crown askew
and cheeks sticky with strawberry jam. She catapults into my arms,
and I catch her, burying my nose in the wild, sweet of sugar,
sunshine, and pure seven-year-old joy.

"You're getting married!" she declares, eyes wide with triumph,
as if I might've misplaced that detail somewhere between coffee
and chaos.

"I am." I crouch down until we're eye to eye. "How do you feel
about that?"

"Happy." No hesitation. Then softer, almost shy, "It's real, right?
They're not just the neighbors anymore. They're going to be ours."

That word sticks in my chest. *Ours.*

"Yes, sweetheart."

Daniel approaches with the solemnity of a tiny psychologist.
"Are you nervous?"

"Not even a little bit. I'm excited. And happy. And ready."

He studies me for a long moment, then nods as if I passed some
secret test. "Good. 'Cause they're ready too. Mr. Leo's been walking
back and forth since forever. Mr. Hudson's been cleaning his workshop for hours. And Mr. Levi keeps looking at his watch, a lot."

I blink. "How do you know that?"

He grins, a little smug. "Uncle Jack's been texting me updates." He holds up his tablet as evidence.

A laugh slips out. "Of course he has."

"Everyone sit," Penelope calls, pointing her spatula at us. "Food's ready, and if Lorna doesn't eat soon, Leo's going to storm over here, and I'm not getting in the middle of that man's food-related panic."

I settle at the table, the kids on either side of me. Archer sets down a plate piled with pancakes that smell of vanilla and cinnamon. Spencer adds berries. Liam pours more coffee.

"These are incredible," I say through a giant mouthful of pancake.

"My family recipe," Spencer says, leaning on the counter. "My gran made them for my mom's wedding breakfast, passed the recipe on to me when we got married." He pauses. "All very traditional, if you ignore the part where Penelope married five people."

Laughter ripples through the kitchen, easy and unforced. This is what I never expected. This casual acceptance, this joy without judgment. My family might be unconventional, but it's mine.

"Tell us about the dress," Charlie says, settling across from me with Summer. "Isla's been cryptic."

"That's because it's so perfect it needs to be a surprise." Isla sweeps back in. "And none of you are seeing it until it's time."

"You haven't even seen it," I point out.

"I helped design it. I've seen the sketches. That's enough." Isla pours herself another cup of coffee. "The grooms had opinions, by the way. Very specific ones."

Warmth creeps up my neck.

Charlie arches a brow. "What kind of opinions?"

"The kind that suggests they've been paying very close attention to what makes her feel beautiful." Isla's grin turns wicked. "And the kind that suggests they have plans for later."

"Later later?" Penelope asks, smirking into her mug.

"None of your fudging business later," I shoot back, which only makes them laugh harder.

Isla produces a smaller box. Inside is a veil, handmade, with tiny dahlia blooms preserved in resin attached to the comb.

It's absolutely beautiful. "Are those from…"

"Your garden. Levi preserved them. Hudson poured the comb. Leo chose which flowers." Charlie's eyes are bright.

"Sneaky bastards." My voice cracks.

I clear my throat, shove another bite of pancake in my mouth. "Okay, enough of that or else I'm going to be crying into my breakfast. What's next?"

Isla pulls out her phone, scrolling. "You finish eating. Then hair. Penelope's handling that. Charlie does makeup. I supervise and make sure no one screws up my vision. At eleven-thirty, you get dressed, and we head to the field."

"Simple. I approve."

"Eat."


The next hour passes in controlled chaos. Penelope attacks my hair with the confidence of someone who's tamed far more unruly things, pinning and weaving until I have no idea what's happening but trust she knows.

Charlie works on my face with an artist's precision, explaining each step. "We're enhancing, not hiding. You're already beautiful, we're making sure Leo, Hudson, and Levi forget how to form coherent sentences."

"Pretty sure they're already there."

She laughs. "Fair point."

"Done." Penelope steps back from my hair. "Don't look yet," she says, turning me away from the mirror.

"When can I look?"

"When you're in the dress," Isla says firmly. "I want you to see the full effect."

"This is worse than Christmas morning when I was a kid."

"Good. Anticipation is half the fun."

At eleven-fifteen, Isla appears with the garment bag. My

stomach flips, not nerves, more a rush of *this is real*, sharp and bright in my chest.

"Charlie, help me with the buttons. Pen, you're on veil duty."

Isla unzips the garment bag with careful hands, and even though I've seen this dress before in fittings and mirrors, sketched and pinned and approved, today it feels different.

Ivory lace that traces every curve, fitted through the hips before flaring wide. The high neckline is elegant and restrained, a quiet contrast to the sheer lace sleeves and the open back that dips low enough to draw stares. No appliqués. No embellishments. Just lace, silk, and skin. Understated. Intentional. Sexy.

The guys are going to lose their minds.

"Okay." I lift my chin, pretending my voice doesn't tremble. "Let's do this."

Getting into the dress is a religious experience. Charlie and Penelope help me step in, careful with the lace, while Isla pulls the zipper up my side with a steady hand.

When they step back, I hesitate, almost afraid to look.

"Open your eyes," Isla orders.

I didn't realize I'd closed them.

*Oh. Oh.*

The woman in the mirror is me, but also not. My hair is swept up with flowers woven through the waves, pieces left loose to frame my face. The makeup isn't heavy or mask-like. Just *more*. My eyes look bigger, the blue-gray more striking. My skin has this glow that might be the makeup or might be the fact that I'm about to marry three men who make me feel desired and loved beyond reason. The dress fits as if it were painted on, hugging every curve before flowing to the floor.

But it's more than that. I look like someone who knows exactly what she wants and isn't afraid to take it. Someone who's done being small and careful and apologetic.

"Fuck," I whisper.

"Fuck is right." Isla's voice is suspiciously thick. "You're going to destroy them, Lorna. Absolutely destroy them." She checks her phone. "It's time. Truck's waiting."


We file downstairs and out into the sunlight, where Leo's truck waits at the curb. Except it's been transformed. Washed to a shine, garlands of flowers woven across the grille and mirrors, sunset-colored ribbons fluttering in the September breeze.

"They did it this morning," Charlie says.

"Of course they did." My eyes sting.

"All right." Isla claps her hands. "Everyone in."

The ride across the property is short, but Isla takes it at a crawl, letting the anticipation settle in my bones. The weight of the dress on my thighs. The scent of flowers drifting through the open windows. The steady rhythm of my pulse.

No cold sweat. No spiraling thoughts. Just this quiet, unwavering truth—I'm about to marry three men who love me. Who choose me. Who see every part of me and want me anyway.

The truck rounds the final bend, and when Isla parks, the world goes still.

Not silent. I can hear everything—the wind whispering through the dahlias, the faint murmur of distant voices, my heartbeat pounding in my ears. Yet the world feels suspended, charged, the way it does right before lightning strikes and even the air forgets to breathe.

"Ready?" Isla's voice is soft, but her eyes are cataloging every microexpression on my face, ready to throw the truck in reverse if I so much as twitch wrong.

"So fucking ready."

Charlie appears at my door, Penelope right behind her, both of them glowing with excitement. "Time to knock them dead, gorgeous."

The door opens and September air rushes in, cool enough to raise goosebumps along my arms. Lace and silk slip over my skin as

I step down, smooth and strange compared to my usual work-worn denim. My fingers catch the fabric without thinking.

"The dress is perfect," Penelope says, adjusting the skirt. "You're perfect."

"I'm about to throw up."

"That's normal," Charlie assures me, squeezing my shoulders. "I nearly vomited on Jack's shoes during our ceremony."

"That's not helping."

"Deep breaths." Isla's hands settle on my shoulders, grounding me. "You've already done the hard part. Today's just the celebration."

Daniel approaches first, Summer's chubby hand clutched in his. He's trying so hard to look grown-up in his little suit, shoulders squared, chin lifted. But when he sees me, his careful composure crumbles.

"Mum?" His voice cracks, eyes going wide. "You look..." He trails off, mouth opening and closing.

"Different?" I suggest gently, crouching carefully in the dress.

"Beautiful." A whisper. "Really, really beautiful. Like in the fairy tale books. A real princess."

Tears prick my eyes. "Oh, my sweet boy..."

"Is that really you, Mummy?" Lorelai stops dead in her tracks. Her flower girl dress in the purple she insisted on is already slightly askew, curls slipping free from the careful style Charlie worked on this morning. She's staring at me with eyes full of wonder, certain I've turned into magic.

"It's me, love." I hold out my hand.

She comes closer in careful, tentative steps, small fingers stretching toward my dress, not quite sure it's real. "You're sparkly," she whispers, awe slipping through every syllable. Her fingertips brush the fabric. "And you don't smell like plants and outside anymore." Her bottom lip juts out, trembling, still deciding whether this new version of me is a good thing.

"It's the special soap Hudson bought me, sweetie." I pull both of them close, inhaling their familiar scents.

"You haven't changed your mind, have you?" Daniel asks, slipping his hand into mine and holding on.

"No, I haven't changed my mind." We've talked about this, over dinner, during bedtime snuggles, in the car on the way to school. Age-appropriate explanations, gentle reassurances. But today is real. Tangible. Permanent.

"Good." The quick, decisive nod is so much like my brother's that it knocks the air from my lungs.

"They're going to be good dads," Lorelai chimes in, bouncing on the balls of her feet. "Can we call them Dad? All of them?"

My heart splits in half and spills glitter all over the gravel. A wet laugh slips out before I can stop it.

"Don't cry, Mummy!" Lorelai says, alarmed. "You'll make your sparkles run!"

"Happy tears." My voice is thick. "The very best kind."

The music begins, a lingering, aching swell that makes my chest go tight because I know Levi picked it. He's been quietly curating this playlist for months, humming under his breath when he thought I wasn't paying attention. This one is all low violin and piano, the kind of melody that slips beneath your skin and settles right over your heart.

"That's our cue," Isla says. "Munchkins, you're up."

Daniel straightens, offering his free arm to Lorelai with surprising gallantry. "Shall we, Lady Lorelai?"

She giggles but takes it with exaggerated propriety. "We shall, Lord Daniel."

They pause at the corner, both looking back at me one more time.

"We love you, Mummy," Daniel says solemnly. "And we're really happy you're happy."

"So happy," Lorelai agrees. "The most happy in the whole world happy."

They round the corner before I can respond, Summer toddling next to them, babbling cheerfully about flowers and pretty dresses.

"Your babies are perfect," Charlie murmurs, leaning in to fix my lipstick.

"They are. How did I get so lucky?"

"Not luck," Isla says firmly, offering me her arm. The solid feel of her grounds me, keeps my legs from dissolving entirely. "You raised them, Lorna. What you see is a reflection of you."

We round the corner and step into view.

The dahlias blaze in the autumn light, gold spilling over everything, turning grass to gilt and faces to art. Every sound sharpens, the collective inhale, the rustle of fabric, someone stifling a sob. My pulse surges, thunderous, swallowing the rest of the world whole.

But it's them who level me.

Leo makes a sound I've never heard from him before. Low and raw, dragged from somewhere deep in his chest. His composure fractures. The way he looks at me is nothing short of devastating. Eyes dark and locked on mine. Mouth parted. He looks ruined. Starved.

Hudson doesn't move. For once in his life, he's absolutely still. No shifting from foot to foot. No nervous energy or bouncing knees. He's frozen in place, tears carving clean lines down his face, his mouth moving but no sound coming out. His fingers twitch as if they want to reach for me, as if it's taking everything in him not to run forward and gather me up.

Levi sways, and Jack's hand shoots out to catch him. He doesn't blink. His eyes are wide and wrecked, pupils blown, lips moving in a frantic whisper. Later, Hudson will tell me he kept saying "holy fuck" and "un-fucking-believable" on repeat, his brain short-circuiting with awe.

My heart answers first. Not with nerves, but with a pull so strong it feels unavoidable. One step. Another. The aisle stretches impossibly long and somehow too short. Each face I pass is a blur of joy and wet eyes. Lach is openly weeping while trying to hold Cam upright. Penelope clutches Archer's hand so tight her knuckles are white. Neighbors and friends surround us, all here to witness this impossible, perfect thing we're doing.

Halfway down, Hudson breaks.

"Jesus Christ." His voice carries, rough and unsteady. "Lorna. Fuck. You're—" The last word breaks apart in his throat.

"Language," Daniel calls out primly, still clutching Summer's hand as she and Lorelai toss handfuls of dahlia petals in wild arcs. The crowd ripples with delight, the tension breaking enough to let joy rush in.

But Hudson doesn't seem to hear. He's staring at me as if I'm a revelation, a miracle, the answer to every question he's never known how to ask.

Three more steps. Two. One.

Isla kisses my cheek, her tears warm against my skin, then takes my hand and places it gently in Leo's.

The moment our hands touch, everything narrows. His hand is damp, fingers trembling as they curl around mine. My unshakable Leo is trembling.

"Hi," I whisper.

"Lorna." My name comes out raw, scraped from the depths of his soul. His thumb strokes over my knuckles compulsively, as if he needs the tactile confirmation that I'm real. "You... Christ. You're here. We're really doing this."

"Where else would I be?"

"Anywhere. My brain kept coming up with scenarios where you realized you could do better and ran." His other hand comes up to cradle my face, thumb brushing my cheekbone with devastating gentleness. "But you're here."

"I'll never run, Leo. I belong to the three of you as much as you belong to me."

Hudson makes a wounded sound, grabbing my other hand like he might fall apart if he doesn't. His grip is tight, almost too much, holding on for dear life. "Hi, beautiful. You look—fuck, there aren't words. I had words. I practiced them. But they're gone."

"That's okay. I prefer you speechless," I laugh.

"Menace." His breath skims my ear as he presses a kiss to my cheek, the word barely a whisper. The kiss is soft, but his eyes burn when he pulls back. "Later, I'm going to peel this dress off you with my teeth."

"Hudson," I hiss, cheeks flaming.

"What? It's our wedding night. I've been thinking about this for a very long time, Snapdragon. I have plans." His grin is wicked, but his gaze is so full of love it nearly knocks me sideways. "Really good plans."

Levi steps in close, careful, as if he's worried one wrong move might break the moment. Or maybe he's the one in danger of breaking. "Can I..." His voice barely clears his throat. His hands are shaking.

"You can do anything you want," I whisper, reaching for him.

He cups my face as if I'm precious. As if I might vanish if he's not careful. "You're absolutely fucking radiant. A poem I've spent my whole life trying to write. Every sunrise and sunset wrapped into one breath."

"Levi." It's all I can manage, my voice thick with emotion.

"I mean it." Steadier now. He exhales and rests his forehead on mine. I inhale him. Ink and paper and that wild, salt-sweet scent that belongs only to him.

"I love you," he whispers. "So much it's rewired my whole damn heart."

"Good. Me too."

Father Calum clears his throat gently, though his eyes are suspiciously bright. "Shall we begin?"

Leo guides me between them, and they form a loose half-circle around me. Our hands stay linked, a quiet chain of connection that runs through all four of us.

"Friends and family," Father Calum begins, voice steady. "We gather today to witness a rare and beautiful thing. Not only a wedding, but the recognition of a family built with intention. With courage. With a love that refuses to shrink itself to fit expectation."

A breeze lifts, sending dahlia petals tumbling. One lands on Leo's shoulder, dark burgundy over the rich brown of his suit. I reach to brush it away, but he catches my hand and presses it to his chest, right over the thunder of his heart.

"Lorna, Leo, Hudson, and Levi have chosen a life that may demand explanation from the world, but requires none between them. They've chosen more instead of less. Love without restriction. Commitment without compromise. Abundance without apology."

My throat tightens. My eyes burn.

"This isn't the easy path. The easy path is well-trodden, clearly marked, and socially approved. But these four have chosen otherwise. They've chosen to carve their own way forward. To redefine what family means. To remind us that love doesn't care about boxes or categories or the comfort of convention."

From his pocket, he draws out a length of cord, deep burgundy braided with glints of gold and silver that catch the light.

"In Celtic tradition, the binding of hands symbolizes the joining of lives. Not ownership, but partnership. Not confinement, but support." His gaze lingers on each of us, steady and full of quiet reverence. "If you would all join."

We adjust our positions, creating an intricate knot of interconnected hands. Father Calum begins winding the cord around our joined hands, over and under, creating a pattern as complex and beautiful as what we're building together.

"With each wrap of this cord, we honor a bond already formed," Father Calum says. "The first—for friendship. The foundation that holds everything else."

The cord brushes my wrist, cool silk against heated skin.

"The second—for trust. Earned through vulnerability, upheld through loyalty. The third—for passion. The spark that drew you together and the flame that keeps you close."

Leo makes a low sound in his throat. Hudson's fingers tighten gently around mine.

"The fourth—for family. Not only the four of you, but Daniel and Lorelai. And every soul here who stands behind this love."

I can feel the thrum of their pulses meeting mine, strong and steady.

"The fifth—for growth. A promise to change, to stretch, to keep becoming—together. The sixth—for challenge. Because every love will face storms, and you have chosen not to face them alone."

Levi's thumb moves across my knuckles, a quiet stroke. A breeze catches the hem of my dress, and dahlia petals swirl around our feet as if the wind itself is offering its blessing.

"And the seventh," Father Calum says, tying the last loop with careful, reverent precision, "for mystery. Because love this profound can't be explained or measured. Only lived. Only treasured."

I look down at our hands, each unique in size and shade, joined by more than the cord that ties us.

"This knot is not easily undone. And neither are you. You've already built a life that speaks louder than any vows. Today is not the beginning, it's the celebration."

Tears are streaming, and I don't bother to stop them. I'm not the only one. Even Leo's eyes shine, his lashes wet as he blinks hard.

"I believe you've each prepared vows. Leo?"

Leo stares at our bound hands for a long moment, jaw working. When he looks up, his eyes are molten, full of love and fear and determination.

"I had a whole speech. Practiced it in the mirror. Levi helped me edit it six times. Hudson made fun of me for using note cards." He shakes his head. "But standing here, holding your hand, watching the kids toss flower petals, looking at you—I don't remember a thing I meant to say. Only that I love you more than I knew a person could."

He takes a shaky inhale.

"Three and a half years ago, I was convinced I'd already used up my share of happiness. That whatever I'd done in a past life must have been terrible, because there was no way I was getting a second shot. Not at family. Not at love. Not at anything that felt like home. I thought wanting more was dangerous. That if I reached for it, it would vanish."

He swallows hard.

"Then we moved in next door, and there you were. Barefoot in the garden, hair glowing, singing to your flowers. And I knew that everything was about to change, it just took a bit longer than I was hoping."

His voice drops, going hoarse.

"And then you trusted me with your children. Do you know what that means to a man who thought he'd never be a father? Who'd buried that dream so deep it hurt to even think about? You handed me that trust as if it was easy, natural, as if I always belonged in their lives."

Daniel lets out a quiet sound beside us, and Leo reaches back without looking, his free hand pulling him close.

"You trusted me with your body, your pleasure, your vulnerability. You let me see you at two in the morning covered in mud and swearing at Mother Nature. You let me hold you while you cried about your past. You let me love you when you were convinced you were too broken for it. And you fell in love with these two idiots, too"—he glances at Hudson and Levi—"which might be the greatest gift of all."

Hudson whispers, "Love you too, you bastard," and several people laugh through their tears.

"And now I remember what I was going to say." He clears his throat. "I promise to be your anchor when storms come, but never your cage. To challenge your stubbornness when needed and celebrate it when it serves you. To teach Daniel everything I know about building and fixing and creating, and probably learn twice as much from him in return. To let Lorelai paint my nails bright colors and stick flowers in my hair and never, ever complain."

That gets a watery giggle from the crowd and a bright squeal of joy from Lorelai.

"I promise to love you, Lorna MacLeod, with everything I have, everything I am, until my last moment and probably beyond, because I'm pretty sure whatever comes after, I'll find you there, too."

Tears slip down my cheeks, quiet and unstoppable. My heart feels too full for my chest.

Father Calum nods to Hudson, who's already crying so openly and unashamedly that several people in the crowd are weeping just watching him.

"Right, so." Hudson swipes at his face with his free hand. "Fair warning, I'm going to ugly cry through this whole thing."

I can only smile at him, words lost to emotion.

"Lorna, the first time I saw you, you were driving that beat-up Volvo down the road, dust clouds billowing behind you, your hair flying out the window as if it had somewhere of its own to be. The kids were in the backseat, singing at the top of their lungs, completely off-key and utterly joyful. You didn't see me standing there. But I saw you. And I knew."

His eyes shine as he smiles.

"That night, you showed up on our porch with a basket of banana chocolate chip muffins, welcoming three strange men into your world as if it were the most natural thing. You handed them over even though you'd been up since five wrangling kids and taking care of your dahlias and God knows what else. You were kind and exhausted and so real it knocked the air out of me."

He pauses, fingers tightening slightly on mine.

"I knew right away I was in trouble. The best kind of trouble."

He shifts closer, our bound hands pulling the others with us, creating a tighter circle.

"In the last eighteen months, you've let me into your sanctuary. Not only your home, though that too, but the quiet space inside you where you keep the softest, most secret parts. The ones you don't show the world. You let me make you laugh when everything in you wanted to cry. Let me love your kids as if they were mine."

His voice catches. He swallows hard.

"I've spent most of my life feeling like too much. Too hyper as a kid. Too distracted in school. Too messy and chaotic and loud to be what anyone wanted long-term. People have always tried to sand me down into a manageable version. But you, you never tried to fix me. You never asked me to be less. You made space for all of me, and then had the audacity to look at me as if all the noise and color and chaos weren't just tolerated, but needed."

I squeeze his hand, trying to pour all my love through that simple touch.

"I promise to make you laugh every single day. To dance with you in the kitchen at three in the morning when you can't sleep, to sing terrible songs until you beg me to stop, to bring joy as a weapon against every dark thing that tries to creep in."

He's barely holding it together, words coming out between gulping breaths.

"Loving you means I get the gift of loving Leo too. You brought us back to each other. You saw a thing in both of us we couldn't quite name on our own, and somehow you made space for it to grow."

He draws a shaky inhale.

"And it means I get to stay close to Levi. My brother. My best friend. The one who reminds me to look closer, to find beauty in the mundane. The one who's seen every version of me and still chooses to show up."

His fingers tighten around mine.

"And I get to be the kind of father Daniel and Lorelai deserve. Not perfect, but present. Not a replacement, but one more person who loves them beyond reason. One more person in their corner. Always."

His voice drops, barely above a whisper.

"And it will be my pleasure to love you with the kind of joy that makes every day feel like the first day of summer break. Forever. No take-backs. No returns. No exchanges."

The sob rips out of me before I can catch it. Hudson grins through his own tears, looking downright pleased with himself.

"Levi," Father Calum prompts gently, wiping at his face.

Levi stares at me for so long I start to wonder if he's frozen. But then he speaks, his voice rising enough to carry on the wind.

"I've written you a thousand poems. Maybe more. Odes to your hands in the soil, earth clinging to your skin because it doesn't want to leave. Sonnets about your laugh, how it bursts out of you unannounced, bright and wild. Epic verses about how your eyes go hazy and glassy when you fall apart in my arms."

"Levi," I hiss, flushing, but he smiles, shameless.

"None of them come close to capturing what you are to me. You're the first person who ever saw all of me and didn't ask for more noise, or fewer thoughts, or a version of me that made people more comfortable. You saw my quiet and called it peaceful. Saw my intensity and met me there without flinching. Saw how I try to make sense of the world in words and asked to read every one."

He lifts his free hand to my face, brushing his fingers across my cheek.

"You gave me a family. Not only you and the children, but Hudson too, my brother by blood who's been trying to save me from my own silence since we were kids, who never stopped believing I had words worth saying even when I'd forgotten how to speak them. And Leo, who became my brother by choice, who saw my introspection and didn't try to fill the silence, who sat beside me in it until it became peaceful instead of lonely."

He takes a breath.

"You didn't just bring us together. You created a space where our grief didn't need to be hidden. You looked at three broken men and didn't see a project to fix or a problem to solve. You saw a family waiting to happen. And somehow, impossibly, you were right."

Tears blur my vision, everything swimming in gold and green.

"You gave me belonging when I'd resigned myself to being alone. You gave me a future when I was still stuck in survival. You gave me words again, Lorna."

He steps closer, eyes never leaving mine.

"I promise to see you, truly see you, every single day. The fire in you that wants to change the world, and the quiet fear that wonders if you ever will. The strength that holds this family steady, and the tenderness that makes it feel like home. Your brilliant, curious mind, rewriting how we understand pleasure and connection. And your beautiful, aching heart, still learning it doesn't have to earn the love it already has."

His thumb traces my lower lip.

"I promise to write you terrible poetry that makes you laugh, and beautiful poetry that makes you cry, and the kind you roll your eyes at when I leave it on the fridge. To read to Daniel and Lorelai until my voice gives out, to whisper stories until they sleep. To love you in every version of yourself, even the ones that forget you're already enough."

His voice dips quieter.

"I promise to love you completely. Without condition. Without end. With the kind of devotion that lives in poems and prayers and the spaces between them. For as long as I draw air, and probably a little while after that."

I've given up pretending I'm not crying. We all have. Even Father Calum has to pause, blinking hard.

"Lorna," he says quietly. "Your turn."

I take a shaky inhale. "A year and a half ago, I didn't just have walls built around my heart, I had them built around my entire life. Around my children. Around the idea that love could ever be safe again. I thought if I kept everything simple enough, controlled enough, nothing could get in. Nothing could hurt us."

I look at each of them in turn. Leo. Hudson. Levi. These men who slipped into the rhythm of our days so effortlessly, as if they were always meant to be part of us. These men who've become home, not a place, but a feeling.

"You three crashed through those walls like they were made of paper. They never stood a chance. Leo, with your quiet strength that made it safe to let go, to let the weight shift off my shoulders and into your hands. Hudson, with your joy that reminded me laughter wasn't a trapdoor, that letting light in didn't mean catastrophe. That being silly was survival, not weakness. And Levi, with that fire in your eyes that taught me intensity could be beautiful instead of brutal. That craving someone down to the bone didn't have to cost me myself."

My voice grows stronger.

"You taught me that love isn't about rationing pieces of myself. It's not a battleground. It's a garden. It expands when it's tended, overflows at the edges, creeps into cracks I didn't know were there."

Daniel and Lorelai are watching with huge eyes, and I smile at them, wanting them to understand, to remember this moment.

"You gave my children three fathers who love them without reservation, without conditions, without limits. Who show them every day that family isn't about blood or traditional structures. It's about choosing each other, again and again, even when it's hard. Especially when it's hard."

I turn back to my men.

"Leo, I promise to trust your strength without losing my own. To let you catch me when I fall but to remember I know how to stand. To match your steadiness with my fire, your protection with my ferocity, your certainty with my faith. To love you through silence and storms, through midnight crises and morning coffee, through every quiet moment that builds a life worth living."

His jaw clenches, eyes bright with tears.

"Hudson, I promise to let joy in even when fear feels safer. To laugh at your terrible jokes and dance to your off-key singing and build blanket forts in the living room even though I'm terrible at it. To match your energy with enthusiasm, your chaos with acceptance, your volume with my own kind of joy. To love you through adventure and stillness, through your highest highs and lowest lows, through every mad, beautiful step in between."

He's full-on sobbing, not even bothering to wipe at the tears streaming down his face.

"Levi, I promise to be your reader, your audience, your safe place to land when the world feels too sharp and bright and loud. To match your intensity with my own, your poetry with passion, your thoughtfulness with intention. To love you through words and silence, through ink-stained fingers and empty pages, through every unwritten verse and half-formed thought that makes you who you are."

His grip tightens on mine almost painfully.

"I promise all three of you to stop waiting for this to fall apart, to stop looking for the catch, the fine print, waiting for the other shoe to drop. To stop apologizing for wanting all of you, for needing this unprecedented thing we've built. To be your partner in creating this life that doesn't look like anyone else's but somehow fits us, tailored specifically for our hearts."

My voice drops to barely a whisper.

"I promise to love you all with everything I have, everything I am, everything I might become. Without fear, without limits, without end. Because you've taught me that love isn't a finite resource. It's infinite, renewable, sustainable. So this is my promise: to keep choosing all three of you every damn day. In the chaos and the calm, in the mundane and the magical. To hold space for your dreams the way you've held space for mine. To grow with you, bend with you, rise and fall and rise again, together."

The silence that follows is heavy and unbroken, as if the world itself has gone still to bear witness.

"Well," Father Calum says, his voice thick with emotion. "By the power vested in me by the gods and Scotland, and in the presence of those who cherish and celebrate you, I pronounce you married. Bound by choice, by love, by the promises spoken and the ones held quietly in your hearts. What you've built, may no one ever tear apart."

He begins to unwind the cord. "The binding is lifted, but the bonds remain." The cord slips free. "And now my favorite part." Father Calum smiles. "Gentlemen, you may kiss your bride."

For a held breath, the world goes still. None of us move. We look, eyes locking, pulses racing, caught in that perfect, shimmering instant where everything we've ever wanted finally aligns.

Leo steps in first, cupping my face in both hands, his thumbs brushing my cheekbones. He kisses me, pouring every vow, every unspoken promise, straight into my soul. It's everything at once—desperate, claiming, impossibly tender. His tongue slides over mine, and I taste salt. Could be his tears. Could be mine. Could be both. When he finally pulls back, we're both out of breath.

"My turn," Hudson says, grinning like he's been waiting his whole life for this. He catches me at the waist and spins me into him, the air rushing out of my lungs as the world tilts. He dips me until my hair brushes the grass and the crowd gasps, a ripple of surprise melting into laughter.

And then he's kissing me.

It's shameless and dirty and pure Hudson, his tongue teasing, tasting, coaxing a moan from somewhere deep inside me. I forget the crowd. Forget the field. Forget my name. There's only the crush of his mouth on mine, the solid weight of his arms holding me like he's never letting go. This is his vow, his brand of devotion, written in touch and tension and the kind of kiss that makes eternity feel not nearly long enough.

"Hello, wife," he whispers against my lips, mischief curling the edges of his smile. "Fancy meeting you here."

I barely have time to catch my breath before Levi's fingers slip into my hair. Gentle, but firm enough to send a shiver racing down my spine. He tilts my head back, guiding me until I'm staring into those storm-gray eyes that have unraveled me a hundred times over.

His mouth meets mine in a kiss that's pure poetry. Unrushed. Intentional. Every movement deliberate, as if he's etching each line of a love letter onto my tongue. There's no urgency in it, only devotion. Forever started the second our lips touched, and he has no interest in speeding it along.

"My love," he whispers, mouth still brushing mine. "My heart. My wife. My always."

By the time he pulls back, I'm flushed and unsteady, heart galloping behind my ribs. I blink, a little dazed, taking in these three men—my husbands. My fierce, tender, maddeningly perfect loves.

And I know without a doubt, I'll never survive on anything less than this.

"FAMILY HUG!" Lorelai's voice cuts through everything, pure sunshine and zero patience.

She barrels into us at full speed, all flying limbs and wild hair, and Daniel's right behind her, trying to look composed but grinning so hard his face might split. We're all tangled together in seconds, a laughing, crying mess of joy.

Three husbands. Two children. One overwhelmed bride. And so much love it might lift us right off the ground.

"Are you happy, Mum?" Daniel asks, his face pressed to my belly, arms wound tight around me.

"So happy I could burst," I whisper.

"Good, me too," Lorelai declares, as if she's solved something. "I'm so happy we'll be happy forever, Mummy."

I look at Leo, Hudson, Levi. At the children we're raising together. At this messy, impossible, imperfect thing we've built against all odds.

She's right.

We will be.

**KEEP READING FOR A PEEK AT
LOVE SEQUENCE BOOK 5 - MILLIE'S
STORY.**

# MILLIE CHAPTER 1

Motor oil and hot metal—that's what home smells like.

Three months in Edinburgh learning the exact tension required to upholster a car seat without creating a single wrinkle, and all I'd really learned is that I'm completely unemployable anywhere that requires you to not swear when you stab yourself with an upholstery needle for the fortieth time. Also anywhere that thinks clouds of Miss Dior and hoop earrings are "unprofessional" or that a woman who shows up in heels can't possibly know the difference between a socket wrench and pliers.

Edinburgh wanted me to pick a side. Girly or grease monkey. Highlights or credibility.

Here? Here I can be both. Here I can show up with grease under my fingernails and lipgloss that tastes like strawberries and nobody treats it like a contradiction. Here I can be exactly myself, which is messy, loud, possibly too emotionally attached to internal combustion engines, and absolutely capable of crying over a rom-com while rebuilding a transmission.

I push through the side door of Montgomery's Garage and immediately know something's wrong. Where's Rory's classic rock?

Where's Dad arguing with Mrs. Abernethy about whether her Volvo really needs new brake pads? (It does. It always does.)

Instead, there's laughter. Deep, American laughter that makes my stomach flip, followed by a softer British chuckle that sounds like money and good breeding.

Nope. Absolutely not. I'm not having a moment over laughter I haven't even identified the source of yet. I'm a professional. A woman with every automotive certification available, who can rebuild a carburetor in her sleep and once cried for twenty minutes after accidentally killing her favorite succulent.

I round the corner into bay three.

Oh, this is a problem.

There's a man bent over Mrs. Abernethy's Volvo, gray coveralls slung low on his hips, white tank top clinging to a back sculpted by actual labor, not gym mirrors. Sweat darkens the fabric, tracing every ridge of muscle. When he straightens, I have maybe three seconds, if that, to take inventory—sun-streaked blond hair, a jawline sharp enough to cut glass, shoulders that have no business existing outside of an action movie, and blue eyes so vivid they scramble my basic grasp of gravity. A smear of grease cuts across his cheekbone, and a thin scar bisects his left brow, giving him the kind of danger-coded beauty that should come with a warning label. When he drags his forearm across his forehead, the motion sends muscles shifting beneath tanned skin, and I have to remind myself, firmly, that I'm a professional adult. Not a hormonal teenager ogling a pin-up come to life.

He's looking at me. Not looking, glaring, exactly like you do at dog shit someone tracked through the carpet.

"You lost?"

American. Of course. The universe has handed me a hot American with an attitude problem because apparently I did not learn my lesson from Marcus in year twelve, or James at uni, or that Edinburgh disaster whose name I have surgically removed from my brain.

"What?"

"Salon's two streets over." He goes back to the engine as if I'm scenery. "Next to the fishmonger."

Did this man just—did a *stranger* just assume I'm hunting for a salon? Heat flares behind my ribs, sudden and cruel, the kind of anger that makes my teeth ache and my vision tunnel. It's the same fury that flattened me when my Edinburgh supervisor suggested I'd be "better suited" to the front office. The same tight, hot knot that rose when Malcom told me I was "too much." The same ache the grief counselor tried to paper over by calling my Bug project a "distraction" instead of what it was, which was survival.

"You heard me." He never looks up. His hand finds a socket wrench with that ridiculous mix of grace and muscle. The sound of metal on metal is absurdly intimate.

A stupid, perfect insult builds inside me, hungry and dangerous, and for a second I almost let it go. I could tell him where to go, in a sentence that would rearrange his face into something less smug. I could slap him, shove him, set the baseball cap in his back pocket on fire if I wanted to be dramatic.

Instead my hands go into my pockets so I don't throw a socket at him. My breath comes out in slow, controlled bursts. The rage is still there, humming, but at least my brain is reminding my limbs that murder in my father's garage would complicate things.

"Oh, hello there!"

A second man slides out from under the Honda in bay two, and honestly, this is getting absurd. No one mentioned the garage had been taken over by the cast of Torque Me, Daddy. His dark hair is perfectly disheveled despite the fact that he's been crawling around under a car, and his coveralls hang open just enough to suggest old money accidentally slumming it. When he stands, I swear I catch the glint of a romance novel being shoved deeper into his pocket— a flash of glossy abs on the cover before it vanishes.

"I'm Archie Sinclair," he says, extending a hand with an accent so posh it makes you think of Colin Firth mid–lake scene. His smile could power the entire village. "And that absolute tosser over there is Keiran Taylor."

When I take his hand, he pauses. "Oh, you've got..." His fingers hover near my ear, voice dropping into something warm and apologetic. "Thread from your jumper caught on your earring. May I?"

I nod, because apparently speech has left the building. His touch is careful as he frees the strand, just a brush of fingertips against my neck, but it sends a ripple straight through me. He smells like Earl Grey and something woody that screams expensive, the kind of scent that belongs to people with family crests. The moment stretches, soft and stupidly intimate, and I realize he's actually paying attention to *me*.

"There we are." He holds up the bit of thread with a grin. "Perfect. Lovely earrings, by the way. Vintage?"

"My mum's." The words slip out before I can snatch them back.

His face changes, just a flicker, but enough to make my throat tighten. "She had excellent taste."

My cheeks go hot. Since when do I blush because someone untangled my earring and complimented my dead mother's jewelry? I've rebuilt engines with Dad. Welded exhaust systems in a pearl necklace. Bled on brake pads and cried over carburetors. I do not blush over basic human decency.

Except, apparently, I do.

"Don't encourage her," Keiran mutters, still not looking at me. "She'll hang around like a stray cat."

The blush dies instantly. My whole body goes cold, then hot, then cold again, like my bloodstream can't decide whether it's molten rage or pure disbelief.

"She?" My voice drops into that quiet, dangerous register Bonnie calls my someone's about to lose a testicle voice. It's gotten me into three fights, out of two parking tickets, and once made a man at a pub apologize for words he hadn't even said yet.

"Garage bunnies." He still won't meet my eyes. Just keeps tightening Mrs. Abernethy's brake calipers, every movement clipped, controlled. "Girls who hang around watching the mechanics. They get in the way. Distract everyone with their..."

Finally he looks up. His gaze travels from my pink heels (yes, I wore them because I felt like it) up my legs, over my body, and stops on my face with an expression so cold it could strip paint.

"Everything."

The word lands heavy, cruel. To him, I'm not a person, I'm the problem in lipstick form. Too proud, too capable, too impossible to ignore. The kind of woman he's already decided to hate.

I've heard this tone before. From the instructor who told me my overalls were "too fitted." From the customer who asked for the "real mechanic." From the supervisor who decided I was "better suited to admin." From every man who looked surprised when I knew the answer before they did.

But somehow, coming from him, it hits different. Like battery acid sliding down my throat.

"I work here."

He snorts. Actually snorts, like I just told him I'm the Queen of bloody England. "Sure you do, sweetheart."

Sweetheart.

The way he says it curdles the air. Not a compliment. Not even condescending affection. Just that casual, lethal drawl that means child. Idiot. Thing beneath my boot.

Here's the thing about me: I don't get angry often. I get loud, sure. I get passionate about whether my plants are getting enough indirect sunlight or if that one Doctor Who episode really counts as canon. I cry at commercials and romcoms and once ugly-sobbed for an hour because I saw a dog that looked like the one we had when I was seven. But anger? Real anger, the kind that makes your hands shake and your blood hum like it's trying to find something to destroy—I save that for special occasions.

And apparently, today's the day.

"I own half this place," I say, each word sharp enough to cut. "Millicent Montgomery. My father's garage. I've been working here since I was eight, which means I was elbow-deep in engines before you even knew what a socket wrench was. I just spent three months in Edinburgh getting certified in automotive upholstery, my seventh certification, by the way, after engine repair, diagnostics, welding, transmission work, electrical systems, and body refinishing.

I point at him. My finger trembles, but it's not weakness, it's voltage. "You're standing in my bay."

The silence that follows is perfect. It tastes like victory, like metal and ozone and the sweet, quiet crumble of someone's assumptions falling apart.

Keiran's face goes through about seventeen different stages of regret. Color drains, returns, and drains again. His jaw tightens. He straightens slowly, wiping his hands on a rag, and I'm pleased to see the faint tremor in his fingers.

"Your bay?" His voice isn't as sure now. It's gone rough, uncertain around the edges.

"Bay three. Has been since I was sixteen and finally convinced Dad I wouldn't kill myself with the hydraulic lift." My smile could slice through sheet metal. "Though I was elbow-deep in transmissions years before that. Dad said I couldn't work alone until I could prove I knew what I was doing. So I proved it."

He swallows, eyes darting like he's recalculating every assumption he's ever made. "Your father hired me and told me to take my pick. He didn't mention having a daughter, or that she already had dibs on bay three."

"He didn't mention hiring a complete asshole," I say sweetly. "So I guess we're both learning things today."

Archie makes a noise somewhere between a strangled laugh and a whispered prayer for mercy.

"Let me guess," Keiran says, and I can see him pulling the pieces of his swagger back on, one by one. "Art history? Fashion merchandising? You said Edinburgh—hairdressing school?"

He thinks he's clever. The kind of man who weaponizes condescension with plausible deniability. What? I was just asking questions.

"Automotive upholstery certification," I say, voice sugar-sweet and lethal. "Which, before you ask, involves understanding vehicle structure, foam density, material stress points, pattern-making, and, shockingly, actual mechanical knowledge, since it requires removing and reinstalling seats, knowing frame architecture, and working around electrical systems. But sure, let's call it playing with fabric if that helps prop up your fragile ego."

"Keiran," Archie says softly, but the word carries weight. It's part warning, part plea. "That's enough, mate."

Keiran doesn't answer. Just turns back to the Volvo, as if I've vanished. As if I was never here at all.

And somehow, that's worse than the insult. Worse than every sneer, every assumption. Being dismissed, made invisible, lands harder than any words could. It hits some old, tender part of me that still believes if I just prove myself enough, someone like him might see me.

But he doesn't. He just keeps working, and I stand there, fury and humiliation burning through the same fragile spot in my chest until it feels ready to split open.

"Millie!"

The door bangs open and Penelope barrels in, arms overflowing with my houseplants—my monstera, two pothos, and a string of pearls all looking like survivors of some botanical apocalypse.

"Thank god you're back," she huffs. "I tried, Mill, I really did, but you know plants and I are natural-born enemies. I think I actually killed the small one. Also, if I smell like smoke, it's because Liam had a little stove incident last night. The house is fine. The paella... not so much."

She stops dead. Her gaze flicks from Keiran, to Archie, then back to me with the kind of raised-brow expression that says we are absolutely talking about this later and there will be wine.

"Oh. Hello."

"Pen, meet Keiran and Archie. The new mechanics."

"Pleasure," Archie says, his voice smooth enough to melt bearings.

Keiran just grunts.

"Right," Penelope says brightly, with the practiced diplomacy of a woman who's handled five husbands and lived to tell the tale. "I'll just get these upstairs before they stage a full revolt."

She walks toward the stairs, and even as she disappears from view, her presence lingers, a quiet steadiness in the air, like the ghost of a hand between my shoulder blades, holding me upright when everything else is trying to push me down.

"Millie Montgomery!"

Mrs. Henderson bursts in like a one-woman parade, clutching her weekly peace offering of baked goods, because in small Scottish towns, gossip and shortbread are the only real currencies. "Back from the big city! Your dad said you'd be home today." Her eyes sweep the room, landing on the newcomers. "And who are these handsome young men?"

I catch the subtle stiffening of Keiran's shoulders as Mrs. Henderson zeroes in, propelled by the unstoppable momentum of a woman who's made it her life's mission to know everyone's business, and, if possible, improve upon it.

"Archie Sinclair, ma'am," Archie says smoothly, bowing just enough to charm without pandering. I notice how he positions himself, gently intercepting her focus, shielding Keiran from the worst of her curiosity. It's protective, almost instinctive, and it does something traitorous to my chest.

Keiran offers something between a grunt and a syllable that could, in theory, be his name.

"American!" Mrs. Henderson's eyes widen as though she's stumbled upon buried treasure. "And English! How exotic. From where, dear?"

"Boston," Keiran says, clipped and unwilling.

"And you?" she turns to Archie, practically glowing.

"London, originally." His smile doesn't flicker. "Though I'm finding Scotland much more agreeable."

"I'm sure Millie will have you both sorted in no time," Mrs. Henderson trills, undeterred by Keiran's obvious discomfort. "Though my husband mentioned you—" she nods toward him "—

keep buying silicone lube from the shop. Very particular about your car, are you?"

Keiran goes still. Archie suddenly finds the wall very interesting. There's something there, sharp-edged and private, and from the way Keiran's jaw locks, it's not a story he plans to share.

The silence stretches taut. I should rescue him. Diffuse the moment. Be the bigger person.

But honestly? After the way he treated me, watching him squirm feels like justice served warm.

"I brought scones," Mrs. Henderson announces, setting a tin on the counter like she's personally rescuing us from starvation. "That one looks like he needs feeding." She gives Archie a once-over that's equal parts judgment and matchmaking, then turns her attention to Keiran. "Too thin, the both of you. You'll waste away if Millie doesn't keep an eye on you."

She finishes with a wink that somehow manages to sound both generous and threatening. The bell over the door jingles in her wake, and the room exhales. The air feels different without her in it, lighter and quieter but still humming with everything she just managed to notice.

I exhale and turn toward the stairs, following Penelope's path with my half-dead plants and the distinct sense that I've just witnessed the opening act of a story I didn't mean to start.

"Come on," Pen calls from the landing. "Let's get these settled before the big one dies out of spite."

I should go. Should follow her upstairs, debrief, scream into a pillow, maybe eat my feelings in the form of Mrs. Henderson's baked goods. But I can't quite make myself move. Keiran's still at it, focused on the car like it's the only thing keeping him tethered to earth. Every motion is clipped, deliberate, charged with what he's not saying. He isn't just fixing brakes; he's punishing them. Whatever's under that armor of arrogance, it's cracking.

Good. Let it.

"Mill?" Penelope's voice softens.

"Yeah. Coming."

I turn to follow her, but as we reach the stairs, Archie says something too low to make out, soft, like a question or a warning. Keiran's reply cuts through the quiet, rough and final.

"Don't."

The word follows me up, sticks between my shoulder blades all the way to the flat.

Pen sets my plants on the kitchen counter with exaggerated care, arranging them like they're sacred relics instead of half-dead foliage. Afternoon light spills through the window, catching the leaves and washing everything in gold and green.

"Well," she says, straightening. "That was something."

"That was a disaster."

"That was a hot disaster." She smirks, holding the pothos under the kitchen sink. "So what was that whole 'garage bunny' comment about?"

"God, you heard that? Apparently women who walk into garages are just there to ogle the help. We're distractions, not mechanics. Decorative problems in heels." I kick mine off, throwing my keys on the counter. "According to him, anyway."

"Ah." Pen's face twists like she's diagnosing an infection. "The American's straight, angry, and definitely allergic to women with opinions. Classic toxic masculinity meets unresolved childhood trauma. Big 'I was hurt once, so now I preemptively ruin things' energy."

"He's horrible."

"He's horrible and you couldn't stop staring at him."

"I was staring in hatred."

"Mmhmm." That knowing hum again, the one that says she's not buying a word of it. "And the posh one?"

"Archie's lovely." I start checking the plants, grounding myself in their small, fixable needs. The monstera's wilted but salvageable, much like my dignity. "Did you see the romance novel in his pocket?"

"I did. Two men on the cover, very muscular, very shirtless.

Honestly, good taste." She grins, then sobers slightly. "They seem close, those two."

"There's definitely something there," I say, though I'm not sure if I mean between them, or under all that noise and fury still burning in my chest.

"What kind of something?"

I think about how Keiran's voice shifted when Archie spoke, how the sharpness dulled, how gentleness crept in around the edges. The way Archie looks at him, all quiet concern and protective instinct, threaded through with something that feels suspiciously like longing.

"I don't know," I say slowly, pruning a dead leaf. "But definitely something."

"My money's on the American being straight and emotionally constipated," Penelope says. "That whole speech? Textbook straight guy who's been burned by a woman and is now taking it out on every woman he meets. Probably got cheated on or dumped brutally. Maybe both."

"Yeah," I say, but it comes out thinner than I mean it to. My chest twists, sharp and unwanted. It's not pity, it's attraction, stupid and traitorous. The kind that kicks in even when your brain is screaming absolutely not. I hate that I feel it. Hate that a man who called me a garage bunny and dismissed my entire existence can still make something low in my stomach spark to life.

I can still feel his eyes on me. That slow drag from my heels to my face.

Penelope checks her phone and sighs. "I need to go before one of the guys actually burns down the house this time. But drinks this week? You can tell me about Edinburgh and why you came back early."

"I didn't come back early."

"Mill." The Look. The one that says she knows I'm lying and she's going to let me lie but we both know the truth and we'll deal with it eventually. "You were supposed to be gone four months. You came back in three. That's the definition of early."

"I missed my plants."

"You missed your garage." She kisses my cheek, and I smell Archer's cologne mixed with her coconut shampoo. "It's okay to admit this is where you belong, love. Not everyone's meant for cities and strangers."

After Pen leaves, I take a slow look around my flat. Every surface is alive with green—pothos spilling from bookshelves, succulents crowding the windowsill, the big monstera in the corner that's been with me since I was nineteen and thought I could grow something good out of grief.

This is home. Not Edinburgh with its spotless garages and people who say "elevated" and "curated" like they invented the words. Not the city where I was always too loud, too much, too Scottish. Here. This messy, motor-oil-scented corner of the world where people know my name and don't expect me to sand myself down to fit.

I trade my day clothes for the real me: coveralls tied around my waist, tank top that says I Know What I'm Doing—Bonnie's Christmas joke that stopped being funny once it became true. I pull my hair back, feel the tension settle into focus. This isn't a costume. This is armor.

Time to check on my girl.

The garage hums when I step inside, quieter now. Music drifts through the air—gravelly, American. Definitely Keiran's playlist. Tom Petty, maybe, or Mellencamp. The kind of sound that smells like gasoline and heartbreak.

Bay five waits at the back, my corner, where my baby lies beneath a rusty tarp. My 1973 Baja Bug, ridiculous, impractical, stubborn as hell. Six years in the making and still not finished. Oversized tires, bright red paint begging for another coat, suspension that nearly bankrupted me.

She's also the only thing I've ever built entirely for myself. Not for Dad. Not for customers. Not to prove a point. Just because I wanted to.

Because I could.

I grip the edge of the tarp and pull it back, slow and careful, the way you'd uncover something sacred.

"That's yours?"

I don't jump. Years in a garage teach you to sense when someone's behind you. The change in air, the creak of the floorboards, the quiet pull of presence. Still, my pulse betrays me, tripping hard at the sound of his voice.

Keiran stands framed in the open garage door, sunlight pouring in behind him and catching on every edge. The glow turns his hair to gold and his skin to warm amber. Dust motes swirl lazily in the light, cinematic and slow, and my traitorous brain takes note of everything, the smear of grease on his cheekbone, the easy slouch against the frame, the way his coveralls hang low on his hips like he was born to make people lose focus.

I need to stop. He dismissed my existence, called me a garage bunny like I was a punchline. He's not someone worth noticing, but my body hasn't caught up to that memo yet.

"We established that I work here," I say, colder than I mean to, "so yes, this is mine."

He moves closer, slow and deliberate, circling my Bug like a shark with a new curiosity. His hand trails along the hood, fingers barely grazing metal I spent months perfecting. The sight makes my stomach twist. I want to slap his hand away. I don't want him touching the only thing in this whole place that's mine, the one thing untouched by anyone else's expectations or mistakes.

"Dual port heads?"

My jaw tightens. "1776cc. Bored out from the original 1600."

"Gear ratio?"

"3.88. Rebuilt the transmission myself."

He crouches beside the car, studying the details, and I watch the change happen. The scorn drains from his face, replaced by respect, maybe, or disbelief that someone like me could build something like this.

"You did all this yourself?"

"Most of it. Dad helped with the roll cage welding, and I had the paint done at a shop, but the rest? Engine, transmission, suspension, electrical—that's all me."

He straightens, meeting my eyes for the first time since he found out who I was. "Why a Baja? Most people give up halfway through a build like this."

Because I needed to build something when my life was coming apart. Because Mum had her stroke and Dad couldn't stop crying and I was seventeen and furious at the world. Because I needed to make something that lived, even when she didn't.

"Because I felt like it."

"That's not an answer."

"It's the only one you're getting."

He steps closer and the scent of motor oil and soap, or maybe aftershave, wraps around me, clean and sharp. Up close, I notice the thin scar through his eyebrow, a small imperfection that makes his face feel less sculpted, more human. His jaw tightens, like he's holding words back, and the silence between us hums, low and electric, alive with everything neither of us will say.

"Most people don't have the patience for a project like this," he says quietly. "Six years is a long time to stay committed to something."

"Good thing I'm not most people, then." I meet his eyes and don't look away.

"No." His voice softens, the edge easing for the first time. "You're definitely not."

The air between us crackles, the kind of charged stillness that comes before a storm. He's looking at me like he's trying to solve something, and I'm trying not to notice how the light shifts in his eyes, washing the blue to gray, like the sky right before it breaks open.

"Keiran?"

Archie's voice cuts through whatever this moment is. He stands in the open garage door, uncertain, his gaze flicking between us like he's stepped into the wrong scene. "Mrs. Abernethy's back for her car."

"It's not ready." Keiran doesn't look away from me.

"I know. I told her that." Archie's tone is careful, his eyes moving between us again. "Millie, would you like me to—"

"She's fine," Keiran interrupts, already turning away.

Archie watches him go with an expression that's equal parts fond, exasperated, and quietly sad. Then he turns back to me, offering a smile that tries for easy but doesn't make it all the way there.

"I'm sorry about him. He's not usually..." He stops, then laughs once, dry and self-aware. "That's a lie. He is usually like that. But I promise it's not personal."

"Feels pretty personal."

"He's had a rough go lately. Not that it excuses anything," he adds quickly. "Just... context."

He moves closer to my Bug, running a hand along the fender with genuine appreciation. "She's gorgeous, by the way. Absolutely stunning. My brother would hate her."

"Your brother's not a car guy?"

"Banking," Archie says with mock solemnity. "Very serious, very polished. Thinks cars should appreciate in value, not drain your life savings." He pulls something from his pocket, and I can't help but grin when I see the cover—two knights, bare from the waist up, all gleaming abs and smoldering intensity. They're locked in a pose that could be swordplay or foreplay. "I'm the family disappointment."

The way he says it, light, but too practiced, makes my chest go soft.

"Why Scotland, then?" I ask.

"Because London's full of people who think dirt is contagious and work is for other people." He grins, and it changes his whole face, brightens it. "Here, the work means something. People bring their cars in because they love them, not because they want to show them off. Plus"—he lifts the book—"Mrs. Fraser at the local bookshop always orders whatever I ask for."

That makes me laugh, unexpectedly. "You just carry those around?"

"Always. Life's too short not to read about handsome men falling in love." He tilts the book toward me. "Have you read this one? Two knights and so much pining you could build furniture out of it."

I laugh. "You make it sound like a medical condition."

"It practically is. Yearning, longing, the whole tragic mess. One of them literally stands in the rain for six chapters waiting for the other to notice him. It's exquisite torture."

We talk books while I check my tools, running my hands over wrenches and sockets to make sure everything's still where I left it three months ago. It's easy in a way talking to Keiran wasn't. Archie's warm, quick, and doesn't make me feel like every word is a test. He moves around the garage like he belongs there, quietly competent, handing me the right wrench before I even think to reach for it.

"What's his deal?" I finally ask, because I can't not. "Keiran's."

Archie's smile falters, softens into wistfulness. "He's been hurt. Badly. Came here to get away from it, whatever it is. He doesn't talk about it." He pauses, eyes distant. "He's not all bad, you know. Once you get past the walls, there's someone... remarkable underneath."

"Those are some tall walls."

"The tallest," he says, with a faint laugh that doesn't touch his eyes. "Reinforced steel, probably. But I've seen him with cars, with engines. He's brilliant, really. Patient. Careful. Everything he isn't with people."

There's longing in Archie's voice, protective, aching. The sound of someone who loves quietly, knowing it's never going to be returned. Before I can say anything, Keiran's voice cuts through the moment.

"We're closing up."

He's suddenly there, all contained tension and quiet anger. He doesn't look at me, just crosses to the workbench, takes the keys from their hook, and pockets them with brisk efficiency. Every movement is clipped, controlled, like he's one wrong word away from breaking.

"I should go anyway," Archie says, checking his phone. "Early morning tomorrow. Mrs. Fletcher's bringing her Morris Minor in." He flashes me a smile that's all warmth again. "It was good to properly meet you, Millie. I'm glad you're back."

"Yeah," I say, and I mean it. "Me too."

When he's gone, it's just me and Keiran and the hum of silence. The setting sun filters through the high windows, turning the garage into a wash of gold and dust.

"You need to leave too," he says, still not looking at me.

"Excuse me?"

"Shop's closed. I'm locking up. Unless you plan on sleeping down here, move."

The casual dismissal hits like a slap, reigniting everything I thought I'd burned off.

"I live here," I snap. "Upstairs. My flat is literally above this garage."

He finally looks at me, expression unreadable. "Then go upstairs. I'm locking the shop."

"That's my father's garage you're talking about."

"And I'm closing it," he says evenly. "You can go up, or—"

"Or what?" I step closer, heat rising up my neck. "You'll what, exactly? Throw me out? Call my father? Tell him his daughter's being difficult in her own building?"

"I'll tell him his daughter needs to learn that just because daddy owns the place doesn't mean she can treat it like her personal playground."

The word hits like a spark to gasoline. Playground. My vision goes hot, sharp around the edges. Years of grease and grit and sleepless nights—reduced to a game. Every certification, every burn, every goddamn scar dismissed like it's nothing. Like the blood under my nails and the hours I bled into this floor don't count because I happen to have a pretty face.

"You don't know anything about me."

"I know enough." His voice is cold steel. "I know you've been working on that car for six years and it still doesn't run. I know you went to Edinburgh to study upholstery because real mechanical work was too hard. I know daddy gave you a garage to play in and you think that makes you special."

Each word slices deep, deliberate and precise.

"You're such an asshole."

"And you're in my way." He gestures toward the door, steady now, all trace of softness gone. "Upstairs. Now."

I should argue. Should tell him he doesn't get to decide what this place means to me. Should tell him that car took six years because I started it three weeks after my mother's stroke, three weeks after watching her die over four impossible days while machines beeped and Dad held her hand and I couldn't fix a damn thing. Three weeks after the funeral, when I wore her perfume and someone told me, at least she's not suffering anymore, like that was supposed to help.

But my throat's too tight. My eyes burn. And I'll be damned if I let him see me cry. I won't give him that satisfaction.

So I grab my bag and head for the door, blinking hard, biting the inside of my cheek until I taste copper.

"You know what?" I turn back, proud that my voice doesn't shake. "I feel sorry for Archie, having to work with you."

Pain flickers in his eyes, anger, maybe both, before he locks it down.

"Archie doesn't need your pity." His voice is low, rough. "Or your attention. So just... stay away from him."

"Or what?"

"Just stay away." It's not a threat. It's softer, frayed, almost pleading. "Please."

The please catches me off guard. But I'm too angry to care what it means that he's asking instead of ordering.

I leave before I do something stupid, before the tears win, before I ask what broke him so badly he can't help breaking everything else.

The stairs to my flat feel longer than usual. My hands are still shaking when I slip inside and turn the deadbolt. The quiet wraps around me, heavy and familiar. And then it hits—all of it. The anger pounding in my pulse. The hurt sitting heavy in my chest. The confusion over why his words still echo in my head.

I pour whisky from Dad's "bad day" bottle, the good stuff he saves for when everything falls apart, and sink onto the couch. Only then do I realize I'm crying.

# MILLIE CHAPTER 2

The Jaguar E-Type is beautiful in the way old things are beautiful when they've been loved well, curves that make you think of Hollywood and martinis, faded british racing green wire wheels that probably cost more to restore than I make in a month.

She's also a complete disaster under the hood.

"Jesus Christ." I'm leaning over the engine bay, and honestly, this is an insult to automotive engineering everywhere. "Who did this?"

"Previous owner's nephew." Dad appears beside me with two coffees, handing me one. "Thought he could save money doing it himself."

"He should be arrested."

The wiring looks like a spider on methamphetamine had a go at it. The carburetor setup is wrong—completely wrong—and someone's used duct tape. Actual duct tape. On a vintage Jag.

"Can you fix it?"

"Can I—Dad. Of course I can fix it. But it's going to take time." I'm already mentally cataloging what needs to be ordered, what can be salvaged, how many hours this is going to eat. "This is a two-person job minimum."

"Good thing you've got Keiran to help, then."

My stomach drops. "No."

"Millie—"

"Anyone but him."

"Keiran's one of the best mechanics I've ever hired." Dad's voice is firm. "And Archie's excellent with electrical systems. This needs all three of you."

"He called me a garage bunny."

"And you called him Satan incarnate in your text to Bonnie. Which she showed me, by the way." He squeezes my shoulder. "I know he was rough yesterday. But he doesn't know you yet. Give him a chance to see what I see."

What Dad sees is his daughter who rebuilt her first engine at fifteen, who spent her teenage years choosing garage time over parties, who came back from Edinburgh early because this place, this greasy, complicated place, is home.

What Keiran sees is some blonde girl playing mechanic.

"Fine." The word tastes like motor oil and resignation. "But if he makes one more comment about my qualifications, I'm using that duct tape to shut his mouth."

Dad laughs and heads to his office, leaving me with the Jag and my impending doom.

They arrive together.

I'm already under the hood, photographing the wiring disaster for insurance purposes, when I hear Keiran's voice.

"That's the Jag?"

"Gorgeous, isn't she?" Archie sounds reverent.

"1963?" Keiran asks.

"'62." I don't look up. "Series One. Which you'd know if you looked at the headlight covers."

Silence. Then footsteps.

"Morning, Millie," Archie says warmly. "Sleep well?"

"Like a baby. A baby who spent all night planning how to fix an engine that looks like it was assembled by a drunk electrician."

"That bad?"

"Worse." I straighten up, and immediately wish I hadn't.

Keiran's in a black t-shirt that looks like it was painted on. He's holding a travel mug that says "I'm Not Always A Dick, Just Kidding Go Fuck Yourself" which is somehow both completely on-brand and weirdly endearing.

Stop it, brain. He's terrible.

"Right." I clear my throat, forcing my brain to behave. "Electrical system's fucked, carburetor setup's wrong, and someone used duct tape on the fuel line which is both idiotic and potentially fatal. We need to strip it down to bare block and start over."

"That's going to take weeks," Keiran says, frowning.

"Two weeks if we work efficiently. Three if someone insists on questioning every decision." I look at him pointedly.

His jaw ticks. "I only question bad decisions."

"Great! Then you won't have any questions, because I don't make bad decisions."

"Everyone makes bad decisions. It's how you respond to them that matters," Archie says, looking between us.

"Lovely philosophical insight. Are we working or having a therapy session?"

God, it's sweltering. Late August in a metal-roofed garage with no air conditioning, and I've been bent over an engine for the last twenty minutes. My coveralls are basically a wearable sauna. I yank the zipper down to my waist and peel out of the sleeves, tying them low on my hips. The air hits my overheated skin and I nearly groan with relief.

Keiran goes completely still.

When I look up, he's staring, not at my face, but lower, his jaw locked tight and darkness flickering in his eyes. My tank top is thin, sweat-damp, and suddenly I'm very aware of how the fabric clings.

Heat crawls up my neck. Great. Add "creepy guy who stares at your tits" to his list of charming qualities.

"You have something to say?" My voice comes out sharper than I mean it to.

His eyes snap to my face, and there's danger in his expression.

Danger that makes my stomach flip in a way that's definitely not fear but might be adjacent to it.

"You should wear more appropriate attire." The words are clipped, controlled. "This is a professional environment."

"It's ninety degrees in here and I'm dressed exactly like you were yesterday—coveralls and a tank top. But please, continue telling me how my body is somehow more unprofessional than yours."

His jaw ticks. "That's different."

"How?"

"It just is."

Classic double standard. His body is just a body but mine is somehow inherently unprofessional. Where I'm supposed to swelter in layers while he gets to be comfortable because my chest is apparently a workplace hazard.

"Right. Got it. Your body is workplace appropriate, mine isn't."

Archie makes a strangled sound. "Bloody hell. Can we—let's focus on the electrical system, yeah? That seems rather pressing."

"We should start with a full diagnostic," Keiran says, voice gone rough and dark. "You can't treat symptoms without understanding the disease."

"It's a car, not a patient," I snap.

"It's a machine that's been butchered. We need to approach it systematically."

He's right. I hate that he's right, but he's right. A full diagnostic will tell us exactly what we're dealing with, what's salvageable, what needs replacing.

"Fine." The word comes out tight. "You handle the diagnostic. I'll keep documenting what we've got."

"And maybe..." He pauses, jaw working like he's chewing on words he doesn't want to say. "Maybe put the coveralls back on."

The heat in my face has nothing to do with the temperature now. "Excuse me?"

"It's distracting."

"My existence is distracting? My clothes? Anything else you'd like me to change about myself to make your workday more comfortable?"

"That's not what I said."

"It's exactly what you said."

"I'll get the wiring diagrams," Archie announces, already moving toward the door with impressive speed.

Which leaves me alone with Keiran's bad attitude.

He sets up the diagnostic computer with efficient, precise movements. His hands are clean this morning, no grease under the nails yet, calluses on his palms from years of work. There's a scar across his left knuckles that's silvery-white and old.

Stop staring at his hands, Millicent.

"You're going to want to check the alternator first," I say.

He doesn't look up. "I know what I'm doing."

"Just making sure."

"I don't need your help."

"We're supposed to be working together."

"Then work. Stop hovering." He doesn't look up from the computer screen. "And stop wearing that perfume. It's distracting."

Heat flares up my neck. "How about you stop telling me what to do?"

"That—" He waves vaguely in my direction. "That cloud you travel in. It's unprofessional."

"Unprofessional. Is that the only fucking word you know?"

"This is a workspace, not a nightclub."

My perfume is Miss Dior. It was my mother's signature scent, the one thing of hers I kept after she died. I wear it every day because sometimes when I'm elbow-deep in an engine, I catch a whiff and remember her laugh.

But I'm not telling him that.

"Right." My voice could cut glass. "I'll stop being a woman. That'll make everything easier."

"That's not what I—" He stops. Runs a hand through his hair, making it stick up. "Forget it."

"Gladly."

We work in brittle silence. Me photographing and cataloging, him running diagnostics. The computer beeps and whirs. My camera clicks. Rory's got the radio on in another bay, his classic rock bleeding through the walls.

"You're not documenting the fuel pump," Keiran says after twenty minutes.

"Already did it."

"I don't see it in the system."

"Because I haven't uploaded it yet," I bite out, clenching my jaw.

"You should upload as you go."

"I upload when I'm ready."

"That's inefficient."

My whole body goes tight, every muscle locked like an over-torqued bolt. "You know what's inefficient? This conversation. I've been documenting car repairs since I was fourteen. I know what I'm doing."

"Could've fooled me."

"What's your problem?" I'm around the front of the car now, in his space. "Seriously. What is your actual problem with me?"

He finally looks at me and anger flashes in those blue eyes. But also heat that makes my skin feel too tight.

"I don't have a problem with you."

"Bullshit."

"I don't know you well enough to have a problem with you."

"Then why are you acting like I personally offended you by existing?"

His knuckles go white around the diagnostic scanner. "Because you're—" He stops. Shakes his head. "Never mind."

"No. Say it. I'm what?"

"Nothing. Forget it."

"I'm what, Keiran?"

The way I say his name makes his expression shift. His eyes drop to my mouth for a second, so quick I almost miss it, before snapping back up.

"You're in my light." Flat. Final. "Move."

Archie returns with the wiring diagrams and an armful of manuals, taking one look at us and immediately sensing the temperature in the room.

"Everything alright?"

"Perfect," I say sweetly.

"Great," Keiran mutters.

"Right." Archie spreads the diagrams across the workbench. "Shall we?"

The next two hours are a masterclass in passive-aggressive teamwork. Keiran questions every wire I trace. I question every connection he tests. Archie plays referee, his posh accent getting posher with stress.

"The green wire goes to the alternator," I say.

"That's not green, that's teal," Keiran argues.

"It's literally labeled 'green' on the diagram."

"Diagrams can be wrong."

"Oh my god."

Keiran leans over the diagram. "I'm just saying—"

"You're always 'just saying.'" I turn to face him fully. "Maybe try 'just shutting up' for a change."

"Maybe if you'd listen instead of assuming you're right—"

"I am right!"

"Bloody hell," Archie mutters. "Can we please focus on the car?"

We both turn to glare at him. He holds up his hands.

"Or not. Continue your marital dispute. I'll be here, actually working."

"We're not—" I start.

"It's not—" Keiran says at the same time.

We look at each other. Look away. The air between us feels charged, like a battery with the terminals too close, one wrong move and everything sparks.

"The green wire," Archie says carefully, "goes to the alternator. Keiran's right that it's more teal than green. Millie's right that the diagram labels it green. Can we move on?"

"Fine," I mutter.

"Whatever," Keiran says.

But when I reach for the wire, his hand is already there. Our barely brush and I jerk back like I've touched fire.

He doesn't.

His hand stays exactly where it is, close enough that I can feel the warmth radiating off his skin. Close enough that if I moved even an inch, we'd be touching again.

"You need to strip this back further," he says, voice low. "The insulation's compromised."

"I was about to do that."

"Were you."

It's not a question. It's a challenge.

I snatch the wire cutters off the bench and strip the wire with more force than necessary. "Happy?"

"Not the word I'd use." But he's watching my hands with an intensity that makes my stomach flip. "Your grip's wrong. You'll damage the wire."

"My grip is perfect."

"No, it's not." He reaches over and wraps his hand around mine, adjusting my position on the tool. "You need to feel the resistance. Like this."

His chest presses against my shoulder. His breath is coffee and something sweet. His hand covers mine completely, warm and callused and steady, guiding the pressure.

This is what intimidation feels like. This is a guy establishing dominance, showing the little lady how it's done. This is toxic masculinity 101, the same power play I've seen a hundred times from men who think proximity equals authority.

But my body isn't getting that message. My body is very interested in how solid he feels behind me, how his voice has gone rough and low, how his thumb is doing something to the back of my hand that definitely could be stroking.

"Feel the difference?" His voice is right by my ear.

My lungs have forgotten how to work. My pulse jumps in my

throat. And my brain, my usually reliable, sensible brain, has gone completely offline.

"Millie?" Archie's voice cuts through the moment, breaking the tension. I should be relieved, but an unwelcome sense of disappointment curls in my chest.

"You've got grease on your cheek."

I step back so fast I nearly trip. Keiran lets go immediately, face unreadable, and moves back to the diagnostic computer like nothing happened.

Archie appears with a clean rag, his smile gentle. "May I?"

I nod, still trying to get my cardiovascular system back online.

He carefully wipes the smudge from my cheekbone, his touch soft and careful. Nothing like the overwhelming intensity of Keiran's hand on mine. This is what kindness looks like—gentle, asking permission, treating me like a human instead of a problem to solve.

"There." He holds up the rag like proof. "Perfect."

"Thanks."

"I think I found the main problem," Archie continues, pointing to a junction box that looks like it's been hit by lightning. "Someone's rewired this completely wrong. It's a miracle this car hasn't caught fire."

We all lean in to look, and suddenly we're all pressed together in the small space around the engine bay—Archie on one side, Keiran on the other, me in the middle like the world's most uncomfortable sandwich.

"That's going to need a complete replacement," I say, focusing on the wiring and not on how much I'm enjoying this.

"Which means ordering parts," Archie adds.

"Which means this is going to take longer than two weeks," Keiran finishes.

We're all thinking the same thing. We're all mentally calculating costs, time, labor. And somehow, being unified in our assessment of this disaster makes the tension ease slightly.

"Right." I step back, putting air between us. "I'll call Henderson's Hardware for parts."

"I'll draft an email to the owner about timeline," Archie offers.

"I'll start on the carburetor," Keiran says.

We separate, moving to our individual tasks, and I can finally breathe again.

Except I can still feel the ghost of his hand on mine. Still feel the weight of his chest against my shoulder. Still feel that electric charge that definitely wasn't about teaching me proper wire-stripping technique.

He's misogynistic. He's an asshole. He's a misogynistic asshole that thinks I'm incompetent.

The fact that he's hot doesn't change any of that.

Mira is the first to break for lunch. She's unfairly gorgeous in that way that makes you question everything you thought you knew about beauty—tall, graceful, with perfect bone structure and eyes that see everything. Today she's in coveralls that somehow look like designer fashion, her hair in a neat bun that hasn't moved despite three hours under a Ford F-150.

"I brought samosas," she announces, holding up a massive Tupperware. "My mother's recipe. There's enough for everyone. I thought we could eat outside, get some fresh air."

"Outside?" Keiran looks skeptical.

"It's a beautiful day. Come on." She's already heading for the side door. "There's a picnic table with a view of the loch. Unless you're planning on working straight through lunch," she says, making a face.

Archie's immediately on his feet. "That sounds brilliant."

I grab my water bottle and follow, leaving Keiran to make his own decision about whether joining us is worth the social interaction.

He follows.

The picnic table is weathered wood, slightly sticky from yesterday's rain, overlooking the loch that's all silver and glass in the midday sun. The air smells like grass and salt water and Mira's incredible food.

"Right," Mira says, opening the container. "We've got lamb samosas, vegetable samosas, and—" she pulls out a second container "—my wife's homemade chutney because she insisted I couldn't serve samosas without proper accompaniment."

"Your wife's a writer, yeah?" Archie asks, taking a samosa like it's made of gold.

"Yeah. Priya writes romance novels. Very successful ones." Mira's smile is private, soft. "She'll probably stop by later with coffee because she's always worrying I'm going to overwork myself."

We eat in relative silence for a few minutes, because the food is too good for talking. The pastry's flaky and perfect, the lamb spiced just right, and I make a sound that's possibly inappropriate for a work lunch.

"These are incredible."

"My mother's recipe," Mira says. "She taught me when I was young. Before—" She pauses. "Well. Before everything changed."

There's a story there, but it's not mine to ask about. Archie seems to sense it too, smoothly changing the subject.

"Do you cook, Keiran?" Mira asks, changing the subject.

"Not well."

"He can make eggs," Archie offers. "Sometimes without burning them."

"Thanks for that," Keiran mutters, but there's no real heat in it.

I watch the easy way they banter, the familiarity in their body language. Archie's whole face softens when he looks at Keiran, goes warm in a way that's almost painful to witness. And Keiran doesn't see it. Or he sees it and doesn't care, which might be worse.

Poor Archie. Stuck in that horrible space of loving someone who'll never love you back because they're not wired that way.

Archie reaches for the last samosa at the same time Keiran does, and they have a brief, silent standoff.

"I'll fight you for it," Archie says, grinning.

"You'll lose."

"I'm scrappier than I look."

"You're about as scrappy as a golden retriever."

"Rude." But Archie's still smiling, still looking at Keiran like he hung the damn moon. "Fine. You have it."

"I didn't say I wanted it."

"You literally reached for it."

"So did you."

"Yes, but I'm graciously conceding."

"I don't want your gracious concession."

"Oh my god." I lean forward. "Split it."

They both look at me like I've suggested something revolutionary. Then Keiran picks up the samosa and tears it in half with his fingers and hands half to Archie.

Archie takes it, their fingers brushing, and a look passes between them that I don't understand. Some kind of private communication that makes Archie's breath catch, makes Keiran's jaw tighten.

Mira's watching them too, a small smile playing at her lips like she knows what the rest of us don't. Or maybe she's happy to witness any kind of affection, even the one-sided kind.

"So, Millie," she says, pulling my attention away. "How's the Baja Bug coming?"

"Slowly. Still needs a lot of work."

"She's been working on it for six years," Keiran says, and it definitely sounds like criticism.

"Six years is nothing for a passion project," Mira says calmly. "My wife's been working on her novel series for eight years. Good things take time."

"Or they're never finished," Keiran mutters into his water bottle.

My whole body goes hot, then cold, then hot again. "What did you say?"

"Nothing."

"No, say it. You clearly have an opinion."

"I don't—"

"You always have an opinion. About my methods, my documentation, my perfume, my car. So say it."

He meets my eyes, and there's sharpness in his expression. "Some projects are passion. Some are procrastination. Hard to tell which is which from the outside."

The anger hits like a piston firing. "You don't know anything about me or my car."

"I know it's been six years and it still doesn't run."

"It runs fine. It's not finished. There's a difference."

"Is there?"

I'm on my feet before I make the conscious decision to stand. "Yeah, actually. One is a process. The other's a failure. But I wouldn't expect you to understand nuance."

"Millie—" Archie starts, but I'm already moving.

"I need to make that call to Henderson's Hardware anyway."

I walk away before I say words I'll regret, before the burning in my eyes turns into actual tears, before I let Keiran ruin my lunch along with everything else.

Behind me, I hear Archie's voice, low and urgent. Keiran's response is too quiet to make out. Then Mira: "Maybe give her some space."

I don't go back to the garage immediately. I go to my flat, to my jungle of plants that need watering, to the silence that's better than Keiran's judgment.

I'm elbow-deep in repotting my monstera, her roots tangled and gasping for space, when a knock rattles the door.

Mira, holding my bottle of water.

"Thought you might want this." She waits for me to step aside, then enters my plant kingdom with the kind of careful respect most people reserve for museums. "Wow. This is incredible."

"It's a bit much."

"It's perfect." She hands me the water. "Drink. Then talk. Or don't talk. Whatever you need."

I drink. She sits on my couch, patient and still, examining my collection like she's genuinely interested in the difference between my pothos varieties.

"He's such a straight boy cliché," I finally say. "The whole brooding American thing. The emotional unavailability. The way he thinks being an asshole makes him interesting."

"Hmm," Mira says, and there's something in that sound, something knowing and amused that I don't understand.

"What?"

"Nothing." But she's smiling slightly. "Sometimes people aren't what they seem."

"He seems pretty straightforward to me. Straightforward asshole."

"Does he?" She stands, moving to examine my monstera. "This one's thriving. You've got a good touch."

"Thanks." I follow her, grateful for the subject change. "That's my favorite. Had her since she was tiny." I trace the edge of a leaf with my fingertip. "He was wrong, you know. About procrastination."

She turns to face me. "He's hurting, Millie. Badly. That doesn't excuse what he said, but it might explain it."

"Everyone's hurting. That doesn't give us permission to hurt other people."

"No," she agrees. "It doesn't. But sometimes hurt people lash out at the things that scare them most."

"I don't scare him."

Her smile is gentle. "Don't you?"

After she leaves, I give it another thirty minutes before heading back down. Armor on. Game face ready.

Keiran's alone by the Jaguar, and he straightens when he sees me.

"Millie—"

"We have work to do." I move to the Jag, focusing on the engine instead of his face. "Let's do it."

"I was out of line."

"Probably. But I don't want to talk about it." I grab the socket wrench, start working on the carburetor mount. "We're here to fix a car. So let's fix the car."

He's quiet for a long moment. Then: "Okay."

We work in silence, but it's different than this morning. Less hostile. More... careful. Like we're both aware that one wrong word could detonate everything, so we're moving slowly, deliberately, keeping our distance.

When I need a tool, he hands it to me without being asked. When he needs me to hold something, I do it without commentary.

It's not comfortable. It's not easy. But it's functional.

And when Archie returns from his parts run, he looks between us with cautious relief.

"Everything okay?"

"Fine," Keiran and I say in unison.

Archie's smile is careful. "Good. Because I've got the new junction box and I think if we all work together, we can have this rewired by end of day."

"Let's do it," I say.

We work. The three of us, moving around each other with increasing coordination. Archie's patient explanations. Keiran's methodical precision. My intuitive understanding of how things should flow.

It's almost good. Almost easy.

Until Keiran needs to show me the proper torque for a particularly delicate connection.

He pauses. Actually pauses, wrench in hand, like he's considering whether this is a good idea.

"Can I show you something?"

The fact that he's asking instead of doing makes my chest tighten.

"Yeah."

He moves behind me, close but not touching, and positions his hand over mine on the wrench. "You need to feel the exact moment when resistance becomes security. Too loose and it fails. Too tight and you strip the threads. It's a balance."

His voice is different now. Lower.

"Feel that?" His thumb presses against my knuckle, guiding the pressure. "Right there. That's the sweet spot."

My lungs have forgotten how to work. Every nerve ending is sparking. My thoughts scatter like stripped screws across a garage floor.

This is what attraction feels like when you don't want it. When it's inconvenient and stupid and aimed at exactly the wrong person. When your body stages a full-scale rebellion against your common sense.

"There." His hand lingers for a second too long. Not enough to be inappropriate. Enough to make my pulse jump. Enough to remind me that whatever this is between us, it's not simple antagonism.

He steps back. The cool air rushes in where his warmth was.

"Got it?" His voice is rougher than it should be.

"Yeah." Mine's not much better. "I got it."

Our eyes meet, and there's heat there. Raw, undeniable heat that he's trying desperately to hide behind professionalism and distance.

"Good work today," Dad says when he stops by at closing. "All three of you. Knew you'd figure it out."

After he leaves, it's just us again. Archie packing up his tools with that careful cheerfulness he wears like armor. Keiran cleaning the workstation with obsessive precision. Me trying to figure out how to navigate whatever this is.

"See you tomorrow?" Archie asks, like he's not sure if we're both going to decide to quit.

"Yeah," I say.

"Sure," Keiran adds.

We leave separately, Archie first with a cheerful wave, then Keiran with his hands shoved in his pockets and his shoulders tight.

I'm the last one out, and as I climb the stairs to my flat, my phone buzzes. Bonnie: How was day two?

Complicated, I type back.

Good complicated or bad complicated?

I think about Keiran's face when he asked permission to show me something. About his hand teaching me torque. About the way he looked at me like I was a puzzle to figure out.

About poor Archie, watching Keiran with that hopeless longing written all over his face.

Don't know yet, I finally respond. Both, maybe.

Interesting. Keep me posted.

I pour myself a whisky—Dad's bottle is going to be empty by the end of the week at this rate—and settle onto my couch, surrounded by plants and silence and the growing certainty that this job is going to be more complicated than I thought.

Tomorrow, I'll figure out how to work with Keiran without wanting to simultaneously throttle him and climb him like a tree.

Tonight, I take care of my plants and try not to think about callused hands and blue eyes and the heat of his body.

Try not to think about Archie's face when Keiran handed him half a samosa.

Try not to wonder what Keiran's running from that's bad enough to make him this mean.

Try not to care.

But the tightness in my chest suggests it's already too late for that.

# MILLIE CHAPTER 3

The Jaguar's brake system is a lesson in British engineering—elegant, precise, and designed to make you question all your life choices when something goes wrong.

"Hand me the seventeen millimeter," I say, arm stretched under the car.

Metal touches my palm. Wrong size.

"That's a nineteen."

"My mistake." Keiran's voice is flat. He's been like this all morning, present but distant, answering in monosyllables, avoiding eye contact.

I slide out from under the Jag to grab the right wrench myself, and move too fast. The creeper shoots out, momentum carrying me further than I intended, and suddenly I'm tipping—

Hands catch my waist.

Keiran steadies me before I can hit the floor. His fingers press against my sides, thumbs resting above my hip bones, and all the blood in my body rushes to meet his touch.

"Easy," he says, voice rough. "You alright?"

"Yeah." But I don't move. Neither does he. "Thanks."

His hands stay exactly where they are for a heartbeat too long, warm through my tank top, firm enough that I can feel the calluses on his palms. Then he lets go like I've burned him and steps back.

"Be more careful."

"I am careful."

"Could've fooled me." But there's no heat in it. The same strange distance he's been maintaining all morning.

I slide back under the car before my face can betray anything, before I can analyze why my skin still feels like static where he touched me.

The morning passes in this careful dance, Keiran and I orbiting each other, maintaining distance, speaking only when necessary. By the time my stomach starts growling, I'm grateful for the interruption.

Mira arrives with her usual Tupperware as Archie returns from the café with sandwiches. We migrate to the picnic table overlooking the loch—me, Archie, Keiran, Mira, Rory, and Tavish joining from the other bays.

I'm half-listening to Rory's story about a customer who thought her engine was possessed (it was mice in the air filter) when I notice it.

Archie and Keiran.

They're sitting close, closer than friends usually sit, knees almost touching. Archie's laughing at what Keiran muttered, and his hand lands on Keiran's shoulder, stays there a fraction too long. Keiran doesn't pull away, but he doesn't lean in either. He sits there, solid and still, while Archie's fingers rest against his collarbone like they belong there.

The way Archie looks at him, god. It's soft. Fond. The kind of look that carries weight.

And Keiran... Keiran's not looking back. He's staring at his sandwich, jaw tight, like he's carefully not acknowledging the touch.

My chest constricts.

"Earth to Millie," Mira says.

"Sorry." I pull my attention back. "Zoned out."

"You've been doing that a lot." Her eyes are knowing. "Everything okay?"

"Fine. Tired."

She follows my gaze to where Archie's now fixing Keiran's collar —such a casual, intimate gesture that Keiran allows. Doesn't acknowledge, doesn't return, but allows.

"Hmm," Mira says, and there's a world of meaning in that sound.

"What?"

"Nothing." But she's smiling slightly, like she knows what I don't. "People are interesting."

The afternoon stretches long and tense. Bay three feels smaller than it did this morning, the air thick with things unsaid. Keiran questions my wiring diagram interpretation. I question his diagnostic conclusions. Archie mediates with increasingly strained patience.

"The junction box needs replacing," I say for the third time.

"I agree. But we should test the downstream connections first." Keiran doesn't look up from his multimeter.

"We already tested them."

"Not thoroughly enough."

"I was thorough."

"You were fast. Fast isn't the same as thorough."

Archie clears his throat. "Right. How about I verify the connections while you two work on the carburetor? Fresh eyes and all that."

"Fine," Keiran and I say in unison.

The carburetor assembly is spread across the workbench in pieces, each component photographed and cataloged. We work in tense silence, passing tools with careful choreography designed to avoid touching.

"Socket wrench."

I hand it over. Our fingers don't touch.

"Needle-nose pliers."

He passes them. Careful to avoid contact.

This is ridiculous. This careful dance we're doing, maintaining distance like we're both radioactive.

"Found the issue," Archie calls from under the car. "Millie was right, the junction box is completely fried. Downstream connections are fine, though. Clean as a whistle."

Keiran's jaw ticks. "Good. We'll order the replacement."

No acknowledgment that I was right. No apology for questioning me. Acceptance and moving on.

I'm about to say something I probably shouldn't when Dad appears in the bay doorway.

"Millie, got a minute?"

I follow him to his office, leaving Keiran and Archie in bay three. Behind me, I hear Archie say words too quiet to make out, and Keiran's low response. The door closes, cutting off whatever conversation they're having.

Dad's office smells like coffee and old paper and WD-40. Photos line the walls—me and Bonnie through the years, Mum before she died, the garage in various states of evolution.

"Mrs. Henderson stopped by," he says, settling into his desk chair.

"Oh god. What now?"

"Wanted to know if you're seeing anyone. She's got a nephew—"

"Dad. No."

"I know, I know." He holds up his hands. "I told her you're focused on your career. That you're young." He pauses, and his expression shifts. "Though I have noticed you spending a lot of time with the new guys."

My stomach drops. "At work, Dad."

"I know that." His voice is gentle but firm. "And I've seen the way you look at them sometimes. Both of them."

Heat crawls up my neck. "Dad—"

"I'm not judging, sweetheart. I want you to be careful. Find someone good when you're ready. Someone solid. A proper relationship, not—" He waves vaguely. "Not whatever you might be thinking."

"A proper relationship." The words taste bitter.

"You know what I mean. One person. Real commitment. Built to last, like your mother and I had." He leans forward. "I don't want you getting any ideas. Those two are your colleagues, and whatever you think you're seeing—"

I barely hear him because I'm still hung up on proper relationship. "You went to Penelope's wedding," I interrupt. "You congratulated all five of her husbands. You smiled and celebrated with them."

"That's different."

"How?"

"Penelope's always been..." He searches for words. "Unconventional. And they're happy, and I'm glad for them. But that doesn't mean it's the right path for everyone. Especially not my daughter."

"So it's fine for Penelope but not for me."

"I didn't say that." He looks uncomfortable. "I want you to be realistic. To not complicate your work life with—with whatever you think might be happening there."

My jaw clenches. "Nothing's happening, Dad. Archie's gay anyway. And Keiran's an asshole who can barely stand being in the same room as me. So there's nothing to worry about."

Dad's expression softens with relief. "Good. That's... good. I want you to focus on your future, on the garage, on finding the right person when the time comes."

"The right person. Singular."

"Yes." He stands, clearly considering the conversation over. "Someone who deserves you. Someone who'll give you the life you deserve."

I sit there for another minute after he leaves, staring at the photos. Mum and Dad, arms around each other, looking at each other like nothing else mattered.

One person. One love. One proper path.

The word proper sits heavy in my chest as I make my way back to bay three.

Archie's gone when I return, headed to Henderson's Hardware

for the junction box and other supplies, according to the note he left on the workbench. Which leaves me alone with Keiran.

Again.

The silence feels different now, charged with Dad's words and my own confusion. I grab my camera and slide under the Jag, needing concrete focus.

I'm photographing the rust damage on the driver's side frame when I become aware of Keiran moving. Not away. Closer.

He's crouched beside the car, supposedly looking at the front quarter panel, but from this angle I can see his eyes aren't on the engine.

They're on my legs.

My shorts-clad legs, specifically. Following the line from my work boots up my calves to where the denim cuts off at mid-thigh.

His jaw is tight. His hands are clenched by his sides. And his eyes—

Heat crawls up my neck. Is he about to criticize my shorts? Tell me they're unprofessional? Add it to his list of everything wrong with me?

I slide out sharply, and his eyes snap to my face.

"Problem?" My voice comes out harder than intended.

"No." But his face is flushed. "Checking something."

"Checking what?"

"The—" He glances at the car like he's forgotten what he was supposed to be doing. "The coolant hose."

"The coolant hose."

"Yeah."

"Which is on the other side from where you were looking."

His jaw ticks. "I was checking multiple things."

"Right." I don't believe him for a second. "Well, don't let me distract you with my unprofessional shorts."

"I didn't say—"

"You didn't have to." I grab my camera and head for the parts washer, needing distance before I say what I'll regret.

Behind me, I hear him mutter what sounds like "fuck" but might be wishful thinking.

The rest of the afternoon passes in uncomfortable silence. When Archie returns, arms full of parts and wearing that careful smile that doesn't quite reach his eyes, the tension actually gets worse instead of better.

"Got the junction box," he announces. "And Henderson had those gaskets you needed, Keir."

"Thanks." Keiran doesn't look up from the carburetor.

"Should I start on the installation or—"

"I'll do it," Keiran says. "You help Millie."

It's not a suggestion. It's a dismissal.

Archie's smile tightens. "Right. Of course."

We work together in relative silence, me writing down a list of what we still need to order, him cross-referencing the parts catalog, both of us hyperaware of Keiran working nearby. Archie's hands are steady, but there's tension in his shoulders that wasn't there yesterday.

"You okay?" I ask quietly.

"Fine." Too bright. Too fast. "Why wouldn't I be?"

"You seem—I don't know. Off."

"Long day." He offers that careful smile again. "Nothing a good cuppa won't fix."

But when he thinks I'm not looking, his eyes drift to Keiran. For a second. Long enough for me to see the expression there, soft and painful and resigned.

By the time closing arrives, I'm more than ready to escape. The ferry to North Uist and Penelope's place feels like salvation.

"I'm hanging out with Penelope tonight," I tell Archie when he raises an eyebrow at my duffel bag.

His face lights up, genuine this time. "Girls' night?"

"Yep. Wine and complaining and probably some of Spencer's cooking if I'm lucky."

"Tell her hello from me."

"Will do."

Keiran materializes from the office, and I try not to notice how his eyes track my movements as I zip my bag.

"You're going to North Uist?"

"Girls' night," I repeat.

"That's a long drive for one night."

"Ferry's only forty minutes. And Penelope's worth it."

He looks like he wants to say more, words hovering on his tongue, unspoken, but Archie's watching us both with that too-perceptive gaze, and the moment passes.

"Be safe," Keiran finally says.

"Always am."

I leave before either of them can see how flushed my face is.

The ferry to North Uist is peaceful in a way the garage hasn't been all day. I stand on the deck despite the wind, watching the water turn silver in the fading light, and try to organize my thoughts into coherence.

Keiran: Hot. Infuriating. Possibly the most emotionally constipated man I've ever met. Shows every toxic masculinity indicator known to science.

Archie: Sweet. Thoughtful. Reads romance novels with shirtless men on the covers. Definitely gay based on, well, on everything.

And the way Archie looks at Keiran? The way his hand lingers on Keiran's shoulder? The careful, painful hope in his eyes when Keiran's not looking?

That's not friendship. That's pining.

Poor Archie. Stuck wanting someone who can't want him back.

By the time the ferry docks, I've almost convinced myself I have this situation figured out. Almost.

Penelope's place is warm chaos when I arrive. Archer answers the door with flour on his hands and a grin.

"Millie! Come in, come in. Fair warning, Sammy's attempting to bake and it's going about as well as you'd expect."

"I heard that!" Sammy's voice carries from the kitchen, followed by laughter from the others.

"It's true!" Archer calls back. He leads me through to the sunroom where Penelope's already set up with wine and that knowing look that says we're having A Talk.

"You look frazzled," she observes, handing me a glass.

"I am frazzled."

"Good. Sit. Talk."

So I do. It all comes pouring out—Keiran being impossible, criticizing everything I do, the perfume comment, the car comment, his general attitude of barely-contained hostility. How he makes me feel simultaneously incompetent and electric. How his hands on my waist this morning felt like they were branding me.

"He's such a fucking cliché," I finish. "The whole bad boy brooding American thing. The emotional unavailability. The toxic masculinity. Don't forget he called me a garage bunny, Pen. On day one."

"Mmm," Penelope says, sipping her wine. "And the other one? Archie?"

"Archie's lovely. Sweet, kind, reads romance novels. Has excellent taste in literature and terrible taste in who he falls for."

"Meaning?"

"Meaning he's clearly in love with Keiran. It's painful to watch, honestly. The way he looks at him when Keiran's not paying attention? The way he tries so hard to be close to him? He's completely gone for a guy who can't give him what he needs."

Penelope sets down her glass. "You're sure Keiran's straight."

"I think so? The toxic masculinity, the way he dismissed me, the whole alpha male energy—he's textbook."

"Mmm," Penelope says again, and there's knowing in that sound.

"What?"

"Sometimes what looks straight isn't."

"No, he's definitely straight. Trust me. I know the type."

"Do you?" She tilts her head. "Or do you know what you expect to see?"

"I'm seeing exactly what's there. Keiran acts like every toxic straight guy I've ever met. Archie acts like every gay man I've known who's pining after someone unavailable."

"Does he?" Penelope leans forward. "Or does he act like someone who reads romance and is in touch with his emotions? Because those aren't specifically gay traits, Mill."

"But the way he looks at Keiran—"

"The way someone looks at someone they care about and worry about," Penelope says gently. "Did he actually say he's gay? Use those words?"

"He doesn't have to. It's obvious from everything—the books, the way he dresses, the way he talks about feelings, the way he watches Keiran like he's the sun."

Penelope is quiet for a moment, swirling her wine. "When I met my boys, I made so many assumptions. Thought Archer was friendly because he's warm with everyone. Thought Spencer was flirting with the waitress when he was working up courage to talk to me. I didn't even realize Sammy and Jamie were into each other, and I thought Liam was completely straight."

"And?"

"And I was wrong about all of it." She smiles. "They were all interested. All scared and confused and waiting for someone else to make the first move. We spent years dancing around each other because we were all too busy assuming we knew what everyone else was thinking."

"This is different."

"Is it?" Her eyes are too knowing. "Or are you so convinced of your narrative that you're not seeing the actual story?"

"Keiran called me a garage bunny, Pen. He criticized my clothes, my car, my methods. He's been nothing but an asshole."

"He's hurting," she says softly. "It doesn't excuse his behavior, but you barely know him, Millie. Maybe give him a chance to show you who he actually is."

The words settle uncomfortably in my chest.

"And Archie." Penelope continues. "The romance novels, the fashion sense, the emotional intelligence—none of those things determine sexuality. They determine personality."

"But the way he looks at Keiran—"

"Could be love. Could be concern. Could be both." She refills my wine. "My point is: you're making a lot of assumptions based on very little actual evidence. Maybe try asking instead of assuming?"

"I can't ask if they're—"

"Why not?"

"Because it's invasive. Because it's their business. Because—"

"Because you're scared," she says gently. "Scared of what the answer might be. Scared that if you're wrong about them, you might also be wrong about what you're allowed to want."

The words hit too close.

"I don't even know what I want," I admit quietly.

"Then maybe start there." She clinks her glass against mine. "Figure out what you feel before you try to figure out what they feel."

We sit in comfortable silence for a moment, and then Liam pokes his head in to announce that dinner's ready. The rest of the evening passes in warmth and laughter and the easy chaos of five men who love each other and their wife without reservation or apology.

When I leave around eleven, after coffee and water and another hour of conversation that's definitely sobered me up, Penelope walks me to my car.

"Stop overthinking," she says, pulling me into a hug. "Start feeling."

"That's terrifying advice."

"It's good advice."

The ferry ride back is quiet, me and a handful of other late-night travelers and the dark water and my spiraling thoughts.

Maybe Penelope's right. Maybe I am making assumptions.

But how else am I supposed to interpret what I'm seeing? The way Archie looks at Keiran? The way Keiran shuts down any possibility of connection? The way they move around each other with this careful awareness?

It looks like unrequited love. It looks like pining. It looks like two people who can't give each other what they need.

But what if I'm wrong?

The question follows me off the ferry, through the dark drive back to the garage, up until I'm pulling into my usual spot and noticing the light still on in bay three.

Someone's here. At midnight.

I move quietly through the side door, instinct making me cautious. The voices reach me before I can see anything, low and hushed.

I shouldn't eavesdrop. I know I shouldn't.

But my feet carry me forward anyway, soft-footed on the concrete, until I can see into the bay.

Keiran and Archie.

They're standing close, too close for casual conversation. Archie's got one hand on Keiran's arm, his face tilted up, earnest and pleading. Keiran's head is bowed, jaw tight, and even from here I can see the tension radiating off him.

Archie says words I can't hear. Keiran shakes his head.

Archie's hand tightens on Keiran's arm. His other hand comes up, like he's about to touch Keiran's face, and—

Keiran steps back. Puts space between them.

The gesture is gentle but firm. Clear.

Archie's hand drops. His whole body seems to deflate.

They stand there in loaded silence, and even though I can't hear what's being said, I can read the body language. The careful distance Keiran's maintaining. The way Archie's shoulders curve inward, protective. The way Keiran won't quite meet Archie's eyes.

This is a rejection. This is Archie trying one more time and Keiran definitively saying no.

My throat goes tight.

Keiran says words too quiet for me to hear. Archie nods. They stand there another moment, and then Archie turns toward the door.

I retreat quickly, quietly, back out the side door and around to the external stairs to my flat. My heart is hammering. My hands are shaking.

I witnessed something private. Painful. Something that confirms everything I suspected.

I don't turn on the lights right away. I stand there in the darkness, surrounded by the shadowy shapes of my plants, trying to process what I saw.

Archie's in love with Keiran.

Keiran's trying to let him down easy.

And I'm somehow tangled up in all of this, feeling things I shouldn't feel, noticing things I shouldn't notice, wanting what doesn't even exist.

I pour myself a whisky in the dark, then finally flip on a lamp. The sudden light makes my monstera cast long shadows across the wall.

My phone buzzes. Bonnie: How was girls' night?

Confusing, I type back. Everything's confusing.

Want to talk?

Not yet. Still processing.

Okay. But Mill? You're allowed to feel complicated things. Even if they don't make sense.

I set the phone down and sink onto the couch, whisky warming my hands.

Allowed to feel complicated things.

But what am I feeling?

Attracted to Keiran despite, or maybe because of, how infuriating he is. Drawn to Archie's kindness and gentle nature in a way that should feel safe, but definitely doesn't. Sad for both of them, trapped in this impossible situation where one wants what the other can't give. And underneath all of that, deeper. Something that pulses every time I'm near them.

Want.

I want what I don't have words for. Something that probably can't exist outside of my head. Something that definitely doesn't fit into Dad's vision of proper relationships.

Something that's probably going to hurt.

But I'm starting to realize that won't stop me from feeling it.

Tomorrow I'll go back downstairs and pretend I didn't see anything. Pretend I don't know about Archie's heartbreak. Pretend Keiran's hands on my waist meant nothing. Pretend Dad's words about "proper relationships" don't echo in my head every time I look at both of them.

Tomorrow I'll be professional.

Tonight, I let myself admit the truth: Whatever's building here, between me and them, between all three of us, it's inevitable.

And I have absolutely no idea what to do about it.

**Millie is available for preorder now!**

Do you want a sneak peek at all of my WIPs? Come join us on Ream where I post chapters as I write them!

# ACKNOWLEDGMENTS

To my family—thank you for surviving the chaos. For months of long days, late nights, and my general disappearance into the world of edits and deadlines. You kept me grounded when I forgot what day it was, and loved me through every exhausted, coffee-fueled meltdown.

And to Lorna—thank you for reminding me that there's life beyond a computer screen. For pulling me outside, for teaching me to love the dirt under my nails and the miracle of something growing just because you cared for it. For showing me the beauty of patience, sunlight, and dahlias.

You've all given me more than I can ever fit into words, and this book exists because of you.

# ABOUT THE AUTHOR

Tucked away in the misty Smoky Mountains with her husband, three kids, and a menagerie of furry companions (three dogs and two cats who think they run the household), Daphne weaves stories that make readers blush, gasp, and fall helplessly in love.

Known for her wickedly spicy romances and vivid imagination, she's been crafting tales since she first learned to hold a pen. When she's not steaming up the pages with her latest novel, you'll find her curled up in her favorite reading nook, devouring books like they're chocolate.

Her mountain sanctuary provides the perfect backdrop for dreaming up deliciously scandalous stories that push boundaries and set kindles aflame. Fair warning: her books are known to cause sleepless nights, excessive swooning, and an insatiable appetite for more.

# ALSO BY DAPHNE LEIGH

Charlie

Isla

Penelope

Stroke of Love